Praise for Reif Larsen's *I Am Radar*

"Big, beautiful, ambitious . . . Radical physicist puppeteers? It takes narrative magic to pull off such a loopy combination, and luckily, Reif Larsen has it to spare. His prose is addictive and enchanting. . . . It's a worthy endeavor that Larsen, who could apply his gorgeous prose to more comfortable literary fictions, is engaging with distant and unfamiliar cultures. . . . The book is striving for something stronger, and Larsen's ceaselessly lovely prose is matched by his many ambitions."

—*Los Angeles Times*

"The promise shown in [Larsen's] first novel is more than fulfilled in the grandly ambitious *I Am Radar*, another masterpiece of geekhood. . . . If Larsen's debut looked like a Donald Barthelme assemblage, this one resembles something by Thomas Pynchon. . . . Larsen's brainy book is no ephemeral performance piece. He grapples with time-honored questions of free will, predestination, man vs. nature, and the tensions between parents and children. But it's the ingenuity with which he does so, rather than the themes themselves, that elicits admiration. . . . *I Am Radar* is a dazzling performance."   —*The Washington Post*

"Set aside for the moment the black baby born to white parents, the avant-garde puppeteers, and the quantum physics that swirl around the whole kit and caboodle. The most interesting fact of Reif Larsen's 600-plus-page novel, *I Am Radar*, is that it reads like something far more compact than its bulk might suggest. There are maps, diagrams, and pictures (e.g., an elephant plummeting from a bridge, a Cambodian prisoner of the Khmer Rouge) that remind one of the visual arrangements in W. G. Sebald's novels. Then there is a deeply patterned narrative that darts easily from small-bore domestic dramas to sweeping historical catastrophes with just the right fillip of silliness and levity to keep the whole text eminently approachable. . . . *I Am Radar* is as easy to enjoy for its swaggering tragicomic spirit as it is to admire for its celestial ambition."

—*The New York Times Book Review*

"Chameleonic, ambitious, epic, fantastical, whimsical, thought-provoking, arcane, philosophical, exhaustive, and completely bonkers . . . It's an estimable, and completely insane idea that has all the hallmarks of a film by Michel Gondry or Jean-Pierre Jeunet, who incidentally also directed the equally dazzling movie adaptation of *T. S. Spivet*. . . . Larsen's fare is unquestionably one of the more adventurous entries into the literary landscape, and his skill and flair for quirky, innovative works that cross over into the historical and the literary will always have an admiring . . . audience. It's a performance, that's for sure, and Larsen is a keen player."
—*The Boston Globe*

"Larsen's is an extraordinarily lush and verdant imagination, blooming wildly on the borders of the absurd and the riotous, the surreal and the ordinary. . . . Quite unlike any [novel] I've read in a long time. One doesn't consume it; one enters it, as part of a literary enactment. . . . Brilliant . . . The effort is well-rewarded: It is both maddening and marvelous. . . . I can't wait to see what he pulls off next."
—*The Cleveland Plain Dealer*

"A story of Homeric proportions . . . It's a wild ride with an unconventional structure and enormous cast of unforgettable characters. Larsen's prose is straightforward and bold, full of sparkling phrases. . . . Wise yet unpretentious, both broad and deep, *I Am Radar* will slake the most unquenchable thirst for storytelling and open the reader's eyes to new possibilities in fiction."   —*Shelf Awareness*

"Sprawling, epic . . . The result is impressive and a little bit wondrous. In a way, the reader becomes part of the story, becoming aware of the observer's effect on the observed. . . . It's an astonishing conceit."   —*The A.V. Club*

"Large, robust, even intimidating: *I Am Radar* is never a laborious read. Sentence to sentence, the reader will find small gems ("How intimate, to trace a person's geography") and beautiful descriptions of typically ugly places. . . . An intelligent and engaging book."   —*Flavorwire*

ABOUT THE AUTHOR

Reif Larsen's first novel, *The Selected Works of T. S. Spivet*, was a *New York Times* bestseller and is currently translated in twenty-seven languages. The novel was a 2010 Montana Honor book and an IndieBound Award finalist; was short-listed for *The Guardian* First Book Award and the James Tait Black Memorial Prize; and was adapted into a movie by Jean-Pierre Jeunet (*Amélie*). Larsen's writings have appeared in *The New York Times*, *The Guardian*, *Tin House*, *one story*, *The Millions*, *Asymptote Journal*, and *The Believer*. Larsen is currently serving as the writer-in-residence at the University of St Andrews in Scotland.

@reiflarsen   ReifLarsen.com   iamradar.net

I

AM

RADAR

REIF LARSEN

PENGUIN BOOKS

PENGUIN BOOKS
An imprint of Penguin Random House LLC
375 Hudson Street
New York, New York 10014
penguin.com

First published in the United States of America by Penguin Press,
a member of Penguin Group (USA) LLC, 2015
Published in Penguin Books 2016

"And Outside," by Milan Milišić, translated by Maja Herman, © 2015
Jelena Trpković Milišić (reprinted from Most / The Bridge Croatian P.E.N. Centre).

Art Production by Maria Cristina Rueda

Image credits appear on page 657.

THE LIBRARY OF CONGRESS HAS CATALOGED THE HARDCOVER EDITION
AS FOLLOWS:

Larsen, Reif.
I am radar : a novel / Reif Larsen.
pages ; cm
ISBN 978-1-59420-616-0 (hc.)
ISBN 978-0-14-310791-0 (pbk.)
I. Title.
PS3612.A773I2 2015
813'.6—dc23
2014036655

Printed in the United States of America
3 5 7 9 10 8 6 4 2

DESIGNED BY MEIGHAN CAVANAUGH

For Holt

CONTENTS

LIST OF FIGURES

I sing the body electric;

The armies of those I love engirth me and I engirth them,

They will not let me off till I go with them, respond to them,

And discorrupt them, and charge them full with the charge of the soul.

WALT WHITMAN, Leaves of Grass

The only thing I am certain of is uncertainty itself and of this
I cannot be certain.

PER RØED-LARSEN, Spesielle Partikler

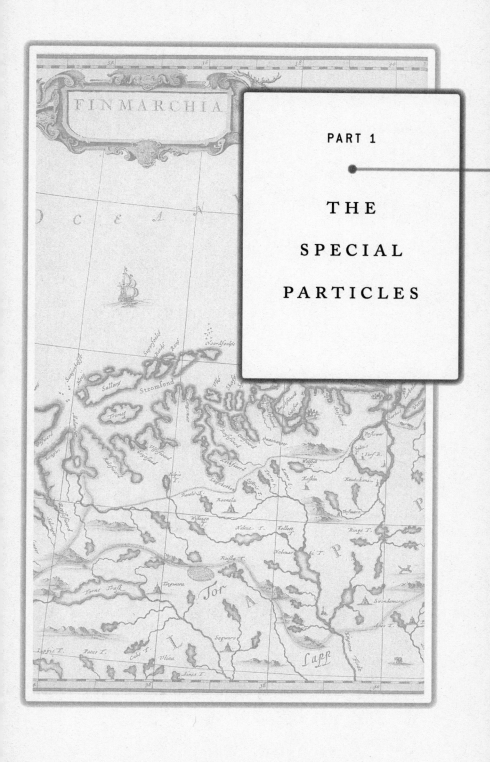

PART 1

THE

SPECIAL

PARTICLES

1

ELIZABETH, NEW JERSEY

April 17, 1975

It was just after midnight in birthing room 4C and Dr. Sherman, the mustached obstetrician presiding over the delivery, was sweating lightly into his cotton underwear, holding out his hands like a beggar, ready to receive the imminent cranium.

Without warning, the room was plunged into total darkness.

Though he had been delivering babies for more than thirty years now, Dr. Sherman was so taken aback by this complete loss of vision that he briefly considered, and then rejected, the possibility of his own death. Desperate to get his bearings, he wheeled around, trying to locate the sans serif glow of the emergency exit sign across the hall, but this too had gone dark.

"Doctor?" the nurse called next to him.

"The exit!" he hissed into the darkness.

All through the hospital, a wash of panic spread over staff and patients alike as life support machines failed and surgeons were left holding beating hearts in pitch-black operating theaters. None of the backup systems—the two generators in the basement, the giant, deep-cycle batteries outside the ICU, usually so reliable in blackouts such as this one—appeared to be working. It was a catastrophe in the making. Electricity had quite simply vanished.

In birthing room 4C, Dr. Sherman was jolted into action by Charlene, the expectant mother, who gave a single, visceral cry that let everyone know, in no uncertain terms, that the baby was still coming. Maybe the baby had already come, under shroud of darkness. Dr. Sherman instinctively reached down and, sure enough, felt the conical crown of the baby's skull emerging from his mother's vagina. He guided this invisible head with the tips of his ten fingers, pulling, gathering, turning so that the head and neck were once again square with the baby's shoulders, which still lingered in Charlene's birth canal. He did this pulling, gathering, turning without seeing, with only the memory infused in the synapses of his cortex, and his blindness was a fragile kind of sleep.

As he shepherded the child from its wet, coiled womb into a new kind of darkness, Dr. Sherman heard a distinct clicking sound. At first he thought the sound was coming from the birth canal, but then he located the clicking as coming from just behind him, over his right shoulder. Suddenly his vision was bathed in a syrupy yellow light. The father of the newborn, Kermin Radmanovic, who had earlier brought a transceiver radio and a telegraph key into the birthing room in order to announce his child's arrival to the world, was waving a pocket flashlight wrapped in tinfoil at the space between his wife's legs.

"He is okay?" asked Kermin. "He comes now?" His accent was vaguely Slavic, the fins of his words dipping their uvular tips into a smooth lake of water.

Everyone looked to where the beam of light had peeled back the darkness. There glistened the torpedo-like head of the child, covered in a white, waxen substance. The sight encouraged Dr. Sherman back into action. He first slipped his finger beneath the child's chin, but when he felt no sign of the umbilical cord wrapped around the neck, he yelled, *"Push!"*

Charlene did her best to comply with the order, her toes curling as she attempted to expel the entire contents of her abdomen, and when the breaking point was most certainly reached, surpassed, and then reached again, there was a soft popping sound and the rest of the baby emerged, the starfish body tumbling out into the dim mustard glow of this world.

Kermin leaned in to catch a first glimpse of his new child. Ever since his wife had come hobbling into his tiny electronics closet, staring at her dripping hand as if it were not her own, time had begun to unravel. The labor had come three weeks early. His fingers—so steady as he mended the cathode ruptures and fizzled diodes of his broken radios and televisions—suddenly became clumsy and numb at their tips, as if they were filled with a thick, viscous sap. In the hospital parking lot, he had taken the old Buick up and over the curb onto a low, half-moon shrubbery, which had not weathered this trespass well at all. As he ushered a blanketed Charlene through the rotating doors, Kermin had looked back at the battered shrubs, lit by the ugly glow of the parking lot's blinking fluorescents, and wondered in that moment if they were prematurely introducing the future into the present.

In the final days of World War II, his younger sister Tura had also been born three weeks early. He and his parents had been fleeing the advancing Communist Partisans for the uncertain refuge of Slovenia and the West when she arrived suddenly, like a sneeze, in the mildewed basement of a Bosnian hotel on the River Sana. He remembered her tiny and pink in their mother's arms, sheltered by a horsehair blanket while they rode in the back of a sputtering diesel truck past homes that burned and hissed against a light rain.

That is my sister in there, he thought, watching the blanket bounce to the staccato beat of the road's potholes. *She was born in the war, but she will not know the war. I will tell her how it was so that we will always have the same memories.*

Tura would not have the same memories as he, nor any memories at all. On the second day, she opened her eyes to the light of this world, but she would not nurse, and so her body grew soft and light like a bird's. One week later she was dead, from an illness that was never named. They buried her in an abandoned vineyard on the outskirts of Zagreb. After the impromptu ceremony, they were walking back to the truck when they discovered an unexploded German bomb lying only twenty meters from her grave.

"Her headstone," his father, Dobroslav, had said, and it was not meant to be a joke, but they all began to laugh, and this felt good until their mother started to weep again. Two days later, she too would be dead, at a checkpoint near Ljubljana. Kermin was too young at the time to understand the particulars, but he knew it was because of something vaguely erotic—something wanted by the trigger-happy Russian private with the moth-eaten beard and something refused by his grieving mother, who was malnourished and weak but who was still and always would be a strong-willed Radmanović woman. His father had just turned from successfully negotiating their passage with the squat colonel, but it was too late; the young Russian guard had already shot her twice through the chest. It was as if the man had meant to push her backwards with the palm of his hand but had simply used the wrong tool. He began to walk quickly away from the scene so his comrades would not see the terror in his eyes. Instead of falling to the ground like a heavy doll, as Kermin had seen the prisoners do at the Chetnik executions, his mother shrank into herself, a reverse blossoming, coming to rest in a sitting position, like a ruminative Buddha. She was already stiff by the time her husband reached her. He sat down beside her and held her hands as though they were quietly praying together. Later, the colonel apologized to his father and promised that the young guard would be executed before the day was through.

Years later, even after he had fled Europe, Kermin's limited sexual encounters—in a Meadowlands parking lot; in a Saigon bordello; behind the vestry of St. Sava's; in the synthetic floral bloom of his dentist's bathroom—these moments of carnal urgency were still inflected with the lingering sense of crossing a hostile border. Until he had met Charlene, his relationships had not gone well.

In the darkness of birthing room 4C, Kermin tried to hold his pocket light steady on his wife and brand-new baby. *All will be fine,* he whispered to himself, *there is no reason to worry.* His own birth had been famously quick and painless. His mother had claimed he leaped out into the world the first chance he got, as if he could not breathe inside her. "I was killing you!" she used to say. Maybe his child would be no different. *Kakav otac takav sin.* Like father, like son.

But even then he could tell something was not right. Under the pocket light's dull beam, the child appeared almost prehistoric. The newborn's skin was covered in a white, gooey plaster, as if he were not a baby but a statue mold of a baby—a golem, complete with tiny plaster penis. Kermin stared. He wanted to press his hand into this creature's clay skin, to test its warmth, but already here were the first signs of life: the statue-child was squirming, clawing for oxygen, expelling the first sticky mew of a cry, his tiny mouth working the air for the solidity of a nipple.

"Why is he like this?" Kermin whispered, his pocket light inadvertently dipping before he righted its beam again. "Why does he look like this?"

Charlene, completely exhausted but wild with muddied adrenaline, tasted the concern in her husband's voice. She tried to sit up.

"What is it? What's wrong? He's a boy? Is he okay?" The words swung and gimballed.

"Don't worry, don't worry. He's fine," Dr. Sherman reassured her, gathering the baby and all of his limbs into a pastel blanket. Instinctively, he took the bright white plastic clamp from the tray and snapped it closed at the base of the umbilical cord. "Preterms are often covered in a substance called vernix caseosa. This protects their skin. It will come right off." In truth, he had never quite seen such a thick vernix coating, but then there had been nothing normal about this night, so he tried not to let his concern reveal itself in the contours of his words.

Charlene's green eyes burned in the light.

"I want him with me . . ." she said.

"You will have him, don't you worry," said the nurse. "You'll have him for the rest of your life."

Before Charlene could process the ominous undercurrent of this statement, the nurse put a hand on her shoulder and gently eased her backwards onto the bed. She smoothed a wet curl of black hair across Charlene's forehead and then adjusted the flow of her IV, opening the secondary port to allow an influx of opioids. Charlene let out a quiet groan and slumped back into the darkness.

"Do we have battery power on the suction?" Dr. Sherman asked.

The nurse checked the machine. "No, doctor," she said.

"That's all right. I'll do it myself."

He took a wet cloth and carefully wiped off the child's mouth and face and then his left arm. The thick layer of vernix came away easily. "You see?" he said to Kermin, but Kermin did not answer. He was holding his pocket light, staring at his son. Where the doctor had wiped away the globular coating, the child's skin appeared very dark—so dark it shimmered purple in the beam of light, like an eggplant. Dr. Sherman looked down and caught his breath. He wiped away more of the white substance. The jet-black umbra of the skin beneath the bright vernix was disarming, as if beneath his covering the child was made only of more shadows.

"He is okay?" Kermin was asking from behind. "He looks . . ." There was not a word for this. And now the first full-force wail from the infant, announcing his own arrival.

"Doctor, should we do an Apgar test?" the nurse asked. The doctor hesitated, mystified, holding the baby up to the beam of light. The body squirmed, half white, half black—a negative image of itself. There was a chance this was all still a dream, though the pain in his oblique muscles told him otherwise. He had lived long enough to know that pain never appears in dreams.

From somewhere down the hall came the sound of urgent shouting.

Dr. Sherman snapped back to life. "It's a boy!" he said, flushing out the obvious. He busied himself with wiping away the rest of the vernix and then snipped the umbilical cord with a precision that calmed his nerves.

"I'll get an Apgar. Can we get some more lamps in here?" He was enjoying speaking aloud. The act of speaking was making this world possible again. "And what the hell happened with the electric? Can someone find out? You would think with all of this modern technology . . ."

"Can I have him?" Charlene said from the darkness.

"We just want to run a few tests to make sure—" Dr. Sherman was in the process of handing the baby off to the nurse when a deep, mechanical moan rose up from somewhere in the building. The central air system shuddered and the ducts began to exhale above their heads and then all of the lights in the room sputtered on, one by one.

Those collected in the birthing room blinked as their pupils constricted with this explosion of photons. Everyone stared at the baby wriggling in the doctor's outstretched hands. In the harsh light of the fluorescents, the infant's skin, marked by the last globs of remaining vernix, was as black as the darkness from which he had just emerged. The umbilical cord and its apparatus dangled white and translucent against tiny, pumping legs the color of charcoal. Such monochromatic contrast appeared manufactured; the child looked like a puppet come to life.

"Why is he . . . so like this?" Kermin finally blurted out.

"I wouldn't worry," Dr. Sherman said reflexively, finishing the handoff to the nurse. "Many newborns have a different skin color when they first come out of the womb. A mark of transition. This will all correct itself."

"Is something wrong?" Charlene asked, drunk on her drugs, her pasty skin flush with the exertion of her labor. She reached for her child, but he was already being wheeled out of the room on a special trolley, followed by the doctor, who began yelling at someone down the hall.

"Is something wrong?" Charlene asked again. "What is that smell?"

"He is . . ." Kermin said, staring at the door, left to wander closed on its hinges. They were suddenly, strangely alone. "He is . . . Radar."

"Radar?"

"His name: Radar."

To her horror, Charlene realized they had never settled on a name. On several occasions they had tentatively circled the topic, but each time, all she could muster was a halfhearted short list of names for girls, and these tended to be lifted directly from famous novels: Anna, Dolores, Hester, Lucie, Edna. Every choice seemed either too obvious or too obscure or both too obvious and too obscure at the same time. How to name someone who existed only in theory? And coming up with a single viable boy name proved next to impossible. You were not just naming the boy—*you were naming the man.* Kermin, of course, proved no help at all; all five of his suggestions had been lifted from an electromagnetic textbook. And so Charlene succumbed to the narrative that they would have a girl and that all would become clear later. The decision of the name had been abandoned for simpler, tactile assignments, such as assembling the crib. They had cleared out space for the nursery; they had bought diapers and a kaleidoscope of onesies; they had inherited an outdated perambulator from her parents; but they had chosen no name. Except now that the baby had arrived (and left again), now that the baby had in fact revealed himself to be a *he,* the absence of a name suddenly took on great significance. *He* could not exist without a name.

"Radar," Kermin said again. "You know, *radar.* Like bats. And aeroplanes."

"I know what radar is," she said. She willed her brain into action. "What about . . . Charles?" Charles had been the name of her preschool boyfriend. He had punched her in the stomach to declare his love. She had not thought of him in at least thirty years, but now his name rose from the depths and became the stand-in for all things male.

"Charles?" said Kermin.

"Yes, he can be a Charlie . . . or Chuck . . . or Chaz."

"Chaz? What is Chaz?"

She sighed. She was too tired for this.

"Okay, not Charles, then. What about your father's name?"

"Dobroslav? This is peasant name."

"I'm being serious, Kerm! What about *your* name?"

His own name was not so much a name as a signal of protest. In the small Serbian village in eastern Croatia where he was born, a name was practically all you had. To know your name was to know your history, your present standing, the circumscription of your future. It was the one thing you could never escape. His father, in a feat of madness or brilliance, had bucked their heritage and invented the name Kermin, in service to no tradition, lineage, or culture. Kermin had thus been both blessed and cursed: his singularity established, he could claim to have never met another with his same name, but he had also weathered a lifetime of confused looks when introduced on both sides of the Atlantic. *Kermit? Like the frog?*

"But listen," he said. "*I* am being serious: Radar *is* name. Have you seen this television program *M*A*S*H?*" He articulated each letter, as if they were made out of wood. "Corporal Radar O'Reilly can sense the choppers before they arrive. It is like he has this ESP."

"We don't want our child to have ESP," said Charlene, bringing her hands to her face. The hospital bracelet white against her wrist. "I just want to see him . . . Where did they take him? They can't just take him like that . . . I want to see him, Kerm. Bring him back to me."

Later, hunkered down in a deserted corner of the hospital, Kermin tapped out a message on his telegraph key, his thumb conjuring signal with the quiver of the smooth brass lever. The clusters of clicks and clats evaporated into the air, invisible pulses slipping out into the Jersey night, to be collected like dew by the radios of those who were listening in the early-morning hours:

—•—• ——•— 4 17 75.

MY SON IS BORN. RADAR RADMANOVIC.
MOTHER IS FINE. BABY IS FINE. I AM FINE.
KAKAV OTAC TAKAV SIN.

73, K2W9

Moments before, the nurse had asked Kermin for the child's name.

"I must type it up," she said. "For the certificate."

He had glanced through the doorway at his sleeping wife.

"Radar," he said, testing the boundaries of truth. "It's Radar."

"Radar?" The nurse raised her eyebrows, unsure she had heard the word correctly.

"Radar," he confirmed, bouncing and recalling his fingers from an invisible barrier. "Like this: *Signal. Echo. Return.*"

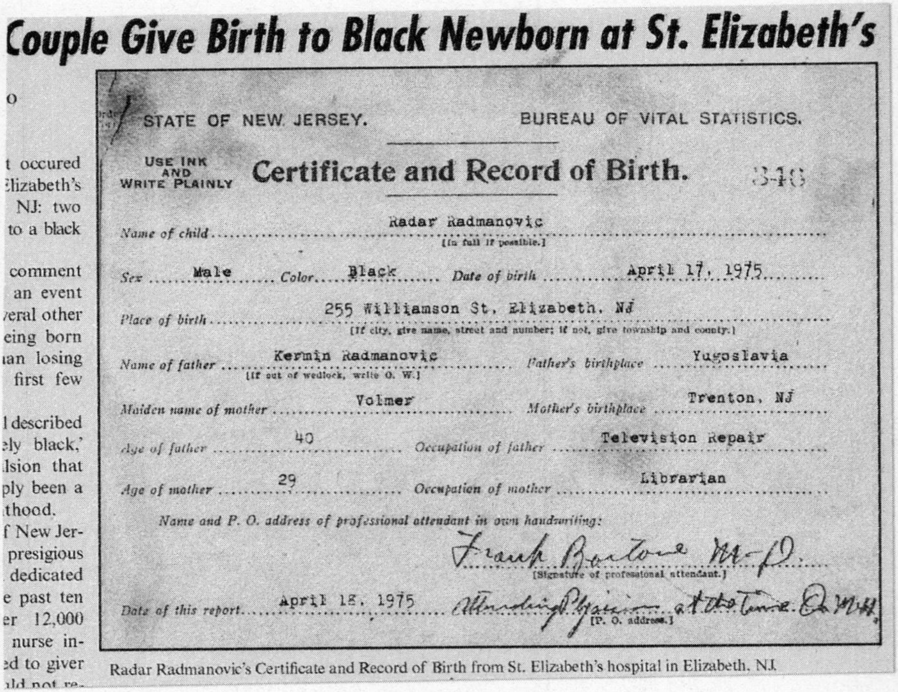

Couple Give Birth to Black Newborn at St. Elizabeth's

o

t occured
Elizabeth's
NJ: two
to a black

comment
an event
veral other
eing born
han losing
first few

l described
ely black,'
lsion that
ply been a
thood.
f New Jer-
presigious
dedicated
e past ten
er 12,000
nurse in-
ed to giver
ld not re-

STATE OF NEW JERSEY.   BUREAU OF VITAL STATISTICS.

USE INK AND WRITE PLAINLY   Certificate and Record of Birth.   848

Name of child........ Radar Radmanovic ....
[In full if possible.]

Sex... Male ... Color... Black ...... Date of birth ...... April 17, 1975 .....

Place of birth...... 255 Williamson St, Elizabeth, NJ ......
[If city, give name, street and number; if not, give township and county.]

Name of father ...... Kermin Radmanovic ...... Father's birthplace ...... Yugoslavia ......
[If out of wedlock, write O. W.]

Maiden name of mother ...... Volmer ...... Mother's birthplace ...... Trenton, NJ ......

Age of father ...... 40 ...... Occupation of father ...... Television Repair ......

Age of mother ...... 29 ...... Occupation of mother ...... Librarian ......

Name and P. O. address of professional attendant in own handwriting:

Frank Barton M.D.
[Signature of professional attendant.]

Date of this report...... April 18, 1975 ...... Attending Physician at the time Q M.H.
[P. O. address.]

Radar Radmanovic's Certificate and Record of Birth from St. Elizabeth's hospital in Elizabeth, N.J.

Fig. 1.1. Radar's Certificate and Record of Birth

From Popper, N. (1975), "Caucasian Couple Give Birth to Black Newborn
at St. Elizabeth's," Newark *Star-Ledger,* April 18, 1975, p. A1

The birth of such an extremely dark baby (described as "blacker than the blackest black" by an overeager *Star-Ledger* reporter) to two white parents was Jersey gossip that could not be kept quiet for long. The news of the birth must have been leaked by one of the orderlies, or one of the janitors, or perhaps even the nurse who had typed up the certificate of birth. Someone had talked to someone who had talked to someone, and suddenly there was a small group of reporters wandering around the maternity ward the next morning asking questions to anyone who would listen: *You're telling me this wasn't just a mix-up, right? The kid could be from another family . . . No? Okay, well, had the mother slept around? All right, all right. Fair enough. So then what was wrong with him? Okay, but what do you call that kind of thing? Was it a disease? What were the chances of this kind of thing happening? Yeah, but ballpark: one in a million? One in a* billion? *How black was he* really? *That black? Like* Nigerian *black? So then, when can we see him? What do you mean? Well, come on now, that's a load of horseshit.*

The day after his birth, the Newark *Star-Ledger* ran a front-page article with the relatively modest headline "Caucasian Couple Give Birth to Black Newborn at St. Elizabeth's." Lacking a serviceable photograph, they settled for a poorly rendered xerox of Radar's birth certificate, as if this was all the proof anyone could need. Across the Hudson, the *New York Post* declared, "Jersey Freak of Nature: White Parents . . . Black Baby!" and then proceeded to give very few details elaborating on their inflammatory headline. Baby Radar, caught in a genealogical conundrum not of his choosing, had suddenly become a cultural touchstone.

Perhaps all of the fuss was due to the alchemy of that particular time and place: eight years removed from the '67 Newark riots, urban white flight was now in full swing. The manufacturing industry was steadily collapsing, leaving New Jersey in the throes of a severe recession. People—both white and black alike—were struggling to come to terms with the great expectations laid forth by the civil rights movement of the previous decade. How would such lofty ideals play out in the banal commerce of the everyday? Had everything changed? Or, as many were slowly realizing, had nothing really changed at all?

No doubt the story also gained traction because the simplest and most obvious explanation for Radar's appearance, the explanation that spawned a thousand breakfast table jokes—a.k.a. "the milkman theory"—ultimately proved inadequate, given the child's coloring. If the people could only have gotten a good look at the baby, they would have understood, once and for all, that mere infidelity could not possibly have triggered such a dramatic swing in color from the whitest of whites to "the blackest of blacks." And yet the people could not get a good look at Radar Radmanovic, because there were no photos of him save a (supposed) shot of his incubator, taken from some distance. With such scant evidence, the public was left to wonder on their own about the nature of inheritance, about what was passed down to a child and what was not, about the chances of such a highly unusual genetic occurrence—if it was indeed a genetic occurrence—ever happening to one of their own children. In the midst of all this, the family remained secretive, declining all interviews, shunning photographers, despite rumors of several five-figure offers for an exclusive photo shoot and rights to their story.

On one of the morning talk radio shows, a then relatively unknown Reverend Jesse Louis Jackson, who was about to embark on the famous ten-day tour of apartheid South Africa that would subsequently springboard him into the international spotlight, weighed in on the case, admonishing the media for implicitly accusing "the black male scapegoat of *raping* another one of its white women."

"This," he said emphatically, "is an act of God, not of one man. This child is *blessed*. I hope the family realizes just how lucky they are."[1]

Radar's story lingered in the Jersey tabloids for only a week or so. Various medical professionals and semi-professionals were called in to offer half-baked theories for what might have happened to the baby—theories that ranged from a rare double-recessive melanism gene expression ("A distant black ancestor come to life!") to toxic waste exposure from one of New Jersey's many Meadowlands industrial sewage dumps ("The child was a mutant!"). After this initial flurry of coverage, however, the story, like all stories, shriveled up and eventually disappeared, and Radar and his condition would not be heard of again until nearly four years later, when Dr. Thomas K. Fitzgerald would deliver his much-anticipated diagnosis, "On an Isolated Incidence of Non-Addison's Hypoadrenal Uniform Hyperpigmentation in a Caucasian Male," in the *Journal of Investigative Dermatology*.

Charlene Radmanovic, for her part, emerged from the afterglow of the birth with a strange olfactory condition, in which everything around her smelled exactly the same, and of such an intensity as to be almost paralyzing. At first the hospital and all of its contents smelled of something approximate to burnt Cocoa Krispies. The night nurse, the squishy spinach greens in her muted meals, the urine-resistant plastic pillows, the television remote buttons—everything was morning cereal, permanently singed and distinctly nauseating. Most distressing of all was that her own son, whom she was eventually allowed to hold, smelled so strongly that she could not be near him for long without becoming overwhelmed by his smoldering stench. It was the worst kind of torture—to be repulsed by the very thing one should love above all else. Breast-feeding felt like the most unnatural act in the world. He would not latch, and she quickly grew too dizzy to persist for long. Her complaints were answered with more painkillers, and when these did not work, a half-blind British otolaryngologist was summoned to her bedside. He prodded her sensory orifices and declared the condition temporary.

---

[1] "Jesse Jackson, Mayor Abe Beame," *The Alex Bennett Show*, WPLJ, April 22, 1975. Radio broadcast.

"A childbirth is an explosion," he said by way of explanation. "Some shrapnel is inevitable, isn't it?"

A week of intensive tests confirmed that everything else with Radar, save his unlikely hue, was more or less normal. A couple of the results were slightly worrisome: the iron content in his blood was elevated, as were his cortisol levels, though neither of these was unusual for newborns recovering from the hormonal starburst of birthing and the violent adjustment to a new world of oxygen and sunlight. Baby Radar also exhibited slightly higher-than-normal blood pressure and suffered from moderately dry skin that required treatment with a prescription lotion. But nothing so out of the ordinary as to point to a cause for his unusual appearance. His hair, present from birth, was soft and black and straight, just like his father's. Indeed, if you could look past his darkness, Radar perfectly resembled a little Kermin: there was the same dimpled chin, the same funicular jawline, the same protrusive brow. If not for their diametric coloring, there would be no question of their relation.

Luckily, the public debate around Charlene's possible infidelity, a debate that had ignited all sorts of heated exchanges about race and sexuality in the local media, had not quite managed to pierce the cocoon of their hospital room. Dr. Sherman had done well to keep the cameras at bay. He was distinctly aware of the care one must take when wading into such a sensitive subject. At the time, comprehensive DNA testing was not readily available, and questions of legitimate parentage could often linger indefinitely. Still, Dr. Sherman thought it his duty to inform them of their options, should they want to pursue certain answers, and so, the day they were scheduled to take Radar home, he called them into his office for a final meeting.

"Here we are!" he said. "Hard to believe it's only been a week."

Charlene looked exhausted.

"What," she asked, bringing a hand to her nose, "do we do now?"

"Well . . ." He thumbed at his pen. "That all depends. I'm not sure if you want to do a test."

"A test?" she said. "For what?"

He paused. "For paternity. There's a new procedure available that uses HLA from both father and baby, but it's expensive, and the lab needs a significant amount of blood to test, so we would need to wait until the baby is at least six or eight months—"

"What're you saying?" she said.

"What am I saying?"

A silence.

Dr. Sherman held up his hands. "Look, I didn't mean to suggest anything one way or another. I was merely pointing out that there are tests out there, should you choose to want to know these things."

Kermin was staring at his wife. She was looking back at him, steadily. After a moment, her eyes filled with tears.

"Kermin," she said, reaching out for his hand. "Kermin. Kermin."

Dr. Sherman decided it was time to start speaking again. "It's all your choice, of course. Regardless, you'll no doubt want to see a specialist about your son."

He handed her a list of referrals, which Charlene accepted, only briefly shifting her gaze away from her husband's face. His eyes had stayed hot, but there was now something dull and sooty around their edges, something she had not seen before, like glowing embers suddenly shushed by a bucket of water.

"One of these doctors I'm sure will help you get to the bottom of what's going on here. Truly, in all my years, I've never seen anything quite like it." He paused, looking at them over his spectacles. "But I say this not to worry you."

That evening, at the suggestion of Dr. Sherman, they left the hospital through a service entrance, so as to avoid any lingering paparazzi. They arrived home to a house that felt like it belonged to a couple of strangers. Everything was familiar but not their own. The curtains were too brown, the forks were too big.

During her first week out of the hospital, Charlene's olfactive focus gradually transitioned from burnt breakfast cereal to something more sinister. Descriptors proved elusive; the closest she could come to describing the stench was rotten meat that had been heavily grilled and then doused with an astringent lemon-scented cleaner. It was a three-toned miasma that pounded her in waves. She tried to nurse her son but would quickly be consumed by an enduring sensation of rotting flesh. One evening, she left him squirming on the bed as she fled to the bathroom, weeping at her own futility.

"Are you okay?" Kermin said through the door, their child in his arms.

"I can't," she said from the other side.

He tried the door.

"Charlene?" he called.

When there was no answer, Kermin clumsily swaddled Radar like a burrito and walked the ten blocks to the A&P, where he bought a case of formula tins. He fed their child in the Shaker rocking chair in the kitchen, the metronome of his son's suckling beating against the static hush of his transistor radio on the countertop. Now and again a Halifax ham could be heard reading verses from *Leaves of Grass* to no one in particular.

At some point, Charlene emerged from the bathroom and stood at the threshold of the kitchen. Father and son had fallen asleep in the chair. She observed them as one observes a painting in a museum, as if she might set off an alarm by venturing too close.

One day, she woke up and found the rotten meat smell had parted and given way to the particulars of the world: she could now smell things individually, though these were warped and amplified a hundredfold. Citrus and all of its iterations triggered a special torment; she was tortured by their downstairs neighbors' heavy hands with the lemon vinaigrette at their weekly family reunions. On one of her first forays into the outside world, she almost passed out on the sidewalk from a single blast of truck fumes. People, too, despite their concoctions of deodorants and perfumes, emitted strong psychological odors, such that she could instantly read a person's mood with a single sniff. She quickly learned how to brave the world with two wads of cotton surreptitiously stuffed up her nostrils.

Yet what was more maddening than this evolving cast of odors was what had remained the same: Radar's smell was the one smell that had not changed since those early days of charred cereal. He smelled exactly as he had the moment he was born. Or: her perception of his smell had not changed since the moment he was born. She was not so naive as to think her perceptions provided an objective dictum on the truth.

As the days and weeks went by, she slowly learned to tolerate her intense olfactive repulsion for him. Such repulsion was not acceptable, she knew—this was her child, after all, her own flesh and blood—and so she willed herself to love the repulsion itself. The dizzier she became, the tighter she held him. *If this was her curse, then so be it.* And yet she also became convinced that if only she could determine what had gone wrong with Radar, then she would also discover the secret to loving him as a mother should. All she needed was a medical diagnosis that could be spoken out loud and everything would be fixed.

They took Radar to each of the pediatric dermatologists that Dr. Sherman had recommended. Charlene expected an answer to come quickly. Surely, science would give them a name for what had happened, some kind of explanation or clinical history. The doctors, however, did not hold up their end of the bargain. They gave the Radmanovics more slips with more references, each of which Charlene diligently pursued. They crisscrossed New York City, visiting a growing list of increasingly suspect specialists who would pluck biopsies from Radar's squirming thighs or rub on seven-syllabled creams that did nothing but irritate his skin. Nothing worked, nor did these specialists seem to have a clue about what, if anything, was wrong. Each doctor, after some fancy medical footwork, eventually admitted he was at a complete loss for an explanation.

Kermin seemed unfazed—content, even—with the utter lack of answers, but Charlene underwent a slow metamorphosis while she waited in all of those waiting rooms. The process began to consume the purpose. She started to collect medical textbooks; she began subscribing to half a dozen obscure dermatology newsletters and journals; she amassed a detailed, cross-referenced Rolodex of doctors' names, which she slowly crossed off one by one. With each successive visit, Charlene became more and more determined to find the root cause of her son's extraordinary condition, though her reasons for doing so were both circular and tautological. *Something was wrong with him because no one could figure out what was wrong with him.* In an African American family, Radar would be a dark, slight-featured baby with unusually straight hair—nothing more, nothing less. The problem (if one could even call it a problem) arose only when you placed him alongside his biological parents.

When Charlene once sheepishly confessed her own smell condition to Dr. Zeikman, a specialist in Queens who was attempting to treat Radar, he told her it was most likely psychosomatic, that she was simply internalizing the situation with her son. This rebuke so shook her that she could not sleep for three nights straight. Could it actually be that her condition was all in her mind? But surely he could tell there was something wrong with her son? This, she had not made up. This—everyone could see. Right?

She called Dr. Zeikman's office several days later, under the pretense of complaining about the peroxide formula he had prescribed for Radar. In truth, she wanted to press him on the extent to which he thought her delusional. If it was not her son but *she* who must be treated, then . . . then what on earth should she do?

The phone in the doctor's office rang and rang until the answering machine clicked on. There was a long pause, and then, in a quavering voice, the secretary announced that Dr. Arnold Zeikman had passed away the night before from a heart attack. All future appointments were canceled.

Charlene stood with the phone in her hand, shocked. She stared at Radar dozing in his bouncy seat. She felt sad for a minute, sad for the briefness of life, sad for Dr. Zeikman's family. But then this feeling was quickly replaced—she was ashamed to admit—by disapproval. Maybe it didn't make sense, but she found herself wondering how a doctor of any skill had managed to die of a heart attack. Shouldn't his alleged expertise on the body's mechanics shield him from his own mechanics ever breaking down?

She put down the phone and went over to her sleeping son. She let the tips of her fingers brush across his forehead. His skin was warm to the touch. He stirred; his lips trembled.

"Radar, my Radar," she whispered. "What have I done to you?"

Well, we just think it's all so crazy," said Louise. "Don't we?"

"*Don't* we?" she repeated.

"We do," said Bertrand. "We don't think it's right."

They were congregated in the Radmanovics' cramped kitchen in Elizabeth. Charlene's parents, Louise and Bertrand, now retired, had just returned from an anniversary trip to Cornwall, and they were sipping tea and eating wine gums as Radar sat at their feet, sucking on a pair of headphones. A stack of dermatology textbooks loomed precariously close to the toaster oven.

"I mean, who's he to tell us there's something wrong with him?" said Louise.

"That's not the point, Mom. We just need to find out what happened."

"Why?"

"If it was your child, you'd want the same thing."

"So what's this doctor going to tell you?"

"I don't know, Mom. That's why he's the doctor."

On a whim, Charlene had recently contacted Dr. Thomas K. Fitzgerald. Based at Harvard Medical School, Dr. Fitzgerald was a veritable rock star in the field. He was the author of the industry standard textbook *Dermatology in General Medicine* and recently the creator of the six-point Fitzgerald Skin Type Classification Scale. His handwritten reply to her query, in which he had expressed great interest in Radar's condition, sat on the kitchen table. The letter, which Charlene had brought to her nose on more than one occasion, carried the faint scent of what must have been the doctor's aftershave—a slightly unpleasant odor, like molding carrots, but the kind of unpleasant one could come to love.

"Was this his idea?" asked Louise, nodding at Kermin.

"No, Mom, it was *our* idea. The man's from Harvard. He's not some quack."

"He's a quack!" said Bertrand, producing various duck noises and pinching Radar's cheek. Radar giggled at the attention.

Her parents' skepticism was not without its effect. The steady drumbeat of professional bafflement surrounding Radar's condition had left Charlene battered by uncertainty. Maybe her mother was right: she did not need another flummoxed doctor, however prestigious, to add to the veritable choir of diagnostic confusion. Charlene silently resolved to file his letter away in Radar's already bulging medical folder and think no more of it.

In the corner of the kitchen, Kermin was only half listening as he worked the dials of his shortwave, trying to catch a signal from Côte d'Ivoire. This was nothing personal. Try as he might, he could only ever half listen to Charlene's parents. They generally meant well, but he found they often fell back into that particularly American stance of self-satisfaction masked as liberal open-mindedness, a brand of moral disembodiment to which he had never quite grown accustomed, despite having lived in the country for more than thirty years.

He quietly swore into the cauldron of static coming from the radio's speaker. The eleven-year sunspot cycle was rapidly declining to a minimum, at which point a year-and-a-half period of near-impossible long-distance communication would descend upon all amateur radio operators. Kermin had cut out a timeline of the last 150 years of this solar cycle from a recent issue of *QST* and thumbtacked it to the wall of his workshop. In blue pen he had cleverly traced how many of the world's disasters—Archduke Ferdinand's and President Kennedy's assassinations, the 1931 China floods—lined up all too well with each electromagnetic trough.

The Volmers, as they always did, mistook his attentiveness to his radio for calculated resentment. They had slowly constructed a portrait of their son-in-law—through the sad summation of pillow talk and unarticulated accusation—as the instigator and primary engine behind "fixing" their grandchild. In truth, they did not like Kermin at all, though they would never say as much, out of respect for their daughter's life choices. His awkwardness in conversation and his habit of dismantling electronics during their infrequent visits allowed them to easily cast him as their Balkan scapegoat. He would return from his radio repair closet and utter whatever was on his mind, even if this was not polite ("You look bad. Are you tired?"). He still dropped his articles and slipped up on his tenses in English, substituting future perfect for present perfect—verbal transgressions that Louise, the former grammar instructor, found obtuse and oddly aggressive. "After all these years in this country, he should at least know how to talk about the future," she had said aloud on more than one occasion. More than anything, they blamed him for sequestering their daughter in the small, nearly impenetrable Serbian Orthodox community in Elizabeth, which was the main reason, they assumed, that she rarely called them anymore.

Several years ago, Charlene had met them at the Newark Museum to see the much-talked-about exhibit of J. M. W. Turner's seascapes. They walked through the show in silence, squinting at chiaroscuro shipwrecks, and afterwards, in the poorly lit museum café with the wobbly tables, she had announced that she was going to marry Kermin, a man Bertrand and Louise had met only three times, to increasingly poor reviews. They had first protested—Bertrand with silence, Louise with cylindrical sentences that went nowhere—and then, with a thirty-year-old look of surrender passed between them, they collectively sighed and wilted into faux-progressive resignation.

"We're happy if you're happy," Louise said finally.

The wedding was an incense-heavy Orthodox affair that her parents silently endured. Soon after, Charlene came down to Trenton to tell them the news: she was pregnant. It was clear to all that the deed had been done well before the nuptials. A silence descended across the room.

"I didn't mean for it . . . I didn't want it like this," said Charlene quietly.

This, too, was digested.

Charlene waited for the wash of disapproval she knew was to come, the chronic sense of condemnation she had come to both begrudge and savor. But then Bertrand rose from the love seat.

"A grandson!" he said.

"We don't know what it is—" Charlene began to say, but he did not seem to hear her. He hiked up his pants and did a little jig on the rug. It was the first time she had ever seen her father dance. He had always been definitively anti-dance, cultivating a proud stoicism in the face of all organized revelry. Now, to see him move like this—giddy, *tout seul,* all hips and wobble—felt so intimate that Charlene almost had to look away. And then Louise got up from the couch and they all came in close and held hands. An impromptu communion for the spirit of her unborn child. Bertrand put on a Smokey Robinson record. Charlene slow-danced with her mother while her father reprised his newfound boogie, adding arrhythmic snaps to his repertoire. They were to be grandparents. Such a promise erased all else.

Thus, when Radar emerged in the midst of a fleeting Jersey blackout, Louise and Bertrand were the first to arrive, white peonies in hand, to greet the baby boy they had already predicted was coming. Like everyone else, they were at first shocked by their grandson's appearance and deeply concerned that something might be seriously wrong. After it had been determined that the child was otherwise healthy, Louise was embarrassed to admit to enjoying a guilty morsel of comfort at the possibility that Kermin might not actually be the father. But this would mean there was an anonymous dark progenitor wandering around somewhere in the belly of the city. Soon they cast all complications aside. This was America in 1975, after all, a land of multiculturalism and acceptance, and Baby Radar was one of their own. Maybe even more so than their own daughter. It was not hard for them to adore him as a counterpoint to Charlene's recalcitrance, so much so that Louise would ache when she was away from her grandson for any length of time. As Radar was ushered around from one specialist to another, Louise became more and more horrified. She vaguely assumed all of this stemmed from some kind of Old World xenophobia on the part of her son-in-law.

What she didn't know, because she never asked, was that her own daughter, not Kermin, was the sole engine behind the quest to find a name for Radar's condition. Kermin had merely become a reluctant follower in their prolonged search for answers. Never once did he lament his son's appearance or complain about the lot that life had given him. In the wake of World War II, after losing his newborn sister and mother, Kermin had fled with his father across a smoldering Europe to Bergen, Norway, where they snuck onto a thirty-foot boat bound for the New World. After six weeks at sea, Kermin had arrived in New Jersey with a bad case of pneumonia and a distinct perspective on that which was worth worrying about.

In the world he had left behind, the differences people used to judge each other, to kill each other, to declare war upon each other—these differences were often largely invisible: religious, ideological, ethnic distinctions not obvious until a name, an accent, or a birthplace was revealed. During the war, the armies wore uniforms that designated them as Partisan, Chetnik, Ustaše, but for the populace at large, one could shape-shift between these definitions, depending on who was knocking on your door. The result of such indeterminism was that in the pre-Tito Yugoslavia from which he had fled, family trumped race, religion, and creed. Above all else, you took care of your own, primarily because you could not be sure about the slippery identity of your neighbor. Kermin had spent only the first ten years of his life in Yugoslavia, but during these ten years he had learned everything there was to know about whom you must protect and whom you must reject, and such lessons can never be unlearned. In his own quiet way, Kermin threw himself into loving his son.

And yet he also knew better than to protest his wife's growing obsession with tracking down a tangible diagnosis. He instinctively understood that her quest superseded the fragile boundaries of their little nuclear family. He, like her, had begun to subscribe to the belief that a diagnosis would solve much of what was wrong in their life, but whereas Charlene hoped such a naming would bring back her child, Kermin hoped it would bring back his wife. He had seen enough suffering in the world to know that Charlene—despite everything— was the greatest prize an immigrant electrical engineer could ever hope for. There were still days when he marveled at his luck: Charlene was beautiful. Charlene was brilliant. Charlene was *his*.

So he would dutifully drive his wife and child to all of their dermatology appointments, sitting patiently in the magazined waiting rooms, listening to ionosphere updates on his handheld. When asked, he would hold his son or feed his son, and when Charlene was busy, he would take Radar to the Ravna Gora

Communications Shop, on Grove Street, where he placed him in a crib among the sea of spare parts as he reassembled radios and pocket TVs, which were his specialty.

It was also Kermin who bore the brunt of scrutiny from the Serbian community in Elizabeth, a community he quietly resented but could not shake. On the surface, Saša and her band of skeptical kerchiefed *babas* were kind and supportive, but he could hear the phlegm-inflected whispers they uttered behind closed doors. There were rumors that Charlene had been seen philandering with black men at certain slick-necked jazz clubs across the river in Harlem.

"Ona voli crni kurac," he overheard snot-nosed Olga say after Easter services. He tried to convince himself it was possible that they were talking about someone else who was not his wife.

On Sunday afternoons, as he and Charlene strolled down Broad Street, they both felt the lingering stares, from stoops and bodegas, from slow-rolling Buicks and the palm-smudged window of Planavic's Diner. The unmistakable wash of gooseflesh that arises from being observed. Despite the pieces of cotton in her nostrils, Charlene still smelled their judgment.

"Zašto je još uvek sa tom kurvom?"

"What did she say?" she asked one bitter January morning as they passed a conspiratorial Iliana and Jasmina eyeing Radar in his carriage.

Kermin looked skyward. "They say . . ." he shrugged. "They say weather is too cold for baby to be outside. They say he will now catch the chill."

"What do they care about our child?"

Kermin shrugged. "In Serbia, it is very bad for baby to catch the chill. They are worrying for us. Our child is their child."

This was no more true than his translations.

At Radar's baptism, the congregation that huddled outside the front steps of St. Sava's was large and unusually restless. Kermin did not know what to make of such an audience. He had barely spoken a word to many of these people. He wanted to understand their intentions as noble, but when he looked out across the crowd of faces, no one would meet his eyes.

On the church steps, Kermin protected Radar from the cold air in the same woolen horse blanket that had sheltered his sister and then him on his journey across the sea. Father Bajac, unusually sober and bright-eyed, held up a hand to silence those assembled. He turned to Kermin and said in Serbian, "On behalf of your son, Radar Radmanovic, do you renounce Satan and all of his services, all of his devices, all of his works, and all of his vengeful pride?"

They were facing west, toward the assembled congregation spilling out into the street, beyond which lay the endless dodecahedral sprawl of America, beyond which, according to the ancient belief, lay the unyielding temptations of Hades's lair. Down one step and to his left, Charlene watched silently. She was neither a Serb nor a Christian, but she had insisted on the baptism more adamantly than he had. His was not a faith but a habit, a reminder of his weakness. Down another step stood the Volmers, grimly, dutifully.

"I do," said Kermin.

They turned to face the east, toward the large double doors of the church. Beyond this, the ocean and the Old World, where his birthplace in the hills of Croatia beckoned. He would not recognize it if he went back now. Such was the blindness of migration.

"Do you unite yourself with Christ?" asked Father Bajac in Serbian. "Do you offer your son into the fold of the Holy Trinity?"

As Kermin felt his son squirm inside the confines of the coarse fabric, he was blessed with the sensation of being present and yet not being present at all. It was a mirrored existence that, as a radio operator, he had become all too familiar with. Every time he worked the dials of his transceiver and cast his hungry net into the invisible RF spectrum, trolling for broadcasts from Guyana or Kinshasa or Battambang, searching for the tender points of his fellow radiomen's aerials, a part of his soul was cast out into this network of signals, even as a part of him remained seated in his workshop. Kermin closed his eyes, and for an instant, the mothballed scent of the blanket became a kind of mnemonic radio, collapsing space and time until he was back inside that Norwegian schooner; the blanket cloaking his fever, the creaking roll and tumble of seawater on the hull, the slow-dance rhythm of an ocean without end. Above, the captain speaking slipshod in his singsong tongue, his father shimmying down the hatch, parting the wool to test the throbbing heat of his contagion. The boat had barely survived the battering of a North Atlantic gale, developing a crack in its hull, before finally limping into New York Harbor on a sublime September morning. Neither father nor son spoke English; in the clerical scrum of Ellis Island, they had lost the acute diacritical mark softening the *ć* at the end of their family name, thereby condemning them to a future of hard-consonant mispronunciation. The *ch* became a *k*—a sign of times to come. But they had arrived. Dobroslav had fulfilled his last promise to his wife to keep their child safe, to deliver him from their devastated homeland to a new world.

Father Bajac cleared his throat.

Kermin opened his eyes, and the wool-scented memory dissolved into the present Jersey nativity scene: the church, the steps, the priest, the crowd shifting in the frigid Meadowlands air. *There is only one* now *now,* Kermin told himself, and yet he still did not believe it.

"I do," he said.

Father Bajac licked his thumb and made the sign of a cross above the baby's body.

"Amen," the congregation called, almost out of relief. The priest motioned for them all to enter the church. Inside St. Sava's, the family circled the copper baptismal font three times as the congregation slowly filed into the knave and heralded the progress of their circumnavigations. Above, a wayward crow that had somehow found its way into God's house squawked and crashed against a window. Everyone stared. A white-robed boy emerged from behind the altar with a broom; he beat at the bottoms of the windows but could not reach the bird. After a while he gave up, and the priest continued, ignoring the creature shuddering in the rafters.

"I'm grateful so many of you are here to witness another child becoming a Christian," Father Bajac said in Serbian, resting his un-Bibled hand on the lip of the font. "This is a rebirth that we all should witness, that we all can learn from, again and again. Jesus teaches us it is never too late for a second chance."

The priest produced a vial from inside his robes and then poured a sprock of oil in the shape of a cross onto the surface of the water. Kermin watched the oil swirl and curl back into itself, like a man slowly placing his arms on his hips. Father Bajac plucked Radar from him, letting the old blanket fall to the ground. He thumbed another cross above the child's head. Radar hung there, quiet and resplendent, and then he was dunked three times. The water gurgled and splashed with each entrance. His pitch-black skin glistened in the hard fluorescent light of the church. The congregation leaned forward as one, peering at the baby, the wafts of incense swirling around him.

Before they fled at the end of the war, Kermin and his mother used to attend the services in their tiny village church outside Knin. He would lean against the folds of his mother's dress, mouthing the words to the Gospels without making a sound, his feet tired from standing so long. They stood for the whole service to show their reverence for God, his mother had explained, and Kermin had nodded as one nods when one does not understand but knows that one should understand. Dobroslav was away, fighting Tito's Partisans way up in the hills with Vojvoda Momčilo Đujić, the famous priest turned Chetnik warrior. Dobroslav was the *vojvoda*'s personal radioman, a source of pride that Kermin reminded the other boys in town of every chance he got. Dobroslav had once told Kermin how the *vojvoda* would sometimes summon him for his radio microphone in their mountaintop bivouac and then proceed to deliver sermons to no one but the empty valley, filling up forgotten frequencies. "My words are only for God to hear," said the *vojvoda*. Retreating deeper into the recesses of his mother's dress, Kermin found himself wondering whether his father and the *vojvoda* were out there now, high up in the mountains, broadcasting one of their radio sermons to a God who apparently could be everywhere and nowhere at once.

4

Charlene awoke in the middle of the night to the sound of an explosion. She shot up in bed, breathing, listening to the chorus of car alarms wailing outside. Next to her, Kermin had barely stirred. She heard Radar give a little hiccuping sob in the other room. She rose. Through the curtains she saw lights flicking on, people emerging onto their front porches.

She went to her son and gathered up his wriggling body. He folded into her, quieting. A small hand tapped at the shelf of her clavicle. She dipped and swayed, mimicking the rocking of a boat, humming a lullaby her mother had once hummed for her. She wondered if there were any words to the song. Outside, a single car alarm still blared through its cycle. She swayed. She was aware of his weight in her arms. She was aware of her arms, the muscles in her arms, holding this weight. She was aware of gravity's pull, of the thousand invisible forces acting upon her.

All of a sudden, she was enveloped by a kind of vertigo—she had felt this sensation before, though she could not remember when. It was a feeling of being not herself, of being trapped in the wrong body, as if she had recently been miscast in a play that was her own life.

She felt herself listing; she was suddenly worried that she would collapse onto the baby. In desperation, she uttered a single sound, something soft and round, like *"Hwah."* And then, just as quickly as it had come, the feeling evaporated, leaving her with only herself again and the hazy memory of a counterfeit existence.

She clutched him. His breath against her neck. Those fierce scoops of oxygen. He was aware of none of her turmoil. He simply was. Breathing.

If only she could just breathe.

When she was sure he was asleep again, she carefully placed him next to his stuffed bear and slipped from the room. Still dressed in her nightgown, she slid into her boots and left the apartment.

As soon as she stepped outside, she smelled it. A stench like singed flesh. Several fire trucks had already arrived. At first she couldn't see what the source of the smell was. She gagged and closed her eyes. Hand over her mouth, she looked up again and realized why she hadn't seen anything. There was nothing there: the giant ginkgo tree across the street, such a familiar anchor to their world, was gone. *Vanished.* A yawning, empty space where its canopy had once resided.

"What happened?" she asked a neighbor who was standing nearby, smoking a cigarette in his bathrobe.

"Lightning," he said. "Freak strike. Could've killed someone."

And now she saw the huge chunks of wood lying all over the road, on top of people's cars. One piece had landed forty yards away in a bed of daffodils. The heat from the electricity had burst the tree like a melon. Against a palette of blue and red emergency lights, she stood with her neighbors and watched as firemen worked at dislodging a missile-size log from Mrs. Garrison's front window. The roar of chain saws filled the night. She tried not to breathe, since every time she got a waft of the smell, she felt as if she might vomit.

Nearby, a bleary-eyed boy stood holding his mother's hand. His face read the twin emotions of terror and fascination as he watched the firemen unwind the destruction. Charlene saw his mother lean over and whisper into his ear. The boy nodded, without taking his eyes off the scene. In his hand he was clutching a little piece of wood. It must've come from the tree. The wind shifted, and Charlene was again hit by a horrific wash of burnt flesh. She heaved and fled back into her apartment building. Through the portal in the front door she looked, but the boy and his mother were gone.

She couldn't sleep. Through the windows she watched them cut up the tree. They loaded the pieces into a truck and hauled them away. She paced. She looked in on Radar. She washed and rewashed her hands. At some point, she fetched Dr. Fitzgerald's handwritten letter from the manila folder. When the sun finally rose, she picked up the telephone and dialed the number beneath the letterhead. It was much too early to call, she knew, and no one would answer, but it comforted her to hear the ringing on the other end. It meant there *was* an other end. The line rang and rang. The rings began to bleed together.

And then: "Hello?"

It was a man's voice. She was caught completely off guard.

"Hello?" the voice said again. She could tell he was getting ready to hang up.

"Yes." She came to life. "I'd . . . I'd like to speak to Dr. Fitzgerald, please."

"Speaking."

"Oh!" she said. It was him. She had not expected it to be him. A secretary, perhaps, but not him.

"Oh," she said again. "I'm sorry to call you so early."

A silence on the other end.

"I'm . . . I'm Charlene Radmanovic. You wrote us a letter."

"*Ah.*" The voice shifted. She could hear the squeak of a chair in the background. "Mrs. Radmanovic. I'm so glad you called."

"Please," she said after a moment.

"Yes?"

"I don't know what to do anymore."

"In regards to what?"

"My son."

"Your son?"

"I need to know what happened."

"Well, that makes two of us."

"I need to know what I did to him."

There was a pause. "Why don't you come up here and see me? We can discuss everything."

Gratefully, she fell into the plush confines of his expertise. Twice a month, Charlene and Radar would ride the train up to Boston, all expenses paid, and visit the doctor's laboratory, inside the twisting hospital complex next to the old city jail. From the moment she sat down in his office, she realized that he was the doctor she had always imagined before all of those useless specialists had unraveled her faith in the medical profession. He maintained a distinct air of calm that was neither contrived nor austere. Though he was already well into his sixties, he seemed both younger and older than this—perhaps it was the way in which he quoted Japanese proverbs with ease while sipping on a can of Tab soda. If he had not been a doctor, she could have seen him as a soft-spoken Sedona guru pursued by legions of followers.

Her many late nights reading textbooks and obscure dermatological articles had turned her into a bit of an expert in the field, and she had already familiarized herself with Dr. Fitzgerald's many impressive achievements. After two years in the Army, a fellowship at Oxford, and a series of high-profile research projects on melanoma tumor growth at the Mayo Clinic, he had become, at age thirty-nine, Harvard Medical School's youngest chaired professor. Now, nearly thirty years later, he had just released a revolutionary schema to classify the color of skin. Designed primarily for dermatologists to diagnose skin types, Fitzgerald's classification system was an attempt to update the largely problematic Von Luschan chromatic scale from 1897, which separated all human skin tone into thirty-six tiers. In the first half of the twentieth century, "respected" anthropometrists like George Vacher de Lapouge and Carleton S. Coon had drawn upon Von Luschan's scale in order to categorize and sublimate racial populations within the extremely dubious discipline of "race science." Following the Holocaust and the events of World War II, Von Luschan's scale had largely been abandoned by the scientific community.

Fitzgerald's system, by contrast, jettisoned such nuanced and largely subjective differentiation for a much more generalized six-point scale, focusing not on racial categorization but rather on the skin's responsiveness to UV light, ranging from Type I (scores 0–6), "pale white; always burns, never tans," to Type VI (scores 35+), "deeply pigmented dark brown to black; never burns, tans easily." To his credit, Dr. Fitzgerald appeared well aware of the great potential for misuse of his schema. In a 1976 *Archives of Dermatology* editorial, in which he elucidated his motivation for creating such a scale, Dr. Fitzgerald also issued a warning, which Charlene had underlined in red pen: "Given the destructive history of trying to classify a person's race based upon various phenotypical attributes, under no circumstances should the Fitzgerald scale be mistaken for any kind of comprehensive racial classification. . . . [Appearance] alone does not dictate an individual's reaction to ultraviolet radiation nor his or her membership in any racial grouping. . . . [The] clues to our composition, more often than not, lie beneath the surface" (Fitzgerald 1976, 142).

"You," the doctor said to Radar on their first visit to Boston as Radar sat in his lap, wondering at the pad of the doctor's stethoscope. "*You* are the most special person I've ever met." He twirled his hands in the air: one finger became two, and then two became one. A simple metamorphosis that made Radar giggle in amazement.

Radar was comfortable with Dr. Fitzgerald from the start, but then he was comfortable around most. Though he was only two and a half, his short life had been one of constant medical inspection, and Radar had become pliable in a doctor's hands. He had come to expect these intrusions into his person, for he had known no other existence than that of the examined. Perhaps because of this, he remained a silent child. Even his cries were fleeting, muted affairs, as if he was reluctant to disrupt the world around him.

"This is fine," said Dr. Fitzgerald. "Many children take a while to find their voice. My mother always told me that I didn't speak until I was three. And you know what? Those were the happiest days of my life. What's the rush to join the chorus? Most of the time, we say nothing of consequence."

During their second visit, after a day of testing basic reflexes, blood work, and UV tests, Radar fell asleep on the doctor's examination table. He appeared at peace, forgiving of all trespasses, and as they admired him, the doctor spoke lovingly: "'Oh, the nerves, the nerves; the mysteries of this machine called man! Oh, the little that unhinges it, poor creatures that we are!'"

Charlene stared. A button depressed.

"Dickens?" she ventured.

He nodded. "*The Chimes*. He's a well I return to often."

This led to a surprisingly impassioned back-and-forth on which was his best work (he: *Bleak House;* she: *Great Expectations*) and whether or not the serialized novel could ever be revived. It was a literary cauldron she had not stirred in years. The talk of books quickened her pulse and dampened the divot just above her lip.

She sat back, marveling.

"What is it?" said the doctor.

"I just hadn't expected this . . . It's not usual that you talk about these things with a doctor," she said. "And I've met quite a few lately. I thought you were all . . ."

"What?"

"Boring?" she ventured.

He laughed. "Most of us are, I'm afraid. You know, it's funny, but I find that books are essential to my profession. I'm a better surgeon if a story has its claws in me. All I need is a little dose of Melville or Dickens and his dirty alleyways, and my scalpel grows steady."

She had a vision of him lounging in his surgeon's gown between surgeries, his feet thrown up on the operating table as he savored the last few pages of *Bleak House*.

"I know I shouldn't admit it," she said, "but a part of me always struggled with Dickens. Sometimes it feels like he's just trying so damn hard. His characters aren't real, you know what I mean? They're like these little parts of a machine. Like that man who just spontaneously combusted in the middle of the book—"

"Krook."

"Yes, Krook. That always bothered me. I mean, it's so careless to make a character disappear like that. Either he wants us to know that it's just a novel and he's in total control or he just wants to annoy us for caring."

The doctor smiled. "As a man of science, of course, I would find it highly unlikely that a person could simply combust into thin air without provocation . . . and yet . . ." He paused, thinking. "The distance between the world within the book and our own world must be exactly right—it cannot be too near or too far. That distance is what I savor: Krook combusts. We see him combust, and his combustion gives me courage. I can walk around it. I can run my hands beneath it. The combustion is here, and I am there. Do you know what I mean?"

"Not really," she said, though she knew exactly what he meant.

He nodded. "If I show you something, will you promise not to laugh?"

"Well, I can try," she said. "I can't promise. I tend to do the opposite of what I'm told."

He bent down and retrieved a typewriter from beneath his desk. Then a tall stack of paper covered in print. Finally, a thick burgundy book. A flicker of the familiar ran through Charlene. He slid the stack of pages over to her.

"I haven't shown this to anyone before," he said. "Not even my wife."

She read the first line aloud: "Happy families are all alike; every unhappy family is unhappy in its own way."

She looked up. "*Anna Karenina.*"

"The greatest novel ever written," he said. "Okay—we can debate it."

"No," she said. "I agree."

"Well, then. We don't have to debate."

She glanced through the stack of pages. It was the entire novel. Typed out, word for word.

"What is this?" she said. *How had he known? This book, of all books.*

"It's a little crazy, I admit, but I suppose I wanted to see what would happen to that distance if I wrote the book myself."

"You've retyped the whole thing?"

"Oh, no. It isn't finished," he said. "I'm a slow typer."

She stared at the pages. She could see places where he had whited out his mistakes. The words bent and swayed in her vision. She had read these words so many times before, but she had never seen them like this. Now they felt entirely alive, ready to jump off the page and fight her with their kinetic energy. She flipped to the last page. The story cut off in midsentence. Why had he not bothered to even finish the sentence? She touched the spot where the words ended, rubbing the paper, as if she could invoke whatever comes next.

"I probably shouldn't have shown you this," he said quickly.

"No—" she said, but he was already reaching for the pages. Their fingertips brushed against one another. A shot ran through her arm.

"Are you all right?" he said.

"I don't know." She suddenly felt ill.

"You don't look well."

He came around the desk and took her wrist in his hand. Two fingers pressed at her pulse. There was certainty in that touch, manifested from a lifetime of expertise. He was counting in his head. The skin where he was touching her felt as if it were burning. She let him lift her chin. He shined a light into her eyes. Her head swam. Something stirred between her legs.

He was old enough to be her father. Older. And yet . . .

"I'm fine," she said, pushing him away. "Really, I'm fine."

She was in such a state that she did not remember the rest of their visit, but as she was leaving with Radar in her arms, still caught in a murky farrago of desire, the doctor put a hand on her shoulder. Again, that heat. Her pulse, beating.

"One more thing," he said.

"Yes?"

"I'm going to need a quart of your husband's blood."

"A quart?" she said.

"I assure you, it's nothing personal. We simply must look at every possibility."

BACK HOME in their apartment, for the first time in more than three years, she stared at the jumble of books on her shelves. She wiped a layer of dust from her abandoned copy of *Anna Karenina*. It was the 1965 Modern Library hardcover edition. A copper stain like a half moon along the fore edge. She opened the book and read the first few lines, smelling the faint tendrils of mildew trapped within its spine, but she felt none of the same electricity that the doctor's facsimile had elicited in her. She slid the book back into its empty slot and scanned the rows of forgotten titles. *The French Lieutenant's Woman. Ada, or Ardor. Hopscotch.* Why had she deserted them so completely? These books, once her lifeblood, had become a graveyard. She could not blame the books for everything that had gone wrong. The books were a smoke screen. The books gave only what they got.

She stood a moment more in front of the bookshelf, then she retrieved the copy of *Anna Karenina* again. She found her old typewriter beneath the bed, rolled a fresh page into the platen, and began to type.

WHEN ASKED, CHARLENE had always explained away her life as a series of false starts that finally had disqualified her from running the race. It was a convenient shorthand metaphor, though, like all metaphors, it was not quite true.

Since childhood, she had combated her low-grade neuroses with the infinite act of indexing. Unlike her older sister Vivienne, who had started dying her hair blond at thirteen and had safely married a Florida real estate mogul by the time she turned twenty-one, wiry, pale Charlene had grown up uncomfortable in her own skin, and yet she seemed to revel in this discomfort, no doubt due in part to a pervasive intellect that she had never quite been able to tame. At age nine, she began collecting obituaries from the *New York Times,* completely taken with the act of summarizing a life in only a couple hundred words. She collected classics of the genre—"Emilie Dionne, 20; Nun, Quintuplet"; "Marion Tinsley, 55; Checkers Champion Who Regularly Beat Men"—and then began to pen her own for (still living) neighbors, friends, and family.

"My little deaths," she called them. *"Mes petites morts."* (She had just started taking French, though she did not pick up on the sexual overtones of her declaration.) Such a morbid fascination had elicited a worried burst of letters from her teacher, until it was determined that this, like everything else, must be just a phase.

Charlene was a voracious, practically manic reader, and her bedroom in the attic had quickly filled with books that threatened to overrun the house. Her mother, Louise, the grammar instructor, recognized the imminent bibliographic chaos brewing above their heads. She warned her younger daughter about the dangers of disorder:

"When you can't find something," she said, "it may as well not exist."

This pronouncement struck an elemental chord in young Charlene. She felt a great panic welling up just beyond the boundaries of her consciousness, so she asked her father to help her build floor-to-ceiling shelves in her bedroom. Charlene then took up organizing all of her books alphabetically by the author's last

name, an incredibly satisfying task that made her fingertips tingle with anticipation of the distinct order she was carving out of nothing. Except that when
she was finished, the allure of such an index was swiftly overshadowed by the
consequent hollowness of the system: the author's name was divorced from what
was actually taking place in the books themselves. *The Age of Innocence,* for instance, written by Wharton, E., was marooned on the very bottom shelf, which
did not seem right at all. She set about discovering a new method of intimate
organization that came as close as possible to mirroring the peaks and valleys of
her own mind. In fact, she was chasing that same first tingle in the fingertips, a
sensation she would never be able to quite replicate. Still, she searched. Painstakingly, over a period of months, she arranged and then rearranged the books
using increasingly obscure criteria: first it was alphabetically by subject, then by
character, then according to a much more mystical system based on how important each book was to her, a scheme that inevitably shifted daily and required
constant tending. She even made a card catalog system for her collection of
books and periodicals and created a ledger book with checkout slips for lending.
Her mother offered to give her an old date stamper from school, but she refused,
instead deciding to steal one from their local public library. It was by far the
worst thing she had ever done, but it made her own library feel bona fide, legiti-
mated by an act of petty larceny. When it was finally all ready to go, she put
posters up at school touting the grand opening of the Volmer Collection Privée.
This was what she called it, thinking herself quite grown up for knowing a
French word like *privée.* On Saturday, she set up a desk by her bedroom door
and waited for the people to come explore her vast, perfectly organized *collection
privée.*

But no one came. No one sought her advice for irresistible summer reads, for
books that could change your life, for books that could make you cry, but in the
way that we love to cry. No one came, least of all her sister, who viewed reading
as a deplorable habit, akin to picking one's nose. That afternoon, her mother
ascended the stairs with a plate of chocolate chip cookies and checked out *The
Phantom Tollbooth,* though Charlene could tell she was not going to read the
book and was just doing it so that the ledger book would not stand empty.

"Where did you get this stamp?" Louise asked as Charlene checked her out.

"Your book is due in two weeks," Charlene said, imprinting the card with great violence.

That evening, as she lay in bed reading *The Scarlet Letter*, Charlene realized she was relieved that the masses hadn't come to pilfer her shelves. Society was the only threat to the sanctity of selfhood: an unpatroned library was an orderly library. Thereafter, lending privileges were suspended for everyone except herself, which was probably a good thing, for her methods of organizing the books continued to change until it was impossible for anyone except Charlene to find the book they might be looking for. Even she struggled with the logic of the system: somewhere in her library she lost her copy of *The Scarlet Letter* and never managed to find it again.

She would graduate summa cum laude from Douglass College in 1966, with a B.A. in English, one of the last all-female classes before the college merged with Rutgers. Instead of listening to her conscience and pursuing a professional life of books, she had decided to test her luck in the big city, selling high-end women's footwear and perfume in a spotless, cathedral-ceilinged department store on Madison Avenue. It was not a good match. It didn't take her long to realize that success at the job was dependent not on sophistication or her instinctual prowess for predicting trends in the sociocultural zeitgeist but rather on wearing the right kitten heel pumps so as to encourage sexual harassment from the boss. Charlene quit her job—dramatically, fittingly—by throwing a rare bottle of Diorissimo across the store, its shattered remains filling the room with the intense velveteen wash of lily of the valley.

She lived, practically for free, in a grimy fourth-floor walk-up in Hell's Kitchen, with two twin Dadaist painters named Lila and Vespers. The twins slept all day in the same bed and, from what she could tell, were locked in some kind of ménage à trois with the same man. Their art, which they worked on in tandem, involved pasting found objects—scissors, thimbles, shoelaces—onto a canvas, painting these objects white and then creating false labels for each item. "Scissors" became "meatloaf," and so on. Charlene was not impressed.

Lila and Vespers also frequently enjoyed "expanding their horizons," as they termed it. Before she met them, Charlene had never even seen a drug. She had drunk in college now and then, but cautiously, for she had never enjoyed relinquishing control, and she sensed her possession of the same gene that had left her aunt in a vodka-fueled stupor in western Pennsylvania. The gene was almost certainly present in her sister Vivienne, as evidenced by her daily succession of postmeridian double martinis.

One evening, Charlene reluctantly tagged along with Lila and Vespers to a party in a Lower East Side basement. The theme was "The Future." The twins wrapped themselves in tinfoil. Charlene went costumeless. At some point Lila or Vespers—it did not matter which—handed her a tab of acid, which she surprised herself by considering for only the briefest of instants before popping into her mouth. Later that night, on the Brooklyn Bridge, she also tried her first quaalude, or what a man in a mustache said was a quaalude. The night was transcendent, but not because of the drugs—she felt as if she had shed a skin, as if anything was possible now.

As she did with everything, Charlene became very obsessed with getting high. It turned into a game, and then it turned into more than a game. Her parents had reluctantly agreed to supply her with a small monthly allowance until she got "her feet back on the ground." She returned this favor by spending their money on cheap Spanish wine and various barbiturates and psychedelics, which Lila and Vespers initially supplied her and which she eventually supplied herself via their contact, a boorish fisherman named Vlada, who most likely was not a fisherman at all. She met people at the parties. *Those parties.* At first she went with the twins and then she went alone. It was just that if you dipped into it, you were utterly consumed. You couldn't go halfway. Charlene felt that she was a part of something very important, something utterly new. This was New York. This was 1967. As the rest of America continued to button its top button, she howled into the night with artists and beboppers and hippies, tripping down the Bowery, high as a kite, debating the ideas of Sartre and Simone de Beauvoir and Hannah Arendt with anyone who cared to listen. She fell in love. She fell out of love. There were a number of men. There were a number of men with mustaches. There was even one woman. And it was this woman who introduced Charlene to Hazel, which is what she called heroin. In retrospect, this was a horrifically innocent moniker. Charlene had always been terrified of needles, but when she felt the drop for the first time, the warmth that erased inside from out, the seven thousand hands upon her, she realized she had found exactly what she was looking for.

It was wonderful. It was wonderful and wonderful and wonderful, until it wasn't wonderful anymore. She quickly burned through her allowance. She sold all of her books to the Strand Bookstore save two—*A Tale of Two Cities* and a recently purchased copy of *Anna Karenina* upon which she had spilled lukewarm tea. The trouble was that even the drugs did not fully extinguish her systemic neuroses, her tingling desire for order. Each morning, she would choose which way to sequence the pair of books. There were only two options, two dichotomous takes on the world. She rearranged them nonetheless. Each was plausible, but not quite true: *Did the city make the woman or did the woman make the city?*

Beyond the confines of that shelf, however, the city itself could not be ordered. The tines of disarray would put her to bed each night, gnawing at the recesses of her mind as she lay there sleepless, and they would greet her each morning when she awoke with a splitting headache to the idling motors of graffitied delivery trucks or the wail of police sirens. Soon the drugs were all there was. Every moment in her day was organized around either acquiring them, taking them, or recovering from their effects. Her body was not so much hers as a vehicle that she occasionally tended. Even the twins, who were some of the most unobservant people she knew, began to remark upon her descent.

In November, after vomiting for the fifth morning in a row and fearing some permanent damage, Charlene finally dragged herself to a hospital. The doctor performed some tests and told her she was suffering from a most common condition: she was pregnant.

"What do you mean, *pregnant?*" she said.

"Do you want me to draw you a diagram?" he said.

As she was leaving, he looked up from his desk. "If I may," he said. "You're now responsible for two people. Everything you put into you, you are also putting into your baby."

Charlene sat in the kitchen with the twins and the malnourished creeper plant, trying to imagine a theoretical child with each of her ghostly mustached lovers, an exercise that caused her to start hyperventilating.

"It's no big deal," said Lila. "We know someone who can fix it."

"He's creepy but cheap," Vespers added. Vespers wore a faux-gypsy rhine-stone headband, even while sleeping. It was a convenient clue for telling the two apart.

Lila handed Charlene the number, scrawled on the back of a prescription bottle. "Don't worry, ShaLa, we've both used him," she said. Charlene had no idea where their nickname for her had come from. They were the kind of people who gave nicknames to mark their territory.

From her lineup of potential progenitors—a shady group whose member-ship grew the more she thought about the extent of her nocturnal encounters—Charlene could not help but gravitate to one man, hoping against hope that it was he who was the father. His name was T. K.—short for what? She couldn't remember anymore, or maybe she had never known. T. K., the black boy from St. Paul, Minnesota, with the warm eyes and the learned prairie laugh, no doubt picked up from one of his white foster parents. Mere months after V-J Day, buoyed by the promise of a new era, they had adopted T. K. after hearing his story on the radio: his birth family had perished in a downtown slum fire, and he had survived the blaze by being hurled to safety out of a fourth-story window into the arms of a firefighter. He was six months old.

At least this is what T. K. told Charlene during one of their precious nights together, lying naked in her bed, ankles touching, the twins arguing loudly about Gauguin in the next room. Charlene had imagined his little Minnesotan family—T. K. and his progressive white parents, dressed in down parkas, sur-rounded by mounds and mounds of snow. He had been first in his class at Humboldt High. Full scholarship to Macalester College. He was one of the smartest people she had ever met, and yet quite clearly sheltered to a fault, for he had been raised on Schubert and Robert Louis Stevenson, had never owned a television, and had never even been out of the state before he left on a bus for Columbia University's College of Physicians and Surgeons, smack in the middle of Washington Heights.

"Whatever were they thinking?" Charlene could not help saying out loud.

Naked, T. K. had looked over at her and asked her what she meant by this and she said nothing, but she remembered feeling a kind of infinite sadness. To let a kid like him, a *miracle* like him, loose in the city? The city relished the chance to eat people like him for breakfast. In the end, of course, she was wrong: it was not him but her whom the city would devour, but she would not understand this until much later, when she was already safely in its belly.

She had first met T. K. at one of those sweaty, drug-heavy midnight Bleecker Street parties, where he had shown up with a fellow first-year med student, looking bewildered and comically out of place in an ill-fitting three-piece linen number, as if he were about to participate in a grade-school ballroom dance competition. She had laughed out loud when she saw him like this, and yet she had also fallen *hard,* very hard—she could not explain why. Encouraged by the lingering buzz of a Nembutal cocktail, she made a beeline across the room, greeting him with an overly familiar kiss and pulling him, despite his earnest protestations, into a round of astrological strip Ouija.

Things had slipped into place that night, as they sometimes do, and they had both surprised themselves by going back to her place and fucking with what she mistook for a mechanical midwestern urgency and with what he mistook for a groovy East Coast blasé. There had been an incredibly awkward moment when he, still naked, had fumbled for his linen trousers and then produced, unceremoniously, a roll of crumpled bills and offered them to her. She stared at him, bewildered, so offended and yet so moved by his innocence that she started to laugh and pushed the money back at him.

"It was a joke," he said hastily, repocketing the bills, though the look in his eyes told her he had no idea what to think. They lay in bed afterwards, and he pointed to every bone in her body and named them for her—every bone, including all twenty-eight bones of the skull. Touching her own cranium with her fingertips, she marveled at the power of the naming: to conjure twenty-eight things when before there was only one.

For two weeks, T. K. occupied her every waking thought. Together they explored the city, laughing at the intricacies of urban density—the joy of a child leaping through an open fire hydrant, a ninety-year-old woman walking five shih tzus, an impromptu performance art–cum–Mod dance contest in the middle of Forty-second Street as taxicabs blared their horns—she seeing it all through his eyes for the first time. She wanted to protect him and she wanted to be ravaged by him. It was the closest thing she had felt to love. She shot up only twice during this time, and never in front of him. It felt like cheating.

Strangely, he refused to take her back to his apartment in Washington Heights. He claimed his place was too small.

"I don't care," she said. "I want to see where you live."

"It's not fit for someone like you," he said and kissed her on the eyebrow, where she had a tiny scar from falling down the stairs as a child.

And then everything imploded, suddenly, as if it had always been meant to implode like this, as if time were only a prelude to all that which must come to an end. He met her outside her apartment one morning and said he could not see her anymore.

"Why?" she said, crying. She felt the panic rising in her chest. And she wanted to ask, "Is it because I'm white?" and she hated herself for wondering this and she hated herself for not asking it.

And he said, "I just need to concentrate more on school," even though they both knew it was not true, and what was true would never—could never—be said.

Years later, she would see him again, after having spent many nights dreaming of his voice, his body, his laugh, after searching for him in the streets, at the parties, on the subways, in the parks, in the shadows of the skyscrapers that towered above her. He came calling on her in New Jersey, quite out of the blue—she couldn't really make out how he had managed to track her down. She was already dating Kermin by then, but when T. K. showed up on her doorstep, it was as if no time had passed. They had sat for a coffee, and she had wanted to ask him a thousand questions—how he had managed, whether the world had defeated him or he had managed to defeat it—but they had not talked about these things or about anything else she could recall. Nor did she ever get to ask him what his initials stood for. Maybe they didn't stand for anything. And then he was gone again, this time for good, and it was as if she had experienced a dream in which she dreamed of a dream she had had long ago.

And so, as she sat in the kitchen with the twins, she made a secret prayer to God or some vague stand-in for God that the father of her unborn child be

T. K. and not Cal, the serial narcissist, or Hector, the Peruvian dealer who had shown her his gun and called her *"mi pequeño coño."*

She considered keeping the child. Raising him alone. She really did. Particularly if it was T. K.'s—she could see herself devoting the rest of her life to raising his brilliant little son. Reading him Robert Louis Stevenson. Telling him about the father he never knew. But then she had a fever dream in which she was trapped in an infinitely long hall of white doors, all of them without doorknobs. Each door was unlocked, she knew, but she had no way of opening them. She woke up sweating, terrified. For the first time, the baby growing inside her felt foreign, thrust upon her by a guiltless world.

The next morning, she called the number the twins had written on the prescription bottle and then rode the subway up to Harlem to the fixer's house. In the subway car, she found herself studying the faces of the weary black men, willing them to be T. K., willing them to come rescue her from what she was about to do.

The fixer's name was Jarmal, and he was not charming in the least. He took her into his living room, where there was a yellowing dentist's chair in the middle of a stained afghan rug. The room's shelving was stuffed with collected Oriental tchotchkes that had been hastily covered in plastic sheeting, creating the impression of an impromptu crime scene.

"Take off your clothes and then take this," he said, handing her a pill.

Afterwards, she was so groggy and in such excruciating pain that she forgot to ask if the fetus had been black, whether you could even tell that kind of thing before a baby was born.

She paid him $75 for his services. All things considered, this seemed like a fairly good deal until she developed an infection one week later that landed her in the St. Luke's emergency room. It was the day before Thanksgiving. Her parents arrived, horrified at the doctor's declaration that their youngest daughter had come within "two hours of dying," whatever this meant. Vivienne even called her on the phone, her honeydew voice mimicking concern, with mixed results. Her sister was cursed with the unexamined libertarian ignorance that only the very privileged could espouse: she believed everything that happened to you, good or bad, was the result of your own choosing. The problem was that in Charlene's case, this was most likely true.

Charlene refused her parents' offer to help her recuperate in their soft Trenton lair and (this part was implied) to take stock of how far she had fallen with a Rutgers degree in hand. Wounded, they made sure she was going to live and then promptly cut off her allowance.

She convalesced back in her squalid little Hell's Kitchen den, hardly leaving her bed for almost three weeks. Unexpectedly, Lila and Vespers displayed some real maternal behavior, checking in with her nightly and bringing her back sad little clumps of foraged groceries. They even chipped in to cover her rent that month. Charlene, feeling the full effects of her withdrawal, pleaded for opioids. To their credit, the twins refused. Charlene became manic. More than once, she seriously considered suicide. Her only solace was a stray cat that frequented their fire escape. She fed him butter pats and named him Bumble Bee—Bee for short. Bee had a gift for non-judgment.

She rediscovered her books. She read and reread *A Tale of Two Cities* and then devoured *Anna Karenina* three times through. The words suddenly all felt new, as if they had been freshly planted on the page. She developed a pathological kinship for Anna's character. Charlene was not deterred by her limited selection; rather, the repeated rhythms of the narratives beat back the wet terror festering inside her chest.

When she was well enough to leave the apartment, she made two decisions: (1) She would find a job, a real job, and (2) she would go clean. Her fortitude on item number 2 felt shaky, so she wrote her intentions for sobriety down onto a piece of monogrammed stationery that her parents had given her the previous Christmas. She initialed the page and then hid it beneath the floorboards of her room.

In fact, it was her fortitude on item number 1 that proved the problem. She was not good at finding a job. There was something liberating about being completely broke in New York. Or maybe she was just lazy. She began spending all of her waking hours at the Strand, reading entire novels as she stood next to the towering rows of shelving. What a strange population haunted those aisles:

maharajas and heart surgeons, shell-shocked vets and Shakespeare scholars, hunchbacked pensioners and schizoid hoboes. Lured by literature or the promise of literature, they came and they usually stayed, and some of them slept and a few of them peed. She read the rest of Tolstoy, then Dostoyevsky, then Dickens, and when she tired of Dickens she turned to Woolf and then Melville. She read the *Iliad*. She read the new Vonnegut. She read *The Crying of Lot 49* and afterwards was so overcome with what we are able to accomplish with the simple constellation of words that she walked right out of the store in a daze, forgetting that she was holding the book in her hands.

A hand grabbed her shoulder. She turned to find a cute, bespectacled young man doing his best impression of an angry manager. He demanded the book back, threatening some kind of intense police intervention. Realizing her folly, Charlene began to apologize profusely, though she also couldn't help but be amused by this man's clear dislocation from the outside world. He was a fish out of water; he belonged back among the books. Relieved, the man quickly dropped his austere routine, and soon they were both absorbed in a cyclical conversation about Pynchon, right there on the sidewalk amid the December rush of shoppers. The bookstore and the city and everything else fell away, and the universe contained only him and her and the delightful possibility of the Trystero all around them. She was not sure how much time had passed, but she surprised herself by asking him for a job. She was good, she said. She knew what the books needed.

The man's name was Petar—it was spelled with an *a,* as she would later come to learn. Needless to say, she was hired. Needless to say, she also began sleeping with Petar. He was kind and gentle and terribly nerdy. Together they got matching tattoos of the Trystero post horn on their ankles. The relationship lasted just long enough to make her believe that she was capable of caring again.

The job itself was a revelation. She loved haunting the bookstore after hours, glimpsing the occasional spine of an old library copy, its Dewey Decimal numbers protected by a crumbling layer of Scotch tape. She began to memorize the index of Dewey Decimal subjects, pairing those numerals with its far-flung content:

813: American fiction

883: Classical Greek epic poetry and fiction

646.7: Personal grooming

179.7: Euthanasia

621.38416: Radio operations (ham)

The system was a salve against the chaos of life, and the disparate glimpses of its calculus made her miss the rigorous order of a true library, where each volume was slotted into place like a giant stopwatch of human knowledge. She realized she had been avoiding her calling. Books, the cataloging of books, that pursuit without end, was the only way to quell the panic.

She applied and was accepted into the master's program in library science at Syracuse. The year was 1969. Back in her parents' good graces, she borrowed their nearly expired woody, packed up everything she owned, which was not all that much, bade the melancholic twins, Bee, Petar, and the great city adieu, and headed north.

It was a tough time to be a librarian. It was never easy to be a keeper of books, but it was particularly tough during that turnover winter of '69, a hinge point when the world rubbed its eyes and realized all was not as it seemed. Students were too busy protesting and talking about protesting to really read anything of substance, and libraries shifted from being quiet places of study to social justice performance spaces and raucous backdrops for self-important sit-ins. The books, poor things, suffered the brunt of this indignity. Various wet concoctions were thrown around in the stacks that should not have been thrown around in the stacks. The books were used as props, shelter, weapons. Precious manuscripts, seen as relics of the establishment, were soiled with palimpsestic hippie poetry and bodily fluids. Students stole everything by Nietzsche and Marx. The entire section on Zen Buddhism (294.3927) disappeared overnight. Charlene found herself shooing away half-naked couples smoking grass and/or fornicating in the stacks on a daily basis. Heavy times. Groovy times. Just not for a librarian. Charlene might've cared more about the whole movement if she hadn't found it all so completely juvenile. She felt like an older sister watching her younger siblings tear apart the house while their parents were away.

There was a professor in her department, H. H., whom she greatly admired. He excelled at that high-wire act—unique to the professorial métier—of appearing both desperately out of fashion and yet also far ahead of his time. A wearer of herringbone tweeds, H. H. had a thick mass of brown hair that, despite vigorous morning placations with a comb, always seemed to untangle gravity's spell by lunchtime. He was a true scientist of books, the only person she had met whom she could definitively call a genius. H. H. was working with a library in Ohio to develop a computerized system that would eventually replace the card catalog. He and Charlene got into endless arguments about this—she defending the sanctity of the cards and he dismissing them as already outdated, an anchor weighing down civilization's eternal march forward.

"Paper will soon be a thing of the past," he said. "It probably already is."

"And so what of the library? Should we just burn down all of our cultural cathedrals?"

"The library is not a cultural cathedral. It is an outdated warehouse." He put a hand on her shoulder. "Progress, my dear. It's the only truth in life. There are some things that you just cannot fight, though I must admit, I find it quite charming when you do."

When Houston Revere, a drawl-edged southerner in her program, asked her if she was sleeping with H. H. yet, she responded with a surprisingly venomous denial.

He held up his hands defensively. "I'll take that as a yes," he said.

On the one hand, it would've been so easy to slide down such a path. Her time in the city had left her with a sexual aptitude that she was not necessarily proud of. She knew that men found her particular mixture of melancholy and candor alluring, but every time she thought of H. H.'s hands upon her (and she would admit, she had thought of those hands, of running her own hands through that pritchkemp mane), she was filled with a sense of terror, of falling backwards into a lake with no bottom. This was familiar territory that she had sworn off for the abstinence of the bibliography. She did not want to turn back. His lingering gaze, despite the heat it elicited in her chest, felt like a force prying her fingers off the tiller.

And so she started sleeping with (it must be said, a somewhat surprised) Houston. True to his southern roots, Houston was polite and oddly balletic in bed, but altogether prosaic. When he came, he sounded like a seagull. It was just what she was looking for. She fought off all uncertainties with the banality of their lovemaking.

Then, in May, the shootings at Kent State popped the balloon of tension that had been steadily inflating that entire spring. Students all across the country recoiled at pictures of bodies lying facedown on the pavement like lonely, discarded mannequins. These pictures were pictures of them: *they* could've been lying on that pavement, with young runaways wailing above them at the bewildered National Guardsmen: *What have you done? What have you done? What have you done*

At Syracuse, the academic pursuit seemed wholly worthless in the face of such mortality, and so the remainder of that semester withered and died with barely a whimper. Exams were optional; students, unsure of what still lassoed them to campus, clustered around boys with guitars on the quad who tried to mimic Dylan's whining pontifications. As she hurried past these sing-alongs en route to the Carnegie Library, Charlene silently tsked their laziness, their disheveled, E-minor self-importance. Where was Homer when you needed him? *Mēnis*—rage so pure it could be felt only by the gods:

Rage—Goddess, sing the rage of Peleus' son Achilles,
murderous, doomed, that cost the Achaeans countless losses,
hurling down to the House of Death so many sturdy souls.

These boys with guitars wouldn't know real rage if it clobbered them on the head. They had no idea. Achilles, who became so intoxicated with *mēnis* after the Trojans murdered his lover, Patroclus, that he killed everyone in sight, and when their bodies choked the waters, he fought the river god, too. Achilles, who finally tracked down Hector, his lover's murderer, and threw a spear straight through his neck, tying him to his chariot and dragging him around Troy for nine days until the mass of flesh became unrecognizable as anything human. *That* was dedication. Not these slow-jam-acoustic-hashish-hippie symposia. This was the curse of the voracious reader, she realized. Real life never quite measured up to the heightened and precise contours of her literary worlds. A real war was never as true as a fictive one.

One night, she was working late in the bowels of the library, reorganizing the card catalog—something she often did when she did not want to face the solitude of her insomnia. The campus was practically empty, so she was surprised when H. H. appeared in the doorway, his tie undone, his hair standing at attention. His car was not working, he said. Would she mind if he waited here with her?

She did not ask what he was waiting for. They spoke briefly of something potentially meaningful, about the viability of protest, about the inevitability of cultural evolution. A theorist was mentioned. There was a silence. She was aware of the space between them. And then he was coming toward her, and she could hear the card rustle in her hands and she could smell the drink on his breath and then he was upon her, with his mouth open and his tongue wandering in circles, and she was receiving this tongue, falling into him, hating him.

"Charlene," he whispered. "I've wanted this for so long."

He undid his corduroy trousers and placed his hand on the back of her head and pushed her down and she took him into her mouth.

IN THE END, she barely slipped out of Syracuse with a degree. Her version of the narrative blamed everything on that night, located his assailment as a kind of anti–deus ex machina, where the universe performed its ultimate act of subterfuge while she was busy trying to play by the rules. It was *analyse réductrice,* but it gave her an excuse to drop the tiller entirely.

She started to drink again, with an enthusiasm honed by a year and a half of sobriety. She bounced around several Jersey librarianships, but she had no appetite for the job anymore. The books mocked her. She now saw the arbitrariness of the Dewey system as an exercise in futility—clearly, it was impossible to classify anything of real consequence. Meanwhile, Louise and Bertrand, once so hopeful for their daughter's turnaround, worried at her sharp descent.

One evening, she was locking up the Hilton Branch of the Maplewood

Memorial Library when she decided to have a few drinks from the bottle of rum that she kept hidden in her bottom drawer. She called up a friend she had met at a disco club on the Bowery and invited him over to the library. They dropped four tabs of Popeye blotter paper and proceeded to spend the rest of the night pulling down books. It was the most fun she had had in years. Running up and down the aisles destroying the system, one volume at a time. The books fell with great drama, splaying open on the ground like slaughtered animals. Then they screwed in the children's section with their socks on, and afterwards it seemed like a good idea to purge the library of its most unworthy members. A small offering to the pagan gods—her own private *mēnis* session. *The Wrath of Charlene.* She started a small fire in a waste bin. She was high, but she knew exactly what she was doing. In went a shelf-ful of mystery novels. An instruction manual on computers. Norman Mailer's *An American Dream.* The volume H from the *Encyclopaedia Britannica.*

"The books aren't burning," she said, staring at her smoldering creation. "They're resisting!"

"You're one wild chick," her companion said to her. He was naked, save for his socks. He resembled a kind of prehistoric hunter.

The books might not have burned in quite the manner she had hoped, but they created plenty of smoke. The fire alarm was soon triggered, flushing them out into the night.

A lone dog walker found them struggling into their clothes on the lawn outside as a yellow alarm beacon beat open the darkness.

"What's happening?" he asked, his terrier standing at attention. "Is there a fire?"

"Don't worry sir," said Charlene. "We are professionals."

Three thousand volumes suffered irreparable smoke damage. Thanks largely to her mother's behind-the-scenes negotiation, *Town of Maplewood v. Charlene Volmer* was settled out of court; Charlene was placed on probation and sentenced to fifty hours of community service. Needless to say, she was also fired. It was an ignominious end to her career as a librarian.

She fulfilled her obligation to the community at the Legion Hall in Elizabeth. On Veteran Career Finder Day, she sat beneath a sagging magenta banner that declared WELCOME BACK BOYS! blindly distributing self-help literature to the hollow-eyed men fresh from the bunkers of Vietnam. In a distinct violation of her probation terms, she was nursing her second flask of schnapps and Kool-Aid beneath the table.

When she looked up again, he was standing at the head of the line. He, back only two weeks from the war in Vietnam. He, standing with hands folded to keep down the shaking, which had started since his return, or at least this was when he had started noticing it. The day he had left, Staff Sergeant Emerson, never known for saying a nice thing about another human being in his life, had squeezed his shoulder and called him the best damn radio operator he had ever worked with.

"What kind of job are you looking for?" she asked, only half registering the darkened eyebrows and the sculpted Slavic rumba-dimple of his chin.

"Radio operations. Repair. This kind of thing," he said. Something in his voice.

She looked through her books for the first time that day. "I'm not sure I have that in my pile right here." A slight slur to her speech. Ready to hand him whatever was on top.

"I know how to do this," he said. "I do not need your book. I know what I want."

"You do?" she said. Her eyes focusing.

"I always know this," he said.

"You do?" she said. Lingering, wondering what was happening to the weight of her body.

"What is your name?" Kermin asked. "I want to know this."

"You do?" she said again, and the thrice-uttered question sealed their fate. It was the kind of collision where there was no time for courtship, where two wounded planets lock into orbit and can never quite free themselves from the insistence of their gravitational pull. *Charlene and Kermin. Kermin and Charlene.* Each would come to understand, in very different ways, that what had come before was only the tuning of the instruments before the real movement began.

What are you writing?"

Kermin was standing in the doorway of the kitchen. She had risen early and was working away at the typewriter.

"Not really anything," she said, flushing. She closed the novel and maneuvered the typewriter slightly, so that its page was less visible to the room. "It's just something for Dr. Fitzgerald."

Kermin nodded. She watched as he began his morning routine. Since Charlene had known him, his breakfast had never varied: white toast, Marmite, slice of cheese, slice of ham, glass of orange juice. He always ate everything until there was only half a bite left, and then he was finished. His consistency was maddening, but then such consistency had also saved her. After so many years of instability, she had come to depend upon that last half-moon of toast remaining on the plate.

"So this doctor," Kermin said, uncapping the Marmite jar. "He is good?"

"Yes," she said. "Of course he's good."

Kermin sat down across from her.

"He's good," she said again, edging the typewriter away.

He took a loud bite of toast.

"So what did he tell you?" he said. Crumbs.

"About?"

"About Radar."

"Oh, plenty of things. I mean, they're still doing tests," she said. "But we're very lucky that he agreed to take on Radar in the first place. I mean, he's the best there is. He's . . ."

She tapped at a key on the typewriter, and a faint *F* thwacked onto the page. She could feel herself blushing again.

Kermin studied her. After a moment, he let his hand drift over to a short-wave radio sitting on the table. A flick of the wrist and the radio came to life. A loud sea of static enveloped them. He slowly turned the dial, stroking the rib cage of the morning's frequencies.

"Kermin," she said. "You'll wake up Radar. He didn't sleep last night."

"This doctor," he said over the noise. "He is the last."

"What?"

"After this, no more."

"Kermin, he's the best there is," she said. "We're so lucky that he even—"

"What did he learn from my blood?" he said without looking up from the radio.

"I don't know," she said. "I didn't ask. They're looking into various genetical possibilities. Something in our DNA. He said it was very advanced science."

The radio hung briefly on two stations at once, both voices vying for supremacy through a canopy of static.

"Kerm!" she hissed. "*Please*. Turn it off."

He snapped the dial. A click. A sudden silence.

IN TRUTH, HER VISITS to Boston were not going as well as she had initially hoped. Although she could not say exactly what it was she was hoping for. The less frequent their appointments, the more fervently she typed. Her *Anna Kare-nina* was taking shape, page by page, and at certain moments, when the beat of the typewriter became like a second pulse, she was blessed with the fleeting sensation that she was the writer of this book, that she, Charlene Radmanovic, was conceiving of Vronsky's torrid pursuit, of Levin's fervent idealism. Or, more precisely: that the real *Anna Karenina* had not truly existed until now, until it had flowed through Tolstoy and then through her and come out the other side. But these moments of transcendent begetting were rare. More often than not, she was aware of herself as nothing more than a scribe, a clumsy regurgitator of words. A book was a dead thing; no manner of resuscitation could change that.

When she finally managed to corner him on the phone, Dr. Fitzgerald claimed he had all the data he needed for his article. The news felt like the thinnest of daggers sliding into the soft space between her ribs.

"Can you tell me what's wrong, then?" she said into the phone.

"Wrong?"

"With him," she said. "With *us*."

"Nothing's wrong. He's a beautiful child."

"You know what I mean."

There was a pause. "We're looking into it. I assure you, we're doing everything we can."

She breathed. Wanting to say things that could not be said.

"When can we come back?"

"There's not really a need—"

"But when?"

He agreed to see her the following Monday. In a panic, she stayed up nearly the entire weekend, desperately trying to finish *Anna Karenina*'s denouement. Once upon a time, this had been her favorite part of the book, for it was that strangely euphoric space in a novel after the main character is gone, where the author can get away with almost anything. When she had read it all those years ago, she had imagined a world after her own funeral, a world where she existed only in memory. But now, charging through these final pages, Levin's protracted exchange with the peasant and his resulting epiphany about his own pious fallibility—a realization that had once struck her as desperately profound—came off as dull and belabored. Maybe it was just because she was viewing everything through the lens of transcription, but when, at 3 A.M., she finished typing out Levin's final declaration to Kitty regarding the power of godliness, she wanted to shoot the man *and* Tolstoy for creating such a blatant mouthpiece. And she hated the doctor for goading her into what she now saw as a fruitless endeavor. It was perhaps the loneliest moment of her life.

The next morning, they took the train up to Boston. When they arrived at Dr. Fitzgerald's office, Radar ran over and punched the doctor in the groin, but playfully, as a kind of familiar salutation.

"Ray Ray!" said Charlene. "Be careful!"

"Doctah Popeye!" said Radar. "Doctah" and "Popeye" were the fourth and ninth words, respectively, in his approximately fifteen-word vocabulary.

"He's been wanting a Popeye Band-Aid. The one you give him after the blood tests."

"This can be arranged," he said. The doctor swung Radar up onto his desk and looked him in the eye. "You've done everything we asked and more. You've never complained once. I think you're going to grow up to do something amazing someday. Mark my words."

Hands fluttering. One became two became one. Radar laughed and did the same back to him, a mirror image: two became one became . . . The gesture fell apart.

"You'll have to practice that one," said the doctor.

A nurse took Radar from the room for a final physical and the prize of a Band-Aid.

Alone again, they sat in silence.

"Is there anything else?" the doctor said.

Charlene took a breath. From her bag she produced the stack of pages. Her stance toward them had warmed somewhat since her low point. She tidied the pile and then slid them across his desk.

"What's this?"

"You inspired me," she said.

He slowly glanced through the pages. Licking his fingers. She tried to read his face.

"I see a mistake," he noted.

"Yes," she said, hurt. "Probably. I just finished last night."

He put the pages down and cleared his throat.

"Charlene," he said and looked up at her. "Is there anything you're not telling me?"

She was startled by his question. "Like what?" she said.

"Really any information can be relevant," he said. "If there's anything you're not telling me, it could delay us from our conclusion."

She considered this. She briefly toyed with telling him about her olfactory condition. She had kept this from him. She had kept many things from him.

"I would tell you anything," she said. "I mean, I've told you everything."

"Have you?" He was coming around the desk.

"Yes," she said, shrinking back into her chair. "I think so."

He was standing in front of her. She closed her eyes. She could smell his aftershave. The hooked barb of musk. She could feel what was about to happen, and she was not sure how she felt about it. But when she opened her eyes again, he had moved to the window. The faintest shiver of rejection.

She went to him. Placed a tentative hand on his shoulder. She could see the false familiar of his reflection.

"Is there something you're not telling *me?*" she whispered.

"Are you acquainted with the principles of uncertainty?" he said suddenly.

"Yes," she said, taken aback. She took her hand off his shoulder. "I mean— no, not really."

"Heisenberg's uncertainty principle," he said. "People are often confused by it. Heisenberg stated that both the position and velocity of a particle cannot simultaneously be known. You measure one, the other will always remain uncertain. The observation affects that which is observed."

"Okay," she said. "What does this have to do with Radar?"

He walked past her to his desk. "This is where people confuse the issue. It's not the act of observation which makes things inherently uncertain—it's the system *itself* which is uncertain. We blame it on us, the observers, but this is merely a convenient excuse, for the uncertainty is actually built into the world. A particle can never have two definite attributes—direction and position. If you define one, the other fades into indeterminism. And so: there is no way to know everything. You must choose your knowledge."

She could feel the tears. She willed them back, but they came anyway.

"But I'm not *asking* to know everything! I'm just asking for this one thing! I don't care about anything else!" she cried. She took a step forward. "Wait, why are you saying all of this?"

"Heisenberg—"

"You don't want to help us, do you?"

"Of course I want to help you. The question is, do *you* want to help you?"

"You never wanted to help us!"

"Charlene."

"You don't care about us!"

"Charlene, listen," he said. "The Japanese have a saying: *Shiranu ga hotoke.*"

"What the hell does that mean?"

"You must be prepared not to know what you want to know," he said. "You must be prepared for the question to be the answer."

The nurse appeared at the doorway with Radar, who was proudly holding up his elbow, recently adorned with a Band-Aid.

"We didn't have Popeye, but we had a bumblebee," said the nurse.

"Popeye is bye-bye," said Radar.

The nurse sensed her intrusion. "Is everything all right?" she asked.

"It's fine. Everything's fine," said the doctor. "We were just finishing up."

Charlene wiped at her eyes and sniffed. Perhaps it was from crying, but she could no longer smell him.

"Come on, Radar," she said. "We're leaving."

"Charlene!" he called after her. "You forgot your pages."

"Keep them," she said without turning around.

IN THE WEEKS and months after, she fell into a kind of mourning. A month passed without any word from the doctor's office. Charlene finally caved and called his secretary, who was polite but evasive. She said Dr. Fitzgerald had gone to Europe to promote his skin classification system. And no, she didn't know when he would return. But she said this in such a way that it was clear she knew exactly when he would return and had been instructed not to share the information.

Two months went by. Then four. What could he be writing? During her visits, Charlene's sense of smell had calmed somewhat, but now, as she waited for his article, it returned with a vengeance. Some days it was so bad she would wear a swimmer's nose clip around the house. She found the mild sense of asphyxiation comforting. After dinner, Charlene would lean out their bathroom window and smoke cigarettes into the night. She had not smoked in years. The smoke tasted awful—the tarry remnants would linger and fester in her sinuses for days—but still she found herself leaning out that window again and again.

Sensing a weight he could not name, Kermin started to sleep several nights a week at his communications shop, tinkering away with dismantled cathodes and diodes and dusty vacuum tubes—the tender ligaments of long-distance communication. When he had nothing to work on, he passed the nights turning black-and-white televisions into color and back again.

Radar turned three. He was constantly speaking now, as if making up for lost time. His finger extended, he pointed at the world around him.

House, he said. *Birdie. Doggy. Raisin. Man. Choo-choo.*

After every word, he would look back at Charlene, seeking confirmation. Sometimes she wondered what would happen if she did not nod in agreement, if she instead taught him all the wrong words for things. What if a birdie became a man and a choo-choo became a raisin? She had the power to completely rewire his perception, to enclose him within a false reality. Except when she started to think about her son's development in this way, she would feel the panic begin to rise—at all the choices she had and hadn't made, all of the thousands of parental failures she would only come to realize later, when it was already much too late.

Time's persistence had slowly dulled her preoccupation with the doctor's verdict. Life settled into the uneasy routine of homebound motherhood, a life she had never thought would be hers. She woke; she made Radar breakfast; she took him nd; she made lunch; she read him a book; she napped with Radar; she went for a walk with Rada ner; Kermin came home; she put Radar to bed; she and Kermin watched television until he began to

Repeat.

Still, even if her day was consumed by the business of mothering, she couldn't shake the feeling that she was still an impostor, as if all of this would be taken away from her at any moment. And a part of her wished it would be, even though she could not imagine her life any other way.

And then, nearly nine months after her final meeting with the doctor, on a day like all the rest, Charlene opened the mailbox and found a cream-colored envelope lying inside.

"Dr. Thomas K. Fitzgerald," read the return address. She caught her breath and then tore open the envelope. The typewritten letter alerted her to a forthcoming article in the next month's *Journal of Investigative Dermatology* concerning their son's "chronic hyperpigmentation." Standing by the mailbox, Charlene brought the paper to her nose. She searched for a hint of the doctor's aftershave but found only the elliptical aroma of ink and his secretary's cheap lilac perfume.

The wait each day for the mail's arrival became excruciating. Charlene began to hate the mailman, shooting him looks of reproach when he did not deliver what she was looking for.

"You cannot fix him," Kermin said out of the blue one night as they sat watching a fuzzy episode of *Three's Company* on the refurbished Zenith television. "He is not broken."

She was so startled by this declaration that she didn't say anything at first.

"You know that's not what I'm trying to do," she said finally.

"I don't know what you are trying to do," he said.

"Kerm," she said as he got up and began adjusting the aerials.

"Kerm," she said. "You have no idea what it's like."

On the television screen, John Ritter dissolved into static and then became whole again. Kermin moved the antennae about like a conductor, quietly swearing to himself, but after a while it was no longer clear whether he was trying to clear up the picture or make it worse.

ONE SATURDAY AFTERNOON, Charlene unlocked their mailbox as usual and nearly cried out. Inside was the beckoning glint of plastic wrap.

"Hey Kermin!" she yelled. She reached for it slowly, her hand trembling. A diagram of a hair follicle graced its cover. She felt herself recoil. Her son's condition was not worthy of the lead article? A finger loosened the plastic seam on one side. She inhaled its pages, again searching for his elusive aftershave, but all she smelled was the buttery, slightly sterile aroma of processed paper and glue.

"Kermin!" she called up the hallway. "It's here!"

She was searching the table of contents for the doctor's name, the electricity flaring out into her fingertips. His name, his name—she wanted to touch his name. And there it was: page 349.

Kermin came down with Radar in his arms. He took a seat on the bottom step.

She read. Neighbors came and went around them. When she was done, she looked up, bewildered.

"So?" said Kermin. "What does it say?"

"I don't know," she said. The article was short. Barely three pages. She had expected it to be longer. She thought real science would demand pages and pages. Not this.

Radar was singing to himself, "Den we all say goodnight bunnee. Den we all say goodnight, goodnight, goodnight."

Kermin rubbed his son's head.

She sat down beside them and read it again. This time, she even read the figures and the footnotes. Radar grew bored and began walking up and down the stairs, counting each railing as he went. Kermin leaned over and looked briefly at the page, then shook his head.

"What does it say?"

"I don't know," she said, exasperated. "I'm not sure it says anything."

Indeed, as far as she could tell, "On an Isolated Incidence of Non-Addison's Hypoadrenal Uniform Hyperpigmentation in a Caucasian Male" was nothing more than a professional shrug of the shoulders. "The unusual uniform darkening in this individual can be linked to a marked increase in melanocyte-stimulating and adrenocorticotropic hormones, though all other pituitary and adrenal gland functions appear normal," Dr. Fitzgerald wrote in his conclusion, hiding behind the oddly disembodied language of the medical professional. "No doubt further genetic studies need to be performed to ascertain the precise catalyst for the over-production of these hormones, which are not present in

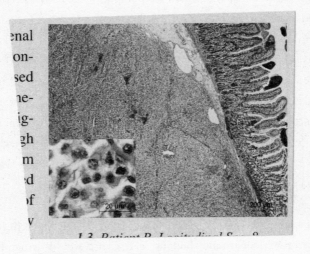

enal
on-
sed
ne-
ig-
gh
m
d
f
v

Fig. 1.2. Patient R, Longitudinal Section 8
From Fitzgerald, T., "On an Isolated Incidence of Non-Addison's
Hypoadrenal Uniform Hyperpigmentation in a Caucasian Male,"
Journal of Investigative Dermatology 72: 351

either parent or gene group. In all other areas, however, the patient is a normal, functioning male infant. Chance transmutation, it seems, has struck again" (354).

"Chance transmutation?" said Charlene. She let out a long, withering breath and covered her face in her hands.

Radar came back down the stairs. "Why mommy sad?"

"I don't know," said Kermin.

"Someone mean her?"

"Come," he said. He took his son by the hand and led him back upstairs.

THE NIGHT AFTER they received the article, Kermin, a man who did not drink but was clearly drunk, barged into their evening bubble bath, shortwave radio in hand.

"There is no more tests!" he said. *"Jebeš ljekare!"*

"Kerm, careful!"

He swayed. *"No more tests,* do you hear me?"

"Okay, calm down. Don't yell so loud."

"And no more doctors!"

"*Okay.*"

"Fuck this Fitzgerald so-and-so."

"Kerm."

"We know more than he does, and we know nothing! If he cannot find such-and-such, then there is nothing to find. *Moj sin je zdrav.*"

He reached into the bathtub to touch Radar's head and tripped, dropping the radio into the sea of bubbles. The shortwave, chattering away, sputtered, slurped, and went silent. Charlene screamed, thinking they would both be electrocuted. She clutched their child to her chest. Radar, dark and radiant against his mother's pale skin, began to whimper. Kermin grasped clumsily at his machine and promptly fell into the bath with them.

A shocked silence. And then Kermin started to laugh. After a moment, Charlene joined him. They laughed and built a tower of bubbles on Radar's head, who waved at his crown. The air parted, the clouds receding. They did not have to fix this anymore.

6

It was a clean break, or as clean a break as you could hope for. In the months that followed, Charlene felt closer than she had ever felt to Kermin. They started sleeping together again for the first time in almost a year, though she still insisted on using at least two forms of birth control.

Perhaps sensing their daughter had turned over a new leaf, her parents offered to help them buy a house, an offer that Charlene begrudgingly accepted. They moved out of their apartment in Elizabeth and into a single-family faux colonial on a tight suburban street in Kearny, away from the Serbian community that had sustained and battered them. The sultry S-curve of the Passaic River formed the real and imagined border between their old lives and new.

Charlene brought all of her books with her—boxes and boxes of them. There was ample shelving in the new house, and she spread out her collection across several rooms, their spines clustered according to color. Visiting the new house, her mother said the library looked like a Rothko painting.

"It's not a bad thing," she said. "Just different."

Soon after, Charlene hung white sheets in front of the shelves, as if to protect the books from an imminent construction project that never came. The sheets, once hung, were accepted and then forgotten, and would remain in place for the next thirty years. To fetch a book, you had to step through the curtain into another realm, into a mausoleum of forgotten bindings.

Kermin also moved his business across the Passaic, to a lonely little block in

Harrison, next to a synagogue and a karate studio. Without the cultural patronage of the Serbs, he had trouble attracting new clients, and what little business which had sustained him in Elizabeth quickly dried up. Kermin sat in his new shop, surrounded by his electronic parts, and waited for the jingle of a bell that rarely came. He was perhaps the best TV-and-radio repairman in New Jersey, but he was not a people person, and the tiny television had not quite caught on in America in the way he had predicted. Americans liked big and bigger, and, most often, biggest. When things broke, they were more likely to buy a new one than fix what they already had.

Once settled into their new home, they enrolled Radar in a local day care. For the first time since his birth, Charlene felt comfortable enough to release him into the care of others.

"He must meet friends, kids, boys, everyone," said Kermin. "So he can be normal."

The day care was a brick-and-pastel compound called Shady Dale Tots. The playground out front was padded. There were two neon turtles you could ride like ponies. The adults at Shady Dale Tots cooed and pinched Radar's cheeks. After his first day, Radar asked Charlene why there were no doctors, only other kids like him.

Her newfound free time terrified her. In the mornings, she would often sit with a copy of the *Star-Ledger,* a perpetually disappointing, perpetually comforting cultural artifact, reading and half reading, taking little sentence-long sips from stories that outlined the misfortunes of others. One morning, after burning clear through the local news, Charlene suddenly found herself in the classifieds—rare territory she usually found a touch gauche, a touch desperate even for her tastes. (*Who would go public with something like that?*) But now, faced with these crowded columns of informal commerce, she found herself voyeuristically scanning the personals and job listings and for-sale items. A thousand potential worlds awaited her attention. The personals were particularly mystifying, for the carefully ascribed acronyms and decontextualized details ("SWDM, 58 seeks SWF for LTR. I'm a Catholic-turned-atheist") made each sound like an encoded diplomatic cable rather than an intimate come-on. In some ways, their impossible brevity reminded her of the obituaries that she had once collected as a child, but these missives were not meant to memorialize a life gone by. The personal ads had been crafted by living, breathing people who were awaiting actual responses. Their summary was like a death before death.

It was then that her eyes fell upon a nondescript ad in the bottom right-hand corner of the page:

DO YOU HAVE A SENSITIVITY TO TASTE AND/OR SMELL?

The International Flavor and Aroma Corporation of Elizabeth, NJ is looking for select, qualified candidates for several entry-level flavorist, perfumer, and quality control positions. Industry and/or science background helpful but not necessary. Apply to: IFAC HR, P.O. Box 4923, Elizabeth, NJ 07207

Charlene read the ad twice through and then once more. She took a pair of scissors and carefully cut it out with four neat little snips. When she was done, the slip of newspaper lay by itself on the table. She fetched a piece of paper, fully intending to respond, but when she tried to write a reply, she found she had nothing to write. After several attempts, she gave up. She hid the ad inside a recipe booklet and tried to forget she had ever seen it.

Still, she realized she needed to find some type of job. Kermin's business was floundering, and even with the financial assistance of her parents (who were incidentally also paying for Radar's day care), they were in increasing need of a steady source of reliable income. Maureen, mother of Bryan, one of Radar's day care buddies, found Charlene a position as a part-time receptionist at the semi-upscale hair salon where she worked. The pay wasn't much, but it kept her busy.

One day at day care pickup, Charlene and Maureen lingered, chatting. Maureen was quietly becoming one of her few confidants. Close female friends were unusual for Charlene, who naturally drifted toward the gruff honesty (and the associated sexual complications) of male companionship. But Maureen was perky and kind and eternally optimistic—everything that Charlene was not.

"I was all, 'If you try that again, we've got a problem,'" Maureen was saying. "You know what I mean, honey? You just can't take that from people."

Charlene, half listening, watched the children. She was aware—not for the first time—of their incredible whiteness. They appeared almost sickly under the fluorescent lights, as if they had never been exposed to the sun. The boy with the bowl cut whose name she could never remember was playing a block game with Bryan. Radar sat in his usual spot in the corner, contentedly rewiring one of his radios. At first the teachers had frowned upon having such dangerous elements in the classroom, but when they witnessed the degree to which Radar was consumed by his electronics, they had reluctantly made an exception.

And then Charlene saw the boy with the bowl cut stop and point at Radar. *He was pointing right at him.* The boy said a word—she couldn't hear what it was, but his face had twisted into a scowl when he said it, giving him a momentarily precocious air of menace. Charlene stood and stared at the boy thrusting his finger in the direction of her son.

That little shit.

She resisted the urge to go over and slap him. Why on earth was he pointing like that? What had he said about Radar?

"Charlene? Are you okay?" asked Maureen. "What is it?"

The boy was pointing, and now he was saying something to Bryan, next to him, and they were both laughing and kicking at the blocks with their little feet. Charlene could not believe it. Bryan was laughing, too. Bryan was supposed to be Radar's friend.

"They're laughing at him," said Charlene.

"At who?"

But Charlene was already running over. She grabbed the boy's hand.

"Never," she hissed at the boy. *"Never, ever do that.* Do you hear me?" The boy looked bewildered for a moment and then began to cry. Charlene plucked up Radar and hurriedly left the room.

"Wait, Charlene! What happened?" Maureen called after her, but she did not stop. She ran to the car and did not bother putting Radar in his car seat before driving away.

SEVERAL WEEKS LATER, perambulating Radar down Harrison Avenue, Charlene was lost in thought when she felt the baby carriage hit something. She looked around and saw a black couple in their seventies standing next to her. The man was holding the chassis of Radar's carriage. Beneath a battered newsie cap, he studied Charlene with sad, elephant eyes magnified by a thick pair of grubby eyeglasses. His knuckles were dry and white with age.

"I'm sorry," said Charlene, thinking she must've clipped them by accident. She tried to push forward but could not break free from the old man's grip.

"Herb!" His wife grabbed his arm and tried to pull it off the stroller.

He pushed her away and lifted a finger at Charlene.

"You got some nerve, you know that?" His voice like a memory, pressing against her chest.

"Herb!" his wife said again. She uncoiled his fingers from the carriage. "I'm so sorry. He doesn't know what he's saying these days."

She took out a handkerchief and wiped his nose. "Come on, love," she said. "Let's go get you some goulash."

Charlene was paralyzed.

"It's not what you think," she finally stammered.

The woman turned and placed her hand on Charlene's arm. Her eyes were warm.

"I think it's wonderful what you're doing, really. God bless," she said. "So many out there who need good homes, no matter what color they is."

THE ENCOUNTER DOGGED HER. It filled the folds of her consciousness. She kept seeing those cataract eyes, large and unblinking behind his Coke bottle glasses. A soft man filled with such malice. She wished she had confessed all to this couple, explained to them what had happened and why, sought their advice, sought their forgiveness. On more than one occasion, she found herself back at the place of their encounter, hoping she might run into them again.

She had always struggled with insomnia, but now she stopped sleeping altogether. After consulting a doctor, she began relying on an array of potent sleeping pills. If she did not take enough, she would not sleep and would wake up nauseated, tired, and depressed. If she took too many, she would pass out and wake up nauseated, tired, and depressed. Every night became an exercise in threading the needle. Days began to blur together.

During a winter playdate with Bryan, she and Maureen huddled on a bench at the playground, watching their parka'd boys attempt to crawl up the red tubular slide, a Sisyphean task that was defeating them.

"He really is gorgeous," said Maureen.

"Who?"

"Radar," she said. "Where did you get him? I mean, where's he from?"

Charlene panicked.

"Originally?" she said, punching at her thighs.

For the first time in many years, she thought of T. K. lying naked in her bed in Hell's Kitchen. She wondered where he was. The great torment of a life unlived. What if things had gone much differently for her? What if life could be ironed out smooth, like a shirt?

The boys finally made it to the top. They came down the slide knotted together, squealing with gravity's delight. Radar raised both of his hands to his mother and said, "We come down, we slip down!" He proudly put his arm around Bryan.

"He's from Minnesota," she said to Maureen, watching her son. "His parents died in a fire. They were Congolese."

As soon as she said it, she realized what a terrible thing she had just done. She instantly wanted to rewind time, to take it all back. But she did not. She left her words hanging there in the frigid air, waiting to see what would happen next, like a child standing over a shattered bowl.

"Oh!" Maureen said after a moment. "I wouldn't have thought. Minnesota! It must've been so cold for him."

"Yes," said Charlene. "It must've been."

The lie sprouted roots. Charlene began telling everyone that Radar had been adopted after a tragic fire in a Minneapolis apartment building. Sympathy was garnered. At first, Charlene hated herself for saying it, but then she became used to it. She slowly shifted from feeling guilty about the moral culpability of her fiction to being afraid of what Kermin would do if he ever found out.

One afternoon, she went to pick up Radar at day care, only to find him crumpled and sniffling in a corner. His eyes were red from crying. Her heart dropped.

"What happened?" she demanded.

"Matt said some hurtful things," said Alison, the teacher.

"I knew it! *I knew it,*" said Charlene. "Who's Matt? He's the one with the haircut, isn't he?"

"We've had a conversation, and Matt's apologized to Radar."

"What did he say?"

"He didn't know what he was saying. He's so young. He's just repeating words."

"What did he say?"

"He called Radar a monkey."

"What?!"

"We've let him know that names can be very hurtful, even if he didn't mean for it to be hurtful."

"He meant for it to be hurtful."

"Matt's a good kid."

"Matt's a shithead," said Charlene. "You have no fucking idea what you're doing, do you?"

She took Radar to get a chocolate-and-vanilla Softee swirl, his favorite. He had a habit of trying to put his mouth around the whole ice cream when he first received it—not to eat it, but just to see if the act could be done.

When they arrived home she saw a letter lying on their doormat. The envelope was covered in several colorful stamps and featured a return address in Oslo, Norway.

"What is dat?" Radar asked.

"I'm not sure," she said. "Someone wrote us a letter."

She debagged in the hallway and opened the envelope.

27 *May 1979*

Dear Mr. and Mrs. Radmanovic,

Please excuse the presumptuous gesture of writing to you directly. You don't know me but I have been following the case of your son since his birth, though from some considerable distance. Several aspects of the case intrigued me as a scientist, writer, and teacher, but until now I have thought it best not to intervene. After giving it some thought, I have had a recent change of heart and deemed it my duty to inform you of an opportunity that may interest you.

In the very north of Norway, there is a community of physicists and artists called Kirkenesferda that have been experimenting with certain electrical shock treatments. This is not their primary business, but among other things, they have discovered a way to profoundly alter the colour of someone's skin using a precise, one-time treatment. The results have been quite extraordinary.

I cannot guarantee success nor can I absolutely guarantee the safety of the procedure, for it has been sanctioned by no health or governmental organization, but I assure you, these people are exact in their studies and have looked into this matter with great detail. Should you be interested in making a trip to visit this camp, please let me know and I can put you directly in touch. I have a relationship with Leif Christian-Holtsmark, the founder, as I used to be a member myself.

Most Kindest Regards,
Brusa Tofte-Jebsen

Charlene put down the letter and stared out the window.

"What dat man say?" Radar said. "*Hello? How are you?*"

They had just done a unit on letter writing in day care, in which they had written to Santa Claus to let him know he could park his reindeer outside their school, next to the turtles, when he was not using them.

"He said . . . I'm not sure what he said. It's from Norway."

"What's Nor*way?*"

"It's by the North Pole."

"Santa write that letter?"

"Not Santa. Someone else who's not Santa."

"Who not Santa?"

"Brusa," she said. And then: "Kirkenesferda." Trying out the name to see if it sounded real. A community of physicists and artists who have been experimenting with electrical shock treatments? In the Arctic? It couldn't be real. But then why would someone invent all of this? As a joke? Was this some kind of weird racist joke? No—it was just too preposterous to make up.

She folded the letter and placed it in a drawer in the kitchen, next to the glue and the spare lightbulbs, as if its proximity to the accessories of domesticity might calm its contents.

When Kermin came home that evening, they sat down to an unsuccessful rendition of zucchini-cumin ragout. Charlene's acute sense of smell had not translated to prowess in the kitchen; her untuned olfactive sensitivity had encouraged a kind of wild and hopeless inventiveness that Kermin and even little Radar usually accepted in resigned silence. This evening, however, Radar, high-chaired, seemed unwilling to play his part. He carefully and deliberately expelled his ragout back onto his plate, giving the eerie impression that he had just ejected something internal and potentially vital.

"Radar!" said Charlene. "Be polite. Chew with your mouth closed."

Radar shook his head and pushed a hand into his regurgitations.

"Do you want to go to bed without any food? Eat like a big boy, please."

"We got a letter from Santa," Radar announced.

"You did?" said Kermin. "What did Santa say? Is he still take suntan in Miami?"

"Noooo," Radar said, shaking his head. He turned to Charlene. "What dat he say?"

"Nothing. Santa didn't write to us," she said.

"He did!"

"Eat your food, please."

"I don't want it!" he said and pushed his plate off the table. It shattered on the floor, releasing a puddle of ragout viscera.

"Radar!"

She grabbed his arm, hard—too hard. He began to cry.

"You've lost your chance to sit at the big persons' table because you're acting like a baby," she said. "Are you a baby?"

"No!" he wailed.

"Then why are you acting like one?"

"*You're* a baby, stupid shitty!" he yelled.

She slapped him. It was the first time she had hit her own child. Afterwards, the palm of her hand—the place where her skin had come into contact—felt as if it were bleeding. Radar's eyes went wide with fright, there was silence, and then he began to wail with everything he had.

Kermin looked at her in surprise. She was having trouble breathing. She was overtaken again by the feeling that she had stepped into the life of another. Kermin picked up Radar and took him upstairs to his room.

"You shouldn't have hit him," Kermin said when he returned.

"I know," she said. "I'm sorry."

"You are okay?"

She noticed her hands were shaking. She wiped them on a napkin. "He had a tough day at day care. They were calling him names."

"Okay."

When he said nothing more, she said, "They called him a *monkey,* Kerm."

"He doesn't look like the monkey."

"Of course he doesn't look like a monkey!"

"They are children. They don't know what they are saying."

"No, they know *exactly* what they're saying," she said. "I can't stand that place. Every time I go there, I want to burn it down."

"Don't do that."

"We're paying a small fortune—"

"We are not paying."

"—to have our child tortured by snobby little white kids. I can't go back. *I cannot go back.* I'll quit my job if I have to. I can take him."

"You can't quit. We need money."

"We'll make money, Kerm. I'll ask for more from my parents if I have to."

He picked up his knife from both ends, as if it were a fragile specimen. "I think soon I will close my shop," he said.

"Close? Why?"

"They are raising the rents." He shook his head. "No one likes these small television anymore."

"To be honest, I'm not sure they ever did." She reached for his hand. "We'll make it work. We can try something new."

"What new? What can I do? I cannot do anything."

"That's not true. You know that's not true. You're brilliant, Kerm."

"In this place, brilliant does not matter. It is lucky asshole who wins. Like Edison. He electrocutes the elephant and says, 'Screw you, Tesla.' And he wins. Tesla is brilliant, but he lose. He talks to pigeons and dies like the poor man."

"But with all the things you know? You could do so many things . . ."

"I am not electrocuting the elephant."

She looked at her husband and then she got up, opening the drawer and retrieving the letter.

"Promise me you won't be mad," she said.

"About what?"

"Maybe we're the lucky ones," she said and handed him the letter.

Kermin read in silence. Charlene watched him. His faced betrayed no hint of expression.

"What is this?" he said finally.

"I thought maybe it was worth looking into."

"Looking into *what*?"

"If there's something that maybe can be done, then I think it's our duty . . . to see what we can do."

He got up suddenly and went to the trash can. He had already opened the lid before Charlene leaped up and grabbed him.

"Don't!" she pleaded.

"It's done. I told you. I don't want any more of this."

"Don't do it, please!" she said, holding on to his arm.

"It is done, Charlene."

He tore the letter in two, three, four pieces. She looked on in horror as he dropped the remnants into the trash.

Before she knew what she was doing, she was in the trash can collecting the fallen pieces, her hands covered in yolk and the thin, wet husk of an onion. She came back to the table and reassembled the sheets. A stain like a sunset.

They sat with the torn-up letter between them for some time.

"Please," she said quietly. "It's just to ask for more information."

He had picked up a radio and was working the dials, though no sound was coming from its speaker.

"I need to," she said. "I *need* to . . ."

"What?" He turned on her.

"I need to—"

"What exactly do you need to do to our son?" He was shouting. She shrank back. She had never heard him shout before. *"I would like you to tell me this, Charlene. I would very much like you to tell me this."*

His face was pink; she could see the whites of his eyes. He looked as though he wanted to kill her, to bash her brains out with his radio. She felt herself adjusting to a world that included such anger.

"Please," she whispered. "Please. It's just to find out information."

"Information? What fucking information could you possibly want?"

"We don't have to do anything. Just find out. I'll feel so much better if I just *find out.*"

The radio suddenly sparked to life. A symphony materialized, much too loud. Charlene winced and put her hands over her ears.

"Kermin!" she yelled. "Shut it off!"

He twisted a knob, but the sound did not go away. An element of whining static was introduced into the whirlpool of woodwinds and strings.

"Kermin!"

The dial turned, and noise engulfed the signal. Static devouring the notes of music. A great wave coming toward them.

"Kermin!" She grabbed at the radio and stabbed wildly at the power button. "Turn it—"

The silence left behind was long and strange, as if the world had been emptied of all sound.

"You don't have to do anything," she said finally. "I'll do it."

"God gave us this. We did not choose," he said. "He chose us. We raise him like this. That is our duty."

"But maybe this letter is a sign—"

"We are not going to make him into some kind of freak, Charlene!"

"He's already a freak," she said quietly.

They stared at each other, wondering at the truth of her words.

"Don't ever say this," Kermin said quietly. "Don't you ever say this about my son."

SHE COULD NOT SLEEP. She lay in bed listening to the occasional hush of the passing motorist. Wondering where they were going at this hour. Wondering if they, too, could not sleep. At a certain point, she realized it was no use. She got up and made herself some peppermint tea. At the kitchen table, she wrote Brusa Tofte-Jebsen a letter. *Dear Mr. Tofte-Jebsen, I am so glad that you . . .* and the rest. When she was finished and the envelope was sealed, she felt a great weight had been lifted from her shoulders.

Three weeks went by before she received a cream-colored envelope covered in lithographed bear stamps.

24 June 1979

Dear Mrs. Radmanovic,

Greetings. I have spoken with Leif and everything has been arranged for your visit. Enclosed you will find three roundtrip airline tickets to Kirkenes. Don't worry, Kirkenesferda has offered to cover the cost of your transport. Leif said he will meet you at the airport.

May I just say that I am so glad you are taking this chance. I am sure you will not be disappointed. Unfortunately, I will be unable to join you at the Bjørnens Hule but I will make sure to get a full report.

Kindest Regards,
Brusa Tofte-Jebsen

What had been merely a declaration of interest had apparently turned overnight into a trip to Norway. The departure date listed on the tickets was in two weeks. She still had no idea what went on at this place, but Brusa's reply served as confirmation enough.

She was just beginning to get excited about the whole venture when, that same day, the doorbell rang. When she opened the door, she found herself staring at a man who resembled something of a disheveled bellhop. He was wearing a burgundy suit and a strange, ill-fitting, fez-like cap that slumped awkwardly down the slope of his forehead, despite the chin strap meant to keep it in place. The man did not look excited in the least to be wearing such an outfit. Before she could say anything, he handed her an envelope and said, "Telegram," then he walked away.

"Wait. What is this?" Charlene said, holding the envelope up. A shy but curious Radar was peeking out from behind her leg.

"It's a *telegram,* honey," the man declared, as if this were the most obvious fact in the world. Then he tromped down their steps and mounted his bicycle, which he had left lying across the sidewalk, leaving Charlene to stare in wonder.

"What's a telly-gram?" Radar asked when they were back inside. "A letter?"

"It's like a letter," she said. "But it's sent by machines."

She would've thought it was all a dream if not for the envelope still in her hands. She brought it to her nose. The paper smelled of oily, metallic parts and oddly . . . *cinnamon.* Telegrams were confusing documents. Their words had traveled great distances, and yet the physical paper had not. This cinnamon scent was Jersey-borne.

She opened the telegram in the kitchen.

Per Røed-Larsen. The name seemed oddly familiar.

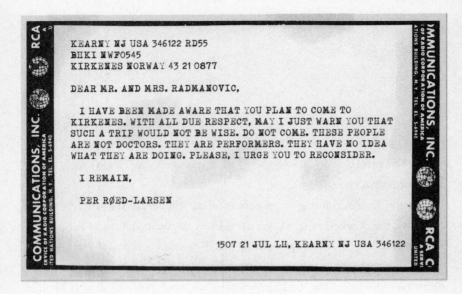

KEARNY NJ USA 346122 RD55
BHKI NWF0545
KIRKENES NORWAY 43 21 0877

DEAR MR. AND MRS. RADMANOVIC,

I HAVE BEEN MADE AWARE THAT YOU PLAN TO COME TO
KIRKENES. WITH ALL DUE RESPECT, MAY I JUST WARN YOU THAT
SUCH A TRIP WOULD NOT BE WISE. DO NOT COME. THESE PEOPLE
ARE NOT DOCTORS. THEY ARE PERFORMERS. THEY HAVE NO IDEA
WHAT THEY ARE DOING. PLEASE, I URGE YOU TO RECONSIDER.

I REMAIN,

PER RØED-LARSEN

1507 21 JUL LH, KEARNY NJ USA 346122

"What dat machine say?" Radar asked.

"It said—well, I'm not sure what it said." She flipped the telegram over, but there was nothing more.

THAT EVENING, while they were watching television, Charlene brought out the airplane tickets.

"I didn't ask for these, I swear. I just asked for some more details," she said. She sat down on the floor in front of his armchair.

He scrutinized the tickets for a long while, turning them over in his hands as if he were judging their authenticity.

"But isn't that nice of them? They're paying for us to come. It must be expensive." She was readying herself for his explosion—to pounce on him in case he decided to try and tear up the tickets.

"I was in Norway once," he said after a while.

"Yes," she said, brightening. "It might be nice for you to go back."

"I don't need to go back," he said.

She placed a hand on his foot. "Kermin."

A silence.

"You really want this?" he said.

She nodded.

"Just to talk to them?"

"Just to talk."

"And then you are okay?"

"And then I'll be okay."

"And then no more?"

"No more." She shook her head. "After this, no more."

"You promise?"

"I promise."

"All right."

"All right what?"

"We can go."

"Oh, Kermin!" She jumped up, hugging him, kissing his rough cheek. "We're just going to find out, I swear. Nothing more. I'll feel so much better then. And I was doing a little bit of reading. It's supposed to be really nice in the summer. Land of the midnight sun and all that."

She did not tell him about the telegram. In truth, she did not know what to make of it herself. So she decided to act as if she had never received it. She hid the telegram in the utility drawer. But soon the drawer felt as though it could no longer safely contain such a document, so she hid the telegram beneath a floorboard in their bedroom that she had pried loose with a hammer. Inside this hole she also put a binder of newspaper articles she had collected about Radar's birth. And the clipped ad for the IFAC flavorist position that she had stashed away in the recipe booklet. When she could not think of anything more to put down there, she hammered the floorboard back into place and covered it with a rug from another room.

7

Kirkenes turned out to be about four hundred kilometers north of the Arctic Circle, the last town in Norway before the Russian border. On the flight from New York to Oslo, they watched an overexposed screening of *Days of Heaven,* in which a man murders his boss in a steel mill and then flees with his wife and daughter to the wheat fields of the Texas Panhandle, only to murder his boss again. At least this is what Kermin thought that the movie was about. There was no sound in his stethoscope-like headset, and he was at a bad angle to watch the dreamy images of the wheat fields burning. There was something uncanny about flying over an ocean while watching wheat fields burn. He looked out the window, trying to catch a glimpse of the ocean that he had once escaped across in the hull of a boat. It was hard to imagine that the small layer of blue far beneath them was the same sea that had borne him to the New World.

Maybe sea and land were not altogether different, he thought, touching the cold glass of the airplane window. Only a small matter of density.

Inside the clean and empty Oslo airport, they blearily drank a coffee and thumbed through a rack of chunky Telemark sweaters before catching a toothpaste-colored prop plane up to Kirkenes. People in line to board the plane stared openly at Radar, until Charlene glared at them, and then they stared at everything but Radar.

The airplane sputtered and bounced against the hidden pockets of turbulence that lay sleeping above the Kjölen Mountains. Radar threw up twice. The Norwegian stewardess smiled as she took the wet airsick bag from Charlene.

"Poor boy," she said. "He is so far away from home, yes?"

They came down in a sea of fog. The airplane descended and descended, and suddenly there was the tiny airstrip. The sun glowing dimly from somewhere behind that suspended scrim of moisture. They collected their bags directly from the plane. Under a light breeze, the air smelled sweetly of wet moss. The handful of other passengers made their way into cars and a small bus headed for town, leaving them alone inside the one-room terminal but for a janitor mopping at a floor that looked as if it had already been cleaned.

"They are meeting us here?" Kermin asked.

"That's what they said."

"There's no one here."

"I can see that, Kerm. Maybe they got the time wrong."

But as she stared out at the fog rolling in waves across the runway, she knew that no one was coming to meet them. There was no such thing as Kirkenesferda. There were no scientists and artists experimenting with electricity up here. There was only tundra and fog and an invisible sun that never set.

"This is Santa Claus house?" she heard Radar say.

"No," said Kermin. "Santa Claus does not live here."

"Jesus Christ," she whispered to her reflection. Her shoulders slumped. They had come this far for nothing.

There was nobody at the ticketing booth. Charlene walked up to the janitor swabbing at the pristine floor.

"Do you know when the next flight to Oslo leaves?" she asked loudly.

To her surprise, he spoke perfect English. "Five hours, ma'am. If the weather doesn't get worse." He looked at Kermin and Radar, sitting on a bench. "Didn't enjoy your stay?"

"No, no," she said, embarrassed. "It's beautiful. There's just been a mistake. A mix-up. We weren't supposed to come."

He nodded. "Same thing happened to me. I'm Swedish. I came here for a woman, but the woman left. I ended up staying. Twenty-five years."

"Is there someplace we can wait?" she asked.

He looked around the room, as if to indicate that this was the extent of the known universe.

It was at this point that a man in a yellow jumpsuit came dashing into the terminal. He appeared quite frantic, but when he saw them, his expression dissolved into relief.

"I'm so sorry I'm late," he said, coming up, breathless. "There was a little problem at the office."

The man was hairless—completely bald, no eyebrows. Charlene guessed he was in his late sixties, though his light blue eyes remained young and bright.

"You're Leif?" said Charlene. He was wearing knee-high mucking boots over his yellow jumpsuit, giving the impression that he had just skydived into a manure field.

"That's not Santa," said Radar, and then hid his face in Kermin's jacket. "Santa has a beard."

"No, I'm sorry to report that I'm not Santa. He was otherwise engaged." The man smiled, extending his hand to Charlene. "Leif Christian-Holtsmark."

"We weren't sure if . . ." she trailed off.

"If I existed? I do. I very much do. My apologies," said Leif, turning. "And this must be the famous Radar. How old are we, little man?"

Radar burrowed into Kermin's jacket.

"How old are you, Radar?" said Charlene.

"Dis many," said Radar, holding up a hand that showed a varying number of fingers, anywhere from two to five.

"He's four." Charlene apologized. "He knows he's four, but he seems to insist on presenting a range of choices."

"It's understandable. One can never be sure," Leif said, and laughed. "But four years old! Now, that is something. Well, Radar, *velkommen til Finnmark*. You are now on top of the world."

He drove them in his battered Land Rover out into a light boreal forest of pine and downy birch. The road hugged the bank of a fjord and then turned onto a small dirt track that wound around several kettle-hole lakes thick with summer algae. The trees began to thin, and they found themselves on a long, flat plain.

"We are right on the edge of the tree line," Lars explained. "To the north is tundra, to the south is the great taiga, which stretches two thousand kilometers into Russia."

The fog burned off. Charlene could see that the ground was marked by splashes of bright lime-colored lichen. It was unlike any landscape she had ever seen before.

"There," said Leif. He pointed up to a raised kame terrace. A herd of bone-white reindeer were tracking their progress. Leif stopped the car and rolled down his window. He was silent.

"Do you hear it?" he said finally.

They listened.

"What?" Charlene asked.

"The reindeer," said Leif. "They have their own frequency. About fifty-eight hertz. Listen."

They listened. After a while, Charlene could hear it, or at least she could imagine hearing it. Something like a moan that had not quite escaped the lips, but rendered simultaneously by hundreds of animals. The sum of a sound never fully finished.

"Santa's reindeer!" Radar yelled.

As if in response, several of the reindeer began to run over the terrace, and soon the whole herd, sensing some unspoken signal, was thundering away as one.

Radar looked heartbroken.

"Don't worry, honey," said Charlene. "It wasn't you. They had someplace to go."

"The Sami have a saying: *'En rein som står stille, er ikke en rein.'* 'A still reindeer is not a reindeer,'" said Leif. "Migration is a part of their being. To move is to exist."

They drove further into the wilderness. Charlene noticed telephone poles running alongside the dirt track, which surprised her, given the remoteness of

*Fig. 1.3. The Wardenclyffe Tower at
the Bjørnens Hule, Kirkenes, Norway*
From Røed-Larsen, P., *Spesielle Partikler*, p. 148

their surroundings. The poles carried a black cable that was as thick as a grown man's leg. Gradually, a tower became visible in the distance. The top of the tower was bulbous; it looked like a mushroom-headed rocket ship.

"What is that?" asked Charlene.

"It's our Wardenclyffe tower," said Leif.

"What's a Wardenclyffe tower?"

"Nikola Tesla invention," said Kermin, craning his head to get a look. "It makes free electricity for whole world. But how did you do this?"

"So you know about Tesla?" Leif said into the rearview mirror.

"Of course. He was Serb," said Kermin.

"And a poor businessman. But he was also the greatest mind of the last two hundred years."

"Wait—free electricity for the whole world?" said Charlene. "Is that even possible?"

"Yes, well, it's all in theory right now," said Leif. "But Tesla's design was quite genius. The towers use the earth like a battery, drawing electricity from deep currents—"

"Intra-crustal telluric currents," said Kermin.

"That's right." Leif paused. "And then the tower transmits this current through the atmosphere. The idea is that everyone has a small antenna on their roof and receives their electricity almost like a radio wave—"

"How deep into ground do wires go?" Kermin interrupted.

"Three hundred meters." Leif smiled. "Deep enough."

The road ended at the base of the Wardenclyffe tower, where there was a cluster of a dozen or so traditional wooden lodges with sod growing on the roofs. Lying between the buildings were large piles of mechanical equipment— ten-foot diesel engines and generators and strange, loop-de-loop electrical transistors. Wires ran from each house into the tower, then back into the transistors, then into totemlike wooden carvings of animals frozen in ferocious poses, their eyes replaced by lightbulbs. They disembarked from the jeep and stood, blinking.

"Welcome to home base," said Leif. "We affectionately call it the Bjørnens Hule, or 'the Bear's Cave' in English. We're somewhere between the Finnish-Norwegian border."

"What do you mean, *between?*" Charlene asked.

"Borders are complicated up here. Especially now. The Cold War has made everything a bit testy. You can't spit near the Russian border without being picked up. But borders are not natural things. Birds do not listen to borders."

"But we're in Norway now?"

"Well, something strange happened. A cartographer made a mistake. The Finns thought the border was one line, the Norwegians thought it was another. Normally when this happens you get a big argument and maybe a war or two because someone is claiming too much, but, typical Scandinavians, both countries have claimed too little. And now there's a space, like this."

He used his fingers to demonstrate:

Finland

Norway

"It's where we get our emblem. The eye." He pointed at the base of a totem pole, where a stenciled eye watched them without comment.

"Over there," he said, waving his hand vaguely, "is the Treriksrøysa. A point where Norway, Finland, and Russia all come together. You aren't allowed to walk around this point fully, like this," he said, promenading his fingers, "because you would violate international law. Wandering in and out of countries. But how about this: at this point, if such a point could even exist, *time fluctuates*. Norway is on Central European time, Finland is on Eastern European time, one hour ahead, and Russia is on Moscow time, two hours ahead. One point, three times. How can that be? And yet we're okay with this being true."

Charlene looked at her watch, suddenly feeling as if she were losing her bearings.

"What time is it right now? I forgot to set my watch." She fiddled with the dial, spinning the hour hand forward.

He shrugged. "In the summer, when the sun never sets, time becomes quite relative."

"Twelve thirty?"

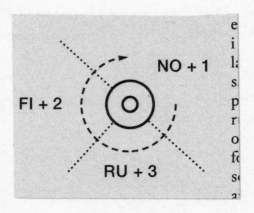

Fig. 1.4. The Treriksrøysa
From Røed-Larsen, P., *Spesielle Partikler,* p. 140

"As you wish." He smiled. "But I'm sorry, I'm being a terrible host. You must be exhausted from your travels. Would you like a sauna? I find it's the only way to cure jet lag."

Caught between a haze of weariness and the urge to follow local custom, Kermin and Charlene, against their better judgment, found themselves stripped and sweating alongside Leif inside a small sauna cabin on the outskirts of camp while Radar slept outside on a blanket in the grass.

The ticking of the sauna's furnace and the resonant smell of the baking cedar planks overwhelmed Charlene's fragile system. She tried to let the heat perform its restorative magic but found it difficult to relax while naked inside a small, sweltering room alongside this stranger. She peeped out through the little window in the door to see if her son was still there, then she cinched the towel tighter around her breasts.

"So how do you know Brusa Tofte-Jebsen?" she asked.

"Brusa and I taught together in Bergen before the war," said Leif. His hairless body glistened pink, his small penis a little mole rat of a thing, which she tried to avoid with her eyes. He did not seem to be sweating.

"I have been to Bergen," said Kermin abruptly.

"Oh?" said Leif. "A beautiful place, isn't it?"

"I don't remember," said Kermin. "It was night and I am sick. We escaped to America. We were not tourists."

"Ah, well, that's a shame. It's funny how beautiful towns can turn very ugly in difficult times. You forget to look at the views, you know what I mean?"

"Then you moved up here?" said Charlene.

"When the Nazis invaded, I had just started my first year teaching physics and chemistry in high school. You can't imagine what it's like to be occupied. We all wanted to join the resistance but didn't know how. It was like a slow death. A silent death. We did simple things, stupid things, like wearing paper clips on our lapels as a sign of protest. We started underground newspapers, declaring all kinds of things. Suddenly you had a newspaper, so you had to have radical ideas to go in the newspaper. Many people think the idea comes first, but it's usually the other way around. You need a place to put the idea before you can have the idea, you know what I mean? But the real turning point was when the quislings wanted all of us teachers to sign a declaration of allegiance. The declaration stated we could only teach Nazi-sponsored topics and such. So we saw our chance—we would take a stand and break our silence. We refused to sign the document. All of us. Without even consulting each other. Seven hundred teachers were arrested, rounded up, and sent up the coast on a small boat. It was packed to the ceiling. Many of them got very sick on the journey. Some even died. Brusa and I worked for a year in the camp up here in Elvenes. Heavy labor. It was freezing; terrible conditions, you know. But we started a few interesting projects in secret, and after they released us, a couple of us ended up staying. And now I have been here for over thirty years."

"Brusa lives here, too?"

"No, he ended up leaving. A disagreement over language." Leif dipped a wooden ladle into a bowl of water and poured it over the stones. A great wall of wet heat rose up and enveloped them.

"Ay," said Charlene. Her head felt as if it were compressing.

Leif did not seem to notice her distress. "You see, here in Norway," he said, "there are actually two languages, two different types of Norwegian—Nynorsk and Bokmål. To an outsider, the differences between them might seem minimal, but there have been years of turmoil and cultural warring over who should speak what, and which is the true language and which is not. It's all a bit silly— I can say this to you now—but back then it mattered a great deal whether 'I' was *jeg* or *eg*. Somehow everything else depended upon this distinction. Did you say *jeg*? Or did you say *eg*? There could be no compromise."

"So what did Brusa say? *Jeg* or *eg*?" she asked, trying to breathe normally.

"Without boring you with the specifics, as a group we chose to speak Nynorsk, which was the language invented for the people, not the elite, who all spoke Bokmål. Bokmål is really a kind of bastardized Danish. And Brusa didn't like this decision, even though we took a vote and it was all done completely democratically. He thought Nynorsk was one man's fantasy. So he left. To tell you the truth, I don't think he ever wanted to stay. He was a different breed than I was. He wanted to be a writer. Some people are meant to do things, and some people are meant to write about these things from a great distance."

The heat was beginning to get to her. She ran a finger across a sweat-soaked eyebrow.

"Brusa seems to admire you a lot," she said. "He was the one who recommended we come here."

"Yes, well, from afar, one can admire one's nemesis."

"Nemesis?"

"Perhaps this is a bad translation. In Norwegian we say *konkurrent*. And this means 'opponent,' but it also means 'someone who is a part of you.'"

"Your English is very good."

"Of course," he said. "I'm Norwegian."

She suddenly had the urge to ask Leif about Per Røed-Larsen and why he might not have wanted them to come, but then she would have had to reveal to Kermin that she had kept the telegram from him. She would have to acknowledge that the telegram had been real.

Instead she said: "So you started a school up here?"

"Not quite," Leif said. He dipped the ladle into the water again. Charlene wanted to tell him not to do it, but he was already dousing the rocks. The air grew thick with vapor. Charlene's head started to swim. "At first, when the war was still on, it was a resistance movement. But not with weapons. We were interested in issues of atomics, theater, the avant-garde. You know, we were still young then. We thought we could change everything by staging a little happening about nuclear fission and cultural decimation on the tundra. There was no audience. No one even knew we existed. But I've come to learn that this isn't how you win a war. And it isn't what the people needed. At the end of the war, this whole area was completely destroyed by the Nazis. Can you imagine? First there was a town, and then there was nothing. Just ashes, bent metal, these terrible memories. For a while there, that's all there was up here. Terrible, terrible memories. We are lucky memories die with those who have them."

The heat was causing Charlene's vision to collapse in on itself.

"I'm sorry. I can't do it anymore. I have to get out," she said. "I'm going to check on Radar."

"Yes, it takes some getting used to," he said. "But it will cure you of almost anything. I hardly notice the heat anymore."

To her horror, she found Radar asleep amid a swarm of mosquitoes. How stupid she had been to leave him unattended! She swatted angrily at the insects. Attacking her poor, helpless child—how dare they? The mosquitoes responded to her attacks by gleefully turning their attention to her.

"I'm sorry," Leif said, emerging from the sauna pink and steaming. "I should've warned you about the *myggs*. They can be nasty this time of year. They have a short period to do their damage, and they take their job very seriously. A reindeer can lose two liters of blood per day."

They flip-flopped back to the main lodge. Now, suddenly, all Charlene could think about were the swarms of mosquitoes dive-bombing their heads. She protectively enshrouded Radar with a towel as they passed a group of men filming what looked like a collection of headless, green-skinned dolls.

From beneath his towel, Radar pointed to the dolls. "Halfway oop or down de stairs," he said.

"Yes. That's like Robin's song, isn't it?" Charlene sang: *"Halfway down the stairs is a stair where I sit. There isn't any stair quite like it."*

"It isn't really anywhere, it's somewhere else instead." Leif completed the verse. "God bless the Muppets, eh? Jim Henson's a bit of a deity around here."

"Where dere heads go?" Radar asked.

"An excellent question, my friend. One that we're trying to figure out as we speak," Leif said. "Do you know where we put them?"

"Nooo," Radar said shyly.

Leif waved at the film crew, but the men were too embroiled in an animated argument to respond. One of them flicked at a green doll, and its body parts flew in all directions. Then the man pulled at an invisible string and the parts returned, the doll whole again. This demonstration calmed the group; they all laughed and then looked up and waved back at Leif.

Charlene noticed a tall, towheaded boy standing among the men.

"Who's the kid?" she asked.

"Oh, that's Lars. The first and only child to be born in the Bjørnens Hule. Fortunately, he has caught the bug from his father."

"Is that you?"

Leif laughed. "No, no. I'm childless, partnerless. My work is my life. My family are these men here. I barely have time to breathe. His father's the famous Jens Røed-Larsen."

"Røed-Larsen?" said Charlene.

"That's right."

"Any relation to Per Røed-Larsen?" She butchered the rolling ø.

"You know Per?" Leif's face clouded over.

"No, no," Charlene said. "I've only . . . I've only read his work."

"And?"

"I'm not sure what to think."

"Per's an interesting character. A bit of a groupie, one must say, though you can't blame him. Jens had a family before he came here. Per is Jens's other son. And then Jens abandoned him for us, and Per has never quite gotten over it."

"Abandoned him?"

"Per stayed in Oslo with his mother. And now he has become obsessed with us. He's writing our history, you see. Writing it before we've even managed to make history."

"So then Lars . . ." She stared at the boy holding one of the green dolls.

"Is from a different woman, yes. Siri. They met here. You'll probably see her around."

"How scandalous," said Charlene.

Leif shrugged. "Strange things happen this far north. I cannot control what others do or say. I can only look after myself."

In the main lodge, they drank black tea and sampled some local Lapland sautéed reindeer meat that smelled to Charlene of old leather jacket and a particular hairspray that she recognized from somewhere deep in her memory. This was undercut by a lingering aroma of ancient peat moss, finished with a touch of lard that had recently turned. She forced herself to try the meat out of politesse. It was delicious. Salty and rich and sweet all at once. It tasted of wet tundra, of pumping leg muscles, of crystallized sweat on the hide.

"Not so bad, yeah?" Leif chewed. "We call it *finnbiff.* An acquired taste, but then everything is acquired north of the Arctic Circle."

"I have a sensitive nose, that's all," she said.

"Alas, I've never had a sense of smell," said Leif. "Though one gets used to it and seeks pleasure in other delights."

Radar licked at the meat on his plate and then recoiled. "Ewwww, 'lectric poop," he said and hid his face in Charlene's lap.

Leif laughed.

"Sorry," said Charlene. "He can be so picky."

"Not at all. The boy knows what he wants, that's all. An admirable quality."

Charlene took a breath. "Thank you, Mr. . . . Dr. Holtsmark, for all of your hospitality." She swept her arm around the room.

"Please," he said. "Call me Leif."

"Okay," she said. "Leif, then. May I ask what you propose?"

"Propose?"

She looked at Kermin. "To do with our son."

He wiped at his lips with a napkin. "Let me show you something."

He got up and fetched a smooth, white rectangular cube with four bolts protruding from two of its sides. He handed it to Charlene. "Do you know what this is?"

Charlene glanced at the cube and then handed it to Kermin, who inspected it closely. After a moment he said, "It looks like voltage switch, but what is this . . . this white box?"

"This is the world's first organic semiconductor bistable switch. Made of polyacetylenes, or *melanin*—the pigments in our skin," said Leif. He took the switch back from Kermin. "The human body is really a wet-tissued machine. It runs on electricity. We've been studying the organic circuitry of the human body for some time, particularly the chemical properties of melanin as a semiconductor. It's such a beauty of a substance. It's not just in the skin—we have melanin in the brain, in the substantia nigra. You find this in the basal ganglia—it's the focal site of learning, reward, addiction, eye movement. But of course, melanin's most visible role is in the dermis, where it performs some of its most remarkable functions, interacting with the environment around us. We're basically covered in a thin coat of 'light radios' that react to UV radiation waves and convert these waves into different energies."

Kermin was sitting very still. Charlene felt compelled to reach out and hold her husband's hand. She felt suddenly close to him. As if the two of them were confronting the world together for the first time.

"So what does this mean for Radar?" she said.

"We've been doing some research of our own here. We were investigating how we might turn a human being into a puppet. To rewire the body so that it is completely controlled by another. You can imagine the theatrical and philosophical fallout from such a discovery. We were deathly excited about the idea, but it never quite panned out. At least not yet. But during the course of our electrochemical experimentation, we did stumble upon several accidental discoveries. We found that with certain electromagnetic adjustments, we're actually able to tune the dial of our melanin light radios—I could turn you into a shortwave radio, for instance, or a telephone, or a television—and we've done this with a couple of our own people. We're pale-skinned, so it's a little more difficult, but Thorgen, one of the puppeteers, was playing Shostakovich for two days straight—except only he could hear it, and it nearly drove him nuts. At first we couldn't figure out how to turn it off, but we've learned more with each experiment. We keep getting better at this."

"His skin was playing music?"

"In a manner of speaking," he said. "His dermis was translating radio waves from a station in Murmansk into pulses that resonated throughout his endoskeleton. His body had become a radio, with receiver, speaker, and no tuning dial, unfortunately. This may come later. But this isn't even the end of what we can do. What's even trickier is to actually manipulate the physical composition of these melanosome radios to our liking. We can change their structure. And thus their appearance."

"Meaning you can change a person's color?"

"Exactly."

"So what's wrong with him, then?"

"You mean what's wrong with your son? This I cannot tell you. Nothing, as far as I can see. But then, it's all how you view it. I cannot diagnose. What I can do is manipulate the proteins in his skin and change the molecular composition of his dermis."

"And you've done this before?"

"Only once, but it worked beautifully."

"Who was it?"

"As a doctor, I'm not at liberty to give you his name, but I will say he was a Negro boy living with the Sami. I'm not sure how he got there. He spoke their language perfectly. And they had heard through the Finnmark grapevine that we were doing these kinds of experiments. And so they came and asked for this. They said it was the child's choice."

"How old was he?"

"Nine or ten."

"And he wanted to change his color?"

"Apparently so. Afterwards, his appearance changed dramatically."

She considered this. "Why did he do it?"

"I think he was confused. He was the only one who looked like he did. He wanted to be one of them."

"But he was only a kid!" Charlene exclaimed. "How could he know what he wanted? You shouldn't just be allowed to change him like that. What if he . . . came to regret it later?"

"I didn't give counseling in this regard. I was merely fulfilling their request."

Kermin shifted in his chair. Radar began to sing quietly to himself, touching his fingers together: "Halfway oop or down stairs, halfway oop or down stairs . . ."

Charlene looked at her son.

"Is it dangerous?" she asked.

"I don't want to mislead you. Everything in life is dangerous. But we're careful men here. I wouldn't expose your child to undue harm. For this I give you my word."

"You *electrocute* him?"

"It's more like a *reverse* electrocution. A negative electromagnetic pulse. We call it electro-enveloping. We would uncharge his subcutaneous layer—specifically his melanosomal proteins—using very precise bilateral voltage switches. We couldn't guarantee final coloring, but"—he leaned back, eyeing them—"we could get it close to his parents. If that's what you want."

Charlene held up her hands. "Well, to tell you the truth, we hadn't even gotten that far. We haven't even discussed it at all."

Leif nodded. "Of course, of course. If it helps to think in these terms: we would be merely correcting a glitch in the system."

Without warning, Kermin stood up, overturning his chair. Radar stopped and stared at his father.

"We don't want," he said. "Thank you, doctor, but we are saying no. To all of this. To everything: thank you, no. Come on, Charlene. We are going."

"Kermin!" said Charlene, standing with him. "The man is just trying to—"

"This man is *crazy*," Kermin hissed. "*Jebeno lud*. I work with electricity all my life and this man has no idea what he talks about. You cannot *uncharge* this thing. He will kill him. Do you understand? *He will kill him. Dead. On je manijak.*"

Kermin picked up his son, who was looking worriedly back and forth between mother and father, sensing the bloom of anger. The knots in their voices.

"Kerm—"

"We are gone," said Kermin, and he walked out the door with Radar in his arms. They heard Radar's quiet cry before the door swung closed.

"I'm so sorry," said Charlene. "We didn't really talk this through."

"Please, please," Leif said, holding out his hand. "He's mad. Okay, no problem. Maybe I came on too strong. In Norwegian we have qualifiers, and I don't know how to translate these into English. Sometimes I get carried away. But believe me, I understand the gravity of this decision. I don't take it lightly, at all. Just keep in mind this is a valuable offer that I'm putting on the table. Think it over. Nothing has to be decided now. You've come such a long way. Relax. Enjoy the famous Finnmark air. There's no pressure to do anything right now. You are my guests. My very special guests."

A CABIN HAD BEEN arranged for their arrival. Radar played with a miniature troll he had found on the coffee table and sang quietly to himself.

"Billy clop gruff, trip trop goat come knockin'. Knock it up my bridge."

Charlene walked slowly around the room, running her fingertips across all the old wooden surfaces. She washed her hands and face. Kermin was busy repacking their things.

"I cannot believe it," he was saying. "What ever happened to Europe? *Drkadžije!* And how do these people make a living? Where does money come from? *Kakvi ludaci jebo te!*"

She came back into the room and ran her hand through her hair.

"Kermin," she said, and she was about to ask why they had come all this way just to do nothing, but before she could even begin, Kermin looked up at her and said, without hesitation, "No," and she knew that he was right. She put her wet hands to her face and tried again, halfheartedly, feeling the tears coming—she was not quite sure why; maybe because she knew it was already over. Her hands were cool and wet against her cheeks, and she knew it was madness. Suddenly she saw herself from a great distance, as though she were standing very still on a stage in an empty theater. How had it come to this? Why had she been so intent on coming here? What had she thought would actually happen?

"Trip trop knockin' on my bridge, Mama!" said Radar, offering up the troll to her.

She took the troll and turned it over in her hands. "So what do we do?" she asked quietly.

"What do we do?" said Kermin. "What we're always doing. We go home. We live our lives like people."

"Okay," she said. "Yes." Breathing. "I should've told you. There was a telegram . . ."

"Telly-gram," Radar cried. "Machine say 'Hello how are you?'"

"Don't worry," said Kermin. "We go home. We forget this."

"Okay," she said. "But we can't just leave, Kerm. The plane is tomorrow. You can't just wait by the door the whole evening with your suitcase. Be gracious. The man just wanted to help us."

"The man does not say what he really wants."

"Just be nice. For tonight, and then tomorrow we can leave. We don't have to do anything. It's a vacation, that's all. Think of it like that. They paid for it. We're on vacation."

He stood still. "For you," he said finally. "And then we go."

"And then we go," she agreed.

They embraced. It had been a long time since they had hugged like this. Radar came over and grabbed their legs. Charlene smelled the beginnings of her husband's beard, the quiet and familiar symphony of waxen musk lingering in the neglected crinkles behind his ears. She had forgotten all this. Routine had a way of erasing intimacy's quiet particulars.

8

The evening came, though the sun showed no intention of setting. Leif, now dressed in a crisp white button-down with yellow trousers and plush leather slippers, served them a delicious dinner of salted herring, a rutabaga-and-carrot puree called *kålrabistappe,* lamb sausage, and a small piece of whale meat, which Charlene tried but could not stomach.

"I'm sorry the others couldn't join us," said Leif. "We're a bit swamped with all of the preparations."

"What're you preparing for?" Charlene asked.

"Probably a great disaster." He laughed. "Would you like to try some aquavit? We make it here."

Kermin refused the liquor, but Charlene warmed and opened with each glass. Radar gave a running commentary on the meal. With theatrical precision, Leif listened to the child's words and nodded his agreement.

"Yes, yes, I'll tell the cook," he said. "I do apologize."

Charlene smiled. She felt free. She wanted to tell this man everything. To kiss his bald head. They did not speak of Radar's treatment. There was no need.

After dinner, they said goodnight to their host and walked into the strange, enduring daytime. On the path back to the cabin, they encountered an older man carrying a stack of books.

"Hello," said Charlene, tipsy.

The man stopped. "You must be our guests," he said and bowed. "Jens. Apologies for the mess. Although they seem to like it messy around here. They are *artists,* you see."

"You're Jens?" said Charlene. "Jens Røed-Larsen?"

He smiled at her mangled pronunciation. "I am."

"Your son wrote to me."

"Lars?"

"No, Per."

He looked at her. "There must be some misunderstanding. I don't have a son named Per."

"Per Røed-Larsen."

"I have a daughter, Kari. And Lars. That's all."

"But Leif said that Per was your son. He's writing a history of this place. He sent me a telegram saying . . ." Her words drifted off.

Jens gave her a kind smile. "Leif says many things. You must remember this about him: he's a born performer. He has a tendency to inhabit others. The Per who wrote to you was not my son. He is another Per."

"What do you mean? Which Per is he?"

"This I cannot say." Jens bowed again. "Goodnight. I wish you a pleasant night's sleep. It can be difficult if you aren't used to the light."

After he had left them, Kermin shook his head. "These Norwegians are such bullshit. They do not look you into your eyes. They are like a cat."

"A cat?"

"They never say what they mean."

Despite being utterly exhausted, Charlene considered taking a sleeping pill when they reached the cabin, fearing the midnight sun might keep her awake. This proved unnecessary: within minutes, she and Radar were both asleep, his head nestled into her belly. Kermin lay down beside her and closed his eyes, but the light seeping in between the blinds pinched at his retinas. The skin of his eyelids was not thick enough.

He shuffled out to the porch and softly twisted the dial of his portable transceiver. The frequencies buzzed and chattered; he tuned the squelch, and his radio locked on to some distant signal before settling again and again into a wash of static. He had expected as much. They were at the end of the earth. He had not brought the dipole multidirectional antenna kit that could reach the horizons beyond the horizon. Perhaps he could tap into the Wardenclyffe tower before they left tomorrow and take a quick peek into the concave Arctic radio spectrum.

Then, somewhere at seventeen meters, a channel crackled. A sign of life. Humans carving out an existence on the pole. It was a garbled Russian weatherman. The Slavic gutturals popped and exploded and then evaporated into the churning shallows of white noise. He kept twisting the dial and caught a snippet of the Jackson 5's "I Want You Back," Michael Jackson's young voice rolling up through the sleeve of static, exercising its magnetic pull before the song fell apart beneath the weight of its own interference, disappearing back into the tundra.

Kermin sighed. He was about to put away the radio when he struck upon an eerily clear broadcast at twenty meters. A chorus of drummers. African, perhaps. The beats were syncopated, hypnotic, the sum of their collective polyrhythms emerging and converging, conjuring a high-pitched harmonic tone that sounded like a wet fingertip traveling along the edge of a singing bowl. The harmonics hovered and bobbed and faded away again into the continuous lurch of the drumbeat. Kermin found himself pressing the radio to his ear and closing his eyes. A vision of whales surfacing on a vast ocean, brackish spray exploding into the air. The weightlessness of the sea.

"They're *noaidi* drums," said a voice.

Kermin opened his eyes and saw a perfectly round head. Their host was leaning casually against the porch rail, like a cowboy in the late afternoon. In one of his palms he held a handful of orange berries. He casually tossed one into his mouth.

"Do you want one?" he said, offering a berry to Kermin. "It's a cloudberry. Very important up here. Cures all ills—even those you didn't know you had."

Kermin shook his head. "No, thank you."

"The *noaidi* is like a shaman for the Sami people. He plays the drum to transcend this world and enter into the spiritual realm of the gods. The skin of the *noaidi* drum is painted with a map of this alternate reality. The shamans use the drums to open the avenues to ascendance."

"And they broadcast this?"

"The Sami are modernizing. They're still the subjugated people up here, but they're not stupid. There's a lot of territory in the north, and not everyone can make the *noaidi* ceremonies. Radios collapse distance."

"Radios transmit across distance. Distance cannot collapse."

"I suppose it's all in the perception, isn't it? The world is as we perceive it. During the war, a radio was the most precious commodity. It was how the underground communicated. It was how a family could hear news from the mainland. The Nazis knew this—whoever controlled the radio waves controlled the means of propaganda. So they seized all the radios in Norway. Except we found ingenious ways of hiding them . . . Disguised as an iron. Or a bedpost. We would hollow out a log and put one inside and then stick it in the woodpile. You just had to remember which log contained the radio before you burned it."

"My father was radioman in the war," said Kermin.

"The most valuable man in the company."

Kermin was silent.

"You don't like me, do you, Kermin? You think I want to harm your child."

"I don't know you, so there is no way to like you or not."

"I didn't force you to come here."

"You are not connecting Radar to your machine," said Kermin. "So stop thinking about this."

Leif smiled. "Would you like to go for a walk?"

"No, thank you," said Kermin.

"Oh, come now, you're leaving tomorrow, you came all this way—why not let me show you around a little? I promise, it'll be worth your time."

Kermin considered this. "I will only go for two minutes," he said. "Then I come back."

"However much time you can spare. Are you sure you don't want a cloudberry?"

Kermin took the berry from his host. It had a sharp sweetness, a soft pinch on the tongue like the white currants back in Croatia, which he would pluck and squish between his fingers before popping them into his mouth. A wisp of memory he could not quite place sifted across his brain.

"It's not so bad," he said.

"Not so bad?"

"Comprehensive." Kermin volunteered the word that Charlene often used with her smells. "Thank you."

"Comprehensive? Okay. Kermin, I like it. You see? Would I lie to you? The cloudberry is *comprehensive*."

Kermin followed Leif down a path lined with large triangular stones that looked like the oldest objects in the world.

"This place was so different during the war," said Leif. "I used to think that war only changes us. But it also changes the land. It changes the rocks and stones around us."

"I was child in the war."

"Your father was a Chetnik, was he not?"

"Yes," said Kermin. "So what?"

"I was simply stating a fact, not making a judgment."

"My father was good man," said Kermin. "He was fighting for his home. He was radioman, not this general making decisions for all of Chetnik army. He did what they tell him."

"I'm sure he did."

"You cannot blame small people for big problems."

"I'm not suggesting your father was a bad man."

"If my father did not fight for Chetniks," said Kermin, "we would not have to run, and we would not go to Bergen and I would not get on this boat to America and then I would not meet Charlene. I would not have Radar. So this all good things."

"And there would be no RGBNN."

Kermin stopped and stared at his host. "How did you know about this?" he said.

"You thought no one was listening, didn't you? We are always listening."

The RGBNN. Kermin had not thought about these letters in some time. A lantern was lit in the recesses of his memory. *How we forget! How we forget everything!*

Kermin had been in America only six months when his father, Dobroslav Radmanovic, brave radioman for the vanquished Chetniks, collapsed and died while waiting in line at the A&P, ground chuck in hand. A brain tumor had been slowly filling the soft space beneath his skull, an artery had burst, and Dobroslav had unceremoniously surrendered his ticket, at the age of thirty-seven leaving his son orphaned and alone in a strange land.

Luckily, the bureaucratic beast that was the Bergen County Department of Human Services had sent Kermin to the Simics, a well-meaning Serbian-Australian couple who lived in a diminutive row house a stone's throw from exit 13 of the New Jersey Turnpike.

Luka, Kermin's new foster father, was quick to denounce the "Chetnik savages," who he believed had given Serbs a bad reputation abroad.

"No offense to your father, but those men are wicked," he said in Serbian. "The only reason to grow your beard this long is because you are shipwrecked. Otherwise, you have something to hide. The Chetnik is the devil sitting on the Serb's shoulder, whispering everything we do not need to hear."

"In *English*," said Weema, Luka's wife, emerging with cocktail and spatula in hand. "Otherwise, the little rooster will never learn."

"In English, in English," Luka agreed. "Everything is clearer in English. Do you know, my little rooster, that it is impossible to tell a lie in English even if what you say is not true? The opposite is true in Serbian: everything you say is a lie, even if what you say is true. And that is the truth."

The Simics had done their best to give Kermin a Normal American Childhood. They had indeed taught him English. They had sent him to school. They had brought him to St. Sava's each Sunday. They had tolerated his strange radio habits. And yet, as Kermin tried to settle into this new life he had inherited, he could not help feeling a great chasm opening up around the question of his father's legacy. Until the day he died, Dobroslav had never once spoken a bad word about either Đujić or the Chetnik cause. Such unequivocalness left his son balancing a degree of cautious reverence for his father's memory with a growing mistrust for the Chetniks themselves, whom he had increasingly come to understand as collaborationist, disorganized, and potentially genocidal. How, then, to reconcile the participation of someone you loved in what was most probably a very bad thing? Could his father still be a good man who had also participated in evil deeds?

Kermin had resolved this, at least in part, by founding the Ravna Gora Broadcast News Network (RGBNN) when he was sixteen years old. Transmitting from his bedroom in Elizabeth, using a homebrewed radio setup, the RGBNN was a short-lived exercise in making right what was once wrong: it exclusively broadcast elaborate (and one must say, incoherent) anti-fascist manifestos that Kermin had penned himself. He would read these aloud over Luka's old Serbian records.

"Ladies and gentlemen, we are all equal rights," young Kermin intoned into his microphone. "No one can tell us how to make difference from others. We are all made from same branches of trees. We are all human branches. Past is past, future is future, man is man, woman is woman."

Any self-consciousness about the clumsiness of these sermons was mitigated by the knowledge that no one was listening to his frequency, and even if they were, they certainly wouldn't know who was speaking. At least this was what he had assumed.

"YOU ARE JOKING ME," Kermin said to Leif, shaking his head. "Truly—how did you find out? No one knows this."

"You know what your problem is, Kermin?" said Leif, smiling. "You keep wanting us to be different, but the more you get to know me, the more you realize that we are exactly the same."

They walked in silence. The light in the sky had grown soft and casual, like the back of a hand. The drumming popped lightly through Kermin's radio.

Leif stopped. "Tell me, Kermin, are you familiar with Heinrich von Kleist?"

"No."

"Kleist wrote an essay called 'On the Marionette Theatre.' Not an essay, really—more of a dialogue . . . in the Socratic tradition. You know Socrates, yes?"

Kermin shook his head. "Not personally."

Leif laughed out loud. "That is a good one. *'Not personally.'* I must remember that one."

Kermin smiled at his unintentional humor. For just an instant, he felt like the smartest man alive.

"Well, I don't know Socrates personally, either," said Leif. "Nor Kleist. But in his essay, two men discuss puppetry, which at the time was seen as a petty craft, performed by unskilled peasants for children and criminals. In many ways, not that different from how it is perceived today, yes?"

"Puppets?" said Kermin. "Like Pinocchio?"

"You see? You think of puppets and you immediately think of children. You have been corrupted by a lack of imagination. Kleist's essay addresses this exact problem. . . . In his piece, one of the men proposes that the puppet, without any awareness of self, is more graceful, *more true,* in the Kantian sense, than any human actor can possibly be. This astonishes his partner, who, like you, has never before considered the puppet as anything but a child's toy. But here, then, is the problem: a human cannot move without also observing his own movement, and in observing it, he corrupts it. A puppet doesn't suffer from this same condition. It's free to inhabit only the movement asked of it, nothing more, and in doing so, the puppet tempts perfection—and, indeed, God himself."

"Without observation, there is no life."

"But how do you know? This is an assumption on your part, yes?"

Kermin turned off his radio. "You are a crazy man."

"No, Kermin, I'm a puppeteer. There's a difference," said Leif. "Come, I want to show you something."

They walked down some steps, through a gate, and to the door of a large house that Kermin had not seen before. Leif paused with his hand on the doorknob.

"Don't be alarmed by what you're about to see," he said. "Your life will never be in danger. Do you trust me?"

"No."

"Fine. Probably better this way," said Leif and opened the door.

The entire house was one large room, with high ceilings and a dimly lit stage at its center, surrounded by several rows of empty chairs. In the middle of the stage stood a bear, perhaps nine feet tall. At first Kermin thought the bear was merely a taxidermied statue, but then he saw its head twist and one of its paws shudder and he realized the thing was alive. He took a step back against the wall.

"Don't be afraid," said Leif. "We've controlled Gunnar thoroughly. He only knows his task."

"He is real bear?"

"As real as you or I," said Leif. "Now I want you to fight him."

"Jesi lud."

"I assure you, there's no danger. Gunnar will never fight back; he has been trained only to defend." Leif picked up what looked like a fencer's rapier. "The point is not sharp, so have no fear about injuring the creature. Your only objective is to try and tap the pendant attached to the bear's chest. If you do this, the alarm will chime and the fight will be over."

"I'm not fighting a bear. He will kill me."

"The bear won't kill you. The bear cannot kill you. For this I give you my word. The only person who can defeat you is you."

"I don't take your word."

"All right, then. We stand at an impasse," said Leif. "If you don't believe another man's word, then what do you believe?"

The question caught Kermin off guard. He had come to Norway hoping that the trip alone would cure his wife of the strange sickness that continued to consume her. He did not know what had gone wrong between them; he could not point to a piece of their life and say, "This is the part that is broken." He knew only that at some point, during some brief, quiet moment when he had not been paying attention, they had drifted off course, and they were now in uncharted waters. Kermin never claimed to know much in this world, but he did know that he must never lose Charlene, that without her he would never be whole again. And so he had tried to come to this place with an open mind, even if he knew in his heart that he had relinquished some vital part of himself by even setting foot here. Maybe this was what love had become: the slow act of giving up more and more until nothing of yourself remained. Yet when Leif had described the procedure to treat their son, something inside of him had snapped and recoiled—not because he believed the procedure wouldn't work or that

Radar might be harmed, but because he knew that there was a very real possibility that it *would* work, and that afterwards, nothing could ever be the same.

Through the shadows of the room, Kermin looked at the bear, who had not moved since their arrival, save for bobbing his head back and forth ever so slightly, giving him an air of reluctant wisdom.

Again the lantern of memory was lit, and Kermin was suddenly taken with a forgotten scene from his past: Once, when he was very young, he was walking through the woods alone, gathering white currants into a thrush basket for his mother's preserves. He had not told his mother where he was going, because he knew she would never have let him go. The war had already been raging for two years, and she had forbidden him to wander, but he had wanted to surprise her with the basketful of currants, to make her smile again, just like she had done before his father left to go fight in the hills. Together they would dip the jars into the boiling water, mash up the berries, and make her famous preserves.

But somewhere along the way, Kermin had gotten lost. Scared and feeling feverish, he had stumbled into an unfamiliar clearing, and there, sitting in the sunlight, working at one of his paws, was a floppy-skinned brown bear. Kermin's first thought was that it must be a man in a bear costume, for the bear's gentle sentience was much too close to his own. And then the bear, startled by his sudden entrance, leaped to its feet and took several tumbling steps toward him. Kermin froze, not daring to move, his basket of currants trembling at his side. He could hear the bear's ragged breath coming in snorts and sniffles. He realized that the creature was trying to smell him, trying to understand what kind of thing he was.

"I'm Kermin," he had whispered. "I'm not a person." He had meant to say "bad person," but the word *bad* had gotten lost somewhere in the space between his mind and his throat.

The bear seemed to hear this. It moved its head back and forth, as if attempting to listen to him from both ears, and then it yawned a slow, wild yawn, peeling back the wet skin around its teeth. Kermin remembered feeling not scared so much as deeply, profoundly amazed that the world could contain both him and the bear at the same time. He hoped then that if his father and the Chetniks ever came upon this bear, they would not shoot it with their guns, but would somehow realize that this bear was a peaceful bear who only wanted to lick his paws and eat some currants and look at the moon.

"Don't shoot him, Tata," he whispered to the bear. "He's not the war."

The bear nodded, turned, and, with one last mournful look in Kermin's direction, disappeared into the forest.

Now, against the glow of that memory, Kermin looked at the bear standing in the middle of the darkened room. Were these two bears related? No. *Impossible*. They were thousands of kilometers from the Balkans. But . . . did bears possess memories, too? Did that bear in Croatia carry with him the image of a child picking white currants? And what of this bear? Would he remember tonight? Would he remember what was about to happen?

He made a decision, then and there: he would fight the bear. It was clear to him now that he had come here for a reason. If he won the fight, then he would know he was on the right course. He would know his cause was just and that he must not sacrifice his son to satiate his wife's despair.

And if he lost? If he lost, he was not sure what he would do.

"Give me this stick," he said to Leif.

His host raised his eyebrows. "So you will do it?"

"If this bear kills me, I will really be pissed off," he said.

Kermin approached the bear, holding the rapier taut by his side. He could see the yellows of the creature's eyes, the glint of the pupils following him across the room. And still the bear did not move; it remained reared up on its haunches, waiting, its head gently moving back and forth. Kermin could see the pendant gleam red against its belly. A smell of oily fur and animal flesh hung thickly in the air.

Kermin cautiously approached. This bear was bigger and blacker than the one from his memory. It continued to stand rigid and unmoving in the middle of the room, undeterred by Kermin's approach. At first wary, but then emboldened by the bear's eerie stillness, Kermin inched closer and then closer still, until he was only four feet away from the creature. The bear towered above him; its massive head swaying lightly on the sill of its thickset shoulders. One swipe of the creature's paw would send him careening across the room and most likely shatter his entire body. The bear stood, immobile, trembling just so. Kermin realized that, unlike in his encounter with the bear in the forest, he could not hear the creature's breath. There was only the sound of his own breathing.

He looked back at his host, who gave him a gesture of encouragement. Maybe this was all a psychological trick. Maybe the bear would never move. He could end this with a single tap. A test of courage and faith. The bear was his *konkurrent*.

He took a deep breath and swung his rapier as fast as he could at the bear's chest. He readied himself for the feeling of impact, but at the very last moment, the bear's paw shot up and parried the blow, pushing the rapier's path down and to the left so that Kermin's momentum carried him forward and onto the floor, where he lay helpless at the bear's feet. He expected the bear to pounce upon him, to tear him to pieces, yet the beast did not move from its upright position.

Kermin got up, burning with the heat of humiliation. He tried again. This time, anticipating the block, he was ready for a counterattack, but this, too, was easily deflected by the bear's other paw. *It could not be!* The bear's reaction time was uncanny. Kermin's rapier zipped through the air, flicking this way and that, and yet every thrust was met with a perfectly equal and opposite block. The bear did not expend one ounce of extra energy; quickly and quietly, he adjusted to Kermin's attacks and moved accordingly. And yet when Kermin made to thrust but did not, the bear would not even flinch.

Life shrank to the singular task of delivering the point of his rapier to its intended target. Everything depended upon this very small piece of physics. And yet he could not do it. He became frustrated, then resigned, then angry, then oddly exuberant. The bear blocked attack after attack, hypnotically countering each and every gesture he performed. The pendant gleamed, remaining untouched.

Finally, after he had lunged and was sent sprawling across the floor for the umpteenth time, Kermin lay on the ground, soaked in sweat. The muscles in his arms were shaking uncontrollably.

"That bear, that bear . . ." he whispered. *"Mamojebac."* He was crying from the pure effort of his defeat.

Leif approached, clapping his hands. "Amazing. We've been here for just over an hour. You possess such great resolve. Such self-belief. It is a rare quality these days."

"This bear is unbelievable," said Kermin.

"Not so unbelievable. I built him myself."

Kermin slowly rose to his feet, his head pounding.

Leif carefully circumnavigated the bear and then approached from the rear, where he casually reached around the giant stomach, as if to hug the beast, before tapping the pendant with his finger. An alarm sounded and the bear froze stiff.

"Every problem must have a solution," he said. "Come here, Kermin. Let me show you."

Still breathing hard, Kermin joined Leif behind the bear. He had removed a part of the bear's fur and was holding the flap open for Kermin to see inside. In the dim light, Kermin squinted and saw the glint of metal—hundreds of intricate gears and cables standing still inside the creature.

"What?" said Kermin.

Among the gears he could see the white stencil of the eye.

"Yes. You see?" said Leif. "Every move was preprogrammed. He knew what you would do before you did it."

"How?" Kermin felt as if he were falling down a deep well.

"He's a puppet. He's a god."

OUTSIDE, THE SUN was finally setting. The dusk, stretched and weightless. Everything smoldering white, yellow, pink. Not so much a sunset as a suspension of disbelief.

"The sun will rise as soon as she sets. Like a breath," said Leif. "To really understand the mind-set up here, you must first understand the light. . . . In the summer, there is no night. We're illuminated for twenty-four hours a day. Our skin becomes confused—you feel alive, like you might never die, as if anything is possible. People don't realize this, but there are many more deaths in the summer than the winter, because people believe they're invincible. In the winter you are much more of a realist. The daylight grows shorter until there is no day at all. But it is not completely dark. There is a wonderful depth to the sky in the winter—the light is almost blue. I feel most at peace then. In the summer I do not sleep, but in the winter—this is when I do my thinking."

They walked. Kermin was still shaken by the image of the bear's metallic innards. There was no life in there, only the click and pop of the mechanism. The promise of movement. The sum of all those gears had equaled his defeat.

He patted his sore hands against his hips and looked up. The sky had turned soft and thick, the light suspended above their heads like a sheet. As if light were a language spoken between heaven and earth.

Kermin realized then that this was the most beautiful place he would ever see in his life. The thought saddened him, for it was an empty beauty, a reluctant beauty, a landscape of longing you did not want buried with you in your grave.

"I've been thinking a lot about the pole," Leif said suddenly.

"What is the pole?" Kermin asked, not quite listening.

"The North Pole. It's a place that often recurs in my dreams. Did you know that at the pole, the sun only sets once a year? A six-month day followed by a six-month night."

"When do you have breakfast?"

"Ah! You are a funny man, Kermin. Most people probably don't understand this about you. When indeed? Two months in? Three months? Or do you go directly to brunch? You can see my dilemma. On the one hand, the pole is a point of infinite possibility. The lines of longitude converge there, and so the North Pole contains all longitudes at once. In essence, you could choose any coordinate with a latitude of ninety degrees north and you would be correct about your position. How to function with so much choice? But then on the other hand, *the only direction you can head is south*. Can you imagine? You have no choice. You *must* head south, there is no other way. Wait—" Leif grabbed Kermin's arm and pointed.

"Look."

They stopped and watched the sky. The sun, perched on the lip of the horizon, seemed to tremble before sliding from view. The world blinked, waited, and then there was the sun again, rising unperturbed, as if it had all been some kind of performance.

Kermin turned and seized Leif's shoulder. They stood looking at each other, caught inside their own magnetic field.

"Will you hurt him?" Kermin asked. His grip was firm, but there was tenderness in that connection, an insistence to the present.

"I will not," said Leif.

"But you can do what you say?"

"I'm not in the business of lying, my friend. I say what I mean."

"I care about him more than anything."

"Of course."

"But I must also take care of my wife."

"Of course you must."

Kermin released his shoulder. "After, how will he be?" he said quietly.

"This I cannot say," said Leif, shaking his head. "But how does that saying go? *'To know the son, look at the father.'*"

They walked on and came to the entrance of another lodge. Another eye above its doorway, staring at them. Leif saw Kermin looking at the emblem.

"If the eye belongs to no one, what does it see?" he asked. And then he opened the door and flicked on the light, which sputtered to reveal a large room filled with shelves of cogs, gears, and pulleys. There were rolls upon rolls of wire and dangerous-looking three-pointed mechanisms and small wooden mannequins contorted into ghastly pirouettes. Kermin looked up at the ceiling. From the rafters hung hundreds of puppets. Hundreds and hundreds of them. All of them headless.

Kermin stared. He had never seen such a collection of wonders in his life.

"As you can see, we're running out of room," said Leif.

"Where are their heads?"

"An old superstition. If you leave the puppet's head on overnight, it may come to life and take its revenge," said Leif. "You must separate the body from the mind."

"And all of this stuff is for making your puppets?"

"Yes. But unfortunately, for our next show we need something more."

"More than *this*?"

"You know how it is. You want what you cannot have. Our next show is about a brand-new idea in theoretical physics called the quark-gluon plasma, a condition that existed briefly after the Big Bang—at least in theory."

"I don't know about this."

"The basic idea is that following the birth of our universe, there was a moment of extremely high temperatures. We are talking *extremely* high, as in never before or since—a singular thermopoetic event. At these temperatures, all matter breaks down into essential building blocks. And for a moment there, right after the creation of our world . . . everything was broken and *everything was the same*. No larger unique molecules, no atoms, no nuclei—just a sea of indistinguishable quarks and gluons. Can you imagine it? The whole universe as a sea of sameness."

"It sounds bad."

"It sounds beautiful. And it sounds a bit like some of the most extreme forms of communism, yes? Complete and utter equality?"

"Communism never works this way."

"Not yet, at least. And I'm not talking about your brand of bourgeois Eastern European Tito communism. This is like window dressing. You must look farther east for the plasma. Burma. The Khmer Rouge in Cambodia. North Korea. China. Well, maybe China no longer."

"So your show is about this? Quark gluton communism?"

"You're good, Kermin. One must say this about you," said Leif. "No, the challenge we face right now is much more mundane. You see, we're building puppets with screens inside of them. Televisions. So they can become anyone they want . . . like an infinite mask. These are certainly our most complex constructions to date. And their circuitry must be able to function in very hot and wet conditions—in the Cambodian jungle, you see, where there's no electricity. We're struggling to make all of this work . . . The wiring is really very tricky. You work with televisions, don't you?"

"Yes."

"Little televisions?"

"Little televisions." Kermin felt a great delight in saying this. "Very mini televisions."

"Maybe I could pick your brain sometime about a few small matters. For instance, we are interested in liquid crystals on plasma-polymerized films. Do you know about these?"

"Of course."

"Of course you do. You see? You and I are not so different."

They stood, staring at the vast collection of puppet detritus. In the middle of the room sat a strange machine that looked like a suspended metal barrel resting on two trapezes, with a large collection of spiraling wires exploding from either end. The barrel was covered in bulbous glass protrusions. Kermin put his hand on one of these glass lumps. It was warm to the touch. He felt a sudden, precise absence in his chest and then his head swam, as if he had been holding his breath for too long.

"What is this?" he asked, withdrawing his hand.

"That. That's a vircator," said Leif. "That is what will cure your son."

9

The next morning, Charlene awoke early to find Kermin already up. Radar was next to him, quietly working on an exploded radio at the little wooden table. It was chilly inside the cabin. Outside, summer snow had fallen sometime during the long, illuminated night. A fresh wet coating of white covered the ground, broken only by a lone set of paw prints that wove and wandered through the cluster of buildings.

"What're you doing?" Charlene said sleepily, coming over to the table.

"We are repairing, aren't we?" said Kermin.

"This radio is broken," Radar agreed.

"I had the strangest dream last night." She yawned. "Did you have any dreams?"

"No," said Kermin.

"No dream," Radar agreed.

"It must be something about being up here. Or maybe it's just all the travel, but I swear, it was so vivid. I was on this boat or barge or something. In the jungle, floating down a big river. And I knew these people were watching me from the trees. I couldn't quite see them, but I knew they were there. And I hear this shout, like a warning, and I expect some kind of attack, but then I look up and I see that the river is ending. Just disappearing into nothing. It's like the water is there one minute and then it's not there. And then, just before I get to the place where the river is ending, I wake up. And you know what's strange? In the dream, it wasn't that I was scared to go through that point of no return—it was that I *wanted* to go through, to see what was on the other side. When I woke up, I could feel this disappointment, you know?"

Kermin looked up at her. "It's okay to give him treatment."

"What do you mean?"

"I mean, we can let him treat Radar. I think it's okay."

"But . . . but you said it was dangerous." She shivered, hugging herself.

"He will be fine. It's what you want. It's what we came here for."

Charlene studied her husband's face. Then she sat down in a chair and pulled Radar to her.

"How're you feeling this morning?" she asked.

"Fiiiineee," he said, electronics in hand. "I like dat man with da white head."

"Who's that?"

"He means Leif. Bald-head Leif," said Kermin.

Charlene laughed. "You do? You like Leif? Crazy old Leif?"

Radar nodded. "Yeah. He makes Kermint go explode!"

"Kermit or Kermin, honey?"

"He makes little green Kermint go explode!" Radar demonstrated with his hands, sending flecks of saliva onto the table.

Charlene smiled. She turned back to her husband, placing a hand on his leg. "Why have you changed like this?"

"It's okay."

"You're doing this for me?"

Kermin nodded. "I want to fix."

"But why now?" She was filled with a sudden wash of uncertainty. "You said you didn't trust him."

"I think we found something here. You said this yourself. Maybe these things happen for a reason. Maybe Leif is not so crazy as he looks. He's giving me his promise."

Radar reached down and plucked up a radio wire from the careful sea of parts.

"No, my little angel," Charlene said, taking the wire from him. "That's not for you."

"Give it!" Radar said, reaching for the wire.

"It's okay," Kermin said, handing the wire back to his son. "He knows what's for him."

"Oh, I don't know," she said. She closed her eyes. "I don't know anymore."

"It is your choice," he said.

She nodded.

"Everything happens for a reason," he said.

She turned to her son. "Radar, do you want to do an experiment today?"

"What's *speriment*?" he asked.

"It's where they connect you to a big machine."

"*Okaaaay*," Radar said. He touched two wires together and made a fizzling sound with his lips. "Connect. Explode!" He burst his hands apart. The wires flew off the table.

"No explode, honey. Just connect," she said.

Radar looked disappointed.

"Thank you," she whispered to Kermin, reaching over and squeezing his hand. "I love you."

"A telegram came," said Kermin.

"When?"

"This morning."

"Who was it from?"

"I didn't open it. It's there."

Before she had even picked it up, she knew.

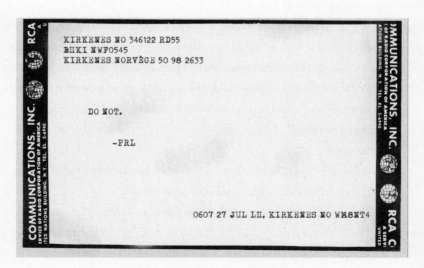

```
KIRKENES NO 346122 RD55
BHKI NWF0545
KIRKENES NORVÈGE 50 98 2633


          DO NOT.

             -PRL




                    0607 27 JUL LH, KIRKENES NO WM8NT4
```

The rest of the day fled toward a distant horizon. By that afternoon everything had been arranged. They stood outside the cabin that housed the vircator. The thin layer of snow had melted into a blanket of fog, relegating the sun to a distant memory. The air against their skin was cool and damp.

Several of the men they had seen before were now milling around, checking wires, writing on clipboards, looking unnecessarily busy. None of the men introduced themselves. Neither Jens, Siri, nor the boy Lars were anywhere to be seen. As preparations were made, Kermin sat on a half-moon boulder some distance away, a radio pressed to his ear, the faint patter of drums emanating from its speaker. Charlene found his newfound nonchalance about the whole matter slightly annoying. She wanted to go over and shake him. *Do you realize what's about to happen? Everything's about to change.*

Leif handed her a large plastic bottle of solution for Radar to drink.

"It's to focus the current," he explained.

"We're going in there?" she asked, pointing to the large cabin.

"*He* will be going in there," he said. "I hope you can understand, but it's not possible for you to be present during the actual procedure."

"But he's my son!"

"I'm sorry."

Charlene thought she would protest more, but she simply nodded, fatigued, haunted by an unsettling feeling that she had seen this all before. The whole scene felt as if it had already happened. She had already been refused entrance to this cabin before. She had already remembered being refused entrance to this cabin before. She tried to shiver away these cycles of recall as she helped Radar drink all of the solution. Then she hugged him and turned him over to Leif.

"Is it painful?" she asked him as he led Radar away.

"Completely painless."

"Are you sure?"

"He won't feel a thing. We don't have nerve sensors for this kind of current."

And then the door swung shut and they were gone.

Charlene was left with her watch and the horrors of time. The next twenty-one and a half minutes proved to be the most difficult of Charlene's life. As Kermin clung to his shitty little radio, she alone faced a thousand possibilities and non-possibilities. She defeated them all and in turn was defeated right back. She wound herself into such a frenzy, she had to take off her shoes. Eleven minutes had passed since that door had swung shut. Still she waited, shoeless, confronting the possibility of a child fundamentally altered. Charlene realized for the first time how lucky she was to have a son exactly like Radar Radmanovic. She would not change one single thing. She would not alter a hair on his head. She wanted to cancel the entire procedure, to yell, *Stop! Stop!* Paralyzed, she did nothing except hate herself for doing nothing, for having done nothing, for having done *this*.

Twenty-one and a half minutes later, Radar emerged. She ran up and hugged him, prodding at his thin little bones until he began to squirm. There was a new scent about him that she could not identify, but otherwise he seemed unchanged.

"Dat machine make me crackle!" he declared proudly.

"He did fine, just fine," said Leif.

"You are still you?" She was weeping at his sameness.

"I need to go the pee-potty," said Radar.

"Thank you, Leif," she said, smiling through her tears.

"It will take some time," he said, misunderstanding her relief. "The effects are not instantaneous."

Kermin stood some distance away, watching Radar and Charlene. He came up and touched his son's head carefully, with the tips of his fingers, as one examines a melon, and then he nodded at Leif and walked back to their cabin.

IN THEIR CLOSING MEETING, Leif warned of the possibility of "dermal peeling" in the coming months and said it was a natural part of the melanosomal adjustment process. Charlene did not believe him, but she could not help loving him for having total confidence in his quack methodology. His faith in electricity was endearing. He had given her the greatest gift by making her realize what she already had.

It was strange, given all the endless space that Kirkenesferda had at their disposal, how cramped Leif's office was. Every shelf seemed to be filled with papers, books, journals, notebooks, boxes of photographs, and reels of eight-millimeter film. There was a pair of limbless mannequin torsos, one of which had its forehead painted with the eye. There was a deflated barrel organ, a whole box of polished black stones, a bushel of branches tied up in the corner, as if a Russian peasant woman had temporarily deposited her burden.

As was her wont whenever a library presented itself, Charlene got up and examined the collection of books. It was often easier to discover someone through his books rather than his words, to see the overlap and divergence between one's taste and another's and then to triangulate the rest of that person's self appropriately. She had slept with plenty of people simply on the merits of their literary curation.

There was no obvious method of organization. Many of the titles were familiar; these were the same books that lived behind the sheets in her own home. Except that here, many of the standbys that had at one time nourished or tormented her were translated into Norwegian. A shadow army of all the classics, rendered through a peculiar Norse lens. She enjoyed trying to guess what each title was. She recognized Turgenev's *Fedre og sønner,* Vonnegut's *Slaktehus-5, eller Barnekorstoget: en pliktdans med døden,* Bulgakov's *Mester og Margarita,* Calvino's *De Usynlige Byer,* Conrad's *Det inderste mørke.* Could these possibly be the same books that she had read? Had he ingested what she had ingested? She realized that with several of these books, she had fallen in love with a translation that did not exist in the original language, a fact that irked her to no end. Staring at this Arctic library, rendered so beautifully in a tongue she did not comprehend, she found herself wondering: When did a book—ushered across linguistic oceans by the unsteady sloop of translation—stop being the same book?

Leif saw her looking at his shelves. "If you can believe it, there used to be about twice this many," he said. "I recently sent a shipment down to Africa, to a monk who is building a library along the Congo River."

"How generous of you," she said.

In contrast to the light chaos that ruled the rest of the room, she was surprised to find one large shelf in pristine order. Everything was arranged in neat little rows, with not one spine out of place. A shelf of twenty-five numbered binders. It was as if this section belonged to another person who was merely renting the shelf space. Charlene pulled down a thin purple volume, feeling almost guilty for disrupting the order.

GÅSELANDET: TEORIER OM IKKE-DELTAKENDE DRAMA OG ERFARRING, PER RØED-LARSEN

She looked at another. This one was also by Per Røed-Larsen. She looked again. Every single book on the shelf was by him. There were hundreds of them.

"Per Røed-Larsen," she said aloud. It was not quite an answer, nor really a question.

"Yes," said Leif. "He has set about the task of writing our history. Though if you ask me, his manner is a bit excessive. Not everything must be documented in such detail. Sometimes a receipt is just a receipt, if you know what I mean."

"Why do you have all of his books here?"

"Per once wrote to me, 'If it is not documented, then it never happened.' Of course, I disagree, but I suppose it's important for someone to record all of this. Sometimes you learn things when you see your work through the eyes of another. It offers a new perspective."

"And Brusa? Do you also have his books?"

Leif walked over to another shelf, one of those that had fallen prey to bedlam. "His works are not as conducive to indexing. They impress an order of their own. But most everything is here."

Charlene looked around the room. "So is anything in here written by you?"

"Surprisingly little. In keeping this place running, performing all of my roles, I can barely find time for myself."

THE FOLLOWING DAY, Leif shepherded them back to the airport. They drove through a tundra of moss and lichen, tinged by tight clusters of black crowberry and nascent birch. The trees gradually grew denser until they found themselves back in the soft pine envelope of the taiga. Kermin sat up front, chattering away with their host about the secrets of miniature-television repair. It was in stark contrast to his silence on the ride in, several days before.

In the back of the jeep, Radar slept in Charlene's lap. Since the procedure, he had been sleeping nearly all the time. Leif had assured them that this, too, was natural.

"His cells are busy at work. It's exhausting to metamorphose—just ask a caterpillar." The joke felt oddly misplaced. "But when the butterfly is revealed, all becomes worth it."

Charlene leaned over and sniffed her son. The new scent had lingered, despite several vigorous baths. A scent gathered in transit. It left her uneasy. Smells are transitory by nature; they should not endure.

At the airfield, Leif wished them well and asked Kermin to stay in touch. "I wish you lived a bit closer," he said. "We could use someone like you on the team. A genius with screens."

"Not genius," said Kermin. "I understand them, like we are friends. That's it. No: like we are relation. We are family, with the same blood."

As Leif walked back to his car, Charlene ran after him. She touched his shoulder.

"Leif," she said.

"Yes?"

"I know who you are."

"Oh? Who is that?"

"I know you wrote those telegrams."

He looked at her strangely.

"Why tell us not to do this?" she said. "And then tell us to do it?"

He carefully removed her hand from his arm and got into his car. "Safe travels, Charlene. Good luck."

"I'm not angry," she said through the open window. "I'm just wondering why someone would do this. Why pretend you are someone else?"

He started up the car but then paused. "My dear, the mask cannot be the player," he said. "And the player cannot be the mask."

As they waited in the terminal for their plane to land, Charlene put her head on her husband's shoulder.

"Thank you," she said.

"For what?"

"For letting us come here." She rubbed Radar's head as he slept in her lap. "I understand now. Things can be normal again."

"What's done will be done," Kermin said as a low whine rose in the distance. "This is done."

Two weeks later, Charlene found a sheath of dried dermis lying coiled around the leg of their armchair. She did not know what it was until she saw that Radar was missing a large patch of skin on his left thigh. The skin beneath was pale and raw. It blushed pink when touched.

Her heart sank.

She called Kermin at the shop, sobbing.

He was unmoved. "Leif's a man to trust. This is what you wanted. This is what he gave you."

"But I didn't want *this*."

"Then what? I gave you everything you wanted."

"Kermin!" she cried. "Oh, Kermin! What have I done?"

Over the course of two months, Radar went through a series of four separate "peels," in which his skin came away from his body in great translucent chunks, like a snake shedding its skin. She would find little pieces of him all around the house—beneath the furniture, caught in the door of the oven, inside her slippers. Like pellucid pages from an ancient tome. The skin smelled of wax and wet burlap and slightly rotten leather, sometimes with the thinnest lead note of citrus, a lemon or kumquat tone. She went around the house collecting the pieces in a small paper bag, which she kept hidden beneath the bed. And then one day she lifted the bedspread and found that the bag had vanished.

Besides making him tender to the touch, the shedding did not seem particularly painful for Radar, though as the skin sheathed off his face and neck, he began to resemble a walking zombie. Since their return from Norway, Charlene hadn't brought him back to the day care. She couldn't even imagine what the other kids would say if they saw him in this condition. The thought made her shudder.

"Why is that like this?" Radar asked one evening. He was standing in front of the mirror. In his hand was a piece of his skin.

Charlene panicked.

"This," she said, hating every inch of her being, "this happens to everyone. You shed your skin. This is part of growing up."

"Okay," he said. "Am I growned up?"

"Not yet, honey. Soon." She brought him close to hide her tears. "Soon."

She didn't dare take him to the doctors, the same doctors whom she knew all too well. She didn't take him even when she noticed that his smooth black hair had started to fall out in quarter-size chunks, leaving him with an uneven patchwork across his skull. She took to combing and recombing the thin hair that remained. When Charlene took Radar outside, she would rub him with lotion and then enshroud him like a mummy in a series of cashmere scarves. It was a ritual Radar came to greatly enjoy, despite the summer heat.

"I am a gift!" he said when she brought out the scarves, holding up his arms. "Wrap me up!" He grew attached to fabrics and the safety they offered—she often found him hiding behind the sheets of her Rothko library, palms on the cotton, humming a little tune to himself.

Kermin was intent on not acknowledging the horror of their son's condition. On more than one occasion, she had to rebuke him when he was about to take Radar out in public without his protective covering.

"This is important!" she said, making sure she left a little space for Radar to breathe.

"He doesn't care," said Kermin.

"People care. *I* care," she said, wrapping.

"I am a gift!" cried Radar.

Each successive shedding left Radar paler than the last, until his skin settled into a slightly yellowish, flushed cream color—a Type I/II on the Fitzgerald

Skin Type Classification Scale, somewhere between the rough-hewn maple of Kermin's unshaven cheek and the cautious milky complexion of Charlene's Franco-Irish-Germanic roots. Certain dark blotches remained around his nipples and belly button and behind his left ankle, where there was a prominent marking resembling the silhouette of a sinking Viking ship. It was like a rebirth.

But the procedure in Norway also led to several serious complications, none of which Leif had mentioned in his debriefing. Radar's skin became incredibly sensitive and subject to severe rashes. His hair did not grow back, and after the final shed, he was left almost completely bald, save for a little patch above his left ear.

"Where is my hair?" Radar asked her.

"Some boys don't have hair," said Charlene. "Like your grandfather."

"*He's* not a boy!"

"He was once a boy like you."

"Okay," said Radar. She could tell he didn't believe her twisted logic.

The media never got wind of this miraculous transformation. There was no reference to Radar in any of the major New York or New Jersey metropolitan newspapers, nor did Dr. Fitzgerald, as least as far as his personal literature suggested, ever learn of his former research subject's "recovery." Not that they would have noticed. The three of them had retreated into a protective cocoon. Some days it felt like the rest of the world barely existed.

About two months after their Kirkenes trip, Radar was busy deconstructing radio receivers in front of the television, watching an episode of *Godzilla*. He was wearing his favorite blue knit cap, which he had taken to doing since losing his hair. From the kitchen, Charlene sensed a misplaced stillness in the air. She came into the room and found her son sitting like a statue, his torso rigid and strangely arched backwards, a motherboard lying in the palm of one hand. And then a wave passed through him, and his entire frame began to shiver and shake uncontrollably, sending him tumbling into the pile of radio parts splayed out before him.

At first she thought he might have electrocuted himself accidentally, but when he continued to shake, she ran over and held him as his eyes rolled backwards and his arms popped and trembled in their sockets. A wilted smell of urine filled the air. She put her hand on his face and felt his jaw balling and grinding into itself with an uncanny mechanical persistence. His hat fell to the ground, revealing the lonely lateral tuft. On the television, the picture of *Godzilla* went soft and then split into a static that pulsed and thrummed with each of Radar's convulsions. A stench of burnt wires wafted through the room.

"Radar!" she screamed. "Radar!"

She comprehended his death with complete clarity. Such finality halted the most basic functions in her body. She could barely breathe. Life without him was incomprehensible. He was all there was, all there could ever be.

"Come back to me," she cried. "I promise I will never let this happen again . . . Come back to me. *Please*."

Eventually the contractions subsided and Radar's body settled into an uneasy quiet. His bald head was covered in a pin screen of sweat. On the television, a commercial showed two blond twins laughing in ski coats as they shuffled gum into their mouths. Charlene held her son and stroked his head. She whispered something small and true into his ear. His eyes slowly came back into focus, darting around the room in fear.

"I'm so sorry," she said. "You're here. You're back. Radar, my love, my sweet, we're together."

Charlene felt a strong urge to yell, but there was no one there to hear her except her limp son and the synchronized twins on the television.

It was his first grand mal seizure. Despite her promise, it would not be his last.

That autumn, Charlene exchanged several heated letters with Leif. The inherent delay caused by the intercontinental postal system left her plenty of time to fill the spaces in between with a vast ocean of anxiety. At first, Leif was sympathetic when he heard of Radar's hair loss and epilepsy. He asked her to describe the symptoms in detail and even to send pictures, which she curtly refused to do. When she accused him of betraying their trust and threatened legal action, he distanced himself from any responsibility and then, around Christmas, abruptly ended their communication altogether. Desperate, she even wrote several letters to the address she had for Brusa Tofte-Jebsen in Oslo, but these all came back RETURN TO SENDER. The trail had gone utterly cold.

With nothing left to do, Charlene unraveled. She quit her receptionist job at the salon. She stopped eating. Soon she was no longer leaving the house. Kermin began taking Radar to his shop every day. He did all of the shopping, the housework, the little administrative tasks of life, as his wife lay prone in bed. He persisted. He persisted and said nothing to her of her descent. There was nothing left to say.

ONE NIGHT CHARLENE AWOKE, shivering. Her body felt as if it were eating itself alive.

"Kerm," she hissed, terrified.

He stirred, mumbling.

"Kermin!"

"Yes?"

"I can't do it." Surprised at her own certainty.

The bedside light clicked on. He blinked, rubbed his eyes in the dimness.

"I can't do it. I just can't," she said. "I'm afraid of what I might do."

"I think," he said after a moment, "it is not a question of *can't*."

"There's nothing I can—"

"It is a question of *must*," he said. "You have no choice. We make him. We make Radar. We did what we did. What is done is done. But he is there, in that room. *There*. He must go and live tomorrow and tomorrow. So you must go and live tomorrow and tomorrow and tomorrow after this."

She stared at her husband. Her eyes welled up. "I *ruined* him."

"No," he said. "There is not just you. There is you and me and him."

She nodded.

"There is *us*," he said.

"Okay," she said. "Okay. What do I do? Tell me what to do, Kerm. Tell me."

"I cannot tell you. Be the person. Love him like always. It is not hard. He is Radar. He is love."

THE NEXT MORNING, she got up and cooked pancakes. Mediocre pancakes—misshapen, singed pancakes—but pancakes nonetheless. There were no complaints. She went over and held Radar so tightly that he complained, "Mommy, you're breaking me!"

That afternoon, she opened up the hole in the bedroom floor. A scent of stillness when the boards came up. A life left behind. She pulled out a folder from the stack and fingered the classified ad for the flavorist job at IFAC.

She sat down and wrote a letter. "*I know you've probably already filled this position long ago but I wanted to offer myself as a possible candidate as I suffer from an extraordinary sensitivity to certain smells.*" She crossed out "suffer from" and wrote "possess." Underlined it.

To her surprise, she received a phone call barely a week later. They were interested. She went to an interview in the International Flavor and Aroma Corporation headquarters, a giant glass-and-steel monstrosity in an anonymous office park off the turnpike. They had her sniff a series of white strips. She closed her eyes and inhaled. Then she used as many big words as she could think of to tell them what she smelled. Her answers astonished them.

"There are only two people in this building right now who could do that, and one of them is you," said a man in a lab coat.

They offered her the job on the spot.

"Apparently they call you *a nose*," she said to Kermin that evening.

"A *nose*?"

"That's the job. You're a professional nose," she said. "We're supposed to make perfumes, or to describe perfumes. Or . . . I don't know. I've never been very good at making things."

"Charlene," he said, coming to her, embracing her. "You are smartest person I know."

"No, I'm not."

"You can make whatever you want. You know this, right?"

"Really?"

"Tell me, what are you waiting for?"

"But—"

"It is time to wake up. Wake up and become the nose."

She became the nose.

It was not an instant transformation. The job offer was conditional: she had to go back to school. Two courses at Rutgers, her old haunt, in organic chemistry and molecular biology, and then a six-week perfumery intensive in Manhattan. She had to learn the names for everything: the pantheon of citric notes, the coarse parade of musks, the natural accordion florals and the synthetic aldehydes, ketones, and terpenes that silently mimicked the sensory world around us. She had to unlace complex bouquets of scents with just her nose and then measure her precision against a gas chromatograph. But she could do what the chromatograph could never do: compose an exact recipe for the smell using fifty words or fewer. Thus, the early draft of a perfume, *zingiberene–pentyl butyrate–thioterpineol–ethyl acetate–2-ethyl–3-methoxypyrazine*, became:

A tender bed of hawthorn, supporting a high trio of grapefruit, Asian pear, and elderberry, with lingering undercurrents of hazelnut and a single, faint note of ginger. A late-summer fragrance, perfect for outdoor events.

She could do this. She could dip her hand into the night-pit of the imagination. She knew all the right words from her previous, foiled career. Life had filled her quiver with the right arrows, even when the target itself had been too far away to see.

GIVEN HER EXTENSIVE BACKGROUND in librarianship, it remains surprising that Charlene never performed a standard literature search on "Kirkenesferda." If she had, she would've discovered that by 1979, there were almost two hundred articles, essays, monographs, or book-length projects that referenced the "experimental puppet troupe," though the vast majority of these were enfolded within a longstanding (and antagonistic) call-and-response between only two authors: Brusa Tofte-Jebsen and Per Røed-Larsen.

After 1979, there was a mysterious, nearly eighteen-year gap in the literature before Per Røed-Larsen published his comprehensive *Spesielle Partikler: Kirkenesferda 1944–1995* (Oslo: J. W. Cappelens). *Spesielle Partikler* is a fifteen-hundred-page monstrosity that details the troupe's four major *bevegelser,* or "movements": the Poselok nuclear fission installation, outside Murmansk, in 1944; the Gåselandet Island Tsar Bomba show on fusion, in 1961, staged during the middle of the largest hydrogen bomb detonation in history; the disastrous Cambodian performance, in 1979; and the abbreviated Sarajevo show on superstring theory, in the ruins of the National Library of Bosnia in 1995.

The book is not easy to get ahold of. *Spesielle Partikler* has been out of print for more than ten years and can be found only with some luck, in certain catalogs and rare Norwegian bookshops, where its list price is often well over 3,500 Norwegian kroner. The sole library copy at the Nasjonalbiblioteket, in Oslo, has been listed as "missing and/or damaged" for years, with no apparent attempt to replace and/or repair the inventory.

If one is lucky enough to track down a copy, *Spesielle Partikler* quickly reveals itself to be a most beguiling piece of scholarship. The rise and fall of the Kirkenesferda puppet troupe is documented in detail, obsessively so, with exhaustive

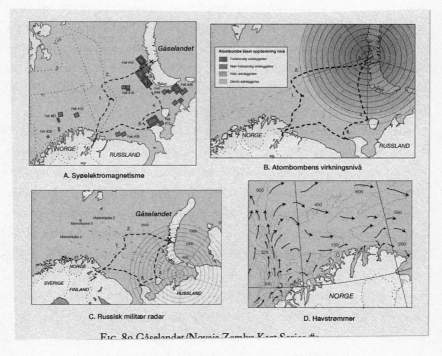

Fig. 1.5. "Gåselandet/Novaja Zemlya Kart Series #4"
From Røed-Larsen, P., *Spesielle Partikler*, p. 221

accounts of each *bevegelse,* including intricate analyses of the scientific concepts involved in the performance; charts and maps documenting the means of transport utilized to move equipment to these remote locations; blueprints and an inventory of materials involved in constructing the troupe's mobile "theater wagon"; and even tables showing the kilowatts used by each electronic puppet-object.

At the end of chapter 18, before turning his attention to the buildup of *Kirkenesferda Fire* in Sarajevo, Røed-Larsen meticulously describes how the December 1979 Cambodia show—performed for the exiled Khmer Rouge leadership in their mountain hideaway north of Anlong Veng—ended in catastrophe, as nearly all of the troupe's members were shot and killed in the middle of the night, including its founder, Dr. Leif Christian-Holtsmark. After this tragedy, Røed-Larsen claims, the Bjørnens Hule was abandoned. The camp was destroyed in a fire in 1982, and its Wardenclyffe tower was dismantled and removed "for international safety reasons," presumably because of its proximity to the Russian frontier, although, according to Røed-Larsen, its circle of concrete feet (with their wires extending deep into the earth) are still visible "somewhere near the Finnish/Norwegian border zone" (295). When Kirkenesferda miraculously resurfaced fifteen years later for *Kirkenesferda Fire,* it would keep its name but no longer be run out of Norway. Its base of operations was now split between Belgrade and New Jersey.

Mr. Røed-Larsen's devotion to his subject is quite evident in the long, digressive footnotes and nearly 340 pages of bibliographic end matter, but even a cursory meta-analysis of his vast collection of sources highlights certain inconsistencies and raises serious methodological questions about his scholarship. Many of the documents he cites either do not exist or are so obscure as to essentially be impossible to review. In his harsh review of *Spesielle Partikler* in the November 1997 issue of *Vinduet,* Tofte-Jebsen asserts that reading the book and its end matter confirmed for him that "the whole endeavor of documentation is a farce, a lie repeated and repeated into the dark" (*"en løgn gjentas og gjentas i mørket"*). "To write is to lie," Tofte-Jebsen writes. "There can be no other way."

Indeed, you would expect such dubious sourcing to cause any serious scholar to dismiss *Spesielle Partikler* outright, but after spending a fair amount of time immersed in Røed-Larsen's bibliographic sleight of hand, a strange phenomenon begins to take hold of the reader: one starts to feel as if one has entered into an uncannily familiar reality with a consistent internal logic all its own—a reality that begins to feel as potentially valid as the one that we now inhabit. Since the *form* of Røed-Larsen's account is so obsessive, so thorough, so exhaustively cross-referenced as to be almost mind-numbing, the overall effect of the monograph is to make one steadily question one's fundamental assumptions about what is and what is not possible, what has happened and what may happen yet. This unease is exacerbated by Røed-Larsen's tendency to use maxims from science in lieu of sectional headings ("3. For Every Action There Is an Equal and Opposite Reaction," etc.). Pairing observed, functional certainties from the world of physics against the most suspect of claims at first creates a kind of conjectural dissonance, but after a while the reader cannot help but wonder how anyone could be so committed to something if it were not, at least in some sense, *true*. Devotion, at its core, must be a kind of truth. In this way, *Spesielle Partikler* can be hailed as an achievement of psychological engineering, if not quite a piece of historiography. It is a proposal of an alternate existence that abuts our own—lurking, never very far away from the room in which we now breathe—and as such, it is also a window, giving us our reflection even as we look through it into an invented world just beyond our reach.

Many years later, in 1998, Charlene Radmanovic would discover a copy of *Spesielle Partikler* inside an unmarked box on her front stoop. There were no postal markings on the package, nor any return address listed. She never told anyone about the book's arrival. After spending some time trying to decipher its contents, she would eventually hide the book in the small, crowded space beneath the floor of her bedroom.

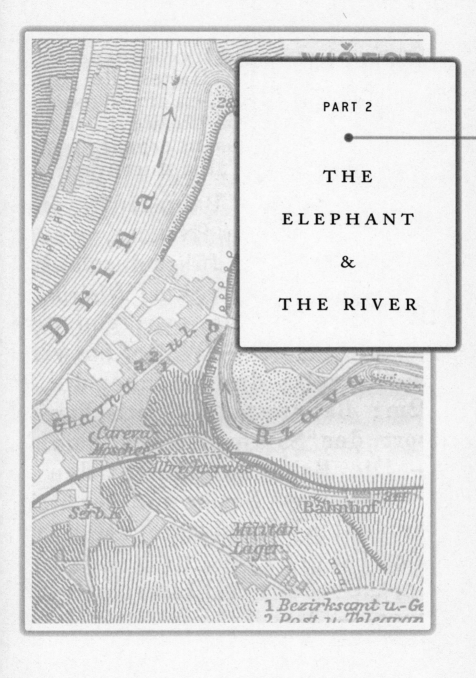

PART 2

THE

ELEPHANT

&

THE RIVER

1

VIŠEGRAD, BOSNIA
April 17, 1975

On the day they brought home his younger brother from the hospital, Miroslav Danilović, barely three years old, swallowed the key to the cabinet that held the family's rifle. The brass key, itself shaped like a small pistol, hung on a hook in the kitchen that was normally out of young Miroslav's reach, but while they were busy fussing with the newborn, he slid over the chair, unleashed the key from its resting place, and promptly swallowed it whole.

"I ate it!" he announced, triumphant, as Stoja nursed baby Mihajlo at her breast.

"Ate what?" said Danilo.

Miroslav showed his father the chair and the empty hook.

The Ukrainian doctor in Višegrad urged patience and calm. The key would pass.

The doctor made a small circle with his thumb and finger. "If it's smaller than this, fine. If it's larger than this, then we'll have problems," he said, which did not really make sense to Stoja, given the irregular shape of the key. Depending on which way you looked at it, the key could be many different keys. There was no telling which one he had swallowed.

Thereafter, Miroslav was forced to squat and shit into a paper bag. Stoja would put Mihajlo down, don her gardening gloves, and search Miroslav's excrement for the offending object.

"You're a good mother," Danilo said to her. "Your patience is a curse."

"I'm a mother," she said, hushing the baby to sleep. "My patience is all I have left."

Weeks went by. The key made no appearance. Miroslav's appetite had decreased since the incident, but he did not seem particularly ill. Nor did he suffer from the kinds of gastrointestinal pains that the doctor had warned them about. After several months, Stoja threw up her hands.

"The key has moved on," she concluded. And so must she. Still, in spite of her reasonable, almost stoic nature, in spite of her declaration that the episode was now closed, Stoja could not shake the lingering threat of that gun-shaped key—for the rest of her life, she was awoken by the same nightmare, in which a metallic bug would crawl up her son's throat, choking him while he slept.

Miroslav, a slender boy to begin with, never fully recovered his taste for food. Getting him to eat became a daily negotiation, involving bribery and complex feats of logical reasoning. A bowl of *pasulj* was traded for an extra half hour of drawing time before bed. In contrast to Miroslav, little Miša—who was not all that little—would eat anything that was put before him, like a goat. This indiscriminateness brought its own problems. Once, when he was four, he ate a whole roast chicken, bones and all. Yet no one was really worried for Miša, even as he cried out in pain on the toilet. Miša was going to survive whatever the world might throw at him. He was born to be a Danilović, with the same protruding jaw, the same large eyes, the same tuberous forehead as his father. If there was a crowd of boys at school, Danilo could always point to broad-shouldered Miša and say, "There—there is my son." And nobody in the village could disagree.

Things had always been different with his eldest. Miroslav did not have the Danilović jaw. His cheeks disappeared into his neck without much enthusiasm. His forehead was long and narrow. While Mihajlo easily became "Miša" to everyone, only Stoja called Miroslav "Miro." Perhaps the diminutive didn't stick, due to his air of unsettling politeness—he would formally address the women of the village as *"Gospođa,"* bowing slightly in the old way, as if greeting them at a ball.

How strange, whispered the people of the village. *Did you know that he's a podmeče?*

This was the unfortunate term for the victim of a maternity ward swap, of which there had recently been several high-profile cases. There was no concrete evidence that Miroslav had shared their fate, but if such a thing was said often enough, it no longer mattered what was true and what was not.

Yes. I heard that. I heard his real mother was a Hungarian Jew.

Their scrutiny did not go unnoticed by Miroslav. Even before his younger brother came along, he had always sensed the narrow chasm of incongruity, the painful gap between himself and the idea of who he should be; yet, being so young, he lacked the language to articulate such existential displacement. To calm his unease, he had taken to playing with wires and string, sculpting tiny men of varying shapes and sizes and naming them all Miroslav. Danilo would help him suspend these figures from the ceiling of his bedroom, like a constellation of possible selves.

Though he was three years Miroslav's junior, Mihajlo Danilo Danilović—known to everyone simply as Miša or sometimes Miš Miš, or even *beba džin,* "the baby giant"—was already four centimeters taller than his older brother by the time he turned six. Whereas Miša spent all his time outdoors, shadowing their father in the fields, killing sparrows with his slingshot, playing football with boys twice his age, there were many days when Miroslav would not even leave his bedroom.

"Children are meant to move," said Stoja, wise as always.

"His mind is moving," Danilo replied, unconvincingly. Indeed, Miroslav was exceptionally bright—this much had been clear from the beginning, and more than one of his teachers had called him the most naturally gifted child they had ever seen—but he was also prone to bouts of melancholy, stubbornness, and obsessive behavior.

Instead of performing his farm chores, he would draw great maps of the Yugoslav People's Army (JNA) fighting off various invading hordes on the walls of his bedroom. At first, this practice was forbidden, but you could steer a horse away from water only so many times. Tired of rapping his knuckles, Danilo and Stoja eventually relented, and Miroslav began covering his bedroom with endless battlefield minutiae as he listened to old Partisan fight songs on his transistor. Every man, every gun, every trigger needed to be sketched, or else they wouldn't exist and that side might lose the war because they were one soldier short. But just as soon as one soldier was added, the tides shifted, and another soldier had to be added to the other side. It was a never-ending task. A perpetual fractal of warfare. The hens would go hungry as Miroslav spent hours rendering the thousands of tiny soldiers, each with gun, trigger, backpack—stars on the hats of the JNA, squares on the hats of the invading foreigners.

No manner of beating could sway the child from his task, and there came a point at which Danilo found it was hopeless. He would be what he would be.

"Feed the chickens, would you, Miša?" Danilo sighed. "I don't know what to do with your brother." And Miša ran off without complaint, eager as ever to please the man he would one day become.

Soon the walls of Miroslav's bedroom could no longer contain the war. He began to build armies of soldiers from screws and paper clips and bottle caps and bits of clay—thousands of them lining his desk and then his floor, arranged into elaborate formations, poised to attack and counterattack. Yet somehow, their static nature bothered him much more than the two-dimensional figures on the walls. Now that his men were rendered in three dimensions, he became all the more aware of their lifelessness. Simply moving them with his hands was both unsatisfying and inefficient: he was always conscious of his intervention, and he could move only a handful of men at a time. He stood at an impasse: how to control his men without implicating himself as the control?

His first tactic employed an old electric football game. When switched on, the vibrating metal pitch would cause his army of wary soldiers to tremble as if possessed by an evil spirit. They would chatter across the board, occasionally colliding with one another in a meager display of hand-to-hand combat. More often than not, however, the random shudderings from the electric game would result in the soldiers spinning in circles before collapsing and spasming in place, seemingly felled by their own volition. Miroslav could not stand such incoherence. He needed to be able to control his men, not watch them suffer the random consequences of electrical pulses. He shelved the game and searched for another way to gain complete command over his domain.

A solution came to him after watching a television program about a Volkswagen assembly plant in Sarajevo, in which cars were swung from station to station suspended on tracks. Inside his bedroom, Miroslav hung a series of coat hangers on four long rods that could slide back and forth using a system of pulleys. He then attached a tiny thread to each soldier and tied these threads to the rods above. In this way, he could manipulate the pulleys to draw the two armies into battle, and while he could move the soldiers only one company at a time, and while their battling was still limited to awkward, imprecise collisions, he could use his imagination to soften the clumsiness of his system and fill in the gaps of real warfare. When a tank blasted an artillery shell into the enemy ranks, he would release a string and a whole swath of soldiers would collapse to the ground, bloodied and wailing. Later, he would tug on the strings, and their souls, as one, would gently float to heaven. This was how he started to give life and death to the lifeless things around him. It was also where he came up against the essential dilemma of the puppeteer: that is, the governance of objects that have no minds to be governed.

From the moment Miša entered the world, he had idolized his brother, despite the vast chasm between their proclivities, outlooks, manners, bodies, and minds. In his eyes, his brother could do no wrong. "Miša would drink Miroslav's bathwater," as Danilo once put it. But such adoration was hardly mutual. Miroslav showed little patience for his brother's clumsiness and lack of imagination. When Miša tried to join in one of his elaborate battlefield maneuvers, Miroslav would quickly become furious at how his brother was breaking the strict rules of engagement or letting the strings get tangled or moving too many men or too few. His hands were much too big for such delicate matters, and there was little room for error with a system as delicate as mass warfare.

"Get out of here, shithead!" Miroslav yelled after another entanglement had halted the battle. Miša, banished and inconsolable, would retreat to the safe space of the chicken coop.

A temporary truce was usually called between the brothers each Christmas. On Christmas Eve, it was custom for the eldest son to go with the father into the woods and cut down the *badnjak*, the oak tree branch that would serve as the Yule log. But Miroslav showed little interest in this tradition, and so it was

Miša who eagerly climbed the tree, bow saw in hand, and felled the branch onto the snowy ground. He would wrap the branch in a blanket like a child and show it to his brother upon his return.

"It's a good one, Miša," Miroslav would say, knowing how much each and every word meant to his younger brother. "You can name him Otik."

"Otik?" repeated Miša in wonder.

"If you wish hard enough, he'll come alive," said Miroslav.

"Okay," said Miša, and off he would go to stare at the branch for hours.

Christmas Eve was also the time to bring out the *vertep,* the traditional puppet theater, which the boys of the town would use to tell the story of the nativity. Children would don paper crowns and fashion wooden swords for themselves, pretending they were the Persian kings on their way to see the Christ child. Predictably, most household *vertep* performances were rudimentary at best, with a few hand puppets utilized in haphazard fashion. Many kids simply used the occasion as an excuse to go around town and sword-fight with one another.

In contrast to those of his peers, Miroslav's *vertep* was a fully automated electromechanical puppet theater with multiple hidden compartments, elaborate lighting and synthesized sound effects, and a loudspeaker from which he could perform the voice of God. His nativity productions soon became legendary in Višegrad, where he would perform several shows to a packed audience in the town square. Miša was his loyal if clumsy stagehand, though this relationship ended one Christmas Eve when Miša tripped and knocked over the entire stage during a matinee.

Afterwards, Danilo found his younger son on the *kapija* of the Turkish Bridge, tears streaming down his face, staring at those oxen hands.

Danilo sat down beside Miša. He was silent, listening to the quiet hush of the river, and then he said, "Your brother is a Danilović, but he is not a Danilo Danilović."

This might have seemed like an odd thing to say had it not been for the convolutions of their family's history: Danilo Danilović's father had also been named Danilo Danilović, as had his father, as had his father, as had his father, Rabbi Danilo, who at one time had been one of only two rabbis living in all of

Montenegro. This history was the source of much contention in the Danilović family, particularly for Darinka, Danilo's now deceased mother, who staunchly denied the presence of Jews anywhere in their lineage.

Rabbi Danilo's ancestors were Sephardic Jews who had been living in Dubrovnik for more than three hundred years before Austrian annexation in 1814 withdrew the few rights granted by Napoleon to the territory's Jewish citizenry. A subsequent confrontation with a Habsburg minister led to Rabbi Danilo's public denouncement, forcing him to flee the city under a cloud of scrutiny. He moved his congregation east, to Perast, on the Bay of Kotor, a calm strip of sea flanked by mountains on all sides, leading some to label it (incorrectly) Europe's southernmost fjord. In the middle of this bay, there was a small island shaped like a waxing moon. Legend has it that the island was completely man-made, created by superstitious fishermen over many hundreds of years, who had thrown a stone into the water every time they left and returned from their journeys. Those who did not add to the pile did so at their own peril and would die terrible deaths, devoured by sea monsters with poisonous horns, it was said. And so an island took shape, and it was on this island that Rabbi Danilo built a limestone synagogue among the linden trees.

Fig. 2.1. "Karta Otičića Abrahama" (1853)
From Mladinov, T. S. (1962), *Židovstvo u južnoj Dalmaciji* 3: 23

"Only God can reach us here," Rabbi Danilo famously said after those gathered had consecrated the temple by circumnavigating it seven times and then throwing a stone into the waters just beyond. Thereafter, every Friday evening, they would hire a local fisherman to row the small congregation (only ten of them had followed the rabbi to Montenegro, the very minimum necessary for a *minyan*) out to the island, now named Otičića Abrahama, to hold Shabbat. Afterwards, they would throw a stone into the bay, and then the fisherman would row them back to town before sunset, two candled lanterns flickering at their helm.

When the Montenegrin state required all of its citizens to take a surname for the 1855 census—to essentially create a history out of nothing—Rabbi Danilo, after some deliberation, assumed the Russian-style patronymic of Danilo Danilović.

"Because I am my own father now," he liked to joke to those assembled on the dock of their little island as they sipped *lozovača* on Sunday afternoons.

The rabbi, to no one's surprise, named his own son Danilo Danilović. And so a tradition was born: Danilo Danilović (the second), a clockmaker, also named his son Danilo Danilović. Danilo Danilović (the third) was a stiff-headed bastard who fought for the First Serbian Army in the Toplica Uprising of 1917. Following the war, he discarded his grandfather's Jewish faith as if it were an ill-fitting jacket, moved to Višegrad, and embraced Christian Orthodoxy. But he did fulfill his duty in one respect: he named his only son Danilo Danilović. Danilo Danilović (the fourth) had slimmer shoulders than his father and spoke in soft tones, like a man delivering bad news. He married a beauty named Darinka, a devoutly religious woman who would not let Danilo touch her during their long forest walks before they were properly wedded. When Germany invaded Yugoslavia and another war began, Danilo joined the nascent anti-fascist Partisan movement recently formed near Mount Ozren. Darinka became pregnant during one of his visits home, and he instructed her, by letter, on what she must name their child in the event that he did not return from the war.

"And what if it is a girl?" she wrote in reply, though her husband would never receive the letter, for he was killed by a sniper in Operation Rösselsprung, in May of 1944.

Danilo Danilović (the fifth), born in September during the middle of an Allied air raid, would suffer from a fear of loud noises for the rest of his life but would also be blessed with the knowledge that all things must end. Darinka raised her son by herself; she taught him, above all else, to be thankful for God's mercy. Her religion had been hardened by her husband's death, and so in the years after the war, when the church was all but banned by the Communist Party, she nurtured her son's faith behind closed doors.

"Tito is confused," she would say to him. "He'll come to find God soon enough. God is the one thing that cannot be forgotten." As living proof of this, she proudly wore her husband's red handkerchief every day. Others assumed that this was to signal her membership in the party, but Darinka knew better—through the presence of a small, nearly invisible cross that she had stitched into one of its corners, the handkerchief represented for her God's almighty omnipotence, even in the depths of a misguided ideology.

Once, on a trip to Belgrade, Darinka took Danilo to see an old illuminated manuscript inside a large museum. It was a book of the Gospels created for Miroslav of Hum, a twelfth-century prince from Herzegovina. At first reluctant and bored by the echoing halls of the museum, Danilo was startled by the

Fig. 2.2. Miroslav of Hum's Gospels (1168)
From Beardsman, T. (1956),
A History of Illumination, p. 144

book's beauty beneath its glass case—he stared at the images of saints grouped in curious orbit around the thick Gothic strokes of the text. The museum guard, perhaps drawn in by Darinka's beauty, offered to unlatch the case and turn the pages of the ancient book. So captured was he by the shimmering images that bent and swayed across the paper, Danilo did not notice the guard leering at his mother as he showed them each page, nor did he notice the man's hand creeping up her thigh or how she let the hand linger for just a moment before discreetly brushing it away. Danilo was too transfixed by the miracle before him: Hum's manuscript made him realize for the first time that if such beauty could exist in the world, then God must exist as well.

They moved to a two-story farmhouse in the hills above Višegrad. Even without a father to guide him, Danilo Danilović sensed the way the earth breathed. He implicitly understood the angle of the sun, how a season always began during the season before, how water did not always run downhill. Holding his mother's hand, he would kneel at the threshold of his bedroom and pray every morning and every night. Before the sun rose on Sundays, they would walk the four kilometers through the pines to attend the small, secret services at the village church, those assembled whispering their prayers to the dusty icons above, which were normally closed and shuttered to keep the party administrators at bay.

During the summer of 1972, Danilo attended an unsanctioned screening of Dušan Makavejev's *W.R. - Misterije organizma* (*W.R.: Mysteries of the Organism*) at the Dom Kulture in Višegrad. He was not even supposed to be there, but someone had told him that they were showing a movie banned by Tito himself and that this movie would most likely change his life. Afterwards, he stood bewildered in a corner, trembling, awash in the utter innocence of his up-bringing. He did not understand all of what he had just seen, but what he did understand made him fearful, and what he did not understand filled him with a great loneliness, as if the world had suddenly left him behind. It was then that a beautiful woman approached him. She was smoking a long, thin cigarette and wearing a JNA army cap. For a moment he was afraid that this was the woman from the movie who had been decapitated, that she had found some way to reat-tach her head and walk out of the screen and into the Dom Kulture.

"You look as if you've just seen a ghost," she said to him.

Her name was Stojanka Stevović. She was from Trebinje. Her mother was a Catholic Croat, her father was a Communist Serb, and she spoke like a Montenegrin, but she called herself a Yugoslav. Danilo was smitten by the strength of her eyes. Every time she opened her mouth, a little vacuum of space opened up inside his chest.

"Don't go with her," his mother warned when it was clear he was going with her.

"Why?"

"She's not a believer."

"That's not a good reason."

"That's the only reason. If you go with her, I will never speak to you again."

He called his mother's bluff and went with her. He had no choice. She had seen him see the ghost. And she went with him, despite her ideological resistance to becoming a farmer's wife. Stoja had always maintained a vague dream of moving to Belgrade and becoming a movie star, smoking her long, thin cigarettes in the Danube clubs as men hung on her every word. She would later say she never made it to the city because she was scared, because she did not trust herself enough to be on-screen, but this was not true, for she trusted herself completely.

Danilo asked for her hand in marriage on the banks of the Drina. It was early evening—the time of day when light moved slowly, laterally, striking the earth with such acuity of angle that everything was forced to step back and glow in wonder. They had just been for a swim, and they lay on the rocks soaking up the last of the day's heat, watching the bugs spiral across the surface of the water, their paths now and again igniting into silver pinpricks of luminescence. Nervous at the absence of words in his head, Danilo wiped some moisture from his lip and tried to say what he meant to say in the right way, but in doing so said it all wrong, which turned out to be the right way after all. Technically, she did not give an answer, but it was clear from her smile and the heat of her silence that she would be bound to him until her last breath.

There was just one problem with their union: when the priest at the local Orthodox church heard of Stoja's questionable lineage, he refused to marry them. Danilo suspected Darinka's influence in the matter, so to spite her, he married Stoja in a civil service, where the Lord's name was mentioned only once, and then only because there was a clerical error in the document read by the flighty municipal clerk.

After a period of time just long enough to make them both nervous that such a thing might never be possible, Stoja became pregnant. When a baby boy emerged into the world—small, thin-boned, but otherwise healthy—Danilo Danilović made a decision that startled even himself: the child would not be named Danilo. They would call him Miroslav, though Danilo insisted that this was not after Miroslav of Hum, creator of the illuminated book that had so transfixed him as a child, nor even—as everyone would later assume—for Miroslav Stevović, Stoja's father. The child was simply named Miroslav, for himself.

"Are you sure?" offered Stoja. "We don't have to. I don't even mind the name Danilo. I married you, after all."

"Every tradition is meant to be broken," said Danilo, though he was not sure—nor would he ever be sure—if such a thing was true.

Darinka, on the other hand, was so upset that she refused to attend the baptism and did not lay eyes on her grandchild for the first six months of his life.

When their second child came along, she again intervened.

"There's still a chance for you to honor your father," she said.

Danilo thought about this long and hard. He came back to his mother with an offering.

"His name will be Mihajlo Danilo. Danilo will be his second name."

"What is a *second* name?" Darinka asked, furious. "And who is Mihajlo?"

"Mihajlo is my son." Mihajlo, the name of no one, and this was exactly the point.

"You're a wicked man, Danilo Danilović. I didn't know this about you until now. You spit on your father's memory. On your grandfather's memory. On all of their memories."

"I hope you'll find room to love them, Mama."

She would not find room to love them, at least not in this life, for she died a week later from a massive heart attack that killed her while she was sitting on the toilet, her skirt at her ankles, the red bandanna with its secret cross still hanging from her throat. The thread of time had been cut.

On Miroslav's fourteenth birthday, Miša gave his older brother a pair of trainers. For weeks, Miša had been bubbling with the excitement of giving this most perfect of gifts.

"He can run everywhere in them," he said.

Danilo remained skeptical. He thought such a gift would be wasted on his eldest, with his staid body and his wandering mind, but in the end, he gave Miša the money and sent him to procure the shoes from the sparsely stocked sporting goods store in town. Miša came back proudly toting his prize, elaborately hiding and re-hiding the box beneath his bed so that his brother would not discover it prematurely.

When Miroslav tore through Miša's ungainly wrapping job that evening, his eyes lit up as he touched the new trainers, gingerly, carefully, as one would touch a newborn animal. The trainers were a pale shade of blue, the color of shallow water in the early morning. Miša's pronouncement proved more true than he could have ever known, for Miroslav had been stuck on a project for several months now: how to perfectly replicate the movement of a man in motion. He had been studying Eadweard Muybridge's famous sequences, frame by frame, trying to build a mechanical automaton that could jog a dozen paces without intervention from its creator.

The problem was proving terrifically difficult. Apparently a team had achieved the feat in Tokyo, but then, this team was Japanese, with all the

Fig. 2.3. Eadweard Muybridge, "Animal Locomotion. Plate 63" (1887)
From Røed-Larsen, P., *Spesielle Partikler,* p. 960

resources afforded the Japanese, and Miroslav was convinced they had cheated anyhow. He was hung up on just three engineering challenges: the balance of the torso, the airborne transition from one foot to the other, and the limited flexibility of the knee joint. As it turned out, these three problematic areas were also the essential components of the humanoid stride. Without them, you merely had a body that tumbled earthward again and again and again.

Yet Miša's gift awakened something within him. The trainers made him realize the solution had been right in front of him all this time: *he* would become the automaton. He did not need to build a running man when he himself could be that man. All he needed to do was separate the *him* part of himself from his body and he would essentially have the perfect robot, one that could mimic nearly all human movement. He would be his own puppet.

Except that excising the *him* from himself—leaving only a body in motion—proved more difficult than designing any automaton. His lanky frame and obsession for repetition made him perfectly suited for cross-country running, but as he covered ever longer distances, he could never quite outrun himself. He went wherever his body went.

I am not the runner, he would repeat over and over again in his head. But he did not believe it. And so he ran farther and still farther, propelling himself forward with an existential urgency that defied both space and time.

At first, Miša tried to run with his brother, but after only a week he found that even he, athletic as he was, could not keep up. Miroslav could run forever. He would run for whole days through the countryside, over mountains, across the frontier and into Serbia, even, drifting through alpine meadows and interrupting the deer and the bears in their slumber. Strangely, his incredible journeys did not increase his appetite. He would run fifty, sixty, seventy kilometers and then eat like a bird. It was remarkable. Energy was not being conserved. Or at least he was drawing upon some unseen source for his perpetual momentum. And still he could not run from himself.

After a while, Danilo and Stoja began to worry. All he did was run. He had no interest in taking part in races for his school; he simply wanted to run alone. His teachers had begun to notice. He no longer turned in work. He slept through class. He talked back. When forced to sit still for any length of time, he constantly tapped his foot in a heel-toe stutter step, as if signaling some kind of code. It didn't matter how bright he was—at this rate he would not make it through his studies.

"I have this feeling," said Stoja, "that one day he might start running and never come back."

What she was noticing without being able to say as much was that with each kilometer covered, Miroslav was running further and further away from the polite little child who had bowed to the women and greeted the postman's arrival every afternoon. With the end of his youth also came an apparent end of his interest in the well-being of others. He was, for lack of a better term, becoming *mean*.

Secretly, Stoja blamed herself. She had given up everything for her children, given up a life that may or may not have come to pass, and she had grown into and accepted this choice until the choice had become no choice at all. But watching her son slip away like this shook her to her core. Stoja, who had never been a true believer, who had grown up a modern secular woman, began stealing out to pray at St. Stephen's alone. She would light a candle at the manoualia and stare into the burning wick. By both being and not being there at the same time, the flame's flicker consoled her.

"We must do something," she said finally to her husband one day. "He's my Miro."

"All right," said Danilo. "I'll handle it."

After one of Miroslav's long runs, Danilo met his son at the top of their road.

"Come," he said. "We're going to a place."

"To what place?" Miroslav asked, breathless. "I need to stretch."

"Come," said Danilo.

"Where's Miša?"

"He's working."

"Can't you take *him* to this place?"

"No."

They took a local grunt bus that hugged the long curve of the river northward and then disembarked at the beginning of an old dirt road, which they started following up into the hills. A thick forest surrounded them. To their left, a small creek bubbled, its waters green with algae.

"Where are we going, Tata?" asked Miroslav. Walking was making him more tired than running.

"Your mother's worried about you."

"She's always worried."

"She doesn't want you to run so much."

"I like running."

"She worries about you. She cannot help herself."

"I know. But that isn't my fault," said Miroslav. "Where are we going, Tata?"

"To the source," said Danilo.

Finally, after about half an hour, they came upon a small, ancient domed building. Moss and a wash of mineral deposits spilled down its weathered sides. Steam rose gently from a broken window.

Danilo gestured at the building. "This is a hammam. Built by the Turks who lived here five hundred years ago. They understood the heat of the waters. It will calm your muscles."

"My muscles feel calm."

"It will calm your soul."

"And what if I am soulless?"

Danilo looked at his son. "We're going inside."

"What's up there?" Miroslav pointed above them, where they could see a large, modern building peeping through the trees.

"Ah! Don't look at that. That's a resort. They built an ugly hotel so the tourists could soak in the hot springs and then eat some *sirnica* in the cafeteria. But this isn't how it's meant to be done. They're stupid. They're only interested in making money. We're going to the real place."

They pushed open the rotting door and shed their clothes and then slid into the ancient, recessed pool. A small stone chute poured water in from the underground hot springs. They soaked. The steam rose around them like silent music, swirling against the arched ceiling above their heads. They breathed, letting the wet silence shift and settle into the pores of their skin.

"Where did you run today?" Danilo finally asked.

"Down to Rudo." Only Miroslav's face floated above the surface, as if the rest of him no longer existed. His voice echoed off the ceiling.

"Rudo?" Danilo raised his eyebrows. "That's a long way."

"Not so long."

"Why do you run so much?"

"I don't know," he said. "It makes me feel good."

They were quiet, and then Danilo said, "When the Turks still ruled this area, that place was called Sokol."

Miroslav made a slight groan that curled and ended in a gurgle of water. His father liked telling stories about old things, things that happened so long ago they did not matter anymore. How often had he heard the story about the first Danilo Danilović, who had defeated the Turks and built a church on an island? One hundred times? Two hundred times? It was enough to drive a man insane.

"Did you know that once upon a time there were two brothers who lived in Sokol?" said Danilo.

"Tata!" said Miroslav. "Please. I really don't want to hear about them. Let's just enjoy ourselves."

"I am enjoying myself," said Danilo. "The brothers' names were Makarije and Bajo."

"*Please,* Tata. No one cares about them. They're dead. They died a long time ago. Let's talk about something real."

"What is real? Soon we'll all be dead. Don't you want to be remembered?"

"I'm sure they'll say the same thing about us—'Why are you telling me this stupid story about Miroslav Danilović? What does this have to do with me?'"

"Just listen to the story. Don't be so critical all the time. It isn't good for you."

Miroslav ducked his head into the water and spat a thin stream across the pool. "Okay, go ahead, Tata. I'm listening. Tell me about Makarije and Milo."

"*Bajo.* Makarije and *Bajo,*" said Danilo. "They came from a poor family. A family with nothing. And so their father, who was a true believer in the mercy of God, sent them away to study at the Mileševa Monastery. This monastery was famous—it was a great honor for them to be admitted there, and the father was rightfully proud. Maybe one day his sons would become priests."

"That is usually why you go to live in a monastery."

"Usually. But these were not usual times. While they were there, the Turks came on one of their *devşirmeler.* You know what a *devşirme* is?"

"Yes, Tata, I know."

"You and Miša are lucky they don't have these anymore. Imagine—just when you were getting comfortable at school, in come the Turks on a *devşirme* and they snatch you boys up like a pack of animals. They do this to all the Christian boys they can find—they throw them into the back of a prison cart and drag them across the country. And behind the cart, a long line of weeping mothers begins to form. The women beg for the return of their sons. They offer anything—money, their homes, even their own bodies. And the Turkish guards keep them back with whips. *Whips!* Can you believe it? The women are bleeding from the whips, but still they follow. And when the cart is full, they return to Istanbul and they force the boys into Islam. They force them to become Islamic priests or warriors. Imagine this! How would you like to be kidnapped and forced to believe in something you don't believe?"

"It doesn't sound so bad. It's a free ticket out of here. And I hear Istanbul was pretty nice back then."

Danilo flicked some water at his son. "Ah! You have no idea. You're too spoiled to even understand what it'd be like. A belief in God is the closest thing to your heart. No one can tell you what to believe. That is the one truth in life. But the *devşirme* was how the Turks kept these lands under their control. They were very smart. They kept us in fear by taking our boys, the same boys who might grow up to cause them trouble. Fear is the most powerful weapon, more powerful than any weapon you can hold in your hands."

He paused. They listened to the water churtling down the chute into the pool.

"So here come the Turks, into the Mileševa Monastery, and they tell the two boys: 'You must come with us.' And you know what Bajo, the eldest, says? He says, 'I'll go. Take only me. Leave my brother.'"

"No way I'd do that. I'd be like, 'Take him—look how big that guy is. Leave me; I'd be a shitty warrior.'"

"Watch your language."

"That's what I would say."

"No, you wouldn't. You'd do the same thing as Bajo."

"How do you know?"

"Miroslav, just let me tell the story. This story has a certain rhythm to it and you're ruining it."

"I'm just saying that you don't know what I'd do."

"So the Turks, they actually listen to Bajo. They take him away to Istanbul and leave Makarije behind. And on their journey back, they of course must pass through Višegrad. But this was before the bridge was built. They have to ferry across the Drina. And the mothers who are following them, they cannot go any farther. They're left weeping on the shore, watching their sons disappear across the river, disappear forever into Islam. And Bajo remembers this image of his mother weeping with the others."

"The mothers could swim."

"That isn't the point. The Drina's too dangerous to swim there. The current's too strong."

"Not so dangerous for a mother who's crazy with grief."

"The mothers don't swim, okay? They're stuck on the shore. Let me tell the story. You can tell the next story, but I'm telling this one now, and the teller gets to make the rules. That's how it works." Danilo paused, scratching at his shoulder as if trying to remember what happens next. "So Bajo arrives in Istanbul and begins to study the Ottoman system. At first he is confused, hopeless. He contemplates stealing a guard's knife and plunging it into his own heart. But one night he's visited by his mother in a dream, and she says that he must survive so that she can one day see him again. And when he wakes from this dream, he makes a decision: not only will he cooperate with his captors—he will defeat them at their own system. And this is what he does. Little by little, Bajo learns their ways. He discovers he has a natural gift for learning their Turkish methods of law. In fact, he's so good that they quickly recognize his talents and they begin to promote him through the ranks. He gains influence with the inner court and develops a reputation for fairness in all matters. As the years go by, he continues to rise, leaving his rivals in the dust. Soon he becomes a governor and then eventually a third vizier and then a second vizier and then finally, after many years, he becomes the grand vizier. He's now the chief adviser to the sultan himself, but everyone knows the grand vizier makes everything happen. And by this time he has a new name: Mehmed-paša Sokolović. Once a poor boy from Sokol, an Orthodox Serb, and now responsible for the whole Ottoman Empire. Rich and powerful, able to affect the course of time itself!"

"So what?" said Miroslav.

"*So what?* Are you listening to anything I've just said? He decided to become someone who no one thought he could be. This, my son, is incredible."

"Not so incredible for the other brother."

"What do you mean?"

"He was left in the monastery. He didn't become the grand vizier. His brother was trying to help him, but he ended up screwing him over."

"Ah! Well, this is where the story gets interesting. Many considered Makarije to maybe not be so wise as his brother Bajo. He was even thought by some to be a little dim-witted. Maybe he was a bit overweight. But he did not do so bad for himself, either. He stayed in the monastery and studied very hard, and slowly he rose up through the levels of the church, one by one. Nothing was given to him by favor, nothing came easily. He earned everything through his patience, through his loyalty, through his utter devotion to God. And at the end of his life, he was ordained as the Serbian patriarch. Saint Makarije of Peć. This is the same Makarije, the same poor boy from Sokol, brother of Bajo. We celebrate his feast on the twelfth of September. Remember, when we roasted Dragan's pig? And Miša caught the rabbits?"

"Miša crushed the rabbits. We couldn't eat them."

"Two brothers in the same family, and each grows up to be the head of a different religion. It just goes to show you that nothing is decided when you're born. Everything is still possible. If you decide to change your life, you can."

"Or maybe everything is decided already. How do you know that they weren't always going to end up like that?"

Danilo thought about this. "That could be. Who's to say how God works his plans?"

"Is that a true story?"

"Of course it's true. Why would I make something like that up?"

"It sounds like bullshit."

"I told you to watch your mouth."

"Sorry, but it does."

"You think I'm lying to you? Then what about the bridge? You think the bridge is a lie?"

"What bridge?"

"The Turkish Bridge! This is Mehmed-paša Sokolović's bridge! He never forgot the dream of his mother saying she must see him again, nor did he forget the image of the women wailing on the banks of the river as he was being taken away. This image haunted him for the rest of his days, and so when he became grand vizier, he ordered a bridge to connect the two sides of the Drina. The sad part of the story is that when he came back to see his bridge completed, his mother was already dead. It was too late. He, too, wept on the banks of the river, and dedicated the bridge to her memory. And it was the story of this bridge that won Ivo Andrić his Nobel Prize. Stories are powerful things. But you knew this. You read his book in school."

Miroslav shook his head. "I pretended to read it. It was too boring to read. All I remember is about that black Arab who lived inside the bridge."

"What? *You didn't read it?* But that book's our history! Andrić is our most famous writer! How could you not read it?"

"How do we know Andrić wasn't also full of bullshit?"

"Miroslav! I won't say it again."

"I'm just saying. That was a novel. Everyone acts like this was true, but no one knows what was really true."

"How can you say this? You can see our history with your very own eyes. You can walk to the *kapija* of the bridge and read the inscription in Turkish from the sixteenth century. You can look out at the river and see. A river cannot forget. It remembers every person who has ever put their foot in it. It's like a book of all time."

"That's not true."

"It *is* true," said Danilo. "And this hammam—the one we're in right now—this was also built by Mehmed-paša. We're sitting in history. We're sitting in the middle of the story. You can feel the water on your skin. So don't tell me this isn't true when it clearly is."

They sat. The waters steamed.

"It's a good story, Tata," said Miroslav finally.

"I'm not telling you any more stories," said Danilo. "You can find your own stories."

Miroslav closed his eyes and thought of the Turkish Bridge, where he had learned to fish with wire and string. He wondered if a river could actually have a memory, then he held his breath and submerged himself in the scalding waters. For the first time in his life, he felt mind and body separating. He had found the secret. He floated above himself, among the clouds of steam, watching his body sink down and down, further and further, three thousand meters into the center of the earth, into a small, hot place from which all things would eventually arise again.

AFTER THE VISIT to the hammam, Miroslav stopped running completely. He hung up his pale blue trainers and did not touch them again. He no longer needed them.

"What did you say to him?" asked Stoja.

"Nothing, nothing," said Danilo. "Children just change, that's all."

"He needs to be with people his own age. He needs a girlfriend."

"Give him time. Boys will be boys."

But Miroslav did not find a girlfriend, nor anyone, for that matter. He became obsessed with building his robots. Soon the house was overrun with little four-wheeled electrical creations. The robots would wheel and bump into walls and fall down the stairs, and sometimes they would make strange noises in the night. He worked three jobs in town just so he would have enough money for his obscure electrical parts, which he ordered from Germany and sometimes Japan, because the Japanese loved robots more than anyone else in the world. He would collect these boxes, with their strange lettering, at the post office in Višegrad, and the postmaster would make the same joke every time about him being an undercover terrorist.

One day, after nearly breaking his neck tripping down the stairs, Danilo stormed into Miroslav's room, the offending robot in hand. "Miroslav! What's all of this nonsense?"

"They're for my show," said Miroslav.

"Things can't go on like this!" said Danilo. Then: "What show?"

"You'll see."

His "show" turned out to be a dark, post-apocalyptic production of *The Nutcracker* in the Dom Kulture that utilized six ambimobile rat robots and twenty-four ballerina puppets manipulated by a modified Jacquard loom. He performed the entire show by himself, his legs pumping the clattering loom backstage as he manically worked a board of remote controls. It was a veritable feat of athletic engineering, and he broke a pinkie on opening night. In spite of the injury and in spite of the Rat King badly malfunctioning and falling off the proscenium into an old woman's lap, the play awed the small audience, for it offered that rare glimpse into a world blessed with only the echoes of humans. After a glowing, if befuddled, write-up in the local newspaper, the story of Miroslav and his performing robots was picked up by the national news station RTV Sarajevo, which referred to him as "Robot Dječak" and "Genij Višegrada."[1]

---

[1] "Robot Dječak," *Vijesti iz kulture,* RTV Sarajevo, March 2, 1987. Television broadcast.

These nicknames would be lovingly recounted and modified at the Danilović dinner table. Even if they did not entirely understand it, Stoja and Danilo could not help but have a certain pride in their son's accomplishment. Maybe he had found his path, however unorthodox. Girls, friends, happiness would all soon follow.

Due to popular demand, *Nutcracker Automata* came back and ran for a week of sold-out shows. It was the kind of production that would still be recalled by audience members many years later. At the final curtain call, Miša was the one to hand his brother a bouquet of roses, and Miroslav responded by having one of the ballerina puppets walk up and stroke his leg.

It was a leg worth stroking. Miša had become a bruising center-back for the junior Drina HE football team. The *beba džin* was feared on football pitches throughout the land. Miša was almost twice as big as anyone on the field yet nimble enough to keep up with the skimpy strikers who tried to negotiate his turf, but more often than not would end up sniffling on the ground.

He was a great fan of Drina HE's senior side, Višegrad's decidedly mediocre semi-professional club. Most of his friends followed the more glamorous Red Star Belgrade, but he steadfastly supported the local team, even if they had finished middle of the table for the past four years. His favorite striker was Vladimir Stojanović, an absurdly talented button of a man who would play well only if he was allowed three and a half cigarettes at halftime—no more, no less. During the war, he would go on to have a successful career for Cosenza, in Italy's Serie B, but for the time being he was happy to wow the home crowd with his God-gifted skill and his occasional histrionics. Stojanović always went to his left foot—all the defenders knew this, and still they could not defend him.

"Always to the left!" Miša would shout as he shot penalties at Danilo, standing in the cockeyed goal that Miša had sloppily painted across the barn. And this meant: *I cannot be stopped no matter what you do.* Miša was not naturally left-footed, but in honor of his hero he trained himself to use only his weaker foot. Eventually his weaker foot became his stronger foot.

For his brother's thirteenth birthday, Miroslav made Miša a mechanical piggy bank in which a football striker shot coins past an inert keeper, the coins always landing in the left side of the goal as the keeper looked on helplessly.

Miša shot every coin he could find into the goal, and when the bank was full, he emptied it and shot them all again.

DURING THE first warm day in April, Miša and Miroslav went swimming in the Drina. Miroslav did not want to go—he was in the middle of working on his next production, a bold, self-penned sequel to *Swan Lake,* but Miša persisted, flicking at the patch of skin above Miroslav's knee until he finally relented. They would swim and then go eat *burek* at the bakery above the bridge. They jogged down their road into the valley, through the farmland, feeling the earth slowly breathing beneath them, now that winter had finally come and gone. It was the first time Miroslav had run in some time, and though he was desperately out of shape, the movement made him miss his long runs, and he vowed to pick up the habit once again. They ran through town and then took the path north, by the shoreline to a bend in the river where the water was deep and still as it eddied back into itself.

Miša quickly shed his clothes and dived into the water. When he came up again, he was almost halfway across the river. For not the first time, Miroslav stopped to admire the physical specimen that was his brother. A sense of pride tinged with jealousy that quickly parted into love.

He took off his clothes and dived in, and the water was so cold from the snowmelt that he felt his heart stop beating for a second. He hung there weightless, half dead. And then he pumped his arms and swam down and down until his cheek touched the river bottom. A thick clump of mud pushed between his lips and into his mouth. An ancient bit of earth, wet from the weight of the water above it. Miroslav held on to the mud, rolling his tongue through it, feeling the muck and the grit separate out against his teeth. Beneath the water, with a mouthful of earth, Miroslav felt strongly that he was of a place, of this place. This sense of belonging made him shiver.

He was in the middle of surfacing when suddenly he felt a hand grabbing on to his leg, dragging him back down. He panicked, kicking out wildly with his other leg at whatever had taken hold of him, but the hand would not let go. What was this? Was the earth reclaiming him for one of its own? Miroslav felt the last bit of air in his lungs draining away. He stopped fighting. He became certain he would die, that he would return to the bottom of the river and lie there forever.

The hand released him. Miroslav pushed upward, breaking the surface and gasping for air, the mud pouring down from his lips. Miša came up next to him, laughing.

"You're such a fucker, Miša," said Miroslav, panting, punching out at his brother.

"It wasn't me—it was the river troll."

"You could've killed me."

"Lighten up, *burazeru*."

Next to where they had dived into the water, a man appeared on the shore. They floated on their backs, and Miroslav felt the anger draining from him. It was difficult to be angry when floating on your back.

He looked back at the man on the shore.

"Miša," he said to his brother. Miroslav started to swim over to where they had left their things, and suddenly he realized that the man was going through their clothes. Even from that distance he could see the man's eyes: wild, like a horse's eyes. The man had to be a gypsy. The gypsy had Miroslav's wallet in his hands; he was opening the wallet and taking out his money.

"Hey!" yelled Miroslav. "Hey, stop!"

He was swimming back to shore when he felt a wave against his side and saw his brother shoot past him. Miša sprinted out of the water toward the gypsy, who looked up, startled at the sight of a giant running at him. And then Miroslav saw that the gypsy had a knife. He tried to warn his brother, but Miša didn't hear him; he ran right at the gypsy and tackled him. They both fell, but Miroslav could see in the way his brother's body recoiled in midair, like a snake's, that he had been hit with the knife.

"Miša!" he screamed. He ran up the beach and saw the blood, saw his brother sitting on the ground in shock, one hand cupped to his chest. The gypsy turned to Miroslav. One of the gypsy's eyes was no good—it was the color of milk and pointed off crookedly to the side.

"*Jebi se!*" yelled the gypsy and wildly whipped the blade at him. Miroslav jumped out of the way, his hands paddling the air to protect himself. His body was suddenly filled with a great electricity, the pads of his fingers throbbing with current. He saw something moving to his left, and then Miša was charging at the gypsy.

"Get away from him!" roared Miša, swinging at the man with one of his hands. The punch missed badly, and then the gypsy was hugging Miša, and Miroslav saw him stabbing his brother in the side of the rib cage, just under his left arm.

Miroslav was overcome by a wash of intense and very clear anger toward this man who was trying to do his brother harm. For the second time in his life, he felt mind and body part ways. He watched as his hands reached down and grabbed the dead limb of a willow tree, grasping the gnarled piece of wood as if he had always known it would be there. He watched himself as he swung the branch with all of his might. He watched as the gypsy, sensing movement out of the corner of his eye, turned back to Miroslav just as the limb came at his head. He watched the look of surprise on the man's face, and then there was a grotesque sound of crunching bone, followed by a soft, inward squish, like a cantaloupe popping, and the man crumpled to the ground and did not move again. It felt as if he should react and writhe and scream from such a blow, but he did not. He was perfectly still. The right side of his face had folded into itself, the blood pouring out of a deep cut just beneath his eye.

Miroslav watched himself standing there, heaving, and then he was himself again. He went to his brother, who was lying naked on the beach. Blood was coming down from the wounds on his chest, across his belly and onto his thighs.

"Are you okay?" he asked, putting a hand on his brother's shoulder.

Miša swore. "Do I fucking look okay to you?"

"Not really."

Miša pulled himself into a sitting position, wincing heavily with the pain. He looked at the gypsy, lying still at their feet. "What about him?"

"Fuck him; we need to get you to a hospital."

"But he's . . . ?" Miša did not have a word.

Miroslav went over to the gypsy. He hovered a hand above his head, as if this would reveal some sign of life. He realized that such a gesture was silly. Before, there had been a living person. Now, it was obvious there was nothing.

"He's dead," said Miroslav.

"Dead?" said Miša. He winced again. "Like *dead* dead?"

"What other kind of dead is there?"

"What do we do? Oh shit. *Shit. Shit. Shit.*"

"Miša! *It's not our fault.* He came at us. You saw it. He had a knife. Look what he did to you!"

"I don't want to go to jail," Miša moaned.

"Miša, calm down. No one's going to jail."

Miroslav looked at the dead man lying on the riverbank. He reached down and searched the gypsy's pockets. He found the money that the man had taken from them, and much more. He thought about it and then took it all. Then he grasped the gypsy's dirty hands and dragged him into the river. The body was surprisingly heavy. When they were deep enough, the water eased the body away, and a slow current began to carry it downstream. The gypsy floated, the river turning him slowly in circles, just the tips of his shoulder blades poking out of the water. They watched until the body disappeared around the bend.

Miroslav came back to his brother. "We don't say anything to anyone about this."

"Ya," said Miša. "Okay."

"Never. I'm serious. It stays here. Nobody can know."

"Ya. Okay. Nobody."

"You swear?"

Miša reached down and wiped the blood off his chest. He offered his hand. "I swear."

They shook.

"Can you stand?" asked Miroslav.

"I think so." Miša got up, wobbling. His face was pale, his eyes loose in their sockets. They dressed carefully. Miroslav tied his shirt around his brother's chest and helped maneuver him back to the road, where a truck from Žepa picked them up and drove them to the small medical clinic in Višegrad.

They told the doctors that Miša had been speared by a bull.

"A bull didn't do this," said the doctor. "Do you think I'm stupid? Are you trying to say I'm stupid?"

Lying on the examining table, Miša looked terrified.

"Do you want us to show you the bull? We can go show you the bull," said Miroslav. "I'm telling you, he was a crazy bull. Someone should really watch out for that animal, because this will happen again."

The doctor looked at him.

"Are you the one who did *The Nutcracker?* With the puppets?"

"Yes," said Miroslav. "And robots. Puppets and robots."

"Did you see it?" said Miša from the table. "It was—*ah!*" He tried to sit up but collapsed back down again.

"You must have a real imagination," said the doctor.

"Not really. It's mostly fixing things. Like you do."

"Okay," the doctor said and smiled. "Fixing things. Well. So do you remember if this bull's horns were rusty by chance?"

Miroslav said he didn't remember. Maybe. They could've been rusty. He couldn't say one way or another. The doctor sighed and ordered that Miša get a tetanus shot anyway, just to be safe.

After stitching up Miša, he gave him a bottle of unmarked pills and told him to take three every four hours for the pain. As they were leaving, the doctor shook hands with Miroslav.

"I hope that bull got some attention, too."

Miroslav realized his hand was still covered in blood.

"The bull's fine. Don't worry about the bull," said Miroslav.

WHEN THEY GOT HOME that evening, Stoja, despite herself, began to weep at the sight of her youngest son wounded.

"A bull?" she said. "What foolishness! You could've been *killed,* Miša. And Miro, you let your brother get into this?"

"He saved me," said Miša. "It was coming back to get me and he scared it away."

"You've got to be more careful, Miša," she said, slapping her thigh. "I swear to God, if something had happened . . ."

"Yes, Mama," he said, and kissed her cheek. "I'm sorry, Mama."

Danilo pulled Miroslav aside. "Who was it?"

"What do you mean?"

"You and I both know there was no bull."

"Tata—"

"I will say this only once, Miroslav. You have only one brother in this world. You have only one family. God gave you only one life. Take care of this. Take care. Someday it'll all be gone, and if you wait until that day to know what you've lost . . . by then it'll already be too late."

That night, Miroslav sat by his brother's bedside. Miša had taken six of the doctor's pills and a shot of *šljivovica,* and now his head was lolling against his pillow. He reached out and tried to hold his brother's hand.

"Thank you, Miro," he slurred. "You really saved me. I owe you so much."

"You don't owe me anything," said Miroslav. "You'd do the same."

"Will you make a show about this one day?"

"About what?"

Silence.

"Oh, okay. I get it. About nothing."

Miroslav patted the soft maw of his brother's palm. "Get some rest."

"I love you."

"I love you too, *burazeru.*"

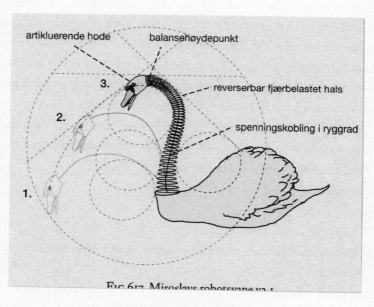

Fig. 2.4. "Miroslav's Robotic Swan v2.1"
From Røed-Larsen, P., *Spesielle Partikler*, p. 962

1. THE TOTAL AMOUNT OF ENERGY IN A CLOSED SYSTEM REMAINS
CONSTANT OVER TIME.

Miroslav's *Swan Lake: Von Rothbart's Revenge,* while praised by the professional
theater critic who had driven in from Sarajevo, was not well attended, and the
preponderance of empty seats during the final performance of the three-night
run sent Miroslav into a post–curtain-call rage. Before anyone could talk him
out of it, he took a hammer to all of his actor-puppets, including the two giant
black-and-white swan robots with their triple-reticulated, reverse-subluxated
necks. This would not be the last time he destroyed his work after a show.

Two weeks later, Miroslav graduated top of his class at the secondary school
in Višegrad, though this came as no great surprise to anyone. Nor was there
much celebration among his peers for this achievement. Despite his relative
fame, Miroslav was not admired by his schoolmates. There were more than a
few rumors about his sexuality.

At graduation, there was an old tradition called *krštenje svinje,* in which students would papier-mâché a live pig with pages from their final exams and then
heave the poor creature off the Turkish Bridge into the Drina. Though the origins of such a practice were unclear, it was beloved by local students, many of
whom had stuck it out through school solely to take part in the ceremony.
Miroslav called the whole endeavor "barbaric" and made a great show of boy-

cotting the festivities, constructing a puppet pig in a field by the church that he slathered in writings by Jean-Jacques Rousseau and then set on fire. Despite the allure of fire and the melodramatic posters that he had pasted around town, no one attended this alternate *krštenje svinje* except Miša, Danilo, Uncle Dragan, and his bewildered twins. Miroslav, again humiliated, vowed never to perform again.

"This town's the worst place in the history of the universe," he said.

"That's a bit extreme," said Danilo. "I liked the pig."

Miroslav's indignation was tempered somewhat by his acceptance shortly thereafter into the University of Belgrade's philosophy department. It was a great honor, for this was the first time in more than a decade that a boy from their village had been accepted into the university. Miša was so proud of his brother that he punched Ratko Obradović in the face and knocked out three of his teeth. Miša claimed Ratko had called his brother a faggot; Ratko claimed the attack was unprovoked.

2. A SYSTEM WILL FOLLOW THE PATH OF LEAST RESISTANCE.

It was the summer of the great drought. More would have been written about this in the history books had it not also been the last summer before the worst war in Europe since World War II. Soon there was barely any water in the mountain streams that fed the Drina; the once great river dropped to the lowest level anyone could remember. If a pig were thrown into the river again, it would likely be killed by the fall. Dead fish rotted on the muddy river shores, and a stench rose up into the narrow alleyways of the old town and hung there for weeks, until the people became accustomed to it. A man can grow accustomed to anything if he lives with it long enough.

Danilo worked long hours in the fields, trying to save the crops. He drilled several wells around the property, attempting to locate an underground spring that never materialized. While Miša recovered from his wounds, Miroslav surprised his father by offering his services, even going so far as to design a "root stimulation machine" that he had read about in an obscure nineteenth-century journal on electricity and mesmerism. He buried a long copper wire in the ground, encircling the rows of wheat with a low-grade current of 19.55 volts, which was supposed to trigger growth and replace the need for water. You could run your hand against the dying husks and feel a tingle migrating up your wrists.

"I'm thankful for your efforts," Danilo said to his eldest son. "I really am. But I must ask you to remove those wires. You're killing my crops."

After this, Miroslav swore off farming for good. He retreated to the back of the barn, where he began building a life-size elephant puppet that could be operated by its rider. He planned to walk it across the Turkish Bridge and then push it into the river, in an homage to Tuffi the elephant's famous fall from the Schwebebahn in Wuppertal. It would be his swan song to Višegrad.

"Why an elephant?" Stoja asked, surveying the huge metal skeleton taking shape in the barn.

"Elephants never forget," said Miroslav. "They've witnessed all of history. Only they can read the river."

Fig. 2.5. Tuffi plunging from the Schwebebahn into the River Wupper (1950)
From Røed-Larsen, P., *Spesielle Partikler,* p. 962

"I see," said Stoja, though she did not. At St. Stephen's, which had become her regular place of refuge, she began lighting a third candle alongside those for her two sons, though even she was not entirely sure if this was for the elephant, the river, or the country.

When Miša had finally recovered, he joined Danilo in the fields again, digging out the ditches, coaxing what was left of the water to run across their land. In the end, it was all for naught: one day the stream finally dried up for good. The grass shriveled and died. Three of their cattle collapsed from dehydration. They found one of them dead in the morning, its hindquarters devoured by a wolf.

3. FOR EVERY ACTION THERE IS AN EQUAL AND OPPOSITE REACTION.

FK Drina HE's ultrafans were known as the Čuvari Mosta, the "Guardians of the Bridge." They had recently aligned themselves with Red Star's Delije ultras, run by Arkan, the notorious criminal turned paramilitary leader. During the last game of the season, a crowd of Čuvari Mosta beat a Muslim man unconscious during a match against Sloboda Tuzla. The man did not die, but he would suffer from chronic cluster migraines and never see out of his left eye again. There was no police investigation. Miša was present for the match, but he claimed he was too busy watching the game and did not even know about the beating until much later. He was much more concerned with rumors that Stojanović had already signed a contract that would send him to Italy.

"He's a traitor!" he wailed. "Doesn't he know he's one of us?"

4. A BODY'S MASS MULTIPLIED BY THE SQUARE OF THE SPEED OF LIGHT EQUALS THE POTENTIAL ENERGY OF THAT MASS.

In the back of the barn, the elephant continued to grow.

5. If Two Systems Are in Thermal Equilibrium with a Third System, They Must Be in Thermal Equilibrium with Each Other.

Most people heard the announcement that Slovenia and Croatia had declared independence from Yugoslavia on the radio. The newsman's disembodied broadcast, quivering the little porous speaker on the mantel, informed them that Tito's kingdom was finally unraveling. The radio gave the news a certain air of inevitability: it felt at once like a tale of fiction and an eternal truth. People could not believe what they were hearing, and yet they also could not remember a time when it had not been so.

In the days that followed, as Slovenia successfully defended itself against the JNA during the Ten-Day War, as tensions rose all across Croatia and tanks were moved into position throughout Dalmatia, people milled around nervously, lingering in bakeries, staring at the bends of the Drina, holding their lovers a second too long. Everyone wondered if Bosnia would get caught in the trouble brewing to the west.

Despite a three-month moratorium on independence, in August war broke out in Krajina between Croats and ethnic Serbs. Each claimed an ancient right to their homeland; each claimed the other had taken what did not belong to him. After the first weeks of fighting—in which almost the entire population of Višegrad did not move from in front of their radios, in which everyone was hungry for any new scrap of detail concerning the distant violence, in which the term "ethnic cleansing" was first used in all seriousness—people began to slowly accept that this would now be a part of their reality. Through the daily rhythm of their lives, they separated themselves from the fighting, hoping it would never come their way. Violence could happen only far away and over the mountains, in the valleys where evil like this had always lurked.

"It's a Croatian problem," one person would say, and wave his hand like a conductor. And his partner would clap, once, twice, as if to wake someone up from a light slumber, and respond: "Yes. Life never changes." But even as they said this, they knew that life always changes, that life had already changed and would never be the same again.

It was also true that certain Muslim residents of Višegrad had already received veiled threats. A crude skull was spray-painted on the Selimović house in Drinsko. And Alija Kujović found a decapitated bat on his doorstep. Perhaps the bat had decapitated itself through a failure of echolocation. But it must also be said that these events were few and far between. The people of Višegrad had lived with their neighbors for a long time, and despite the vague rumblings of nationalism, there was still a pervasive belief—based on the slow thrum of proximity, based on the cushion of a handshake repeated ten thousand times—that everyone in their heart was decent and that a man could not turn on another man he had known his entire life.

6. THE FORCE OF FRICTION IS INDEPENDENT OF THE APPARENT AREA OF CONTACT.

That whole summer, the brothers did not speak of what had happened on the riverbank.

For Miša, such silence was an attempt to erase the event from his memory. If it remained unspoken, then maybe it had never happened at all. He played football and worked in the fields and fell in love with a girl from town who kissed him on a rock by the riverside and then broke his heart when a week later she was seen with an older boy on the same rock. But when the darkness came, he could not forget: he would dream of the gypsy's body drifting in the current, the slight, tetrahedral mounds of the shoulder blades peeking above the water, the man's long hair floating on the surface of the river like a black jellyfish. In the dream, he would run out into the river and lift the man's head from the water and find that he was not a gypsy at all—he was Miroslav. He would cradle his brother's head and then look back to the shore and the gypsy would be standing there naked, laughing at him.

For Miroslav, the memory of the killing was more complicated. He knew that he would never be able to forgive the world for directing such violence at his kin, that there was no way to return to the neutral ignorance that had enshrouded his life thus far. On the one hand, the echoes of the attack brought with them a great sense of shame and guilt; he could not rid himself of the feeling that his actions were somehow to blame for the natural and political disasters that were slowly enveloping their world. He was not superstitious like his poor *baka* back in Trebinje, who crossed and recrossed every threshold twice so as to confuse the trailing spirits—he did not *actually* believe in curses, and yet he was fairly certain that it was he who was directly responsible for the evil that everyone felt blowing in from across the river. He could not explain this knowledge in any rational terms, though he felt it in his heart, and this angered him. Why must he be the one who was held karmically accountable? Weren't there much worse people in the world than him?

In his darker moments, as he lay awake on his back at night, the guilt was not what lingered. Tucked beneath the guilt was a longing—a longing to feel it all again, to be enfolded in that giddy sensation of mind and body bifurcating, of himself other than himself, of watching his person strike the gypsy down with such ease it made his bones ache. This division was what he had been searching for in each one of his plays—he relied on the services of puppets and robots to perform this cheap trick of displacement—but in that moment by the river, he had needed nothing but himself. *He had been the other.* Puppets—glorious and profane—were no substitute for the real thing.

7. THE FORCE WITH WHICH TWO OBJECTS ATTRACT EACH OTHER
   IS DIRECTLY PROPORTIONAL TO THEIR MASS AND INVERSELY
   PROPORTIONAL TO THE SQUARE OF THE DISTANCE BY WHICH
   THEY ARE SEPARATED.

Work on the elephant stalled. Lacking one of its ears and a proper sheath of skin, it languished in the nave of the barn, silent and immovable. This picture of incompletion, of an animal half-realized, slipped Miroslav into despair. He feared he would never create anything again. The carcass presided over a tribunal of failure.

One day, when he felt himself on the edge of madness, he wrote a letter to Professor Darko Zunjić, in the philosophy department at the University of Belgrade, asking him if he wouldn't mind providing a reading list of essential titles in hermeneutics and continental philosophy.

"It's bleak out here," wrote Miroslav. "I hope you understand. I'm primarily a puppeteer, but the puppets have stopped speaking to me. So now I'm at a loss. I'm interested in anything that deals with consciousness, reason, and/or death. Thank you very much in advance. Regards, Miroslav Danilović."

To his great surprise, Professor Zunjić sent him a battered box full of his personal books.

"May they change you as they have changed me," read the note. "See you in the fall." Professor Zunjić asked only that he return his books when he arrived in Belgrade.

Miroslav was so moved by this gesture, by the cracked binding of the books, by the wild, illegible notes in the margins, by the infectious evidence of a mind at work, that he spent his whole summer working his way through the box as his father and brother slaved away in the fields, trying to save what could not be saved. Aristotle, Kant, Kierkegaard, Heidegger, Derrida, an American named Richard Rorty—he did not understand all of what was in the box, but what he did understand made him hungry, and what he did not understand made him hungrier still.

"What are those books about?" Miša once asked him after coming in from a day of digging ditches. There was a palm print of mud on the left side of his neck, as if the earth itself had tried to strangle him.

"Nothing much," said Miroslav. "You could go through life and never read Heidegger and you would still be fine. You would probably even be better off. You could just go about the act of being without worrying what that meant."

"So then why do you read them?" Miša asked.

Miroslav thought about this. "Well," he said, "I guess I'm afraid."

"Afraid of what?"

"What is anyone afraid of, Miša?"

"I'm not afraid of anything. Spiders, maybe."

"I'm afraid of a world without meaning."

"Okay."

"I'm afraid of our capacity for self-deception. I'm afraid of being without being. I'm afraid of dying alone."

"I would never let you die alone," said Miša.

"I love you, Miša, but we all die alone. They never tell you this in school, but this is the only truth you can depend upon. Solitary demise."

"But then you still go to heaven. And heaven is full of people."

Miroslav smiled. "And then you go to heaven, Miša. Full of people. It's true. There's always that. Although you could go to hell."

"Lots of people there, too," said Miša. "You'll never be alone."

8. An Object in Motion Will Stay in Motion Unless an Unbalanced Force Acts upon It.

One evening in early August, Danilo knocked three times on Miroslav's door.

The sequence was like this: - - - such that the last knock seemed like it would never come, and then it came.

There was no answer. Danilo cautiously opened the door and found Miroslav reading on his bed.

"Why didn't you answer?" he asked.

"Why did you come in?"

Danilo had noticed a shift in his eldest son. Long ago he had given up on his being a productive participant on the farm, and he had accepted this loss because Miroslav was destined for great things—opportunities were open to him that Danilo had never had for himself. And yet he sensed something impure in his son's heart—he no longer looked at you when he spoke, and when he did, his eyes appeared heavy and resigned, the kind of look Danilo recognized in an ailing animal.

Danilo came over and sat on the bed. He put a hand on his son's foot.

"Tata, what is it?" said Miroslav. "I'm busy."

"Tell me what is on your mind."

"What do you mean?"

Danilo remained quiet. He left his hand resting on his son's foot.

Finally Miroslav closed his book. He sat like this for a while and then looked at his father.

"I think I'll go to Belgrade next week," he said.

"So soon?"

"I need to leave."

"But it might be dangerous there. They're saying it might be dangerous."

"I can't be here anymore."

Danilo picked up the book.

"*Prolegomena to Any Future Metaphysics That Will Be Able to Come Forward as Science*," he read out loud. "Immanuel Kant." He opened to the first page and tried to read a few sentences. "So you like this?"

Miroslav shrugged. "Kant's all right. He wrote his first book and no one understood it, so he tried again with this one. It's better."

"What was he saying?"

"He was trying to work out a theory that could apply to everything."

"And did he?"

"Not really. He was wrong. I think he knew he was wrong even as he was writing it."

"It's easy to be wrong," said Danilo.

"He didn't know at the time how important he was going to be. When he was living, he wasn't *Kant*. He was just another German philosopher trying to write down his ideas."

Danilo closed the book.

"Maybe you should wait before you go. Maybe it's better to stay until we know what will happen."

"Well, we cannot know what will happen," said Miroslav. "So does this mean we shouldn't do anything?"

"I'm asking you not to go. I know I can't tell you to stay, but I'm asking you, as your father, not to go. Just for now. Please. We need you here."

"You don't need me here. I don't do anything."

"That's not what I'm talking about. Your brother needs you."

"Have you seen him? He doesn't need anybody."

"It's just for the fall. Then we can talk about all of this again."

"Tata. I can't. You know I can't."

Danilo opened the book again. "Tell me, why do you hate it here so much?"

"You wouldn't understand."

"Not if you don't give me a chance."

"Have you ever woken up and felt like you're being suffocated by your own lungs?"

Danilo thought about this. "God's with you. He's always with you, wherever you go."

"You can't prove it."

"I don't need proof. I've always had proof. The world is my proof."

"I'm suffocating, Tata. I'm suffocating with each breath. Every day I'm here, I'm reminded of me."

"But you *are* you."

"So you see my problem."

"Wherever you go," said Danilo, "you cannot leave those lungs behind. So you better get used to them."

9. ALL CHEMICAL PROCESSES ARE REVERSIBLE, ALTHOUGH SOME PROCESSES HAVE SUCH AN ENERGY BIAS THEY ARE ESSENTIALLY IRREVERSIBLE.

On the seventeenth of August 1991, Miroslav loaded a single battered suitcase, the professor's box of philosophy books, and a jar of his mother's *slatko* juniper preserves into the luggage compartment of the express bus bound for Belgrade. The four of them stood together awkwardly, saying nothing until Miša went to his brother and hugged him.

"Burazeru," he said. "Will you come back?"

"Of course I'll come back," said Miroslav. He pointed at their parents. "Take care of them."

Miša nodded, tears in his eyes. "I'll miss you."

As the bus pulled away, he ran alongside it, banging on the luggage compartment before flashing his brother the peace sign, although he could not see through the glare whether Miroslav was looking back at him. The bus upshifted and moved out onto the road. Danilo hugged Stoja, who wept heavily in his arms. Then he walked back to their car before the bus had even passed the old pump station, leaving his wife and son standing alone to watch its final disappearance.

10. ANY EFFECTIVELY GENERATED THEORY CANNOT BE BOTH CONSISTENT AND COMPLETE.

After his brother left for the city, Miša shaved his head and began calling himself Danilo.

Like his father and his father before. And his father before and his father before that. He gave no reason for this change, but he no longer responded to Miša or Mihajlo. On several occasions, he expressed his desire to visit his older brother in Belgrade. Stoja forbade it.

"You must stay close," she said. "I'm not going to lose you, too."

When it was clear this was not negotiable, he took a mug and threw it at the wall with such force that it left a hole in the plaster in the shape of a sinking ship. Later he would apologize, crying like a baby, surprised by the permanent wake of such fleeting rage.

Stoja could now be found most days at the church. She went to confession every day at 11 A.M., though there was never anything to confess. Her husband was a religious man, but even he sensed something was amiss in the persistence of her visits.

"You know God is everywhere?" he said. "Not just at St. Stephen's? We can pray here as well."

Her collection of candles had grown. Now there were ten that she lit each day in the manoualia. In her mind, each candle no longer represented an individual prayer; rather, it was their collectivity that came to stand in for all things. Ten candles would be lit—no fewer, no more. She would stay until they had all burned right down to the wick, until she could hear the hiss and see the puff of smoke that signaled their extinction.

If you had asked her long ago, at that Makavejev screening in the Dom Kulture, whether she thought she would be one of those kerchiefed *babas* who whittled away their days praying in church, she would've laughed at you. And yet sometimes we become the person we most dread. Or maybe we dread most the person we know we are to become.

11. THE PATH TAKEN BY A RAY OF LIGHT BETWEEN TWO POINTS IS THE PATH THAT CAN BE TRAVERSED IN THE LEAST TIME.

On the first of October, the JNA began its seven-month siege of Dubrovnik, Croatia's Adriatic jewel. It was a symbolic attack, for the town was without strategic importance; the siege was intended solely to damage Dalmatia's biggest tourist attraction. Of the 824 buildings in the old town, 563 were hit by shells, and 114 people lost their lives during the bombardment, including the poet Milan Milišić, translator of *The Hobbit* and close friend of the writer Danilo Kiš. Milišić died in his wife's arms after a 120-millimeter shell landed on the threshold of their kitchen at No. 7 Župska Street.

His second-to-last poem was titled "And Outside":

In the room it is night
And it is day outside

The three tumble outside
And the table sniffles inside

Something new is going on outside
In the room, only partially

There is no window in the room
That can be seen from the street.

12. EVERY INDIVIDUAL POSSESSES A PAIR OF ALLELES FOR ANY
PARTICULAR TRAIT. EACH PARENT PASSES A RANDOMLY
SELECTED COPY OF ONLY ONE OF THESE TO ITS OFFSPRING.

(Mihajlo) Danilo Danilović began spending all his time with his friends from
Čuvari Mosta, who had become increasingly radicalized since the outbreak of war.

With the beginning of the new season, football matches were now highly
choreographed scenes of nationalism and elaborate xenophobia. Arkan guided
the discourse from his refuge at the Cetinje monastery. New banners were
unfurled, listing the populations of Croats in various towns in Krajina; these
numbers shrank with each passing game. Chants were repeated and repeated
again until they became something close to true. At halftime, as Stojanović—
who still remained despite the rumors of his imminent departure—puffed his
three and a half cigarettes in the locker room, the crowd, hands held high,
thumb and two fingers extended in the Chetnik salute, gloried in the singing of
"Vostani Serbije" ("Arise Serbia") and "Marš na Drinu" ("March on the River
Drina"):

Poj, poj Drino, pričaj rodu mi
Kako smo se hrabro borili
Pevao je stroj, vojev'o se boj
Kraj hladne vode
Krv je tekla
Krv je lila
Drinom zbog slobode.

Sing, sing, Drina, tell the generations
How we bravely fought
The front sang, the battle was fought
Near cold water
Blood was flowing,

Blood was streaming
By the Drina for freedom!

It was an old song written by Stanislav Binički to honor the Serbians who had fought the Austro-Hungarians in the Battle of Cer in 1914. But this old song had been given new life and new meaning by a group of frantic young men inside a half-empty stadium.

Blood was flowing, they chanted. *Blood was streaming by the Drina for freedom!*

Danilo the elder did not approve of such appropriation.

"Those idiots," he said to his son. "They have crazy ideas in their heads. They're talking about medieval battles and old wars that have nothing to do with us."

"You're the one who's always saying history is so important."

"Not when you make it up! Those people have no idea about history."

"Tata, we've got to protect ourselves. You saw what happened in Krajina. The same thing'll happen here if we're not careful."

"I didn't see anything in Krajina. I've never been to Krajina."

"The Muslims have an army. They're organizing a jihad."

Danilo stared at his son. "You're not allowed to go to any more games."

"What? You can't do that!"

"I can do whatever I want. I'm your father, Mihajlo. You are fifteen years old. You know nothing."

"My name's Danilo."

"Your name's Mihajlo."

"My name's also Danilo. You gave me this name. You can't deny that."

"Why do you want to be Danilo all of a sudden?"

"Why did you name me Danilo?"

"It was for your grandmother."

"You see. Everything has a reason."

Danilo pressed his hands together. "Be careful, my son. Be very careful with this."

"We're making a stand, Tata. Someone has to. At least my boys believe in something."

"Please. It's not about believing," said Danilo. "Belief on its own is a house with no foundation."

13. ALL PARTICLES EXHIBIT BOTH WAVE AND PARTICLE PROPERTIES.

On October 16, somewhere between twenty and one hundred fifty people (depending upon whom you talked to), most of them Serb, were systematically massacred in Gospić by an elite Croatian military unit nicknamed Autumn Rain. The massacre was in apparent retaliation for the murder of Croatian civilians by Serbian rebel forces several days before in Široka Kula. The Gospić victims were doused in petrol and burned, then buried and hastily concealed under an uneven layer of concrete, although this would become known only much later, in evidence given at the 2004 trial of General Mirko Norac at the International Criminal Tribunal for the Former Yugoslavia (ICTY) in The Hague.

14. THE ANGLE OF REPOSE IS EQUAL TO THE MAXIMUM ANGLE AT WHICH AN OBJECT CAN REST ON AN INCLINED PLANE WITHOUT SLIDING DOWN.

Danilo Danilović never attended another Drina HE match. He never saw Stojanović go to his left again. He did not need to. Čuvari Mosta had joined with the newly formed Serbian Radical Party (SRS). Meetings were now held in the basement of the municipal hall. Old flags were hung on the walls, ceremonial rifles placed on the table. "Marš na Drinu" was sung to the accompaniment of a wheezing accordion. There was talk of forming a local militia, of strategies for self-defense when the war came to the valley.

Not long after, Danilo and two other boys from Čuvari Mosta took a bus to Užice and tried to enlist in the JNA. The recruitment officer, who was from Višegrad, recognized Danilo from primary school, and would not take him.

"I admire your initiative, Mihajlo. The army needs people like you. But you're still a child. Come back when you're of age and then we can talk again," said the officer.

"My name is Danilo, sir," said Danilo.

When Stoja came back from the church and heard what had happened, she flew into a rage.

"What were you thinking?" she screamed at her son. "You cannot fight!"

"I'm trying to help the country!" he yelled from the doorway. "I'm trying to actually do something! You'd let us just die here."

"If you go," she said, "I will never forgive you." She came over and embraced him like a tree, and he stood there and let her hold him and cry two long wet spots into his chest.

"Oh, my baby boy," she whispered.

"Mama, I don't want to die alone," he whispered to her.

15. At Any Junction in an Electrical Circuit, the Sum of Currents Flowing into the Junction Equals the Sum of Currents Flowing out of the Junction.

The next day, a day of chilly, unending rain, he was gone. He left without saying goodbye.

16. The Position and Momentum of a Particle Cannot Be Simultaneously Measured.

Later, after Vukovar fell and was cleared of its Croats, after the massacre at Ovčara, there were reports of Danilo Danilović doing strange and terrible things for Šešelj's White Eagles in Voćin and then Bokane. Legends began to circulate about his strength, his courage, his ruthless innocence in battle. It was said that he could not grow a beard but that he was the size of two men. It was said they called him the *beba džin.* It was said that he locked an entire village of Muslims outside of Brčko in their six-hundred-year-old mosque and then burned the building down, shooting those who tried to escape, calmly and without malice, like a child reciting a poem.

But these stories would all develop and emerge slowly, over time, and the sources of such reports were unreliable at best, as the ICTY would later discover when it attempted, unsuccessfully, to assemble evidence for an indictment of Mihajlo Danilo Danilović for crimes against humanity. The facts, if there were any facts, were difficult to establish beyond a reasonable doubt. Who had actually lit the match, and who had ordered the match to be lit? Perhaps many people had lit the match at once, or perhaps the match had simply lit itself.

17. The Rate of Change of Angular Momentum About a Point Is Equal to the Sum of the External Momenta About That Point.

After her son left Višegrad, Stoja went to St. Stephen's and would not leave. In the evening, her husband found her crouching next to the manoualia, surrounded by hundreds of candles. He tried to bring her home, but she insisted on staying through the night.

"He'll die without me," she said. "Both of them will die without me."

"You can't stay here," he said. "There's no place to sleep."

"I won't sleep."

"Come home."

"Home?" she said. "Where is home?"

He left her kneeling on the floor of the church. That night, he finally managed to reach Miroslav on the phone in Belgrade. This in and of itself was quite a feat, for ever since Miroslav had left for the city, phone calls had come few and far between. University life was busy, he said. He didn't have time for country chitchat anymore.

Danilo told him of Miša's enlistment with the Chetniks.

"I know. He wrote me a letter."

"When?"

"A while ago. He told me it was his calling."

"His *calling*?"

"That's what he said."

"He wrote you a letter and you didn't tell us?"

"Why should I? The letter was to me."

"He's your brother, Miroslav."

"I know who my brother is."

"He'll get himself killed . . . he has no idea what he's doing. And fighting with a bunch of savages? Have you heard the stories of what they've done?"

"Miša has more courage in one pinkie than the rest of us will ever have."

"He's not Miša anymore. He calls himself Danilo."

"You named him Danilo."

"I named him Mihajlo. Danilo was only for my mother."

"He's going to be fine. Stop worrying. Worry about the poor Croatian idiot who meets Danilo Danilović in the middle of a field, man against man. Worry about him."

"Your mother's upset. She's at the church. She won't come home now that you're both gone."

"Tell her to stop worrying so much."

"Will you come back home? Just for a weekend? It would mean so much to her."

"I'm busy," said Miroslav. Then: "I'll see what I can do."

18. At the Level of the Subatomic, the Laws of Classical Mechanics Begin to Break Down.

It was late October by the time Miroslav came back to Višegrad. The air had already turned cold; the birds had stopped singing. People tightened their scarves against the early chill of winter. Though Stoja had agreed to sleep in her own house, she spent nearly all her waking hours at St. Stephen's. News of her son's visit briefly lured her back. She busied herself preparing the house, baking fresh bread, turning and re-turning the sheets. They waited at the kitchen table, listening to the tick of the clock. When he finally arrived, late in the evening, they couldn't believe their eyes. He wore tight-fitting, peculiar clothing and what looked to be eye makeup. Stoja would later say that he resembled an exotic bird caught in an oil spill.

"Miro," she said. "How are you?" Her voice quavered.

"Fine. I'm fine, Mama."

Danilo brought out the *šljivovica,* which Miroslav took down in one go. Danilo refilled his glass and gave his shoulder a squeeze.

"Welcome home, son."

Miroslav again dropped back the *šljivovica* without pause.

"Easy," said Danilo. "There's time."

"So you're happy?" said Stoja. "What've you been doing with yourself?"

He brought out a black box about the size of a milk crate, which he placed carefully onto the dinner table. A black velvet curtain flowed down from one side. He ducked his head underneath the curtain for a moment, fiddling with various unseen things before reemerging and motioning for his father to put his head beneath it.

Once inside, Danilo found himself in complete darkness. It was like diving into a deep well. He fought the urge to whip the curtain off his head. He waited. Nothing happened. He breathed. He could smell the stuffiness of his exhalations.

"What am I looking at?" he asked from beneath the curtain.

"Patience," he heard from somewhere in the world beyond.

And then, from out of the gloom, he saw tiny figures appearing. A bird. Shivering. It was a crow, pecking nervously at the ground. Looking up at him, pecking again. The movements were so natural—the bird was alive, but it was impossible for this bird to be alive, because it must've been less than a centimeter tall. Pecking. Ruffling its feathers. The beat of a heart.

The whole scene gradually became illuminated. A wooden farmhouse. The walls streaked with age. A woman emerging, kerchiefed. Danilo marveled at the detail. He could see her breathing. She swept the threshold with her little broom, rested a moment on its handle, looking up at the sky. Danilo tried to look up with her, but he realized he was not part of the scene. He felt altogether massive, a clumsy, towering presence in this minuscule world. The woman shook her head, gave the threshold one last sweep, and then disappeared back into the house. From somewhere off to the side he heard the rustle of wind in the trees, though he could not decide if this was from her world or his own.

Footsteps. A man came from around the corner of the house. Bearded. Wearing a peasant's cap, with a rifle draped over his shoulder. When he saw the crow, the man stopped. Silence. Then the man's arms, tiny, moving, lifting the gun, aiming. The crow looked up and saw the gun. The bird lifted its wings, but it did not fly.

Then: everything went black. The kind of black that happens just after a dream. Danilo heard the sound of two gunshots. He jumped, peering into the dark, trying to see the body of the bird. He couldn't see anything. He breathed. He could feel his pulse thumping. He waited.

The curtain was lifted off his head. A rush of light.

"So?" said Miroslav.

"How did you make it so small?"

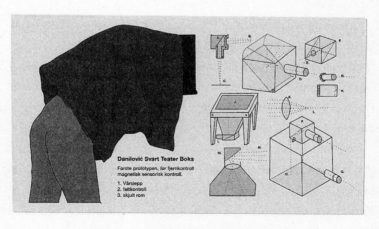

Fig. 2.6. "M. Danilović's Black Box Theater"
From Røed-Larsen, P., *Spesielle Partikler*, p. 974

"It's not that small. We're big, is all."

"Where are the strings?"

"There are no strings. But what did you think?"

"I've never seen anything like it. That bird? What happened?"

"It's a secret, Tata."

Stoja donned the curtain and viewed the scene. She came out, blinking, tears in her eyes.

"We've missed you so much, Miro," she said.

"Don't call me Miro," he said.

THE WEEKEND WAS UNPLEASANT for all. After the brief magic gifted by the black box, Miroslav seemed to slide backwards into the safety of unpleasantries. He drank often and in great amounts. He swore. He did not help to clear the table. He had begun smoking, which he did indoors, without asking for permission, leaving his cigarette butts strewn about the house. It was as if their son had been replaced by another, a copy that was not quite right.

"Does he have an accent?" Stoja whispered to her husband as they lay in bed.

"It's not an accent."

"He smells different."

"It's the city."

"Do you think he's taking drugs?"

"It's the city."

"He might have an accent."

"He doesn't have an accent."

During dinner on the second night, Danilo looked over and noticed his son's hands were shaking.

"Your hands," said Danilo.

"My hands?" said Miroslav, and for the first time he looked like their child again.

Danilo went to pour his son more *šljivovica,* but Stoja grabbed his arm and shook her head.

"Your elephant's still in the barn," said Danilo. "What shall we do with it?"

"My elephant," said Miroslav, shaking his head. "My elephant. You can burn it."

"You don't want it?" said Stoja.

"No."

"I thought you were going to walk it over the bridge," said Danilo.

"I can't stand that fucking bridge," said Miroslav.

"Watch your language," said Danilo.

They ate the *burek* in silence.

"Has Miša written to you again?" asked Danilo after a while.

"Has he written to you?"

"No."

"He must be busy, then."

"Too busy for his own mother?" said Stoja.

"You know there's a vast fucking world outside of this little shit town of yours."

"Miroslav!" Danilo yelled. "Don't speak to your mother like this."

Miroslav offered a smile. "Sorry, Mama. I haven't heard from him, either."

"I light a candle every day," said Stoja. "He doesn't know what he's gotten into."

"He's okay, Mama. He's okay. You can stop lighting your candles."

She nodded. She wiped at her eyes and split open a piece of bread. "And you've met girls in Belgrade?"

"I'm not looking for girls, Mama. I have an audience. This is much better than girls," he said. "They're hungry for something new. And I give them something new."

"Is that right?" she said. "So you're learning new things?"

Miroslav leaned back in his chair. "Yes, many things. I'm learning that nearly everyone is an asshole. And I'm learning this country enjoys fucking itself in its own ass."

Danilo put down his fork. "I won't say it again. Watch your mouth," he said. "This is still a house of God. We'll not tolerate such language. If I hear it one more time, you can find your own roof to sleep under."

"A house of God?" said Miroslav.

"When you're under my roof, you follow my rules. You can go back to the city and live however you like, but here you show respect."

"Tata, wake up! This town is full of whores. The city is filled with hypocrites. The priests are war criminals, and the war criminals are priests. So good luck with your whole house of God there. This house will be the last one standing when everything around it fucking crumbles into shit."

Danilo stood up, furious. "Get out."

Miroslav picked up a piece of bread.

"This is where you came from, Miroslav Danilović. This is the house you came from. Don't ever desecrate your own home. Now get out."

Miroslav rose from the table.

"Danilo, we can't—" Stoja began.

"You are a Danilović," he said to his son. "You will always be a Danilović."

"Believe me, I know. Why do you think I left?" He kicked his chair and stalked out of the house.

Miroslav spent an hour shivering in the barn with the ghost of the elephant. Once he had calmed down, he came back and knocked contritely on the door of the house. Stoja answered.

"I'm sorry, Mama," he said. "I didn't know what I was saying."

"Miro," she said. She reached across the threshold and took him in her arms. "My baby."

Danilo came down and saw them like this. He put his hands on his kin and whispered his love. The three of them stood together in the doorway until the cold wind blowing into the house forced them to swing the door shut.

THE NIGHT BEFORE MIROSLAV was to return to the city, Stoja wept in bed.

Danilo tried to reassure her. "It's natural. He's making his own way. He needs to separate himself from us," he said.

"But he's my son! He's Miro! How can he be like this?"

"Give him some time. You'll see."

"Miša is God knows where," she said. "And Miroslav's here, in this house, but he feels even further away. What have we done to deserve this?"

Danilo put a hand on her stomach. "No matter what he says, he will always be . . ." And he had meant to say, "your son," but he did not say it.

19. THE ANGLE OF INCIDENCE EQUALS THE ANGLE OF REFLECTION.

That January, a cease-fire was finally declared in Croatia. Televisions were filled with images of UNPROFOR's bobbing Blue Helmets moving in to manage the peace. Despite the bleakness of winter, everyone's mood began to lift. Maybe this would be the end.

Life had grown more and more difficult on the farm. There was an increasing shortage of goods, and prices had risen. Without enough hay for the winter, they had been forced to sell all except two of their remaining cows. Then Danilo fell one morning on the ice and injured his leg. He limped around, trying to keep up with the work. Stoja was forced to abandon her daily vigils at the church and run the farm herself. She built her own manoualia and iconostasis in the barn next to the elephant.

Miroslav called to say he would be coming home for Orthodox Christmas, surprising them both. After his last visit, Stoja had been afraid that he would not come back.

On Christmas Eve, the three of them sat in the kitchen as a light snow fell outside. Stoja served tea and then sat down next to her son.

"Let's talk like adults," she said.

"Fine," said Miroslav.

"Your father won't say this, but he needs your help. It's been very hard with his fall, and without Miša here to work—"

"Danilo," said Miroslav.

She took in a little breath and then began again. "I know the university's important for you. I can see you've learned things. But we need you here. You can go back to Belgrade when everything's normal again. We all must do our duty in difficult times. God bless us, we'll get through it."

"I never would've guessed," said Miroslav.

"What?"

"That you would be the one to go so God crazy," he said. "Him maybe, but not you."

"I was always a believer. I just didn't realize when I was younger, that's all. We're foolish when we're young. We're blind to the truth."

"Miša's gone," said Danilo from the other end of the table. "We could use a hand here."

"That's not my fault. Don't put that on me. Miša left because he wanted to leave."

"It's not for forever," said Stoja. "Just for now."

Miroslav formed a beak with his fingertips and pinched his tea bag.

"Asking me to come back here's like asking me to take a poison that'll slowly kill me. Is that what you want?"

"We're all taking the poison," said Danilo.

"What's all this about poison?" cried Stoja. "What about us? This is your home. It's your duty to come home."

"Come help me chop the *badnjak*," said Danilo. "Just like you and Miša used to do. We can do it together."

Miroslav smiled a long, sad smile. "You're still looking for your *badnjak*, aren't you, Tata?"

"What happened to you, Miro?" said Stoja.

"You and me, together," said Danilo. "We'll find a nice *badnjak*. I know the perfect tree where we can find one. Then you can do a *vertep* performance, just like the old days."

Miroslav shook his head. "It's too late, Tata," he said. "It's too late for all of this."

THE NEXT DAY, Stoja rose early and collected the water from the well. She made *krompiruša* pie and *sarma* and roasted the *pastrmka*. She rolled the dough for the *česnica* bread and placed the traditional coin inside. Danilo hummed to himself and went around sprinkling the hay on the windowsills. Then he went out and chopped down the *badnjak* himself.

Miroslav came down late in the morning, a bag slung over his shoulder.

"I have to go back," he said.

His parents stood in the kitchen, dumbfounded.

"But the meal . . ." his mother began.

"It's Christmas!" said Danilo. "You can't leave now."

"What about the *česnica*? We must see who gets the coin!" said Stoja.

Miroslav shook his head. His eyes were heavy. "I have to get back," he said.

"*Miroslav,*" said Danilo, raising his voice. "You must stay! You cannot go!"

"Sorry," said Miroslav. "Now one of you can get the coin."

He hugged them both once and then turned and left his home for the last time.

20. WHEN TWO PARTICLES BECOME ENTANGLED, THEIR SHARED STATE IS INDEFINITE UNTIL MEASURED.

Two months later, Bosnia declared independence from Yugoslavia, and the war came to Višegrad. The town was overrun by the JNA; huge tanks squeezed down the narrow streets, flattening signposts, crushing flowerpots. Danilo tried to call Miroslav in Belgrade, but he could not get through. The lines had been cut. He wrote to him on several occasions. He was not a writer, but he tried to write nonetheless.

From a letter dated April 19, 1992:

> *There is no telling what might happen in the future. Normal people have become sick in the head. They are pushing the Muslims out of town. The army is here now but they will leave soon. After that, no one knows what will happen. . . .*
>
> *Why don't you ever write to us? Your mother is worried. She prays for you every day in the barn. It's too dangerous to go to St. Stephen's anymore.*

We miss you. We miss both you and your brother. I pray we will all be together again.

> *Love, your father,*
> *Danilo*

From a letter dated May 21 (?), 1992:

The JNA have left. . . . We heard their tanks going by at night. When I went down the next morning, I found they had knocked over our fence. There was garbage everywhere. It is a mess. They say bad things will happen. . . . Maybe you should come back home. It is best for us to be together. We can celebrate your birthday together. I hope you are safe in the city. I have not heard of how things are there. Your mother sends her love. Write if you can. We miss you.

> *Love, your father,*
> *Danilo*

From a letter dated June 25, 1992:

We tried to call you yesterday for your birthday but the lines are still cut. We lit a candle and said some prayers. We are always praying. We think of you every day. Things are very difficult here. You can't imagine. The White Eagles have moved in. They are in charge now and they are very terrible. The worst kind of evil. I can't believe Miša would know them. . . . They told the Muslims to move back into town and then they began to kill them. Every night, they say. They line them up on the Turkish Bridge and then shoot them or cut their throats and then they throw them down into the Drina. Sometimes they push them over the bridge while they are still alive, and they let them swim and then they shoot them. I saw blood on the bridge last week. Lots of it. I could not look. It is madness, Miroslav. The river does not forget. . . . I think it is best if we move to Belgrade with you. The Serbs in the town are safe for now, but what if the Bosnian Army hears of what is happening and does the same to us?

Do you want your parents thrown off of a bridge into the river? Do you want our throats cut like animals? . . . Your mother is not the same as she was. I worry for her. I worry for us all. Please, write to us.

Love, your father,
Danilo

21. THE ENTROPY OF ANY ISOLATED SYSTEM NOT IN THERMAL EQUILIBRIUM ALMOST ALWAYS INCREASES.

These letters no longer exist.

4

S toja," said Danilo.

"Stoja," he said again.

Above them, the great elephant loomed against the flicker of the candles. A line of saints stared at his wife, who was kneeling, hands clutched in prayer.

"You have to move to live," he said.

He put a hand on her shoulder. A dankness in the air.

"Please," he said.

"Where can I go?" she said, staring at the saints. "It's too dangerous to go anywhere."

"Just don't go into town. Take a bicycle. You can ride to the river. The weather's nice today."

"I don't have a bicycle."

"Take Miša's. Ride to the river and then come right back. It isn't far. It'll be good for you. You've got to move around or else you'll shrivel up into a nothing."

"I like being here."

"If you don't want to do it for yourself, then do it for me."

SHE CHANGED into a summer dress. She put on earrings. Danilo found the red bicycle in the shed. He inflated the tires. He lowered the seat with a wrench and squeezed a drop of oil into the gears.

"You see?" he said, spinning the pedals. "Like new."

"I haven't ridden in years," she said. "Since I was a girl."

"You don't forget," he said, kissing her forehead. "Go. I love you. Take care. And bring your ID card. They're checking everyone these days."

She followed the road down into the valley. The air felt cool and light on her face. Danilo had been right: she had lost herself somewhere along the way. The barn, the candles, the elephant—it was a trap, she could see that now. She smiled, feeling the ground slip beneath her. She felt as though she could ride clear across the world like this. If she could just keep riding, everything would be normal again. And when she went back home, she would find that both of her sons had returned, and they would run out of the house to greet her.

As she got down to the main road, she saw a car stopped in front of four men armed with machine guns. She caught her breath. The men had strung barbed wire across the road. They were talking to someone in the car, which she could see was stuffed to the brim with suitcases. Through the back window she could see a small white dog. It seemed to be barking, but she couldn't hear any sound. One of the men saw her coming down the road on her bicycle, and he waved with his gun for her to dismount.

"Oy," said the man, approaching her. He was wearing camouflage and a traditional Šajkača army hat, like the ones she remembered seeing in history books. This had to be one of those White Eagles that everyone was talking about. She had never seen one of them up close before.

"What's your name?" he said. He had a splotchy mark on his temple, the color and shape of an overripe raspberry. She could see how young he was. Young and foolish, just like Miša.

"Stojanka Danilović. I live there," she said and pointed back to where she had come from. She wanted to tsk this boy for dressing up in such a stupid costume. For playing games. Why had his mother let him do such a foolish thing?

He asked to see her ID card. Stoja reached into her pocket, but even as she did this, she realized she had left the card on her bureau. She had picked up the card and then set it down when she put on her earrings. She could see the card lying on the wooden bureau. She could see the grainy photograph staring back at her, her smile that was not quite a smile. She hated that picture, though Danilo had said it was not far from the truth.

"I don't have it," she said, her heart dropping. "I left it on the bureau."

"What?" he said, moving closer.

As calmly as she could, she explained to the young man that she was the wife of Danilo Danilović, that she lived just over the hill, that she had not planned on seeing anyone, she was merely trying to ride to the river, "to get the air back into my lungs." This was how she said it. She was a Serb in good standing, she said. She was an Orthodox Christian. A believer. Had he not seen her holding vigil at her manoualia in St. Stephen's? She pulled out the little silver cross around her neck to show him. A gift from Danilo. She had never been more grateful for it than now.

She thought that everything would be right then. This stupid boy would understand and let her go and she would turn her bike around and tell Danilo all about this. *The White Eagles are everywhere!* she would say. *And they are using children to fight for them!*

But the young man did not wave her through. He looked concerned. He took a step forward and grasped the cross in one of his hands. He was close to her now. She could smell the rancid stink of alcohol and dried meat on his breath. *God bless, how could they let such a boy drink?* The boy's fingers, covered in a deep layer of grime, fumbled with the small silver object. He turned the cross over, as if to find proof of its authenticity on the reverse side. When she looked up at him, he was not looking at the cross but at her.

"Please," she said quietly. "God bless."

"You're a liar. I can hear your accent," he said and ripped the chain from around her neck. Her head snapped forward. She could feel the burn on the back of her neck where the chain had split.

"Please. Listen. I'm a Serb. I promise," she said, and tried not to let the fear split open the seams of her words. What he heard was true: she had been born in Trebinje, near the Montenegro border, and so her accent was foreign. Not quite foreign, but peculiar.

Oh Danilo, Danilo, what shall I do? This boy has no idea!

"You're lying. You carry this cross to hide yourself." He held up the necklace. "You should be ashamed."

"I'm a Serb, I swear to you. I'm a devout Christian. I hadn't been until recently, but now it's all I have. My sons left me. My youngest is your age. He's fighting like you."

"You're an old, filthy, lying whore is what you are," the boy said. He stepped forward and grabbed the space between her legs. The force with which his hand moved emptied the air from her lungs. His lust, fetid, like a whiff of curdled milk. The blindness of his fingers, kneading at her. He brought his mouth very close to her ear, breathing raggedly, the raspberry splotch on his temple trembling with each pulse. She was gathering her strength to scream when he pushed her to the ground.

"Here's another Turkish whore for Lukić," he said to the others.

"Fine, fine," said one of the soldiers. "Let's go back. It's enough for now."

They loaded her into the back of the truck with a mother and a daughter whom they had taken from the car. Stoja recognized them from the market. They were Muslim, she knew. The mother's name was Remiza. Remiza was holding on to her daughter's hand so hard that her knuckles were turning white. Remiza's husband stood by the car and watched them go, his hands on his hips, his face registering nothing at all.

The truck drove through the valley and then turned up a steep road. A stream flowed nearby, the water thick with bright green algae. There was no wind in the trees, and she could smell the thickness of the minerals in the water. Stoja tried to smile at Remiza, to let her know that she was with them, but the woman held on to her daughter and looked right through her.

They came to a hotel, looming in a clearing of the forest like the hull of a great beached ship. The facade of the hotel was bright white, the top floors lined with concrete balconies, their railings painted red. All of the curtains behind the balconies were drawn closed. From somewhere there came a cry, and then silence. Around the hotel, men lay sleeping, sunning themselves. Some wore ski masks pulled up above their faces. Stoja had heard of this place. Before the war, people had come to heal themselves in the thermal pools. They had come from all over, as far as Austria and Hungary and Romania. Somewhere nearby, the Turks had built a hammam hundreds of years ago. The waters from inside these mountains could supposedly cure all ills.

As they pulled into the parking lot, Stoja saw a girl come out onto one of the balconies. She had short brown hair, cut close to her head. The girl watched them come to a stop in front of the hotel and then disappeared back into the room.

As soon as they were stopped, a man with black paint on his face came at them with a machine gun and ordered them off the truck. Remiza began to weep. She begged the man to take her but leave her daughter. The man leaped up onto the back of the truck and rammed the butt of his gun into her head. He did this easily, without effort. Remiza fell down onto her side. She lay there, unconscious. Her daughter collapsed onto her, weeping.

"Shut up," the man said to them. "When we want you to talk, we'll ask you to talk. But we'll never ask you to talk, so you will never talk."

He grabbed the girl by the back of her neck and pulled her off the truck. Then he turned to Stoja.

"Please," she said. "There has been some mistake. I'm a Serb. I'm like you."

"You're nothing like me," said the man.

The last thing she saw before the darkness came was a red car driving up the hill, and in that split second she could not help but hope that whoever it was had come to rescue her.

IN THE AFTERNOON, when Stoja had still not returned, Danilo grew nervous. Maybe she had gone back to the church? He should have figured as much. Then he found her ID card on the bureau. He stared at her picture.

"Stoja," he said.

Their truck was not working, so he ran over to his cousin Dragan's house and asked him for his car. Dragan insisted on coming along. They first drove to the church but found it locked. They tracked down the caretaker, who opened it up for them, but the church was empty, the candles unlit. Danilo's mouth went dry.

They slowly drove down the road that led to the river.

"There," said Danilo, pointing. "Stop."

It was Stoja's red bicycle. Leaning against a tree, as if waiting for its rider to return. An open suitcase lay by the side of the road, its contents strewn into the ditch. Children's clothes. A little doll made of sticks and strings sat by one wheel of the bicycle.

They searched up and down the road. All the way to the river and back, until it grew too dark to see. Their headlights began to make every mound, every irregularity, look like a possible body.

"She's not here," said Dragan. "Maybe she went into town."

"Why would she go there?" said Danilo. "I told her not to go there."

"Maybe she had dinner with a friend?"

"I told her not to go there. I told her just to the river and back." Danilo brought his hands to his face. "Oh, this is my fault. It told her to go."

"It's not your fault, cousin," said Dragan. "We'll find her."

They drove into town. Past burnt and gutted houses. A couch sitting upright against a doorway. The streets were deserted. Dogs running around, searching for scraps.

A soldier came up and waved for them to stop.

"There's a curfew," the soldier said. "Go home."

"I'm looking for my wife." Danilo leaned over to the window. "She was bicycling today. She hasn't come back. Her name's Stojanka Danilović. Have you seen her?"

The soldier stared at him. He looked shocked. Then he raised his gun and pointed it at them. "You can't be out now. Go home."

"But she's my wife! She left her ID card. I'm very worried she—"

"We've got to go back," said Dragan.

"But I'm just worried something's happened to her. Have you heard anything?"

"No one is allowed to be out." The soldier's eyes flicked back and forth between them. He was young, with a birthmark on his temple. They heard him click off the safety of the rifle.

"Danilo!" said Dragan. "We can come back in the morning."

They left the car at Danilo's house. Dragan tapped his cousin on the shoulder.

"Everything will be all right," he said. "What did your mother say? 'The Danilovićs are survivors.'"

"My mother was a liar."

Danilo fell asleep sitting up, in a chair facing their bed. Before the sun had fully risen, he awoke, made himself some coffee, and washed his hands. Then he took down an alabaster jar that they kept hidden inside the ceiling. Inside the jar was a roll of deutsche marks. He took all the money and his wife's ID card and drove Dragan's car down to the police station in town, where he waited all morning for them to open.

At eleven o'clock, a large man pulled up in front of the station in a small blue VW Golf. The man looked tired. He spent some time in the car before he struggled to pry himself from the front seat. He headed to the locked door of the police station. Danilo got out. He tried not to run.

"Please," he said, approaching the man. "My wife has gone missing."

The man showed no interest in this news. He busied himself with unlocking the door.

"Please," Danilo tried again. "There's been a mistake. We're Serbian. Here's her card."

"I don't know anything about this," the policeman said. "Why are you telling me this?"

Danilo took out half of the money in his pocket and showed it to the man. "Please," he said. "There's been a mistake. Can you help me?"

The policeman, who walked stiffly, as if one of his legs could no longer bend, took Danilo down the block to an old hotel that smelled of dried sweat and blood sausage. A small radio was playing Herzegovinian folk music in one corner. The policeman left Danilo sitting in the lobby and headed upstairs. When he came back down, he said, "Lukić will see you." He stood, waiting. Danilo reached into his pocket and gave him several more bills. The policeman left without giving any further instructions.

Danilo waited in the lobby. Men came and went, many of them bearded. They wore all sorts of military uniforms. Sometimes their tops did not match their bottoms, as if their clothes had become mixed up in the wash. Many of them wore the patch of the White Eagles, and almost everyone carried a gun. He did not see the young man who had stopped them the night before.

Finally, one of the men came into the lobby and motioned for Danilo to stand and follow him up the stairs. The man, smoking a cigarette, roughly patted Danilo down for weapons, then he pushed him into one of the hotel rooms.

Lukić was a large, clean-shaven man, with a broad, flat nose and surprisingly soft eyes. He looked like a father who had not yet become a father. He smiled slightly when Danilo entered the room, and Danilo saw the flash of a rotten tooth that had turned blue. Lukić sat in an armchair. He wore camouflage pants and a grey sweatshirt that was marked by several indecipherable stains. The bed next to him was covered with ammunition and handguns of varying sizes. Danilo briefly wondered if this was how he slept, in a sea of bullets. On the table next to the bed, a lone plastic flower stood at attention inside its vase.

In a voice that he tried to keep strong, Danilo said that he had known Lukić's uncle in grade school.

Lukić smiled. "Pluto."

"Yes, Pluto," said Danilo. "He's a nice man."

"He was a terrible man. A sadist. But he's dead now," Lukić said with a smile.

"Oh. Well. I'm sorry to hear this," said Danilo.

"What can I do for you?"

He told Lukić that he was looking for his wife, Stojanka, who had disappeared the previous day. He explained that her two sons had moved away; one had joined the Chetniks up in Croatia—he lingered on this word, *Chetniks*—and the other had moved to Belgrade to study at the university. His wife had been distraught for several months. It was unlike her to be so on edge. She was just going out for a little bicycle ride to clear her head and she forgot her ID card. Simple as that. He didn't care what had happened. Or who had done what. He just wanted to bring her home.

Lukić listened politely and took Stoja's ID card when Danilo showed it to him. He studied it closely, holding it up to the light.

When Danilo was finished speaking, he reached into his pocket and took out the money, which had somehow gotten wet. Lukić took the damp deutsche marks from him and dropped them on the bed without looking at them.

"Go on," said Lukić.

Danilo shrugged. "There is nothing more to say."

Lukić picked at something beneath his fingernail and suddenly made a little chuckle, as if he had just remembered a joke. Then he looked Danilo in the eye.

"Okay, so first you must know this: I like you," said Lukić. "I like that you came here and had the courage to talk. So this is why I'll tell you what I will tell you now. Otherwise, you have to know, you'd already be dead. So today is your lucky day. This is the first thing you must know."

Then he went on to talk about the war for a while, about the justness of their cause but also the difficulties of conflict, about how sometimes things happened that were regrettable, and that no one could be said to be responsible for these things when they happened in the heat of battle. It was difficult enough to maintain order in a town when no one knew whom to trust. Mistakes would inevitably be made. It was the way of things. But they were doing their best. Višegrad was in very good hands, this much he could say.

Danilo grew impatient. "So then you know what happened to her?" he said.

"I'm not saying that; I'm just saying you must understand the circumstances. We're looking after many people right now. We're making sure this country's safe to live in. It's not an easy job. The Turks let this place go to shit. So you must understand our situation."

"But she's done nothing!" said Danilo, exasperated. "Stoja's innocent!"

"I understand your opinion. But I must disagree. She was without ID, as you say."

"I told you. She forgot it. She was just—"

"And, as you say, she looks like a Turk."

"I didn't say that."

"She even talks like a Turk. And this is not my fault. This, of course, is asking for trouble. You can imagine how difficult it would be if all the Turks had no identification and they claimed they were not Turks and we had to check each one. It would be madness. It would not be good," Lukić said, but very kindly, as if he were doing Danilo a favor. "You have to understand the Turkish mind. I understand this mind. It's my business to understand the Turkish mind."

"What have you done with her? Please? Just give her back. I just want her back in the house. She's a good woman. Her sons went away and—"

"Why would you let a woman out like that without an ID? Don't you love your wife at all?"

Danilo fell to the floor. He clasped his hands together. "Please. I just wanted her to get some air. She was not herself . . . she was praying all the time . . ."

"Look, look. I'll see what I can do," said Lukić sympathetically. He placed a hand on Danilo's shoulder. "But if you want my opinion, it was her own fault for coming from a mixed family. This was a disaster waiting to happen."

Danilo stared up at him. He was filled with a sudden, unbearable hatred. He had never before felt such venom in his blood. If he had had a knife, he would've plunged it into this man's heart.

"Not all of it is your fault," Lukić was saying, "but you must think about these kinds of things before you marry a woman like that."

"Like what?" Danilo could feel his body shaking. He was worried what he might do next.

Lukić studied him calmly. "A man can never change who he really is."

"People change all the time," said Danilo. "I've seen good people become very bad."

"Maybe they were bad to begin with," said Lukić. He picked up one of the guns from the bed and began to play with it. "We're making right what was wrong. That's all. Nothing more. Now get out before you disappear. I'm being so nice right now my balls are beginning to hurt." A man came back into the room. He grabbed one of Danilo's arms and hinged it up into his back, painfully.

They pushed him out into the street. He stumbled, righted himself, and then let himself fall. He felt as if he could destroy a thousand men if only he had the strength. But he did not have the strength, and so he sat on the sidewalk next to a bright red Passat and wept. He wept for his wife, and he wept for the town that was once his home, the town that now watched him silently.

Danilo got up and began to walk through the streets of Višegrad. Only a few souls had ventured outside. He passed the Dom Kulture and the restaurant where Darinka had taken him on his sixteenth birthday. He passed the town square where his boys had put on the Christmas *vertep* performances. He passed the sporting goods store where Miša had bought his brother those blue trainers. It was now closed for good, its shelves overturned, its windows broken.

He came upon a woman selling ragged beets from a basket. Danilo handed her a coin and smiled through his tears.

"Be well, Danilo Danilović," she mumbled.

With the beet in his hand, he came around the corner, and there was the bridge. Mehmed-paša's bridge. Empty. As always, the Drina flowed silently beneath. Not for the first time, Danilo was struck by the feat of building such a massive stone construction all those years ago. He thought of all the lives sacrificed in order to erect a road from this side to the other. Danilo made his way out to the *kapija,* halfway between the two banks. He did not care if they shot him. To die crossing the bridge—this could be the most noble of all deaths.

They did not shoot him. He stood with his beet and placed his hand on the cold stone of the bridge, scrubbed clean of its blood. He watched the river. A few pages from a forgotten book were floating on its surface.

"Stoja," he said. And he knew then that she was still alive.

THAT NIGHT, HE AGAIN tried to call his son. The phone line clicked and popped, but finally, through some miracle of the wires, his call connected. Miroslav's roommate picked up. He said Miroslav had moved out of the flat two weeks earlier. He didn't know to where. He didn't have a new number.

"This is an emergency," said Danilo hopelessly. "I need to know where he lives. Who knows where he lives now?"

"No offense to you, but your son's a bit of an asshole," said the roommate. "He didn't pay rent for six months, so we kicked him out."

"He's a good boy," said Danilo. "It's not easy."

"He's a dick. I'm not saying it's your fault. Some people are just dicks," the roommate said and hung up.

. . .

Two days later, Danilo awoke to Dragan knocking on his door.

"They found her," he said.

"Where?"

"In the river."

"In the river?" said Danilo. "Are you sure it's her?"

"They say it's her."

"Did she suffer?"

"She's not suffering now."

"*Oh, Stoja!*" He leaned against the threshold. "*Stoja, my Stoja.*"

His cousin kissed his cheek, and the two men stood like this for some time.

The police, who supposedly had found the body in the river and deemed the death an accidental drowning, had sealed the body in a coffin and then delivered the coffin to the town morgue, with strict instructions to keep the coffin shut.

"I'd like to see her," Danilo said to the mortician when he went to identify the body and sign the paperwork.

"I'm afraid that's impossible," said the mortician.

"But how do I know it's her?" said Danilo.

"She's already been identified."

"But what if she's not dead?"

"She's dead. It's my job," said the man. His voice turned soft and instructive as he handed Danilo the papers. "I know this can be difficult, but you must sign here, please. The signature is the first step in the process."

At the funeral, Danilo wore his only suit. Stoja had helped him choose it for their wedding. Only Dragan, his parents, and a handful of friends attended. Stoja's two boys were not present to see their mother being put to rest. Their closest neighbors were also conspicuously absent, perhaps fearful of how their presence might be interpreted by Lukić and his men.

SOMEONE HAD NESTLED A vase of wild lilacs into the dirt of the freshly dug grave. The doll made of wood and string that they had seen next to the red bicycle was sitting against the vase. There was no note.

Halfway through the service, it began to rain. The priest paused in his sermon to look up at the sky. His tongue slipped out between his lips and caught a drop of water, and then he bowed his head and began again.

5

L ess than a month later, as an unusually cold, early fall descended upon them, Danilo sold his last cow to Slavko Novaković.

"Where are you headed?" Slavko asked, rubbing the side of the animal.

"To find my son," said Danilo.

He found locks for the farmhouse and the barn. He had never locked these buildings before, and the click of the mechanism made his blood run cold. Before he closed up the barn, he stood before Stoja's altar. The wax frozen into white rivers. He looked up and saw the elephant watching him through the dust-filled darkness. He touched its lone ear. A certain kind of warmth.

"Someday, you will walk the bridge," he said. "I promise."

He took down one of her icons and slipped it into his bag.

At the bus stop, two idle young men in White Eagle uniforms sat on the hood of a car, picking at the remains of what looked like a chocolate cake. They watched the line of people shuffling onto the bus. As he boarded, Danilo glanced back. One of the men blew him a kiss.

MANY HOURS LATER, after passing through what seemed like dozens of army checkpoints, in which IDs were shown and reshown and a man he did not recognize was dragged screaming from the bus by his legs, they finally arrived in the city. Rolling past row after row of tall buildings, Danilo realized he hadn't been to Belgrade since that trip with his mother to see the illuminated manuscript forty years ago. Had it really been that long? He tried to decide what was worse: having never left Višegrad or not realizing he had never left Višegrad.

He was gathering up his two small bags from beneath the bus when he heard someone yell his name.

"Danilo! Danilo Danilović!"

He turned and saw Ilija Dragonović trundling toward him in a suit that could barely contain his great body. Ilija was a distant relative who had left for the city twenty years ago. Danilo had written to him about his arrival but had never received a reply.

"Danilo Danilović!" Ilija hugged Danilo as if they were brothers. "Welcome to Belgrade. Everything is such shit, but welcome."

Ilija was over two meters tall. He was a former basketball player who had flirted with playing on the national team before a blown-out knee destroyed his jump shot. Now he made a living selling washing machines.

"Business is no good," he said, weaving his car through the crowded streets. "No one wants to buy a new unit. Do you want to buy a new unit? No, because maybe a bomb will fall on your house tomorrow and then your new unit is totally fucked. I understand. But I'm still pissed off—WATCH OUT, LADY!" He swerved, then smiled at a terrified Danilo. "It's important to remind people of life, yes?"

They arrived at Ilija's warehouse in Vračar, where Danilo would stay until he got his feet on the ground. When Ilija rolled up the graffitied garage door to the storage room, Danilo saw a small army cot among the stacks of plastic-wrapped washing machines. He could see his breath.

"There's a shower and toilet in the back," said Ilija. "Hold down the handle for at least three seconds; otherwise it all comes up again. It's not the good kind of déjà vu."

"Okay," said Danilo.

"I used to come here to think," said Ilija, lighting a cigarette. "But I don't think anymore, so there you are."

"Thank you," said Danilo. "It's only for the time being. Until I find Miroslav."

"You know, I was so sorry to hear about Stojanka," said Ilija. "I always liked her. She was a beautiful woman."

"Thank you, Ilija."

"Shit, man," said Ilija, shaking his head. "I just can't believe it. One day she is here, and then she's gone."

The warehouse was sandwiched between a tennis club and a train yard filled with rusting boxcars. The nets at the club had all been taken down for the season, but despite the frigid temperatures, a single old man still showed up each day in tennis whites to serve a bucket of balls across the court. Danilo would watch him rumble through his routine, tightening and snapping his body like whip. The balls made a light and easy sound coming off the man's racket. Every serve looked good, but then, there was no net to halt the ball's progress.

It was freezing in the storage room. There was a single radiator that sputtered and spat but only grew tepid to the touch. Danilo shivered through the nights, and, in an act of midnight desperation, he ripped open a carton of hand towels and carefully spread them over his blanket in rows, like uncooked bacon. He lay on his cot in the darkness, mummified and alone.

Soon after his arrival, he took a bus over to the university at Studentski Trg. The bus was shockingly crowded. Danilo found himself standing with his face inside another man's armpit, barely able to breathe. After two minutes he knew he would die inside this bus along with everyone else. He looked down and saw a small child crammed among a sea of legs, twirling a leaf between his fingers.

When the doors finally opened, he tumbled out into the air of the world, gasping. He vowed never to take another bus again. He would walk one hundred kilometers if he had to. Grateful to be alive, he circled the Brutalist buildings of the university square, trying to find the philosophy department and a clue to his son's whereabouts. Next to a bookstore, there was a two-story mural of a man entering a doorway at the end of a long path. The man appeared decapitated, for his head had already disappeared into the darkness of the doorway.

Danilo asked a student lounging beneath the mural whether he knew Miroslav. Who? Miroslav Danilović. He did not. Danilo asked another, with similar results. Maybe Miroslav had never even come to the university. Maybe he was no longer in Belgrade.

He was just about to give up when he saw a man wearing eyeliner and army fatigues, smoking a cigarette and rolling a ball across his hands, theatrically, as if he was doing it for money, though there was no place to leave money. If anyone knew where Miroslav was, it would be this man. As Danilo approached, he saw that the man was really no more than a kid.

"He's the puppeteer, right? Who never says anything?" the kid said after Danilo asked him about his son. He did not look up from his ball play.

"That's right," said Danilo, wondering if this was true. "Where does he live?"

"He was in the papers for something or other," the kid said, still rolling his ball. "He became kind of famous."

"What do you mean, *kind of famous?*" asked Danilo.

But the kid didn't know anything else. He hadn't seem him around in months.

"When you're in the paper, I guess you don't have to go to school anymore."

"But where does he live?"

The student shrugged. He stopped moving the ball across his hands. From out of his bag he produced a lackluster ferret, which he held up to Danilo, as if offering it to him for a good price.

AROUND HIM, the city practiced a restrained form of agitation. International sanctions and the toll of an uncertain war had led to a volatile hyperinflation of the dinar. Money that was worth something this morning might be worth nothing this afternoon. It seemed like every couple of months the government would revaluate the currency at a rate of 1 million to 1, so that everyone would instantly become a million times poorer than they had been the day before. The government was thus forced to issue larger and larger denominations; this culminated in "the poet of sympathy," Jovan Jovanović Zmaj, having the unfortunate distinction of appearing on the five-hundred-billion-dinar note. The constant uncertainty brought about by these daily fluctuations and the imminent threat of another devaluation left people in a perpetual state of apprehension, as if they were awaiting a terrible diagnosis from their doctor. They tried to go about their daily business, sipping coffee in cafés, window-shopping the wide promenade of Knez Mihailova, but no one bought anything. They were playing the role of citizens in a city that no longer belonged to them.

The little money Danilo had brought quickly evaporated, even when he was not using it. He would often see little torn-up bits of the old currency blowing through the streets like pollen; it was as if an entire civilization had once lived here but now was gone forever. One department store, in a gesture of black humor, wallpapered its window displays with the worthless dinars, a pink-and-violet iconostasis of fallen Yugoslav heroes: Zmaj, Tesla, Andrić, a mournful Communist child staring into the future.

Grocery stores, more often than not, had no food on their shelves, and the little food they did have cost almost a month's wages. Danilo stopped eating at night. He would lie on his cot wearing all of his clothes, shivering, reading from his Bible and praying as his stomach growled in protest. To think: a farmer who could not even feed himself. It was the worst humiliation imaginable.

He began to smoke. He, who had never smoked a cigarette in his life, even as every man in Yugoslavia had merrily puffed away. And now, when there were practically no cigarettes to be had, he had begun to smoke.

"It's a beautiful habit," said Ilija as he lit Danilo's Marlboro. "Forget what the doctors say. They are just jealous. Smoking keeps you healthy as a bull."

After observing others sifting through trash—respectable people, men in suits, women in hats—Danilo began to follow suit, searching for items that might be bartered for food and cigarettes. Old kerosene lamps. Broken radios. Tailors' dummies. Cracked spyglasses. Only Gazur, the kind, paunch-laden owner of the Rijeka Café, on the River Sava, would accept his hodgepodge of defective items in exchange for a glass of black currant juice and a bowl of fish stew. It was clear that Gazur had no use for such things, but without fail, whenever Danilo showed up on the terrace, he glowed and began humming old folk songs.

"Would you like a table with a view?" Gazur would ask, relieving him of his latest tawdry procurement. All of the tables had a view of the river, the same view, but nonetheless the question gestured at a rare kind of decadence.

"Please," said Danilo. "And a glass of black currant juice."

"Of course! The usual!" And Gazur would go to the kitchen and order the busboy to come out with his accordion and play a song, and Danilo would sit there drinking his juice and then quickly suck on his cigarette so that the smoke entangled with the dying sour notes on the back of his tongue. Danilo could not even say he liked the flavor of smoke and currant together, but he found himself compelled to create this pairing every time, as if pressing at an old wound.

"The river's beautiful, yes?" Gazur would say.

"Yes."

"And the music?" The busboy was earnestly banging out the Macedonian song "Zajdi, zajdi, jasno sonce." Darinka had sung this song to him at night when he could not sleep.

"The music is nice, thank you."

"Eder likes the turbo-folk, but I tell him, 'No, you must play the old ones. Play the old ones so we don't forget.'"

Danilo often wondered, as he watched the river and thought of all that had gone on in the past year, what the source of Gazur's kindness was. It would have been much easier to let him starve with the rest.

HE SPENT HIS DAYS wandering the city, searching the unhappy faces for a version of his son. Once, an old woman carrying a basket of stuffed rabbits came up to Danilo on the street. She touched his hand, startling him with the sudden intimacy of this contact.

"My son," she said, peering into his face.

For a moment he wondered if this woman could be Darinka, whether there had been some colossal mistake and she had never in fact died—she could not die, because she wore the red handkerchief with the little cross. Yet this woman was not wearing a red handkerchief. And then he saw in her eyes that even as she was staring at him, she did not see him. She had the eyes of a child. She was a vagabond. A miscreant. Did others now see him this way, too? When they passed him in the street, did mothers pull their children closer and avert their eyes?

After another moment, the woman let him go. He watched her shuffle away, orbiting a telephone pole before dissolving back into the weary stream of men.

SLOBODAN MILOŠEVIĆ'S FACE was everywhere. Those imploring eyes, the certainty of his uncertain gaze. You could find him splashed across billboards, newspapers, and television screens as he declared one victory after another for Mother Serbia. Yet Danilo also heard a surprising amount of dissent with Milošević's version of events on his little radio in the warehouse. He listened as academics and activists argued passionately about the injustice of such a war.

"We are witnessing a state suicide. The snake has bitten off its own head. These are the spasms of an animal that is already dead," a poet said during a talk show.

One night, in a vision probably informed by his flat's frigid temperatures, Danilo dreamed he was hiking through snowcapped mountains with Milošević. They were trying to find his wife's body. Only Milošević knew where the body was hidden. They kept walking and walking, and Milošević—sipping from a bottomless thermos of tea—kept promising that the body was just over the next rise, but that summit would only reveal more mountains that closely resembled those from which they had just come. Eder, the busboy from the Rijeka, was also there with his accordion, trying to keep up with them. Eventually he fell in the snow, his accordion making a last gasp as he collapsed, and they left him where he was.

Finally, Danilo turned on his guide, ready to kill him with a knife that had appeared in his hand, only to realize at the last moment that it had not been Milošević this whole time, but Miša. The last image before he woke up was his son's terrified expression as the blade came down upon him.

6

The next morning, a scissor-sharp October morning, Danilo drifted through the city toward Nikola Pašić Square and the Parliament building, as if to confront the real Milošević about Stoja's whereabouts. With the last of his money he bought some warm nuts from a one-eyed vendor of uncertain descent, possibly a Gypsy, possibly a Turk.

"Please enjoy," the vendor said with great kindness.

Danilo was studying the majesty of the olive-colored Parliament dome when he noticed a small group of onlookers clustered just off the square, next to a children's playground. The crowd was focused intently on something in their midst. Danilo walked over, casually munching on his bag of nuts, letting their oily warmth settle into the foundation of his teeth.

When he got closer, he caught his breath.

The crowd was assembled around a black box. A man was hunched next to the box, his head covered by a velvet curtain.

Danilo ran up to them.

"Miroslav!" he yelled. Those assembled stared at him warily.

"Miroslav!" he called again. He grabbed the man beneath the curtain and pulled him up. It was an old man with a gold tooth.

"Did I do it wrong?" said the man.

"Where's the puppeteer?" asked Danilo.

The man looked confused. "I'm sorry. I did not have enough," he said.

"What?"

The man pointed to a handwritten sign propped up on the ground:

I WILL BE RIGHT BACK.

FEEL FREE TO WATCH THE SHOW.

PLEASE, BE GENTLE WITH THE BOX

AND ONLY 1 AT A TIME.

SUGGESTED DONATION:

Next to the sign was a little wooden cashbox with a slit on top.

"Is that Tesla?" said Danilo.

"It means ten billion dinars. That's the note Tesla's on," someone said behind him.

"That was the old bill. Tesla's on the five-thousand-dinar now," said a woman.

"No, it's the thousand-dinar bill," said another. "But it's worth more than before."

"No. That was the old currency."

"Well, it's too much, whatever it is. Who would pay that?"

"It doesn't mean that," said a man with a mustache. "It's not referring to *money*. It's a metaphor. It means you must bring your imagination to the box. That's what my friend said."

"Can I see?" said Danilo to the old man whom he had interrupted.

"There's a line," said the woman.

"But my son made this."

Their collective groan made it clear that the people did not believe him. Embarrassed, he slipped behind them, awaiting his turn, glancing around nervously, half expecting his son to materialize out of the city at any moment.

Nearly everyone put something into the cashbox, though it was clear that most were just getting rid of old worthless bank notes, whether they featured Tesla or not. They would then hunch over, duck their heads beneath the black curtain, and emerge five minutes later wearing a dazed look. One woman waited for her friend to watch, then they embraced and moved to the nearby playground, where they spoke excitedly, occasionally gesturing at the box. After watching the show, the man with the mustache circled the box six or seven times, inspecting it from all angles before finally shaking his head and walking away.

When it was finally his turn, Danilo bypassed the cashbox altogether, not caring what the others might think, and hastily threw the curtain over his head.

He was met with darkness and silence, tempered only by the faintest of rumbles from the city beyond. Danilo was suddenly struck by how vulnerable he was, crouched like this in the middle of the street. Anyone could come up behind him and punch him, rob him, kill him. There were others to protect him, to shelter him, but maybe they were pointing at him as he stood beneath the curtain: *That one. He's the crazy one. He's the one who didn't pay. Him. Take him.*

He waited patiently, but the darkness remained. Perhaps the box was broken. Perhaps the whole point was to get strangers to crouch down in this ridiculous posture, to pay money, thinking some little entertainment was coming simply because others had done it before them, but in the end there was no entertainment, and this expectation of entertainment was what had so upset people.

And then: soft music, coming from just in front of his ear. The sound of a few violins joined by a pair of cellos and then an accordion. The music felt very close but very far away at the same time. The song being played was familiar, though Danilo could not name the tune. Maybe it did not have a name.

The darkness was softening. But this was not quite right: the darkness was no longer darkness. There was a feeling of rising from the depths. A sense of shape. An awakening into form.

A scene appeared before him. Danilo could see a river. Not an image of a river, but *an actual river.* He could see the water moving, turning back into itself as water does. There was a river somewhere inside that box. But how could it be? From where, and to where, did it flow? And now he could see there was a bridge over this river. Not just any bridge: *the bridge.* The Turkish Bridge. Tiny, resplendent, complete with its *kapija,* and the central pillar beneath with its grated opening, inside which a black Arab was supposedly imprisoned. It was the one detail Miroslav had remembered from the book. Had he also included a miniature Arab inside that pillar? An Arab who stared longingly at the river that flowed into the distant sea?

Danilo began to cry. How he missed his home! How he missed her! How he missed the life they had once lived!

He was again taken by the scene. How on earth had Miroslav made a river inside a box?

Something was moving slowly into the frame. At first Danilo could not tell what it was, but then he saw it, unmistakable and true: an elephant. Yes—there was the trunk, the flapping of the ears. A tiny elephant, no more than five centimeters tall, walking along the road. It was all so real, so perfect—the way the elephant leaned heavily into each step, the left front leg slightly lame, the little tail now and then fluttering away at the invisible flies. Its walk was a kind of dance, in time to the lilt of the music. And as with the box he had seen back home, there weren't any strings. No wires or tracks or anything to betray the presence of a controller. The elephant moved on its own. Although this was not quite true: the elephant had a rider on its back. A minuscule man with a whip. The rider was directing the elephant to walk across the bridge. Danilo sensed some hesitancy in the animal, as if it knew what would happen next. Would the bridge hold? It must. It had been used for so many years. Hundreds and hundreds of years. But then Danilo remembered that this bridge was not the bridge back home, that this bridge had not been built by the hands of slaves and artisans and soldiers and thieves. This bridge could fit in his lap, and so: could this bridge, this whisper of a bridge, hold an elephant ridden by a man?

Danilo noticed then that the elephant was not right. Half of its body looked as if it had been eaten away by wolves. There was a great hole in its stomach, and you could see inside it, even as it was walking past the last building and onto the first stretch of the bridge. There were no guts or blood inside the animal, only metal, mechanics, pulleys. He noticed then that the elephant had only one ear.

Yes. He understood now. This elephant was the elephant in the barn. Incomplete, but complete. Moving. *Walking.*

He leaned in, staring at the rider on top, who was no taller than a thimble. He could almost see it. He cursed the age of his eyes. He squinted. *Yes.* It was. *It had to be.* It was his son. Beneath the black curtain, Danilo crossed himself twice.

The elephant had arrived at the center of the bridge, next to the *kapija*. It stopped, flapping its ears. The music, too, hung still, waiting. The tiny Miroslav seemed to gesture with his whip, and then the elephant shook its head and Miroslav gestured again and whipped the elephant's back, and slowly the animal turned, shuffling to its left, placing one, then two of its feet onto the bridge's parapet. The violins rising, urged on by the hook-slant caress of the accordion.

"No," he whispered.

The elephant seemed to hear him, for it paused, its body open to the world, straining. He could see the whirring gears inside its rib cage. The music gathering force, the cellos working themselves into a frenzy, the violins everywhere at once, and then the creature was lifting itself, up and over the parapet, and Miroslav was urging it onward, whipping the creature with a whip the size of a thread. The music crescendoed as gravity caught the elephant and it started to fall toward the surface of the water and then—

Black. The violins sounded once more and everything went quiet.

Danilo waited for the light to return, but there was no more. A click from somewhere in the darkness, a flipping of a switch. He could hear the muffled traffic again. The show was over.

He lifted his head from beneath the curtain, blinking at the dingy city that greeted him. A woman with several shopping bags full of bottled water looked at him impatiently. He stepped aside so that she could have her turn.

DANILO WAITED by the black box all day. There was always a small line of people, and passersby would see the line and stop and talk and then begin to wait themselves. Occasionally children would swing on the swings in the little playground and then come over, curious, and they too would put the curtain over their heads and watch the show, and some would come out crying, running back to their parents.

At one point, a photographer came up and snapped photos of the box and of those waiting to see it. Shortly after, a group of soldiers, on their way to guard the Parliament building, stopped and examined the box, poking at the curtain with the muzzles of their guns, though none of them stayed to watch the show.

Some patrons put money into the little wooden box. Some did not. One man slipped in a letter. Danilo began to predict who would give money and who would not. There was a recurring conversation about what was meant by the picture of Tesla and, by extension, how much the show was worth.

"Nothing is worth anything," a woman in dark glasses declared, and she looked as if she meant it, though she stayed to watch the show three times.

Danilo himself rewatched the elephant perhaps a dozen times. Each time, it was the same: the creature reached the point of falling and then the scene went dark, never allowing the animal to complete its fall. And there was never any evidence of previous falls. He began to look for clues, to watch the rider's movements, to stare at the meticulously rendered houses in the background. He noticed more things: laundry drying on balconies, a crow watching from a nearby tree. After witnessing the interrupted fall for the fifth time, he knew the movements and the timing so well, it was like watching a recurring dream. After a certain point, he could not be sure it was not a recurring dream.

Miroslav never showed. Danilo marveled at how he could leave something so remarkable and precious out on the street like this, where anyone could steal it, where anyone could take the money in the wooden case, even if this money did not amount to much. And yet the box remained. Where was the creator of all this? No one could say. The sign, it turned out, was a lie: he would not be right back.

Night fell. Danilo was hungry. The vendor selling nuts had already packed up his cart, but Danilo did not dare search for food, fearing that as soon as he left, his son would come back and fetch his box.

The streetlights sputtered, popped on, one by one. Danilo sat on the sidewalk, watching the box. The number of people on the street had thinned. A policeman came up to him and nudged him with his baton, telling him to move on.

"I'm waiting for my son," he said.

"Where is he?"

"He told me to watch his puppet box while he was gone." He pointed across the street, though the black box had been swallowed by shadows. The policeman looked confused.

"Have you seen it?" said Danilo. "It's really something. My son is a great artist."

"Get out of here, old man," said the policeman.

Danilo drifted to a park across the street. From such a distance, he could just barely make out the silhouette of the box. He was hungry and cold. He sat on a bench and felt sleep coming, though he was afraid to close his eyes. Finally, reluctantly, he walked back through the city to his storage room, which felt comparatively balmy. The little sleep he got was interrupted by an insistent vision of his son coming to take the box away in the middle of the night, leaving nothing behind but an empty sidewalk.

At first light, he jumped up and ran back to Nikola Pašić Square. To his relief, the box was still there. The same sign, the same wooden cashbox, although when he shook it, he found the cashbox was empty. *Someone had taken the money!* Or maybe Miroslav had visited while he was gone. The thought gave him hope. There was no line to view the box, so Danilo dipped his head under the curtain and waited for the elephant to appear.

As soon as he entered the curtain, he noticed that the smell had changed. Or maybe it was the darkness itself. He waited. This time, when the music came, there was only a lone cello, surfacing from the deep as the light gradually rose. It was the same Turkish Bridge, the same small Drina, though the water was darker, reddish this time, filled with the mud from a heavy rain.

There were people on the bridge. The sky had changed. By the pinkness of the stone, Danilo guessed it to be early evening. He had been to the bridge many times at this hour; it was one of his favorite times to visit, to feel the valley slinking toward nightfall.

Fighting the soft blur in his eyes, Danilo squinted and saw that the people on the bridge were soldiers. He recoiled. They were White Eagles. The soldiers were standing and talking, their guns slung casually across their backs. But surely they could not see him. They were inside, and he was outside. He leaned in again, marveling at their littleness, the independence of their movement. Who controlled these men? If he reached out and smashed them with his hand, would they fight back? Would they shoot him with their tiny guns?

And then he saw the blood. The bridge was stained dark crimson with blood. They were standing in the blood, talking casually, smoking.

The cello dipped and swirled with the muddy current of the river.

A woman appeared. From the near bank, where the elephant had walked the day before. She was running, looking back in the direction from which she had come. Her clothes were torn, and she was wearing no shoes. She moved quickly, up and onto the bridge, in the direction of the soilders. Danilo wanted to warn her not to run toward them.

Turn back! Don't run over there!

She saw the soldiers standing amid the blood and stopped. She was already a quarter of the way across the bridge. She looked back in the direction of Danilo.

He saw then that the woman was his wife.

Stoja.

Good God, Stoja! Turn back! Run! Get out of there!

The men approached her.

"Turn around! Run!" he yelled, his voice damp and close beneath the cloth.

Stoja froze. The cello, waiting, held its note. She looked up at the sky.

"I'm here," he said. "I can see you, Stoja. I'm here with you."

She did not hear him. The cello sounded a ferocious chord, and Stoja bowed her head and ran toward the bridge's parapet, one foot on its top, and then she leaped. Her body making an arc in the air, gravity's rainbow catching her in slow motion—yes, Danilo was sure that she was falling more slowly than normal. She splashed into the water. The White Eagles were running to the parapet, guns drawn.

"Stoja!" he yelled.

He saw her surface and begin to swim. The sound of tiny gunshots. He winced, transfixed, but she continued to swim until she reached the central pillar of the bridge, with the small grated opening above. This was the buttress that held the Arab. She grasped the stone, pulling herself from the water. The men were looking down at her, aiming, ready to kill her. And then, at the last moment, she slipped through a narrow opening and disappeared into the bridge.

"Stoja!"

His hand thwacked against a thin pane of glass. He swore he could see the figures jostle, as if an earthquake had hit—the bridge trembling, the White Eagles confused—but then the lights and the music abruptly cut out and everything was black again.

Something had gone wrong. It was not meant to end like this.

He took off the curtain, touched the box, looking for her, for a sign, then got back inside the curtain. He waited for ten minutes, but the show would not go on. After hesitating, he shook the box with both hands. A faint rattle. He had broken it. And now Stoja was trapped. She was trapped inside the bridge with the Arab. What would he do to her? Was she safer in there than outside, with the soldiers? He contemplated ripping the whole thing open to rescue her, but instead he fell to his knees and prayed.

Eventually others arrived to see the box. Some he recognized from the day before. Some had been told about the elephant and were eager to see it for themselves. But everyone who put their head under the curtain waited and waited, and nothing happened. And even then, more people came, having heard rumors of the wonders inside the box. They too waited in vain.

"It must be broken," one said to his companion.

"You were telling me a lie, weren't you? You were teasing me," said the companion.

"I was not. I swear. Yesterday there was an elephant. You wouldn't believe. It was alive. I swear to you."

"Maybe no one paid enough money," someone said. "Typical. People are selfish."

"I paid!"

"I paid twice!" said another.

The crowd grew restless, and Danilo, feeling infinitely guilty for having caused all of this, found himself trying to calm a woman down.

"The show will be on tomorrow," he said.

"How do you know?" she asked.

"It's my son's show."

"Who's your son?"

"Miro." He wasn't sure why he gave only his son's nickname, but there it was. Others came up to him with questions. *How did he do it? What was the secret?*

He tried to answer as best he could, until he saw an angry man in a beard go up to the box and shake it violently.

"All right!" he yelled to everyone. "The show's been canceled for today. I'm sorry. We've had technical difficulties. Please come back tomorrow. I'm sorry for the inconvenience."

"Who are you?"

"I work for the artist."

"Who's the artist?"

"His name is Miro."

"Where is he now?"

"He's gone to get new parts. Please. Come back tomorrow. Everything will be fine tomorrow."

They left, eventually, grumbling. Danilo found an old newspaper and a pen and wrote out CANCELED TODAY and posted it on top of the sign. Then he went across the street and waited.

Someone tapped him on the shoulder.

"I'm going, I'm going," said Danilo.

It was a reporter. The man wanted to know whether it was true that Danilo worked for Miro, the artist who had made this cabinet of wonders.

"Cabinet of wonders?" said Danilo.

"That's what they're calling it. What would you call it?"

"That sounds good to me."

"Can you tell us more about Miro?"

"He was born in Višegrad."

"But how does he do it?"

"Do what?"

"Make them move like that? There are no strings."

"You can't *see* the strings."

"So there *are* strings?"

"You'll have to talk to him about that."

There were more questions, but, realizing he might have already said too much, Danilo declined to answer them. He told the man to come back the next day. "The artist will be here tomorrow and will be happy to answer any questions."

"I think your Miro will be a famous man someday," said the reporter as he left.

Night fell again. The streetlights came on. Danilo had brought warmer clothes this time, and he settled down in the park, a good ways from the box and the playground, but not so far that he couldn't see it. He waited, watching the changing of the guards in front of Parliament. An ambulance went by. More policemen. At some point, without meaning to, he drifted off to sleep.

When he awoke again, it was still dark. His body was freezing. He opened and closed his fingers and slapped at his legs, trying to conjure some kind of circulation. The soft halo of a streetlight caught the outline of a feral dog slipping into the park. The dog threw him a glance before trotting off. The streets were empty save for the guardsmen in front of Parliament and a lone taxi driver asleep in his cab.

Danilo walked over to the box. He noticed immediately that his announcement about the cancellation had been removed. There was only the original sign. He looked around but saw no one. Then he ducked beneath the curtain.

The darkness had shifted again. He heard gypsy music. Two horns. The quiver of a drum. An accordion.

The lights rose. Again, the bridge.

There were two figures on the bridge. Not soldiers this time. The blood had been scrubbed away. Only a faint stain remained. Danilo rubbed his eyes, shivered. Trying to blink away the blur. The men, familiar but too small to recognize. He thumbed out the sleep and looked again.

Yes.

It was Miroslav. An older version of Miroslav, to be sure, but there was no doubt it was him. The angle of the jawline. It did not change, even at such a size.

Next to him, a big mass of a man, rendered in miniature. Those shoulders. Such shoulders. Danilović shoulders.

Seeing the two of his boys together, moving together, made him wish they all could be together again. If they were together, then they would all get through this, he knew.

He wanted to tell them that their mother was trapped in the bridge beneath them, but Miša and Miroslav were bending over, lifting something up. It looked to be a body. A body of a man! Who was he? But it was all too quick. They were heaving, rolling the body up and over the wall of the bridge. The body fell. Danilo half expected the scene to cut off then, but the man continued to fall, and there was the sound of a splash and then the body was floating in the river. Danilo again wondered how he had created such a river. *A river with no beginning or end?*

His sons stood on the bridge, watching the body float out of the frame. A flock of birds moved past overhead. Miroslav turned away, but Miša remained, staring at the river. Then black.

In the darkness, Danilo suddenly felt very cold. He remained crouched as he was, wrapping the curtain around himself, shivering. The show did not start again.

He didn't know how long he had been like this, his forehead resting against the glass of the box, when he felt a hand on his back, lifting the curtain up and over him. Maybe the police would take him to prison, where he could get warm again. He felt as if he would never get warm again.

Outside, the first rays of sun were already reaching across the sky.

"Tata?"

He looked up, confused, and through the dim light of dawn he stared into the face of a man who vaguely resembled his son. The man had a beard and long, greasy hair beneath a white fedora, but the eyes had not changed.

"Miro," he whispered.

"Tata."

"I found you."

"What're you doing here?"

"I'm sorry. I was the one who broke the box. I was trying to catch her." His voice cracked. He swayed on his numb feet, nearly tumbling backwards into the street.

"It's okay, Tata." Miroslav grabbed him, hugging him. "It's okay."

"I saw her in your box," Danilo whispered. "I was trying to catch her."

"It's okay."

"She's inside the bridge."

"Who?"

"Stoja."

"What're you talking about, Tata?"

"She's dead. Your mother's dead."

Miroslav released him. *"What?"*

"But I saw it in your box. The Chetniks . . . She was running, and she jumped . . . and now . . ." A sob, long buried.

Miroslav was staring at his father.

"But you must've known!" said Danilo. "Tell me you know. Your mother was in the box. She jumped off the bridge. I saw it . . ."

"That wasn't her. It was just a woman."

"But it *was* her! I saw her go into the bridge."

"They aren't people, Tata. They're just puppets."

7

They went down the street to a restaurant called the Double. They were the first customers of the day; the waitress, still sleepy-eyed, nodded and made a gesture with her hand that meant they could sit anywhere. Miroslav took off his wool coat and placed his fedora on the seat next to him, as if saving it for another. The waitress came over and they ordered two bowls of hot *pasulj*. After a moment's hesitation, Miroslav called her back and added a shot of *šljivovica*.

Danilo considered his son. The long, greasy hair had grown prematurely thin at the top, and the skin around his eyes was ashen. He looked as if he had not slept in weeks. Danilo spotted a single white hair in the middle of his beard. He resisted the urge to reach across the table and pluck it out.

"Miroslav," he said, and he was not speaking to his son but to time itself.

Miroslav smiled weakly.

"I'll also have a *šljivovica,* please," Danilo said to the waitress. He realized he had no money.

"I can't afford this," he said shamefully.

"It's okay, Tata. They know me here."

The *šljivovica* came and they clicked glasses. Miroslav downed his in one go; Danilo sipped the liquor slowly.

"So," said Miroslav. "Tell me everything."

And so Danilo began to speak. About the resort hotel where the White

Eagles took the women. About Lukić. About the funeral to which no one came. The anonymous delivery of flowers. He did not mention the sealed casket, that he had never seen the body with his own eyes.

The soups arrived, but neither man touched his bowl.

"This hotel's the same one we saw that day, above the hammam?"

Danilo nodded.

"I can't believe it," said Miroslav. "I can't believe she's gone."

"I should never have told her to take that bicycle," he said. And then it hit him again, as it had hit him, as it would hit him. He rubbed his eyes.

"It's not your fault, Tata." Miroslav reached across the table but did not touch his father.

"I told her to get outside. She was so sad to see you boys go . . . you can't imagine," he said. "She was in the barn, praying every day. She never went out anymore."

"I'm sorry," said Miroslav.

"*Oh, what did she do to deserve this?* She was so kind."

"I know."

"You don't know. You've no idea," said Danilo. "You weren't there! Where were you?"

Miroslav was silent.

"I'm sorry." Danilo exhaled. "I miss her. I want to see her smile again. That's all I want. I would like to see her smile once more."

He covered his face again, but the tears came down through the little spaces between his fingers. He took out a handkerchief and wiped his eyes, then he lit a cigarette.

"You smoke now?" said Miroslav, incredulous.

"It's a strange city."

"*Danilo Danilović is a smoker.* I never thought I would see this day. Can I have one?"

"It's good to see you," said Danilo, lighting his son's cigarette. "I've been trying to find you. You're all I have left."

"There's Danilo."

"Who?"

"Miša."

"Yes, *Miša*," Danilo sighed. "But where is Miša?"

"You haven't heard from him?"

"I haven't heard from anyone."

"He wrote to me a while ago. But nothing since then."

"Sometimes I worry he's gone too."

"If something happened, I would know," said Miroslav. "He's just busy, that's all. He's fighting a war. Someone needs to fight the war, otherwise there'd be no war." A little laugh.

"Someone should tell him about his mother. How do we get word to him?"

"I don't know," said Miroslav. "I make a point of not talking to those people."

Danilo looked down at his soup and suddenly felt a sharp pang of hunger. He realized he had not eaten in almost a day. He picked up his spoon and began scooping the soup into his mouth with short, quick strokes.

Miroslav watched him. "You're hungry."

"It's a strange city," Danilo said through a mouthful of soup.

They slurped at their *pasulj* in silence.

"I feel like I've never eaten before," said Danilo.

"I know what you mean."

"A reporter asked me yesterday how you did it."

"Did what?"

"Those boxes. How you made them."

"Oh, yes. They always want to know. What did you tell him?"

"I said they should ask you."

"I was already on the cover of the paper."

"I heard about that. Was it for the boxes?"

"No. For a piece of graffiti."

"Graffiti?" said Danilo. "You got into trouble?"

"Not really. A little. But people viewed it like a kind of art."

"What was the graffiti?"

"It's not important. People were just looking for a phrase. And I gave it to them. I gave them an anthem."

Danilo considered this. "You should see the people when they come and look at your boxes. It's like they've seen a ghost. They don't know what to think. I watched them for a whole day."

"I know. I'm watching too."

"You are?"

"Of course. You think I would miss it?"

"You were watching the last few days? From where?"

"I have a place."

"Then you saw me?"

"Yes."

"So why didn't you come and say something?"

"I don't know." Miroslav shook his head.

Danilo stared at a little globule of spilled soup seeping into the white tablecloth. "You said they weren't real people."

"They aren't."

"But I saw you. I saw you and Miša throw that man into the river."

Miroslav's eyes went wide.

"I saw you in the box," said Danilo. "You threw him off the bridge. You turned and Miša stayed. I saw it."

Miroslav stared at his father. The corner of his mouth was quivering. He suddenly looked angry, as if he might strike his father, and then he said, very quietly: "I killed him, Tata."

Danilo nodded. "Only God can save us now," he said and crossed himself.

"No. You don't understand. It was true. I made this all happen."

"Made what happen?"

"I killed a gypsy. I killed him and then I pushed him into the Drina."

"What're you talking about?"

"You're the only one who knows. Besides Miša. I killed him. And then the war came."

"Miro, what are you talking about?"

"That day Miša was stabbed. It wasn't a bull. It was the gypsy."

Danilo's face fell into comprehension. He folded his arms. "I knew it wasn't a bull," he said.

"He had a knife and he was robbing us. And then he attacked Miša, and I killed him. I took a tree branch and I crushed his head. And then I pushed him into the river."

"Who was he?"

"I don't know. A gypsy. But I killed him. I made all of this happen. I'm the one to blame . . . for Mama . . . for everything."

"Stop it," said Danilo. "You can't think like this. It's not how it works. Do you know how much evil there's been in this country? It's not any one man's doing. It's the work of many. None of us can say we're innocent anymore."

"But it's because of me! I started it. *I know this*. It's why she died. Something needed to happen. Something needed to be taken away again. *That's how it works*." His voice was rising. The waitress was staring at them.

"Miroslav," said Danilo. "Only God knows how it works."

"There is no God," said Miroslav.

"Miro—"

"I don't believe what you believe."

Danilo was too tired to argue. "Okay," he said. "Okay. I've missed you, my son. How are you feeling? You look tired."

"The boxes tear me apart. They're very difficult to make. I leave a part of myself in them."

"I can imagine," said Danilo. He thumbed at the droplet of *pasulj* sitting on the tablecloth. "Wait—when did this happen?"

"When did what happen?"

"You and Miša. With the man by the river."

"I told you. It was last April. Before the drought."

Danilo thought about this. "That must've been the Selimovićs' son. That was Mahir. He was found downstream, near Žepa. Everyone thought he was the first."

"Mahir?"

"Didn't you hear about that?"

"No."

"You remember Mahir, though."

"Mahir?"

"You went to primary school with him. Everyone thought the Serbs had killed him. He was the first Muslim to die in the Drina. After him, there were hundreds. There was a man in Žepa who would fish them out of the river every day and then bury them. That's all he did. He would give them a Muslim burial. Mahir was the first person he buried."

Miroslav blinked at his father. "Yes, but the man I killed was a gypsy. I know who Mahir is, and this wasn't Mahir."

"He was found in the river, downstream. His head was knocked in. You don't remember this? They said he was the first."

"It wasn't Mahir."

"Okay," said Danilo.

"It wasn't Mahir."

"Okay," Danilo said again. "It wasn't Mahir."

Miroslav stared at his soup.

"Your brother has done far worse things than you," Danilo said quietly.

"You don't know that."

Danilo reached across the table and touched his son's hand. The nails were bitten to the quick, the palm soft and damp. Such a foreign hand.

"Miroslav," he said. His son was crying.

"Miroslav!"

His son looked up at him.

"Your mother loved you. To the very end. I know this. There's evil in this world, and we cannot solve this evil, but don't forget your mother. Don't forget her. Speak her name to everyone you meet. We must not forget her, even if this is all that we can do. She's the reason I live now. She's with me when I wake up, when I take a step, when I take breath into my lungs. You may not believe in a God, but I do. I do, and He tells me that she's here. She's with us. I saw her in your box. I see her everywhere."

Miroslav held his father's hand. "Will you tell me a story, Tata?"

Danilo shook his head. "I've no more stories to tell."

AFTER THAT, THEY MET every week. When the weather became warmer, they would walk along the Danube, past the shuttered houseboats, pausing to watch the children do their exercises in the fields. Danilo would occasionally ask what his son was doing, but Miroslav would say little, only that he was working on "a show that was going to change everything."

When Danilo was not with his son, he spent much of his time alone in the storage room, reading his Bible and smoking. In one corner he had set up a little altar to Stoja, with a photograph of her taken one Christmas, smiling next to her two boys. To one side was the icon he had taken from the barn and a couple of candles that he had swiped from a local church.

The weeks and months passed. Without running water or a proper razor, he grew a beard, just like his son. Ilija began to call him Moses.

"Hey Moses, we need to get some culture!" Ilija declared one morning after rolling open the garage door to the warehouse. "No more praying."

Danilo blinked at the rush of light. "What culture?"

"*Museum* culture," said Ilija. "Otherwise we'll forget we're a *civilized* people."

"I don't forget."

"Well, *I* forget," said Ilija. "And if you spend enough time with me, you'll forget too."

But the source of their culture, the National Museum, was closed.

The sign on the door read:

WE'RE SORRY, BUT DUE TO BUDGETARY CUTS THE MUSEUM IS OPEN ONLY ONE DAY A WEEK, OR BY APPOINTMENT.

It did not list which day of the week the museum would be open.

"Complete and utter bullshit," said Ilija to the guard out front.

"I just do what they tell me," said the guard.

"Can we make an appointment?"

"You have to do that before you come."

"I want to make an appointment with you."

"It's impossible."

"Listen to me: nothing is impossible. If I've learned anything from the washing machine, it's this. Together, you and I can make a deal."

"I don't know anything about that," said the guard.

"Do you know about *this?*" Ilija said. He handed the guard a wad of bills. The man looked around, pocketed the money, and then opened the door.

"We can be open for a little bit," he said.

They walked up the grand staircase, past a series of towering marble sculptures, past a shuttered ticket booth, into a room with a vaulted glass ceiling. They were completely alone.

"Imagine. This is my palace, and I'm the king," said Ilija.

"Why are you the king?"

"You can be a prince," said Ilija. "Believe me, it's a much better job. You have no responsibility. All you have to do is make love to beautiful women and ride your horse in the parade."

They wandered through the halls. Their solitude made the great works of art at once personal and impossibly distant, as if they had broken into another man's house and were perusing his private collection.

They stopped in front of *Composition II,* by Mondrian.

Great blocks of color. A perfect field of red.

"I've wasted my life," said Ilija.

It was the sound of their feet on the polished floor that made Danilo remember Miroslav of Hum's illuminated manuscript. This was the same museum he had visited as a child.

He found the book inside a glass case in the same room on the second floor where he had seen it forty years ago. Open to the same page, even. The saints, lugubrious, resplendent as ever. Aware of all that had gone on, but unchanged in posture and expression.

His mother had stood right there.

"Do you see, Ilija?" whispered Danilo. "It's from 1186."

"I keep telling you: we come from great people. Look at this book we made," Ilija said, his face glowing from the light coming off the page. "We've just lost our way. That's all."

He put his hand on his heart and began to sing "Uz Maršala Tita."

"What're you doing?" said Danilo. "This is a museum. You can't sing in here."

"This is our palace. As king, I can do whatever I want."

He began to sing again, louder this time, and after a moment of staring at his friend, Danilo joined him. Together they belted out Tito's anthem, serenading Miroslav's saints, who looked bemused and even a touch flattered:

Rod prastari svi smo, a Goti mi nismo.
Slavenstva smo drevnoga čest.
Ko drukčije kaže, kleveće i laže,
Našu će osjetit' pest.

Of an ancient kindred we are, but Goths we are not.
Part of ancient Slavdom are we.
Whoever says otherwise slanders and lies,
and will feel our fist.

Danilo made an appointment to return. And return again. Just so he could stand near the book. He even took Miroslav to see his namesake's manuscript. His son was underwhelmed.

"You named me after a tyrant."

"I didn't name you for him."

"It doesn't matter who you named me for. I'm still named after him."

"Forget him and just look at the book."

"That's not how it works. The book is nothing without its maker."

DANILO RETURNED so many times to see Miroslav's Gospels that the museum staff got to know him well. The guard who had first let them in was named Boris.

"Hey, Dino," said Boris. This was what he called him. "Dino, *you* should work here."

"What do you mean?"

"I mean, you should work here. They got someone else, but he's a drunk. He can't hardly stand up. You can stand up, right?"

"Yes."

"It's a lock. The job's yours, I'm telling you."

So Danilo became a guard at the museum. They gave him a uniform with a tie clip. It was two sizes too large, but it was still a uniform with a tie clip. On the day the museum was open to the public (this changed regularly, but usually it was a Tuesday or a Wednesday), he had to work all three floors, though he would always try to maneuver himself to the station on the second floor when a patron came through. He liked to be there when they walked into the room containing Miroslav's Gospels. He would quietly stand at the doorway, watching them watch the book. If visitors looked particularly transfixed, he would go over and offer to show it to them.

"I don't normally do this," he would say.

Then he would carefully lift off the glass case, put on a pair of white gloves, and turn the pages of the great book for them. He was fairly sure that if his boss caught him doing this, he would be fired instantly. But it was worth it.

"It's from 1186," he said to a young woman and her son.

"It's beautiful," said the woman. "Isn't it beautiful, Danilo?"

"Yes," said the boy.

"His name is Danilo?"

"It's a family name," the woman said.

The three of them stood and stared at the book in silence.

A YEAR WENT BY. The dinar—now the novi dinar—had stabilized, officially pegged 1:1 to the deutsche mark. After bouncing around on several astronomical banknotes, Nikola Tesla now presided calmly on the five-novi-dinar bill. Though there was still a shortage of food, and though public buses were still stuffed dangerously full of people, and though there were still only a few cars on the streets because of the oil embargo, people had grown used to the struggle of wartime life. There was even a kind of humorous nostalgia for it, although the war was not over. Turbo-folk singers lamented the end of difficult times that still remained.

On four separate occasions, Danilo had written Miša a letter to explain all that had happened. He had sent these to a variety of Srpska army bases in eastern Bosnia, but none of the letters had gotten through. This became evident when Miša again wrote to Miroslav in the late spring, saying he had been stationed above Sarajevo next to the 1984 Winter Olympics bobsled track, where he would loft mortars down into Stari Grad. He said he was now being moved to Srebrenica, where there were "still some problems to be solved." The joyous news of his son's still being alive was tempered by these details of his involvement in the horrors of war.

> *I might be able to get some time off and come see you in Belgrade soon if things don't get busy again here. There's never time to leave because the fight is too important right now. . . . Commander Vukov says we are close to winning.*
>
> *If you speak with Mama or Tata, tell them I say hello and I love them. I wrote to them but wasn't sure if they received my letter. I hope they are fine.*

> *Your brother,*
> *Danilo*

"He still doesn't know," said Danilo when Miroslav showed him the letter. "In his world, she is still alive."

He thought of his letters lying in bags in the back rooms of Srpska army bases as mortars rattled the ceilings. He thought of those bags, filled with undelivered letters, filled with impossible truths.

IN LATE JULY, Danilo and Miroslav met at the Rijeka. Miroslav ordered a cappuccino and Danilo ordered a black currant juice. As soon as they were sitting, Gazur sent Eder out to play his reluctant accordion, a rendition of "Stani, stani Ibar vodo." Danilo, thinking Miroslav would not approve, was about to wave Eder away, but his son's expression seemed content with the music.

It was early evening. They smoked and watched the light come in off the Sava. A lone canoeist was working his way northward to the point where the two rivers met. It occurred to Danilo then that all rivers were the same river.

"I heard from Miša again," said Miroslav.

"Why doesn't he ever write to me?"

"He did write to you. He doesn't know you're in Belgrade."

"He didn't mention Stoja?"

"No."

"What about that mess in Srebrenica?"

"He didn't say anything about that. He said he had been blessed by a priest and that because of this, a Muslim soldier had fired at him from close range and missed. He said he was down in Žepa and even got to swim in the Drina, but he didn't make it to Višegrad to see you."

"I'm not in Višegrad."

"He doesn't know that."

"Višegrad," said Danilo. "I wonder what's become of it."

"But he sounded fine, considering."

"Mihajlo. *Danilo.*" Turning over the name. "What could I have done?"

"Don't worry, Tata. He'll be all right."

Danilo shook his head. "You can tell they aren't saying what happened in Srebrenica."

"An American said ten thousand Muslims were killed in six days. They were hunting them in the forest. Children too."

"Good God." Danilo closed his eyes then shook out another cigarette. "Miša didn't say anything about that?"

"It'll all be finished soon. Before the year's out," said Miroslav.

"You think so?"

"Milošević's pushing his luck. Even Clinton—*dickless, prickless Clinton*—won't be able to put up with him much longer."

"I never knew you were such an optimist, Miro." Twining the smoke with a sip of juice and wincing at the terrible beauty of it all.

Eder started in on "Ajde Slušaj, Slušaj Kaleš Bre Anđo," and Gazur came over with two slices of cherry *štrudla.*

"A gift," he said. "Compliments of the house."

"I might be dead without that man," Danilo said as he watched Gazur waddle away. "Everything has been compliments of the house."

"Well, it's a big house. You know he runs one of the biggest black market rings in the city."

"No!"

"I thought you knew. It's how he and Ilija know each other. Why do you think he has so many compliments to give?"

"Gazur? But he's such a good man."

"To you, maybe."

"I don't believe it."

"They say he was born a Jew but renounced his faith."

"Now you're lying."

"This is only what they say."

Miroslav seemed to grow serious. He took down the last of his cappuccino and then looked at his father. "Look, Tata. I have to go away for a while."

"What do you mean?"

Miroslav looked over at Eder on the accordion. "You can't tell anyone," he said. "No reporters. Not Ilija. Not anyone."

"Where are you going?"

"Sarajevo."

Danilo blinked. "Sarajevo? But it's under siege."

"Oh, is it? I hadn't heard."

"It's not safe, Miroslav. You've seen the pictures. They're shelling it from—"

"Tata, it's not safe anywhere. The Americans could drop a bomb on us right now. So should we not sit here? Should we not sit here and take our drinks because of a bomb that may never come?"

"But you can't even get near there. How will you get inside the city?"

"You can always get inside. Getting inside isn't the problem."

"And then? And then what're you going to do?"

"Tata, I need you to promise you won't say anything. I mean, it would be very bad if they found out I told you."

"If *who* found out? What are you talking about, Miroslav?"

"I need you to promise."

"Okay," he said. "I promise. I won't say anything."

Miroslav shifted in his chair. "Last year I was contacted by some men who are living in the United States. They're a very important group—they've done incredible work all over the world. I saw a video once of this miniatures installation they did in northern Russia in the 1960s. It was in the middle of a nuclear test explosion. The installation was destroyed by the blast. You can see the bomb and then the blast coming . . . Well, it changed everything for me. I mean, you see something like that and it's as if there's your life before and then your life after. Things could never be the same again. And I knew what I was supposed to do."

"You mean make those boxes."

"Yes, but it's more than that . . . It was like I saw the world in a different light, a different set of possibilities. Suddenly there was a way for me to be me."

"And so these people . . . they contacted you?"

"They had heard about my work through a professor in the philosophy department here. He knows these guys, he's a great admirer of theirs, and now they asked me for help putting on their show in Sarajevo. I mean, it's a huge honor. These are my heroes."

"But of all the places in the world, why would you want to put on a show in Sarajevo? You could be killed!"

Miroslav shook his head. "Oh, never mind, Tata. Forget I even told you."

"I'm sorry," said Danilo. "Where are you going to do it? On the street? Are there snipers?"

"We're performing in the National Library. It's burned down, but the shell of the building's still there. It's a magnificent space. Here, look." He slid a photograph across the table. "Can you imagine?"

Danilo examined the photo. "You'll put a black box in *there*?"

"No, no. They have a whole show. They'll use some of my technology, but they have an agenda. They have a whole plan."

"What's the show about?"

"Many things. It's about many things."

"Like what?"

"Like many things. String theory. Neutrinos."

"Neutrinos?"

"Invisible particles that pass through everything."

Fig. 2.7. *National Library of Bosnia and Herzegovina, Winter 1993*
Photo by R. Richards, from Røed-Larsen, P., *Spesielle Partikler,* p. 988

Danilo returned the photograph. "Can't you wait until the war is finished to do this?"

"No. It has to be now. That's the whole point."

"But do people really want to watch something like that during a war? If I'm trying to survive, maybe I just want food and water instead of a show about neutrons."

"Neutrinos," said Miroslav. "But this is what this group does. The whole performance is what it is because of where it's taking place."

"Well, it doesn't sound right to me."

"Fine," said Miroslav. "It doesn't sound right to you. Let's just forget it, okay?"

"Okay."

They ate the pie and smoked and listened to Eder working the accordion.

Gazur came over. "How is the *štrudla?*"

"Delicious," said Danilo.

"The river's beautiful today, isn't it?"

"It's always beautiful."

"Your father's a real man," Gazur said to Miroslav. "I meet a lot of men, but none like your father. The world needs more men like him, wouldn't you agree?"

"He's a real man," Miroslav agreed.

"Father and son." Gazur smiled. "It's good to see."

When he had gone again, Danilo turned to Miroslav. "He's really into the black market?"

"He's the biggest there is. He has a whole warehouse of guns. Drugs. Prostitutes. Everything."

"Gazur," said Danilo, shaking his head. "What next?"

After a while, he said, "You know, back home, your elephant's still in the barn."

Miroslav laughed. "That old thing. I told you to burn it!"

"I'll never burn it. So long as I live. Stoja's altar is there."

Miroslav nodded. His face grew somber.

"I miss her," he said.

"Yes," said Danilo. Then: "This group from the U.S., they like you?"

"They said I was the best they've ever seen."

"They did?"

"It's a chance of a lifetime, Tata. It will be my greatest achievement."

"I'm proud."

"Thank you."

"You've become a man now."

"Why does everyone keep saying that?"

"You'll be careful?"

"Of course, Tata," he said. "I'm always careful."

"I can't lose everything again."

8

The next week, Danilo found a homemade postcard slipped beneath the door to the storage house.

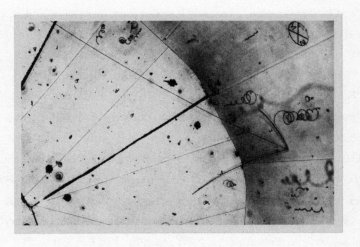

Fig. 2.8. Postcard of Neutrino Collision, Hydrogen Bubble Chamber (1970)
From Røed-Larsen, P., *Spesielle Partikler,* p. 991

At first he thought it might be from Miša, and his heart began to race, but when he flipped it over there was no stamp or address, only the minuscule handwriting of his eldest:

Vratiću se uskoro.

—M.

"I'm sorry," said Ilija later that day at the Rijeka. "Where did he go?"

"I'm not supposed to say."

Ilija looked down at his hands, then reached into his bag.

"I wasn't going to show you this. A friend found it. From last year. You said Miroslav had been in the papers."

"That's right."

Ilija handed him a rumpled copy of *Naša Borba,* a leftist monthly.

On the cover was a picture of Miroslav and an older man, each holding a pipe; Miroslav's was grotesquely larger than the other man's. The older man was wearing some kind of peasant's costume. He looked strangely familiar. The two men stood next to a wall, which was covered in a black-and-red graffito.

"Ja nisam takav sin oca," it read—"I am not my father's son." This was also the title of the article.

"Who's that other man?" said Danilo.

"He looks like you, doesn't he? That's what I thought."

"But what does it mean?"

"Everyone said this was a big antiwar statement. I thought it was stupid. I didn't realize it was him."

Danilo read the article. In the accompanying interview, Miroslav claimed his graffito was not a play on the common phrase *"Kakav otac takav sin"* ("Like father, like son"), but rather that he was paraphrasing another famous graffito, seen on the crumbled wall of the Berlin Zoo in the aftermath of World War II: *"Sind wir mehr als dieses Erbe . . ."* ("We are more than this gift . . .").

N.B.: *But this doesn't seem like a paraphrase.*

M.D.: *Well, exactly, exactly. We can no longer paraphrase our parents' generation. And the generation before. We see what happens. We repeat their mistakes. Carnage.*

N.B.: *Would you say you have a political agenda?*

M.D.: *I have no agenda. I'm an artist.*

N.B.: *Surely everyone has an agenda, whether they're willing to state it publicly or not.*

M.D.: *My job is to make my work. The audience can decide what it means. I can't control their reaction.*

N.B.: *Do you think the artist becomes more critical to society in wartime?*

M.D.: *The artist is always critical to society, even though the artist must end up hating society. War happens when society forgets its artists.*

N.B.: *War happens for many reasons.*

M.D.: *War happens for only one reason: we cannot see past our own death.*[2]

"No offense, but your son has always rubbed me the wrong way," said Ilija when Danilo looked up from the paper. "I never knew where he stood. I never saw him with any girls."

"He's a good boy."

"Yes, yes, of course. I meant no offense," said Ilija. He grunted, clapping his hands. "Aye. I'm so constipated I could punch a horse. Gazur! Gazur . . . come here. Do you have something to get this train started again?"

DANILO BEGAN to collect newspapers. He started listening to the radio again. There were more reports of mass graves being found in Srebrenica. Even some of the Serbian press began to call it an atrocity, though others claimed it was revenge for a previous massacre performed by the Muslims. Perhaps sensing an endgame, Milošević had begun to slowly distance himself in his speeches from Radovan Karadžić and the Bosnian Serbs.

But no news came from Sarajevo. No news of a show in the library that was no longer a library. Danilo lay on his back and listened to the radio, but there was nothing. No mention of either of his sons. He lay among the washing machines and smoked and listened and waited.

Then, on August 28, a 120-millimeter mortar fell onto Mula Mustafe

---

[2] M. Bozović, "Ja nisam takav sin oca," *Naša Borba*, April 4, 1993, 5.

Bašeskije Street, just outside the busy Markale Market, in the heart of Sarajevo. Thirty-seven people were killed, and nearly one hundred wounded. The news over the radio was sketchy at first; the newsman initially claimed the attack had been perpetrated by Bosnian authorities on their own people, to garner sympathy from the international community. This would later be meticulously refuted during the 2006 ICTY appeal case of Stanislav Galić via a thorough analysis of the depth of the impact crater (22cm ±2cm), the angle of descent (60° ±5°), the bearing of the shell (20° ±3°), and the charge of the mortar (0 ±3), narrowing the Markale projectile's origins to two possible positions above the city, both of which were held by Srpska troops in August 1995.[3]

Prompted by the Markale massacre, on August 30, after years of waiting on the sidelines, NATO began Operation Deliberate Force, a comprehensive air offensive against Bosnian Serb positions. Belgrade ground to a halt, wondering if the bombs would soon drop on them.

DANILO SAT in the Rijeka, listening to the peculiar silence of the city. Even Gazur's customary cheer came off as oddly hollow.

"The river's still beautiful," he said. "No matter what happens."

"Where's Eder?"

"He left. He didn't want to play the old songs anymore. So he quit and went to war." Gazur waved his hand dismissively. "*Bah!* Now he can play all the turbo-folk he wants. This war kills me."

"But a war can also be profitable, yes?" said Danilo.

"Nothing is worth the price of life, my friend. I would trade everything I have for peace tomorrow."

Danilo drank his black currant juice and smoked. He put his hand on the morning's newspaper but did not open it. The night before he had dreamed he was floating down a river. Not the Sava or the Drina, but a mighty river in a

---

[3] *Prosecutor v. Stanislav Galić,* appeals judgment, International Criminal Tribunal for the Former Yugoslavia, IT-98-29-A, November 30, 2006.

jungle. At some point he looked up and saw that the river abruptly vanished into thin air. In the dream, he wondered if he was actually inside one of Miroslav's black boxes. Whether he was tiny now. He had awoken just before he got to the point where the water ended. He did not get to see what was beyond the box.

Ilija came out onto the terrace.

"Ilija," said Danilo, surprised. "Come, join me. Let me tell you about my dream. You can tell me what it means."

"Hello, friend," said Ilija.

"There's no music. Eder has gone to war . . ." He saw the expression on Ilija's face. "What is it?"

"Your son," said Ilija.

"My son?" Visions of Miša, shot in a field. "Which son?"

"Miroslav."

"Miroslav?"

At this precise moment, Gazur came up to the two men, but, seeing their expressions, he froze, understanding everything, and withdrew.

Ilija wiped some sweat from his brow and grimaced. "I'm so sorry, my friend," he said. "They found him in his flat. They said he had suffocated."

"Suffocated?" Danilo's body froze. "How?"

"That's all they said. My friend's a policeman. He called me just now. I went to the warehouse to find you." Ilija shook his head. "This world is such shit."

"But he was supposed to be in Sarajevo! Are you sure it was him?"

"A neighbor found him in his flat. The door was open."

"What happened?"

"I don't know. My friend didn't know anything more. He's expecting you to call." He handed Danilo a slip of paper.

Danilo looked at the number. "He didn't even tell me he was back!"

"I'm very sorry, my friend," said Ilija. "I wish I could do something more. His body is at the morgue in St. Sava's hospital. I can drive you there if you'd like."

Danilo sat. The breath was gone from his lungs.

"Danilo," said Ilija. "I can drive you."

"No," said Danilo. "I'll go myself."

"This is no time to be alone, my friend. Life's too short for this. We must be together."

"Please," said Danilo.

Ilija stood and then bowed in the old way. "Well, you know where to find me. Anything you need. I am here for you. No joke. Anything I can do." He walked over to Gazur, and the two men talked and shook hands.

Danilo left money on the table, even though he knew that the juice, as always, was on the house. As he was leaving, Gazur approached, but Danilo ignored him. He kept walking across the road to the railing overlooking the Sava. A tugboat was crawling upstream, tugging nothing but itself.

Danilo imagined the river inside a great box. Imagined himself in the box. Imagined men beneath a black curtain looking in at him as they stood on a street corner.

He began to take off his clothes. Piece by piece, until he was in only his underwear. Then he climbed over the railing, struggling with his stiff leg. He jumped. The water was cold, not entirely clean, syrupy against his skin. He pushed himself out to where the current was and then floated on his back and thought about letting himself sink.

When he looked back at the bank, he could see Gazur, waving his hands, the white city rising up behind him.

SOMEWHERE ALONG THE WAY, Danilo had lost the policeman's number. He did not go to the morgue as he knew he should. Instead he went to Miroslav's flat in Voždovac. A small part of him hoped that Ilija had been mistaken, that the police had been mistaken, that *someone* had to be mistaken and that he would knock on the door and Miroslav would be sleeping and he would take a while before he opened the door, blurry-eyed, angry at the awakening, and Danilo would gaze upon him and the two would embrace and everything would be as it once was.

The door to the flat was just a door. Nothing to indicate that anything unusual had occurred on the other side. Danilo realized he had never actually been inside the flat. On several occasions he had met Miroslav here and they had gone out together on a walk, but Miroslav had never invited him to come in, a fact that now seemed odd.

Danilo knocked. There was no answer. He tried the doorknob and, to his surprise, found it to be open.

The flat was nearly spotless. As if someone had come in and swept the place clean. Surely this could not have been how Miroslav lived? If anything, his son thrived in a space bordering on the edge of chaos. Getting him to clean his room as a child had always been an affront to his sensibilities.

Danilo walked through the flat, laying his hands on the surfaces. There was a table with an empty bowl on it. A bottle of old milk in the fridge. The bookshelves were empty, save a single xeroxed article. Danilo picked it up. Something by Werner Heisenberg.

Where were all of his son's books? He must've had books. He remembered seeing many books through the door the last time he was here.

A typewriter sat on a desk, a blank sheet of paper tucked in its roll. Danilo pulled out the sheet and found on its reverse side a small eye printed on the top of the page:

In the bedroom, a cheap bureau reinforced with tape. Also empty. The bed had been stripped. Danilo got down on all fours and looked beneath it. Nothing, except a landscape of lint and a stray yellow tube sock. He reached out and took hold of the sock. Squeezed it.

Danilo stood up. He sighed. He tried to imagine his son sleeping on this bed, opening the refrigerator, spending many late nights working on his black boxes. Had he made them here? Had he assembled all of the little pieces on this carpet? Had he breathed in his magic, closed the lid of the box, watched the elephant leap from the bridge for the first time?

Such miracles in such an ordinary place. He suddenly felt very close to Miroslav, closer than he had ever felt before. He rubbed his beard and inhaled.

On his way out, he opened the closet. Like everything else in the flat, it was empty. There was only the top of a yellow tracksuit hanging from a plastic hanger. Danilo was just about to close the door when something caught his eye.

On the shelf behind, in the shadows. He leaned in closer, blinked.

It was him. *It was Miroslav.* Tiny and true, no more than two centimeters tall, as if he had escaped from one of his boxes.

"Miroslav!" he said.

Miroslav did not move. He was lying on his side, his expression frozen in amused wonderment. Danilo saw then that a little white string was attached to his belly button. He followed the string. It ran down to the floor of the closet. Danilo got down on his knees. The string ended at the belly of another tiny man, also lying on his side.

"Miša!" he whispered.

Miša was in his uniform. His eyes were open but contained no life.

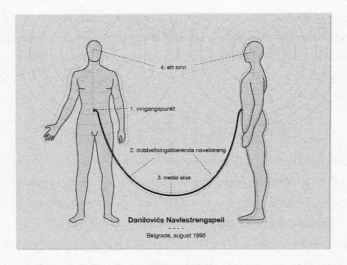

Fig. 2.9. "Danilović's Umbilical Mirror"
From Røed-Larsen, P., *Spesielle Partikler,* p. 973

For the second time in his life, death would not reveal itself to Danilo Danilović. The pretty young mortician at the morgue in St. Sava's smiled sympathetically and said that his son's case was still under review, and the body was not able to be viewed. This was how she put it: "not able to be viewed."

"But he's my son," said Danilo, a level of desperation in his voice. "He's my son. Do you understand? Please. If I cannot see him, how do I know he's dead? You must understand." He looked around at the rows of metal drawers. "Which one is he in?"

"He's not here," the mortician said kindly.

"Then where is he?"

"I'm not sure," she said. "He's with some specialists."

"Are you not a specialist?"

The mortician gave him a strained smile. "You will see him soon," she said reassuringly.

This turned out not to be true. According to the records, an error in the paperwork had caused the corpse to be transferred to Višegrad, and it was subsequently lost in transit. But in that moment, against all his instincts, which wailed for some kind of proof, Danilo brought his hands together and tried to believe what she told him.

The mortician showed him to the exit. They paused in the hospital lobby.

"Do you know how he died?" asked Danilo. "He was younger than he looked. He was still very young. Maybe he wasn't eating well. His mother was always worrying about this."

"We don't know yet," said the mortician. Her mascara was smudged beneath her left eye. "It looks like he just stopped breathing." She touched his arm in the same way Stoja once had. "I will try and find you some answers, Mr. Danilović. I know how hard it can be."

Danilo nodded. He wondered what life would've been like if he had had a daughter instead of a son. If this woman with her smudged mascara were his daughter; if they could have dinner together later at the restaurant around the corner as they always did; if she would bring her boyfriend for him to meet for the first time; if this boyfriend were charming but reserved, nervous that he would offend her father, of whom he had heard so much; if, only months after this first dinner, she would announce to him that she would marry this man and he would approve, first in words and later in spirit, ushering her down an aisle before men and God himself; if, barely a year later, there would be a baby cradled in her arms, the husband standing at a safe distance as the grandfather leaned in close, knowing that life spills across generations in the simplest of ways, and as Danilo touched his grandson's tiny sea-creature fingers, his daughter would look up at him and say, "His name is Danilo."

"Oh, I almost forgot," said the mortician. She reached into the pocket of her lab coat and handed him a small ziplock bag. "I was asked to give this to you."

Inside the bag there was a small metal key.

As Per Røed-Larsen points out at length in *Spesielle Partikler* (pp. 693–705), the official police report on Miroslav Danilović's death is a curious document. While it offers seemingly superfluous details about the "deceased wearing [the] lower half of [a] yellow tracksuit, seated in front of a bowl of milk," it remains vague about the actual cause or essential circumstances of the death itself. One of the officers who signed the document, Officer Stanislav Radić, was later dismissed from the police force under suspicion of extortion and bribery. Miroslav's obituary in *Naša Borba,* the only Serbian paper to carry an announcement of his death, was brief, if complimentary, mentioning the graffito and the cult of the black theater boxes. It did not reference a theater project in Sarajevo.

Røed-Larsen elaborates on Miroslav's role in *Kirkenesferda Fire,* that group's famous Sarajevo performance, which ran for only four nights in the eviscerated shell of the National Library of Bosnia, from August 24 to 27, before it was cut short by the Markale marketplace massacre. He writes:

> *[Miroslav] was perhaps the most talented of all the puppet-makers . . . more so, it could be argued, than Ragnvald Brynildsen, the original, or even Tor Bjerknes, who so beautifully oversaw the design of* Kirk Tre *in Cambodia with Kermin Radmanovic. What separated Miroslav [from the others] was his erasure of the connective tissue between puppet and puppeteer. His objects moved without*

intervention; they literally took on a life of their own, in which the puppeteer
became just another spectator to the miracle at hand. (999)

Per Røed-Larsen, for all his thoroughness, fails to mention what happened to the rest of the family. After the war, Danilo Danilović moved back to Višegrad. The farm had been untouched in his absence—all was accounted for except one thing: the elephant had vanished. He would eventually sell the farm and move to a house not far from the bowed shadows of the Turkish Bridge, which he would visit each evening until the day he died.

Mihajlo Danilo, his only remaining son, lived in semi-hiding as a bricklayer in a hamlet outside Belgrade, occasionally writing to his father. He returned once to Višegrad for a reunion of sorts, but neither father nor son could say he recognized the other. Eventually his underground network of supporters began to unravel and he was forced to flee to Argentina, where he worked reshelving books at a municipal library, even though he could not read a word of Spanish. Over the years, many of his friends and colleagues, former paramilitaries and Srpska army officials, were arrested and brought to trial by the International Criminal Tribunal in The Hague. Mihajlo Danilo was never captured. He remained at large, existing only in the memory of those who had once known him.

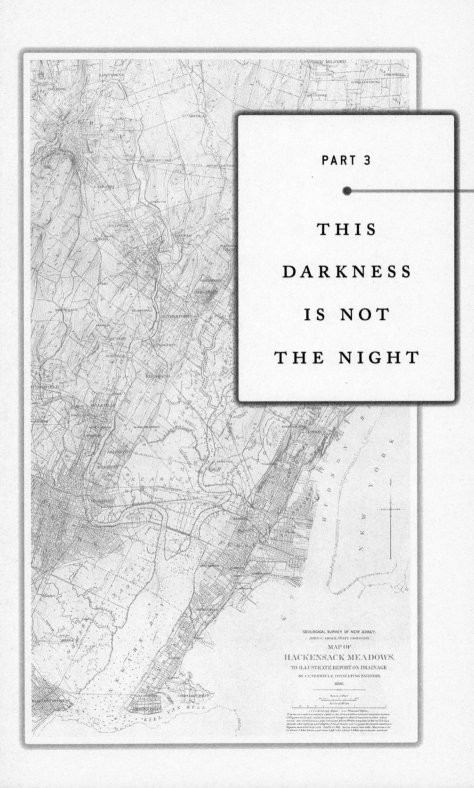

PART 3

THIS

DARKNESS

IS NOT

THE NIGHT

GEOLOGICAL SURVEY OF NEW JERSEY.
JOHN C. SMOCK, STATE GEOLOGIST.

MAP OF

HACKENSACK MEADOWS,

TO ILLUSTRATE REPORT ON DRAINAGE

BY C. C. VERMEULE, CONSULTING ENGINEER.

1896.

KEARNY, NEW JERSEY

August 10, 2010

On the day that would change everything thereafter and much of what came before, Radar Radmanovic rose before his birdcall alarm clock could tweep out its dreaded tree swallow soliloquy and stumbled into the shower. He closed his eyes as the warm curtain of water enveloped him, letting his forehead come to rest against the same geodesic turquoise tiles that had counseled his bathing for the past thirty years.

The horror. Last night he and Ana Cristina had gone on their fourth date—fifth if you counted their Slurpie meeting on the A&P loading dock, which Radar often did. After each of these dates, he would wake up the next day panic-stricken and horrendously embarrassed, positive he had done or said something that had subsequently ruined his chances of ever seeing her again.

That was my last glimpse of paradise, he would always think, just as he was thinking now, forehead pressed against tile.

Indeed, his relationship with her was one of the universe's great mysteries: why would beautiful, lovely Ana Cristina—with her duotone lipstick and those impossible hoop earrings and that smile (so effortless!) that revved his transmission and numbed his knees—why would a girl like that stick around with a guy like him? It defied all rational thought. Unless of course she was perpetuating their connection merely to gather amusing stories that she could later share with her *muchachos*—but such mean-spirited behavior was not like her. No, not like her at all—Ana Cristina was a giver, not a taker. This he had learned as they sat side by side in darkened movie theaters (four times now!) watching terrible movies, his leg inches from hers; he, petrified, unable to listen to a single line from said terrible movie as he contemplated when and if and how he should fulcrum his arm up and over and around her shoulders.

And last night he had finally done it. He had counted to three (or four—he couldn't remember now) and his arm had shot into the air completely without grace, bordering on some fascist salute, but somehow when it had fallen back to earth it had found an uncertain home around her frame, and it was as if she had been waiting for that arm, because after a moment she had let her head fall— no: *drift*—onto his shoulder. And then, while Radar was pleading for his body not to shut down, something monumental had transpired. He couldn't even satisfyingly reconstruct the minute procedures that led up to its apotheosis, but somehow, *they had kissed*. They had actually kissed. Briefly, her lips had grazed his. It was an event he once could've only dreamed about, during all those commercial transactions at the A&P. He had pined after her for months as she plied her trade in checkout lane number 2 before he had finally worked up the nerve to ask her out in what would be one of the most awkward date proposals known to mankind, and now—

Sweet Jesus!

He stood in front of the bathroom mirror and gargled the yellow mouthwash that he hated but continued to buy. The reflection that regarded him, with a degree of curious disgust, was not the reflection of a handsome man. Bald since birth, jaundiced, a nervous, *torsadée* curvature to his spine that caused his whole body to naturally list to starboard—he would be the first piece of merchandise plucked off the assembly line by a disappointed quality control. And yet, here he still was, rattling down the line, unplucked.

And they had kissed.

Radar returned to his bedroom and dressed slowly, like a man dressing for a funeral. He knew he should feel ecstatic, that this should be the single greatest morning of his life, that he should be singing arias, and yet he could not dispel this lingering sense of dread.

As he struggled into his jack-o'-lantern socks, the alarm clicked on again and the tree swallow began to maniacally twitter out its wake-up call. He made no move to switch it off. The swallow should suffer as he suffered. The swallow should feel the full weight of living on its little swallow back.

While the bird tweeped and tweeped, he went over to the bedside table and opened his *Little Rule Book for Life,* a hot pink journal he had bought for $1.99 at Dollar Daze, and into which he added, on average, one rule per week.

He wrote:

Rule #238. Don't do it because you can. Do it because you must.

He wasn't sure if this was even true, but it sounded good, and it gave him a little dose of precious momentum. He underlined "must." Twice.

Do it because you must.

The double underline was clearly redundant, the two lines canceling each other out with their excess of enthusiasm, like giving the double middle finger to someone in very close proximity. He tried crossing out one of the lines.

Do it because you must.

He sighed. Such a collision of failed revisionism was a fairly decent summary of his life up until this point. No matter. He donned his fanny pack and trucker's cap, finally slapped the tree swallow out of its misery, and pattered down to the kitchen.

Two Grundig Ocean Boy radios were blaring away simultaneously in the middle of the breakfast table, flanking a morose-looking ceramic pig centerpiece. An uncapped jar of Marmite, like an offering to this altar of sound, sat next to a plate of half-eaten toast. Clear evidence his father had been on the early-morning prowl. Radar sat down in front of the twin radios, trying to parse the dueling signals in his head. It was an exercise in the impossible. His father was constantly haunted by the thought that he might be missing an important bit of news on a station he wasn't listening to, so he often had at least two radios going at the same time, though sometimes it could be as many as six. Kermin claimed an ability to pay attention to multiple signals at once, but Radar had a working theory that his father listened to them all so that in the end he wouldn't have to listen to any of them.

Radar killed one of the Ocean Boys and skizzered the dial of the other to WCCA 990 AM, the financial news station where he worked as head engineer. A familiar prattle of market indices spilled forth from the speaker. *Good.* All was well at transmission. He clicked off the second radio. He admired the vacuum of silence left behind before he lacquered a healthy dollop of his father's Marmite onto a slice of seven-grain. Radar hated the Marmite like he hated the mouthwash, but family ritual often trumped logic, and Kermin kept a vast supply of the awful stuff close at hand. As rule #98 stated, *Belief is 90% proximity and 10% conviction.* (Well, maybe the nihilist arithmetic in that one needed to be massaged a bit. It was probably closer to 70/30.)

His mind drifted back to the sequence of the night before. It was not that anything had gone wrong, per se. At least nothing that he could put his finger on. They had even kissed again when they parted ways outside the movie theater. It was a tentative kiss, but it was a kiss nonetheless, one that suggested a future filled with more such kisses.

He cringed again. It was not just that his measuring stick for physical contact was akin to that of a middle schooler—it was that literally every time he opened his mouth, a disaster was waiting to happen. Case in point: While he and Ana Cristina were waiting in line to buy popcorn, Radar had panicked, thinking they were not chatting as much as normal people on normal dates did. So he asked her: "Have you seen any good television movies lately?"

What? Even as he was saying it, he saw that such a question was already dying and curled up in a fetal position on the floor. What an unfathomable idiot he was. He had meant to say "television shows," but then his mind froze and he transitioned midsentence into "movies," perhaps because they were in a movie theater, which unfortunately resulted in the very narrow category of made-for-television movies. Very few made-for-television movies were good—it was like starting a race with your legs tied together. Radar knew this much, even though he was not really one for television, which was why his original question had been flawed from the very beginning. He wouldn't even have been able to sustain a conversation if she had said something like "I enjoy reruns of *Friendship*." (Was this even the name of a television show? Or was it merely a complex and precious phenomenon that could develop between two people?) All he could have responded with was "Yes, well, my father enjoyed *M*A*S*H,* and I watched fuzzy episodes of *Muppet Babies* for a time on one of our many pocket televisions when I was younger, until my father went crazy and destroyed them all. You see, in his heart I think he was still a radioman, just like his father, and just like me. Maybe he was protesting the death of listening. Do you like to listen? I do. Not to brag, but I would call myself a professional listener."

But he said none of this. Just the dead television-movie question lying on the floor in front of them. To her great credit, Ana Cristina, looking puzzled, had just laughed in that way she did (where everything in the world seemed both terribly unimportant and important at the same time) and said he was "such a weirdo." He could not disagree.

Radar bit into his Marmite toast and chewed through his distaste.

She would break up with him today. He just knew it. And truthfully, he probably deserved it. It had been an amazing ride, but the dream could not last forever. She had most likely realized—somewhere in the middle of that kiss—what a terrible kisser he was, what a fumbling, mechanical albatross he was, and, by natural extension, what a terrible mistake this whole endeavor had been. She had realized (and one could not blame her) that things could never work out between a perfect little slip of creation like herself and a malfunctioning human-shaped fabrication like him. But she would be gentle about it. The next time he called or went into the A&P, she would get that sad, inevitable look in her eyes and then she would say, "Radar, we need to talk," and he would try to take it like a man. In truth, he wasn't sure how he would take it.

"Have *you* seen any good television movies lately?" he asked the melancholic pig centerpiece on the breakfast table. If only he could pretend he was a normal person. He didn't even have to *be* a normal person; it would be enough just to *act* like a normal person. Artificial intelligence experts had long ago given up on creating actually intelligent robots—their goal was simply for robots to be-have like intelligent beings.

"Television movies?" a woman's voice said from behind him. "I can't say that I have."

Radar wondered briefly if he had been teleported back into his date, whether he was reliving some parallel existence, some second chance where he could be the suave Casanova he had always dreamed himself to be. But this fantasy instantly evaporated as soon as he turned around. There stood his mother in her lab coat.

"I haven't seen a good movie in ages," she said, already rummaging through her vast cabinet of tea above the stove. "Have you?"

The cabinet held all sorts of incredibly rare samples from around the globe, one perk of Charlene's position as head quality-control aromatist at the International Flavor and Aroma Corporation, a position she still held despite reaching and now surpassing the age of retirement. Every morning, she selected her steeping ingredients based upon an elaborate but completely arbitrary formula guided by the phase of the moon, barometric pressure, karmic vibration, and whatever particular ailment she happened to be suffering from. Foot pain required two laces of Tasmanian kelp, a dash of white asparagus extract, and a pinch of powdered tiger shark cartilage. Indigestion called for a teaspoon of fiesole artichoke leaf infusion, two pinches of gentian and *Codonopsis* root, a drop of bee saliva, and a generous handful of Israeli black horehound.

"What *is* a television movie, anyhow?" she said. She put the kettle on and began assembling a small collection of glass jars on the countertop. "Is that a movie that's *made* for television or a movie that is just being *shown* on television? Because I think there's a difference."

Radar sighed. "I wasn't talking to you, Mom."

"Oh," she said. She crumbled an oolong base into the strainer. Some unidentified twigs. After a moment she said, "May I ask whom you were talking to?"

"I wasn't talking to anyone. I was recounting."

"You were *recounting*," she said. Half a dozen little red chokeberries disappeared into the strainer. "Recounting what, exactly?"

"Nothing."

"What kind of nothing?" They had lived together long enough that lying had become an exercise in futility.

He sighed. "I went on a date last night. And I was recounting one of the many ways I screwed it all up."

"A date?" she said, raising her eyebrows. She sniffed at a jar that looked to contain the remains of a dead bat.

"*A date,*" she said again. "Well, what makes you think you screwed it up?"

He didn't want to be having this conversation. "I don't know—maybe because I say all the wrong things? Maybe because I'm the most awkwardest person on the planet?"

"How long have you known this girl?"

"Uh . . . about six months. She works at the A&P."

"What's her name?"

"Ana Cristina."

"And how do you feel about her?"

He rubbed his face. "Mom?"

"I mean, is she worthy of my boy?"

"She's only the best thing that's ever happened to me. It's not a question of whether she's worthy of me; it's whether she and I belong in the same galaxy."

"Hm." She considered this. "Well. Be careful."

"*Be careful?* That's your advice to me? *Be careful?* Thanks, Mom."

Time had a funny way of playing its hand. Charlene's quarter-life audacity had slowly wilted during her middle years into a near constant low-grade anxiety at the various provocations of modern existence. Once upon a time, she had dropped acid and nearly burned down a library, but now just answering an e-mail could be enough to send her into a state of panic that she placated with her teas and dream catchers. As their little family had grown into each other, as life had begun to arrange itself so that it became impossible to escape their own nuclear dysfunction, as the time for Radar to move out had come and gone (and then come and gone again), Charlene still maintained that she was the normal one, that she was the one holding it all together, when in fact the converse was closer to the truth. Yes, she lived with two men caught in varying states of electromagnetic purgatory, but she had chosen this life, and as much as she might have claimed otherwise, she took courage from the stagnation of this purgatory. Every complaint she leveled their way also had the effect of steadying her wobbly rudder. They were her Pleiades. Without them, darkness would overtake her night.

"I only mean that women can be complicated," she said, breaking off some aspect of the bat body and dropping it into the tea strainer. "I should know. I used to be one."

"You're still a woman, Mom."

"They'll say one thing to your face, but what they're really thinking is something else entirely."

"She's not that kind of girl, Mom. Seriously, she's wonderful. And honest. And . . . and . . . I don't know. She's just . . . *her*."

"I'm sure she is. I'm not saying you shouldn't go out with her," she said. On the stove, the kettle had already begun to shudder. "Just know that every time she opens her mouth, it's an opportunity for her to lie to you."

"Thanks. I'll take that into consideration."

"Not that this is always a bad thing. Sometimes a lie can be just as good as the truth."

"Uh, I'm pretty sure that's not true."

The kettle came to life and whistled its disapproval. Charlene looked surprised, as if this boil did not happen every single morning, scooped up the pot, and layered the water through the strainer in an overly ornate spiral. Her mug of choice featured an orgy of rabbits engaged in various balletic sex acts, though after twenty years of use, the humping bunnies no longer registered as carnal agents, save to the rare houseguest, who could be forgiven for staring at Charlene's crockery in fascinated horror.

"Oh, I was meaning to ask you," Charlene said, ushering strainer and mug to the kitchen table. "I have to get a new cell phone this afternoon. What's that one you recommended again?"

"I didn't."

"Didn't you?"

"I don't have a cell phone, Mom."

It was true: despite his clairvoyance with all things electronic, cellular phones had always struck him as a gaudy and unnecessary technology. He did not want to be constantly at the mercy of others. And why pay a cell-phone company ridiculous amounts of money each month when there was plenty of frequency in the 1-to-250,000-MHz spectrum open for the taking? Radio signal felt much more organic—like swimming in the ocean versus swimming laps in a tiny pool, though he didn't know how to swim, so he couldn't be sure if such an analogy was entirely accurate.

"And why *don't* you have a cell phone?" she said. "What's wrong with you?

You and your father, both of you." She took a sip of tea and wrinkled her nose. "Oh, God, this stuff is *awful.*"

"It smells awful. Was that a *bat?*"

"Bolivian chinchilla," she said. "It's good for bile flow."

"*Chinchilla?*" he said, recoiling. "As in those cute little guys with the crazy soft fur?"

"The ones I use are female."

"How am I supposed to tell that to my friends? 'Yeah, and that's my mom, who drinks *chinchilla tea.*'"

"Which friends are these?"

"Okay, there's no need to rub it in."

She took another sip. "But really, why *don't* you get a cell phone?"

"I don't *want* a cell phone."

"So then how am I supposed to call you?"

"You can call the station. We've managed without a cell phone for all these years."

"And what about when you're not there?" she said. "You know, for when something comes up?"

"Like what?"

"*I don't know.* Everyone has cell phones. It's a part of life now. All the kids—it's how they communicate. With the text message," she said. "How are you supposed to talk with this girl if you don't have the text message?"

He sighed. "Morse code worked just fine before text messages came along."

"*Morse code?* Honey, I hate to break it to you, but that's not the way to a girl's heart. This girl you're seeing—what's her name again?"

"Ana Cristina."

"I'm betting Ana Cristina probably doesn't have a ham radio station in her bedroom," she said. "You have to *adapt.* You have to learn to speak her language."

As much as he hated to admit it, she had a point. Ana Cristina was an avid texter and expert multitasker. She could carry on a perfectly coherent conversation with him while she also navigated through dozens of electronic communiqués on her device.

Charlene took another sip of the tea and grimaced. "I'm going to get you and your father cell phones this afternoon."

"Please don't," he said.

"It will just be for emergencies, but if you like it, then you can start the text messages. I'll even do the text with you."

"That's not how you say it. You don't *do the text* with someone."

"Well, how would you know? You don't even have a cell phone."

"Don't get me a phone, Mom. Please?" he said. "I like my life just the way it is."

"No . . . no, you don't," she said, almost ruefully. "No one likes their life just the way it is."

The transmission site where Radar worked—indeed, the sum of his life—was located in the Meadowlands, a yawning swath of New Jersey marshland crisscrossed by countless highways and train lines and looping, arterial interchanges, all feeding into the great megalopolitan hydra of New York City. The mosquito-laden swamps were a sprawling back stage for the city, the many container ports and truck depots and train yards housing the props that fueled Manhattan's insatiable appetite for citrus delicacies and all manner of combustible fineries. The Upper East Side bodega could not exist but for the generosity of the Meadowlands warehouse. *Enter, stage left:* orange juice from Florida, pineapples from Costa Rica, strawberries from California, tulips from Holland, chicken thighs from Colorado, crates of gum and chips and Mango Tango Dragonberry iced tea. The Meadowlands was the triage point for the inevitable daily deluge of Chinese-made trinkets: handbags and wigs and tampons and dog muzzles and yoga mats and mouse pads and tube socks and Happy Meal figurines. A whole warehouse annex devoted to nothing but boxes and boxes of shrink-wrapped Happy Meal figurines. It was all threaded through the odorous palette of these marshes, beneath the cold, wet tremble-cord of the Hudson River, and up into the waiting mouth of the lonely city denizen.

Aside from providing a perfect habitat for bloodsucking insects, the brackish Meadowlands water was an ideal conductor of AM radio signal, and if you drove the turnpike from here to there during a heavy summer night, you might see those morose clusters of radio towers, blinking their lanky presence to any wayward planes. The WCCA 990 AM transmitter site, perched on the shore of a lagoon, hidden from the world by a forest of reeds, was a thirteen-and-a-half-minute bike ride from their periwinkle faux colonial in Kearny and a seventeen-minute ride from the A&P Express where Ana Cristina worked. This velocipedal commute through the swamps was usually his best thinking time of the day, a kind of moving meditation, as he found the forward momentum and solitude of his transit allowed him to carefully inflate the vision of who he was and who he might want to be, even if this vision would inevitably collapse as soon as he stopped pedaling.

Radar had written half a dozen mediocre poems about his bicycle, affectionally named Hot Lips Houlihan, after that temptress nurse on *M*A*S*H*. Hot Lips was an Optima Stinger double-suspension custom recumbent with low-point tiller steering. He had blown six months' salary on the rig four years earlier, and it was the one choice in life that he had never regretted, even in his darkest hours. She boasted more electronics than a small airplane: he had installed a reinforced plexiglass dashboard on top of the stem, upon which sat two transceivers, a decommissioned SRC ground surveillance radar dish, a portable shortwave multiband radio, a Shocker DX locomotive horn, an AmpliVox fifty-watt megaphone, and a plastic hula girl. Above the luggage compartment on the back, he had an extended whip antenna and a multidirectional yagi molded into a swivel plate that rattled behind him like exotic plumage.

As he rode to work on this strange day, this day of potential conquest mired in the foreboding of potential defeat, he sought comfort in Houlihan's shortwave, which he gently tuned to Radio Skala, a distant signal originating all the way from Belgrade. Somehow the station perfectly utilized the ionosphere's reflective properties to skip over the Atlantic and right into his lap. The song came on and he recognized it immediately as one of his favorites: "Stani, stani Ibar vodo," about a lovesick country boy who has a conversation with a river about his darling. How fitting. He liked listening to the music of his people as he rode through the damp material excess of the Meadowlands, broadcasting the wisdom of suffering to trucks filled with capitalism's runoff. No matter if the music tendered a history he was not entirely sure was his own. But whatever. Today he needed all the Balkan armor he could muster.

"Smrt fašizmu, sloboda narodu!" he yelled to the swamps.

As is the case with many children of immigrants, particularly those whose sole immigrant parent married an American, Radar knew only a little of his inherited language, gleaned mostly from when his father would produce an incredible string of Serbian swear words, often in the shower. (*"Da ideš u tri pizde materine!"*) Sometimes his swearing was correlated to his level of annoyance, but more often than not, he swore just because he could. If there was one thing Serbs could never abandon, it was their dangerously poetic and casual manner of cussing. It was not uncommon for his father to toss out the phrase *"Jebem ti supu od klinova Isusovih!"* which translated roughly as "Fuck the soup made from the nails of Jesus's crucifixion," and not think twice about it, even if in English he was unfailingly polite. Radar had never heard him curse even once in English. Serbian remained his language of expression, his private lounge of paroxysms. Thus, after a childhood of exposure to such intricate verbal execrations echoing across his subconscious, Radar could understand the language much better than he could speak it himself.

The Radmanovics had visited Belgrade only once, in 1989, at the invitation of a distant half relation, Julija Maravić, who showered them with kindness and warmth despite having never met them and maintaining only a tenuous familial connection to Dobroslav, Radar's grandfather. It did not matter: they were part of the family, and she would've jumped in front of a train for them. She had said as much on their last night there. This backdrop of extreme hospitality made Radar's experience with the rest of the population all the more confusing.

"Hej Marko, gle ovog američkog šupka—izgleda ko majmun oboleo od raka," a pudgy man with a shaved head had said as Radar was lingering with his parents in front of a fruit stand in Žarkovo Selo. Radar's comprehension of the language was hazy at best, but he knew that this man was talking about him to his friend Marko and that whatever he had just said to Marko was not a very nice thing to say. Clutching his two malnourished beets, Radar was left with that very acrid, mothballed sensation of self-recognition that the Germans no doubt have a word for:

Übernachredenfremdschämlähmung (n.)—*the feeling caused by knowing someone has insulted you even as the slanderer(s) remain(s) unaware that you have seen/heard their insults quite clearly. The consequent self-pity, combined with an embarrassment for the slanderer(s), will often freeze the victim into a state of weary acceptance, such that he or she ends up doing nothing to address this trespass. Ex:* While waiting in line for the bathroom at the restaurant, Günther felt a passing sense of Übernachredenfremdschämlähmung when he spotted his waiter spitting into his liverwurst sandwich. Upon returning from the loo, Günther ate his sandwich in silence, despite feeling as if he might throw up at any minute.

Beets in hand, Radar had felt the dull heat of transcultural ignorance wash over him. This fat, odiferous skinhead in his ill-fitting patterned short-sleeve and his sniveling sidekick Marko were supposed to be his people! Still, despite the Serb's tendency for simultaneous compassion for the family and xenophobia toward the other, Radar felt that there was an ancient knowingness to the Balkan way that he found inexplicably seductive. *Yes, yes:* he realized he was being just as reductive with his Old World nostalgia as the Serbs themselves. But let us not forget rule #55: *Dreaming is the first step to knowing is the first step to dreaming.*

AT THE WCCA TRANSMISSION SITE, Radar relieved Gary on the night shift.

"Knock yourself out, man," said Gary. Gary said this every morning.

Radar checked the Interplex circuits and restarted the backup microwave systems. He read the weather report live on the air at thirty-three minutes past the hour and walked the rickety catwalk out into the swamps to inspect the twin three-hundred-foot radio towers aging gracefully against the sky.

"Do it because you must," he said to their soaring heights.

He sat in front of the stacks, listening to the financial news drone on and on. Occasionally he twisted a knob to tweak the signal. He got up and paced. He sat down again. He could not dispel the feeling that something was not right between himself and Ana Cristina. This feeling festered and metastasized and grew horns, until he finally broke down and dialed her cell phone from the station landline. It rang a painful number of times before going to voice mail.

"Hi, hi. Hello!" he said, trying to sound cheerful. "Ana Cristina? This is Radar. Hi. Just checking in. Saying hi. It was fun last night. I hope it was fun for you, too. Even if that movie was kinda bad. Well, terrible, really. One of the worst. But—*okay*. Nothing really to report here. Just—give a call at the station if you get a chance. Okay, bye. Bye. Talk to you later. Bye."

Wow. That was ugly. Next time, he needed to remember to hang up before the beep, lest he break her voice mail with his social ineptitude. In fact, the call only served to heighten his unease. She was working today at the A&P. Maybe he could just pop over and say hello? It was clearly forbidden to abandon the station during the middle of his shift, but then this was a borderline emergency.

He checked and rechecked the signal. Everything was fine. Really, what were the chances of the station imploding during the short time he was out? He would be gone forty minutes, tops. No one would have to know.

"Look after yourselves, all right?" he said to the racks of machines.

He took a deep breath and slowly backed out of the station, closing the door behind him. He paused, listening, and then went out to the shed and fetched Houlihan, his noble steed. Once more, he clicked on his bicycle's radio, calling upon Radio Skala's infusion of Old World pluck to show him the way forward. The Guča trumpets and the polyrhythmic hither-thwack of the tapan drum blasted forth from the megaphone, weaving its mournful cocoon. Radar wheeled onto the main road and began pedaling fast and easy, bobbing his head to the beat, feeling his skin prickle and ping with the music.

The simple act of transporting his body from here to there did much to calm him. He regained some of his much-needed confidence. Yes, he, Radar Radmanovic, was a conqueror of hearts. *Un conquistador!* Ana Cristina was Mexican, or at least her estranged father was Mexican and still lived there, in a town called San Cristóbal, which was very beautiful, apparently. This was one of the first things he learned when he had finally worked up the courage to engage her in conversation at the checkout till. ("It's beautiful there," she had said while ringing him up. "But I can't take his shit no more.") Many of their first conversations had occurred like this, in the fragile space between the checkout beeps.

All time was created equal, he knew, but this time between the beeps had been strange and long and wild time, around which the rest of his day had revolved. *Oh, Ana! Ana Cristina! Do not abandon me now!*

When the automatic doors to the A&P Express hushed open and the sweet, stiff hand of air-conditioning slapped him across the jaw, Radar caught his breath and stopped. There she was. In checkout lane number 2. Wearing those same hoop earrings, painfully beautiful as usual. He watched as she risped off a receipt and handed it to an elderly man in a fedora. Radar's carefully constructed Houlihan-chutzpah collapsed like a house of cards. The universe could never support such an imbalanced union between him and her. He almost turned around and left right then and there. He would've, too, if not for the telling taste of bitter lemon on the back of his tongue.

Oh, crap. He knew exactly what would happen next: a fine-toothed gear fell out of the compartment in his heart and bounced against his ribs, zippering past his groin, down the hollow tube of his leg, before finally settling into the little microphone of his toe. The electric system in his body fluttered, he was enveloped in that familiar, cinnamon waft of doom, and then everything fell away. His vision skittered and finally blinked off. There was only his underwater breath, loud and echoing in the tunnel of his ears. The faraway world floated silently just beyond the cocoon of his perception. A hummingbird against his neck. He waited. And then: that peppery feeling of awakening. The wires sparkling with current. His wrists on fire. His vision whooshing in from the edges. He was back.

A petit mal seizure. Induced by stress or breakdancing or certain dog-whistle frequencies. More and more frequent now that he had stopped taking his meds. After ten years, he had finally decided that the meds essentially took the *he* out of *him*. He had begun to miss himself, flawed as he was. According to his parents, he had been blessed with epilepsy since birth, one of the many symptoms of his very particular affliction—an affliction so particular that the doctors had named it for him: Radar's syndrome. Radar had spent his whole life seesawing between pride and shame for this personalized diagnosis, which he tempered by referring to it only as *"me problems,"* usually in an embarrassing faux Jamaican accent, usually in the dying swoon of the evening, and usually when he was alone, which was usually always.

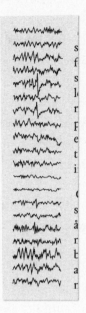

Fig. 3.1. "Petit mal #7"
From Wolcott, D., and Henry, H., *Epilepsy & Seizures,* vol. 3,
as cited in Røed-Larsen, P., *Spesielle Partikler,* p. 884

The diagnosis did bring up a seemingly larger philosophical question: How many medical cases were required for a condition to be officially deemed *a syndrome*? If there had been only one incidence of the disorder in the history of the universe, was it still worthy of the title? Or was it just another example of extraordinarily bad luck? The underlying assumption behind the doctor's diagnosis must've been that his luck would eventually be shared by others, that no experience could *possibly* be that unique, so we might as well go ahead and call it a syndrome now, because somewhere down the line there was going to be another poor sucker with exactly this same set of symptoms: the epilepsy; the sallow pallor; the comprehensive alopecia (save his patch—*"me patch!"*); the partial left-side paralysis; the irregular dark splotches on nipple, calf, and groin; the complete lack of social proficiency.

Meanwhile, Radar had been standing still long enough that the automatic doors decided he was no longer human, or, at the very least, no longer relevant, a nonmoving object that could safely be closed upon. And so they closed, only to squawk open in protest as they crashed against his backpack, the impact dislodging Radar's mesh trucker's hat, which was spray-painted with his call sign, K2RAD, in bright red, "urbanized" lettering. He had just purchased this very cool personalized accoutrement from a graffiti artist on the street in Newark. At the time, he remembered wondering why everyone did not transform their lives using one of these hats, which so effortlessly announced to the world one's *hipness totale*.

The automatic doors shuddered in horror as they slowly returned to their open position, watching him.

Radar quickly bent down to fetch his fallen cap. He glanced up to see if Ana Cristina had noticed his baldness. She had not. She was still busy with Fedora Man.

"Sorry," he muttered to the doors. He said this to be nice, though he knew it was their fault. They lacked vision, flexibility, long-term goals.

One of the checkout women turned and stared at Radar standing in the doorway.

"Your doors," he said nervously, trying to dispel the growing disquietude of the situation. He corrected the bill of his hat.

The checkout woman, who he believed was named Lydia, though he had never sought out her services, yelled, "You in, you out? We lose the cool when you stand there."

"I'm in," he said and took a step forward.

But once he was in, he found himself wondering what he should do. He couldn't just march right up to Ana Cristina and ask her if she still wanted to be his girlfriend. He had to act casual. He needed to fetch some product so he had an excuse to approach the checkout counter. He picked up one of the yellow shopping baskets and began to wander the aisles. *What should he get?* A seemingly simple question that suddenly felt freighted with significance. Small flecks of panic began to run up and down his legs. He started to sweat into his crocodile boots. His limp grew more pronounced. He needed to pick something. *Anything.* In an act of desperation, he grabbed a jar of guacamole, only to realize once he was already in line that this was a stupid thing to purchase on its own.

Guacamole needed a delivery device, like tortilla chips or a piece of celery. But now it was too late. He was already in Ana Cristina's line. There was no turning back.

"I can take you over here," said Lydia. Checkout lane number 1 was empty.

Radar shook his head.

"I can take you here," she said again, louder this time, thinking that perhaps he had not heard her. Clearly Lydia did not know that he and Ana Cristina were not just commercial acquaintances. Her ignorance made him even more paranoid: clearly Ana Cristina had kept their relationship secret from her co-workers. Clearly she was embarrassed about him.

Radar panicked. He could feel the heat in his face. "My knee," he said to Lydia, pointing. "My knee is broken." Which, in a way, was true.

Lydia looked at him strangely, but then a shopper coming from the deli section approached her till and the crisis was narrowly averted.

When it was finally his turn to check out with Ana Cristina, he became flustered again. How on earth was he going to do this? He set his yellow basket on the floor next to the counter.

"Hi," he said, more to his basket than to her.

"Hi," she said.

He couldn't properly read her tone, so he stole a glance at her. She was wearing the dark lipstick again. It covered only the edge of her lips; on the inner part, there was a softer shade of burnt sienna, and the duotone reminded Radar of the interior pattern of his mother's still-operational 1976 Oldsmobile Omega, an image that should have dispelled the sexiness of her lips but somehow only enhanced it.

Briefly stunned by her chromatic splendor, he bent down and picked up the jar of guacamole from his basket. The basket was covered in a thin brown film. This was the subtle, pernicious ooze of a thousand shoppers' products—wet bags of cabbage and salami cold cuts and leaky containers of mayonnaise. *I cannot be that ooze,* he thought. *I must be the guacamole and not the ooze.*

He came up, guacamole in hand, and said, "I am the guacamole!"

Idiot!

Ana Cristina froze, confused.

"I mean . . ." He tried to recover. "I mean, it was fun last night."

"Yeah," she laughed nervously. "You were sweet."

"I was?"

"Yeah. I was gonna call you when I got off. Are you free tonight?"

Radar was so stunned by this reply that he felt his entire body go limp and realized too late that the guacamole had slipped from his grasp. He watched in horror as it rolled along the very edge of the counter in an excruciatingly slow display of physics and then fell and fell and fell until it shattered onto the floor in an octopus splatter of tomato chunks and processed avocado solution.

Radar and Ana Cristina both stared as the puddle slowly grew before their eyes. A green paradise island of guacamole.

"I'm sorry," said Radar. "I'm so, so sorry." He could not bear to look at her, so he instead fixed his gaze on the rack of Dentyne Ice gum, which caused a strange sensory dissonance: the promise of spearmint paired with the vulgar wafts of salsa fresca and avocado preservatives.

"It's okay," he heard her say. "It's no problem."

He stole another quick glance at her and saw that she was not in fact angry, but still smiling, almost laughing, as she thumbed at the microphone above the register. "Javi, Enchanted Valley Light Guacamole spill, checkout 2." He was amazed at the specificity of her announcement, the natural roll of the word *guacamole* off her tongue.

"Do you want to get another one?" she asked.

"Another what?"

"Another guacamole?" There it was again. He could listen to her say that word all day.

"Not really," he said. "You really still like me? Even after everything?"

"Of course," she said. "Why would I not like you?"

"I don't know," he said. "Because?"

"What is there not to like?"

"Oh, plenty, believe me."

"You're like the nicest boy I ever met."

"I am?" he said.

"Cutest *and* nicest." She hesitated, wiping back a stray hair. "Do you want to meet my mama? She's cooking tonight."

"Your mama?" His heart soared.

Javier showed up with a mop and bucket. Fifteen-year-old skinny boy Javier. The wolf. He who did not rid the baskets of their ooze. He who carefully launched his coagulate hair heavenward with a pound of toxic gel, he who always kept a white shirt tucked into the back pocket of his shorts, as if he were ready to change at any moment and enter a televised street fight. When had the bad blood started between them, really? Radar had never said a word to Javier, and yet he sensed evil in those bony, slumped shoulders. Maybe he was being unfair. Maybe he was being racist. Maybe Javier was a nice kid. Maybe Javier was in love with Ana Cristina.

And now Javier was mopping at the spill, and Ana Cristina was saying something to him in Spanish, and Radar was straining to pick up its meaning. Javi sighed and propped the mop against Radar and left the scene. He was now pinned to the rack of Dentyne by the mop handle.

"Do you want me to clean it up?" he asked.

Ana Cristina shook her head. "No, no. I told him to get a paper towel. For the glass," she said. "So, can you come tonight? No pressure or anything, but she asks about you all the time, and I was like, *Okay, mama, all right already, you can meet him, jeez.* She's going to cook her empanadas. They're really good."

"Empanadas?" he said. *Asks about me all the time?* "I would love to. Nothing would make me happier."

She smiled and then leaned across the conveyor belt and took his hand, just for a second, but her touch sent such a strong electrical current through his body that he thought he might have another seizure.

Javier returned, paper towel in hand. He scowled at Radar as he got down on all fours and began picking up the pieces of glass.

Radar. *Un conquistador.* A man among men.

Do it because you must.

He swept the mop handle aside and carefully sidestepped around the guacamole explosion.

"Good day, Javier. Sorry about the guaca*ma*-ole," said Radar, completely butchering the Spanish accent.

Javier looked up and smirked at him, but Radar did not mind the smirk, nor anything at all, really, for he felt as if he were walking on air.

"And I will call you later," he said to Ana Cristina, loud enough so that he could be sure Javier heard it. "About the *empanadas*."

Then he turned around in slow motion, imagining that he was in a movie with a band of Guča trumpeters serenading his exit.

But he had not gone more than two steps before he became fearful that this whole scene had not really happened, that he had imagined it all, and that he was actually still standing in the doorway experiencing another one of his little deaths.

As Per Røed-Larsen notes in his introduction to *Spesielle Partikler,* the diligent historian often "struggles to work out the details of the hazy *then* when all we have is its faint, dying echoes in the muddled *now*" (28). How, then, to accurately capture all the twists and turns of young Radar's life when the public record offers us such scant insight into the mechanics of our character's psyche? There are really only a handful of sources we can turn to after the relative supernova of his birth, a few specks of data rather than a rich portrait of a New Jersey juvenescence, and, lest we wade into total conjecture, we must make do with what we have.

After Dr. Fitzgerald's article in the *Journal of Investigative Dermatology,* there were no more professional writeups concerning Radar—a search for "Radar's syndrome" in the medical databases turns up a giant, singular blank. His haphazard medical file does indicate a long history of epilepsy, dating back to a first episode at age four, with several major hospitalizations following his grand mal seizures, approximately once every four or five years. The doctors' notes for these hospitalizations are cursory, noting "left-centered asymmetric claudication," "near alopecia totalis," and a "jaundiced xanthoderma," though from the lack of follow-up on these slightly disturbing observations, it seems clear that Radar was not under the care of any single primary pediatrician, but rather a revolving cast of disparate emergency room doctors, who had neither the time nor the inclination to assemble a working medical history. At age twenty-three, after a particularly vicious grand mal in which Radar almost bit his tongue in half, he did have an MRI at St. Elizabeth's, the results of which showed some "abnormal dark spots" on his temporal lobe, the part of the brain concerned with, among other things, temporal perception, spatial organization, and object recognition. Following this MRI, it appears he began taking a prescription for Zarontin (ethosuximide), an anticonvulsant, for a period of approximately ten years, though this prescription ended with no follow-up medications prescribed.

Beyond this, there is only a cluster of peripheral sources, which, when viewed in sequence, offers the briefest of glimpses into a restless teenager testing the limits of his great, strange electromagnetic gift.

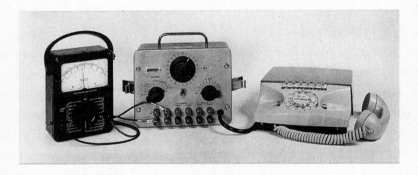

Fig. 3.2. "Blue Box from Modified Western Electric Test Equipment"
From R. Radmanovic's NJ Science Fair Project, 1988 (disqualified)

Exhibit A:

During the summer of 1990, the New Jersey Bell pay phone on the corner of Midland Avenue and Forest Street was the target of repeated "phreak attacks," whereby more than two hundred free long-distance calls were made over the course of three months. The pay phone was eventually removed. "Phone phreaking"—the practice of exploiting the telephone system via unauthorized means—was invented in 1957 by Joe Engressia Jr., a.k.a. "Joybubbles," a seven-year-old blind boy with perfect pitch who discovered that when he whistled a 2,600-Hz tone into the phone, the call would temporarily disconnect and then search for a new trunk line, allowing him to make another connection to any number in the world, completely free of charge. Joe also figured out how to dial a number entirely by whistling—in essence, he had taught himself how to speak a rudimentary form of "telephone." Based on Engressia's breakthrough and several technical documents inadvertently leaked by Bell Systems, subsequent phreaks in the 1960s and '70s developed and refined a device called the "blue box," which utilized the 2,600-Hz trunk switch tone to quickly and easily reroute calls from one line to another.

In the case of the Midland Avenue pay phone, calls were made to nearly every corner of the globe, including New Zealand, Norway, France, Thailand, Kenya, Brazil, and Ascension Island, in the middle of the Atlantic. Numerous "reverse link-ups" were also placed from this phone, in which the system was manipulated so that two distant pay phones would call each other, ringing continuously until a bystander on the street picked up the phone and found himself or herself talking to an equally confused citizen on a completely different continent. Officer Burberry, the author of the Kearny Police report on the incident, writes that "[the] perp dialed [a] 1-800 number repeatedly using [a] so-called 'blue box' to switch to [a] different number, e.g. in Texas." As if Texas were as far as Officer Burberry could imagine. What Officer Burberry did not mention was that a traditional phone phreak's blue box no longer worked on the New Jersey Bell system in 1990. In the Midland Avenue case, the perpetrator must have been using either a highly sophisticated terminal device or—in the tradition of Joybubbles— some other unprecedented means to communicate with the vast inner workings of the telephone network. The case would remain unsolved, and though the phone itself was removed, the phone booth remained, becoming a kind of obscure mecca for certain members of the phone phreaking scene.

Exhibit B:

On the evening of June 17, 1990, approximately seventy-eight separate car alarms were set off, which led Officer Burberry (who was not having a good summer) to conclude that "an individual or group of perps" was going around "disrupt[ing] or tamper[ing] with the vehicles' anty-theft [*sic*] devices." Yet none of the vehicles in question were found to have any damage or exhibited any signs of tampering. Stranger still, the alarms themselves could not be turned off by normal means. Mechanics were required to physically disconnect the alarms from the batteries in order to quiet the cacophony of sirens that had begun to drive Kearny residents into hysterics. It was as if the alarms had been instructed to simply wail of their own accord. It is unclear whether Officer Burberry and his team (Johnson, Altez, et al.) connected this incident with the ongoing investigation of the Midland Avenue phone phreak case. A simple map, however, might have provided them with valuable evidence: if they had merely traced the route of these car alarm incidences, they might have noticed that the path of aural carnage forms a slightly deflated horseshoe beginning and ending at the Forest Street block between Midland and Oakwood Avenues, adjacent to the phreaked pay phone and also the location of the Radmanovic residence.

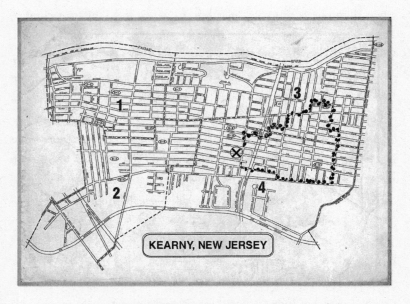

Fig. 3.3. Car Alarm Incidents in Kearny, N.J. June 17, 1990
From Radmanovic, R., *I Am Radar,* p. 288

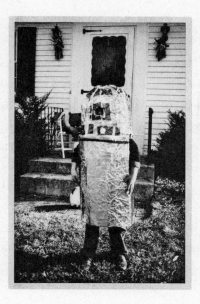

Fig. 3.4. "R2-D2, Halloween, 1988"
Pasted into R. Radmanovic's *Little Rule Book of Life*

Exhibit C:

In the Kearny High School faculty meeting minutes dated November 1, 1990, chemistry teacher Emily Gagnon relates an incident of "bullying" that took place at the school on Halloween. The details are hard to fully make out from the meeting's rather perfunctory notes, but it appears that sophomore Radar Radmanovic, dressed "again" in a tinfoil R2-D2 costume, was "found by a member of [the] janitorial staff" trapped in a "dumpster behind [the] gymnasium." When pressed for details, Mr. Radmanovic would not elaborate on how he had gotten there. The incident led to a larger discussion at the meeting about bullying at the school, with a host of faculty members chiming in on the perceived severity of the problem. Perhaps most troubling was Ms. Gagnon's comment, recorded in the minutes, that this was "not [the] first time [we've found] Radar in [the] dumpster."

Exhibit D:

On the afternoon of December 5, 1990, a varsity basketball game inside the Kearny High School gymnasium was interrupted when both teams and the majority of the three dozen spectators experienced what was described in the police report as "cramping" and "diarrhea-like symptoms." This turns out to be polite language for what was in essence a mass crapping of the pants. A barrage of ambulances and even a P3 CDC hazmat team from Long Island were summoned, and rumors of a "killer virus" whipped through the community like wildfire, but doctors could find nothing wrong with the victims beyond a lasting case of public humiliation and a newfound appreciation for the daily operations of the lower intestine. Curiously, none of the city's tabloids carried the story, ignoring a golden

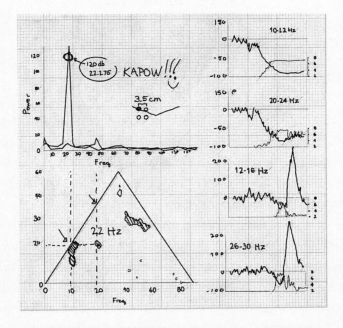

Fig. 3.5. Sample Tests, KHS Gymnasium PA System (March 1990)
From *Notebook of R. Radmanovic*

opportunity for near-infinite scatological punnage. Only WWOR-TV, a local outfit broadcasting from Secaucus, mentioned the incident, briefly, during its evening newscast—and even they neglected to dispatch an on-scene reporter. Neither they nor anyone else, apparently, looked into the possibility of the so-called infrasonic "brown note," rumored to be somewhere around 22.275 Hz, effective when broadcast at levels of at least 120 decibels. The elusive brown note was purportedly experimented with by the French during World War II and is currently used by certain elite Japanese SWAT teams, although there has never been any official documentation of its effective implementation. Nor did anyone bother to interview Radar Radmanovic, the installer and student operator of Kearny High School's highly sophisticated (some might say excessive) public address system, who also happened to be working the scoreboard for the game that afternoon.

Exhibit E:

Finally, there is the now mostly forgotten "Vladi Affair" from December of that same year. Those living in New York City at the time may remember that for a series of three consecutive days right in the middle of the Christmas rush, the newly installed Sony Trini-lite JumboTron at One Times Square displayed a strange series of interference patterns—including clips from *3-2-1 Contact* and various Run-D.M.C. music videos, but most famously a grainy feed of a mildly beleaguered goldfish with a black spot on its forehead, swimming in circles to Shostakovich's Symphony No. 7 ("Leningrad"), which played from a hidden speaker that would take the authorities a day and a half to locate. The iconic image of this fish limping to moribund Soviet nostalgia persisted for almost seventy-two hours, evading the best efforts of the JumboTron's engineers to correct the malfunction. A December 17 New York *Daily News* article surmised that some "hacker" (an early use of the term, at least for the *Daily News*) had managed to create an "off-site remote control" and taken command of the television, despite the fact that the screen was not actually connected to any VHF or cable receiver system but instead received its data from prerecorded LP-size "optical discs." The *Daily News* noted that the goldfish had already caused "several car accidents" and that the NYPD, Port Authority, and the FBI were all investigating the crime. On the fourth day, the giant screen at the junction of Broadway and Seventh Avenue was unplugged, an act that met with some popular outcry, as the goldfish—by this point nicknamed "Vladi" by a popular on-air personality—had gained a cultish following among commuters and tourists alike, perhaps buoyed by the recent dramatic fall of Communism. When the JumboTron was finally turned on again two days later, the interference patterns had ceased and did not resume again, though it is debatable whether this was because the JumboTron's engineers had discovered a way to block the incoming transmissions or whether "the hacker" had ceased his malicious activity. Regardless, the crime remained unsolved. Years later, you could still find certain street kiosks selling T-shirts of the goldfish's pixelated image, with the caption VLADI LIVES! printed in some heavy-handed pseudo Soviet font.

Fig. 3.6. "Something's Fishy on Times Sq. Jumbo TV"
From New York *Daily News,* Dec. 17, 1990

Of course, if the authorities had checked the attendance sheet for Kearny High School, they would have discovered that Radar Radmanovic had been absent from school on the three consecutive days of the JumboTron's disruption. There also exists a photograph of Radar sitting at his home-brewed ham radio station in his bedroom, giant ear cans on his head, delivering an enthusiastic thumbs-up to the camera. In the background, perched precariously on a transceiver, a mildly beleaguered goldfish is clearly visible. The goldfish matches—in demeanor and appearance, including the single black spot—the famous Vladi, though on the back of the photograph Radar has written R.I.P. DOBROFISH, suggesting that the fish was named for Dobroslav Radmanović, the man responsible for bringing their family to the New World before collapsing in a grocery store checkout line, ground chuck in hand.

Other items from the R. Radmanovic file seem important to highlight: Radar graduated from Rutgers, although, due to an apparent computer glitch, he actually graduated twice (if on paper only), with a dual degree in religious studies and electrical engineering, summa cum laude each time, making him the most decorated undergraduate in the history of that school. Such illustrious qualifications landed him a job directly out of college as the WCCA Belleville Transmission Site assistant manager of operations. Now, after thirteen years of exemplary work, he was head engineer of transmission. During that time he had been named employee of the month fourteen times for the Green Channel Network, a midsize regional media conglomerate that spanned the tri-state area as well as parts of western Massachusetts. No other employee had received the honor more than twice. And yet, once he had become master of the transmission site, Radar had not moved up in the corporate hierarchy, despite repeated offers of upper-level management positions. Eventually, the GCN executives had simply stopped trying. Apparently their savant engineer preferred to stay where he was, in the swamps, conjuring signal.

The employee-of-the-month awards were not undeserved. In truth, he probably should have won the accolade every month, but then, this would not have been good for company morale. Radar was that good. A bona fide professional. No—what was the step above bona fide professional? A natural. *A motherfucking sorcerer.* He would glide his hands across the stacks of panels, checking the levels, whispering a knob here or there, often with eyes closed, adjusting the modulators and repeaters and phase monitors as if he were playing a perfectly sculpted contrapuntal fugue. In that precise moment of propagation and frequency, amplitude and scissor-slip wattage, he was the Buddha himself sitting beneath the electrical bodhi tree.

Radar's unique spiritual connection to the machines also made it difficult to find another human who enjoyed working with him in that swampland radio outpost. He had gone through no fewer than twenty-one partners in his thirteen years, from poor old Ernie Bailey to his current co-workers, Gary "Knock Yourself Out" Balkin and Moses "Mo' Money" Rodriguez. The managers seemed willing to accept this revolving door of placeholders in order to keep around an employee who looked mostly humanoid but functioned more like an extension of their radio transmission system. On his watch, *they had never lost signal.* Not once. How this was possible, the station execs in Manhattan could not say. Every station lost signal—it was the way of the world, of the incoherent spectrum, of the random grumblings of electrons, but Radar was always able to anticipate these electromagnetic hiccups and swivel the backup systems accordingly. It was as if he could look down the barrel of time and see into the future. Even his seizures at the workplace, of which there had been several, had never disrupted his craftsmanship. He would wake up on the floor of the transmission site, sweating and sore, and the fearful machines would be calling to him, wondering how he was doing. They had looked after themselves while he had shifted into another plane. They had felt his contractions, felt the throbbing agony of his synapses, but they had not faltered in his absence. They had his back. They would always have his back.

PEDALING BACK to the transmission site after his near miracle encounter at the A&P Express, Radar was initially ecstatic over Ana Cristina's invitation, but as the sulfuric breeze from the swamps blew against his face, a little sandcastle of belief begin to melt inside his chest. There was nothing quite like imagining one's life through the eyes of another to effectively initiate an irreversible, existential nosedive.

Radar sat in the station cockpit, surrounded by his instruments, and tried to figure out exactly why he felt so depressed. Ana Cristina had invited him to meet her mother! To eat empanadas! Surely this was a good sign. Surely the fact that she was offering to introduce him to kith and kin meant she wanted to keep him around. And that gesture, that touching of his hand at her workplace, no less, meant she was comfortable enough for their relationship to be semi-public, for Lydia and Javier to know of their shared *amour*. And yet, what did he have to share, really? When Ana Cristina's mother peered at him over a plate of steaming empanadas and asked him what he had done with his life, whether he was happy with who he had become, whether he was ready to share this happiness with her daughter, what could he possibly say?

For the first time in his life, he realized this: he had been following a path that was not his. He was living the life of another man. It could be said without exaggeration that he was perhaps the best radio engineer in the world, but his heart was just not in it. He did not love what he did. He did it only because he could. And this, he realized, was no reason at all.

Do it because you must.

He remembered a late-summer excursion to Manhattan the previous year in which he had observed an inverted *petite chinoise* acrobat spinning plates on a street corner in the Lower East Side. It had been appallingly humid out, but the woman—bedecked in a gleaming white rhinestone costume that appeared out of place against the buttery grunge of the summer sidewalk—was so focused on her revolving tableware that it was as if her body had melted away into the heat, or at least her body could not be separated from the task at hand. Radar sensed that the ring of people who had stopped to watch were doing so not because of her enthralling acrobatics (though her acrobatics *were* enthralling), but because of their collective awareness that this woman, in that moment, could only be doing *exactly what she was doing*. The laws of the universe had determined it. Transfixed, Radar had waited in line to dump all of his change onto a plate, a plate that had struck him as painfully ordinary and dull, lying so still on the ground. Afterwards he had swerved back into the traffic of humanity, filled with a strange mixture of exhilaration and dread that he would never be able to achieve the elemental beingness of that plate spinner.

Seated in his station chair now, recalling the image of those gleaming, whirling plates, Radar picked up a pen and slowly started to trace a little oblong
circle onto a legal notepad. With each added revolution, the circle became more
and more perfectly circular, all those wonky, globular loops adding up to something whole and proportional and right, and this summation comforted him.

Rule #49: Many imperfections can and may lead to perfection.

Soon the flimsy yellow paper grew thick with ink and finally tore open, so
that now he was drawing circles on the page beneath. If he drew enough circles,
maybe he could burrow right through the earth into its molten center and then
through to the other side, into the V-necked alpine valleys of Kyrgyzstan. That
could be nice. Maybe he could start over again there. He could be a more perfect
version of himself.

Distracted by his existential malaise, he wandered into the engine room and
lay down next to the big, purring vacuum capacitors that expelled so much electromagnetic energy into the air that the temperature of your skin went up by
two degrees and began to tingle. This was the voltaic green room where the
radio signal huffed and puffed and readied itself for the great scream. The station's transmitters took the thinnest trickle of signal and blew it wide open,
turned it into a hundred-mile-wide fire hose, an explosion of invisible waves
licking the surface of the city, shooting through seawater and brickwork and
grocery bags and into the antennae of the thirsty radios, their transistors reshap-
ing the signal into a wiry, pulsing frequency that sent speakers quivering into
long streams of S&P numerals.

Radar lay on his back eating an apple and swinging a fluorescent light tube
through the air like a lightsaber. The tube lit up magically every time it swung
close to the huge, humming induction box.

Dim.

Now glowing.

The world, thick with current.

Dim.

Now glowing.

Like a heartbeat. He wanted to make Ana Cristina glow like this.

Radar sighed. He pulled himself off the ground and was just about to go check on control when it came. Usually, he had an inkling that a seizure was on its way as he was filled with a fleeting sensation akin to reverse déjà vu—a remembrance of things future—but this time he had only a whiff of lemony lilac in the back of his throat and not even a pretense of falling before he was already out, down this time—*really, really down.* As in: *kill the lights down.* Not a petit mal, but the full monty. Usually petits came and went, but sometimes they were a sign that a storm was on the horizon, and apparently this was the case today. His last thought was of the cruel misfortune of life: *Oh, why today of all days should I suffer such a fate? On this day of imminent empanada conquest? Please don't let me hurt myself too—*

He awoke in total darkness.

Every part of his body ached. For a moment he wondered if he was dead. But could death really be this painful? Once you got through the difficult part of dying, surely they should at least cut you some slack and make you comfortable? No, death was too simple a solution for his lot. He would live and he would suffer.

He tried to deduce his condition. From what he could tell, he was lying on his back, covered in what felt like a thin layer of sweat. He could also feel that his underwear was soaked through. A familiar, swiftly cooling sensation. When he rolled his tongue across the roof of his mouth, he tasted the metallic tang of blood.

He tried to sit up. His head pounded. The sound of crackling glass beneath him. Something wet and squishy against his hand. This, he realized, was the apple core. He reached out and felt blindly through the darkness, felt the cool perforations in the metal wall. He was still in the engine room. So he was definitely not dead. But . . . the lights were out. *Strange.* He wondered how long he had been in there. Was it nighttime? Surely someone would've found him by now. Where was Moses? He sat there in the darkness, listening. An absence. The great capacitors around him, normally so full of life, were cold and quiet.

He wiped the blood off his chin. *That's weird,* he thought, *because if the capacitors are quiet, then that means—*

Panicking, he stumbled to his feet, groping around in the dark for the door to control. He hit his head on a low ledge and then finally managed to locate the handle of the door, which he opened to find a darkened control room. A small window in the corner provided the only light. At least it was still daytime outside. But why were all the lights out? He stood, listening. The speakers, lifeless. Not even a hint of static. Nothing.

The signal! The radio signal is dead! The one thing he was supposed to be able to do in this world and he had failed at doing it.

He fell over himself trying to get to the stack, punching at the backup microwave channel to get it up and running, but he quickly found that none of the systems were online. The power. The power was out. He was disoriented, but he knew this shouldn't be happening. They had two fancy backup generators that should've automatically kicked on at this point. In the dimness, he stumbled toward the generator room, his vision wobbling dangerously before he leaned over a trash can and vomited up the apple and the remnants of the Marmite toast.

The generator room was also dark. The twin Generacs simply lying there. He tried to manually start them with a pull cord, but, try as he might, he could not get them to catch. He bent over, panting. The oddest sensation of stillness. He placed his hand against their circuitry, closed his eyes. It was the same feeling he had had in the engine room. An utter absence.

He wandered back into the darkened control room and picked up the phone. There was no dial tone. He clicked the hook switch several times, but the line was dead. *Damn.* He had no way of letting the station in Manhattan know what was going on. Maybe his mother was right: he should get a cell phone. For emergencies like these.

He looked at his calculator watch. The screen was blank. He squeezed and re-squeezed the mode button, to no avail. Had the watch just run out of batteries? This would be an amazing coincidence. He looked up at the clock on the wall. Its second hand was motionless, the time frozen at 2:44. The exit sign was also dark.

What the hell was going on? And why had everything stopped working—him included—at exactly the same moment?

He felt his way over to the bathroom and, out of habit, flicked on the light switch. Nothing happened. So he was forced to peel off his urine-soaked jeans in the darkness, tripping over the toilet as he hopped up and down on one foot. He fumbled for the faucet and, to his relief, found this working as usual. *Thank God.* Civilization had not completely disappeared. Using a damp paper towel, he awkwardly wiped at his groin. He changed into the extra pair of sweatpants he kept in his cubby in case of just such an accident, rinsed out his mouth, and gargled some of that horrific-familiar yellow mouthwash. The alcohol stung where he had bitten into his tongue.

Through the dimness, he peered at himself in the mirror. He could just make out the contours of his outline. It was faint, but it was an outline nonetheless. He was still Radar.

He went back into the control room, examining the racks and racks of state-of-the art equipment. Everything completely dead. He touched the cold chassis of a phase modulator, then leaned in and smelled its circuits. No semblance of signal. Minutes earlier, this stack had been brimming with carefully choreographed current. But now? A wasteland.

He was suddenly reminded of the last blackout, in 2003. By coincidence, he had also suffered a grand mal then, just before the power went out. He had been riding his bike when he smelled a scent of burning lilacs and was taken by that feeling of tumbling back into himself. He had just managed to pull over to the side of the road when he felt himself actually tumbling over his bike and into the reeds. He woke up covered in mud, bleeding from a crescent gash in his arm. A wary duck was eyeing him from a little spit of marsh water just beyond. He nodded to the bird, conspiratorially, as if what had just transpired had all been on purpose. The duck had nodded back.

That night, when the lights had not come back on, Radar had wandered the darkened streets alone, pining for lost current. As New Jerseyans partied around him, grilling their defrosting meats and retiring to make blackout babies, he had communed with utility poles, pressed palms to traffic lights, searching for any errant scraps of wattage. *The grid, the grid.* How he missed the grid. He vowed never again to take that cushion of electricity for granted. Thereafter, he carried a AAA Energizer in his fanny pack as a kind of talisman against the darkness.

Now, sitting alone in the dim control room, filled with a growing feeling of helplessness, he excavated the battery from its pouch and began rolling the cylinder between his palms, warming the metal.

What should he do? He was a radio engineer with no radio frequency to engineer. He idly turned on the portable shortwave that he kept on his desk but found that this, too, was dead.

How could everything have gone dead at once?

Battery in hand, he stepped outside, blinking in the bright sunlight. At least there was still that. It was a beautiful summer day, if only a touch humid—the kind of day that makes you forget the taste of all other days. The sky was a sheet of uninterrupted blue, infinite and resilient and altogether unaware of the dark, broken machines that lurked indoors. He spotted a black plume of smoke rising from somewhere to the west, in Kearny. Such black-looking smoke could never be a good thing. The burning of that which should not burn.

Radar gingerly made his way out onto the creaky catwalk that led across the swamps to the base of the transmitters' twin antennae. The antennae soared above him, two latticed, triangular fingers pointed heavenward. He sensed their silence, the absence of signal emanating from their tips.

But their silence was not the only silence. From this vantage point, the Meadowlands was normally a humming palace of movement, of planes and trains and automobiles sliding through on their way from here to there. Yet the familiar river of sound from the turnpike was gone. He listened. Birds hummed and twittered across the swamps. No sound of freight. No burring upshift of tractor-trailers. From somewhere in the distance, he heard the call of a police siren. And then, overhead, the muffled *wup-wup* of a helicopter.

Something was very wrong. This was no ordinary blackout.

Beneath the sagging catwalk, the marsh water was muddy and thick, covered in some kind of plush, aromatic slime. An iced tea bottle floated, half-submerged, its label bleached pinkish white by the sun. Like the flesh of a made-up cadaver. At the end of the catwalk, he startled a great blue heron into flight. He could hear the bird's wings beat against the air as it circled him once, twice, before heading off east, across a calligraphy of islands.

There were only two scenarios that Radar could think of that would cause not just the electric grid to fail but all electronics to stop working instantaneously. Radar had written a paper in college on the first possibility: a huge coronal mass ejection (CME) from the sun, a solar flare so large that it could disrupt modern microprocessors. The last such major CME had occurred in 1859, when a series of solar flares precipitated an unprecedented geomagnetic solar storm, dubbed the Carrington Event, after British astronomer Richard Carrington, the first person to observe and describe the flares. The resulting storm caused havoc in telegraph systems throughout the world, disrupting messages and giving operators powerful electrical shocks. The aurora borealis was seen as far south as the Caribbean and was so bright that people could read newspapers by its light in the middle of the night.

There were all kinds of prediction models for what would happen to the modern-day electrical infrastructure in the event of a solar storm as massive as the Carrington Event—predictions that ranged from the vaguely inconvenient to the totally catastrophic. In truth, no one knew what would happen to a society so dependent upon the semiconductor if the sun unleashed its rage again. But there was just one problem with the solar flare explanation: they were currently in a low point of the eleven-year sunspot cycle, so it was even more highly unlikely that such a highly unlikely solar storm had occurred.

Which left the only other known explanation, a possibility so outrageous that Radar could barely comprehend it: a nuclear bomb had been detonated above the earth's atmosphere, and New York had just experienced the devastating effects of its electromagnetic pulse.

"Jesus," Radar said, his brain already making room for the impossible.

4

The world would be crippled. Food and water would instantly be in short supply, particularly around the metropolises, where on any given day, consumables kept on hand could support the populace for three days, maybe four, *tops*. An EMP was so devastating because it fried all electronic circuitry, and without electricity, the density of urban populations was a death sentence. Refrigeration and air conditioning would be gone. Water pumps gone. Communications gone. Most cars and trucks and planes and trains would be fried, too, as virtually every modern automobile depended on a microprocessor-driven computer system. *Everything* depended upon the microprocessor. He thought of Grandma Louise, stranded by herself in her little house in Trenton. Old people would be the first to go, along with the sick and the weak. *People like him . . .*

Radar closed his eyes.

Calm down. Maybe he was wrong about all this. Maybe something funky had gone down at the station. Some weird surge of current. Maybe no one else was affected. No need to panic just yet.

First things first. If there *had* been a massive EMP, he needed to make sure his family was okay. His mother was probably still at work. His father would be in his radio shack at home as usual, no doubt having a conniption at the mass death of all his electronics. He would find his mother, and together they would head home. *Yes.* This seemed like a sensible plan. One thing at a time. He thought of Ana Cristina in the A&P and wondered if she was safe. He would check on her later.

He left a note for Moses on the off chance he came into his shift as usual, though he was fairly sure this would not happen. He had the feeling that nothing would be as usual ever again. He locked up the station and went out into the heat of the day. Already, refrigerators would be warming—millions of pounds of food slowly spoiling. Entropy would eventually reign supreme. It was the beginning of the end.

He fetched Houlihan from the shed. Sadly, just as he had feared, when he tried to coax one of her transceivers to life, he found that her onboard electronics hadn't been spared.

"Rest in peace, Houlihan," he murmured, observing a moment of silence at the handlebars.

Then he gripped the pedal with his crocodile skin boot, took a deep breath, and headed out into a changed world.

On Belleville Turnpike, he quickly came upon a tractor-trailer stopped in the middle of the road. Its driver had opened the hood of the cab, but he now stood off at some distance, smoking and staring out across the swamps.

"You're the first person I seen come down here," the man said. He looked tired and unshaven. "I never even looked at this place before. All kindsa birds."

"Is your truck dead?"

"Everything's out. Radio doesn't work. CB. My cell phone won't even turn on." He held it up. "You know what's going on here?"

"I think it was an EMP."

"An EMP?"

"An electromagnetic pulse."

"Okay," the man said, scratching at his chin with his thumb. "How's that?"

Radar took a deep breath. "It's usually caused by a nuclear-powered bomb exploding above the atmosphere. Gamma rays from the blast hit atoms in the atmosphere, knocking out electrons, which causes a huge surge of energy directed toward the earth. It's called the Compton effect. The pulse instantly overloads circuits and fries anything with a semiconductor. Including your truck. Including your cell phone. Including just about anything."

The man nodded, absorbing this information with surprising calmness. Pulled at his cigarette. Squinted at the sky.

"So how come we still standing here if they nuked us?"

"An EMP bomb is detonated above the atmosphere. There's no nuclear fallout or physical damage from the blast. The primary weapon is the pulse. Depending on where it was, how many there were—that kind of thing—the whole country could be paralyzed."

He gestured at Radar's bicycle. "You're smart. At least that thing still works."

"The human body isn't affected by an EMP. At least, not directly."

"Not directly?"

"There was some study that said eighty percent of the population would die within six months of a massive nuclear EMP."

"Damn," the man said. "Okay."

"Sorry. I don't mean to scare you, but this could be really serious."

The man sighed, turning his phone over in his hand. "I'm guessing these things don't come back to life, then?"

"I'm afraid not."

"I'd like to call my wife. She's gonna be worried."

"I know what you mean. I'm trying to track down my parents."

They stood, watching as a pair of house sparrows spun above them. The man sucked on the last of his cigarette and threw the stub to the ground. The ember skipped and rolled across the pavement like a furious insect.

"So how come I ain't never even heard about this EMP?" the man said. "Seems kind of important to keep the citizens informed of that kinda thing."

"The government's report on an EMP attack came out the same day as the 9/11 Commission's report."

"Bad timing," the man said, shaking his head. "You know, my niece was born on 9/11. Sweetest little thing. She still doesn't know."

RADAR PASSED three more cars stalled in the middle of the road, their drivers nowhere to be seen. A Jeep Cherokee had driven off into the reeds. Its front bumper was submerged in water. A man dressed in a Hawaiian T-shirt sat on the ground next to the Jeep, looking bewildered but otherwise unharmed.

Radar slowed. "You okay?" he asked. The man didn't seem to hear him.

Schuyler Avenue was a mess. As soon as the threat of vehicles had been removed, the street quickly became the domain of the pedestrian. It felt like a carnival, except that people were wandering around, appearing alternately elated and terrified. An old man with a fierce underbite was warbling out "Amazing Grace" on a street corner, the hat in front of him overflowing with coins. Nearby, a policeman argued animatedly with a group of construction workers who were all holding their hard hats in their hands, as if they had stumbled into a funeral. Radar passed by the day care center and saw the children busy with their games in the playground, blissfully unaware as their teachers stood whispering in conference by the seesaw.

He made his way across town, weaving around more stalled cars. Perhaps seasoned from the blackout seven years ago, a number of storeowners had already set up grills in the street, and the air was filled with the heavy scent of cooking meat. And yet the mood now was decidedly different from 2003. Coming on the heels of 9/11, that blackout had felt like a paradise of good vibes and bonhomie as soon as people found out that the grid had failed not because of any attack but rather as the result of an accident. *Imagine that: an accident!* Such happenstance sounded a citywide time-out to the regularly scheduled grind and gave everyone permission to become everyone else's best friend, lover, or a cappella partner singing early Guns N' Roses ballads. But now, as Radar bicycled down Schuyler Avenue, he sensed a degree of collective worry he had not witnessed since the day the towers fell. This feeling of foreboding appeared fundamentally connected to the categoric failure of people's smartphones, which many clutched tenderly, as if they were holding recently deceased pets. Others simply gazed at the sky.

Radar passed a restless crowd of people all staring in the same direction. He looked and saw that someone had smashed the front window of the liquor store. The pavement was covered in broken glass, and a few shattered bottles were strewn across the sidewalk. A policeman had his gun drawn and was standing over a man who was handcuffed and lying facedown on the pavement. Radar tried to catch a glimpse of the man's face. Was he a crazy person? Or was he just a normal guy who had suddenly panicked and gone for the booze? There was a strange tension in the air. The crowd took a couple of steps forward and the policeman, sensing this, waved his gun above his head.

"Get back!" he said. Then he said something into his walkie talkie, but Radar could plainly see that it was not working, that the policeman was just doing this for effect. Somehow this posturing made the situation all the more scary. Even the police had to pretend they knew what was going on.

Soon we will all be lying on the ground in handcuffs, thought Radar. *Either that or the police will be the ones on the ground.*

With a shiver, he started to wheel away from the scene, but then he felt a hand on his shoulder. He nearly jumped. He turned around and saw a ponytailed man in an oversize AC/DC shirt.

"You want some ice cream?" the man asked.

"Ice cream?" Radar repeated. The question seemed at once preposterous and perfectly appropriate. He saw now that the man was towing a wagon filled with large buckets of ice cream, their sides perspiring in the summer heat.

"Think about it, man. It might be your last chance."

"Uh, no thanks," said Radar. "I'm good."

This answer left the man looking incredibly distraught. Radar peeled away from the sad sight of the man tugging at his ice cream wagon and rode on. A couple of blocks later, he passed a car accident, slowing when he saw the swath of blood on the street.

"Can I help?" he asked a large woman in yellow. Her shirt was covered in bloodstains.

"They just took him to the hospital," she said. "Some guy's VW was still working, and they just put him in there and took him."

"Was he okay?" Radar asked.

"I don't know," she said. She brought a hand to her face. She was shaking. "I don't know."

"Are you okay?" he asked.

"Does your phone work?"

"I don't have a phone."

"I don't know what I'm going to do," she said. "I want to call my daughter, but I can't find a phone. I need to talk to her and tell her." She started to cry. "I just need to hear her voice."

"Everything's going to be fine," he said. His mother was right: sometimes a lie was better than the truth.

GIVEN THE CHAOS in the streets, he decided to take the back route to his mother's office. This was a bit of a misnomer, for in the Meadowlands, there really was no front route. It was a land of back doors and frontage roads and side entrances. Radar first cut through the rail yards, passing a group of engineers circled around an inert locomotive. Then he zipped over the old plank bridge to the dirt service road that followed beneath the turnpike. The highway remained astonishingly silent except for a series of helicopters hovering overhead. This gave him hope. If these helicopters still worked, then maybe all was not lost.

At the padlocked gates of the power substation, which was no doubt powerless, he sliced across two abandoned lots, swerving around a scattering of hypodermic needles and a few gulls working at a dead muskrat carcass. He slipped through a peel hole in the NJ Transit fence, across another set of rail tracks, past the rusted shell of a Chevy Nova that he had named Cassiopeia—in honor of glimpsing that celestial cluster from this very spot one miraculously dark night—until he emerged out onto a road that wound lazily through an organized skirmish of industrial parks. A few cars were stalled on the side of the road. People were sitting on the closely mowed grass in front of the corporate parking lots. A few were walking away from the buildings carrying all of their belongings. One man was pushing his office chair, stacked high with boxes, his tie undone. He looked almost content.

Ahead loomed the great gleaming silver behemoth of the International Flavor and Aroma Corporation. A perfect box of a building. All mirrors and secrets. It was here that 60 percent of all flavors and smells in America—including the never released Chanel No. 7, the irresistible saccharine mortar filling for Oreos, and the curiously embedded maple syrup taste in McGriddles—were designed, carefully tested, and then mass-produced for taste buds and quivering olfactory epithelia all across the universe. Whenever you popped open a bag, chances are that first whiff, that first familiar sizzle of brackish powder on the tongue, had been sourced from a vat of clear somewhere inside of this magic mirror box.

The parking lot in front of the building was full of people milling about. Someone had brought out a portable grill and was poking at a large amount of meat that gave off a fruity kind of smell. Several half-empty cartons of anonymous soda lay on the pavement nearby. More boxes of cookies, crackers, and various condiments were scattered around. These had to be IFAC's test products. In a blackout, they were deemed fair game for consumption.

A group of women in lab coats had set up a table and chairs and were busy playing what looked like gin rummy. Another woman, in a power suit, was sitting on the back of a pickup truck, crying hysterically as a shoeless, heavyset man tried to comfort her. The whole scene had the feeling of a birthday party for someone who was probably dying.

Radar stopped his bike.

"Have you seen Charlene?" he asked a black man picking at a paper plate full of sausage.

"Charlene?" he said. He pointed to an empty parking space. "She drove out of here."

"She *drove*?" Radar said. "What do you mean, *she drove*?"

"Yeah, it was the craziest thing. We're all stuck here, right, I can't even get my engine to turn over, and she comes out and starts up the Olds, no problem. We thought she'd been messing with our cars just to prove a point. It's kind of funny, when you think about it. We've been giving her grief about that car for years, but now who's laughing? I guess that's just how karma works. She drove five people home and now she's a hero. She said she was coming back for more."

The Olds! His mother still drove an oyster grey Oldsmobile Omega that she had acquired the year after his birth. It had upwards of 200,000 miles on it, but she refused to trade it in.

"Why change?" she would ask defensively whenever the topic of getting a new car came up. "Why are we always changing? Just because we can? When something works, let it be, I say." Another example of her coin-operated wisdom that sounded good at the time but was contradicted by the rest of her behavior.

The Olds. *Of course.* It was premodern circuitry.

"A mechanical ignition," said Radar. "Brilliant."

"What?"

"Her car," he said. "It doesn't rely on a computer to run it. That's why it survived the pulse."

"She probably knew something we didn't. I always said that about her. Woman knows something we all don't. And now she's the only one who can get the hell out of here."

"I'm not sure there's anywhere to go."

"Someone was saying not everywhere got hit. They say the city's fine. I mean, they don't have power, but their phones work. Not like here."

"The city didn't get hit?"

"That's what someone said."

How could that be? Did this mean there hadn't been a nuclear explosion?

"You said my mom was coming back here?" said Radar.

"Charlene? Wait, she's your *mom?*" The man squinted at him. "Oh, okay. Okay—I can see it now."

"We don't really look alike."

"Hey, my mom's half Japanese, but you look more Japanese than I do."

"I've gotten that before."

"People are crazy. They think all kinds of things," the man said. "So yeah, your mom *said* she was coming back here, but you know Charlene—she says a lot of things."

Radar debated waiting around. But no. He should check on Ana Cristina and his father. If Charlene had a working car, she'd be better off than all of them. Either that or she'd become a target. The thought made him shiver.

ON HIS WAY HOME, he stopped by the A&P. To his relief, he found no evidence of looting. No broken windows, no goods strewn about the parking lot. The place was locked up and dark inside. He put his face up against the now

helpless automatic doors and could just make out the darkened aisles of products. The pyramid of Pringles cans. The empty checkout counters. The place
where Ana Cristina normally stood. Was it only this morning that she had
asked him to come over for empanadas? It seemed like ages ago. A lifetime ago.
He wondered if she was still inside. He knocked. Waited. No answer. He tried
to pull open the automatic doors, but they wouldn't budge.

"Ana Cristina?" he called. He knocked.

A person appeared in the darkness. A man. Radar tensed, ready to rush in
and tackle him, to demand to know what he had done with his girlfriend, but
as the figure approached, Radar saw that it was only Javier.

Javier unlocked the doors and pushed them open.

"Hey," he said.

"Hi," said Radar.

"You want some?" Javier held up a bottle of water.

"Thanks," said Radar. The bottle was ice cold. "Is Ana Cristina around?"

"She's inside," said Javier.

"She is?" His heart soared. "She's okay?"

"She looks okay."

As they were speaking, a Montclair Police car rolled by with lights flashing.
The sight of a working police cruiser was startling, given all of the inert vehicles
Radar had just seen. The car pulled into the A&P parking lot.

One of the police officers leaned out his window. "What are you doing here?"

"I work here," said Javier.

"What's your name?"

"Javier Valdes." He pulled an apron from out of his back pocket and held it
up as evidence.

"And who are you?" the policeman asked Radar.

"He's okay," said Javier. "He's my boy."

"Well, be careful," said the policeman. "We got a lot of reports of looting. It
might start to get dangerous around here. I'd lock up and get home if I
were you."

As they drove off, Radar said, "Montclair must have electricity."

"Yeah, everyone does except us," Javier said.

"How do you know?"

Javier led him back into the store and locked the doors behind them. They walked through aisles of darkened products. Radar could hear the squeak of their shoes against the floor. Javier pointed to a radio sitting on one of the checkout counters. Next to the radio, sitting on the ground, holding her beloved cell phone, was Ana Cristina.

"Oh, hi," he said, a wave of relief sweeping over him. He kneeled down beside her. "Are you okay?"

Her face instantly changed when she saw him. She wrapped her arms around him and they hugged like this. A small kiss. She was crying.

"Are you okay?" he asked again.

"Yes," she nodded. "My phone's dead."

"We were just listening to the report," said Javier.

He reached over and turned on the radio. The sound of a voice. A miracle of a voice.

"How does it still work?" said Radar.

"I don't know. I found it in the walk-in," said Javier.

"The walk-in?"

Of course. The walk-in freezer had acted like a giant Faraday cage, shielding the radio from the pulse. Why hadn't he thought of doing this? A simple container of nonferrous metal. A shield. He could've saved everything. Houlihan. The station.

They stood listening to the voice on the radio which was speaking in an urgent, clipped tone.

A curfew has been declared for eight P.M. tonight in Essex, Bergen, and Hudson counties. Martial law and a state of emergency remain in effect. Boil advisory for affected areas. The governor's office is discussing a mandatory evacuation for the affected areas as soon as tomorrow morning. Until then, the governor asks that people limit travel to only essential activities. Senior citizens and those in need of assistance can relocate to several emergency shelters at the designated—

There was a pounding on the glass doors at the front of the store. Radar looked up in terror. He could see the silhouette of a man peering in at them. He was once so critical of those sliding doors, but now they were the only thing between them and what could be a panicking populace.

Javier clicked off the radio. "I'll go see," he said. He got up and walked toward the front.

"He's brave," said Radar.

"He's a kid," said Ana Cristina.

Javier had cracked open the doors and was speaking with the man outside.

"Where's Lydia?" Radar asked her.

"She freaked and took off," said Ana Cristina. "I should've done the same thing."

"You're a good employee."

"Yeah, right," she said. Then: "I hope my mama's okay."

"I bet she's okay."

"She gets nervous."

"We probably aren't doing empanadas tonight, are we?"

She reached out and took his hand. They sat like this, hand in hand, and Radar could've sat like that forever, as the world slowly crumbled around them.

Javier had closed the door and was going back to the drinks aisle. He fetched two large bottles of water and brought them back to the man.

"What do you think's going to happen?" whispered Ana Cristina.

"I don't know, but I don't want anything to happen to you," he said. "I'd do anything for you."

She smiled. "You're so cute."

"I should go check on my dad." He sighed. "He's probably flipping out right now."

"Can I meet him sometime?" she said. "I mean, if we get out of this?"

"Yeah," he said. "He's a little weird. Actually, just to warn you, both of my parents are kind of strange."

"They made you, didn't they? They can't be that bad."

He was caught again by her belief in him. She actually cared. This was something you could not fake.

"How should I get in touch with you?" he said.

"I don't know, text me?" she said. "I'm gonna try to get a new phone. I feel, like, *naked* without it." She flipped open the blank display.

"I will," he said. *I'll do the text with you.* "I think I'm gonna get my own cell phone, especially after this."

"You are? Wow. Welcome to the twenty-first century, Radar."

"I know, right?" he said. "See you soon?" Feeling bold, he leaned in and kissed her, and she kissed him back, and for a brief second, everything was right.

When he stood up, Javier was standing beside him.

"Oh, hi," Radar said self-consciously. "I was just going. Everything okay up there?"

"He wanted some water. He was going to pay like twenty bucks for it, but I just gave it to him," he said. He looked down at Ana Cristina. "Don't tell the boss, okay?"

Radar walked with Javier to the doorway.

"She likes you," said Javier.

"She does?" A crinkling in his chest. A great roaring in his ears.

Javier nodded. "She's like the nicest girl I know, so don't mess with her, okay?"

Radar realized that what he had seen before as a scowl was merely Javier's look of concentration. Scrutinizing a world that was not inclined to like him.

"You're a good man, Javier," he said, offering his hand. "I'm sorry for misjudging you."

"You and everyone," said Javier. "My mama said I'm a good book with a bad cover."

"Yeah," said Radar. "Me, too."

RADAR'S BLOCK WAS TYPICAL of the compressed suburbia you found in Kearny and its environs, where each house rested its chin on a cursory, heavily manicured front yard. On the Fourth of July, Halloween, and Christmas, these diminutive front plots became engulfed by blustery displays of patriotism or typhoons of cobwebs or animatronic Santas that rotated creepily at the waist.

Once upon a time, Kermin had been an eager subscriber to such pageantry.

"We are engaged in *uspon*. One day we will have in-ground pool," he used to say, blinking Rudolph lawn ornament in hand.

The *uspon*. The great climb. Kearny and all the contiguous suburbs just west of the Meadowlands were on a subtle incline such that its residents were forever aware of their precious bodily fluids slowly draining into the swamps. The unspoken immigrant objective was to claw one's way up to higher and higher elevations, until you eventually graduated to places like Montclair, Livingston, and Maplewood, places far away from the swamps, where one could live in landscaped, cul-de-sac bliss and dig a large, kidney-shaped hole for one's turquoise-tiled swimming pool. Sinking your pool belowground was the ultimate sign that you had joined the *buržoazija* and reached the end of the road, baby. A true *Amerikanac* could command the earth itself.

But while Kermin might have at one point subscribed to the *uspon*, dreaming of diving boards and paying pool men to suck the scum from his tiled oasis, somewhere along the line to *buržoasko blaženstvo*, probably right around the time when he shuttered his repair shop for good and hermited himself from the world, the dream had stalled for the Radmanovics, leaving them stuck halfway up the hill, their fluids still draining into the marshes. They weren't *in* the shit, but they weren't that far from it, either. Kermin had signaled his surrender by abandoning first the yearly Rudolph lawn display and then the front-yard maintenance altogether. Oh, if only Deda Dobroslav could have seen this sad display of stalled momentum, this lingering proximity to the shit. To have fought so long against the Communists, the fascists, his own people; to have lost and lost again; to have escaped and fled across a continent and an ocean; to have come so far, only to die in a checkout line and deposit his legacy on the lip of these swamps, a toxic vortex whose centripetal forces would prove too powerful for his offspring to overcome.

Yet seeing Forest Street now, urged into fellowship by the sudden disappearance of electricity, Radar could not help but feel a sense of pride in his home. Why would you want to live anywhere else? The street resembled a collegial, if slightly disorganized, family reunion. Kids squealed in the middle of the road, letting slapshots ricochet against overturned trash cans. Bella and Milos, bedecked in sun hats and matching Hawaiians, presided over the ceremonies from their customary lawn chairs; the Andratti boys tossed a pigskin to their brother in the wheelchair; Genevieve paced worriedly among her gargantuan sunflowers. Mr. Neimann, their next-door neighbor, with his Gorbachev-like wine stain, was waving furiously at a smoking grill with a spatula.

"Rib eye?" he called as Radar went past. "We were saving it for a special occasion, but this seems like as good a time as any."

"Maybe later," said Radar. "Have you seen my father?"

"I haven't seen him in weeks," he said. "I did hear some kind of bang out behind your house, next to that tower of his. Loud as hell. I was going to go see if everyone was all right back there, but then the lights went out and I forgot all about it."

"I'll go check it out," said Radar. "You heard any updates about the black-out?"

"Bob Deacon said they found out what made it happen."

"What was it?"

"He didn't know. He just said they figured it out." Mr. Neimann lifted the lid of the grill and stabbed at the meat. "You sure you don't want to take some of this home? It might cheer ol' Kermin up. I worry about that man sometimes."

"Thanks. I'll go ask him."

"God bless," Mr. Neimann said. "Anything you need, you let Jean and me know. We're here to help."

He made an awkward salute with his spatula. Radar returned the gesture with equal ineptitude.

THE OLDSMOBILE WAS NOT out front. His father's Buick was in the drive-way, but Charlene was nowhere to be seen. Radar suddenly felt responsible for her. What if a band of hooligans had commandeered her Olds and she'd been left to wander the streets among the panicked mobs? He feared she would not fare well.

"Kermin!" Radar yelled as he opened the front door, though he knew his father was probably not in the main house.

"Kermin!"

He was already walking back through the kitchen, opening the sliding glass doors to the backyard and his father's domain.

If undersize front yards were the superego, the mantle of decorum, a way to impress and reassure the viewing public that everything was under control, then backyards were the id, the palace of dreams, the impossible private oasis, a five-and-a-half-minute power ballad of whatever this homeowner would do if he or she had one thousand acres of good, clean American soil. The backyards of metro New Jersey contained patios and boat ports and decks and gardens and shrines and doghouses and water features and toolsheds and bocce pits and basketball courts and chicken coops and bonsai nurseries and ancient cannons and a pantheon of wonders that spring from the lavatic recesses of the soul.

In their own backyard, there was a path—carefully lit at all hours by theatrical clamshell lights—that led to the "playpen," as Charlene called it, the radio shack into which Kermin had retreated, full stop. The shack itself was not very remarkable except for its outsize appendage: a giant 119-foot antenna tower with multiple dipoles and rotatable reflectors mounted up and down its trunk. Even Radar, supposed champion of wave propagation and far-flung DXing, would have been the first to tell you that the tower was obscene and unnecessary, its soaring reticulation shivering upward like the twisted hand of a dying corpse. Here, writ large, was the conundrum of the amateur radioman's antenna: there were always more signals to catch, always that obscure 5.910-MHz radio wave from Papua New Guinea that could be corralled with just the right forty-five-foot parallel yagi. And so the antenna would grow, collecting its metallic progeny, until it threatened to collapse under its own excess. When he had installed it ten years earlier, the neighbors all served complaints and held town meetings and tried to sue Kermin, but he had done his homework: as long as the tower was under 120 feet and posed no immediate health risk, it was perfectly legal. *God bless America.*

On the day it was finally complete, when the cranes had left and the very last dump truck had hauled away its load, Kermin, bleeding freely from the forehead after being stabbed by some errant antenna spoke, came into the living room and announced: "We are now part of the world."

The opposite was true. One year later, he finally shuttered his shop, a business that had been failing steadily since its opening. It could now be freely said out in the open: the Sony Watchman™ had been a flop. Kermin, long blind to the writing on the wall, had been slow to adapt to new, successful technologies. For years, Ravna Gora Communications had languished as one of those sad, musty repair stores with no one coming or going save its hunchbacked owner, haunting his collection of junk like a ghost of spare parts past. After the shop's closure, with no real reason to leave the house, Kermin had hunkered down in his shack at the base of that monstrosity. He now left their property only to fetch an obscure part at J & A Specialties Electronics or to walk the banks of the Passaic River when a technical problem was particularly vexing.

The strange thing was that for all of their supposed overlap in interest and expertise, Kermin would never talk with Radar about his work in the shack. Radar had learned long ago to stop asking. He had also accepted that no matter his own qualifications, he would never gain entrance into that sacred ground. Such a prohibition might've seemed gratuitous once upon a time, but now it was just another fact of life. The closest he had come was several lingering peeks when the door was momentarily left ajar, before Kermin noticed the trespass and snapped the door shut like a lizard's mouth.

"This world is so big," he once said. "I just want one space that is only mine."

After the tower went up, Radar had asked if he could tap the mighty antenna to service his own modest ham station in his bedroom. Kermin had refused. Late one night, Radar tried to run a discreet coaxial line into the tower's box, but Kermin found it on his inspection rounds the next day and ripped up the cable.

"We must not let others do work *we* should be doing," Kermin said, dangling the offensive wire like a demised serpent.

"But I'm your son," said Radar.

"This is the lesson: find your own frequency," said Kermin. "If you want tower, buy tower, and place tower next to mine. But please don't cast signal shadow. And you might want to make less than ten meters high so the neighbor won't get feisty again."

Radar never did end up building his own tower.

ON THE DOOR TO the shack, his father had hung the alphanumerics of his call sign, K2W9, carefully burned into a board of stained maple alongside a framed picture of a cartoon radio tower expelling boisterous, parenthetical signals. Radar rapped out a *K, dah-dit-dah* —•—, on the door. In the past, confronting the shack had always been a reminder of the balance of power in this world, for it was still a forbidden place, a monument to his father's tenuous generational hold on the reins of authority. But now that the current was gone, the shack suddenly seemed sad and useless, its antenna a ridiculous hubristic appendage. What would he find inside? His father weeping amid a sea of dead receivers?

Radar knocked again. *Dah-dit-dah* —•—. *Dah-dit-dah* —•—.

No answer. All was quiet.

He tried the door, assuming it would be double-bolted, but found, to his surprise, that it was unlocked. He tentatively pushed it open. His internal motor hiccuped, upshifted, spinning its gears at this rare chance to glimpse the shack's coveted interior.

"Hello? *Tata?* You in there? There's been a . . ."

An intense wave of burnt metal wafted out from the gloom. He coughed, reeling backwards. The smell made him shudder and gag at the same time.

"*Tata?* Are you okay?" he called into the gloom, knowing even as he said it that if anyone was inside there, it was highly unlikely they would be okay. He lifted the collar of his shirt above his nose and ventured forth.

"*Tata!*" he yelled.

The open door let some light into the hut's darkened interior. The place looked like a disaster zone. Several large shelves had collapsed, spilling heaps of equipment onto the floor. Nearly every surface was covered with electrical components—buckets of antennae, spare parts, wires dangling from the ceiling, all manner of radios in various states of decay. Radar peered into the darkness. Nothing appeared to be on fire, but the smell of cordite was incredibly strong. One wall was completely black and scorched.

In the middle of the room, Radar spotted a giant machine. A long series of interlocking metal cylinders ending in a large cone. It looked like a futuristic ray gun. Radar took a step forward. What the hell was this thing? He noticed that the end opposite the cone appeared heavily damaged. The metal was twisted and gnarled. This must have been what he smelled. It looked as if there had been some kind of explosion.

Radar carefully approached, fearful of another blast. He put a hand on the smooth barrel of the machine. There were three main parts to it: the end that had burst open, the middle series of cylinders, which were covered in a sea of wires, and then the cone, which was made of a very fine mesh.

Could it be? Radar closed his eyes. Counted to three. Opened them again. The machine was still there.

All at once, he realized he had seen this machine before. It was in a science magazine that had been floating around their house for years.

But no. It was preposterous. He could not believe it. This was from a science fiction movie. It couldn't be real.

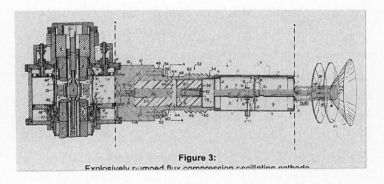

Fig. 3.7. Explosively Pumped Flux Compression Oscillating Cathode Electromagnetic Pulse Generator
From Radasky, W. (2005), "Non-Nuclear Electromagnetic Pulse Generators," *Journal of Electrical Engineering* 27: 24–31

And yet all the proof was here: the exploded flux compression generator that would precipitate the massive blast of electrons, the barrel-like vircator to shape this blast into a brief, powerful pulse of microwave energy, and the conical antenna to diffuse and direct the pulse. He would never have thought it was possible to build a machine like this without massive governmental support, yet here it was. Not only had his father built it (*Where had he gotten the parts?*), but it had actually *worked*. The pulse must have been magnified by the giant 119-foot antenna above the shack and been broadcast across a huge area.

Holy, holy crap.

His father, Kermin Radmanovic, had caused the blackout.

5

And yet his father was nowhere to be found.

"Tata?" he called again.

Nothing.

What the hell had his father been doing? Why had he built this thing? The whole idea of an explosively pumped flux compression generator was that it would *explode*. Didn't he realize this? Didn't he realize the potential devastation? Did he *want* to cause such devastation?

"Tata!" he coughed.

Maybe his father had been blown into a corner and was now knocked unconscious—or worse. He ventured deeper into the room but saw no evidence of Kermin, only more piles and piles of electrical junk. There was an overturned barrel full of various antennae that looked like an arsenal of medieval sabers; a collapsed rack of plush leather earphones; boxes of shattered vacuum tubes; rolls and rolls of wires of all different gauges; a collection of old World War II cryptography machines; and, across one low shelf, a solemn procession of microphones from every era since the dawn of broadcasting, now covered in shrapnel from the blast.

It was then that he looked up. He made a little gasp and tripped, falling backwards against the wall. *Bats.* The ceiling was filled with bats. There were hundreds of them. The bats were getting ready to sweep down and attack him. He instinctively covered his face.

But there was no attack. In fact, they did not move at all, so, after catching his breath again, Radar stood up and took a closer look. They weren't bats at all—they were birds. Hundreds of tiny birds. *Thousands* of tiny birds. All dead. Hanging upside down from strings attached to their feet. He now saw that a number of the birds had been blown around the room during the explosion—he could see them on the floor, littered across the shelves.

Yet there was something wrong with the birds. Not just in their deadness—their bodies were not right. Then Radar realized what it was: *the birds had no heads.* Every single one of them was headless. This couldn't have been caused by the explosion alone. He picked up one of the creatures and touched its feathered wing. The joints were soft and supple; the wing bent perfectly against his hands, swinging up and down as if under the influence of an invisible breeze. He had always figured taxidermied birds would be stiff and immovable, but this one was like a little bird robot. He looked into its neck and saw the glint of metal and wire.

What had been going on in here? Electromagnetic pulse generators and flocks of headless robot birds?

"Tata!" he called. "Kermin!"

He shivered. Despite the heat, he suddenly felt chilled and overtaken by the distinct sensation that he was performing some kind of trespass. He dropped the bird and slowly backed out of the shack, slamming the door behind him. In the yard, he stood, breathing, trying to reconcile what was in there with what was out here.

Mr. Neimann had mentioned that he heard a loud bang right before the lights went out. He had also said they had found the source of the blackout. What if the authorities were already on their way? Their entire block would instantly be swarming with FBI agents, CIA, military—*everyone*. His father would be labeled a whack-job terrorist. He could already see the *New York Post* headline:

BIRD-CRAZY BALKAN MAN DETONATES E-BOMB,
CRIPPLES NEW JERSEY

And where *was* Kermin? Had he panicked when the explosion went off? Maybe he was hiding somewhere. *Yes. Of course.*

Radar ran into the house, shouting his father's name.

"It's okay, Tata. I saw the machine. I know what happened," he said. "It's okay—you can come out now."

He checked every room in the house. He checked the basement. He looked under the couches, in the attic crawl space, behind the shower curtain. His father was nowhere to be seen. He must've fled. Or maybe he was injured and had gone to the hospital?

He heard a car door slam out front. *The police! The police had found them already.*

Suddenly he was the one looking for a hiding place. *The basement!* Behind those boxes of his childhood Erector Set! *Quick!*

There was no time to lose, and yet curiosity drove him into the front parlor, where he hunched on Kermin's favorite beige couch and parted the linen curtains. He just wanted to see the scrum of SWAT trucks, to see how many guns they had trained on the house. He wanted to see the police tape cordoning off the crowd of anxious, disbelieving neighbors. He wanted to see polite Mr. Neimann's expression when he heard the news that Kermin, kind old Kermin, was a wanted terrorist.

But there were no guns. No SWAT trucks. There was only the Oldsmobile.

It was Charlene. She was speaking with Mr. Neimann on the sidewalk, gesturing at the car. Mr. Neimann, still holding the spatula, was nodding like a good neighbor.

Radar collapsed back into the couch. Suddenly the question now became: What should he tell her? The truth? That her husband had blown up New Jersey, kept a shackful of headless birds, and was now on the run from the authorities? What would this do to her?

As much as she might argue otherwise, his mother was a fragile woman. Radar had the feeling that she had spent much of her life running from a part of herself, a dark part that had never seen the light of day. While he was away at college, she had battled through multiple bouts of depression, and there were a couple of times when things had gotten really bad, when she had slipped all the way to the edge, when he was terrified that he would wake up to a call in the middle of the night and she would be gone. That call had never come, but the edge was still there. The edge was always there. The threat of her relapsing had created a strong gravitational field around their little family and was part of the reason he had never left home.

He went to the kitchen and sat down at the table. The twin radios, now silent, still flanked the pig centerpiece. His father's plate and its lunula of forgotten toast. Nearby, the humping-bunny mug, which housed the cold dregs of his mother's chinchilla concoction. The props of a marriage at equilibrium.

This house. How funny, this house. How funny this house was just another house, and yet it contained all of this.

Outside, the light was beginning to soften. He wondered what time it was. A pang of hunger. He looked at the clock on the wall. Two forty-four. Like all clocks, it had stopped at the moment of the pulse. He guessed it must be at least eight o'clock.

He heard the front door open and close.

"Radar?" his mother called.

"I'm in here, Mom."

"Radar?"

"In here."

She was still wearing her lab coat, which was covered in great big streaks of muck, as if she had been thwacking her way through a dense forest. There was a small cut across her forehead.

"Are you okay?" he asked, standing.

"Oh, Radar!" she said, her eyes sparkling. "I was out there. You should've seen me. I was *out* there."

"You look like you were out there."

"It was *absolutely* wild."

"The Olds worked, huh?"

"Oh, it was beautiful. What *justice*. I mean, to drive around all these fancy cars—these BMWs, these Mercedes. I just lay into my horn. I had no shame. I think I drove six people to the hospital. Everyone thought I was a doctor because of my coat. But it didn't matter, I was just out there. Helping people. Doing my duty. I haven't felt this good . . ." She shook her head. "But it's the strangest thing. My sense of smell is gone."

"Gone?"

"Well, not *gone*. You know me. But not like it was. I can't feel a room anymore." She sniffed.

"I'm sure it's just stress," he said. "How bad is it out there?"

"Well, for the most part, everyone's helping each other out. But even in the last hour, it's been getting worse. People were starting to act a little crazy. Like it was the end of the world. Who knew a simple power outage would cause such a panic?"

"It's not just a simple power outage."

"A policeman even tried to take my car. Can you believe it? But I told him, 'No. No way—this is my baby.' He even had the nerve to pull out his gun and tell me the roads were closed and that I *had* to give him the car, by law, but I didn't fall for any of that crap."

"So what did you do?"

"Well, I drove away. What was he going to do, shoot me?"

"A policeman pulled a gun on you and you just drove away?"

"They can't just do whatever they want."

"Uh, they declared martial law. They actually *can* do whatever they want."

"*That's my car.* I was helping people. I wasn't causing trouble," she said. "I stuck by that car for thirty years; I should at least be able to keep it when the going gets a little rough."

Radar smiled. "I never would've thought, Mom," he said. "I didn't know you still had it in you."

"Just wait until I tell your father about all this. He probably didn't think I had it in me, either. Where is the old man, by the way?"

Radar blinked.

"I bet he's in a foul mood. Is his playpen in ruins?"

Radar felt his gears hiccup. Did she know?

"What do you mean?" he said.

"All those electronics he has out there! People were saying everything got fried. You've got to feel for the man."

"Oh. Oh, yeah," he said, relieved.

"How's your station?"

"Same as everywhere. The pulse took out all the circuitry. We hadn't protected it properly," he said. "It's my fault."

"How were you supposed to know about something like this?" Charlene got up and started walking toward the backyard. "Well, I suppose I'll have to talk him down myself."

Radar leaped up. "Don't!"

"What?" She looked surprised.

"He went out."

"He did? Where?"

"I don't know."

"What do you mean, *he went out?*"

"I mean, he just disappeared."

She shook her head. "I'll tell you what—that man. I love him, but that man will drive you *nuts.*"

Radar considered telling her everything. About the EMP. The birds. He opened his mouth but couldn't bring himself to speak.

"Well, I for one am going to lie down," she said. "When he comes back, tell him I'm upstairs and he's responsible for dinner."

"Dinner might be a problem. We might be facing a lot of problems."

"I'm sure we will, but I'm going upstairs," she said. "I'm going to take a Valium and put my feet up so that when the end of the world comes I'm at least feeling relaxed."

RADAR DID NOT DRINK, but as day faded into night, as what was then faded into what will be, he pulled out a dusty bottle of his father's *šljivovica* and poured a thumb or two into one of his old *Star Wars* glasses. As Mr. Neimann had said, now seemed like as good a time as any. And in some strange way, it felt as if he was lighting a homing beacon for his father, even though Kermin also rarely drank. The *šljivovica* was saved for only momentous occasions— births, deaths, graduations. *Blackouts.* He sipped the *rakija*, waiting for someone

to walk through the front door. Kermin? The authorities? Surely any investi-
gator with half a brain would be drawn to the house with the absurd, 119-foot
antenna that towered above the entire neighborhood?

Yet the front door remained closed. Eventually, after two more thumbs of
šljivovica, feeling the quiver of wire in his blood, he lit a dusty candle from their
dining room table and headed out to the backyard again. Dusk had already
descended on the neighborhood, leaving the houses oddly dark. A sound of
sirens rushing a street or two over. He listened, but they did not stop in front of
their house, instead Dopplering away to a distant disaster.

When Radar opened the door to the shack, he was again hit by that pungent
odor of things burning and now burned. The bird bodies still hung above him;
the light from the candle elongated their limbs into a latticework of ghoulish
shadows.

He stepped over the detritus and made his way to his father's cluttered desk.
Tacked to the wall just above, two framed black-and-white photographs hung
cockeyed. One showed a young Nikola Tesla, looking heavily eyebrowed and
manic under the glare of a flashbulb of his own invention. The other was a
grainy snapshot of Deda Dobroslav, posing triumphantly on some anonymous
mountaintop in Bosnia during World War II with Vojvoda Đujić and a heavily
bearded band of Chetniks in black sheepskin *shubaras.* He leaned in closer to
the photograph. In the foreground, Dujić, their talismanic leader, was holding
an absurdly long rifle in one hand. This picture must have been taken early on
in the war, when hope still carried the day and weary warriors could pause in
their day's pursuit to taste the sun's riches on the top of a mountain. Crouching
beside the cluster of barbarian warriors, his grandfather was the only man
without a beard, his face burned dark from the sun. Radar sensed an aura of innocence emanating from those eyes, no doubt enhanced by his giant radio backpack. The resident communications geek. Some things never changed. Though
the photograph was blurry, Radar could just make out Dobroslav saying something into the mouthpiece of the radio. Was he actually communicating a message as the camera shutter clicked open? Or was he simply hamming it up
for the photographer? Somehow, this picture had survived the war and then
made it halfway across the world to America. The captured photons of that fall

morning still held true, seventy years later, suspended in silver gelatin, framed above the desk of a radio shack in New Jersey.

It was as he had written once. *Rule #48: History persists.*

He walked back over to the pulse generator. Touched its hull. He was suddenly taken by a chill, a feeling of emptiness. He looked down and saw something lying on the ground. A little figure. A man, made of sticks and coiled twine. He picked it up, turning it over in his hands. He thought he had seen such a figure before, though he could not remember when.

In one corner of the room, Radar caught sight of a large metal trunk. He touched its side, confused at first, before he realized what it was: a Faraday cage. *Of course.* His father must have known the potential consequences of his machine, even if he was perhaps not quite aware of how wide-ranging those consequences would be. But he would have at least wanted to protect his own equipment.

Radar looked around the shack. It sure seemed as if he had left a lot out in the open, to simply be fried by the pulse. Maybe he hadn't really known what he was doing. Certainly he hadn't considered the role the giant antenna would play in broadcasting the pulse. But all of this—this explosion, this pulse—did not seem like his father's behavior: his father did not *affect* things. His father simply *was*—observing, listening, grumbling. He was a passenger, not the driver. Maybe he had seized the wheel for one brief and terrible moment?

Radar unlatched the trunk and opened its lid. A little gasp. It was indeed a trunk full of riches. There were flashlights and radios and small televisions (apparently he had not thrown all of these out). Earphones. A calculator wristwatch. A cell phone (so his father did have a cell phone!). A Taser. An old IBM laptop. A digital camera.

Just then, released from its cage, one of the transceivers began to beep. The noise sounded foreign to his ears, and Radar realized he had already mentally adjusted to a world devoid of such electronic sounds. He picked up the radio and found that it was connected to an old Vibroplex Morse key—what they called "a bug" in the business. The transceiver must have been in CW mode. The beeps he was hearing were in Morse code:

— —•— ••• •—•• —•— ••—— — •—— ———•— ——•— — ••••

It had been a while since Radar last used Morse, but it was a language deeply ingrained in his psyche. When he was five years old, he had learned the code in just one day, and for weeks afterwards he would speak to people only in Morse, annoying everyone but Kermin to no end.

Radar quickly translated the signal in his head:

QSL K2W9 QTH?

These were the so-called Q Codes—abbreviations developed by CW operators as shorthand for common phrases. QSL meant "Acknowledge that you receive this message." K2W9 was his father's call sign. QTH? meant "What's your position?"

This was most likely one of his father's ham friends. He probably just wanted to chew the rag about the blackout, not knowing that Kermin was, in fact, the cause of it all.

Radar picked up the paddle key. Positioned thumb and forefinger. The lingering twitch of the first dash. The code came back fast. He realized how much he had missed it. The secret to Morse code was not the length of the *dits* and the *dahs* but rather the length of the spaces in between.

——•— ••• •—•• ——•— •—•——•• he tapped, the letters coming out neat and clean. *QSL QRZ?* This was an acknowledgement of message and a request for the identity of the caller.

There was a pause. And then: ————• •————••—— This meant: *9 12.*

What was this? There was a chance he was hearing it wrong, that he was out of practice, but he didn't think so, as the sender on the other end had a tight, clear delivery, and Radar could generally understand him perfectly. "9 12" in old Western Union 92 Code meant "Priority business. Do you understand?" It was unusual for anyone to be using such antiquated lingo, but then Kermin kept strange friends.

Two can play this game. Radar tapped out *13,* Western Union for "I understand."

The reply came after a moment:

QRZ WHERE IS K2W9?

His interlocutor obviously was not fooled. Like every CW operator, Radar had his own particular "fist," or accent, that no doubt diverged from his father's. It was like a sonic fingerprint. A trained ear could hear the difference between two Morse operators within the first few dashes. Radar wondered about the deviation between his father's fist and his own. Was he more forceful? His father lazy and self-assured? Well, he would just have to come clean.

QRZ K2RAD, HIS SON, he tapped out. *K2W9 IS MISSING.*

He waited. A long pause. Maybe he had scared him off.

Then: *WHAT HAPPENED?*

He responded: *DON'T KNOW. I'M IN SHACK. QRZ?*

He didn't want to get into the whole pulse generator situation, lest this person decide to report it to the police and ruin everything.

VIRCATOR? EXPLOSION? came the reply.

How did they know?

WHO ARE YOU? Radar tapped.

Pause.

A FRIEND. WHAT ABOUT BIRDS?

Radar looked up at the creatures hanging above him. *So they knew about this as well.*

THEY SURVIVED, he wrote. *WHAT ARE THEY?*

I WILL COME OVER.

Here? Radar looked around. Kermin wasn't even here to defend himself. It was a disaster. He couldn't have anyone here.

HOW YOU KNOW K2W9? he tapped.

WE WORK TOGETHER.

WHY DID K2W9 HAVE VIRCATOR?

Pause.

FOR THE SHOW.

WHAT SHOW?

Another pause.

I'LL COME AND GET BIRDS.

NO. Radar was suddenly annoyed at the stubbornness of these beeps. Who did this person think he was?

IT'S IMPORTANT, came the response.

K2W9 MUST AGREE, he tapped.

WHERE IS HE?

I DON'T KNOW.

A long pause.

Then: *K2RAD, YOU COME HERE. WE WILL SHOW YOU.*

SHOW ME WHAT?

THE HEADS. BRING A BIRD.

WHAT ABOUT K2W9?

There was no answer.

DO YOU KNOW WHERE HE IS?

WE ARE AT XANADU P4 D26 came the answer.

Radar took a scrap of paper and wrote this down.

XANADU P4 D26? QSD?

IN 1 HOUR. 73 SX.

"73" was a sign-off. Radar felt himself panicking.

WHAT IS XANADU? he tapped frantically. *ROAD? STREET?*

There was no answer.

WHICH BIRD?

Silence.

R U THERE? But it was already clear that whoever it was had slipped back into the vast, blank spectrum of night.

"Xanadu?" Radar said by candlelight. "P4 D26?"

He studied the scrap of paper. It was clearly a code of some sort. He had flirted with cryptanalysis in college, and now his mind jumped to possible encryption methods: could it be an alphanumerical substitution cipher? Maybe "Xanadu" was the keyword. Or maybe it was a columnar transposition coordinate system? Or a modified Nihilist symmetric encryption cipher? Or was it a chess move, and the board was some kind of map? It would take him days—*weeks*—to crack. He did not have weeks. He did not have days. He looked at his watch. He had about fifty-three minutes.

There was, of course, still the minor dilemma of what to do with the smoking gun of the pulse generator. With his father nowhere to be found, should he take the liberty of dismantling and destroying the evidence? Sooner or later, the authorities would triangulate the origin of the blackout to their house and they would all—he and Charlene included—be in serious, *serious* trouble. Radar decided to leave it for the time being. He would come back and handle it shortly, but first he needed to find Xanadu and try to track down his father.

But where could his father have gone? Kermin never went anywhere. That shack was his den. If ever he strayed too far (read: ten blocks or so), he always came rushing back to its safe haven.

Radar went over to the Faraday trunk and proceeded to pilfer it. At this point, he no longer cared what Kermin thought—after nearly blowing up New Jersey, his father had lost the moral high ground. Radar took the flashlights, the radio, one of the pocket televisions, the calculator watch, and the cell phone. He put on the watch and stuffed the rest into a backpack. He also carefully picked out three birds from the ceiling. He tried to choose three varying specimens, but to his eyes, at least, they all looked fairly similar.

Tata, what the hell were you going to do with these things?

Radar took one last look at the carnage of the shack's interior. This, the epicenter of the Great Jersey Blackout. Would they one day write a book about this room? Radar shook his head. Just before leaving, he felt compelled to pick up the stick figure he had found by the vircator and put this into his backpack as well. Then he closed the door behind him.

Xanadu, Xanadu . . . What was Xanadu?

He had heard this name before. In a movie? Or was it a book? He cursed his ignorance of pop culture. His time was ticking away. He looked at his watch. It was 8:23 P.M. He estimated he was already down to forty-five minutes.

The house was dark. He lit another candle and headed upstairs.

"Mom?" he called.

She was lying on her bed, listening to a hand-cranked record player crackling away on the floor. The windows were wide open. There was a collection of uncapped sniffing bottles on the bedside table.

"He still isn't back?" she said.

"No," he said.

"I wonder where he's gone off to?" she said. "Obviously he feels no obligation to protect his own family."

"I'm sure he has good reason."

She shifted on the bed. "This is his favorite piece," she said.

"What is?"

"Caruso singing 'Una furtiva lagrima.' We used to take this out and listen together after you had gone to sleep. We would hold hands. Can you believe it? *Holding hands,*" she said. "I pulled out the record player and thought that if I played it, I might lure him back."

So they both had their homing beacons: his was liquor; hers was music.

They were quiet, listening to the aria. Caruso sustained, inspected, and released a high note out through the windows and into the ether.

"Where could he be?" she said. "I don't have a good feeling about this."

"It's going to be okay," he said. "You'll see. There'll be some explanation and we'll all laugh about this later."

Charlene reached over and sniffed one of the bottles on her bedside table.

"I still can't smell a thing," she said.

"I'm sure it'll come back." He went over and sat on the bed. "You did really good today, Mom. You helped a lot of people. Tata would be proud."

"Are you sure he's not in his shack?"

"I—" He again thought about telling her all. "No. I checked."

He lay down beside her. His parents' room had morphed and changed colors and layout over the years, but lying on his back now, he was able to recall all of those nights when he would burrow down between his parents after having a nightmare, Kermin sideways and snoring, Charlene rubbing his back and humming a little lullaby. In his memory, this room was a place no nightmares could penetrate.

After a final exhortation from Caruso, the aria clicked to an end. The needle shifted into an endless groove, spinning around and around. Radar got up, cranked the box several times, and then flipped the record to the other side.

"It's amazing the things that still work now," he said. "Maybe we'll become a mechanical society. Everything will be hand-cranked."

"Do you think we'll ever get the electricity back?" she asked.

"I think so," he said. "The city already got its power back. But then, I don't think the city got hit like we did."

"Ha! *Of course.* The city will always have its power."

"Mom," said Radar, "what's Xanadu?"

"Xanadu?" she said. "You mean the poem?"

"The poem?"

She began to orate in a faux British accent:

In Xanadu did Kubla Khan
A stately pleasure-dome decree:
Where Alph, the sacred river, ran
through caverns measureless to man
Down to a sunless sea.

"What is that?" he said.

"Coleridge," she said. "I wasted my time in college writing a useless thesis about Coleridge and narrative fragmentation."

"It doesn't sound so useless."

"Oh, it was. I think the title was 'Completion as a Function of Interruption' or some nonsense like that."

"But is Xanadu an actual place?"

"I think it did exist in China once upon a time."

"But I mean, we couldn't actually go to Xanadu now, right?"

"No, but then, that's the whole point. It's something not real . . . The poem was famous in part because it was incomplete."

"How do you mean?"

"Coleridge claimed he had been reading this book about Kublai Khan right before he smoked some opium and then he fell asleep. And while he was sleeping, he had this very vivid dream about a poem . . . a complete poem, in five parts . . . something like three hundred lines long. And so he wakes up and begins writing it all down. But then the doorbell rings and a visitor from Porlock interrupts him. The visitor stays for about an hour or so, and when Coleridge finally gets back to writing the poem, he's forgotten the rest."

"So what did he do?"

"He left it as it was. At least that's what he claimed. A lot of people think he made the whole story up, but I guess I just loved the idea of this mysterious visitor from Porlock coming in and interrupting genius at work. It's the idea that if only we hadn't been interrupted, then we could've accomplished our magnum opus . . . but in the end, we come to realize that the interruption is the work itself." She paused, opening and closing her hand like a jellyfish. "Did you know that in *Lolita,* Quilty checks into the hotel as 'A. Person, Porlock, England'?"

Radar was suddenly struck by the depth of his mother's knowledge. He realized he had never once asked her about her college thesis. He had always dismissed her as his slightly less hapless parent, when in fact, here she was, a walking literary encyclopedia, a font of information, untapped for all these years. How had he never quite understood this? Perhaps because proximity—contrary to popular belief—did not breed clarity. Her habits were not habits, but merely the backdrop for his own upbringing, quite literally: for as long as he could remember, sheets had obscured all of the bookshelves in the house. He had grown up thinking of books as something dirty, to be kept but never shown, which might explain why as a teenager he would regularly develop random erections in the school library. But these books, her books, hidden as they were, had all been considered, read, placed in an order dictated by a mind at work. For the first time, he saw her as a fully functioning being, someone other than just his mother.

"A. Person, Porlock, England," he repeated.

"When I first read that, I almost died. It was like Nabokov and I were living in the same world. We were not so different, he and I. We both had our Porlocks."

"Someone said they would meet me at Xanadu." He reached into his fanny pack and took out the scrap of paper. "Xanadu P4 D26."

"Sounds very Dadaistic."

"I think it's some sort of code."

"You mean like *spies?*" she said.

"Some kind of transposition cipher or something."

"Or maybe they were talking about Xanadu."

"What do you mean?"

"You know, *Xanadu*—that monstrosity by the football stadium."

"What monstrosity by the football stadium?" Radar said. A dim light flickered in his head.

"You know, *the mall*. Xanadu. The building with the awful stripes?"

The awful stripes. Yes. Why hadn't he thought of it before? *Xanadu.* The answer had been staring him in the face the entire time. *Of course.*

"It's the mall!" he whispered.

"It's an abomination," she said. "Have you seen that thing?"

She was right. It *was* an abomination. Billed as "the largest mall in the world," the hideously gargantuan pajama-striped mega shopping complex sat at the confluence of the New Jersey Turnpike and Route 3, just across from the newly constructed Meadowlands Stadium, a stone's throw from the Hackensack River. One day soon, Xanadu promised to offer six million square feet of glory for the entire family, including an indoor ski slope, a skydiving tunnel, a skating rink, a water park, and a three-hundred-foot Ferris wheel that orbited a giant Pepsi symbol visible for twenty-five miles on a clear day. The only problem was that it looked like a day care turned terrorist detention center and had been languishing, empty, for years now—ever since its primary backers, Lehman Brothers and the Mills Corporation, had both gone belly up. Xanadu had been renamed Xanadu Meadowlands Mall, which was then shortened to Meadowlands Mall, which had recently been rechristened again as the American Dream Meadowlands Mall. But Xanadu would always be Xanadu.

"I need to go," Radar said suddenly.

"To Xanadu?"

"I'll be back. I swear. I just need to go." He kissed her forehead. "Thanks, Mom."

"What did I do?"

"Everything," he said. "I'm lucky to have you."

"Don't go," she said. "Not you, too."

"But I'm going to find out what happened to him."

"At *Xanadu*?"

"That's all I've got right now."

She stared at him and narrowed her eyes. "What aren't you telling me?"

He realized his folly. She was his wife, for God's sake. It was a bond of intimacy, however flawed, that he would probably never experience. She had a right to know.

He sighed.

"Kermin was the one who caused it," he said.

"Caused what?"

"The blackout."

"Kermin? As in *my husband*?" She blinked. "How?"

He shook his head. "It's complicated. But when I went into the shack today, I found an electromagnetic pulse generator. It's very powerful. It had exploded, and it must've sent out a pulse that was amplified by the antenna in our backyard."

"Is he okay?" Her voice rose.

"He wasn't in there."

"But why would he do something like that?"

"I don't know. I got a message on one of his radios to meet this guy at

Xanadu." He reached into his backpack, pulling out the little figurine. "And I found this. Have you ever seen it before?"

She took the stick figure from him. Touched its face with her fingertips.

"It's strange, but I can't feel him anymore," she said. "I can't explain it."

"We'll find him. I'll go to Xanadu and then I'll check the hospitals if I have to. He didn't go far. He *couldn't* have gone far."

"The hospitals?" she said.

"I don't think it came to that, but we have to be open to—"

"Wait, don't go," she said suddenly. She dropped the figurine and grabbed his arm, her fingers digging into his skin. "Don't."

"*Ow,* Mom. Let go. *Easy.*"

"Please," she said. "Don't go. You're all I have left."

"It's gonna be fine, Mom. He'll turn up. You know him. He probably freaked out when the pulse happened."

"No," she said. "You don't understand. I should've listened to him . . . and now it's too late."

He was trying to pry off her fingers. "Mom, just let go for a second."

"He was right the whole time."

He stopped. There was a note of surrender in her voice that had caught his attention. Her hands suddenly went limp.

"Right about what?" he said.

"Oh, my sweet," she said quietly. "I can't believe what I did."

"What did you do?" he said. "You're kind of freaking me out right now."

She was very still. Her eyes, looking out into an invisible distance.

"I . . ." her mouth opened, hung there. "I almost killed you."

"No, you didn't," he said. "You saved—"

"*I did!*"

Startled, he looked at her. The moment hung, swayed, tottered. Almost on cue, the record began to skip.

"Your *seizures,*" she whispered.

"*Oh, Mom,*" he said. "*Stop.* I can go back on my meds if you—"

"No, you don't understand. *It was all my fault.*" Her eyes were filling with tears. "Your seizures, your hair. Everything. It was all because of *me.*"

He got up to fix the record. When he clicked the needle into a new groove, Caruso's tenor again filled the room. The lightness of his voice drifting over a pincushion of notes.

"Mom," he said, still from the floor. "A lot's just happened. Tata's not here, I understand. But don't be too hard on yourself, okay? Just go easy. They'll put the power back on, we'll find Kerm—"

"You're not listening to me."

"I *am* listening to you."

"No, you don't understand," she said. "You were *black*. I mean, when you were born, you were black."

"Wait," he said. *"What?"*

All at once, he was overcome by a deep and acutely painful sense of déjà vu. As if she had already told him this. As if he had already sat by this record player, listening to this exact melody, looking up at his mother as she sat on the bed in this precise way. It had all happened before. It was as if they were merely rehearsing lines from a play.

"What do you mean, I was *black*?" Hearing himself say the words again for the first time.

"I don't know why I did it. He told me not to go." The glint of tears on her cheeks.

"Did what?" he said.

She got up from the bed.

"Did *what*?" he repeated. "What the hell are you talking about?"

"I just needed to find out what had gone wrong." She was moving the bed-side table, the smelling bottles tinkling against one another, one spilling onto the floor, filling the room with a strong scent of lilies. The candle trembled.

She was down on her hands and knees, prying at a loose floorboard.

"Hey, Mom. Don't do that," he said. "What're you doing?"

He was about to go over and stop her when the board came up and then she was reaching inside the floor and pulling out something from the depths. A folder. Manila. Dusty. She wiped it off, came over, laid it in his lap.

"What's this?" he said.

"It's for you," she said.

Black Baby's Condition Remains a Mystery

By THOMAS SNYDER

It's been just over a week since Radar Radmanovic was born, but in many ways we are still just as much in the dark about the origins of the child's unusual appearance now as we were then. The latest statement released by St. Elizabeth's hospital merely says, "We pride ourselves in our patient's privacy. The family asks not to be contacted or bothered at this time."

The details about Baby Radar are scarce. He was born with an unusually dark skin pallor to two caucasian parents just after midnight on Thursday, April 17. The mother, identified as Charlene Volmer Radmanovic of Elizabeth, NJ, has claimed that her husband, Kermin Radmanovic, also of Elizabeth, NJ, is the biological father. As many in the media have suggested, such a claim seems dubious at best, given the child's appearance, but Baby Radar's skin color also would seem too dark for a black father and white mother.

Indeed, that "extremely black" skin tone has led several doctors to offer a variety of theories, including mutant melanin mutation.

"It's not unprecedented," Dr. Adam Tuleridge of Albany Medical Center said in an interview. "One occasionally comes across melanin discrepancies or mutations that can give a baby a very different coloring than either parent. Normally we see the reverse—a lightening, various forms of complete or partial albinism. I must say, complete hyper-pigmentation is quite rare."

Quite rare to the point of having no cases on record, hyper-pigmentation, as Dr. Tuleridge points out, is usually only partially expressed on a patient.

"Usually you'll see hyper pigmentation around the nipples, the hands, the face, the genitals," said Dr. Anne Figaro. "You almost never see complete uniform hyper-pigmentation."

Other theories about the child's appearance include an allergic reaction to oxygen, radiation poisoning, a form of Crohn's disease, or an as-yet unheard of double recessive gene, though this would have surely expressed itself prior to this single case.

Regardless, the baffling nature of the story has kept it firmly in the public's eye in the past two weeks. Seemingly everyone has become a medical expert and will happily offer

Fig. 3.8. "Black Baby's Condition Remains a Mystery"
From the *New York Post,* April 25, 1975

Inside, there were pages and pages of newspaper clippings. He moved over to the candlelight and squinted at the text, though, again, he already somehow knew what he would find. "Caucasian Couple Give Birth to Black Newborn at St. Elizabeth's," "Easter Miracle in New Jersey," "Doctors at a Loss to Explain Child's Appearance." He saw his name. His parents' names.

His hands felt as if they were not his own. He saw a copy of a birth certificate, the blurry picture of a baby lying in an incubator. He had seen this picture before. He felt a rushing sensation in his ears. Another burning wash of the familiar frissoned his body's circuitry.

"I've never shown this to anyone," she said.

"This . . ." He tapped the picture of the incubated baby. "This is me?"

"Not even Kermin," she said.

"Why didn't you ever tell me about this?"

She didn't say anything.

He felt the heat in his face. "Why the fuck didn't you tell me about this? I mean, this seems *pretty fucking important,* right? Pretty fucking important to let your son in on . . ."

"I know—"

"Were you just never going to tell me?"

She was weeping suddenly, uncontrollably, and his anger parted as he watched her crumple onto the bed.

"Hey," he said softly. "Hey, all right. It's okay."

"Your father . . . Your father didn't like to talk about it," she said finally, wiping her face. "So we just left it. We left it and hoped it would go away."

"But—" He was staring at a journal article, "On an Isolated Incidence of Non-Addison's Hypoadrenal Uniform Hyperpigmentation in a Caucasian Male." A diagram of skin cells surrounded by a mote of long, polysyllabic words. "I don't understand. Why was I *black*? I mean, how is that even possible?"

She slid down beside him on the floor. Put her hand on the page, touching a cross-section of dermis.

"It was just the way of things," she said slowly. "There were theories. There were theories, but no one could prove anything."

Radar looked over at the record spinning in circles. Caruso's voice was full of quiet counsel. He blinked, trying to make room for this. Trying to imagine himself emergent, a black newborn.

"Fuck," he said.

"I know, I know."

"So then . . . wait." The wheels spinning. "What does that make Kermin?"

"What do you mean?"

"Is he my father?"

She was silent.

"Mom."

"There were tests. They tested his blood."

"And?"

"The doctor said he was your father."

He turned. "But I'm asking *you*. Is Kermin my father?"

"Yes! Yes, of course. I mean . . ." She sighed. She rubbed her face. "I don't know. I mean, I didn't want to believe it."

"Didn't want to believe what?"

She was silent.

"Didn't want to believe *what*, Mom?"

"It was just one night. He only came back for one night," she said quietly.

"Who came back for one night?"

She turned back to him and closed her eyes. "Oh, Lord."

"*Who* came back for one night?"

"I never knew his real name. T.K. That was it. I had known him from before—when I first moved to New York. And then we lost touch. And right when your father and I were getting married, he came back. He showed up on my doorstep one day." Her eyes glazed over. "He was from Minnesota. He had a laugh. He had a way of laughing . . ."

"He was a black guy?"

She nodded.

"Holy shit," he said.

"I still couldn't believe it. Even when you came out how you did. *Maybe it's just a coincidence,* I thought. And then there was all this coverage about you, and I thought for sure that he would show up and say, 'That's mine, that's my kid. Give me back my kid.'"

"But I was your kid too."

"Yeah, but for a while it didn't feel like that."

"And so did he?"

"Did he what?"

"Did he come back?"

"No."

"And you never tried to find him again?"

She shook her head.

He looked down at the diagram of the skin cell. Trying to imagine T.K., this black man from Minnesota, from whom he had possibly sprung.

"Did Kermin know?" he asked quietly.

"I don't know," she said. "He was so quiet. That was his way of getting through things. But he always knew more than he let on. I mean, how could he not know, right? You would look at you and you would look at us, and it was obvious that something had gone wrong."

"Why didn't you tell him?"

"If you don't want to believe, if you do enough *not* to believe, if you see a doctor and he tells you a whole other possibility . . . then you believe what you want," she said. "But your father . . . he was so . . . so *patient*. He loved you from the moment you were born. He always loved you, even when I couldn't take care of you. Even when I fell apart. He never stopped loving you."

"But," Radar said, suddenly feeling dizzy. "But . . . I'm not black anymore."

"You've got to understand," she said. "I became obsessed. I became obsessed for all the wrong reasons . . ."

"So what happened?"

"I just got this idea in my head that there was a solution. Some kind of medical solution."

"What do you mean, *medical solution*? My father was black. What other solution could there be?"

"I didn't see it like that. It was like that wasn't an option. That was impossible. Everything else became possible. I was searching for the possible. And then we found these people . . ."

"What people?"

"You're going to hate me if I tell you."

"I'm not going to hate you," he said. "What people?"

She closed her eyes, took a deep breath. "Well, we saw all these doctors, and no one could tell me what had happened to you. And then, out of the blue, I get this letter. And it was from these people. These scientists. They were in Norway. They said they could help us. And we shouldn't have . . . but we did."

"Did what?"

"We took you there and . . ." She grimaced. "And they *electrocuted* you."

"I'm sorry, you *what*?"

She took his hand. "Oh, Ray Ray, I didn't think it would actually work! We were just there to—I don't even know. But it *did*! It did work! I mean, it made you look how you are now, but it also gave you everything else. Your epilepsy. Your hair. *Everything.*" She was losing it again. "And it was all . . . all my idea. It was all my *fault* . . . Oh, my sweet. My *sweet*. I'm such a bad person. I'm wicked. I'm such a wicked, selfish person."

He was trying to understand. He no longer cared if she was falling apart or not. This was his life. This was about him. "I still don't get it," he said. "They *electrocuted* me? How?"

Hearing the hardness in his tone, she took a gulp of air and tried to bring herself back. "Your father, he would be—"

"My father?"

"*Kermin* would've been able to explain it much better than I could, but they connected you to this machine, like a pulse generator . . . This is what made me think of it, after all these years. And they zapped your skin . . . I didn't understand it all. But look, that's the point—*there was nothing wrong with you.*"

"I was black."

"You were *perfect,* honey. Kermin said this, he kept saying that you were just fine as you were, but I didn't listen to him. I wasn't listening to anyone. I told you, I got totally crazy with this idea that there was an answer that could make everything better, and then that answer became this thing that we did to you." She paused. "I was terrified of being a failure. Of being a mother who couldn't take care of you. Of anyone. And so I did this thing that was exactly the thing I didn't want to do. That's always been my problem: I figure out what's exactly the worst thing to do, the thing that will ruin everything else, and then that's what I do. It's cowardice, is what it is. And after doing what I did to you . . . for many years, I couldn't even look at myself in the mirror. I hated myself so much, it hurt just to get up in the morning. But your father . . . he always stuck by me. Even when I couldn't bear living another day. He told me we still had you. And it was true. We had you. We have you. *Oh.*"

She reached out for him, but Radar got up, the clippings spilling across the floor. He went over to the bed and fell backwards onto the comforter. Breathing. Trying to let it settle. He stared up at the ceiling, recognizing the same pattern of cracks from his childhood. The cracks resembled a wounded whale.

The whale had been wounded for many years. He could hear his mother sniffling on the floor below.

"So," he said slowly. "So . . . I was born black? Like *actually* black."

"No," she said. "You were born dark. Very dark. But that's the point, honey: You're weren't black. You weren't anything. You're Radar! *My* Radar. You've *always* been my Radar. You're perfect."

He lay there, hearing her words drift over him. But instead of feeling a great and terrible anger, as he had first expected he might feel, he was filled with a terrific sense of lightness, as if his whole body were lifting off the ground.

"I'm black!" he whispered to the wounded whale.

"No," Charlene cried. She came up to him on the bed. "You aren't black."

"I'm black!"

"You are *not* black, honey. That's not what I meant to say. I meant to *apologize*. I meant to say that I'm sorry . . . I'm so incredibly, *incredibly* sorry for what I did. I've managed to live, but only because I had to. I don't think I can forgive myself. And . . . and I don't expect you to forgive me, either. But just know I love you. I've always loved you," she said. "I can't imagine my life without you."

Radar saw himself lying in the bed, saw the two of them in this little dim room surrounded by a great, dark city. As if every moment in his life had merely been a prelude to this moment. All at once, the world felt right. Knowable.

"I just didn't want it to be a secret anymore," he heard her say. "It all seems so pointless now. What was I trying to do?"

"It's not pointless, Mom," he said. He sat up. His arms felt limber. He felt as if he could scale a mountain. He reached for her wet face and kissed her on the forehead. "Thank you."

She looked bewildered. "You aren't mad?"

"I don't know," he said. "I feel like I was asleep. And now I'm awake."

She studied him. "I could've so easily killed you," she said. "Oh, I can't even think about it."

"I'm not dead."

She nodded, biting her lip. "I know."

"I'm alive." He *felt* alive. More alive than he'd ever been before.

"I know."

"Mom."

He hugged her, and she fell into him. They were like this for some time, listening to the hollow click of the record player, the scents of lily around them, and then he broke their embrace.

"Listen, I'm going to go find him. I promise I'll come back, okay?"

"I don't think you'll find him."

"*I will.* I'll be back in a couple of hours, I promise. Just stay here and don't go anywhere."

"You'll be careful?" she said. "You want to take my car?"

As soon as she said it, she winced. Radar had never gotten a license because of his epilepsy.

"Thanks, but I'll bike," he said.

"I'm sorry," she said. "I forgot."

"It's okay," he said. "It's probably easier to bike at this point anyway. They'll never find me."

He reached into his backpack. "Here. Here's a flashlight. And I'll light some more candles."

"It's okay. I can do it."

"You're sure?"

"I've managed this long. I can fend off the beasts for one more night." She picked up the figurine and placed it on the bedside table, next to the sniffing bottles. "He'll protect me."

Radar gathered up the folder, aware again of the hole still looming in the floor.

"Can I keep this for a little bit?"

"Of course. It's yours. I've been saving it for you."

He went over and placed a hand on her shoulder. She took hold of it.

"Come back, please," she said. "Don't leave me alone."

"*Mom.*"

"You promise you don't hate me?" she whispered.

"I wouldn't change a thing," he said. "Not one thing."

7

Out on Forest Street, Radar emerged into a darkness he did not recognize. He realized he had never seen his neighborhood in such a state, released from the angular confines of the streetlights. Above, he could see stars, stars that had never been there before. But no: they had always been there; they had just been hidden by a scrim of light. To see the stars, you must be able to first see the night.

"Hello," he whispered heavenward. "Welcome to New Jersey." And when he said this, he knew he was actually talking to himself.

To the east, a faint, withered glow. So. The city had already gotten its power back, while they were left to suffer in the dark. But what a dark it was. A dark beyond reproach. The kind of dark that was, is, and always will be.

Since he was little, he had maintained a fraught relationship with the dark. Darkness had come to represent not the cyclical arrival of the night, but rather his periodic forced flights from consciousness. To feel the darkness creep into the edges of his vision meant that an involuntary departure from his body must soon follow. Darkness meant the absence of time. Or, more precisely: the absence of him from time. The world continued to spin without him, he hanging suspended between this universe and the next, waiting for the darkness to beat back its retreat and the light to take hold of him again. He had thought a lot about that world—the world that continued to spin while he was gone, the world that did not include him. It was almost impossible to comprehend. The observed could not exist without the observer. If he removed himself from the equation, what remained? The equation could not hold.

Once, when he was five, while they were waiting in the emergency room after one of his grand mals, Radar had turned to his mother.

"Why do I disappear like that?" he asked.

It was a complicated question. Or maybe it was a simple question. Regardless, Charlene had not prepared an answer. The query triggered the first of what would become a long series of awkward explanations that his mother revised and honed over the years. These explanations hinged upon the continuous misuse of phrases like "You're such a special child" and "There's no one quite like you" and, worst of all, "It was God's choice." Radar could sniff the stink of these answers but could not decipher why his mother was being so shifty. Kermin never ventured into such fraught territory. He had a habit of leaving the room when questions arose about Radar's condition. Finally, Charlene's explanations had culminated in that glass cathedral of a term, "Radar's syndrome." *His* syndrome. When she stumbled upon this conceit, she immediately put all of her eggs into this basket, realizing its genius, for the diagnosis was essentially a tautological conversation stopper. Everything could be blamed on the syndrome. The syndrome could explain all, and yet the syndrome itself could not be explained.

Alone in the middle of Forest Street, Radar shivered. There was no such thing as Radar's syndrome. There had never been a syndrome. There was only him. He was free.

He switched on a flashlight and split open the darkness. Using a bit of duct tape, he strapped the light onto the front of Houlihan's dashboard. A droopy, but serviceable, headlight.

He took out Kermin's portable transceiver and clicked it two slots to AM mode. After checking to see if WCCA was up and running (it was not), he trolled the frequencies until a woman's voice sprouted from out of the bed of static:

Jersey City, Newark, and several other towns in Essex, Bergen, and Hudson counties continue to reel from the baffling blackout that has plagued northern New Jersey today. Experts are now calling the incident "not an accident" and a "deliberate attack." Authorities are still mystified as to why all electronics in the affected zone have also failed, leading some to believe a so-called e-bomb was detonated in the region. Members of the police and fire departments would not comment on the source of the blackout, saying their primary task was to keep people safe and help return essential services to operation. But as National Guard troops flood into Newark this evening, many government agencies, including the FBI and Homeland Security, have sent in representatives to help solve the mystery of why and how the electrical grid was so paralyzed in today's incident. A warehouse in Paterson was briefly surrounded by law enforcement officials, but this turned out to be a false alarm—

Radar clipped off the radio.

Jesus Christ. They were coming. They were coming, and he was abandoning his mother alone with a stick figure. How could he do such a thing? He needed to defend her against the troops. He stopped and turned the bike around. A soft glow emanated from the bedroom window upstairs. The distant cajolement of Caruso hitting a high note.

No. He had to keep going. If he didn't, he would never know.

She would have to fend for herself.

"I'm sorry, Mom," he said. "Stay safe."

He put his crocodile boot into the pedal clip and pushed forward. His headlight bounced slightly, spooling forth its little patch of light, and he followed, soothed by the simple feeling of movement through space and time. After hearing such a vastly revised version of his birth, his questionable lineage, his apparent electrocution, the true source of his condition, he had expected to feel overwhelmed, askew, for his elemental sense of balance to be forever changed. But in truth, he did not actually feel all that different. Rather, he felt like himself—only more so, as if he had just come up for air after holding his breath for a very long time.

He glided down the darkened street, following his little bouncing patch of light. *Rule #4: We will be what we are, and what we are is what we will be.* No matter if his parents had electrocuted him in Norway. No matter if he had lost his hair, had developed epilepsy and an eternal sense of inadequacy. No matter if

Kermin was not his real father. All that mattered right now was following this little patch of light to Xanadu. Everything would work out if he could only get to Xanadu.

He had been bicycling for only a minute when he came upon a red-and-blue blur of lights strobing across the neighborhood. Two police cars were parked nose to nose. A roadblock.

An officer got out of one of the cars and motioned for Radar to stop.

"There's a curfew," the officer said. "You can't be outside right now."

He could see, against the psychedelic wash of the police lights, that the officer was a black man.

"All right," said Radar. He felt a very strong impulse to tell this man everything that had just happened—how he had just found out that he was also black, or at least had been born black. He knew such a declaration would most likely not go over very well and possibly get him into a lot of trouble, so he just stood there, slack-jawed, staring at the man.

"Did you hear me? You can't be outside right now," the officer repeated, a hint of irritation in his voice. "You've got to get home."

"All right," Radar said again. *Do not say that you are black! You may want to say this right now, but this is not how people talk about these kinds of things.*

"Sir, did you hear what I said? You cannot be out right now. You've got to go home."

"I'm going home," Radar said suddenly. "I'm headed there right now."

"What were you doing?"

"Me? I was . . . buying a chicken. For my mother."

"A chicken?"

"Yes. My mother loves chicken." *Oh no.*

Radar had always been a terrible liar. The effort of fabricating even the smallest of untruths immediately sent him into a surreal tailspin. His lies could never be simple; they quickly ballooned into elaborate explanations that soon popped under the weight of their own flawed logic. When he was six years old, he had told his first real lie after shoplifting a pack of size-C batteries from the Korean bodega down the road. Kermin had caught him guiltily stroking the alkaline wonders on their porch.

"Where'd you get those?" his father had asked, standing very tall and still.

"From . . . the battery man," Radar said without thinking.

"Battery man? What is that?"

"It's a man . . . He gives you batteries. He gives batteries to everyone." The lie grew and grew before their eyes, yet even little Radar knew the world couldn't sustain such a character. Batteries were a precious commodity, not something that could be gifted to strangers by some Peter Pan of electricity.

Now, as the red and blue lights illuminated the police officer's expression of blatant incredulity, Radar felt the same sinking feeling in his loins. He knew he would crumple under the lightest of cross-examinations. He would never be able to sustain a narrative in which his mother loved chicken so much that she would send him out on a long excursion in the middle of a blackout. It was hopeless. They might as well arrest him right now for perjury, libel, and slander.

Much to Radar's surprise, however, the officer seemed to relax and then waved him on.

"You better get the old lady some chicken," he said. "But be careful, you hear? Lot of ways to get hurt right now."

"Yes, sir. Of course, sir," Radar said. He wanted to hug the officer, and again had this dangerous impulse to declare his newfound identity as a black man who was no longer black. Again, he resisted the urge and instead asked, "Did they figure out what happened yet?"

The officer shrugged. "I'm just doing what they tell me."

"But do they think it was a terrorist?"

"Look, I don't know any more than you, son. And frankly, I don't give a damn if it was al-Qaeda or the Russians or who now. I'm going on my seventeenth straight hour."

"I don't think it was a terrorist," said Radar. "I think it was an accident."

"Well, that's some kind of accident," the officer said. "How 'bout we just keep moving and keep this street clear, all right?"

"Yes, sir," said Radar. He wheeled his bike a couple of paces and then turned back.

"I'm with you," he said.

"All right, son," said the officer. "We're with you, too. God bless."

"God bless."

After this, Radar switched off his headlight and rode on, commando style. Whenever he saw a blockade or an emergency vehicle, he would veer onto a different block, weaving his way northward. At some point he realized he did not actually know how to get to Xanadu and East Rutherford. In his haste to leave the house, he had consulted neither map nor atlas to untangle the web of highways and byways that knitted the Meadowlands into an impenetrable tapestry of cloverleafs and interchanges. Once he got far enough north, there was actually no way to safely cut east across the swamps by bike. Xanadu mall was not a biking destination. There were no bike paths in this land of automobiles, NJ Transit, and the occasional Boston Whaler.

He had actually been to East Rutherford only once, when, as a twenty-four-year-old, he had attended a Bruce Springsteen concert at the Continental Airlines Arena. He had gone alone, and from the highest possible point in the stadium he had watched the Boss roll and tumble and sweat and stir that magical Jersey elixir with his golden Telecaster, and afterwards, streaming out of the stadium with the rest of the blissful New Jerseyans, he had felt a great pride for his home, as if this were the one true place on earth. The concertgoers had a dazed look on their faces, as though they had just witnessed Jesus turning water into wine, and maybe they had. For one night, at least, the Boss had transformed those swamps into a paradise. After that show, Radar never had the desire to go see another concert. Sometimes, glimpsing the divine just once was enough.

But now, trapped by the constricting geography of wetland and darkness, he was not sure which way to go. He tried to conjure a mental map of the Meadowlands, tried to picture Bruce's voice calling out to him from somewhere in the middle of all that night.

He rode on, blindly, past rows and rows of darkened homes, past a cemetery, past a silent gas station, through an intersection filled with stalled cars, past an empty city bus frozen like a submarine in the middle of the road. Everything and nothing looked familiar—it was all part of a long and endless Jersey sprawl.

He was just about on the verge of giving up and seeking help from some bystander when out of the darkness he saw an oasis of red light appear. It looked at first as if an alien ship had landed, but as he got closer he saw that it was in fact the sign for Medieval Times, that beloved Lyndhurst medieval-themed dinner theater that featured live jousts as you downed your mutton and gruel. The sign was such a startling sight, after he had seen no lights at all, that Radar nearly crashed from the beauty of it. He felt like a caveman witnessing fire for the first time.

Radar had staged his birthday party at this establishment every year without fail between the ages of ten and fifteen. The number of friends in attendance had slowly dwindled from eleven the first year to only one in that final year—a snotty, heavily myopic boy named Jurqal, who had an unhealthy obsession with anything to do with the Middle Ages. Radar had not been back since. Even now, seeing the glowing Gothic letters in front of two armor-clad knights preparing to collide in mid-joust instantly brought back the same bitter, coppery taste in the back of his throat—a Pavlovian recall of the rejection he had experienced years ago when confronting Jurqal's sole RSVP.

But how had Medieval Times kept their lights on? What kind of electric sorcery were they practicing inside there? He stared at the letters, hot and proud against an unending sky.

Medieval Times! they shouted. *Medieval Frickin' Times!*

More important, he now knew where he was. The entrance to the highway was just beyond. It was the only way across those swamps, and he decided to risk it.

Rule #34: If the choice is between no and yes, choose yes (unless you must choose no).

He turned on his headlight and hit the on-ramp at full speed, weaving around three stalled cars. And then he was on the highway. It was a rush. As he passed more stalled cars, he slalomed between the stripes of the centerline, then drifted to the breakdown lane. How often did one get to bicycle down a highway like this? The world was his private playground.

He noticed the cars beginning to thin out, and then he was passing a tow truck as it was levering up a sedan. Next to the truck was a police car.

Drat! He looked in the dentist mirror attached to his helmet and saw the police car start up and turn around behind him. Lights ablaze. It was coming for him. Ahead, the highway was completely open, devoid of cars. A prison. He saw the stiff rumba of red lights blanket his world as the police car came up right behind him. The car gave him a quick *woop woop* of its siren: • •, a careless little "I" in Morse code.

The car's loudspeaker came to life: "Please pull your bicycle to the side of the road and dismount."

Radar responded to this directive by bicycling harder, swerving this way and that, like he had seen gazelles do on the savanna.

"PULL OVER TO THE SIDE OF THE ROAD! THIS IS NOT A REQUEST! THIS IS AN ORDER! YOU ARE NOT ALLOWED TO RIDE A BICYCLE ON THIS ROAD! PULL OVER NOW!"

Up ahead, he saw the highway slope down a grassy knoll. An idea occurred to him. He had once seen a pretty awesome getaway performed by a cyclist in a movie on one of his father's pocket televisions. He was not sure whether such a maneuver could work beyond the confines of a two-inch screen, but at this point anything was worth a shot.

Radar slowed his bike and pulled over to the breakdown lane. The police car rolled to a stop behind him. In his dentist mirror, he watched as the officers slowly got out of their car. It was then that he remembered that the getaway he was thinking of had actually been performed by a man on a motorcycle and not a recumbent bicycle.

Crap. Well, it was too late now. He couldn't risk getting caught. Not now. Holding his breath, he waited for the policemen to approach, and when they had almost reached him, without warning, he swung his bike to the right and pedaled down the grassy slope, which led to a darkened little outcrop of bushes. Behind him he heard the policemen yelling and he winced, half expecting a volley of bullets to come flying his way, but then he was riding through the trash-covered underbrush, the branches and bracken whipping at his windshield. He went up and over a culvert before spotting a chain-link fence up ahead. He was certain he was going to crash into it and that would be that, but at the very last possible moment he saw a small hole in the fence, which he just managed to steer through, only to suddenly feel himself go airborne, launched without warning off a four-foot ledge. Time stood still. In midflight, he prepared himself for the spectacular wreck that was sure to follow, but somehow, miraculously, he managed to land on two wheels, swerving wildly before righting the ship. His jerry-rigged flashlight went flying off his bicycle, the hula girl shuddered, and he heard something snap in the chassis, but he paid no heed, and pedaled on like a demon, following the road as it cut beneath the highway through an underpass.

He glanced in his dentist's mirror. He could see neither the police officers nor much of anything, really. It was dark. Truly dark beneath this underpass.

Holy mother of God. His heart was pounding, but he continued to bicycle forward as best he could, hoping not to crash into the walls of the tunnel.

"Blow me shivers!" he said, out of sheer nervous energy, the words echoing off the concrete underpass.

It was not quite the line he imagined he would say if this were a book or a movie, as it sounded more like the catchphrase of a randy pirate, but it was all he had to offer.

Rule #101: We are more than our words & our words are more than us.

Somehow, he emerged from the underpass without calamity. He was just beginning to wonder where the hell he had ended up when he reached the top of a slight hill, and there, looming ahead of him like a giant oasis, was the Meadowlands Stadium and the mess of the Xanadu mall behind it, all aglow in construction lights.

In truth, he had expected another seizure to overtake him. There were way too many signals going on inside his brain for there *not* to be some kind of electrical malfunction. He waited for the darkness to come calling, but nothing happened—besides the percolation of adrenaline streaming down his legs, he actually felt okay. Better than okay. *Like a frickin' champ.*

Blow me shivers!

As he bicycled into the mall area, he was astonished by the vast amount of light illuminating every square inch of the road, the construction site, the building, the parking lots. At some point he must have passed beyond the boundary of the pulse, across an invisible barrier that separated the worlds of light and darkness. He stared at a streetlight as it buzzed above him. Such a simple thing, but a miracle nonetheless. The blackout already felt like a dream.

The mall complex was a maze of construction fencing and trailers and backhoes and dump trucks parked at odd angles. Radar glided among them all, trying to remain inconspicuous as he cut through various work zones abandoned for the evening. As he approached the behemoth of Xanadu, its hideous striped siding glowing eerily in the light, he wondered how on earth he was going to find the sender of the message amid all of this. Charlene was right: the place was not even open yet. You could spend days wandering its cavernous interior. It was not even clear how you entered the complex, considering that much of the building was blocked off by an imposing moat of construction barriers. The developers were insistent on this point: *You can look, good people of New Jersey, but you better not touch.*

Fearing that the police from the highway might reappear, Radar decided it was best to get inside as quickly as possible. He doubled back along the frontage road and found an unmanned gate in the chain-link fence. After stopping his bike, he discovered, to his surprise, that the padlock had not been secured. Maybe the contractors had grown complacent. He squeaked open the hinges of the gate, shuffled his bike inside the barrier, and closed the gate behind him.

He was in.

Ahead, he saw the entrance to one of the multilevel parking structures that cradled the mall in a great cement palm. Above him, a massive red-and-yellow-striped structure turned and inclined skyward, like a giant HVAC duct. This had to be the indoor ski slope. According to the plan, people would come and park in these lots on blistering ninety-degree days, they would come and rent skis by the hour, they would ski up and down an artificial hill chilled to subfreezing temperatures inside this giant HVAC duct, and they would laugh and high-five each other's gloved hands and say, "Friends, this is really living." Radar had to admit it sounded pretty nice. Particularly the friends part.

He bicycled beneath the ski slope and down into the yawning mouth of the parking garage. Once inside the darkened lot, he saw the blinking lights of a security vehicle coming from the other end. But by this point, he had become a professional at avoiding the Man. He veered sharply to the right and stopped behind a dumpster, breathing hard. The yellow security lights slowly approached, illuminating the cavernous garage in a lazy, sweeping motion. They came up next to him and paused. *They must have seen him.* He clenched the pedal with his crocodile boot, ready to flee, but then the lights began to move again, fading away into the darkness of the lot. He exhaled.

Where to?

He rooted around in his fanny pack, searching for the scrap of paper with the code on it. He came across the piece of paper with Ana Cristina's number on it. The sight of those numerals buzzed his wires. How far away she seemed now! He hoped she was still okay, that her mother had not flipped out. He felt a strong urge to see her, to be near her. Soon. But first things first.

After some more rooting, he found what he was looking for:

XANADU P4 D26.

P4 D26? *What could it mean?* It could be anything, really. He was not a professional code breaker. There were not enough letters to do a letter frequency analysis. He needed some clue, a crib to crack the code.

Dejected, he dismounted his bicycle, swung out the kickstand, and sat down on the ground. He was exhausted. He was exhausted and he was in the middle of a parking garage beneath some abandoned mall, caught on a wild goose chase for a mystery acquaintance of his father's. It dawned on him that he might in fact be in the completely wrong place, that *this* Xanadu might not be the Xanadu in the coded message. What then? He had abandoned his mother for nothing. Left her to the wolves as he whiled away the time in a concrete bunker.

He shook his head and looked down at his sad, imperfect body. Who was he kidding? He was still Radar. Just because he now knew the truth of his origins didn't discount all of his defects. He was still broken.

And that was when he saw it: there, between his legs. In yellow paint.

C21.

For a moment he was confused. And then he realized what it was.

Of course. He looked up and saw a sign hanging above him. PARKING LEVEL 2. It was not some complicated cipher text. Xanadu P4 D26 was a parking space.

Radar jumped back on his bike and took the spiral ramp down and down to the grey semi-darkness of parking level 4, an apparently forgotten domain lit only by the glow of an orange exit sign pointing to nowhere. Well, at least there was that, even if it did point straight at a wall. He had learned not to take illu-mination for granted anymore.

What could possibly be down here?

Nothing, it seemed. He slowly rode through the empty lot. *A. B. C.* There were a few lonely traffic cones. A turquoise port-a-john.

He reached section D, a remote corner of the parking lot. 7 8 9 10 11 12 . . . 22 23 . . .

He stopped. There, in the dimness, was one of the most peculiar sights he had ever seen.

It was a *tiny house*. There was no other way to describe it. A single-story house—perhaps ten feet wide, complete with shingled roof, white lace curtains, and gutters—built on top of a small four-wheeled trailer, sitting in the middle of parking space D26. A yellowish glow came from within.

Radar closed his eyes and opened them again. The house was still there. *Could it be real?* He parked his bike and approached cautiously.

This, he decided, must be his Xanadu.

After a moment's hesitation, he walked up the three stairs to the front en-trance. On the door he spotted a brass plate and the symbol of an eye.

He stood, took a deep breath, and then rapped out his father's initial: *dah di dah* —•—.

8

C ome in!" said a voice.

Radar cautiously opened the door. The house was composed of only a single room. The room looked to be a workshop, much like his father's radio shack, lit by an overhanging light and filled with all manner of mechanical parts. In contrast to the chaos of his father's workspace, however, this room was infinitely organized. Hundreds of little wooden drawers lined the walls, the contents of each carefully labeled—*eyes, twine, feathers, bones, hex flanges, cross dowels, 2" lite-tooth gears, 1" lite-tooth gears,* and on and on. Everything clean, accessible, in its place. A perfectly slim bookshelf in one corner. On the opposite wall, a constellation of tools hanging inside their outlines. It felt as if he were looking at a dictionary of existence, as if this room contained a specimen of everything in the world, like a Noah's Ark of Man's March of Progress.

An incredibly tall blond man stood in the middle of the room, his head nearly touching the ceiling. He was surveying what looked to be a multiplicity of bird heads spread out across a worktable. Nearby, a pudgy man with long, greasy hair sat at a workbench, inspecting something under a magnifying glass. Radar recognized him as Otik Mirosavic, one of only a handful of people whom Kermin might've called a friend.

A symphony was playing from some hidden radio.

"Shostakovich," said Radar.

"'Leningrad,' number 7," said the tall man, smiling. "Well spotted."

"I used to have a goldfish who loved Shostakovich."

"A discerning beast," said the tall man, holding out his hand. "You must be Radar."

He was dressed in a tight-fitting yellow tracksuit that matched the tone and timbre of his wheat-colored hair and beard, both of which were trimmed to the same impossibly short length; it was as if he were wearing the world's thinnest, fuzziest helmet.

"Yes," said Radar, shaking the man's hand. "I'm Kermin's son." He said it reflexively but then wondered if it was true.

"Lars Røed-Larsen," the man said, his tongue curling expertly around the contours of the name.

"Lars *Rlood*-Larsen?" Radar tried to mimic the articulation.

Lars smiled to indicate that he had gotten it wrong but that he was not going to be a stickler about such things.

Otik looked up from his workbench.

"Hello, Radar," he said in a thick Balkan accent. "Where is Kermin?"

"I don't know," said Radar. "I was going to ask you."

"I'm afraid we're a bit in the dark," said Lars. He scrunched his nose. "Sorry, bad metaphor. We're as uninformed as you."

"You don't have any idea?"

"One could always guess, but—"

"But you knew about the vircator."

"Of course we knew about vircator," said Otik. "I *designed* vircator. I gave him all of these plans. Without me, he would have nothing."

In truth, Radar had never liked Otik. He and Otik must've been about the same age, except Otik looked at least fifty, with a large gut that he did no favors for by wearing ill-fitting, faded Serbian rock T-shirts. His face, flushed from misuse, was long and ugly, and his balding head was accentuated by a crown of oily, chin-length hair. Charlene and Radar used to have a running joke in which they would ask Kermin whether or not Otik had had his heart attack for the day yet.

Otik had immigrated to New Jersey sometime during the war in the

1990s—from exactly where, and under what circumstances, was unclear. It was also unclear what he had done in Serbia, just as it was unclear what he now did in Jersey. He supposedly taught the occasional class at Bergen Community College in computer science and sometimes continental philosophy—these pedagogical ventures inevitably resulting in long rants to Kermin about the idiocy of today's youth. Sometimes he and Kermin would play dominoes in the backyard and complain about the general disintegration of government, culture, and footwear. Radar had even seen the two of them disappear into the radio shack together, an event whose significance was not lost upon him, considering he had never received a similar invitation. Why did Kermin choose to spend time with Otik rather than his own son? Was it because Otik spoke the mother tongue? Because Otik laughed like a wounded hyena? Because Otik did not remind him of his failed parenting?

All of which is to say that Radar could not help but feel a needle of jealousy when he spotted Otik in this most spectacular of rooms, sweating away at the workbench in his Rambo Amadeus T-shirt. Mr. Mirosavic had again beaten him to the punch.

"I didn't know it was you on the line, Otik," said Radar. "I would've been a little nicer."

"I didn't know it was you, either."

"I said it was me."

"Yes, but who can we trust this days? You say it's you, but who are you? I cannot know—"

"All right, Otik," said Lars. "Let's be gracious hosts. Consider the circumstances."

"I'm not egregious, I just explain—"

"Otik, *enough,*" said Lars. He turned to Radar. "He means well, really. He's just a bit gruff, that's all."

"I understand. My father's the same way."

"Your father." Otik shook his head. "*Ispario je.* I will miss him. I will miss his bones."

"What?" said Radar.

"Please, sit," said Lars.

"What did he say?"

"Ignore him. He has a flair for the dramatic," said Lars. "I'm afraid all I can offer you is some cold coffee. We can stick on a fresh pot if you'd like."

"I'm fine, thanks," said Radar, glaring at Otik. He looked around for a place to sit, though there was none.

Seeing his confusion, Lars took up a bucket of parts, dumped them loudly on the floor, and handed the bucket to Radar.

"I'm terribly sorry," he said. "We don't usually have visitors."

"You weren't easy to find," said Radar. "P4 D26?"

"We like it that way," said Lars. "The management company doesn't bother us. We don't bother them. It's a nice little arrangement."

"Do they know you're here?"

"*Someone* knows we're here."

Radar sat down awkwardly on his bucket before he remembered his cargo.

"I brought you some birds," he said, removing his backpack.

"Oh, good," said Lars. "Good. Otik will be pleased. Did you hear that, Otik? He brought us some birds."

Otik looked pleased. He leaped up as best his body would allow and trundled over.

Radar opened the backpack. "I wasn't sure which one to get, so I just grabbed a couple."

He carefully handed each bird over to Lars, fearful that they had somehow been damaged in transit, but Lars did not even look at the birds before passing them on to Otik.

"Can I ask what these are for?" said Radar.

"They're for the next *bevegelse*," said Lars. "The next movement."

"The next *what*?"

Lars look surprised. "Your father never told you?"

"Told me what?"

"About Kirkenesferda?"

"Kirkenesferda? What's that?"

Otik clapped his hands. "You see? Kermin says nothing. I told you. So we say nothing."

"My dear Otik," said Lars. "It's not possible——"

"Wait, what do you mean, *movement?*" said Radar. "What was that word you used? *Bay vay ghoulsa?*"

Lars looked at him sympathetically. *"Bevegelse.* It's what we call our shows," he said. "These birds you so kindly brought over represent years and years of work."

"They are bitch to make one," Otik agreed. "They are really bitch to make two thousand."

"It's true. Your father has done an exemplary job," said Lars. "You see, about five years ago, Otik here finally figured out how to entangle particles." He gestured toward a tube on Otik's workbench that looked like a smaller replica of the pulse generator in Kermin's workshop. "We place these entangled particles into a chip inside each of the bird's heads. Once it's in place, the birds will be forever linked."

Radar blinked. "I'm not sure I follow."

"The birds are puppets," said Lars. "Entangled puppets."

"They are *entangled,*" said Otik.

"Yes, you keep using that word, but I have no idea what it means," said Radar.

"You know: *entangled,*" Otik said again.

"I actually don't know. Like *strings* entangled?"

Lars sighed. "Of course. I apologize. We get so caught up in our little world." He picked up one of the bird heads. "Entanglement is a quantum phenomenon. Two particles interact and become linked in perpetuity, even if the two particles are millions of light-years apart."

"How?" said Radar.

"Yes, *How?* is the question. Einstein shared your skepticism. He called it *'spukhafte Fernwirkung'*—'spooky action at a distance'—and when people proposed the existence of entanglement, he said it was impossible. But here's the thing: entanglement *does* exist. Scientists have proven this to be true. They've managed to entangle particles in the lab, although they're not very good at it. In fact, they're quite clumsy," said Lars. "But recently scientists have discovered that all kinds of quantum reactions actually happen in nature . . . It's how photosynthesis works, it's how our smell works——"

"Our *smell?*" said Radar.

"Olfaction operates via quantum electron tunneling—we actually smell a molecule's vibration and not the molecule itself. But what's particularly interesting for our project is that we've discovered how birds navigate the magnetic field of the earth using a form of organic quantum entanglement inside their eyes."

"Inside their *retinae,*" Otik chimed in.

"We've known for a long time that birds have this ability to sense the earth's magnetism, but we haven't known the mechanism for *how* they can sense this magnetism, particularly because the earth's magnetic field is so weak . . . You would need very precise equipment to measure it. Well, it turns out birds have a series of special cells in their eyes—"

"*Retinae,*" said Otik.

"In their *retinae,* in which photons—that is, *light*—will excite a pair of electrons into a state of entangled superimposition. These two entangled electrons then act like a very sensitive compass, and this is how the birds navigate the poles. They can actually *see* geomagnetism." He paused. "So. This was the secret. Why reinvent the wheel when nature has provided the apparatus for you? We extracted the protein from the bird's eye, modified it using a fiber-optic coupler, and then placed it into the microchip. In essence, Otik has managed to build a rudimentary organic quantum computer. The secret was to put a part of the bird into the machine. Quite elegant, yes? *The bird in the machine.* For our purposes, it's really all we need. Our show relies on building a flock of puppets that all move in conversation, no matter where they are in the world. One is entangled with the next, who is also entangled with the next, who is entangled with the next and so on. It is a kind of collective consciousness. A *bounded* swarm, if you will."

Radar glanced at the birds, lying inert on the table. "They can actually fly?" he said. "I mean, really fly?"

"They can. But flying's really the least of our worries. A purely mechanical problem. People have been building flying machines for ages. Our dilemma is one of *groupthink.*"

"And you can control them?"

"Only initially. We control the first input, the spark—*'Tilt up 68, bearing 128, thrust 4.'* And then they're set free and must discover their own path after that. The question will be if we can train them en masse to participate in the movement. But in the end, the birds will decide together."

"So they control themselves."

"There's been much debate in Kirkenesferda over the years about what constitutes a puppet, whether we must be in constant control of the object for it to be called a puppet, whether a robot or an automaton is a puppet even if it moves under its own volition. Much has been written about this distinction—by my stepbrother and others. This is the kind of thing that keeps me up at night. We're testing the boundaries of control. Of who controls what. About what control *is*. About whether control is even *possible*."

Otik was slipping something small and fragile into one of the bird heads.

Lars shook his head. "Otik, let's not do this right now."

But Otik would not be deterred. He connected a set of wires and then snapped the head of the bird onto the body. He then repeated this preparation on a second bird. His hands were working quickly, massaging the necks of the creatures with an unexpected tenderness. Back at his workbench, he opened a laptop and began to peck away at the keys, muttering to himself.

"Otik, please," said Lars. "Let's leave it."

Otik slapped a final button and raised his arms in triumph.

"Let's dance, baby," he said, turning to face the birds.

They waited, Radar holding his breath. Shostakovich played on in the background. Nothing happened. Radar glanced over at Otik, whose face had turned sour. They waited some more. The birds lay still on the table.

"Bem ti sto majki!" said Otik, deflating back into his seat. "I told you it was problem. I told you before: *amplitude shackles are such bullshit.*"

"And welcome to life at Xanadu," said Lars. "We spend most of our time attempting to figure out how we just screwed up. It's a game of outrunning our own failure."

"Kirkenesferda," said Radar, stumbling over the strange word. "Wait. Are these the same people who electrocuted me?"

Lars sighed. "First of all, I want you to know I had nothing to do with your

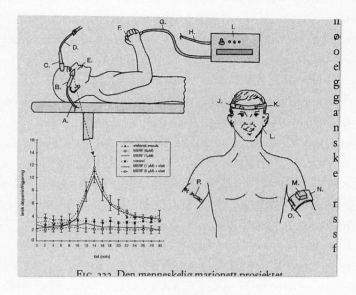

Fig. 3.9. Notes from Den Menneskelig Marionett Prosjektet
From Røed-Larsen, P., *Spesielle Partikler,* p. 493

electro-enveloping. I was only ten years old at the time, so I plead the ignorance of youth."

"Electro-*enveloping?*" Radar said.

"The technology came about accidentally from Kirkenesferda's investigations into some old Tesla designs. After *Kirk To,* they began looking into organic circuitry so as to try and make the human body into a puppet of itself. It was an attempt to circumvent Kleist's dilemma. An awareness of ourselves as an actor on the stage inevitably corrupts the essence of our movements. We think, and therefore we cannot just *be. Den Menneskelig Marionett Prosjektet* was meant to rewire the body so that another could control our movements, just as if we were a puppet. The project did not pan out, but many other discoveries came from this."

"Like how to *electro-envelope* someone's skin," said Radar.

"Well, yes. Among other things. But really, they had no idea what they were doing. The technology was primitive, brutally so. Let me tell you this: what they did to you was not right. Leif should never have offered his services. He was charismatic and excitable, but he was also a schizophrenic delusional. At the time, I worshipped him. Everyone did. And everyone wanted to believe in what he said, but now I see that he was just a boy playing with a toy, and this toy should never have been used on a living human being, and certainly not a child. I'd like to think that Kirkenesferda's come a long way since then. We've matured—spiritually, morally, karmically."

"I'm sorry," said Radar. "I'm still not quite following you. What *is* Kirkenesferda?"

"It is most important group in all of performance history," said Otik, looking up from his workbench.

"Well . . . let's stay modest, shall we?" said Lars.

"It is truth," said Otik. "You want to argue about this?"

"What he means is that their contributions have often been overlooked."

"It's not what I mean," said Otik. "I mean they are most important group in history."

"Your father played an important role."

"It is truth," said Otik. "Your father, he had so much talent. He was the best."

"He was?" said Radar. It was only after a moment that he heard the past tense in Otik's words.

"So much," said Otik, shaking his head. "So, so much. *Genius.*"

"But what do you mean, *was?*"

"Ah, let's not quibble about semantics. Otik's English is not the best," said Lars. Otik opened his mouth, but Lars held up a finger in warning. "I'm going to put on some coffee. Anyone for coffee? Radar?"

"I actually don't really drink coffee," said Radar. It was true: coffee, like alcohol, caused his already malfunctioning body to go into overdrive.

"In that case, I'll just drink yours," said Lars. He busied himself with an electric kettle. "So how would one describe Kirkenesferda? I think Per called us a 'metaphysical army of Arctic puppeteers,' but of course that's a ridiculous explanation. Per has a tendency to overstate his case."

"Who's Per?" Radar asked.

"Per Røed-Larsen. My stepbrother." Lars went over to the bookshelf and took down a mammoth beige book. He handed it to Radar. "He's written the most comprehensive history of Kirkenesferda, even if most of it's not quite true. He and I don't speak anymore, but I must say his work's impressive, if perhaps overly critical, although I would be, too, if my father abandoned me for some metaphysical army. I don't mean to go all Freudian on you, but Per was a little obsessed. He elected himself the primary Kirkenesferda historian, much to the outrage of Brusa Tofte-Jebsen."

Radar leafed through the book, staring at the pages and pages of graphs and tables. A whiff of the familiar. He felt as if he had held this book before.

"Your father abandoned you?"

"No. He abandoned Per and his sister. You see, in 1939, my father, Jens Røed-Larsen, was one of the most important nuclear physicists working in Norway." Lars came over and flipped to a page in the book. "There. That's him. Per claimed he was on track to win the Nobel Prize, but I'm not sure about all that.

Fig. 3.10. Jens Røed-Larsen at the Bjørnens Hule (1968)
From Røed-Larsen, P., *Spesielle Partikler,* p. 96

Anyway, when the Nazis invaded, Jens was forced to flee to Stockholm with his wife, Dagna, and their baby, Kari. Both the Germans and the Allies of course wanted him for their nuclear weapons programs, but he refused. He was something of a die-hard pacifist at the time. But while he was hunkered down in Sweden, he heard whispers about this avant-garde performance group working on the Russian frontier, in Lapland. They were supposedly making a courageous stand against the war through these art pieces centered around the physics of the nuclear bomb. You've got to remember that the bomb at this point was only a dream, a terrifying possibility on the horizon. Hiroshima was still two years away. My father's interest was piqued. He heard this group were in need of a nuclear physicist on the team, so, in 1943, he essentially left his family and traveled up to Kirkenes. You can imagine what a difficult choice this was."

"Why did he do it?"

"I still don't know, really. War causes strange things to happen. People's priorities shift. I suppose he came to think that this cause was something pure, something effectual. Still, I can't imagine. It was quite a dangerous trip for my father. You see, the Nazis still controlled the entire North. The whole reason they were occupying Norway in the first place was so they could produce heavy water to make an atom bomb. But my father risked it anyway. He was guided by a small band of Sami. They say it was bitterly cold—one of the worst winters on record—and he lost two toes in the process. But he made it. They took him over the mountains and then down into Fennoscandia to the Bjørnens Hule. My father then worked on *Kirk En* in 1944, the first of the two nuclear events."

The kettle began to shiver.

"You sure I can't interest you in some?" said Lars. "I get it from this great little place by the docks in Constable Hook."

"No, thanks," said Radar. "Did you say *nuclear* events? You mean like *bombs*?"

"Heavens, no." Lars laughed. He took out a small French press. "Not bombs—*happenings. Movements. Kirk En* took place in Poselok, before the war was even finished. This was the whole reason my father was invited up north. It was an installation largely about nuclear fission, but also about longing and witnessing and infinity, I believe, but then, this is just my interpretation. Per, of course, disagrees with me. One of my great regrets is that I never got to see it. They never even took photographs. Can you believe it? All that work, and no evidence of its existence. Sometimes, in my more skeptical moments, I wonder if it even happened. But it must've been beautiful—I can picture it in my mind very clearly—a small, isolated island in the Arctic, perhaps twenty meters across. A forgotten shred of land. There's a chance no human had ever even set foot on the island until they staged this miraculous event. 'A silent, devastating critique of our obsession with manipulating *natura* into instruments of mass execution,' writes Per. I think that's well put."

"So what was the event?"

"No one actually witnessed it, so all we have left is the description," said Lars, pushing down the plunger of the French press. "Two hundred and thirty-five jars, arranged in a perfect circle. The jars were all filled with heavy water allegedly stolen from the Nazi plant in Vemork. Inside each jar, three tiny dolls are floating. The dolls are designed to have the exact density as the heavy water, and so they appear essentially weightless. And in the middle of the circle, two

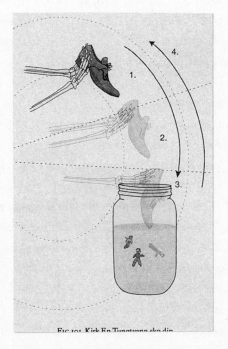

FIG. 101. Kirk En Tungtvann sko dip

Fig. 3.11. **Kirk En *Heavy Water Shoe Dip***
From Røed-Larsen, P., *Spesielle Partikler,* p. 154

hundred thirty-five beautiful puppets, made from fox skeletons, mounted on tracks, each with a single shoe cradled in its arms—"

"Wait, I'm sorry—no one ever even *saw* the show?" said Radar.

Lars smiled. "Apparently two Russian fishermen eventually did discover the installation sometime in the eighties. You can imagine their surprise. *Bože moj!*"

Otik snorted. Lars looked over at him.

"What?" said Otik. "It is funny when you speak. *Bože moj!* You are funny."

"So," said Radar. "I don't mean to be rude . . ."

"Please," said Lars, pouring the coffee into his mug.

"You're saying your father left his family to put together an installation with jars in the Arctic that no one saw except two Russian fishermen?"

"Forty years later, yes."

"Forty years later."

Lars smiled. "When you put it like that, it does sound a bit awful, doesn't it? But you've got to understand that at the time, it was much more serious. It felt like a matter of life and death. They truly believed they were changing the course of history by staging such an event."

"Of course they were changing history," said Otik. "It is no doubt."

"But no one ever saw it!" said Radar.

Otik turned around. "You don't know anything, do you? You are like little child."

"Please," said Lars, holding up his hands. "It's a fair critique. And it's a critique that's been leveled at Kirkenesferda by more than a handful of scholars. Many have called us the worst kind of self-satisfied, pretentious time-wasters—creating our art while others die. Sometimes I harbor these same doubts myself. But then I think back to what Leif said all those years ago: that we were circling around something essential, something far too beautiful to abandon—'an eternal object,' he used to call it. He used to say small things affect big things, just as big things affect small things."

"This is true," said Otik. "Small and big."

"Okay," said Radar, eyeing Otik warily. "So then what happened next?"

"After the war, my father moved back to Oslo with his family for a time. He took up his old position at the university again. He went through his routine, taught his courses, but everyone said he wasn't the same man. He always had his eyes pointed northward. Per was born in 1952, but even this couldn't keep him there. My father left maybe three years later for Kirkenes. He couldn't escape it, I suppose. And he essentially abandoned the family, the toddler, the job, everything. You can imagine the effect this had on Dagna. To be left by the same man twice. She never recovered."

"So you had a different mother?"

"I did. Her name was Siri. My father met her at the Bjørnens Hule. He had been living up north for ten years or so. This was after they had already staged *Kirk To,* in 1961. My mother joined them in 1968 or something like this. I'll have to look at Per's book. She was the only woman in the camp."

"Why did she come?"

Fig. 3.12. Frame still from Kirk To, *Gåselandet*
From Røed-Larsen, P., *Spesielle Partikler,* p. 230

"Oh, I don't know. She was a hippie. A Norwegian hippie. You know—long dresses, no bra, the whole gambit. But beneath this flower-power routine, she was a fiercely intelligent idealist. She was a set designer. Just brilliant. She had seen the famous nuclear bomb footage of the Gåselandet performance at some drug party in Oslo and decided this was what she wanted to do. And when she showed up at the camp, you can imagine . . . There was a kind of brutal competition for her affection among the men. Some of them had not seen a woman in years. And yet it was Jens, the old professor, who won out. I don't think my father was really even interested in meeting a woman. A part of him was still in love with Dagna, and he must've felt great guilt about leaving Kari and Per behind. But Siri was Siri, and he couldn't resist. I'm glad he didn't. I wouldn't be here otherwise."

"So when did my father come in?"

"Your family visited the Bjørnens Hule in 1979. This was when Kermin first met Leif."

"Who's Leif again?"

Lars flipped though the book and pointed to a picture. "Leif Christian-Holtsmark," he said. "He was one of the founders of Kirkenesferda. Him and Brusa Tofte-Jebsen. And then Brusa left after a disagreement about the group's future, so really Leif became our spiritual mentor for many years. He was the heart. Leif asked your father to help him out for *Kirk Tre,* the Cambodia movement in Anlong Veng."

"Cambodia?"

A weary look came across Lars's face. "It was the first time they did a movement in a place of active warfare. Everything changed after that."

"And my father went, too?"

Lars shook his head. "No, thank God. But he made the puppets. They were incredible."

"Incredible," Otik agreed. "Most."

"They had screens for heads. It was very complicated, very time-consuming. They were these fantastic creatures with essentially infinite faces. The puppet could become anything you wanted it to be," said Lars. "And they were magic. Absolute, utter magic. I wish you could've seen them. Some of the most beautiful objects ever made. Here—here's a drawing from Per's book. It doesn't really do it justice."

Otik came over and looked at the image with them. "It changed my life when I see this," he said. "I remember someone showed me this photo and I think, 'Ah, okay, everything is possible now. I must work like son of bitch.'"

Radar stared at the image of the thin little puppet-man with the circular television screen for a head. So simple, yet captivating, even in this black-and-white iteration. He imagined the puppet-man moving, eyes blinking on the screen. The slow bend of his arm, the nod of the head. His father had made this. Something approximate to pride stirred inside of him.

"So then?" he said. "What happened in Cambodia?"

"Oh," said Otik, returning to the workbench.

"Oh?" said Radar. He looked over at Lars and saw a slight grimace pass over his face. The mood in the room shifted.

"Why do you always ask these questions?" said Otik. "You are like child with all of your questions."

"I'm sorry," said Radar. "I didn't mean to—"

Lars held up his hand.

"It's okay. Of course you didn't." He sighed, running a finger around the rim of his mug. When he looked up again his eyes were heavy. "It wasn't good."

"It was beautiful," said Otik.

"Only in theory."

"In more than theory. Anlong Veng was most important event in twentieth-century performance."

"It was a human catastrophe," said Lars. "The only thing we can be grateful for is that your father wasn't there. Only his work."

Radar was silent. The music on the radio encountered a brief batch of static. Strings evaporating.

After a moment, Lars began speaking again. His gaze had moved to some distant point, far away from the room. "We got in. It was a bloody miracle that we got in at all, thanks to Raksmey."

"Raksmey?" He had heard this name somewhere.

"Raksmey Raksmey," murmured Lars. He stopped and closed his eyes.

"You see?" Otik said to Radar. "You see what you do?"

Lars shook his head. He took a sip of coffee. "I lost everything that night," he said quietly.

"I'm sorry," said Radar. "I didn't mean to bring it up."

Lars looked up and smiled weakly. "Of course, everyone assumed it was the end. I mean, there's no way to recover from something like that. And your poor father . . . he had no idea what had happened. I was stuck in Thailand in government custody. I turned eleven while I was there. And then, out of nowhere,

Brusa Tofte-Jebsen reappeared. He'd been out of the picture for years. He'd been writing his articles about Kirkenesferda, of course, but I'd never met him before. And he just swooped into Bangkok and got me out of there. I don't know how he did it . . . Per claims he paid a one-hundred-thousand-dollar bribe, but Brusa always denied it. As you can imagine, I was in complete shock. For years. After losing both of my parents like that . . . There was talk about sending me to live with Dagna and Jens's old family. But the relationship wasn't good with her, so in the end, Brusa ended up adopting me. He was also the one who contacted Kermin and told him what had gone down in Cambodia. I think it was hard for your father, being so distant, not knowing what to do . . . He had put so much energy into a show that had ended with all of these people getting killed."

Radar's throat went dry. He wanted to ask what had happened in Cambodia but didn't dare.

"So that was it?" he said. "The group was finished?"

"No," said Lars. "You would think so, but no. Years later, I attended school at Columbia University, in New York. I was studying Portuguese literature, of all things. Writing a thesis on Fernando Pessoa and all of his heteronyms. But who should walk into my dorm room one afternoon? Kermin Radmanovic. I don't know how he found me, but he just appeared in my doorway and said, 'I want to do another show.' No 'Hello, how are you? By the way, I'm sorry about your parents, I'm sorry about Cambodia.' Just this announcement. And of course, I was angry. You can imagine. I mean, who the hell was this fucker, and why was he bringing up all this painful shit that I had tried so hard to forget? Truthfully, I wanted to punch him in the face. I think I almost did. But he was insistent. He stayed, and we began to discuss his ideas. He came back the next day, and the next. And after several weeks I realized that I had been waiting for him to come through that door ever since Anlong Veng. It was my destiny to perform another movement."

"And then your father called me," said Otik.

"Otik was not Otik back then. His name was Miroslav Danilović." Lars looked over at Otik. "Am I revealing too much?"

"Yes." Otik shrugged.

"Your name is Miroslav?" asked Radar.

"Not anymore," said Otik. "Names can die like people."

"Okay," said Radar. "So how did you first meet my father?"

"I was living in Belgrade during the war," said Otik. "I was at university working on some little performance here and there. Mostly like street shows. Your father has seen my work in some magazine or something like this, and when I hear he was one who did show in Cambodia, I was excited, because he is my hero. So we become pen pals. And then he explain what he want to do in Sarajevo and I think, *Oh, man, he is so crazy,* but good crazy, you know? And he want to pull off this something that is so unbelievable—like *no shit* unbelievable. So I just said, 'Why not? Of course I work with you, you crazy motherfucker.'"

Lars nodded. "Your father proposed a performance in the Bosnian National Library, in Sarajevo. The library had already been gutted by firebombs several years earlier. At the time, Sarajevo was still under siege, so you can imagine it was an incredibly complex production and a wildly dangerous performance. Just to get the equipment in there was a ridiculous undertaking. We had to bring our own electricity, everything. It's true that Kermin never went halfway on anything."

Radar tried to decide if this was true. "When was this?" he said.

"Back in 1995."

Radar remembered that the summer before his sophomore year in college, Kermin had left on an extended trip to Europe. He had supposedly been visiting friends in Italy who were displaced by the Yugoslavian war. At the time, Radar had been worried because his mother was in one of her depressions, and he didn't want her sitting around the house alone. So he had moved back home while Kermin was away. Radar tried to imagine Kermin caught in the middle of a war, staging a show in a bombed-out library in Sarajevo, while he and Charlene sat at home playing Scrabble. *Why hadn't he shared any of this?* He had come back tired, bearing some sad Italian gifts of biscotti and cheese, but otherwise none the worse.

"He never mentioned anything to us," said Radar.

"I'm sure he had his reasons," said Lars. "There were security issues, particularly coming on the heels of Anlong Veng."

"And Sarajevo? Did it happen?"

Lars looked at Otik. "In many ways it was the masterwork. Per said as much in his book. Brusa agreed. Otik brought a level of technical complexity we'd never seen before. He works in miniature. Otik, would you show him the . . . Oh, never mind. We'll show you later. It will blow your mind," said Lars. "But the other big difference with *Kirk Fire* was that we had a *public*. We had an actual audience . . . for the first time in Kirkenesferda's history. The public came the first four nights of the run, despite the sniper fire and the shelling. They risked their lives to sneak into this destroyed library to see our show about superstring theory. So in this respect it was—"

"It was bad," Otik said suddenly, looking up from his birds. "I screwed it up, and Thorgen was killed by sniper. Then there was bombing in Markale. No. We had to stop. It was too much."

"It wasn't entirely your fault."

"Don't bullshit me, Lars. I don't need your bullshit right now."

"We had to get Otik"—Lars corrected himself—"*Miroslav* out of there. He was in poor health."

"The black boxes, they were killing me, slowly," said Otik. "Every time I make one, I must leave part of me inside box. And so my body goes like *this*. I used to be very thin, if you believe."

"He had also been found out by certain security forces," said Lars. "It wasn't safe for him anymore. So we brought him back to a new life with a new name."

"You brought him *here*? To New Jersey?" said Radar.

"You could do worse."

The music on the radio had shifted into a march. The rattle of a snare as an oboe urged them onward.

"I had no idea," said Radar. "I can't believe he kept all of this from us."

"He was a private man. He kept things from everyone."

Radar thought about this for a moment.

"Do you realize he caused the blackout?" he said.

Lars and Otik looked at each other.

"We had a hunch," said Lars. "We couldn't be sure, but when I heard there'd been an accident, I figured as much."

"I just don't understand why he would build something like that without thinking about what could happen? I mean, he must've known he would fry the whole electrical grid. What was he trying to do?"

"He didn't build the vircator to fry the grid," said Lars.

"What was he doing then?"

"He built it for you."

"For *me?*"

Lars sighed.

"What do you mean, *for me?*" said Radar.

"We've been experimenting with vircators for some time now." Lars pointed at the machine next to Otik. "And the more we researched this, the more Kermin became convinced that a high-energy pulse was the secret to reversing the effects of your procedure."

"My procedure?"

"Your electro-enveloping. Kermin thought that if he just found the right energy and focus, then he could cure you—"

"*Cure* me?"

"Or at least cure your epilepsy," said Lars. "Okay, it's crazy, but it's not as crazy as it sounds. There's evidence that epilepsy is a quantum phenomenon. But we told him it was a bad idea, particularly because there was no way to know—"

"I tell him so many times this is bullshit, bullshit, bullshit, bullshit," said Otik, looking up from his work. "Like *total* bullshit. *Even* if we identify the coherence, seizure is *huge* reaction. Not some small event. But Kermin, he's so . . . I don't even know this word."

"He's stubborn," said Lars.

"Yes, stubborn, but more sneaky than this. In Serbian it is called *zadrt*. Like he is hypnotize."

"He was building his own vircator," said Lars. "He didn't tell us as much, but we had our suspicions. Particularly when he stopped letting Otik come over. He was assembling the birds, he was showing us his work, but on the side he was building his own private EMP generator. We were on the outside, just like you. And we certainly didn't know how far he'd gotten or how powerful it was."

"Jesus," said Radar.

The vircator had been for *him*. To *cure* him.

"Obviously, he underestimated the strength of the pulse," said Lars.

"But how do you build something like that and not know it's going to screw everything up? He must've caused like billions of dollars in damage today. He probably *killed* people."

"Yes," said Lars. "It's most regrettable. He's disrupted our work as well. Ten years of planning have all gone out the window."

"What planning?" said Radar.

"Nothing is out the window," Otik said from his bench. "We still go."

"We're not going, Otik," said Lars. "We need Kermin."

"No. He blows it. We get birds and we go. Alone."

"We can't go. Not before we find Kermin and make sure he's okay. We owe this much to him."

"You were one who said this boat sails only tomorrow," Otik said to Lars.

"Yes, but we can't just go without him. We can't do it alone."

But Otik had turned back to his computer and was no longer listening. He was typing intently, whispering something inaudible to himself.

Lars smiled. "I'm sorry," he said. "As you can see, you've caught us at a tricky time. Clearly Otik and I need to discuss a few things here. We were supposed to catch a ship bound for Africa tomorrow morning, but your father's . . . *untimely disappearance,* shall we say, has complicated matters considerably."

Radar felt a quiver of guilt. "I should go. I should go look for him," he said.

"I'm not sure that's wise," said Lars.

"I have to," said Radar, suddenly feeling antsy. "I thought he might be here, but I've got to find him. My mom's waiting alone at home right now. I just worry he got into some trouble."

"As you wish," said Lars, bowing his head.

Radar got up to leave. "Thanks," he said. "Good luck with your—"

"I am telling you! *Genius!*" Otik yelled.

He punched a button and jumped to his feet with surprising dexterity for someone of his girth.

The light flickered above them, and the march on the radio slowed. Radar felt a hum across his skin, and it was then that the two birds on the table quivered and came to life. They leaped up into the air, spinning around each other, up and up until they crashed against the ceiling, plummeted, rebounded, and smacked against the wall, toppling over a jar of screws, a folder exploding into a cloud of papers. The birds rounded each other, eyes unblinking. They careened into the ceiling again and tumbled down, but just before they hit the ground, they swooped up again. And now an understanding emerged between the two and they began to circle the room in tandem, the oboe on the radio offering a cushion to the sound of their wings against the air, the bare lightbulb gently rocking back and forth in time to the birds' revolutions. The three of them stood below, watching the pair act and react, react and act, until Otik yelled something in his language that Radar could not quite understand. Otik twisted and leaped like an animal in pain, and then he was at the door to the house, flinging it open with great drama. One of the birds sensed this expansion of space and immediately whipped out through the open door, leaving the other to circle the room alone. The difference between one bird and two was immense. After several more revolutions, the lone bird stopped in midair, hanging there motionless, as if it had forgotten what to do next. There was an impossible pause, a flagrant denial of gravity's embrace, and just as the bird began to plunge back to earth, it regained itself, remembering, and now it was turning and swooping out through the open doorway. They were both gone just as quickly as they had come to life, and before Radar could ask if what he had just seen was real, Otik was already running out after them, whooping, the sound of his voice echoing against the walls of the garage until this, too, faded away into just the soft question mark of the oboe playing its final notes on the radio.

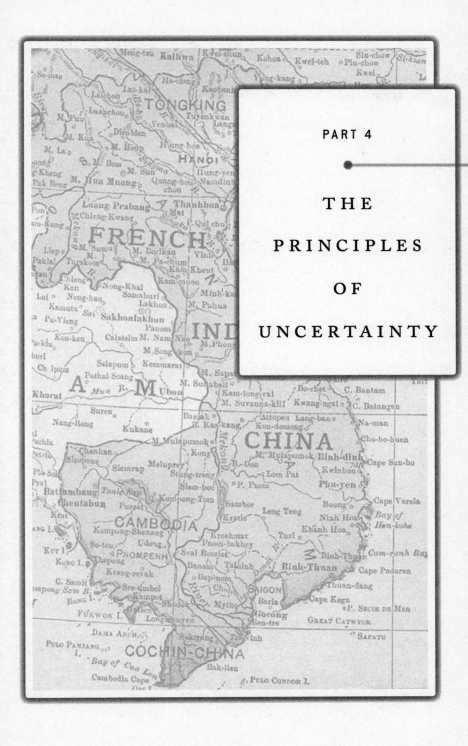

PART 4

THE

PRINCIPLES

OF

UNCERTAINTY

La Seule Vérité Plantation,
Mekong River,
French Protectorate of Cambodia
March 2, 1953

Tien was squatting on his haunches in the shade of a banana tree, smoking the last of his three cigarettes, trying to ignore the heat that was beating down on him in waves. He had been up since before dawn, when the mists still hung heavy, tapping 445 rubber trees by the light of a kerosene headlamp that burned hot against the skin of his forehead. The trees could only be cut in the cool dawn air, when they would bleed enough to fill the collecting cups before their spiral incisions dried up in the tropical sun. Tien had half an hour remaining before he had to brave the midday heat and begin the collection, retracing his route from that morning. He could no longer separate this cycle from the pulse of life itself: *Cut, drain, retrieve.* Repeat. It was as natural as breathing.

He took another drag from the cigarette, slowly, longingly, a breeze bending a twig, and then he heard a noise coming from the ditch behind him, a sound like the hushed whistle of a teakettle left to simmer on a stove. Tien ran the back of his thumb against his lip and shook the ash from the tip of his cigarette. He did not move. It was too hot to move, too hot for anything except that which was absolutely necessary. In heat like this, you had to decide your actions long in advance.

The sound came again, insistent, louder this time. Tien closed his eyes, the image of a woman coming into his mind: a torso, naked and white in the light, a shawl of saffron dragged across the thin curve of her shoulders. The woman turned her face toward him, and that elemental ache returned, but then the vision evaporated as the sound came a third time, now forming into a cry that could only have arisen from the lungs of a human. Tien exhaled, carefully stubbed out his cigarette, and placed it into an overflowing tin can, the label peeled clean. He got down on all fours and peeked over the edge of the ditch, afraid of what he might see.

What he saw stunned him: a naked baby, floating in the scoop basket of a conical sedge hat. The child, exposed to the heat of the sun, was shriveled, a deathly pale yellow-green, the size and color of a pomelo fruit. Too tiny to be alive. But it *was* alive: now it was moving an arm and again making that strange whistling sound.

"Come," Tien called to the others. "Come. Come quickly. Look what I've found."

The others looked, blinking in wonder. It was agreed: this was the smallest baby they had ever seen. It was agreed: the child would not survive.

Tien fished the hat from the water and wrapped the baby in his red checkered scarf.

"Go get Suong. She can give him some milk," he said to Keo.

As they waited, there was much debate among the men. *What to do? Was it a test? A trap?* The baby looked Cambodian, perhaps Laotian, and the first thought was that it must've been one of the workers on the plantation who had delivered the baby and then abandoned him. This theory was passed around and digested and eventually rejected. None of the women workers had been far enough along to deliver even a baby as tiny as this.

Suong arrived at the ditch, the sweat catching in the crinkles of her eyes. It was much too hot for a child to be in the sun. She took him to the shade of the banana tree, where she coddled the child, pinching at the diphthonged knees, the miraculous little legs, no bigger than her fingers. The child's coloring was all wrong—he was suffering from disease. She lifted him to her breast, humming a wordless song, but he would not take the nipple.

"He's sick," she said. "He's too small to drink. He will die." Her tense shifted. "He's dead."

AT LEAST this was the version of events described in Brusa Tofte-Jebsen's obscure novella *Jeg er Raksmey* (Neset Forlag, 1979), which utilizes the usual mixture of pictures, diagrams, and prose that was so popular in Scandinavian literature at the time. Yet *Jeg er Raksmey* was also another sad example of a book written but hardly read; it sold barely half of its listed first run of 750 copies before the rest were sent to the pulper in Lysaker. The slim book did have one notable (if not surprising) reader: Per Røed-Larsen. In a section of *Spesielle Partikler* entitled *"En elementær partikkel er en partikkel som ikke kan brytes ned til mindre partikler"* ("An elementary particle is a particle that cannot be broken into smaller particles"), Røed-Larsen devotes a mind-boggling amount of time and space refuting the factual basis of Tofte-Jebsen's story, despite Tofte-Jebsen's making no claim that his book is anything but fiction. Røed-Larsen disagrees. "[*Jeg er Raksmey*] is near-truth posed as fiction and I can think of no worse crime," he writes. "It has thus become my beholden duty . . . to set the record straight. We must stick with the facts and only the facts" (591).

In particular, Røed-Larsen is bothered by Tofte-Jebsen's claim that the child was discovered in a floating hat. In building up a case against such an origin story, Røed-Larsen references (among other things) the improbable buoyancy quotient of a newborn's (even an unusually small newborn's) staying afloat inside the leaky and unstable containment vessel of a palm-leaf *nón lá* hat (591–93). Much more likely, Røed-Larsen argues, was that the child was given directly to Tien by one of the women on the plantation, sans floating hat.

No matter. Regardless of how he was discovered, what cannot be disputed is that the child had chosen a most unusual landing point for his entrance onto the stage. Owned by the de Broglie family for three generations, La Seule Vérité was one of the few French rubber plantations still operating along the banks of the Mekong. In 1953, France was already seven years deep into its dirty war with the Viet Minh, unable to relinquish its Indochine colonies without a pro-

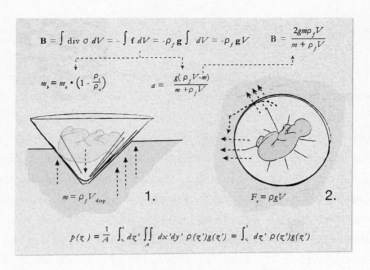

Fig. 4.1. Nón lá *Hydrostatic Buoyancy Analysis*
From Røed-Larsen, P., *Spesielle Partikler,* p. 592

tracted, bloody fight that would culminate the following spring on the slopes of Dien Bien Phu. La Seule Vérité, perched on an oblong bend in the river, was both of this empire and wholly separate from it, a place that had gracefully excused itself from the normal laws of both space and time.

After some discussion, the workers decided to present the baby-who-was-dead-but-not-dead-yet to the manager of the plantation, Capitaine Claude Renoit. Capitaine Renoit had lost a leg early in the war and had come to La Seule Vérité to sulk and wax on about the decline of everything that once was great about the land. But he was an honest man, and he treated the workers as well as they could hope for. He did not believe in an excess of suffering, and so he would know what to do with the child. If he gave permission for the little thing to die, then the child's spirit would not blame them when it found no place to rest.

Renoit was sitting on the patio, thumbing at a glass of Courvoisier, the ledger sheets splayed out before him. A fleeing diplomat had given him the bottle in Saigon for services rendered on the battlefield, and Renoit had been saving the cognac for a special occasion ever since, but it was becoming more and more likely that he would die before a worthy occasion came, so he had broken the seal and let the old liquid cut through the heat of his body. These grapes were from Napoleon's time, when empires were carved with simple gestures of the hand. Renoit found himself wondering whether, if the worst were to happen, he would kill himself or let another man have the pleasure. He had seen enough to know that in every death, someone suffered and someone triumphed, and often those two were the same person.

He was startled out of his reverie by a group of coolies coming up the hill from the rubber fields. Someone must have died again. This was both annoying and somehow exhilarating.

We're still making the rubber. We're still dying to make the rubber. It didn't matter what the ledger sheets said. *La mort est notre mission civilisatrice,* Renoit thought, and took a sip of the cognac.

When presented with the baby, Renoit, like all the others, was taken with the child's almost mystical diminutiveness. Its fingers like tiny spiders, toes like grains of rice.

"What the hell do you want me to do?" Renoit said to Tien, who was offering the child with outstretched arms, like a gift. "He's one of yours. *Fais-en ce que tu veux.*"

Tien bowed. His heart sank. As he feared, the blood would now be on his hands. He turned away, sheltering the child, who had suddenly grown quiet, as if sensing the imminence of his doom.

It was then that Jean-Baptiste emerged from the main house. He was carrying a wireless, intently swinging its long, spindly antenna toward the sky, fishing for an elusive, invisible signal.

"Why ever did we get this thing? I wasn't worried about receiving the news before," he said. "But now I can't seem to live without it."

Jean-Baptiste saw the crowd of workers around Renoit.

"This heat's miserable. Even the radio waves have wilted." He paused. "Did someone die?"

"Not yet," said Renoit.

Tien's hopes rose. He offered the baby, still wrapped in his scarf, to the master of the house.

Jean-Baptiste studied Tien closely.

"Whose child is this?" he said. He put down the radio, still expelling its plush blanket of static, and took the small creature in his hands.

"Whose child is this?" he said again.

Tien bowed. "He is yours, Monsieur de Broglie."

2

As Tofte-Jebsen points out, it might at first seem curious that Jean-Baptiste de Broglie, reluctant sovereign of La Seule Vérité, would be one of the last remaining *kmaoch sbaek sor* ("white ghosts") in the twilight of a dying empire, especially considering his almost total indifference to the actual business of running a plantation. But dig beneath the surface and you will discover an uncommon resolve; Jean-Baptiste, willingly or unwillingly, had inherited that strange but effective colonial alchemy of nostalgia, loyalty, and imperial duty.

Jean-Baptiste's grandfather, Henri de Broglie, had been part of the first wave of eager settlers to the newly formed French Protectorate of Cambodia in the 1870s. Henri was an early champion of the magnificent ruins of Angkor, and through a series of articles in respected periodicals such as *Le Globe* and *Le Petit Parisien,* he had helped to popularize their "rediscovery" among Western audiences. At the time, the temples still fell under the jurisdiction of the Kingdom of Siam, and Henri was part of the diplomatic delegation that had negotiated their successful return to the Cambodian people.

"The Khmers are a friendly but short-sighted race," he wrote in an editorial in *Le Petit Journal.* "If they are to achieve anything in the future, they must see what magnificence was possible in the past."

Along the way, Henri had forsaken Catholicism for his own Westernized version of the local Theravada Buddhism: he borrowed selectively from Khmer traditions but also subtly aligned spiritual enlightenment alongside the tenets of Rousseau's rational enlightenment. For Henri, ascendancy to nirvana meant total mastery of one's own domain using the latest advances in technology. It was a convenient alteration: such cultural blending allowed him to shirk responsibility for his actions by locating himself in the ethically ambiguous space between the colonizer and the colonized.

While on a tour of Brazil in 1882, Henri visited a rubber plantation and witnessed the cultivation of hevea trees. He watched in fascination as the men made a V-shaped incision into the soft bark of the plant and then siphoned the milky sap through a half-moon spout into the hollow shell of a coconut. Later, Henri would dip his hand into a great steel drum of warm latex, the rubber coating him like a second skin. Sensing his guest's great admiration, the plantation owner gave Henri a pair of black rubber boots that smelled of wet ash.

"I am certain that nearly all of man's inventions in the next 100 years will be made of this material," he later recorded in his journal. "There is a life to its texture that brings me great comfort."

He brought back a jar full of hevea seeds and a notebook of instructions for its cultivation, and founded La Seule Vérité in the heart of the colony, on the banks of the Mekong, the great river that would deliver his crop to the world. The plot was expansive but perhaps two hundred kilometers farther upstream than it needed to be. This choice, like all others, was made defiantly, *un défi du cœur.*

"The river is the spine of the colony, from which all life comes and goes," he wrote. "My house is built between the fourth and fifth vertebrae. . . . And the view does not disappoint."

Sometimes the surface of the river was so calm and wide, one could not believe there was any movement at all—it resembled not a river but a thousand-year-old lake. This curving stretch of the Mekong, like the bend of a woman's knee, inevitably affected all those who passed through it. Either they fell in love with the way *les heures* bubbled and moaned here or else they urged their *capitaine* to push through to the next turn, wondering who would ever choose to live in such a place.

The house itself was a lavish, two-story affair built of Italian marble and local rosewood, surrounded by rolling bushes of bougainvillea. It was one of the first rubber plantations in all of Indochine, and for years it stumbled along, producing little from immature trees for a nearly nonexistent Asian market. Henri, undeterred, continued plotting his rise to wealth and fame, writing at length of rubber's sturdy flexibility, extolling the great rubber farms of Brazil, Java, and the newly formed Congo Free State in Africa.

Henri was a notorious cataloger. He recorded nearly everything that went on at La Seule Vérité in obsessive detail, documenting tree height, wages, temperature, flooding, bird species, even his own bowel movements. Fearful that someone might get hold of these notes and decode his secrets, Henri kept the large calfskin tomes locked in a vault. Years later, when his son and then grandson were able to glimpse their contents, such worries seemed superfluous: the ledgers did indeed contain a wealth of information, but their system of organization was beyond mortal comprehension. Columns of numbers, labeled only with a series of initials, would intersect graphs and tables of equally opaque figures. An unidentified chart could just as easily have been referring to kilograms of rubber output as to kilograms of excrement produced. Henri's system existed only in the world of the system itself.

Henri married a Khmer woman from the north named Kolthida. Unlike in the British colonies, where race lines were drawn quite clearly, such intermarriages were not unheard of in French Indochina, but the union did not help Henri's reputation in Saigon as a rogue colonist who had lost himself with the natives upriver. Yet Koko, as she came to be known, would quietly prove her detractors wrong: she spoke good, clean French and quickly mastered the intricate art of judging the world from beneath a parasol. Her wardrobe featured full-length corsets, ordered specially slim and narrow from Paris, and she subtly inflected her formal ensembles with a touch of tasteful local flair—a bright Khmer scarf or a snail shell bracelet that clicked and tinkled as she strolled the paths. On the mantel in the drawing room she installed two traditional *Lakhon Khol* masks from the Reamker epic: Sophanakha, the demon seductress, and Hanuman, the noble monkey warrior. The masks smelled of blood, but Henri eventually grew accustomed to this.

Like her husband, Koko managed to toe the finest of lines between the *exploiteur* and *exploité:* she ran her house with an iron first, commandeering the servants in a stiff mixture of French and Khmer, and surprised their respected visitors from Phnom Penh by playing a repertoire of jigs on a piano that was always slightly out of tune from the constant damp. These visitors would later remark in private to Henri what an admirable job he had done with the native woman. He accepted their congratulations—for him, the miracle was not that Koko had adapted so well, but why such adaptation did not take place all across the colony.

"Nearly anything can be cultivated anywhere, given the right care and attention," Henri said to his bemused guests. "Certain environments demand more care and attention, but this is not a failure of the cultivar. Any failure lies squarely on the shoulders of the *cultivateur.*"

Then he would take them through the young hevea grove. The trees were planted at precise distances such that no matter where one stood, the rows would form and re-form into an infinite kind of order. There was no way to unbind them.

Koko bore Henri a son, André, who, despite his Khmer lineage, looked very much like a round-faced Frenchman left out in the sun to ripen, a true *Indochine français.*

Henri would not live to see his grand vision come to fruition. On December 31, 1899, five minutes before the dawn of the new century, he succumbed to a swift and brutal case of hemorrhagic dengue fever. The servants, unsure of what to do, lit off the fireworks anyway. The explosions flushed open the night, momentarily revealing the great jungles beyond before their dying embers streamed down into the cool, black river, where they hissed and sizzled into silence.

On New Year's Day, as word of Henri's death spread up and down the river, more news came to join it: Koko had disappeared during the night, taking with her a box full of jewelry and several thousand francs. Despite some efforts by colonial forces to locate her, she would never be seen or heard of again. There were rumors, of course: that she had fled to Paris and had opened a successful Indochine-themed lounge and nightclub; that she had been murdered for her jewels by a group of masked men near the Laotian border. One story even claimed she had used witchcraft to assume the appearance of a white man and now ran a nearby plantation.

"The only way you can still tell who she once was," said one of the characters in Tofte-Jebsen's novella, "is to catch her sleeping and shine a torch into her eyes. A person can never change their eyes when they dream" (56).

André de Broglie, barely nineteen years old and now an orphan, was left to manage the plantation on his own. Luckily, his hand was steady, and the fledgling century would witness the swift rise of an automobile driven on the rubber pneumatic tire. Seemingly overnight, the global demand for latex exploded. La Seule Vérité—primed by Henri's hubris for just such an explosion—eventually grew to thirty thousand hectares, with a workforce of more than six hundred indentured Vietnamese laborers.

When he was twenty-four, André floated down to Saigon and returned with a wife standing upon his prow. Eugenia was the eldest child of Pierre Cazeau, the stately, arrogant owner of the Hôtel Continental, on rue Catinat. She was also deaf. Her tutors had spent the first thirteen years of her life attempting to teach her how to speak like a hearing person, as was dictated by the popular pedagogy of the time. Her tongue was pressed, her cheeks prodded, countless odd intonations were coaxed forth from her lips. Cumbersome hearing horns were thrust into her ears, spiraling upward like ibex horns. It was a torture she finally rejected for the revolutionary freedom of sign, which she taught herself from an eighteenth-century dictionary by Charles-Michel de l'Épée that she had stumbled upon accidentally on the shelf of a Saigon barbershop.[1] Based on the grammatical rules of spoken language, L'Épée's Methodical Sign System was unwieldy and overly complex: many words, instead of having a sign on their own, were composed of a combination of signs. "Satisfy" was formed by joining the signs for "make" and "enough." "Intelligence" was formed by pairing "read" with "inside." And "to believe" was made by combining "feel," "know," "say," "not see," plus another sign to denote its verbiage. Though his intentions may have been noble, L'Epée's system was inoperable in reality, and so Eugenia modified and shortened the language. In her hands, "belief" was simplified into "feel no see." Verbs, nouns, and possession were implied by context.

---

[1] "So unlikely as to approach an impossibility," writes Røed-Larsen of this book's discovery, in *Spesielle Partikler* (597).

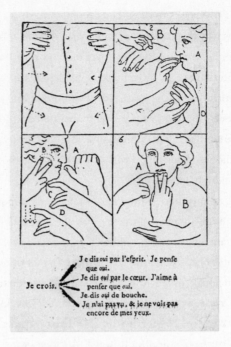

Fig. 4.2. L'Épée's Methodical Sign System
From de l'Épée, C.-M. (1776), *Institution des sourds et muets: par la voie des signes méthodiques,* as cited in Tofte-Jebsen, B., *Jeg er Raksmey,* p. 61

One could not quite call her beautiful, but the enforced oral purgatory of her youth had left her with an understanding of life's inherent inclination to punish those who least deserve it. Her black humor in the face of great pain perfectly balanced her new husband's workmanlike nature. She had jumped at the opportunity to abandon the Saigon society that had silently humiliated her, gladly accepting the trials of life on a backwater, albeit thriving, plantation. Her family's resistance to sending their eldest child into the great unknowable cauldron of the jungle was only halfhearted—they were in fact grateful to be unburdened of the obstacle that had kept them from marrying off their two youngest (and much more desirable) daughters.

André painstakingly mastered Eugenia's language. Together, they communed via a fluttering dance of fingertips to palms, and their dinners on the veranda were thus rich, wordless affairs, confluences of gestures beneath the ceiling fan, the silence broken only by the clink of a soup spoon, the rustle of a servant clearing the table, or the occasional shapeless moan that accentuated certain of her sentences, a relic from her years of being forced to speak aloud.

Eugenia began to paint. She painted the rows and rows of rubber trees. She painted the bougainvillea. By torchlight, she painted the flowers of the *Epiphyllum oxypetalum* cactus that bloomed only once a year, and only at midnight. Her paintings were better than they should have been, primarily because of her unusual color palette: nothing appeared as it should. Colors were reversed, dulled, heightened. Eugenia claimed that this was how a blind person would see the world if he or she were to suddenly gain sight.

André had inherited the de Broglie curse of recording everything possible. In the vault next to his father's giant calfskin books, he began to accrue his own ledgers. Unlike his father's records, André's notes were organized, fastidious, and—perhaps most important—*legible*. Yet even his rigorous accounting did not always tell the full story, either. For instance, when he wrote, *"1906 – 8 personnes contractent la syphilis,"* he did not recount that one of these eight cases was actually himself, and that the source of the outbreak was a prostitute who had arrived from Phnom Penh under the guise of being one of the worker's sisters attempting to escape a battered marriage. The prostitute then proceeded to purvey her services for a month before she was found drowned in the Mekong, her mouth stuffed full of stones. Her death was dutifully noted in the tally for that year without comment: *"mortalité totale – 26 (1 de vieillesse, 5 du paludisme, 2 de la dengue, 4 d'une maladie cardiaque, 7 d'une pneumonie, 3 de la tuberculose, 3 de causes inconnues, 1 par noyade)."* Flip forward a few pages and you will find the total profit for this year as well: *"1,931,398 FF"*—an astounding amount, considering time, place, and circumstance.

As their fortune grew, André remained keenly aware that he was reaping the delayed fruits of his father's persistence, that nearly every one of his triumphs was not the result of his own doing but rather a by-product of his predecessor's brilliance. Yet instead of neutering his sense of achievement, such knowledge exonerated him from ever having to find his own way. His destiny had set him free. Henri's gravestone, which André paid a visit to every Sunday, presided over the plantation from a hilltop. Its inscription, a phrase of the Buddha's that a local boatman had reportedly recounted for Henri, read thus:

CE QUE TU AS ÉTÉ DÉCIDE DE CE QUE TU ES.
CE QUE TU FAIS MAINTENANT DÉCIDE DE CE QUE TU SERAS.

Tofte-Jebsen translates this as: "What you are is what you have been. What you'll be is what you do now" (89).

Jean-Baptiste, full of jaundice, came forth into this cauldron of patrimony and newfound wealth in the monsoon season of 1907, nearly killing his young mother in the process. He was a sickly child, whose first years were marked by a succession of illnesses that kept him bedridden and unable to venture outdoors. A hawkish, unpleasant French tutor (Tofte-Jebsen assigns this tutor no name or gender) was brought in from Phnom Penh to teach Jean-Baptiste in his bedroom, which became a sanctuary not just for restless sleep but for intercontinental and even interstellar travel through the crates of books that arrived on the slow boat from Paris. He developed a devout love of reading, devouring the tales of Robert Louis Stevenson, Rudyard Kipling, Victor Hugo, and Alexandre Dumas by candlelight as lizards flicked across the ceiling. Later, he read Keats and Blake and Coleridge and pined for an English countryside he had never seen. He wished desperately that he had grown up in the open expanse of the heathered moorland instead of the equatorial cage of Indochine.

And all who heard should see them there,
And all should cry, Beware! Beware!
His flashing eyes, his floating hair!
Weave a circle round him thrice,
And close your eyes with holy dread,
For he on honey-dew hath fed,
And drunk the milk of Paradise.

When he was thirteen, having outgrown his tutor's expertise, and being well enough to weather the dangers of the outside world, he requested admission to the Collège Lanessan, in Saigon. Eugenia remained reluctant; she worried not just for her son's fragile health but about exposing him to Saigon's colonial aristocracy. Yet André supported the idea: it was evident that in this new world born from the ashes of the Great War, the successful businessman had to possess not just local wisdom but worldly knowledge—*mondanités,* as the French say. Perhaps he saw a lack of *mondanités* as one of his own shortcomings—André much preferred to stay at home, tending the books rather than searching out inspiration in some remote corner of the globe. He knew such complacency soon would not be enough: the owner of a plantation in Indochina now needed to understand the shifting markets in Europe just as well as the flooding cycle of the Mekong. Morse's telegraph, Marconi's radio, and now the proliferation of Bell's telephones—which had just begun appearing in the more stylish salons of Saigon—these were all contributing to a swiftly shrinking globe. André was a child of the last century, but his son was coming of age in a new age.

When Jean-Baptiste was fourteen, he made his first journey to Europe. He and Eugenia—who also had never ventured out of the colonies—traveled by steamship to visit Monsieur Pascal Vernon, a distant uncle in Paris. On the occasions when her son was either unable or unwilling to act as her interpreter, Eugenia communicated by using a little writing pad that hung around her neck. Although slightly involved, such a method of communication seemed to curry her favor wherever they went. Tofte-Jebsen claimed that the pad from that trip remained intact many years later, providing a kind of oratory receipt of their travels: *"Allons nous asseoir près de la fenêtre?"* . . . *"Cette crème brûlée est passée"* . . . *"Pardon, mais que cet homme est bête."*[2]

Jean-Baptiste's intoxication with La Ville Lumière was evident in his short (but precise) journal entries. After managing to skip the lines at Notre Dame due to his mother's *"déficience,"* he called the famous cathedral *"splendide"* and *"comme un cauchemar plaisant."* He wondered about the similarities of the gargoyles to *"les démons d'Angkor."* They also managed to jump the queue at La Tour Eiffel, which he labeled *"majestueuse, mais incomplète."* Yet his real attention was drawn back again and again to the nature that cushioned the more

---

[2] The existence and persistence of such a pad is briefly disputed by Røed-Larsen (598).

famous aspects of the urban landscape. He filled an entire sketchbook with renderings of the city's trees in autumn—the chestnuts of Montmartre, the long rows of London planes lining the Champs-Élysées, the distinguished canopy of a weeping willow guarding a curve of the Seine like a great Chinese firework frozen in mid-explosion. He came to realize, even before he could articulate the thought, that a place was defined by the manner in which it came up for air.

Tofte-Jebsen lingers (96) on an account of a strange episode that occurred the day before they were to head back home. For the first time since her enforced oral schooling, Eugenia encountered another deaf person, at the Marché aux Fleurs et aux Oiseaux at the Île de la Cité. The woman was a Parisian, out on a Sunday to buy daffodils for her apartment. At first excited for such a meeting, Eugenia animatedly began to sign a barrage of questions and comments, only to be met by confusion. Soon the pad was brought out and it was determined that the woman could decipher only one in three of Eugenia's signs. The reasons were manifold: L'Épée's dictionary, from which she had taught herself sign, turned out to be very much out of date, long ago cast away for the more modern and practical LSF (la Langue des Signes Française). She herself had greatly manipulated L'Épée's turgid system to make it more streamlined, largely abandoning his strict adhesion to oral grammar. On top of this, her own realization of each of L'Épée's signs, taken from two-dimensional, static diagrams, was a singular interpretation. She had taught herself in isolation, with no one to learn from or to converse with. She had thus invented her own dialect, a dialect so particular as to be incomprehensible to all others. Her language was uniquely her own, an island of marooned expression.

This discovery sent Eugenia into a deep depression, which lasted the entire journey back to Indochina. Not only was she an outcast from the society of the hearing; she was an outcast from her own kind. She vowed never again to venture abroad. La Seule Vérité became her only domain.

In contrast to his mother, Jean-Baptiste could not be contained. After that first taste of Paris, he traveled abroad every summer, initially with Uncle Pascal and then on his own, visiting much of Europe, including those English foothills that he had so often dreamed about. His travels then took him farther afield: to North America, where he visited New York City, Niagara Falls, and the Grand

Canyon; to Brazil, where he floated the Amazon and saw a vast array of flora, winged fauna, and flesh-eating fish; and to India, where he fell ill in Calcutta, remaining bedridden for three weeks, suffering from feverish flashbacks to his immobile childhood and the stale, molding odor of his tutor's breath as he (or she) read to him from Plato's *Republic*.

André, at first supportive of his son's boundless interest in the world, soon grew worried that he might one day leave and never return. It was his hope that Jean-Baptiste would absorb a certain degree of *mondanités* but then eventually grow tired of such adventures and settle down to the more mundane task of managing the planation. André therefore tolerated his son's sojourns as long as he attended to his schooling and was home every Christmas.

The schooling, of course, was not a problem—Jean-Baptiste was a naturally brilliant student. When he turned seventeen, he was one of two dozen in the colony offered a place at the Sorbonne.

Once back in the heart of Paris, Jean-Baptiste quickly dropped the course in economics that he had qualified for and instead took up philosophy, specializing in metaphysics, while also making the occasional informal foray into medicinal botany during his free time. He would spend his afternoons in the botanical gardens, splayed out on a bench reading Kant and a young German philosopher named Martin Heidegger.

When his head grew too full with questions of phenomenological hermeneutics, he would stroll through Jardin des Plantes and sketch the curated flora from far-flung lands, including those from his own. The plants' structural certainty soothed him in the face of great doubt. On each of his annual returns to Indochina, he would bring back a new specimen for the gardens of La Seule Vérité. Eugenia became his horticultural partner in crime, and together they cultivated a collection of more than two hundred exotic plants that rivaled the great botanical gardens of Saigon. Her surreal chromatic paintings of the flowers hung throughout the house, presenting the unsuspecting visitor with a mildly hallucinogenic experience.

In 1931, Jean-Baptiste helped design the Indochina Pavilion at the Colonial Exposition in the Bois de Vincennes. A reconstruction of Angkor Wat's central tower complex was built next to a Laotian fishing village and an exact copy of

*Fig. 4.3. Pavillon de l'Indochine à L'Exposition Coloniale
Internationale de 1931, Bois de Vincennes, Paris*
From Tofte-Jebsen, B., *Jeg er Raksmey*, p. 98

La Seule Vérité's rubber-processing hall, where the latex was squeezed into sheets and then hung to dry. Jean-Baptiste oversaw its re-creation. Forty full-grown hevea trees were shipped in from Brazil and planted in their orderly rows. At first they would not bleed, so a mixture of goat's milk fortified with flour was concocted to mimic the appearance of fresh latex.[3]

The organizers of the exhibition asked Jean-Baptiste to give several on-site lectures about the biological wonders of Southeast Asia, and it was during one of these lectures, which was halted prematurely by a rare tropical downpour, that he sought shelter beneath the Angkor Wat simulacrum with a pretty woman who shyly introduced herself as Leila Cousaine. She was from Normandy. She was in town with her parents for their annual shopping excursion, and a friend had told her about the wonders of the exposition, which she had decided to reconnoiter for herself. She admitted her admiration for his talk and said she had always dreamed of traveling the world but lacked the valor and

---

[3] Røed-Larsen takes issue with Jean-Baptiste's involvement (601), citing Catherine Hodeir and Michel Pierre, *L'Exposition Coloniale* (1991); Sylvie Pala, *Documents: Exposition Coloniale Internationale* (1981); and Sylviane Leprun, *Le Théâtre des colonies* (1986) as providing no mention of a rubber plantation at the exposition's Indochina Pavilion.

constitution to do so. Jean-Baptiste noticed immediately that the color of her eyes did not match—her left was a luminous shade of aquamarine and her right was a reddish flint tone that had a way of catching the light at certain angles. He wanted to ask her about this particularity but instead made a hasty and embarrassed dinner invitation for the following evening, which she accepted on the condition that her father gave his consent.

They dined at an art deco brasserie in Montparnasse. The meal was halting and awkward—Jean-Baptiste oscillated between lecturing her on plant species and asking questions that came off as impertinent. After a while, he fell into a kind of half silence marked by inappropriate humming. Leila, clearly intimidated by her partner, spent most of the meal with eyes downcast, answering his queries without enthusiasm. Toward the end, as they waited for a pair of crèmes brûlées that couldn't come fast enough, Jean-Baptiste, thinking nothing could make the evening go worse, mustered up the nerve to ask her his original question, albeit without asking a question at all.

"Your eyes," he said.

"My eyes?" she said, glancing up at him, briefly revealing the pair of mismatched wonders before maneuvering her gaze once again to the hem of the tablecloth.

"They are . . ." He drifted. "I've never seen them before."

"Of course you haven't seen them before. We've never met before yesterday, Monsieur de Broglie."

"Yes," he said, embarrassed. "I suppose we haven't. But your eyes are different. That is, they are different from each other."

"My mother says they make me look wolfish."

"Wolfish? Heavens, no. They're beautiful," he said. "Truly. I could live a thousand years and never see something so beautiful."

She blushed and flashed him a cautious smile, her first true smile of the evening.

"The Cambodians believe the eyes never change," he said. "You can go through an infinite number of reincarnations, but your eyes will always remain the same. It's how we recognize our friends and enemies across time. So perhaps you came from two different people. Or one person and one wolf."

She laughed, miming a snarl and raising a mock paw. The moment vanished just as quickly as it had appeared.

"Will you ever go back?" she asked, recovering. "Back to Indochina, I mean."

"Of course," he said, still staring at her lips. "It's my home. My father and mother are still there. They expect me to come back."

"Yes, but how do you *know* it's your home? You seem so at ease here."

"I feel at ease here."

"Then your home is where you were born?"

He shook his head. "Your home is where you will be buried."

"That's a little morbid, isn't it? I mean, for me, a home is where I shall want to live."

He straightened his napkin. "Forgive me."

"For what?"

"I'm not used to a lady's company. I grew up under isolated circumstances. You must have thought me a worldly gentleman, only to be sorely disappointed when you met the insensitive impostor before you."

"On the contrary," she said. "But then you must find *me* so boring. 'Une petite nonne normande,' as my sister says."

"Not at all," he said quickly. "It's not every day that you meet a wolf."

That night—in the transience of that snarl, in the delicate collision of their words—a mutual acknowledgment of need was established. Not quite love, but something more useful, which would eventually grow into a kind of interdependence. On paper, such a thing was not all that different from love.

Leila came to tolerate Jean-Baptiste's habit of leaving a conversation in midsentence to examine leaf structure and, as it turned out, such tolerance was just enough. They were married in 1933, in the gardens of the Muséum National d'Histoire Naturelle, in front of her family and a small collection of scientists and acquaintances from the colonies. Eugenia and André elected not to make the trip.[4]

During those fleeting years in Paris, as fascism began to rear its ugly head to

---

[4] Røed-Larsen claims they were actually married in the spring of 1934, citing an *attestation de marriage* he tracked down at the bureau de l'état civil in the Mairie du 11e.

the east, Jean-Baptiste lived a charmed life of fitful ideas. He started and did not finish a thesis on Heidegger (*Dasein, Terreur, et le Regret du Colonialisme*) and then started and did not finish a thesis on epiphytic orchid propagation. Everything was captivating from a distance, but as soon as he got too close to a topic, his interest began to wane. He enjoyed dropping in at the laboratories of the Polytechnique and listening to lectures on physics and astronomy by the visiting scholars, because most of what they said he could only marginally understand, and this kept him hungry.

One of these lectures was given in the dead of winter by Georges Lemaître, a bespectacled, portly priest from Belgium who was the first person to propose that the universe was expanding, much to the twin annoyance of the Catholics and Einstein, who both claimed that Lemaître was meddling in territory beyond his comprehension.

Monseigneur Lemaître's talk at the Polytechnique was on how one might go about calculating the precise age of the universe, an act he did not see as being at odds with his faith. As he put it: "Even God enjoys a birthday party. One common mistake is to attempt to solve scientific problems with religion and religious problems with science. Each must be solved in the state in which it arises."

Impressed by Jean-Baptiste, who lingered after the lecture and asked several probing questions about measuring stellar luminosity, Lemaître invited him to attend an atomic physics conference in Copenhagen the following week.

Jean-Baptiste took the sleeper up to Denmark, and over the course of four utterly chilly, utterly magical days, he rubbed shoulders with some of the greatest minds of a generation—men like Niels Bohr, Werner Heisenberg, and Wolfgang Pauli, who were ferociously negotiating the framework of quantum mechanics over stale pints of lager at the Hviids Vinstue, a poorly lit pub that smelled like the bilge of a ship.[5]

The crew of physicists did not seem to mind that Jean-Baptiste was not a

---

[5] In one of his more passionate dissents, Røed-Larsen claims there is no evidence that such a conference ever took place in Copenhagen during the winter of 1937, pointing to, among other things, the fact that Niels Bohr was in the middle of a world tour at this point, engaged with visiting the USA, Japan, China, and the USSR. "Unless, of course," Røed-Larsen writes facetiously, "Tofte-Jebsen is writing of another Bohr, another Copenhagen, a parallel Bohr in a parallel Copenhagen . . . in which case I can offer no comment" (604).

scientist, that he was instead a middling botanist and deficient philosopher who hailed from an Oriental plantation. Such credentials appeared, rather, to gain him credence in their eyes; his place outside of their discipline encouraged them to use him as a confessional booth for their unformed theories. After the day's formal sessions, he would find himself in intimate interlocution with the men as they strolled through the streets of the city, lit brightly by a constellation of white lanterns, their conversations dancing across a range of quantum theories that would set his head spinning. At the Hviids Vinstue, he was often used as a prop when someone was trying to illustrate a particular point. Sometimes he was an electron, sometimes a fermion, sometimes a vast celestial body. They would orbit him in circles, knocking over chairs, spilling beer, laughing at their own audacity, all the while arguing about charge, position, spin. His involvement in these impromptu demonstrations—even simply as a flexible bit of mass—gave him goose bumps. Pauli teasingly referred to him as "Your Highness." Heisenberg ignored him. Bohr—Bohr was the best of the lot. Bohr knew, in that way that few great men do, exactly how much of the universe could never be understood at all. The limits of the known world did not bother Bohr—instead, he viewed our peaceful coexistence with the unknown as a testament to the capacities of the human mind.

"If you admit you are uncertain," he said once, "then you are that much closer to certainty."

Tofte-Jebsen recounts how, on the final evening, the conference members had paid a visit to the university's cyclotron, a sleeping giant of a machine that struck Jean-Baptiste as "the altar of the new secular religion" (107). Afterwards, he found himself back at the pub, deep in an argument with Bohr about the nature of free will. The others, exhausted by the week's negotiations, had already headed home, but Bohr persisted, and Jean-Baptiste got the feeling that it was strictly for his benefit, though he was unsure why such a genius would want to spend any time with a colonial dilettante like himself.

That evening, a pipe had burst in the flat above, and the pub was unusually humid. Every now and then, little drops of condensation would fall upon their heads and into their beer mugs.

"Are you comfortable with complementarity?" Bohr asked him.

"I'm not sure . . ." Jean-Baptiste's English was excellent, but around Bohr he always felt a bit like a child again.

"Most people aren't. They don't want to hear about something being both true and not true at the same time. They don't want to believe that Schrödinger's cat can be both dead *and* alive until the moment they open the box. Most people don't want to push their minds to accept both possibilities at once. But for me, such concurrence is beautiful—necessary, even. The universe is not based on truth but on *possibility*."

Jean-Baptiste took a slow drink from his mug. "But surely there are things that are just true? What about the forces that govern us? Laws? Causality?"

"Causality is a siren. She enchants and she tames," said Bohr. "Look at Einstein. He's come undone. He's trying to explode our framework, and he's convinced he will, all because he cannot release himself from the temptations of locality. He cannot free himself from *If this, then that*. Don't tell me it's a failure of imagination. Don't tell me it's because of the numbers. I'll tell you what it is: we are confined to consequence. We can survive the *now* only because we claim to know what comes next. We are terrified of the truth: that by saying *If this*, we have already destroyed *then that*."

Jean-Baptiste shook his head. "Your entire framework is based on the unobserved theory—"

"Observation is precisely the problem. Observation, as we understand it, is the nemesis of understanding," said Bohr. "We're *obsessed* with this act of witnessing—yet witnessing is an action that irrevocably affects the subject. As it turns out, we can only *witness the witnessing*."

Jean-Baptiste left that evening—damp and bewildered, his core shaken by the steadiness, the utter generosity, of Bohr's belief in the uncertain. On the train back to Paris, he sat in a state of agitated confusion, nursing a brandy as the lowlands slid past. Yet he had never felt more alive. It was as if he had suddenly jumped orbits and could now feel the heat of the sun against his skin.

"I DIDN'T OPEN IT," his wife said as soon as he came through the door. She pointed to a telegram from Saigon that was propped up on the dining room table.

He sat down, laced open the envelope, read the fifteen words, and then read them again.

It was midafternoon, but the sun had already begun to sink. Jean-Baptiste left the house and walked through the cold and empty streets, following a familiar path through the Cimetière du Père Lachaise. The dew had frosted in the grass. In a hickory tree, a lone raven pecked at its feet, its brethren having left long ago for balmier skies. At some point, Jean-Baptiste placed his hand on the surface of one of the gravestones. To his surprise, he found the stone warm to the touch.

"What will you do?" Leila asked when he returned. Her voice revealing the slightest tremor.

"There's nothing to be done," he said. "I must go and take my place."

His father, André de Broglie, was dead.

Leila did not try to dissuade him. She packed her possessions into a pair of steamer trunks, and together they made the long, grueling trip to La Seule Vérité. A journey is never measured by its distance alone, but rather by its chapters: they took the overnight train to Marseille; then a steamer to Saigon, stopping in Alexandria, switching boats first in Bombay and again in Singapore; then a riverboat up the Mekong, pausing in Phnom Penh for supplies before heading on to the plantation that was to be their new home.

Eugenia welcomed her son's return, if only for the company he provided. She had never harbored the same grand illusions about the de Broglie lineage as her husband did. For her, the rubber plantation, even during its heyday, had been something to tolerate rather than celebrate. Deafness was a shroud that had taught her to study life's details while always ensuring she could never fully touch them, and this distance had afforded her a shrewd kind of wisdom. As Tofte-Jebsen writes, "She haunted a stage not of her own design" (110). Eugenia had known for a long time that her only son's heart was not in the business, but she could not bring herself to release him from his burden. Selfishly, she wanted him close, to suffer as she had suffered.

If Jean-Baptiste ever resented the millstone of his familial duty, he did not express it. He buried his father on the hilltop, next to his grandfather, in a quasi-Christian ceremony that also incorporated local animistic funeral rites performed with incense and flowers freshly cut by André's distraught workers. They had clearly loved him. When Jean-Baptiste walked past them they would bow, tears in their eyes. At first he tried to go out of his way to be friendly with them, telling jokes, querying them on their work, even joining them for the early-morning tap, but after being met with only confused silence, he eventually stopped trying. Knowing he could never fill the gulf left behind by his late father, Jean-Baptiste delegated responsibility for the day-to-day rubber operations to a young, wily Algerian man named Raouf, whom he brought in from Phnom Penh, meanwhile busying himself with a series of complicated projects that became less and less relevant to the family business.

The combination to the vault containing all of the ledger books had somehow been lost. Jean-Baptiste considered blowing open the door but instead had it moved by fifteen men to the basement, where it would stand unopened for forty years. He bought another safe, the same model, and put it in the old safe's place, though he never used it.

"If they have come this far, a safe will not stop them," he said to no one in particular.

His first item of business was to construct a telegraph line. The line would cut east through the jungle, meeting with National Road No. 7 down to Kratié, before heading twenty-five kilometers south through the rice fields into Vietnam, to the northern station at Saigon. The construction of the line took six months and came at an enormous expense: Jean-Baptiste hired two teams of three hundred laborers to work from either end and spent nearly a quarter of the family's savings on the project. When it was finally finished, he sat in the telegraph room beneath the stairwell in the main hall and breathed deep. The smell of blood in the wires.

Jean-Baptiste tapped out a message to Monseigneur Lemaître, the astronomer-priest in Brussels, and imagined the electromagnetic flashes hurtling their way through the thick foliage. The quiver of signal. The promise of contact. He was a part of the world now.

Under Lemaître's distant instruction, Jean-Baptiste built a domed rosewood observatory on the hilltop shared by his grandfather's and, now, his father's gravestones. The dome rose up like a moon, a wooden effigy to the invisible planets suspended above. Two months later, the telescope arrived from Paris, lashed like a cannon to a barrel-stave barge that was filled with bleating

Fig. 4.4. Jean-Baptiste de Broglie to Georges Lemaître, telegram, July 16, 1938
From Tofte-Jebsen, B., *Jeg er Raksmey,* p. 113

livestock. The device was installed inside the observatory with much fanfare, an ancient Khmer man bowing a high-pitched tune on a three-stringed fiddle, and awed locals came from miles around to look through its eyepiece at the rings of Saturn. Jean-Baptiste began taking meticulous notes on the rotation of the constellations, the regularity of comets, and a star that Lemaître had informed him was about to disappear, had in fact already disappeared—they were watching a death from the past, echoed across the great expanse. After barely a full moon cycle, however, the novelty of the telescope had worn off and Jean-Baptiste grew bored with his astronomical observations.

One morning, he was leafing through the pages of a French science journal when he came across a dazzling array of radiographic photos: bony hands with wedding rings, open-mouthed skulls, a bullet lodged inside a buttock. He had stumbled upon his next calling.

"These rays have a very high frequency—four times that of visible light, and so they can penetrate where light cannot," he wrote to Lemaître. "I mean this with no offense, but to see inside the depths of a human body is even more exciting than glimpsing the heavens. It's almost enough to make me believe in God again. To think: it's all right here, right in front of us. We need only make it visible."

He constructed a giant but erratic Tesla coil in their wine cellar and then connected this to a footlong cathode ray tube that he had ordered from Tokyo.

The results were far from immediate as the coil sparked and churned, causing the radio receiver in his study to erupt into static, and the cutlery in the corner of the cellar to take on an ethereal glow. It was not an exact science: he blew through three transformers and constantly overwhelmed their fragile power supply, which had been tenuously wired only a year before from a hydroelectric dam on a tributary of the Mekong. Gradually, though, after much experimentation, he began to home in on the correct amount of voltage needed to operate the X-ray tube with some precision.

His wife became his primary subject. At first, the intensity of the X-rays was either too powerful or too weak, the images coming out white and misty, as if her body were suspended in an English fog. In time, he figured out how to master the machine. The first clear photograph was of her hand, with the darkened orbit of a wedding ring just visible—a re-creation of the photo he had first seen in the journal. Ignoring her protests, he hung this in their bedroom.

"I feel like I'm witnessing my own death," she said.

"Nonsense," he said. "You're witnessing your life."

Despite her hesitancy at being documented so intimately, he X-rayed every inch of her skeleton again and again. Fully clothed, she lay on the examining table as he unveiled her with his machine. He could hear her breath before the X-ray sprang noisily to life, shuddering, groaning, sending its stream of photons flying into her body. Afterwards, he would develop the images alone in the red-tinged darkness of his closet, the negatives emerging wet with solution, his hand trembling as he handled the proof of his wife's conquest. He had ventured where no one had ventured before, including himself, for their actual love-making was a passionless, fumbling affair, done under cover of night. Jean-Baptiste hung the ghostly X-rays of his wife's bones in the hallways, the drawing rooms, even the bathrooms—an ethereal gallery of possession.

Meanwhile, Leila suffered. From the beginning, his wife had been a poor match for the tropics—she pined for the familiarities of home, for the comforting spray of the sea during her walks along the bluffs. She could not grow used to the heat, the damp, the insects, the constant smell of cooking rubber, the natives that watched her every move. Her melancholy was stoked by a long correspondence with her mother in which she savored the most banal news from their village. A dog had borne puppies. Her niece had made a paper hat for Bastille Day. The house at the end of the pier had collapsed during a storm. Jean-Baptiste could not appease her homesickness, even as he imported maps of the Seine's curvatures and the Channel Islands, novels, fine linens, silverware, oil pantings, and custom-made marionettes crafted in the finest workshops of Paris. Their drawing room became an elaborate museum of his placations, but no earthly object could quell her misery. Yet when Jean-Baptiste offered to take Leila to Paris and Normandy for Christmas, she refused, oddly, saying there was too much to be done at the plantation. In the end, she spent the holiday doing nothing except writing her letters back home and reading the same Russian tragedies over and over again.

Leila and Eugenia tolerated each other, but in private each complained of the other's shortcomings. Eugenia viewed her daughter-in-law as a spoiled priss who lacked both backbone and a sense of humor, while Leila saw her mother-in-law as a terrifying, controlling matriarch who heard more than most hearing people and cared only for her spooky portraits of phantasmagoric flowers. Leila had done her best to learn Eugenia's obscure language of signs, but it was as if Eugenia willfully chose not to understand Leila when she signed, shaking her head and insisting that her son act as their translator.

Leila's despair grew with each passing year, for despite their awkward attempts beneath the mosquito nets, no child came therefrom. Jean-Baptiste's mother was strangely content with the absence of any progeny, despite the uncertainty that such a scenario brought to the question of inheritance.

"You must at least be where you are," Eugenia signed to her son. "And she is no place at all." Though the matter was a delicate one, a doctor from Phnom Penh was brought in to examine Leila. He could find nothing wrong.

"Sometimes one simply cannot," the doctor said over tea. "It's the way of things."

Jean-Baptiste became intent on fixing the problem, not necessarily because he wanted a child but because there was a problem to be fixed. Having heard the amazing tales of traditional medicine passed among the workers, he eventually sought advice from a *kru Khmer,* a local shaman. Jean-Baptiste was not enthusiastic about the fact that their inability to conceive would almost certainly become common knowledge among the workers, but in his mind the potential for success outweighed this invasion of privacy. The *kru Khmer,* after visiting with Leila one afternoon, prescribed a fertility tea made of palm root and *Psychotria* bark.

Even Raouf weighed in on the matter: "You must have more sex."

"Thank you, Raouf, but this is none of your concern."

"You must have *much* more sex."

Tien, a hardworking young foreman whom Jean-Baptiste had come to trust, delivered the shaman's tea to Leila each morning, laying down a paper-thin orange tablecloth and pouring the kettle with much formality. He would sit with her while she sipped the tea and nibbled the lemon cakes that were baked to temper the bitter taste of the bark. In this way, Leila began to learn Khmer. The mornings were marked by Tien's lilting singsong voice entwining with her laughter. She was a fast learner, and soon they spoke only in his native tongue, the tea left to simmer, untouched.

"Khnhom sraleanh anak," she said to Jean-Baptiste. "This means 'You look like a beautiful flower.'"

After encountering a group of young students walking upstream to the regional lycée, Leila became excited at the idea of using her newly acquired language skills to teach the children French. Jean-Baptiste, relieved that his wife had expressed interest in anything besides the Normandy postal system, arranged for Tien to shuttle her by riverboat up to the school three days a week.

It was an instant revelation. Her whole demeanor changed. She began standing upright, carrying herself with a newfound determination. Her eyes burned, full of life. Once again she started to dress smartly, taking particular care with her hair and makeup. She was now often gone late into the evening, returning home exhausted and content.

"They know so little," she breathed beside him in bed. "But then, they also know so much. Sometimes I don't know who's learning more—me or them."

"My darling," he said. "I am so glad."

His wife now taken care of, Jean-Baptiste turned back to his own projects. He briefly flirted with the idea of building a cyclotron like the one he had seen during the conference in Copenhagen, but after some investigations, he resolved himself to the impossibility of its creation in such a remote location. Soon after this, the telegraph line to Saigon stopped working. Somewhere in that vast jungle, there had been a breach in the wire. The telegraph room in the main hall fell silent. When an engineer was sent out to ride the entire length of the line and came back without locating the rupture, Jean-Baptiste resigned himself to defeat. If the world would not have him, he would not have it.

"HOW'S SHE GETTING on at the school?" Eugenia signed to Jean-Baptiste as they all sat at the dinner table one evening.

"Mother," Jean-Baptiste signed. "Really, how am I supposed to know this?" He turned to Leila, who was sitting beside him. "She wants to know how you are faring at the lycée?"

"Oh," said Leila. "Fine."

"Very well, thank you," she signed to her mother-in-law, though Eugenia looked on blankly.

"That is, the children are wonderful," she said aloud.

"Ask her which child holds the most promise," Eugenia signed to her son.

"Mother," Jean-Baptiste signed back. "Ask her yourself. She can sign. You know this."

"They are all clever," Leila signed helpfully. "They make me happy."

Eugenia shook her head, swallowing a small bite of pork shoulder. "There's always one who stands above the rest," she signed to her son. "Tell her to be truthful with us."

"I couldn't follow," said Leila. "What did she say?"

"I said you must not lie to us. We are your family," Eugenia signed.

"What's she saying?" said Leila. "I can't follow when she goes so fast. Something about the family?"

Jean-Baptiste sighed. "She's excited for you. She said she wishes she had your patience."

Eugenia bristled but said nothing. Leila, aware that she was being sheltered, resorted to her nervous habit of turning her wedding ring in circles. Jean-Baptiste rose from the table and switched on the Zenith. A symphony by Schubert came on, full blast. The strings pulled and churned. The radio had become an instrument of retaliation, a playground beyond his mother's perception.

IT WAS NOT LONG after this that Eugenia followed her daughter-in-law to work. She waited for Leila to disappear down the river, then unmoored one of the dugouts and paddled after them. She had never been out in the river alone before, and she found navigating the boat difficult, for she could not balance her strokes to make it travel in a straight line. The bow always wanted to go one way or the other. Though the red waters appeared glassy, the current was deceptively strong. By the time she had rounded the bend, she was already sweating into her dress, and her boots were soaked with river water brought in by the bite of the paddle.

She looked for Leila's boat at the school's dock but could not find it, nor did she see Tien coming back her way. She continued slowly upriver, past the school and its overgrown landing strip, and she was just about to turn around, thinking she had simply missed them in passing, when she saw the boat, tucked into a little cove, half hidden by the sagging branches of a river palm. With some trouble, she beached her dugout close by and stepped out into the muck. She saw no sign of Leila or Tien anywhere, so she carefully followed the path up from the cove some ways into the forest. Thinking she had made a wrong turn, she decided to turn back to her boat, but then she spotted the outline of a hut through the dense foliage. She approached, quietly, pausing outside. Lacking any aural faculties, she did what she always did: she turned to her other senses. Eugenia sniffed and smelled it immediately: the distant, sweet fragrance of opium, a scent she had not smelled since her days in Saigon. Above her, the forest moved, birds twittered, twigs crackled, but inside her head there was only the silence and the wet fragrance of the drug, and she closed her eyes and she was a small girl again, staring at her mother lying on the bed next to a man who was not her father. The heat, the stillness of the room, the light from the blinds streaming across their bodies.

The walls of the hut were made of dried leaves wrapped tightly into bundles using a kind of vine. Finding a small gap in the wall, Eugenia hiked up her dress and leaned in close. Her vision adjusted to the darkness of the interior.

Shapes emerged—forming, unforming, forming again. She blinked and returned her eye to the peephole. There was Leila, lying on a blanket, the hourglass of her buttocks white against the hut's soft gloom. A candle flickered. Eugenia shifted her position to gain a better view. She gave a little gasp. Leila was wearing a mask. Eugenia recognized it as the mask from the drawing room, the black Sophanakha demoness, grotesquely missing both ear and nose. The dark head was much too large for her slender white frame; occasionally her head swayed with the weight of the wood. In front of her, he moved, shirtless and also masked, dancing, a monkey warrior, his simian face frozen in a horrible grin. The man glided around the room and then came to her and grasped the end of a long pipe. Delicately, he twisted the bowl flush into the candle's flame, working at the white glob of opium with a pin before swinging the mouthpiece to her, like a flute. The pipe disappeared into the mouth of the mask. She pulled, released, her shoulders shrinking with the exhalation, and again that elemental smell rose up and took hold of Eugenia's consciousness—strong and sweet, seemingly everywhere and nowhere at once. The silence in her head roared.

Eugenia watched for some time, long enough for the masks to come off, long enough to know how far this had come. She felt oddly calm, filled with a sense of the familiar, as if she were watching a ritual she had witnessed many times before. She left only after Leila was asleep and he had risen and was moving toward the door. She ran then, not caring if they saw or heard, tripping once, the leaves in her hair, her boot unlaced, her elbow bleeding into the silk of her dress. She jumped in the boat and pushed off, and she did not paddle, but let the river take her back home as she breathed and stared at the grey silence of the sky.

That evening, a storm moved in. The three of them ate dinner on the porch as the rain hammered at the corrugated tin roof. Leila seemed unusually nervous. She apologized, claiming she was not feeling well, and requested to be excused early, but Eugenia put a hand on her arm and signed that she had something to say. Leila's eyes smoldered in the candlelight. She looked back and forth between husband and mother.

"It occurred to me today," Eugenia signed, "that we should start our own school."

"A school?" Jean-Baptiste signed. "Here?"

Leila's eyes widened with surprise. An uncontrolled shiver passed over her.

"Yes. Right here. Leila's no doubt developing considerable expertise at the lycée, but why not utilize her talents closer to home? Where she could have more control over the lessons and would not have to travel so far every day?"

A silence filled the room. Outside, the rain drummed at the roof.

"Well," said Jean-Baptiste, looking at his wife.

"We certainly have the space," Eugenia reminded them.

"I think it's a brilliant idea," said Jean-Baptiste. "I love it. What do you think, Leila? Could you manage?"

Leila looked down at her hands. Her cheeks were flushed.

"I'm not sure," she said. "They need me up there. I couldn't just abandon—"

Eugenia rapped the table, catching them both off guard. "I'm sure they'll make do," she signed. "Just think of the possibilities!"

"She's right, you know. This could be a great opportunity. No offense against your lycée, but the French colonial education system's a failure."

"On what grounds can you say that?" said Leila.

"The great mistake of the French is to re-create France in Indochina," said Jean-Baptiste. "We must instead teach them *éléments* of science and rationalism, yet modify the course in such a way that the Khmer might understand. We'll use their terms. We'll use their beliefs. We'll make the course of study relevant. This is how you reach and change the native mind."

"We already have a little revolutionary on our hands, don't we?" Eugenia signed. "Maybe there'll be room for my son at this school. That is, if she agrees to it."

A gust of wind rose and extinguished one of the candles, a thin thread of smoke curling and dissolving into itself.

"How can you be so sure you can change a native mind?" Leila said, her face now in half shadow.

"You can always change a mind," Eugenia signed. "A mind is there to be changed."

"Please excuse me," Leila said, laying down her napkin. "I'm not well."

After she left, Jean-Baptiste sipped cognac in the library while his mother worked on her embroidery. Outside, the storm had begun to fade.

"I'm sure she'll come round once she feels better," he signed. "It's a wonderful opportunity to make a real difference. We should have thought of this long ago."

"Good ideas take time," Eugenia signed as she tautened the thread.

"About that man who takes her to work . . ." she signed.

"Tien?"

"I've caught him thieving. The masks on the mantel. I think we should fire him."

"Thieving?" Jean-Baptiste got up to look. The masks were indeed gone. "Are you sure, Mother? Tien has been with us since birth. This place is his home."

"Maybe he's become too comfortable."

"But where would we send him? This is the only life he knows. And he cares for Leila so."

"That is precisely the problem."

"Mother, you mustn't always take your misery out on others," he signed.

The needle stopped in midair.

"I'm sorry," he said aloud.

"I'm only reporting what I see. I'm not telling you how to run your own plantation." The needle plunged again.

"I appreciate your candor, Mother. It's true. Sometimes we may lose our way. God knows I have."

He lit a cigar and studied the empty mantel, listening to the last of the rain and the quiet thrush of the needle and thread.

THE NEXT DAY, Jean-Baptiste called Tien into his cluttered office.

"I have been informed of your theft," he said.

Tien bowed his head. Slowly, he fell to one knee and then the other. He brought his hands together in prayer but said nothing, simply remaining motionless in this position.

"Oh, for heaven's sake, stand up, Tien," said Jean-Baptiste. "I'm not going to punish you. We all make mistakes. And I'm not going to ask why you did it. You know it's wrong. But this place cannot run without you. If there's something you need, please just ask me. I will give you anything within my power."

Tien looked at him, stunned. "You will not kill me?"

"Kill you?" Jean-Baptiste laughed. "Are you mad? We aren't barbarians. No, Tien, your conscience will provide all the punishment required."

Tien began to quietly weep into his hands.

"Pull yourself together, man. It's all right. Forgive and forget," said Jean-Baptiste. "Listen, we're starting a school. Here at the plantation. So Leila will no longer need your ferry services. You'll have more time for your work here."

Tien bowed, wiping at his face with the back of his sleeve.

"And Tien? Return the bloody masks. They have some sentimental value, I think, though I can't recall what that is."

Tien left the office, bewildered and teary-eyed. He promised to work hard, to do good, and to never betray his master again. The next day, the masks were returned, smelling of a scent that would gradually fade with time.

AFTER SOME ENCOURAGEMENT, Leila eventually warmed to and even embraced the idea of a school on the plantation grounds. They made a clearing in the forest next to the rubber house and built a one-room schoolhouse—LA SEULE ÉCOLE, read the wooden sign that hung over its entrance. Thirty-five little desks and a chalkboard arrived from Saigon by riverboat. The first day, there were already too many children for the desks; those who could not sit stood patiently in the back as Leila drew out the French alphabet and gestured at the letters' bulbs and cursive tails. When she came to the S, Leila wiggled her index finger like a snake, hissing conspiratorially, and the children covered their mouths and laughed. She already had them. She spoke their language and the children loved her, and she loved them back.

That first semester before the rainy season, word spread quickly of the smiling white woman with two different-colored eyes whose school was open to all. Soon, a hundred children were crowding into the small room, struggling to get a glimpse of the board. Eventually the desks were cast aside and the children sat in neat little rows on the floor. Jean-Baptiste's grand visions of a Khmer rationalism were never quite realized, but nonetheless, in only a few short months, the students made great strides in their writing and arithmetic. Some began to read. Even Tien and the men would come to listen to her during their lunch break, a look of amusement covering up the awe at what they were witnessing.

"However could I have lived without this?" Leila said to her husband as they prepared for bed one evening. "They feel like my own."

Jean-Baptiste smiled. He reached for her hand.

"My dear," he whispered.

"Thank you for being so patient with me," she said. "I know I'm your burden."

"You're my gift. My wolf."

"I haven't been true to you."

"We're all trying. I know it isn't easy. We're all trying. It's the best we can do."

She extinguished the lantern and then she came to him, her hand moving quickly inside his pajama bottoms. He inhaled, sharply. Her forwardness caught him off guard, for they had not been together in some time. She shivered out of her chemise and rose up, white in the moonlight. He whispered a word and fell backwards into the bed. A dead lizard had dropped onto the mosquito net, its silhouette like a dark star against a white sky. He closed his eyes and raked his hands against her back. Beneath the skin, he could feel the heaving roll of her bones. Bones he knew better than his own.

LEILA'S COLLAPSE CAME just as the second semester was beginning. She was standing at the blackboard, writing the word *l'honnêteté,* applying the *accent aigu* on the third and final *e,* when she shuddered and fell, striking her chin on the edge of her desk. She lay on the ground, lifeless, a thin trickle of blood running from her nose and down to the point of her lips. The children crowded around her. They whispered to themselves, some held hands, a few began to cry. Then, from out of nowhere, Tien appeared. He held Leila's head in his arms, wiping away the blood with his scarf.

"*Khnhom sraleanh anak,*" he said tenderly. "*Sophanakha.*" There was a growing pool of blood between her legs. He picked her up in his thin arms and carried her back to the house.

"She shouldn't work so hard," Eugenia later signed to her son in the hallway outside their bedroom. "Some people aren't designed for the stress of the tropics."

"Stop." Jean-Baptiste signed.

"She doesn't belong here."

"Stop," he said aloud, grabbing her hands. "She needs us. Please understand. I need you to understand."

Eugenia's diagnosis proved premature. Leila could barely rise from bed. It was not simply a matter of stress or jungle fatigue. Nor did it appear to be malaria or any of the more common tropical maladies. Her skin became translucent, her lips dull and grey. She developed large, pus-filled blisters up and down the length of her arms and legs. Her back began to peel in large sheets, making it extremely painful for her to lie supine.

The doctor was brought back in from Phnom Penh. The man spent some time examining her, taking notes, asking her questions. She was conscious but feverish. Her answers emerged as half sentences, words without tethers.

After some more prodding, the doctor came downstairs, shaking his head.

Jean-Baptiste offered him some brandy, an offer he refused, pondered, and then accepted. Eugenia watched as the two men sipped their drinks.

"What did you find?" asked Jean-Baptiste.

"She was pregnant," the doctor said. "I couldn't say for sure, but it was early in her term. Two months at most. The child's gone. I'm sorry."

"Pregnant?" Jean-Baptiste said, bewildered, nearly dropping his glass. "But she never told me."

"I'm not sure she knew," he said.

"So this is why she's sick?"

The doctor shook his head. "There are a number of diagnoses I could give you. Smallpox, pemphigus, shingles. But none of these are quite right. Has she been exposed to anything unusual recently?"

"Only the children," Jean-Baptiste said. "Maybe she contracted something from them."

"But there have been no outbreaks in the population that you know of?"

Jean-Baptiste stared at him. "She was pregnant?" He put his head in his hands. "Good God. We were going to have a child?"

Eugenia touched the back of his neck. She made a small sign against his skin with her fingers. He was trembling.

The doctor walked through their house with his glass of spirits, rubbing his beard. He lifted up the arm of one of the marionettes and let it fall. He put a finger to the missing nose of the Sophanakha mask. He leafed through several of Jean-Baptiste's science journals. At one point he stopped in front of a wall in the drawing room, where a framed X-ray of Leila's radius hung in a golden frame.

"What's this?" he asked.

"An arm," said Jean-Baptiste.

"Your wife's arm?"

"Yes. Why?"

The doctor left without pronouncing anything definitive, only that he had read about several cases of patients becoming sick after being exposed to high doses of radiation from an X-ray machine. Their symptoms were similar to Leila's.

"I'm no expert," the doctor said. "But there seems to be some destructive force hidden within the ray itself. An invisible killer."

After he was gone, Eugenia sat with her son, whose eyes had lost all life.

"Your machine's not what made her sick," Eugenia signed. "I know it. She has a weak constitution."

Jean-Baptiste shook his head. "She's stronger than you will ever know, Mother."

During the night, he went down to the cellar with a candle and directed its glow at the chassis of the defunct X-ray machine, now covered in a spectral scrim of spiderwebs and dust. There was a metallic scent of blood in the air. He ran his hands over the cool wires of the Tesla coil and then took a hammer and smashed the tubes one by one, the glass jumping and tearing at his wrists. He fell to the ground, weeping, wiping the blood from his hands across his eyes, nose, and mouth.

Upstairs, he knelt by his wife's bedside. "I'm sorry," he said. "I never meant for it to be like this."

"I've betrayed you," she whispered. "I am the wolf."

. . .

EUGENIA, WHETHER OUT of guilt or obligation, began tending to her daughter-in-law day and night, dabbing at the dark fluid that trickled from her nose, changing the dressings on the lesions, and reading to her from the lavish collection of novels that filled the house's study. Her voice was at once too loud and too soft, the words helpless newborns, but Leila listened and smiled and held on tight to Eugenia's hand.

Jean-Baptiste stalked the grounds like a ghost. Every part of the place now pointed to his folly, to his childish insistence on tinkering with the unknown. Everywhere he went, he could not escape his own shadow. With the telegraph line long dead, he was forced to write to a friend in Paris, Dr. Luc Jeunet, who he remembered had been one of the doctors to treat the great Madame Curie when she had become ill.

I fear I may have inadvertently poisoned my wife with the X-rays from my machine. I know now I was playing with an invisible kind of fire. The images were so brief. How could they have such a profound effect on her tissue? From what I understood, it takes prolonged exposure, years, to become dangerous. Nothing so fleeting. Yet words cannot describe the terror and shame that I now harbor in my soul if my actions are indeed the cause of her rapid decline. Please let me know what treatment course we should pursue and whether anything can be done.

I await your timely reply, JBdB

Desperate for any help, he once again sought the services of the *kru Khmer.* The shaman was a round man who seemed to smell unusually bad, but there was an air of wisdom in his movements that was both disquieting and comforting at the same time. The man had lived a thousand lives and had forgotten nothing.

He spent nearly ten minutes pressing at Leila's skin, until she groaned. Eugenia, furious, sent him away.

"Why do you let that fraud into our house?" she signed.

Yet the shaman returned the next day, this time accompanied by Tien. He brought with him a small pouch of bark and roots that, despite Eugenia's protestations, they concocted into a thick soup. The room became filled with a decaying, earthen odor. Leila tilted her head up to meet the bowl. She struggled to take only a few sips of the foul-tasting brew. Then the shaman removed a series of small glass cups from his bag. He lit a match inside each, heating the air within before bringing one of the cups to each of Leila's lesions.

"What is he doing?" Eugenia signed from the corner of the room. "How can you let him do this?"

"The cups," Jean-Baptiste pointed. "What are they for?"

"She is too hot," said Tien. "He is making her cool."

Eugenia blew out a sound of disapproval.

"How do they expect to make her cool with hot bark soup and matches against her skin?" she signed.

The shaman produced a coin from his pocket, said some words in his language, and began dragging it across Leila's forehead, between her breasts, down her arms.

"She is hot," Tien said. "She has the hot wind inside her. We must release the wind."

Eugenia could not take it anymore.

"Stop this at once!" she said aloud. She seized the shaman's hand and pushed him away. The coin fell to the ground, rolling beneath the bed. He stared at her with a look of curious amusement and then carefully bowed and left the room.

"Mother," Jean-Baptiste said, stooping down to retrieve the fallen coin, "this is their way. They have been doing this forever."

"It isn't *our* way," she signed. "I won't let my daughter be scraped to death by some witch doctor."

"The coin's French," he said, holding it up to the light.

"I don't care what it is. This cannot go on any longer."

"Please," he said. "Please. We need all the assistance we can find right now. Let them do what can be done."

After this, Tien came every day with the shaman's soup. Under Eugenia's disapproving eye, he rubbed the coin against Leila's forehead and the space between her shoulder blades. Yet Tien was painstakingly tender with his ministrations: he would speak to each part of her body and carefully roll her over, as if turning over a very delicate manuscript. Her body emaciated and weak, Leila could no longer eat the soup, but he served it to her anyway, in careful little spoonfuls. The soup dribbled down her chin, coming to rest in the hollow of her neck before he wiped it away with a small cloth he kept in his back pocket, all the while singing lullabies to her in Khmer.

"Send him away," Eugenia signed angrily. "We all know his coin does nothing. I'm fine managing her myself."

"He cares for her," Jean-Baptiste signed to his mother. "He brings her hope. He brings me hope. And maybe this is enough."

"I don't trust him. I've never trusted that one," she signed. "There are things you don't know." She stopped, glancing over to Leila's bed.

"You think me a fool," he said. "I am not a fool."

The next day, a monk dressed in saffron and umber robes arrived from upstream. He was standing at the bow of a small boat, carrying a gnarled stick in his hands. Thin as a rail, he looked nearly a hundred years old, but his gaze was steady and clear. Tien greeted the monk at the dock and led him by the arm to the main house. They talked quietly, as if they had known each other for a long time.

"It is a great honor," Tien said to Jean-Baptiste. "He has come a long way."

"Why is he here?" asked Jean-Baptiste.

The monk settled in by Leila's bedside with his eyes closed, sitting very still. Eugenia watched him wearily, several times shooting an exasperated glance in Jean-Baptiste's direction. And then the monk took Leila's thin, yellowing hand. He looked up at Eugenia and smiled.

"She is at peace," he said. "She is ready for the wheel to turn."

The following morning, as the sun rose over the vast rows of rubber trees, the wheel turned. At the exact moment of her death, she was alone, and when the living returned to her bedside shortly thereafter, they found the faintest smile on her lips, as if she had known this would happen all along.

4

Though local custom dictated that the body be put on display for seven days before being cremated, Jean-Baptiste made arrangements to have Leila buried immediately, next to the de Broglie men on the hilltop by the observatory. A large crowd had gathered for the ceremony. The plantation workers were there, but so were the schoolchildren, and more came from the forest, streaming in from every direction. The monk mingled among them, chattering softly, clearly displeased with the break from tradition.

"He says her soul will not be able to escape if we put her in the ground," Tien said to Jean-Baptiste.

"What do you think, Tien?"

He put his hands together and bowed. "Madame has her own beliefs."

"And she's my wife. Tell him that. *She's my wife*, Tien. Tell him we're not like you. Tell him we don't believe in reincarnation. Tell him we only believe in what we can see."

Jean-Baptiste read a passage from Corinthians and a short excerpt from one of Darwin's notebooks. (Tofte-Jebsen does not identify which.) He gestured for the monk to say a prayer. The monk stepped forward and bowed, but did not speak. He began to make slow, lazy motions with his hands, like birds coming to roost.

"What's he saying?" Jean-Baptiste signed to his mother.

"He doesn't speak with his hands," his mother signed. "I don't understand."

It was conveyed that the children would like to sing a song. They gathered shyly, the littlest ones in front. A nervous silence. And then they began. A lullaby: "Au clair de la lune." The volume was all wrong, words were mispronounced, the thread was lost and verses repeated, but the effect was instant and unmistakable. It melted those assembled like a great wave. Jean-Baptiste wept openly. Next to him, Eugenia leaned into her son, trembling. After the children were finished, they heard a commotion behind them. The crowd parted and revealed Tien on the ground, inconsolable. Tears were streaming down his face. Two workers with scarves wrapped around their heads took him by the waist and led him away.

Jean-Baptiste drafted a letter to his wife's family. It would be the second most difficult letter he ever wrote. He apologized for taking their daughter to a foreign land. He told them about the school that she had started. How much the children had loved her. About their song at her funeral. He told them she had not died alone. He said he would send them a small pension as long as he was able. He mentioned nothing of the radiation, of the machine in the basement that could see through their daughter into the worlds within, of the baby that had not come into the world. Inside the envelope he enclosed the small French coin the *kru Khmer* had used to treat her.

After only two days, a letter from Paris arrived on the mail boat. At first he thought Leila's parents were already replying, that somehow the laws of space and time and steamship had collapsed, but then he realized the letter was not from them but from his friend Luc, the doctor. The letter began with a description of the chaos in the city, the sense of an imminent Nazi invasion.

I envy you to be so far away from this mess in your little jungle paradise, but then I hesitate to call it a paradise with this news of your wife's illness. The list of symptoms you describe match those we have seen in our patients exposed to a high level of radiation. Radium used to be a commonly prescribed treatment, but as we have learned more of its effects, we now know how serious acute radiation poisoning can be. You are correct in asserting that the severity of the poisoning usually corresponds with the length and amount of exposure, and so I think this good news in your wife's case. Her exposure was not prolonged, and if radiation is indeed the culprit, I see no reason why she won't recover. Regardless, I would not be too hard on yourself. You did not know of its effects, just as many before you did not know.

We must all be in a mood of forgiveness these days as ordinary men have been pressed to make extraordinary decisions. Many of the physicists have already fled to London and the United States. Bohr's still in Denmark—he refuses to leave despite the German occupation. There are rumors that the United States and Britain are already developing a powerful bomb built on the process of irradiating atoms. The Germans may build one too, and no one wants to be forced to work for them. I do not doubt if it will be built—it is only a question of when. Once it gets the bit between its teeth, there's no stopping the horse.

What a mess we've created in this gentle world we used to call home.

Well, take care. God bless & best of luck. May we all make it out of this alive.

Yours, faithfully,
Luc Jeunet

It would be the last letter he received from Paris for nearly six years. One month later, the Nazis were marching past the London plane trees on the Champs-Élysées.

Perhaps Jean-Baptiste should have left then, and given up on an enterprise he had never believed in. But he did not leave, and he did not give up, not as the war in Europe spread across the world and the Japanese lay claim to the peninsula. The news of the silent takeover came in rumors and hearsay from the perpetually cheery boatmen who plied the Mekong. It did not seem to matter to them who was in charge. The French *colons* were still running the day-to-day operations in the capital, but the Japanese were the new masters. "*Sdech muoyo-thngai,*" the locals called them. "King for a day."

At La Seule Vérité, the world remained unchanged. Their little patch of earth remained. Day fell into night and back into day. The trees were cut and bled, the latex collected, pressed, dried into strips, and stored in the warehouse.

Jean-Baptiste began to smoke. The opium was brought up the river from the Kampong Cham poppy fields by a toothless man who laughed at every utterance Jean-Baptiste made. Sensing his mother's disapproval, he never smoked in the house, only in a remote hut on the outskirts of the property where he couldn't hear the sound of the machines or the tap, only the birds and the rain and the beat of his own heart. Occasionally a worker would join him with a pipe, but most often it was just him and the trees and the dull sense that what had begun had already ended.

The monotony was broken one day when a military patrol boat hushed around the bend of the Mekong, the imperial flag of the red-spoked sun flapping damply at its stern. A Japanese naval officer wearing a peaked hat bowed formally to Jean-Baptiste as he mounted their dock and introduced himself in polite but halting French as Lieutenant Sakutaro Matsuo. Jean-Baptiste returned the bow and invited the lieutenant to take a brandy with him on the porch.

As they sat sipping the Darroze Bas-Armagnac from Château de La Brise, their bodies enveloped by the jungle heat, Jean-Baptiste studied his guest. Matsuo refused to take off his hat, even as sweat began to run down the arrowhead of his temples and along the thin eave of his jawline. The slim mustache balanced on his upper lip could not hide the rawness of his youth. Jean-Baptiste sensed a lingering, misplaced terror beneath the lieutenant's pristine movements, beneath the tightness of that button-snap collar. It was the kind of terror men spent their entire lives trying to ignore.

Matsuo straightened, as if remembering his duties, and laid out the demands of the occupying forces: Jean-Baptiste must hand over his entire rubber supply to the Japanese army and continue to produce for them indefinitely or else face certain arrest.

"They will send you away to work on the Burmese Railway," said Matsuo. "It is a long railway. It is never finished."

"Excellent," said Jean-Baptiste. "I love projects that have no end."

The man's pinkie had begun to quiver. Jean-Baptiste wanted to reach across the table and still this tremor.

He smiled, assuring the officer of their cooperation.

"We don't want trouble," he said. "I don't care who flies the flag, just as long as we're able to make our beautiful rubber. I live only to make that rubber. We'll do what we can. Here, have some more Darroze. They say it opens the heart. God knows when we'll get it again."

"Thank you," said Matsuo, though he looked as if he had had quite enough.

The lieutenant sweated into his uniform as Jean-Baptiste, with great flourish, signed all the requisite documents.

"I see the Japanese are as fastidious with their documentation as they are with their own mortality."

"Pardon?"

"Tell me," said Jean-Baptiste. "Do you think you'll ever see Japan again?"

The young man look startled.

"I do not know what you mean," he said.

"Japan, your home."

"This *is* Japan."

"Is it?" Jean-Baptiste laughed. "I hadn't heard. Maybe you'll do better here than we have done."

"What have you done?"

"Too much," said Jean-Baptiste. "Or perhaps not enough. Well, my dear Sakutaro, if this is your home already, then I insist you spend the night."

"My orders—"

"To hell with your orders. You're in the jungle, my friend. There are different rules here."

The lieutenant seemed to be weighing his options. "My boatman—" he said.

"We'll take care of him. He'll get on with the workers. They like news that they don't make up themselves."

In the end, Matsuo reluctantly relented. After dinner was served, Eugenia excused herself, sensing that this dance did not include her. Jean-Baptiste and the lieutenant sat long into the night. Jean-Baptiste did most of the talking, recounting the story of his life, of other lives, of lives never lived, placating the young man with the last of the Darroze and, when this ran out, some half-turned merlot, and, when this was gone, an old bottle of Cordon Bleu that he found in his laboratory. When there was nothing left to say or drink, the two men, having come to an unspoken understanding, stumbled up to Jean-

Baptiste's room, where they shared a pipe of opium and spent the rest of the night together.

The next morning, Lieutenant Matsuo, eyes bloodshot and uniform askew, skipped the elaborate array of quail eggs and split pomelo for breakfast, hurriedly boarded his boat without further comment, and disappeared down the channels of the Mekong to wherever he had come from.[6]

The rubber they produced for the Japanese during the war years was weak and unstable: Jean-Baptiste had ordered his men to interrupt the coagulation process by pouring in a peroxide solution so that the latex would snap under any sort of duress.

"They'll never land their planes on tires made from this," Jean-Baptiste said to Tien as they stood over the bubbling vats of latex. "But then, I suppose their planes were never designed to land, were they?"

"Why do we make this if it is no good?" Tien asked.

"Sometimes when something is bad, it can be good," he said. "You understand?"

Tien rolled his head slowly from one shoulder to the other, an ambiguous gesture of comprehension. "And when something is good, it can be bad," he said.

Jean-Baptiste laughed. "Yes, Tien, that is probably more the truth of it."

TOWARD THE END of the war, the Japanese, sensing their own demise, briefly turned over power in Cambodia and Vietnam to local governments. Cambodia became "Kampuchea" and roman lettering was abandoned for Khmer script. The arrangement lasted less than a year, however, before the French *colons* finally managed to reestablish control of the peninsula. Yet the damage was already done. In Vietnam, the Viet Minh, having tasted independence, and now

---

[6] "Another fabrication," writes Røed-Larsen. "There is no record in the Japanese Imperial Army Hall of Records (大日本帝国陸軍記録図書館, Tokyo) of a Lieutenant Sakutaro Matsuo stationed in French Indochina during the years 1940–1945. There is a Warrant Officer R. Matsuoka and a Captain T. Matsumoto, but I must assume that neither of these are the man in question, unless of course Tofte-Jebsen can provide evidence to the contrary" (610).

backed by a steady stream of armaments from China and the Soviet Union, refused to fall back into *imperialisme* as usual, and so another war began. Grenades were thrown into movie theaters, roads attacked at night, garrisons shelled from the safety of the jungle. The slow noose began to tighten. All wars end badly, but with this war there could be no doubt of its outcome.

The bend in the river persisted. The news whispered up the Mekong was never good, but the remoteness of their location, a result of Henri's reckless imagination, now insulated them from all conflicts. King Sihanouk was busy negotiating Cambodia's independence from France and had largely managed to avoid becoming embroiled in the war between the Communist and colonial forces by using a shifting veil of neutrality that had left Phnom Penh's French population in limbo. There had been whispers of insurgencies—one plantation upstream in Phumi Hang Savat was razed, its owners stabbed and disemboweled, their kidneys reportedly eaten raw by members of the guerrilla army Khmer Issarak.[7] This story, told often and in graphic detail, did much to hasten the shuttering of homes along the river as families retreated to the relative safety of Saigon, where they would dream often of the land they had abandoned in the heart of the colony. Once considered too docile to pose any real problems to remote colonial rule, the Cambodians, now led by their young and crafty king, were embracing a new age of self-government. Abroad, potent seeds of malcontent were also being sown: a nascent Khmer Communist movement incubated in Paris, where a handful of Khmer students—including the soft-spoken Saloth Sar, who would later assume the nom de guerre Pol Pot—were beginning to debate how best to graft Marxism onto the slippery landscape of their homeland.

Yet even in this volatile climate of the early 1950s, as the Cold War giants began to take sides in Southeast Asia, as Sihanouk navigated a perilous transition to monarchical rule, as the floods came and went, when everything and nothing seemed possible, Jean-Baptiste did not budge. Occasionally they could hear the rumble of guns in the far distance, and once an Issarak rebel group

---

[7] The Phumi Hang Savat attack is challenged by Røed-Larsen, who points to the absence of any record or testimony of such an event. "Historical fiction disgusts me," he writes. "No—*all fiction*, no matter its time or place, sends me into an existential tailspin. Why invent? Why invent when so much of the truth—*the real truth*—remains unknown?" (618)

moved through the plantation in the night and stole some chickens, but in general, the violence did not pierce the sheltered confines of their universe. It was as if that idle bend in the river provided them with an invisible, protective force field.

Still, Jean-Baptiste was not blind to the danger that lurked all around them, and at his mother's prompting, he broke the silence of the severed telegraph by buying a wireless radio transceiver that he could use to contact Phnom Penh in an emergency, though if they were to be attacked, it was clear no radio would ever save them.

When Raouf the Algerian caretaker left to fight for his homeland in North Africa, Jean-Baptiste brought in Capitaine Claude Renoit to manage the business—or what remained of it. Capitaine Renoit was a one-legged war veteran. He meant well but lacked any sense of urgency when it came to the whole enterprise of rubber, and this suited Jean-Baptiste just fine. Operations became haphazard, shipments irregular. Tien and the men still bled the trees and loaded the stacks of latex onto barges, but it was all done out of tradition and not necessity. The center was no longer holding. Maybe the center had never held.

Eugenia, whose health had begun to decline but whose energy had not, spent her days painting the same *Paphiopedilum appletonianum* orchid plant. She had set up her easel and paints in the old telegraph room, and though Jean-Baptiste thought it ridiculous that she would squeeze herself into the smallest room in the house when they had so much space at their disposal, Eugenia claimed the tightness of the quarters gave her an urgency that she translated onto the canvas. She was prolific in her output: some days she would produce three or four paintings of the flower, all wildly different, all exactly the same. The paintings began accumulating in the warehouse, next to the racks of latex—shelves and shelves of the same blossom, repeated in every imaginable color, its two sagittal petals outstretched in greeting or malice, depending upon the canvas. When he gave a tour of the plantation to the rare visitor, Jean-Baptiste liked to joke to their guests that they were in the business of modern art making, merely amusing themselves now and then with some light rubber production. This was not far from the truth. More than one visitor left with a surreal orchid rendition tucked beneath his arm—whether out of guilt, appreciation, or morbid fascination, it was never clear.

"I'LL NEED A VAT of rubber," Jean-Baptiste informed the Capitaine one day. "About seventy-five liters."

"Seventy-five? That will take a couple of days . . . weeks, maybe."

"Is this not a rubber plantation? Are we not supposed to have rubber in bountiful supply?"

"Well, yes . . ." Renoit seemed embarrassed. "We'll see what we can scare up. May I ask what you will be using it for?"

"To make a rubber mold."

"Of what?"

"Of myself," said Jean-Baptiste. "I'm making a dummy. For medical purposes."

The first rubber mannequins to emerge were white, grotesque beings with elephantine arms and strange leaks spilling from their hips. The clay that Jean-Baptiste was using for a cast could not hold the heated rubber; it seeped and bubbled and broke free from its confines. After this failure, he sent away for a bronzed mold of himself to be made in a navy foundry in Saigon. A month later, he received the molding, along with a note:

Très joli corps. Je l'épouserais volontiers. X

The bronze worked magnificently. He finally managed to find the right mixture of rubber and solution to give the mannequin a lifelike texture. When he made his first fully formed being, it was as if he had given birth. Jean-Baptiste painted the body white, then filled in the details of the face, taking care to get the coloring of the lips just right. For some reason, the lips suggested life more than any other aspect. Once the being had life, he went about giving it death: he painted on the telltale burns and lesions resulting from radiation poisoning. He wrote up a key for the mannequin, explaining each manner of wound, each degree of burn in relation to the amount of radiation exposure. He made four of them, each more convincing than the last, and then sent these radioactive dummies to four of the major French hospitals in the colonies.

"In the event you should have a case of acute radiation syndrome," he wrote. "These models will instruct you on the symptoms of exposure. They are my gift to your institution."

He did not have to wait long for a reply. The hospitals wrote back quickly, thanking him for his dummies, effusive about their usefulness. In fact, all four—plus the teaching hospital in Saigon—requested more mannequins, but would he mind not decorating them with any symptoms? The hospitals wanted them for more general purposes, and plain white dummies would suffice.

Jean-Baptiste had found a new calling. The dying plantation briefly came to life again as the source of the region's rubber medical mannequins. A small force of the workers, including Tien, were trained in casting the mannequins and painting on a face that vaguely resembled a sleepy Jean-Baptiste. Every month, the piles of bone-white bodies were loaded onto a boat that floated down the Mekong with its curious cargo, inspiring strange legends in the villages of a white sorcerer turning men into dolls—particularly after one boat capsized and the dummies were found floating in the river for weeks afterwards. The mannequin trade proved fleeting, however, for soon the hospitals claimed they had enough, that in fact they had *too* many; they had dummies coming out of the closets, and they were getting in the way of the live patients. Please, they wrote, would he cease and desist his shipments, for the safety of everyone involved? Reluctantly, Jean-Baptiste put the production plans on hold and La Seule Vérité slipped back into its eddy.

Sometimes, in the early evening, before the night grew too thick, Renoit, Eugenia, and Jean-Baptiste would congregate wordlessly in the living room and play a few records on the phonograph. After a few minutes it was always necessary for someone to get up (usually Eugenia, oddly, since she was the only one who could not hear the music) and fan the revolving vinyl so that the record would not warp and melt in the heat. After a while, even she stopped attending to the apparatus, and eventually the records began to melt, one by one, the music evaporating into a nighttime chorus of crickets.

5

Tofte-Jebsen sums it up nicely: "The child, as only a child can do, changed everything in an instant" (122).

After Tien had turned over the baby and left with the other men for the afternoon collection, Renoit and Jean-Baptiste sat on the veranda, sipping the remarkable cognac and staring at the tiny infant. They had placed him in a fruit bowl, because they did not know where else to put him. Perhaps sensing a shift in the mood, Eugenia shuffled outside from her telegraph studio and saw the baby squirming among the tangerines.

"What is that?" she signed.

"That? That's a baby," said Jean-Baptiste. "A *human* baby," he added.

"To whom does he belong?" She carefully lifted the child into her arms.

"He's mine, apparently," said Jean-Baptiste.

"He's sick," she signed to him with one hand. "Where did he come from?"

"From there." Jean-Baptiste pointed to the rubber trees. Or the sky. It was not clear.

"He's going to die, you know," said Renoit. "I wouldn't get too attached. It will only lead to suffering."

"We're all going to die."

"*Touché,* my friend," Renoit said, conducting a finger through the heat. "She is brief, this life, and then she leaves us when she realizes her mistake."

"What shall I call him?" Jean-Baptiste asked.

"Something native," said Renoit. "Something easily said and easily forgotten."

"André," Eugenia said aloud.

Jean-Baptiste was briefly caught off guard by hearing the name of the patriarch spoken in his mother's curious, flattened speech. *André*.

He shook his head slowly. "No," he said. "Raksmey."

"Raksmey?" said Renoit. "Isn't that a woman's name?"

"There was a student named Raksmey. Leila often spoke of him. I believe it means 'ray of light.'"

"Ray of light?"

"He needs a doctor," Eugenia signed. "I'll get on the wireless and summon Dr. Moreau."

"Raksmey de Broglie?" said Renoit.

"It doesn't sound right, does it?" said Jean-Baptiste.

"Are you listening to me?" Eugenia signed.

"Anything can sound right if you say it enough," Renoit laughed. "The French have learned this over many years."

"Then he'll be Raksmey Raksmey," said Jean-Baptiste. "He came from himself."

He looked around for the subject in question, but the baby had already disappeared with Eugenia into the coolness of the great hall.

FOR THE FIRST WEEK, the child did not eat. Bound to the fate of his discovery, Tien came by every morning to check on Raksmey's progress. On the third day, he arrived bearing a cradle that he and the others had fashioned from rubber wood. Leila's old dressing room, unused for years, was hastily converted into a makeshift nursery. Suong came in the mornings with her cousin to breastfeed the infant, but he still would not take her milk.

"He won't survive," she said. "He doesn't want this world. He's waiting for the next."

Yet he did not die. He did not eat, but he did not die. He persisted—a silent newt, wriggling, only now and then emitting his shrieking whistle that raised goose bumps and brought everyone in the house to a standstill. Who was this creature? And from where had he come?

Eugenia's bond with the little one was instantaneous and deep. She slept beside him on a rickety cot and connected a string between his ankle and the first knuckle of her pinkie. When she felt a tug in the darkness, she would come to him and hum songs without pitch, deep songs, songs that slept in the marrow of her bones. Her previous indifference to Leila's infecundity melted away as her heart was thawed by that peculiarly intimate distance of grandparenthood. It was true: all she had wanted was this.

"At some point during the first of those long nights," writes Tofte-Jebsen, "with the string stretched taut between them, the question of who Raksmey Raksmey belonged to, a question that would linger on in the patronymic repetition of his name, became irrelevant. He was theirs. He was hers. He was all she had" (123).

The child floundered at the brink of death's door, and Jean-Baptiste lost his lifelong ability to sleep soundly through the night. When he did manage to doze off, he found himself dreaming of Bohr inside that humid Copenhagen pub, drops of condensation swelling and descending upon them. Bohr, who had finally escaped Nazi-occupied Denmark in the middle of the war, who had fled to America, where he reluctantly consulted with Oppenheimer on the bomb that was to be dropped halfway across the world, thirty-five hundred kilometers northeast of La Seule Vérité on a bustling port city in southern Japan shaped like the tail of a bird. Jean-Baptiste thought he had felt his teacup tremble that day, felt the earth wobble and wander on its axis. What had gone through Bohr's mind when he heard the news? When he saw the images of shirts burned into backs, of faces removed, of the miles and miles and miles of torn wood and concrete rubble? Of the single domed building at the epicenter that had somehow managed to survive the godly forces at work? What had he thought then? That the hands of men had banished indeterminacy? That from that point forth, nothing would be left to chance? Once again, we had become the masters of our own world. There was nothing we could not know.

Or maybe he had thought: *Now we can know nothing.*

One night he was awoken from one of these dreams—of Bohr, of mushroom clouds, of what exactly he could not remember—by the child's cries. He went to the nursery and found Eugenia still asleep. The string had fallen from Raksmey's ankle. He thought of waking his mother but instead went to the baby, scooped up all of that uncertainty with both hands. The baby fell quiet. He could feel its warmth, feel its breath against his neck. He thought: *This boy is breathing. This boy is alive. One day he will become a man like me.* And it was then that the idea first came to him. He held the baby and walked out to the veranda and listened to the insects calling open the night. A flash of heat lightning. He brought a finger to the child's cheek. *Raksmey. Raksmey Raksmey.* The idea circling in his mind. After a while, he returned his son to the nursery, retied the string, and fell back into a restless sleep, believing the idea would fade into the darkness.

Except that when he awoke the next morning, the idea was still there. It lingered. And grew. He was haunted by its possibility. He could not look at the child without being consumed by everything that could be done. He paced the veranda, sweating, mumbling beneath his breath. So taken was he that he could not sleep a wink the following night. He knew that the window to make such a decision was narrow, that time was already being wasted, and so the next evening he went to the hilltop where Leila lay beside his father and his grandfather and watched as the first stars appeared. He asked for his wife's permission. He did not say anything aloud, but asked in his mind. He waited. He heard nothing. Felt nothing. There was no one there. Just him and the stars, emergent. It was enough.

Jean-Baptiste hurried back to his study. Under the light of a single candle, he wrote the following on a sheet of La Seule Vérité letterhead.

I, Jean-Baptiste de Broglie, on this date, 27 August 1953, do hereby declare my intentions for the child Raksmey Raksmey, found on the property of the rubber plantation La Seule Vérité in the French Protectorate and Kingdom of Cambodia:

1) If the child survives, it shall be my ambition to train and nurture him with a singular goal: to become Cambodia's first native quantum physicist, in the humanist mold of Niels Bohr. This will be an exercise in testing the boundaries of predetermination, and, while being far from conclusive on the absolute nature of free will, shall at least form a body of evidence that will allow us to debate what is bound to chance and what can be dictated a priori.

2) To this end, I shall document my raising of him henceforth in the utmost detail, the sum of which I hope will provide a valuable resource for future researchers. Every bit of input—be it gastronomic, intellectual, or spiritual— shall be entered into the ledger. Time will tell if this equation will eventually lead to the output of a physicist—not just a meddling scientist, but a great one, one who changes the very course of history.

Signed and witnessed by me alone,
JBdB 27/8/1953[8]

He creased the paper twice with his thumb and sealed it inside an envelope using the plantation's wax stamp. He then placed the envelope into a carved wooden box that he hid beneath a loose floorboard. He went to bed that night and slept soundly for the first time in days.

Jean-Baptiste decided to tell no one of his intentions; he only let Eugenia know that he would be keeping a detailed journal of the child's behavior.

"His behavior? How can you think about such things when we don't even know if he will survive?" she signed.

"We all have our ways," he said. In his notebook, he entered:

09:04, R.R. REFUSES MILK, FLEXES TOES.

The following morning, Tien brought the *kru Khmer* over to the house. To both of the men's surprise, Eugenia embraced the shaman.

"Please help us," she said aloud. "Please."

She turned to Tien. "Thank you," she said.

He bowed. When he looked at her again, there were tears in his eyes.

---

[8] Røed-Larsen notes that such a document, if it indeed ever existed, was never recovered.

The *kru Khmer* determined that the baby's wind had grown cold from a premature birth. He was trying to grow smaller so that he might be able to crawl back into the womb. The forces inside him must be warmed, to reverse this trend and encourage the child to start eating the food of this world. This was done with a hot green liquid smeared across his body and a single needle, exposed to the heat of a flame and then plunged into the bottom of his neck, just above the small lump of his seventh cervical vertebra. Eugenia, clearly taken aback at the sight of the piercing, did not protest. A prayer was intoned. Incense lit. More prayers. Another coin was produced, this time of ambiguous origin, and rubbed in spirals down the child's back. From somewhere outside, a monkey squawked in surprise. The smoke from the incense shivered and righted itself again.

All of this was recorded in Jean-Baptiste's little black book. Life happened twice: once in real time and again in the book.

The next day, the child took Suong's breast into his mouth and began to nurse. This, too, was noted. Eugenia, previously never one for celebration, hiked up her skirts and began to dance with her son in circles, her old body flush with new life.

The *kru Khmer* returned, but unnecessarily so. The sickness had been lifted. Raksmey grew stronger; his skin shifted from yellow to a shimmering light brown. By the third week, he had gained a voice and begun to cry like a normal infant, on average 16.5 times a day, Jean-Baptiste noted. He also noted at what point Raksmey could follow a finger across his field of vision (2.5 months), at what point the baby could recognize movement and then a specific object at ten feet (3.5 months), fifteen feet (3.9 months), and twenty-five feet (4 months). He recorded precisely when Raksmey sat without aid (6.2 months), gained independent dexterity of his limbs (7.3 months), began to crawl (9.8 months), stood without assistance (12.5 months), and then began to walk (13.9 months).

He bought an unwieldy German reel-to-reel Magnetophon left over from the Japanese occupation and recorded hours of Raksmey's sounds. High-pitched squeals, exploratory *ohs*, and wet, boneless words, not unlike his grandmother's speech. All of these he categorized according to frequency, length, vowel type. Using this data, he created a massive wall chart of Raksmey's preverbal musings,

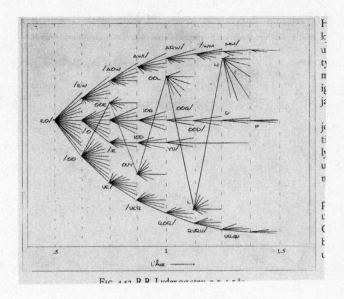

Fig. 4.5. "R.R. Sounds & Noise, 0.5–1.5 years"
From Røed-Larsen, P., *Spesielle Partikler,* p. 588

a flowing sea of intonation. The chart would survive until the very last days of La Seule Vérité.[9]

When he was not recording, Jean-Baptiste would sit and read to Raksmey from the great novels of his youth. *Les Misérables. A Tale of Two Cities. Gulliver's Travels.* When he felt the narratives were growing too fantastical, he would switch to papers on quantum mechanics, though often he could barely grasp what he was reading himself.

"Why read to him like this?" Eugenia signed. "I can understand more than he can, and I can't hear a word you're saying."

"Information is conserved," said Jean-Baptiste. "Everything I say finds its way in there, and everything that goes in will eventually come out. We may not fully understand it yet, but I'm convinced that nothing can be lost."

"The child cannot even speak!"

---

[9] Amazingly, both Tofte-Jebsen and Røed-Larsen agree on the existence of such a chart.

"Speech is not a prerequisite for comprehension. I think you, of all people, would be the first to agree."

"If I've learned anything in my life, it's that comprehension is not an idea, it's an act," she signed, her hands shimmering back and forth. "You must be able to use what you understand."

"It's not as simple as that. You cannot ascribe a timeline to understanding. When we learn, when we act, when we speak—we draw upon a lifetime of experience. Who knows the origin of our thoughts? They come from deep places, from before we knew what to call them. I'm merely enriching the foundations of the subconscious from which Raksmey may draw his later conclusions."

In the nursery's newly installed bookshelves, Jean-Baptiste began to assemble the library for Raksmey's education. He also selected objects from his past projects and placed them around the room: the telegraph switch, the Tesla coil, a small telescope, a copper-wire mobile, a shortwave radio. He filled the nursery with exotic succulents and orchids from their botanical garden and installed a portable Victrola that alternately played Bach and several rare shellac recordings of Khmer and Vietnamese stringed music. On the mosquito netting above his son's bed, Jean-Baptiste painted Greek constellations and famous equations from physics:

$$\lambda = h/p \qquad \Delta x\, \Delta p \geq \hbar/2 \qquad \lambda = h/p = h/mv\sqrt{(1 - v^2/c^2)}$$

"He is sleeping in his father's museum. You're going to suffocate him."

"Not suffocate. Elucidate. *Illuminate.* You remember I spent my own childhood trapped in a bedroom, but my mind was able to roam free."

Luckily, Raksmey, unlike the youthful Jean-Baptiste, was not bound by illness and could flee the confines of his bedroom. Though unusually small, he overcame the sickness that marked his birth and grew into a bright-eyed, curious toddler. As soon as he gained bipedal mobility, he could not be corralled for long. There were many times that Eugenia or Jean-Baptiste turned their back only to find that Raksmey had run outside, deep into the gardens. And soon they had no choice but to let him run.

Jean-Baptiste's black notebooks began to gather on the shelf in his study, at the rate of two per month, which later became three and then four. Either there was more to look for or Jean-Baptiste was learning how to look.

Tofte-Jebsen includes a sample of his observations:

- RR's eyes are a light shade of brown, like almond paste. Seem to be lighter than when he was born. As far as I can tell, both are the same color, though the outer ring of his right iris is darker, giving the illusion of a protruding pupil.
- RR's hair is almost jet black, natural counterclockwise swirl, splotch of lighter hair on the back/left side of his head, about 4 cm down from crown. present since birth.
- food preference (at 1 year) rice w/ pork, bananas, and jackfruit. will refuse water spinach, bok choy, and most greens. (I don't blame him.)
- a mole. nape of the neck, recent. possibly where the needle went in?
- always sneezes in twos, half-second interval between. never three, like me.
- birthmark on left ankle, just above the talus bone, in the shape of a longtail boat w/ square sail. simple. beautiful. → ◗)
- RR can wink his left eye, but not his right, seems to happen more frequently when tired.
- his first word is not a word: a salute, as in "hello" in sign language, which he performs when E. walks into room. she returns the sign, cups hand to face, then rocks, "my lovely son." he giggles. for him, gestures are words, words are gestures. (131)

At two years, Jean-Baptiste took his son's measurements with a tailor's tape:

1. Length: 78cm tall.
2. Weight: 10.3kg.
3. Left pinkie: 2.75cm.
4. Right pinkie: 2.7cm.
5. Penis: 2.1cm.
6. Circumference of head: 53cm.

This last measurement Jean-Baptiste found particularly interesting, for it was slightly above average, which was quite incredible, considering the diminutive size of the boy's body.

"It's a good thing. We must put the entire universe inside of it," Jean-Baptiste said to his mother. "Lemaître says it's expanding."

"His head or the universe?" Eugenia signed.

"The mind is the last frontier, Mother."

"How about we leave his head alone?" she signed. In her language, the sign for *head,* a sweeping of the pointer finger around the face that ended at the temple, was very similar to the sign for *dream,* except that the circle moved away from the head, ending with the fingers pointing toward the heavens. Her gesture fell somewhere between the two, an ambiguity that Jean-Baptiste did not ask her to resolve.

"I cannot stop," he signed. "This is like asking a man to stop breathing."

Raksmey became trilingual and bimodal: Jean-Baptiste instructed Suong and Tien to address Raksmey in Khmer, while he spoke in French and occasionally English to the child, and Eugenia communicated with him exclusively through sign. By 2.5 years, Raksmey already had a working vocabulary of four hundred fifty words in French, one hundred words in English, at least three hundred signs, and sixty words in Khmer, though this was only an estimate, given that Suong and Tien were less than exact with their observational notes and exit interviews. Raksmey put what he knew to good use: he was already utilizing sophisticated, multi-morphemic constructions ("Tien go to work, he cut the tree when it cold"). Jean-Baptiste noticed that Raksmey had developed a subtle stutter when speaking in French, such that when he would stumble on a word, he would often introduce Eugenia's sign language to talk around it.

Throughout Raksmey's fourth year, Jean-Baptiste began to engage him in a series of science experiments usually done only in primary and secondary schools—measuring the point of vaporization, testing Hooke's law with springs, mapping electrical fields using a voltmeter. In the half hour before lunch, they would go out into the forest and Jean-Baptiste would drill Raksmey on various species of plants in the garden. Together they would do drawings of leaf structure and take rubbings from the bark. Raksmey was left-handed, though

Jean-Baptiste purposefully trained him to use both hands during his writing and experiments. He continuously used advanced-level vocabulary around the child and noticed a 15 percent retention and reuse of new terms within a week of their introduction. Soon Raksmey began acquiring vocabulary at an exponential rate, beginning with five to ten words per week and quickly advancing to twenty to twenty-five words per week by year's end.

Eugenia, at first disapproving of Jean-Baptiste's neurotic methods, eventually acquiesced. "Thus, they settled into their de facto roles," writes Tofte-Jebsen. "He became the instructor of the mind, while she became the silent nurturer of the heart" (140).

"You can't hear sounds?" Raksmey asked her once. It was a watershed, duly recorded in Jean-Baptiste's notebook. Evidence of a *theory of mind:* he understood his grandmother as a being unto herself, one who operated under a different set of rules.

"No," she signed. "That's why I have you." Thereafter, she and Raksmey

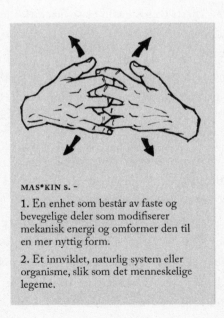

MAS•KIN S. -

1. En enhet som består av faste og bevegelige deler som modifiserer mekanisk energi og omformer den til en mer nyttig form.

2. Et innviklet, naturlig system eller organisme, slik som det menneskelige legeme.

Fig. 4.6. "Sign for Machine"
From Tofte-Jebsen, B., *Jeg er Raksmey,* p. 149

played a game in which she asked him, "What do you hear now?" and he would tell her, in sign and spoken words and also movement, like a little play.

"There are machines in the rubber house," he said, signing the word for *machine*—interlocked fingers, palms turned to the chest. "They sound like . . ." And then he danced up and down with his arms in the air and shook his head back and forth, blubbering air out through his lips.

"Thank you," she signed, laughing. "I understand now."

When he was not working with his father or explaining the world of sound to his grandmother, he spent much of his time alone. He had trouble relating to children his own age, and most were not sure how to approach him. He looked like them, but he was clearly not one of them.

One day Raksmey came home crying.

"What is it?" said Jean-Baptiste. "Are you injured?"

"He's not injured," Eugenia signed. She got down on one knee. "What did they say?"

Raksmey wiped his eyes. "Prak called me *barang*."

"That's ridiculous," Jean-Baptiste said as he noted this in his book. "Do you know what this means?"

Raksmey shook his head.

"It's a butchering of the word *français*. It's spoken by people who have no idea what they're talking about. *Barang* means anything which is not them. Are you a Frenchman?"

"I don't know."

"Of course you aren't. You're as Khmer as they are."

"But he called me that."

"You must learn not to hear them," Eugenia signed.

"No," said Jean-Baptiste. "You must learn why you are right and they are wrong."

Later that evening, Eugenia brought up the idea of sending him to the regional lycée, which had shut down during the war but had recently been reopened by a pair of American missionaries.

"It might be good for him to be around more children. We don't want him to grow strange."

"You don't understand the project at hand," Jean-Baptiste signed. "Raksmey's not going to be just another boy sitting on a mat, repeating his times tables to some Bible-thumping American from Texas. He's destined to become the most famous person Cambodia has ever produced."

"He'll certainly be the most famous person *you* have ever produced," she signed, fingers slapping palms.

"I can see your sarcasm, thank you. But we cannot trust his future to a middling lycée in the middle of nowhere. We must control as much of the input as possible. These are the critical years."

"You're mad, Jean-Baptiste!" she signed. "You cannot control him like this! Why must you try to control everything?"

"I'm not trying to control everything. Only one thing. And if I can't determine the outcome . . . well, then this is almost as interesting as if I can."

"He's a child! Not an experiment!"

"All children are experiments, whether they like it or not. Most are just very sloppy experiments."

"You're a selfish man, Jean-Baptiste!" she signed. "When did you become so egotistic? You were not like this as a boy."

But the experiment continued. There could be no stopping the experiment. At 4.2 years, Jean-Baptiste noted, Raksmey had developed an imaginary companion, Rasey. Initially Jean-Baptiste thought of informing his son of the nonexistent nature of Rasey, but Eugenia pleaded with him not to. "He doesn't have anyone else; at least let him have this."

"But it's no one! He doesn't exist!"

"He exists for your son. Who are we to argue? To him, Rasey might be more real than we are."

And so, real or not, Rasey became part of the household. They even laid out a place at the dinner table for him, making sure never to serve him any vegetables, for apparently Rasey was allergic and could die if he accidentally ate even one. Like Eugenia, Rasey was also deaf; he did not speak, but he could (conveniently) read minds. As they learned from Raksmey, Rasey had a habit of getting into trouble—he would often get lost in the jungle, fight tigers, hop on the backs of eagles, and dive with sharks in the ocean. It was difficult to tell Rasey not to do these things, because he would pretend he couldn't hear you (which he couldn't).

"It's very frustrating," Raksmey told them. "He's like a child."

"Isn't he a child?" Eugenia asked.

"No," said Raksmey. "Rasey is forty-seven years old."

Jean-Baptiste reluctantly recorded Rasey's many adventures, recounted in exquisite detail by Raksmey, who had realized long ago how to take advantage of having a resident scribe registering his every move. Jean-Baptiste did not like including such fictions, but he came to accept them as psychological data rather than simply fantasies. It was a slippery distinction: everything was data, yet not everything could go into the notebooks.

On one occasion, Raksmey came into his father's study and pointed to one of the first medical mannequins.

"Who is that?" he asked.

"Well, I suppose . . . I suppose that is me," said Jean-Baptiste. Indeed, there was a distinct resemblance.

"And what are those, Papa?" Raksmey asked, pointing to the shelves of notebooks. There were now hundreds of them, stretching from floor to ceiling, an intimidating fortress of black spines.

"Those are you," said Jean-Baptiste.

Raksmey seemed content with the answer. "There are many more of me than you, yes?"

When he was not busy with his studies, Raksmey would roam the property, often following Tien around like an obedient dog, watching carefully as he tapped the trees and collected the sap. Tien showed him how to apply just enough pressure to the curved blade with the pad of his thumb to slice through the bark into the soft layer of phloem that lay beneath. A streak of white fluid would appear in the wound and run down the spiral groove.

"The tree must bleed, but not bleed too much," Tien said, and Raksmey would nod.

Tien even made Raksmey his own little bucket so that he could take part in the collection. Despite his heavy load of latex, Tien always found a way to hold the boy's hand wherever they went. Jean-Baptiste noted this bond with a touch of envy. Their connection was easy, gentle, unspoken—everything that he and Raksmey were not. Sometimes Jean-Baptiste saw them resting their heads together, talking softly in Khmer.

"What were you two speaking about?" he asked Raksmey once.

"Nothing so important," said Raksmey. "Tien was telling me stories about the beginning of the world."

"You know those stories aren't true."

"Yes," Raksmey nodded. "But I didn't want to make Tien sad."

When it was too hot to do anything else, he would lie on his back in the river as the women chattered and washed their clothes. There was an old rope swing tied to an ancient bombax tree that allowed him to swoop out and release into the deeper part of the river. He would expunge all breath from his lungs and let himself sink and sink until his face came to rest on the bottom, and sometimes he would even let a bit of mud come in between his lips. A part of him wanted to live down here forever, to never go back up to the world of his father's constant observation.

When Tien was in a good mood, he would take Raksmey across the widest part of the river on a bamboo raft to a thin little island that Raksmey had dubbed Rak—the one place on earth where he could make all the rules. The

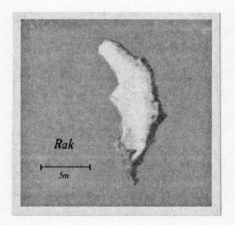

Fig. 4.7. "The Island of Rak"
From Tofte-Jebsen, B., *Jeg er Raksmey,* p. 153

trouble with making rules was that you then had to follow them. On one of his first visits to the island, Raksmey had decided that only Rak could be spoken on the island of Rak. Rak was a language consisting of just one word—*Rak*—which stood for everything. At first, this limited their conversations.

"Rak," said Raksmey.

"Rak," Tien agreed.

But after a while, a certain freedom and understanding came from such limitations. There was no need for any other word.

"Rak," said Raksmey.

"Rak," Tien agreed.

A river carp that Raksmey had named Rak could usually be found lazing in the shallows of this island, pecking at the insects that skittered across the surface of the water. Raksmey sometimes wondered if it was the same fish that he saw each time or whether there were many Raks inhabiting this role. He wondered if this mattered.

When he was not out on the river, Raksmey particularly enjoyed climbing the bony lattice of a strangler fig that had engulfed an old rosewood tree in the lower gardens. Thirty feet off the ground, he would call down to them, "Ha-ha! You can't get me!"

"We *can* get you," Jean-Baptiste said to him from below. "But we're choosing not to at this very moment."

"Rak!" Raksmey yelled.

"What did you say?" Jean-Baptiste called.

"I think you may have a little athlete on your hands," said Renoit, coming up from behind him.

"No," said Jean-Baptiste, shielding his eyes from the sun. He made a notation in his book. "We do *not* have a little athlete."

"He climbs like a monkey."

"Bodies wither. Intellect persists."

"All I know is you can't keep a good man down. If he wants to be a climber, he'll find a way to be a climber."

"You've no idea what you're talking about," said Jean-Baptiste. "Be careful up there, Raksmey!"

"Rasey says he won't come down," Raksmey yelled from above. "I must observe him and make sure he doesn't fall."

"Rasey does not need to be observed! Come down right now," Jean-Baptiste called up.

"Or maybe a wrestler?" said Renoit. "The little man would be a son of a bitch to bring down in a match—"

"Claude!" Jean-Baptiste turned upon him. "Don't joke about this. This isn't a kind of game. This is my son."

Renoit held up his hands. "I'm envious of such possibility. To think: a lifetime of mobility. How quickly it fades when that which is dear is stolen from us." He slapped at his wounded leg. *"La liberté est un fugace don."*

Despite Raksmey's inclination to spend his days in the trees, Jean-Baptiste's rigorous methods of education had created a brilliant mind. Or rather allowed an already brilliant mind to blossom. By the time he was seven, Raksmey was reading well beyond his age. He, like his father, was a swift reader, who could take in books just as quickly as they were put before him. And yet he appeared indifferent to their contents.

"What did you think?" Jean-Baptiste asked after Raksmey had devoured Saul Bellow's new novel, *Henderson the Rain King,* in a day.

"Boring," Raksmey said with a shrug. "Too much talking."

"Human discourse is important. It cannot all be chasing lions and such."

"Can I go out and play?"

"Complete your experiments first," said Jean-Baptiste, shaking his head. "You can make a lion out of words, you know. More powerful than any beast in the jungle."

"Yes, Papa," said Raksmey.

The years passed, marked only by the notches in the trees and the cyclical monsoons that broke the heat for three months every year. Eugenia's vision began to fade and Jean-Baptiste fell and broke his ankle, which slowed him considerably. He and Renoit would limp around the plantation and bicker at each other. In other ways, time stood still at La Seule Vérité, as it always seemed to do. Tofte-Jebsen puts it rather elegantly: "If you stared at a river long enough, you started to believe that the water, and not the earth, was the one true thing" (160).

Much to Jean-Baptiste's delight, Raksmey began to show a natural inclination for the sciences, moving through advanced textbooks with ease. Their science lessons were conducted in Jean-Baptiste's basement laboratory, the same laboratory that had housed his many failed experiments. Raksmey, unlike his father—who was impatient and often allowed his mind to wander—was a born experimentalist. The two of them took up Jean-Baptiste's old radiation research, dusting off the jars of radium, even building a linear particle accelerator that utilized new superconductive technologies Raksmey had discovered in a science journal. While his father had been interested primarily in documenting radiation's destructive effects, Raksmey became fixated on the beneficial powers of the radiation beam in decreasing tumor size. His methods were much more disciplined than Jean-Baptiste's—there was always a control, always a second and third retrial, even if the results were favorable. In short, he was not just curious—he was a *scientist*. After a while, Raksmey was making observations about radiation treatment that Jean-Baptiste had never come close to considering, tuning frequency, wavelength, and fractionation to the specific types of cancerous tissues. Jean-Baptiste noted each of Raksmey's discoveries in his notebook, and next to one he could not help writing an overeager underline: *Ça se passe*.

Still, everything that Raksmey did, even if procedurally defined by great discipline, was also inflected by a sleepy indifference, a weary adherence to the rules, as if he were performing for an audience that had not shown up. He would go about his work with quick, precise movements, but there would be no joy on his face, no excitement at the possibility of discovery.

Jean-Baptiste also noticed that Raksmey had a habit of whispering to himself while he worked. Eventually he realized that Raksmey was actually communicating with Rasey, who had not been banished by the blossoming of Raksmey's intellect, but instead had morphed into a subtle, constant presence, a benign sounding board of knowledge. Watching his son move with equal parts meticulosity and insouciance, Jean-Baptiste found himself oscillating between awe, frustration, and jealousy, as if Raksmey knew a secret that none of them were in on.

"Do you enjoy this?" he finally asked his son one day. Having donned lead smocks, they were exposing a rat's splenic tumor to radiation from Raksmey's linear accelerator while modulating the degree of fractionation by quarter steps.

"Enjoy what?" Raksmey asked, intent on aligning the beam.

"The lab? Our work? *Science?*"

"What is it, Papa?" Raksmey looked up. "Have I done something wrong?"

"No. You haven't done anything *wrong.* I just want to know your desire. What do you want to be?"

"I want to be like you."

"No, you don't. You have a much better chance than I do."

"Chance for what?"

Jean-Baptiste sighed. "Maybe it's time."

"Time for what?"

"For you to go away."

"Away?"

"To school."

"Are you angry with me, Papa?"

"I fear I can no longer give you what you need."

"Papa!"

Raksmey ran to his father and hugged him. Their embrace, weighed down by the clumsiness of their lead aprons, felt oddly disembodied. Later, Jean-Baptiste would comb through his notebooks and confirm what he had suspected in that moment: it was the first time he had ever hugged his son. He had no rational explanation for this, only that maintaining the necessary distance between the observer and the observed—the fact that he always carried notebook and pencil in hand so as to be ready to capture life's spontaneities (like an embrace) in real time—had prevented him from actually embracing his son in real time. He did not note this absence in his notebook.

The rest of that day, Raksmey was unusually quiet, glumly stalking through the house. In the afternoon, Jean-Baptiste saw Tien and Raksmey paddling across the river to their island.

"What did you say to him?" Eugenia signed.

"That it might be time for him to go to school."

"To school? But you were against sending him to the lycée!"

"Not just any school. To Saigon. To my school. They've changed the name to Collège René Descartes, but it's still the same place."

"Saigon?" she said aloud. "Is it safe?"

"Of course it's safe. It's Saigon."

"The Americans have moved in."

"The Americans will make it safe."

"The French did not make it safe."

"The French are fools. The Americans are much more practical."

"You really think they are any different from us?"

Jean-Baptiste, caught in the quicksand of his thoughts, did not respond.

At dinner that night, Raksmey broke his silence.

"I'll go," he said. "I want to go."

Eugenia let her soup spoon clatter into her saucer. She flipped her hands on the edge of the table, palms down, a gesture that could've meant "stay," or "death," or nothing at all.

"It's for the best, I think," said Jean-Baptiste, nodding. "You've outgrown us. Sooner than I thought. They have resources that we don't have here."

Raksmey was staring at his grandmother, who was staring at her hands.

"Will I make friends?" he asked.

"Of course you'll make friends," said Jean-Baptiste. "Everyone makes friends someday."

"But what if they don't like me?"

"The only reason they wouldn't like you is if they're jealous of you."

Eugenia abruptly got up from the table and left the room.

"Did I say something?" said Raksmey.

"She'll miss you. She doesn't have much in her life, and when you leave she'll be alone again."

"You'll be here."

"It's true. Sometimes I forget about me."

Raksmey was quiet. Then he said: "Tien said the world is a big *and* small place."

"Did he?"

"He said as soon as you think you've seen everything, you realize there's much more to see and you'll never see it all. And as soon as you think you'll never see anything, you realize everything's the same," he paused. "Is that true?"

"Tien can be a wise man when he wants to be," said Jean-Baptiste.

"But he said he's never left here. So how does he know all of this?"

6

There were no openings at Collège René Descartes.

"But in the tropics," writes Tofte-Jebsen, "no never means no" (173). Given Jean-Baptiste's unique legacy as one of the school's best pupils, and given his generous offer to fund a new library, the rector was able to make an exception and set aside a place for Raksmey Raksmey de Broglie. (The last name had been added on the forms to gently remind the administration of his heritage.)

Inquiries were also made about the safety of the journey down the Mekong. News of the security situation, received from boatmen and garbled reports over the wireless, was unreliable and dependent on whoever was doing the reporting. There had been rumors of government instability since President Ngo Dinh Diem's assassination the previous year, of American planes dropping bombs in the north, of Chinese troops amassing at the Laotian border, of Vietnamese Communists attacking monks, of Khmer insurgents attacking supply routes— but then, there had always been rumors. If repeated often enough, a rumor could become truth; if repeated still more, the news would drift back into the uncertain realm of rumor. "Reality," Tofte-Jebsen wrote in a 1976 letter to *Orientering*, "has little bearing on truth; truth is instead a confluence of time and story."[10]

It was decided that they would all make the trip together, as both Eugenia

---

[10] This was rebutted, tongue in cheek, by Per Røed-Larsen in his epistemological essay "Levetiden på sannheten" (1978): "Time and story have little bearing on truth; truth must be, by definition, a confluence of reality and reality alone" (24).

and Jean-Baptiste realized they had not left La Seule Vérité in the decade since Raksmey's arrival. Eugenia, who had just turned seventy-nine, was not in particularly good health, and Jean-Baptiste thought she should stay behind, but she would not hear of it. She insisted on seeing Raksmey delivered safely from the jungles with her own eyes. Secretly, she also wanted to revisit the city of her childhood one last time so that she could make a kind of peace with it. Her parents were long dead; her sisters, having left for Paris decades before, were also dead. The city was not the same city that had tortured her so, but she still wanted it to see her, to see how she had survived and outlived them all. She thus requested that they stay at the Hôtel Continental, her family's old establishment, now under the ownership of a shady Corsican mafioso and renamed the Continental Palace.

At the docks on the morning of their departure, Tien held Raksmey close. He pressed something into his hand and bowed to the little boy, who solemnly returned the gesture.

"Rak," he said.

"Rak," Raksmey agreed.

When they were on the boat, Raksmey signed to Eugenia, "Rasey is staying here with Tien so he won't get lonely."

As they made their way down the huge, muddy river, weaving past nameless islands, the channels splitting and splitting and coming together again, Raksmey spent the entire trip perched on the bow, watching the landscape slip past. He saw workers hunched thigh deep in rice fields, herds of weary, low-backed buffalo, men tossing nets into the shallows, packs of children waving frantically as they passed. It was his country, yet he had never seen it. He knew the half-life of radium 225, but he did not know the curves of the Mekong, the scent of rotting cassava, the sweeping glint of sunlight across the floodplains of Kampong Cham. Hundreds of villages dotting the vast basin. Specks of people fanning out across the paddies, swaying against the heat of a flickering horizon. A long, spindly bamboo bridge filled with bicyclists and women with fruit on their heads. Raksmey asked no questions, merely watched, the faintest of smiles hanging on his lips, the spray from the river occasionally leaping over the bow and wetting his brow.

They reached the wonder of Phnom Penh in the late afternoon. The ringed spires of the wats and the Royal Palace rose through the thin layer of smoky sweat that hung across the city. The smell of something metallic and unburnable, burning nonetheless. After docking their boat, they shuffled through the throngs amassed along the riverfront to a four-story guesthouse on the boulevard near the place where the Tonle Sap spilled out into the Mekong.

That evening, Raksmey held fast to Eugenia's hand on the way to the restaurant as bicycles and motos sped past, clipping at their heels. Having known only the rhythm of the rubber trees, he was paralyzed into a kind of awed silence by this swarm of fluctuating humanity. There were more people here on a single street than he had seen in his entire life. Hawkers wielding dripping pig heads yelled out prices to an indifferent crowd. A boy, not much younger than Raksmey, tore by them after a loose chicken, diving beneath a car to snatch at the terrified bird. Loud pop music played from an open window. A crowd of young monks in orange robes enveloped them and then moved silently on: an oasis of calm amid the urban hustle.

"What do you hear?" Eugenia signed to him as they wound through the city.

Raksmey closed his eyes to listen, and promptly tripped over a curb.

"Careful," Jean-Baptiste said. "In a place like this, you must keep your eyes open. Always open."

Raksmey stopped, listening. He tried to pick out one sound, but there was simply too much.

"I hear everything," he signed to Eugenia. Then: "I don't hear anything."

"Yes," she signed. "I know what you mean."

Later he sat at the window of their guesthouse, staring at the twinkle of streetlamps. A lone firework exploded above the river. Someone moaned from another room. Cars honked and zipped by along the boulevard. The scent of spilled gasoline wafted up from below. Next to the window, a strip of sticky flypaper whispered in the breeze. A fly had recently gotten stuck and was buzzing loudly in short, frequent intervals.

"There's so much," said Raksmey.

"Try to get some sleep," said Jean-Baptiste. "Tomorrow will be even longer."

"It's funny to think this place was here this whole time," said Raksmey, touching the trapped fly.

THE NEXT DAY, they departed before dawn, pushing out into a misty river that prevented them from seeing more than fifty meters ahead. Soon the fog burned off, but the current—unsettled by some unseen force—became choppier. The river appeared to be flowing both ways, so their progress was slow and laborious. At one point they rounded a bend and came across a Buddhist wat in flames, the temple rippling against the jungle heat, the monks running to the river for water.

"What happened?" Raksmey asked.

"I don't know," said Jean-Baptiste.

When the monks saw their boat, they began to jump up and down, calling out for help.

"We should help them," said Raksmey. He looked down and saw ash floating on the surface of the river. A half-burnt page.

Jean-Baptiste shook his head. "We can do nothing."

"Why?"

But his father gave no answer.

After an eternity, the river opened and parted into the salamander islands of the delta. They passed clusters of floating markets teeming with long-tail boats, bunches of fish hanging from their sterns. They passed a large container ship that had become beached on a sandbar, its crew lazily playing cards on the deck. One of the men formed an imaginary gun with his hand, aimed, and shot at Raksmey as they went by.

Finally, as the sun began to sink behind them, they could see it: the place where all things went, the great expanse of the South China Sea.

Raksmey turned to his grandmother. "You cannot see the end," he signed.

"We must have faith," she signed. "If there was no end, then all of the water would flow out and the ocean would be empty."

The wind picked up. It began to rain. They sought shelter in the boat's little cabin, listening to the raindrops hammer at the thin metal roof. Raksmey curled up in Eugenia's lap and quickly fell asleep to the lull of the motor and the roll of the waves against the hull. A leak from the roof began dripping onto Eugenia's head, but she did not move, fearing she would disturb the child. The water collected and ran down her neck. She put her hand on the bulb of his cheek and smoothed his hair.

"Little one," she signed against his skin. "How do you say goodbye?"

Hampered by a steady headwind and a whipping rain that increased in intensity as they worked their way up the coast, they arrived in Saigon late that night, cold and hungry, caught in the middle of a tropical downpour. It was too late to head to the *collège* as planned, so they hurriedly loaded their luggage into the back of a tuk-tuk, clambered into another, and directed this little caravan directly to the hotel.

Much was as Eugenia remembered it from her youth, though the facade now read CONTINENTAL PALACE in an art deco sans serif and the street signs were all in Vietnamese, an attempt by the state to shed the language of its colonizers. They stood, waterlogged, in the bright white-marble lobby, blinking at the legacy of Pierre Cazeau's audacity. A group of American officers emerged from the elevator, holding their hats in their hands. One of them delivered a punch line and the rest burst into laughter.

"This is where your grandmother grew up," said Jean-Baptiste. "She was high society."

"High society?" Raksmey repeated. "What's this?"

Eugenia wobbled, steadied herself, and then tumbled over their luggage and onto the floor.

"Grandma!" Raksmey yelled.

The American officers came rushing over to help.

"I'm fine," she signed, shooing them away. "It's been a long trip."

They did not understand her signs, so they lifted her up and placed her in a plush chair next to a palm plant. She was annoyed at all the attention, but her face had drained of its color and she'd begun to shiver uncontrollably.

"Someone should call a doctor," one of the officers said loudly.

"I'll do it!" yelled another.

"Does she speak English?" asked another.

"She does not speak. She's deaf," Jean-Baptiste said in English.

"Deaf, eh? My old lady's deaf," said the officer. "*Selectively* deaf."

"Let's get you upstairs, Mother," Jean-Baptiste signed. "You shouldn't have come to Saigon."

"I'm *fine*," she said aloud, but her voice quavered, and she did not protest when a bellhop brought over a wheelchair.

When they got her into the room, it was discovered that she was already running a high fever. The doctor arrived, bearing pills and a hot water bottle. Swaddled inside the blankets, a shell of herself, Eugenia was too weak to complain.

Raksmey sat by her bed, staring at his grandmother, lying prone beneath a headboard of two ornamental dragons locked in combat.

Eugenia moved her hands from beneath the covers. "Don't look so worried," she signed. "It doesn't suit you."

"Your father owned this hotel?" he signed.

"Yes," she signed. "This was back when the French were in charge. My father was a . . ." She paused, her hands searching for the word. She waved her fingers and floated her hands upward. "He was a proud man. He was used to getting his way."

"When did he die?"

"In 1911. Four years after your father was born. He never met Jean-Baptiste. I don't think he wanted to meet Jean-Baptiste."

"Why not?"

"Sometimes we're related to people purely out of chance. We don't love them; they're simply there, like the forest."

"He was mean to you?"

"Not so mean. He didn't understand who I was, that's all. We can't expect people to understand all the time, can we?" She closed her eyes. "Tell me, Raksmey, what do you hear now?"

The answer to their game felt vitally important. As if he could make everything better simply by giving the correct response. He closed his eyes and imagined a world where there was nothing but sound. Nothing but the compression of air molecules, bouncing this way and that. No light, no objects, no jungle, no animals, no love, no fire, no death. Only sound.

He listened and heard piano music drifting down the corridor. A woman's laughter, rising, joined by a man's, before both fell silent again. The faint ting of the elevators opening and closing next to their room. The rattle of silverware on a cart in the hallway. Rain tiptoeing against a windowpane.

How to say this to her? He scratched his nose and took a breath, then he put his mouth up to her ear and hummed. He hummed, and from his lips he gave her everything he heard. She smiled, her eyes closed, taking in the little boy's vibrations.

THE NEXT MORNING, she was gone. The bed was neatly made, and there was no sign of her anywhere in the room or the hotel. The staff in the lobby had not seen her come or go.

Jean-Baptiste was furious.

"What was she thinking? Wandering off like that in the middle of the night? Unwell? Deaf and blind? Doesn't she have any sense at all?"

After giving a description to the hotel manager and a representative from the police, he told Raksmey to gather his things.

"We will not let the lunacy of an old woman derail the whole purpose of coming here."

"But what if she's in trouble?"

"Don't worry about her. You've got enough to worry about. We came here to get you to school, and that's exactly what we'll do."

"But—"

"Raksmey, she'll be fine. Has she ever not been fine? She's going to outlive us all. We're going. No arguments."

Saigon was in a state of low-grade unease. The president's assassination in a U.S.-backed coup had created a vacuum in the country's leadership. On nearly every corner, young policemen in oversize helmets stood at attention, thumbing at their surplus Kalashnikovs. On the way to the *collège,* they passed three jeeps carrying American troops, their faces set in hard expressions, their skin pasty in the gleam of the morning sun.

Raksmey watched from the back of the tuk-tuk as they crisscrossed the broad, palm-lined boulevards, weaving through waves of traffic, gliding through the roundabouts like electrons circling a nucleus. He tried to chart their route, but he could not read the street signs. It was the first time he had encountered a language he did not understand.

"What does that say?" he asked Jean-Baptiste, pointing to a bright yellow banner above a shop.

"I don't know."

"Why do they write like this?"

"Because they're Vietnamese. Because they're trying to be their own country now."

"Why don't they speak Khmer?"

"Vietnam's a different country than Cambodia. Everyone has their own language."

Raksmey thought about this. "If I'm Cambodian, why don't I go to school in Cambodia?"

"A fair question," said Jean-Baptiste. "I suppose it's because I went here once upon a time, before it was Vietnam. And because you are my son. And sons do what their fathers did."

Looking above them, Raksmey noticed a complex system of wires connecting all of the buildings. The wires came together in tangled bunches, following the roads, exploding apart, rejoining again.

"What are those?" he asked.

"Electricity," Jean-Baptiste said. "Telephone. Telegraph. This is what makes a city possible."

"Don't people make a city possible?"

"Yes. You're right. People *plus* electricity make a city possible."

"And food."

"And food."

"And language."

"Yes, Raksmey, we could extend this list indefinitely. To include everything in the city. The list would fill the city itself."

Raksmey was quiet as they moved through the streets. He could drive like this all day. One among many.

"I like you, Papa," he said after a while.

THE RECTOR OF COLLÈGE René Descartes was a young, exuberant Vietnamese man named Han Mac Than, who had taken control of the *collège* the year before, just after President Diem's assassination. Monsieur Than wore circular glasses that were too small for his face and a white three-piece suit that was too large for his slender frame. He combed his hair long and to the side like the young people did, but he had a purposeful, self-assured air that put both Raksmey and Jean-Baptiste at ease, though for different reasons.

"We are on the verge of a new era," he said to them in his office. "Independence has given many Vietnamese a fresh perspective on life. This is a very important time. We must make our own way. There can be no more excuses for failure. You cannot blame the Frenchman. Blaming the Frenchman is like blaming a ghost. There's nothing there. The only one you can blame is yourself."

"You can still blame us," said Jean-Baptiste. "I give you my permission."

The rector looked confused, then he laughed, quickly and uncomfortably.

"Of course," he said. "I understand you're joking now. We can all make many jokes now."

"Just as soon as the Americans leave."

"Ah," the rector said, opening his hands. "What can I say? Saigon is a popular place. Many ideas, many forces at work, not all of them . . ." He turned to Raksmey, who had remained silent throughout their conversation. "It's a good place to come and study. Do you like to study?"

"Yes, Monsieur," Raksmey said quietly.

"And tell me, what is your favorite subject?"

Raksmey looked at his father. Jean-Baptiste motioned for him to speak.

"Molecular physics," Raksmey whispered, shrinking down into his seat.

Monsieur Than raised his eyebrows. "Well, welcome to René Descartes, Raksmey."

"I've left my instructions in here," said Jean-Baptiste, sliding a thick envelope across the table.

"Instructions?"

"Raksmey is used to a rigorous education program. Obviously this school will represent some kind of break from that, but I'd like to ensure as much continuity as possible. There are certain . . . *aspects* of his development that I'd like you to keep track of."

Monsieur Than leaned back in his chair. "Many parents are nervous when they first drop off their children here. They wonder, what will we do to them? Well, I can assure you he will be in good hands."

"Read the materials. This is a little different. I've been involved in a . . . project."

"We aren't going to turn your son into a Communist, if that's what you're worried about, Monsieur. We believe in a basic set of ideals, but we also teach open-mindedness. Tolerance. It's the only way this region will survive."

Monsieur Than offered to give them a tour of the grounds, but Jean-Baptiste explained that his mother had gone missing and that he must get back to the hotel.

"I'm sorry to hear this," said Monsieur Than. "But Saigon is not such a big town. I'm sure you'll find her."

"I'm sure," said Jean-Baptiste.

Outside, he paused at the gates of the *collège*.

"Please, take care of him," he said to the rector. "He means a great deal to me. You'll quickly see the caliber of child you have on your hands."

"It's what we do here," said Monsieur Than. "The future of this country depends on them."

"He's Cambodian."

Monsieur Than smiled. "I don't discriminate. Cambodia's problems are our problems. And our problems are Cambodia's. We're all in this fight together."

Jean-Baptiste bent down to Raksmey. "And you take care of them. Be nice. Chew with your mouth closed. Don't show off."

Raksmey looked at his father, his eyes wide with terror.

"Don't worry," said Jean-Baptiste. "We'll find her." And he hugged his son for the second time in his life.

THEY DID NOT FIND HER. Two weeks went by. Despite a citywide search, despite inquiries into various underground factions that might have had grounds to kidnap her or worse, Eugenia remained missing. All avenues of inquiry turned up nothing. Even the American army had been sent notice of her disappearance and were on the lookout at their checkpoints around the city and as far north as Bien Hoa.

That first morning after Eugenia disappeared, the maid had discovered something unusual inside the bed: a smooth, polished stick figure, wrapped in a roll of twine that had been threaded through pieces of bone-white seashell. When shaken, the figurine made a thin rattling noise. Jean-Baptiste had never seen this wooden effigy before and was convinced it could not have been in his mother's possession. He propped it up by the window, and though he was not a religious man, he took to kneeling in front of the stick creature each evening and praying for her safe return.

He spent several days searching the city from the back of a tuk-tuk, scanning the sea of faces. Every old white woman he spotted from a distance caused his pulse to quicken, even if he also knew, in his heart of hearts, that it was not her, that it would never be her. This simultaneous expectation and resignation wore him to the bone. Eventually he stopped looking.

Jean-Baptiste also began to worry about his son. He did not want Eugenia's disappearance to have a negative effect on Raksmey's first days at the *collège*. In fact, the more he was away from Raksmey, the more nervous he became that Monsieur Than had not properly studied his instructions. Vital aspects of his development might even now be going unnoticed and unrecorded. The possibility drove him mad. This initial break-in period was crucial for developing Raksmey's positive attitude toward an institutional education. How could he have left such important data collection in the hands of others? His notebooks would suffer, were already suffering.

In the middle of his third week in the city, he returned to the school. He found Raksmey on the sporting grounds, playing football, a game he had never taught the boy. He realized there was so much he had not done, a million opportunities not taken, a million chances for growth lost and gone forever. *What a ruse! What a sham—to raise a child when failure is almost certainly guaranteed!* He very nearly turned around then and there, to leave and never to return, but Raksmey spotted him on the sidelines and came running over.

"There you are," said Jean-Baptiste. "How're you getting on? Do you like football?"

"Yes," said Raksmey, flushed from his exertions. "Did you find Grandma?"

Jean-Baptiste got down on one knee. "Yes, of course," he said. "She had just gone out to find her old house, and she had gotten lost. How silly of her. Apparently she had left a note for us but it had slipped underneath the bed."

Raksmey studied him. "But she was sick."

"You know your grandmother. She's never one to let anything keep her down," he said. "Have you made any friends here?"

Raksmey shrugged. "Some of the boys are mean."

"Yes, well, this happens, unfortunately. And I'm afraid it won't change, wherever you go. These boys are scared of their own deficiencies."

"Yes, Papa."

"How are the studies? Are they difficult?"

"They put me with the oldest class in science. It's a bit easy. But the boys laughed at me. They said I was *un phénomène de la nature*."

"Well, that doesn't sound so bad," said Jean-Baptiste.

Raksmey blinked at him.

"Okay, go out and play. Score some goals!"

"They won't let me score," Raksmey said and ran off.

Monsieur Than joined him on the sidelines. He was carrying a rolled-up umbrella, even though the sky was clear.

"You were right," said the rector. "Raksmey is most unusual. I don't think I've ever encountered a student quite like him."

"You need to protect him. The other children don't understand."

"Boys can be like that. We'll make sure he gets the attention he deserves."

"Did you get my instructions?" Jean-Baptiste asked.

"Yes, I wanted to talk with you about this—"

"I've been thinking," said Jean-Baptiste. "I believe this break has caused too much discontinuity in the experiment. I'd like to do the observations myself, at least for the first month or so. Then I can train one of your own teachers to pick up after me. But it's critical right now—"

Monsieur Than cleared his throat.

"Monsieur de Broglie, I admire what you've done with Raksmey. You've clearly taught him a great deal. But you've sensed there are things that . . . that you cannot teach him. This, I assume, is why you've brought him to us."

The whistle blew. Raksmey had fallen. He looked over to where Jean-Baptiste and the rector were standing and then pulled himself up. Another boy slapped him on the back of the head. Jean-Baptiste instinctively cringed.

"I realized I could not be everything for him," Jean-Baptiste said, staring at the boys milling about. "He needs socialization with other children."

"Among other things," said Monsieur Than. "He also—and please do not take this the wrong way—he also needs to be away from his father for some time."

Jean-Baptiste took a step back. "What do you mean? I made him into who he is!"

"No, Monsieur de Broglie, you did not make him—"

"Where would he be without me?"

"Nor did his mother make him. Nor did God, nor Buddha, nor whomever you ascribe your ascendant powers to. Raksmey can only make himself, and in order for him to do this, your project—as honorable as it is—must end here. I won't force you. You're free to withdraw Raksmey from the *collège* at this very moment. But if you choose to keep him here, if you truly wish for us to be partners, then you must agree to entrust him to us and to let him go. I would ask that you leave and visit us again in four months. I know this may seem harsh, but it's absolutely necessary. For you as much as for him."

JEAN-BAPTISTE STAYED in Saigon for two more weeks. At night, in search again of that beautiful, horrific sensation *du familier,* he began to frequent an opium parlor in District 5. The door was tended by a madam named Phuong. She never smiled as she took his money. The dimly lit parlor, which consisted of a damp cement room adorned with a meager collection of pillows and dull green army mattresses, was populated by potbellied French colonials who had lost their way; sleepy-eyed American servicemen on R&R, happy enough to wax melancholic about the impending war; the occasional Chinese diplomat who took his drug and said nothing at all.

Jean-Baptiste lay there in the gloom and thought of his wife, of his mother, of his father, of Raksmey, of Tien, of the river and the jungle, the jungle that had become his jungle. He thought of everything that had come to pass, all the words spoken and not spoken, everything said and done and never done, and the promise of a forgiveness that would never come. The depth of his loneliness surprised and soothed him. Stumbling home from the parlor late one night, his left hand bleeding from an incident he could not recall, he realized he would always be alone—that he *had* always been alone.

There was nothing left but to leave.

"Please," he told the hotel's concierge. "If my mother shows up, tell her to wire this number in Phnom Penh. They'll get word to me. Give her this letter. Tell her I'm not angry. Tell her I love her."

"Monsieur," the concierge said, bowing.

"You'll tell her?"

"Monsieur?"

"You'll tell her everything?"

The concierge bowed again. "I will try," he said.

Jean-Baptiste packed his bags and hers, including the little wooden doll, and started back to the place from which he had come.

7

MARCH 1975

There were only five other people on his flight to Phnom Penh, and none appeared to be Cambodian. Raksmey squinted out the airplane window at the rolling green expanse of his country. He had not been home in eleven years. The plane lurched, then steadied itself. In the distance, something burned, the smoke pooling pleasantly in the air. From this height the world was in miniature, like a museum exhibit, content with its own beauty, wanting of nothing.

After his passport was stamped by a plump, bored army officer, Raksmey wandered through what looked to be an abandoned airport. Inside the main terminal, a series of plastic buckets filled with greasy mechanic's tools were lined up next to a deserted security checkpoint. Nearby, a lone worker mopped at the floor, though the floor appeared to be clean.

As he was walking past the shuttered airport café, Raksmey heard someone call his name—once, twice. He turned, and there was Tien, standing in a white short-sleeved shirt and slim blue slacks. The two men embraced, laughed, nearly falling into a dusty ficus tree.

"You survived?" Tien asked in Khmer, holding on to Raksmey's shoulder as if he might fly away.

"Survived what?" Raksmey answered in French.

"Sometimes the Khmer Rouge shoot at planes coming to land." Tien switched to French.

"No one told me this!" said Raksmey.

"Better not to know," Tien smiled. "How is life in Europe? You are a big man now?"

Raksmey held up his arms. "Not so big."

"Where do you live?"

"Geneva," said Raksmey. "Switzerland."

"Your father . . ." His voice caught. "He said you are working inside a tunnel. Like a rabbit."

"It's a collider. A big tunnel, like a circle," said Raksmey, tracing a loop with his finger. There were new lines beneath Tien's eyes and across his forehead. "Things here are not good?"

Tien shook his head. "Not so good. Maybe you should not come."

"I had to come."

Tien smiled, nodded. "Yes," he said.

"Rak," said Raksmey.

"Rak," said Tien.

THEY WALKED OUT into the heat. Raksmey almost gasped as the heavy air strangled him. His pores flexed open, his breath shortened, his pupils dilated and then contracted with this sudden transfer of energy. The molecules in his skin began to sputter and churn, tuning themselves to the temperature of the world, and yet his body settled into an enduring weariness, his walk morphing into an improvised lean. It was out of this paradox—of quick molecules and slow bodies—that the great, beautiful sadness of the tropics arose, causing men and country alike to fall and rise and fall again. When Raksmey felt this familiar malaise, felt his skin both alive and dead, he knew he was finally home.

Tien hailed a tuk-tuk. They wove through a quiet, sullen Phnom Penh. Women hanging up laundry eyed them warily as they passed.

"You live here now?" asked Raksmey.

"I'm having trouble," said Tien. His voiced quavered.

"I brought you something," said Raksmey. From his pocket he produced a coin. He placed it in his friend's palm. "Rak."

Tien stared at the little silver circle. His eyes grew moist.

"The world is not so big," he said.

"Very small, in fact," said Raksmey.

They rode through the city, past a marketplace that had been bombed. Streaks of soot rising from broken windows.

"Tell me, Tien, did he suffer?"

Tien shook his head. "No. He did not."

"You saw?"

"When he went, he went like this." He clapped his hands around the coin.

"Tell me, Tien. Tell me everything. I want to know."

AND SO ENDS that slim little wonder that is *Jeg er Raksmey*. In a review of the novella in *Vinduet*, Røed-Larsen declares this ending "a curious failure of invention for a man whose only gift was an overactive imagination" (125). Other reviews complained about how such an ending left too much unexplained. Dagfinn Møller writes, in the final issue of *Profil*, that "this last line . . . a plea for information, for anything concrete . . . becomes the voice of a reader left in the lurch" (102).

Tofte-Jebsen never responded publicly to these criticisms, but in a lecture at the Bergen Offentlige Bibliotek in 1983, he advanced this theory of fiction making:

> *If you grow too comfortable with your book, I say dismantle it* ("demontere det"). *Put it into a paper bag and heave it out the window . . . no matter if it hits someone in the street. You have to clear the decks before you grow complacent. If you've lived with even one eye open you'll know what I'm talking about—change is the only force that keeps us alive.*

He then, it is said, walked out in the middle of the lecture.

Regardless of Tofte-Jebsen's motives, if we are to discover anything more about Raksmey's story, we must turn exclusively to Røed-Larsen's account in *Spesielle Partikler*. Keep in mind that Røed-Larsen's Raksmey is not Tofte-Jebsen's

Raksmey (and vice versa). We thus may sense a distinct break in character. To make matters worse, Røed-Larsen points to the nearly impossible challenge of establishing facts in post-independence Cambodia, renamed Democratic Kampuchea. After seizing power in April 1975, the Khmer Rouge regime famously declared that time had been reset to "Year Zero," effectively wiping the slate clean of all Western influence, including historical written records.

Despite such formidable historiographical conditions, Røed-Larsen has done a remarkable job piecing together a crude timeline of Raksmey's whereabouts from 1965 to 1979, which we may now summarize here.

In the mid-sixties, Raksmey spent three years at Collège Réne Descartes, in Saigon, under the personal tutelage of Rector Than; by all accounts, he excelled magnificently. When the American war in Vietnam began to accelerate, Rector Than had Raksmey graduate early, at age fifteen, while simultaneously convincing the admissions office at the École Polytechnique, in Paris, to admit him, despite his young age. Jean-Baptiste did not come to Saigon to see his son off. Instead, he sent him a letter, a copy of which apparently found its way into Per Røed-Larsen's possession and was translated in *Spesielle Partikler* (640):

10 August 1968

Dearest Raksmey,

You must forgive me. I have not been well & am only now recovering from my illnesses. Please do not see my absence as having any reflection on my feelings towards your departure, which I regard with utmost excitement & pride. I have been getting updates from Rector Than about the rapid progress of your application. Your acceptance to the Polytechnique comes as no surprise, though I must admit it does bring me into a certain state of rumination.

You no doubt realized my great aspiration for you to become a physicist, an aspiration that guided the movement of my hand in nearly every choice I made while raising you. I recorded your progress in the volumes upon which I now gaze, volumes that seem lifeless without their subject. I now see this singular mind-set for what it is: a foolish defense which offered me shelter from myself.

By sticking to my regime, I could deflect the fear I felt as my love for you grew. When we found you, you were so small, so sick, in the very borderlands of quietus. If only you could have seen the impossibility of your own existence! Your continued survival, against such odds, was extraordinary, & transformed us all—some for the better & some, like myself, I fear for the worse. My wife—whom in my head I still consider your mother—has never left me, & her legacy was alive & well when you floated by in your basket. My project was my way of rescuing you, but it was also my way of rescuing me.

Please, Raksmey, my dearest Raksmey, I beg for your forgiveness & I urge you, as you depart on the biggest journey of your life, to forget all that I have taught you & to listen only to the voice inside your own heart, if such a feat is still possible, given all the damage I have wrought. I am a selfish old man, a jealous, vindictive fool, who had no business doing what he did. Know that whatever path you choose, I will love you no less or no more. I am sorry for what I have inflicted upon you & no doubt what I will continue to inflict with the legacy of my actions. Nothing would make me so happy, or serve me so justly, as to see you decide to take up the profession of a cobbler, a mechanic, or a composer. Anything but the methods of science that I so bound you to.

Be well, my dear Raksmey, Raksmey. I have given you all & here I have nothing left to give.

With highest admiration,

your father,
Jean-Baptiste de Broglie

In the fall of 1968, Raksmey traveled to Paris to begin his studies at the École Polytechnique. He did not return home before this journey. Indeed, since that boat trip down the Mekong with his father and grandmother, Raksmey had not set foot in Cambodia.

Save his impeccable school transcript, not much is known about his time in Paris, about how young Raksmey navigated the trials of a large urban university in the late sixties, about whether he experimented with drugs, sex, or *le rock and roll,* or whether he simply stuck to his studies, as his prodigious academic record suggests. He took an average of eight classes per semester and graduated in four years, with a highly unusual dual master's in quantum devices and applied particle physics. He also hosted a weekly classical music show on the university's radio station, called *La Vie Rallentando*. What is most interesting is that Raksmey seemed intent on ignoring the advice of his father, which came either too late or too early. He would become Cambodia's first (and only) particle physicist.

Accordingly, Raksmey promptly began work on a doctoral degree in quantum electrodynamics at the Polytechnique. He was offered, after some testy political negotiation within the department, a coveted fellowship at CERN, the international particle physics laboratory straddling the border between France and Switzerland. Only twenty-one at the time, Raksmey was the youngest doctoral student in CERN's history. Under the mentorship of the theorist Dr. Abdus Salam and the experimentalist André Rousset, Raksmey wrote his dissertation, "On the Electroweak Interaction of Neutrinos with Quarks via Z Boson Exchange," utilizing experimental research from CERN's newly constructed Gargamelle bubble chamber. Several key points of Raksmey's dissertation would later contribute to Dr. Salam's winning the Nobel Prize in physics in 1979.

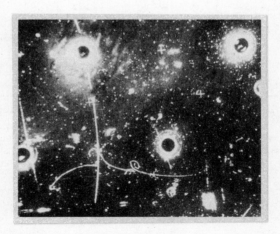

Fig. 4.8. "A neutral current event, as observed in the Gargamelle bubble chamber"
Image from R. Raksmey's 1974 dissertation, "On the Electroweak Interaction
of Neutrinos with Quarks via Z Boson Exchange,"
as reproduced in Røed-Larsen, P., *Spesielle Partikler,* p. 651

Raksmey was quite clearly an eager and brilliant disciple of Salam, but he also struggled with social interaction. He had a small collection of English poetry in his apartment, as well as "several novels by Latin American authors" (653), including Julio Cortázar, and he enjoyed listening to Bach, Debussy, Shostakovich, and Britten. When not doing lab work, he often went hiking alone in the Swiss Alps.

In *Spesielle Partikler,* Røed-Larsen also cites rumors—although these remain unconfirmed—that Raksmey developed an intimate (possibly sexual) relationship with an older man, Dr. Alan Ferring, who was visiting the Gargamelle team from Berkeley, California. This relationship—if indeed it existed at all—must have been brief, for in September 1974 Ferring returned to his wife and family in California. Dr. Ferring apparently refused to be interviewed for Røed-Larsen's book.

This much we do know: on March 2, 1975, Raksmey flew back to Cambodia after hearing news of his father's death. Raksmey was listed in the passenger

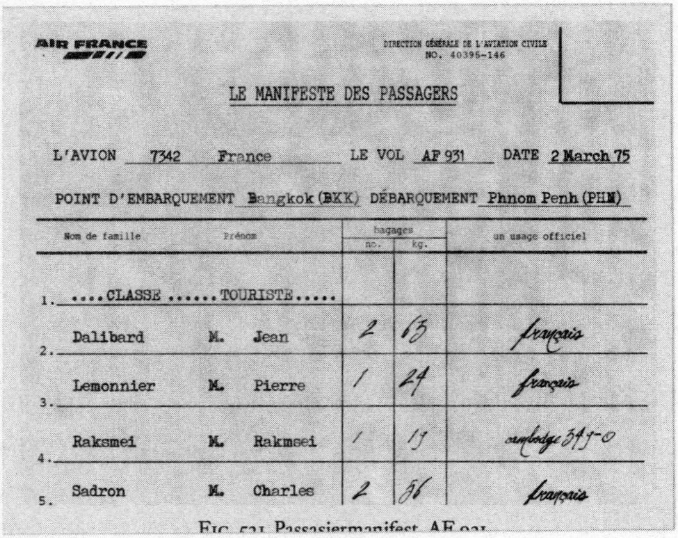

AIR FRANCE

DIRECTION GÉNÉRALE DE L'AVIATION CIVILE
NO. 40395-146

LE MANIFESTE DES PASSAGERS

L'AVION 7342 France LE VOL AF 931 DATE 2 March 75

POINT D'EMBARQUEMENT Bangkok (BKK) DÉBARQUEMENT Phnom Penh (PHN)

	Nom de famille	Prénom		bagages no.	bagages kg.	un usage officiel
1.	....CLASSE	......TOURISTE.....				
2.	Dalibard	M.	Jean	2	63	français
3.	Lemonnier	M.	Pierre	1	24	français
4.	Raksmei	M.	Rakmsei	1	19	cambodge 345-0
5.	Sadron	M.	Charles	2	56	français

Fig. 4.9. Manifest from AF 931, Bangkok–Phnom Penh, March 2, 1975
From Røed-Larsen, P., *Spesielle Partikler,* p. 670

manifests of the Air France flights from Paris to Bangkok and from Bangkok to Phnom Penh—Flight 931, one of the last commercial flights to land in Cambodia.

Regarding the circumstances of Jean-Baptiste's death, Røed-Larsen, lacking much concrete evidence, contends that a small squad of Khmer Rouge troops, possibly heading southwest from their camp in Ratanakiri, near the Vietnam border, came upon La Seule Vérité by accident. Their movement was in the context of a larger dry-season mobilization of Khmer Rouge troops to Kampong Thom before a final push toward Phnom Penh down Highway 5.

According to Røed-Larsen, the encounter at La Seule Vérité was not without precedent. During the two years before, there had been plenty of fighting in the area between Khmer Rouge rebels and various divisions of Lon Nol's woeful Khmer National Armed Forces. In 1973, an American B-52 had mistakenly dropped a payload of phosphorus bombs on the lycée, only three kilometers upriver, killing seventeen schoolchildren and the two missionaries from Texas. The school had burned for three days. Yet for the most part, La Seule Vérité had remained relatively unscathed by both the American war in Vietnam and the civil war raging in Cambodia. Rubber collection had completely ceased about five years earlier, following Capitaine Claude Renoit's suicide, in 1969, and only a skeleton crew of five or six men remained with Jean-Baptiste at the time, maintaining the grounds, cooking, and ostensibly providing protection from hostile factions. On several occasions, representatives from the undermanned Cambodia National Army had recommended that Jean-Baptiste abandon his home and retreat to Phnom Penh, as they could no longer guarantee his safety. He had politely but firmly dismissed their counsel each time.

What happened on the night in question is not known. Tien managed to escape, but the plantation was burned, and it is unclear what was rescued from the fire. One can assume that all of Jean-Baptiste's notebooks on Raksmey's development—numbering perhaps 750—were destroyed, though less certain is the fate of André's and Henri's ledgers, which presumably remained locked in the basement safes. And what of Jean-Baptiste's wager with himself concerning the fate of his only son, squirreled away in a rosewood box beneath the floorboards? Or the *Reamker* masks on the mantel? Or the strange wooden

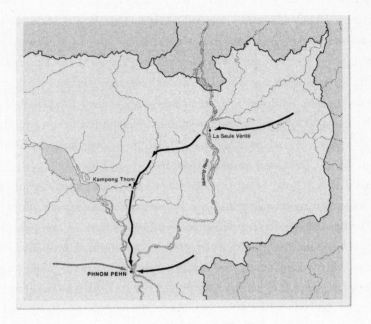

*Fig. 4.10. Map showing movements of Northern Sector Khmer Rouge
rebels from Ratanakiri to Phnom Penh (January–April 1975)*
From Røed-Larsen, P., *Spesielle Partikler,* p. 650

puppet discovered in place of his mother, which had found a home next to the inkwell in his study?

In the years of conflict that followed, the plantation was used as a refuge for several Khmer Rouge divisions, vagrants, and later, for those fleeing the regime. Over the course of this period, the grounds were apparently picked clean. Røed-Larsen recounts how, many years later, in 1995, the property was examined by a ministerial housing inspector and the resulting report made no mention of a safe in the basement or any miscellaneous scientific equipment. The property was valued at 290 million riel, or about $75,000, a prohibitive price to anyone but the most elite provincial ministers.

Not surprisingly, given the site's obscure location and the country's ongoing economic woes, the property was never redeveloped. The state attempted to seize the plantation on several occasions, but the estate's legal status remained unresolved, particularly since Raksmey Raksmey de Broglie was never officially located. Many travelers on the Mekong have remarked at the unusual sight of the main house's grand ruins, just visible from the river, surrounded by rows and rows of overgrown hevea trees. Locals pass along several competing stories about its onetime inhabitants, involving sorcerers, the CIA, and even Pol Pot himself. The name La Seule Vérité has been completely lost to time.

After landing in Phnom Penh in March 1975, Raksmey attended a brief funeral ceremony for his father inside a small wat near the university, as it was no longer possible to travel back through Khmer Rouge territory to the plantation. The Mekong was now mined all the way up to the Laotian border. Days after this, flights out of the country were suspended, and Raksmey was prevented from returning to his lab in Switzerland. He and Tien shared a small flat in the Khan Chamkarmon district of Phnom Penh for a little over a month, waiting, with the rest of the city, for the imminent arrival of the Khmer Rouge. No one knew what this would mean, though many diplomatic organizations, including the U.S. embassy, took no chances and evacuated all of their members.

Finally, on April 17, 1975, trucks and tanks full of battle-weary Khmer Rouge soldiers streamed into the city down Highway 5 and "liberated" Phnom Penh. They were met by a jubilant populace, who hoped that this signaled the end of the endless civil war. Peace could now prosper in a region that had not seen peace in many years. It was not long, however, before Cambodians came to terms with the reality of these liberators. Within days, the entire city—all two million inhabitants—was ordered to leave for the countryside. The Khmer Rouge had begun its surreal war against time.

In pursuit of a total socialist order that eradicated the individual and shunned all Western influence, the Khmer Rouge bombed the national bank and symbolically burned its currency in the streets. They turned the National Library into a horse stable and pig farm, and nearly all of the books—both Khmer and French—were indiscriminately destroyed or used for cooking fires, toilet paper, or rolling cigarettes. Røed-Larsen includes a famous photograph of three young Khmer Rouge cadres standing around a torn-up copy of Dante's *Inferno,* smoking cigarettes rolled from its pages, a look of weary amazement in their eyes.

Knowing that religious traditions could pose the most serious threat to their plan to socially engineer the populace, the Khmer Rouge forced the Buddhist monkhood, the spiritual backbone of Khmer society, to disband. Their sutras were seized and burned; their wats were turned into granaries or fish sauce factories, the altars pushed aside to make room for great barrels of fermenting anchovies. The Khmer Rouge leadership wisely co-opted several familiar Buddhist notions—such as selflessness and transcendence—for use in their extreme form of Marxist ideology, with spiritual nirvana replaced by the perfect embodiment of the state, Angkar.

Yet monks were by no means the only targets of the Khmer Rouge. Intellectuals, academics, artists—anyone with a perceived connection to the West, including those spotted simply wearing spectacles—were all rounded up, tortured, and, in most cases, summarily executed. Eventually, in a sign that the system was rotting from within, the paranoid Khmer Rouge leadership began to turn on their own ranks, arresting hundreds of Khmer Rouge cadres suspected of being traitors to the Angkar cause. Those who did the arresting were then arrested, and so on.

Røed-Larsen wonders (656) why, given their disdain for historical transcripts, the Khmer Rouge kept such comprehensive records at the Tuol Sleng, or "S-21," security prison, a former Phnom Penh high school that had been converted into a torture camp. The place was run with astonishing efficiency by Comrade Duch, a former mathematician. Perhaps sensing the chasm left by the erasure of the written word, Comrade Duch began to forge a new history, a new kind of truth.

The S-21 documentation division, including a young photographer named Nhem En, meticulously recorded every arrival to the camp. Following strict orders, Nhem En would remove the new prisoner's blindfold and then take a series of photos: facing the camera, in profile, occasionally from the back. After a prominent prisoner died of torture, he would also take postmortem photos, the pools of blood like black ink against the white cement floors. Nhem En faced immediate execution if the photos were not up to Comrade Duch's exacting standards. He thus took great care with the lighting, the placement of the prisoner in the frame, the shallow depth of field. His art kept him alive, but it also became something alive itself.

Of the seventeen thousand prisoners who passed through Tuol Sleng, only seven survived. Nhem En's black-and-white photographs of the prisoners remained in a file cabinet in the school's old cafeteria after the Khmer Rouge fled the city, though at some point the photographs became separated from their files, so many of the images live on in a liminal, unidentified state. A man resembling Tien is pictured among these photographs, #4816, although, without proper documentation, one cannot be sure if it is actually him or someone else entirely:

Fig. 4.11. Tuol Sleng prisoner #4816
From Røed-Larsen, P., *Spesielle Partikler,* p. 658

Yet even just this act of immortalizing a prisoner in a photo, filled with its soft palette of greys and marked by the subject's vacant stare of simultaneous comprehension and disbelief, was more attention than the vast majority of the regime's victims received. Most were never documented by their killers. They slipped into death anonymously, silently, leaving no proof of their existence or of their abrupt demise.

It is here that Røed-Larsen (and by extension *we*) enter the realm of conjecture. Following the "liberation" of Phnom Penh, Raksmey was able to disguise himself as a peasant and evade execution, presumably because he was mostly unknown to the population. After walking out of the city with the rest of its inhabitants, he was sent to work up north in the rice fields in the Preah Vihear region, near Tbaeng Meanchey district. He survived only by completely abandoning his identity and pretending he was deaf and mute—for more than two years, he did not speak. It must be said, his deafness was a dangerous choice, for those with disabilities were also culled. Raksmey, however, compensated for this with tireless work in the fields, and thus ingratiated himself with the Khmer Rouge district leaders, who were less ruthless than in other sectors. As Røed-Larsen writes, "Cruelty is always local . . . [it] depends not upon the system which creates it but the hand that serves it" (660).

In the evenings, Raksmey would smile and clap as his exhausted comrades chanted songs pledging their allegiance to Angkar. When the Khmer Rouge cadres gave lectures on the triumphs of the Kampuchea state, Raksmey made sure his head was downcast, his eyes dull and empty, so that the chiefs would not detect any hint of life or understanding in them. He thus lived two lives: a life inside the crevices of his mind, where he unwound particles and debated the theories of subatomic quantum mechanics late into the night with an apparition of Dr. Salam, and another that comprised his outward actions during the day, where he was deaf and mute. A simpleton. Eager to please, eager to serve the great and powerful Angkar. Even in the darkest hours of the night, he made sure that his two lives never crossed paths, never greeted each other.

"Angkar!" he would yell with the others in a mangled voice of incomprehension. It was the only word he allowed to pass his lips—two declaratory vowels draped in vague consonants. It was not so much a word as a breath and release: "Ang-*kar*! Ang-*kar*!"

During the monsoon season of 1977, he and two others managed to escape their work camp by foot, over the Dângrêk Mountains and into Thailand. One of the men died en route after stepping on a land mine, and the other succumbed to illness as soon as he reached the safety of Thailand.

In Bangkok, Raksmey took up a research assistantship in the physics department of Chulalongkorn University for Dr. Randall Horwich, the friend of a colleague at CERN. Dr. Horwich must have been surprised at who had crawled into his lab from Democratic Kampuchea, which at the time remained an impenetrable mystery to the world. It was a fortuitous arrival that would help to jump-start Dr. Horwich's career. Together, they co-published an important theoretical paper in 1979 on the mass of up quarks in the *Pakistan Journal of Pure and Applied Physics*. This paper precipitated Dr. Horwich's move to CERN in 1980, where he would work on the UA1 experiment, which definitively discovered W and Z bosons and won its research heads a Nobel Prize.

If nothing else, Raksmey's reentrance into the world of record keeping did yield valuable evidence of his survival: along with the theoretical paper, Per Røed-Larsen managed to track down his letter of hire at Chulalongkorn, several pay stubs, and a university work transcript. There is also one improbable document that stands out from the rest: a handwritten letter, purportedly written by Raksmey to his friend Sébastien Ouellette, a fellow researcher at CERN.

The letter is dated April 18, 1975:

My dear Sébastien,

The Khmer Rouge have finally arrived in Phnom Penh. Yesterday everyone was very glad to see them, people were clapping and cheering in the streets. Many think this is the end of the war though I fear for the worst. . . . I tried to speak with one of the soldiers but he only screamed at me to back away. His eyes were dead. When I saw this, I knew very bad things are ahead. These soldiers have not been trained to run a country. They are trained to kill. Maybe I'm wrong about this. I hope. I hope.

I'm mailing you this letter on the off chance it will get out of Cambodia. Most probably it will never arrive. I miss you and our laboratory in the fields. It feels so incredibly far away right now. What a privilege it is to work there. If anything happens know that I will never forget you.

Fondly,
Raksmey de Broglie

P.S. I had the strangest dream last night. It was very vivid. I was on a river, lying in a boat. I'm not sure what river. It wasn't the Mekong. But then suddenly I felt as if I was no longer alone. I felt another person was with me— there was no one else on the boat but I felt whole, as if I had found my other half. When I woke up this morning I was still filled with this feeling of completion. I wonder what it means? Maybe I am just suffering from nerves.

Miraculously, this letter survived, according to Røed-Larsen, although it was delayed somewhere along the way and was not delivered to CERN until five years later.

Per Røed-Larsen also includes a telegram sent to Raksmey while he was staying in Bangkok. The telegram was sent from Kirkenes and received on November 10, 1979:

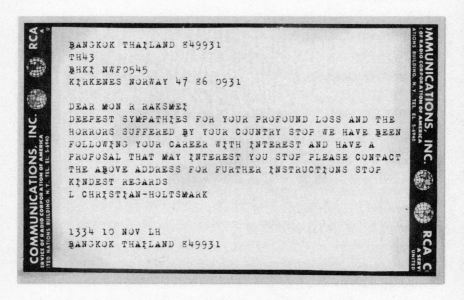

```
BANGKOK THAILAND 849931
TH43
BHKI NWFO545
KIRKENES NORWAY 47 26 0931

DEAR MON R RAKSMEI
DEEPEST SYMPATHIES FOR YOUR PROFOUND LOSS AND THE
HORRORS SUFFERED BY YOUR COUNTRY STOP WE HAVE BEEN
FOLLOWING YOUR CAREER WITH INTEREST AND HAVE A
PROPOSAL THAT MAY INTEREST YOU STOP PLEASE CONTACT
THE ABOVE ADDRESS FOR FURTHER INSTRUCTIONS STOP
KINDEST REGARDS
L CHRISTIAN-HOLTSMARK


1334 10 NOV LH
BANGKOK THAILAND 849931
```

Fig. 4.12. The initial telegram, November 10, 1979. The only surviving piece of communication between Raksmey and Kirkenesferda.
From Røed-Larsen, P., *Spesielle Partikler*, p. 670

8

After some negotiation, including several telephone calls, Dr. Christian-Holtsmark gradually made clear to Raksmey the extent of his request. Raksmey was to help negotiate their passage to the highly secretive "Camp 808," just north of Anlong Veng on the Thai border, where the Khmer Rouge had retreated to a jungle base following the Vietnamese invasion. It is unclear how much Raksmey came to understand, over the course of these transmissions, the extent of Kirkenesferda's ideology or motives, or what they planned to do once they had entered the camp. These telephone calls were not recorded, nor did Raksmey keep any journal or notebook, so Røed-Larsen is left to speculate why, given his horrific experience at the hands of the Khmer Rouge regime, he would have agreed to place himself so dramatically in harm's way on behalf of an unknown group. Røed-Larsen is quick to stress that, once onboard, Raksmey was not merely a hired gun, as Kirkenesferda did not believe in mercenary fixers. Writes Røed-Larsen, "From the minute they landed, [he] was accepted into the group, full stop, as an equal player . . . Kirkenesferda's eighth official member" (675).

Raksmey met Kirkenesferda at the Bangkok airport the day after Christmas. The team consisted of Dr. Christian-Holtsmark, the de facto leader of the troupe and director of the show; Tor Bjerknes, the primary puppet-maker; Ragnvald Brynildsen, Tor's mentor and aging Kirk patriarch; Professor Jens Røed-Larsen, who was responsible for the theoretical physics in the show; Siri Hansteen, his wife, who had designed much of the mise-en-scène; and their child, young Lars Røed-Larsen, puppet savant and torchbearer for the next generation.

In Bangkok, they hired two canopy trucks and drove to Sangkha, just north of the Choam border crossing into Cambodia. At the time, the Thai military were collaborating closely with the exiled Khmer Rouge army, providing cross-border supplies and support in exchange for a political allegiance that would act as a buffer to the perceived threat of a growing Vietnamese empire. It was critical for Thailand that Cambodia function as a self-governed country with an actual populace and not just as a cavernous Vietnamese puppet state. Such a calculated realpolitik approach had already led to horrific humanitarian failures, as many Cambodians who had fled the Khmer Rouge to the relative safety of Thailand were now forced at gunpoint to return to their homeland. Military trucks dropped them at the border, often in the middle of the minefields, leaving the refugees paralyzed in a state of territorial limbo: they could go neither forward nor backward, and so they remained exactly where they were until starvation eventually gave them the courage to test their fate in the sea of mines.

Raksmey turned out to be a wise choice as both guide and counselor: somehow he managed to coerce and/or bribe the Thai border guards into letting him and the other performers through the blockade and into Cambodian territory. The rough track into the mountains wound through several live minefields, and it was not unusual for them to pass half-exploded cows or carts blown to bits, their onetime owners nowhere to be seen. After crossing into Cambodia, Raksmey again managed to convince the Khmer Rouge soldiers guarding Camp 808 to let them through. Røed-Larsen explains:

> [Kirkenesferda's entrance] seems entirely improbable until you consider that at the time the Khmer Rouge were attempting to boost their image as one of the legitimate government factions that would take part in the anti-Vietnamese Coalition Government of Democratic Kampuchea (CGDK). . . . Realizing any hope in future political viability lay with disassociating themselves from their failed occupation, [Pol Pot and his loyalists] rebranded the Khmer Rouge as the Party of Democratic Kampuchea (PDK) and embarked on a (short-lived) PR blitz to counter the reports only just now

beginning to emerge of genocidal horrors during their three and a half years in power (681).

One must thus assume that Kirkenesferda caught a murderous regime in a unique window of existential recalibration. Khieu Samphan, the prime minister of Democratic Kampuchea—once upon a time one of the most secretive governments in modern history—was now the charming public relations figurehead attempting to resurrect the PDK's image. Barely a month after Kirkenesferda's unprecedented visit in December, he would invite a group of prominent Western journalists to dine at 808.

"Reality was suspended," recalls Henry Kamm of that trip, in his book *Cambodia: Report from a Stricken Land*. The *New York Times* journalist describes his strange January 1980 sojourn to 808's oasis of indulgence in a region of squalor:

> The Khmer Rouge guest camp was the very latest in jungle luxury. That evening the soldier-waiters filled the table with platters of Cambodian, Chinese, and Western dishes of infinite variety and saw to it, following the prime minister's discreet, silent commands, that the visitors' plates stayed filled. The best Thai beer, Johnnie Walker Black Label scotch, American soft drinks, and Thai bottled water were served; the ice to cool them, which also must have been brought in from Bangkok hundreds of miles away, never ran out. The contrast between the real Cambodia and the holiday resort atmosphere was shocking (178).

Kamm makes no mention of Kirkenesferda's visit only a few weeks prior, which is no wonder, for Samphan and the rest of the Khmer Rouge leadership would have done their best to eradicate all evidence of the disastrous events that transpired on December 30, 1979.

Like Kamm, the theater troupe encountered moments of surreality during their visit. Each member of the troupe, upon entering the compound, was issued a "Democratic Kampuchea" visa, written in flowery Khmer longhand by an old Khmer Rouge officer with beautiful penmanship. The man lingered over this job of drawing up visas, as if this were the last good deed he might do in the world. No matter that Democratic Kampuchea existed only in the minds of these men.

At some point, an offer was made by the troupe, translated by Raksmey, to provide some evening entertainment in the form of a puppet show. Questions were passed up the chain of command, and some superior, probably Khieu Samphan himself, granted permission. Never mind that such artistic practice had been banned in Democratic Kampuchea while the Khmer Rouge was in power, or that most puppeteers and actors in the country had been murdered. In this time, at this mountain base, such a show apparently was a welcome treat for the weary Khmer Rouge contingent.

Kirkenesferda's entrance into the jungle compound must have been an odd spectacle. Who knows what these battle-hardened cadres thought as the theater wagon rumbled into camp. The wagon and generator were set up in a little clearing next to the rusty radio tower that the Khmer Rouge was using to communicate with its Chinese allies as well as the remaining far-flung Khmer Rouge factions along the Thai border. Chairs were assembled for the audience, and several rudimentary floodlights were installed as house lighting.

The view from 808 was spectacular. Perched on the edge of a steep precipice, one could see for miles and miles into the heart of Cambodia, a land now enduring mass displacement, famine, and widespread disease due to its hosts' astonishing negligence of the citizens' most basic needs. Presumably, such a spot was chosen for security reasons, but the stunning vistas on that evening, particularly as the sun set against a jungled horizon, brought both visitor and host to congregate at the overlook point, lending an air of contemplation to the proceedings as they silently admired nature's vast depth of field.

At first, the guests were treated well, if not quite up to par with Kamm's profuse testimony. They were fed a robust meal and given plenty to drink, mingling with Khieu Samphan, Ieng Sary, and several paunchy Khmer Rouge higher-ups. The mood was described as "festive and expectant" (694) about the upcoming show. Raksmey was very much in the middle of it all, dressed now in the simple black outfit of the Kirkenesferda puppeteer, which was reminiscent of the black uniforms formerly worn by their Khmer Rouge hosts, who now sported the dull hunter green of the jungle rebel. Perhaps the Khmer Rouge wardrobe shift was another effort by the rulers to distance themselves from their disastrous years in power, though many still wore the familiar red-checkered *krama* of the revolution. The puppeteers wore simple black masks around their necks. When the time came, they would disappear behind their puppets.

Raksmey mingled, joking in three languages, steering the conversations, complimenting the officers, saying little about himself or his acquaintances. He negotiated a starting time for the performance, the practicalities of electricity, housing, protocol. As darkness descended and the floodlights went up, Raksmey directed people to their seats. He was the perfect mediator. It was as if he had been training for this evening his entire life. Writes Røed-Larsen, "though [Raksmey] was the group's newest addition, on that night he was also their most essential member. . . . (For the moment at least), he was Kirkenesferda's lifeline" (703). It must be noted that the ease with which he took up this ambassadorial role was in marked contrast to the shy reclusion in which he had lived while at CERN, listening to Britten's *Les Illuminations* on repeat until the vinyl had begun to erode.

Despite Raksmey's social high-wire act, there were two circumstances beyond his control that would later lead to catastrophe. The first was that, unbeknownst to him, Tor Bjerknes had wired a telegraph key into the Khmer Rouge radio tower. This was to beam out the somewhat superfluous and altogether harmless signal "What hath God wrought?" on an obscure frequency. Transmitting this echo of Morse's first telegram in 1844 was a practice that Kirkenesferda had maintained before each of their *bevegelser,* or movements, to date. However innocuous the signal, permission was not requested from their hosts, and Raksmey had no knowledge of the wiring or the transmission.

Second, and perhaps more serious, was the coincidental and unannounced visit of Pol Pot himself to the camp, a visit that, due to security concerns, not even Khieu Samphan had been made aware of. Pot normally lived two hundred kilometers to the south, in the Cardamom Mountains, in a top-secret Khmer Rouge compound called Office 131. He presumably had made the risky and arduous trip to 808 in order to discuss political strategy with Samphan and Sary face-to-face. Pol Pot must have been surprised to see that in his absence, a theater troupe had been invited to perform at the camp, but we cannot know his initial response, since prior to the show there was no witnessed confrontation between Pol Pot and Samphan.

The great irony is that Kirkenesferda—as they would do for their *bevegelse* in Sarajevo sixteen years later—had theatrically "reserved" certain seats in the audience for the major political players in the current conflict. There was a seat set aside for former U.S. president Richard Nixon; for Prince Norodom Sihanouk; for Chairman Mao Zedong and Vietnamese prime minister Ho Chi Minh, both already deceased; for Thailand's acting prime minister, General Kriangsak Chomanan; for Hun Sen, the Vietnamese-installed head of state in Cambodia; and for Pol Pot. These were meant to be symbolic, a kind of "meta-material extension of the stage" (718), as Røed-Larsen terms it, but just before the curtain went up, the real Pol Pot emerged from a building and took the seat reserved for him, causing a stir in the audience, which also was unaware he was in camp. Raksmey was the only one who saw what had happened. It would only be after the show that the troupe's other members discovered that Pol Pot was in attendance.

What happened next is covered in some detail by Røed-Larsen, who, as always, takes great pains to document every second of each of Kirkenesferda's *bevegelser*. *Kirkenesferda Tre* was to be the troupe's most complex creation to date, though the show would start ordinarily enough. When the curtain opened, traditional Khmer shadow puppets made from tanned buffalo hide appeared against a white screen. A scene from the epic *Reamker* play unfolded, in which the ten-headed monster Krong Reap, disguised as an old man, kidnaps the beautiful Neang Seda. The *Reamker* is a Buddhist adaptation of the Hindu *Ramayana* and a mainstay of Cambodian theater. As was custom, the play was accompanied by a live, but hidden, four-piece Khmer *pinpeat* band, even though this music had not been heard by many of those present in more than four years. At this point, one cannot help but wonder what the audience of fallen Khmer Rouge elites were thinking: here was a traditional Khmer art form, part of a rich cultural heritage that they had attempted to eradicate during their time in power, now being enacted for them. The play itself was amusing—"the hijinks of disguise [is a] universal wellspring of humor" (722)—and apparently soldiers were laughing at the antics of Krong Reap trying to behave like an old man.

Fig. 4.13. Traditional Khmer Lkhaon Nang Sbek, featuring a scene from the Reamker *epic.*
From Cohen, M., *"Khmer Shadow Theatre,"* p. 187

If this puppetry was vaguely confrontational in its very reenactment, this was by far the least controversial aspect of the show. The piece quickly veered off the rails: in the middle of the scene, metallic bird rod puppets came down from above and began to attack Krong Reap and Neang Seda, ripping off pieces of their arms and legs and gathering them into a nest. The birds sported antennae made from television radials, beautifully latticed rice paper wings, and flowing tails of magnetic cassette tape and pocket-watch gears, and they wielded "abnormally long and crooked beaks cut from shellac records and whalebone" (735). The Khmer shadow puppets, or what was left of them, fled the stage.

For those familiar with the *Reamker* epic, the performance of which could often stretch to twelve hours, this aerial attack by apocalyptic Frankenstein birds was an affront to the very form of Lkhaon Nang Sbek. Before the Khmer Rouge came to power, the *Reamker* was performed by a wide range of puppeteers, actors, and dancers, from regional groups on up to the Royal Cambodian Ballet. While each performer was allowed a certain personal flourish, it was also critical that they stayed within a strict, familiar framework. Every Cambodian knew the story by heart, so it was not uncommon for audience members to leave and return over the course of the day, instantly recognizing where they were in the story. Thus, the manner of Kirkenesferda's narrative disruption was deeply forbidden. The group had painstakingly honored the form with their meticulous reenactment, only to completely disregard it with their experimental blitzkrieg.

Soon the birds returned with more items for their nest: tiny musical instruments, presumably taken from the *pinpeat* band, who had begun to stop playing one by one as the birds stole their instruments, until only a fiddle remained. Left alone, the fiddle started to play wild, chaotic strokes—an excerpt from John Cage's *Freeman Etudes*.

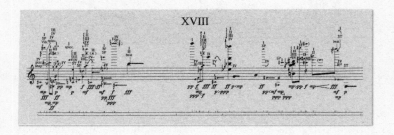

Fig. 4.14. Notations from "Freeman Etude #18," by John Cage
From Røed-Larsen, P., *Spesielle Partikler,* p. 749

The birds brought still more things to the nest: numbers, pieces of mathematical equations, Greek symbols. When the nest had grown to tremendous proportions, it began to tremble and then exploded, sending the birds flying offstage. The fiddle music ceased. The stage went black except for a single red spotlight. A mist appeared, and then puppet figures, dressed in those same familiar black outfits of the Khmer Rouge, began to move around the stage, their faces masked by *krama* scarves. One by one, these scarves came off, revealing tiny television screens instead of faces. Each screen showed the curiously gentle visage of Pol Pot, smiling, nodding, on a loop. There were two dozen, then three dozen Pol Pot figurines wandering around the stage, smiling, nodding to one another.

Each of these puppets, designed by Kermin Radmanovic and Tor Bjerknes,

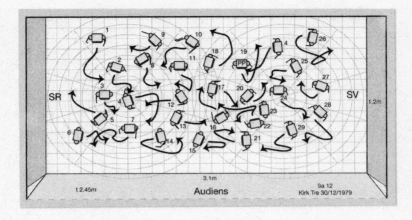

Fig. 4.15. Figure of Sequence 9a, 12: "Intermingling puppets,
cascading, choreographed Brownian motion."
From Røed-Larsen, P., *Spesielle Partikler,* p. 768

was an astonishing work of art—the inner mechanics of their one-off design were complex beyond belief. But while exceedingly intricate, each puppet had also been carefully designed to withstand the rigorous environment of the humid jungle, for a single short circuit would have ruined the entire choreography of the show.

The fiddle music returned, amplified and warped, as if fed through a synthesizer. The lights shifted, flickering; the steam billowed toward the audience. The Pol Pot puppets started to vibrate with increasing violence, and when the boiling reached a certain point, they collapsed onto the stage. An 8mm projector began projecting video of marching troops from Maoist China, superimposed on diagrams from Henrik Bohr (Niels's son) and H. B. Nielsen's "Hadron Production from a Boiling Quark Soup" (*Nuclear Physics,* 1977), depicting the dissolution of quark soup bubbles and hadron decay immediately following the Big Bang.

As the smoke began to clear, the puppet bodies rose up again, but now their robes had come off, and the figures were revealed to be birdlike themselves—half avian and half humanoid, a circulatory system of electrical wires and twine

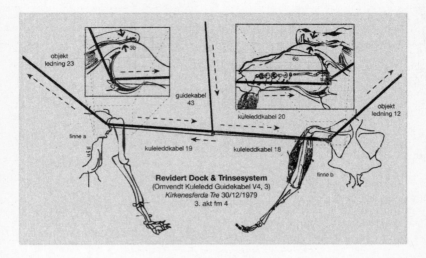

Fig. 4.16. "Revised Dock & Pulley System. Reverse Ball & Socket Joint Guywire v4.3."
From Røed-Larsen, P., *Spesielle Partikler,* p. 777

intermingled within their skeletons. Yet by all accounts, what was astonishing about this part of the show, from both a technical and an emotional standpoint, was that the body parts of the figurines began to interchange: arms were traded between figures, heads were swapped. The stage, as Røed-Larsen writes, "had become an elaborate marketplace of beingness" (776).

While this flurry of exchange took hold of the puppets, the footage of Pol Pot's face on the headscreens being passed back and forth was gradually replaced by images of prisoners from S-21, photographs that had been released only months before. The Khmer Rouge leaders were staring into the eyes of the very victims they had helped to execute. Yet these victims were not dead; they were performing in an act "of nostalgia-play, re-animation, re-appropriation . . . the executed dancing for the executioners" (828).

Slowly, the trading of body parts diminished and each figure became identifiable again. The music stopped. The figures collected toward the front of the stage and formed a line, facing the audience. Their screens flickered and then, as one, displayed a long equation:

An expression of the uncertainty principle in harmonic analysis.

One of the puppets in the middle of the equation's head was not like the others. His screen still showed a cheerful Pol Pot—the puppet had in fact been displaying this image the entire time. In an unsettling act of coordinated scrutiny, all the other puppets turned their screen heads toward him. Then his screen went blank, except for a dot, which winked out the Morse code:

• — •— — •• •—•• •—•• ••••• •— •—•—•• •—•—• • —• •— — —•—• •—•• —•

Curtain down.

"A terrible silence followed," writes Røed-Larsen. "You could hear a sewing pin drop—if such a sewing pin had still existed in Cambodia" (788). Everyone turned to Pol Pot, the impromptu guest of honor, in order to read his response to such an audacious display of insubordination. The small man sat perfectly still, and then his face broke into a broad grin and he started to clap, vociferously, as the Khmer Rouge were prone to do during important ceremonies. A sigh of relief must have passed over Khieu Samphan and his comrades. Everyone stood, joining in the applause. The crucial moment had passed.

Under orders, the assembled Khmer Rouge soldiers dispersed, preparing to secure the camp for the night. The Kirkenesferda troupe quietly went about the mundane task of disassembling their lights and packing up their theater wagon, though their heads and hearts were no doubt buzzing with that unique post-show mixture of adrenaline, sadness, hunger, and relief. Once they were finished, a Khmer Rouge cadre escorted them to their quarters.

Shortly after this (Røed-Larsen does not offer an exact amount of time), Ieng Sary approached Raksmey. His demeanor had changed drastically. He was now furious, and he accused the group of being CIA operatives.

"I have read my history," Røed-Larsen reports Sary saying to Raksmey (801). "I know the puppeteers of Europe were also spies. They were the only ones who were allowed to cross over borders, because no one suspected them." As evidence, he produced part of the telegraph wire that had been connected to the radio tower. Caught unaware, unsure whether such a wire was a fabrication, Raksmey did his best at damage control, assuring his hosts that if the wire had indeed existed, then certainly no message had been sent, and that their position had not been transmitted to a foreign entity (as Sary claimed). Raksmey promised a full report on the wire's purpose. Sary, threatening imprisonment or worse, reluctantly retreated to discuss the situation with the senior Khmer Rouge officers, including Pol Pot, who presumably had been behind this sudden change in attitude.

Raksmey went directly to Dr. Christian-Holtsmark and informed him of the accusations. The troupe's leader admitted that while the wire had been real, the transmission had been purely for dramatic purposes and had not contained any intelligence information. Tor Bjerknes was also alerted. He apologized for not asking permission before connecting the telegraph.

As they debated what to do, the group became aware of an intensifying light, at just the same time that young Lars Røed-Larsen raced into their guest hut and declared that the theater wagon was on fire. The entire troupe went outside to see that, sure enough, their wagon—the summation of years and years of labor—was now in flames, guarded by a ring of stiff-jawed Khmer Rouge guards. There would be no intervention. Their work was gone. Abandoning camp then and there was considered, but they discovered that their trucks had been moved to an unspecified location. The consensus was that they should wait until morning and then decide how to proceed.

The next few hours were restless ones. No longer was this regime a distant surrogate for reckless ideologism—"what was once theoretical had become intensely personal . . . their hosts had become their potential judge, jury, and executioner" (822).

Sometime during the night—Røed-Larsen places it at 2:20, though this is without supporting evidence—Raksmey was visiting the outhouse when he met up with a young and frightened Lars, who, like the others, could not sleep and was additionally suffering from an upset stomach due to the foreignness of Khmer food. Raksmey reassured Lars that everything would work out in the end. At that point, the two of them heard "a series of loud pops" coming from the direction of the guest quarters. Lars attempted to run toward where his family was sleeping, but, realizing the pops were in fact gunshots, Raksmey instinctively held him back, pulling the boy into the shelter of the forest. Knowing that the group had been ambushed, Raksmey made the decision to take the by now extremely distraught Lars out of the camp immediately. They snuck through the forest, around the guard post, and headed back in the direction of the border. Avoiding roads and buildings, they did not have an easy time of it, and suffered multiple lacerations from barbed wire, vines, and low-hanging branches.

When they were only a hundred meters from the Thai border crossing, Raksmey stepped on a land mine. His left leg and part of his pelvis were liquefied by the explosion, and the left side of his face was partly sheared off. Hearing shots behind them, he waved for Lars to continue and leave him where he was. After attempting to drag Raksmey several meters, Lars finally gave up and, covered in blood, stumbled to the border crossing, where the stunned Thai officials took him into custody.

Buried at the end of a long footnote on page 845 of Røed-Larsen's book, there is a subtle shift in perspective that is quite easy to overlook:

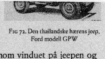

frem til grensepasseringen der lamslåtte tjenestemenn tok ham i varetekt. Etter å ha krysset grensen, satt Lars i baksetet på en jeep og forble stille til tross for en kryssild av spørsmål fra en thailandsk offentlig tjenestemann, om hva som nettopp hadde skjedd på Vamp808. På et tidspunkt fløy en sommerfugl gjennom vinduet på jeepen og landet på kneet hans. Skapningen flakset med vingene og skalv. Det var et bilde jeg aldri vil glemme.

Fig 72. Den thailandske hærens jeep, Ford modell GPW

(Once across the border, Lars sat in the backseat of the government jeep and remained quiet, despite the barrage of questions coming from a Thai official, who was demanding to know exactly what had just transpired at Camp 808. At some point, a butterfly flew through the jeep's window and alighted on his knee. The creature flexed its wings and shivered. It was an image I would never forget.)

Did you hear it? The sudden presence of that "*jeg*" haunts me. The rattle in the engine. Perhaps I am misreading what was only a minor typographical error, but the appearance of the first person is so unexpected and so out of place in the context of the book's fifteen hundred pages that it calls into question nearly everything that has come before and everything that comes after. *It was an image I would never forget.* Who, may I ask, is the *I* here? Is it Per, the author? Is it Lars, the subject and stepbrother? Is it both author and subject? Or is it someone else entirely? That lone *I,* sounded like a trumpet at dusk, makes me long for a voice, a motive, a warm body beneath this ocean of words.

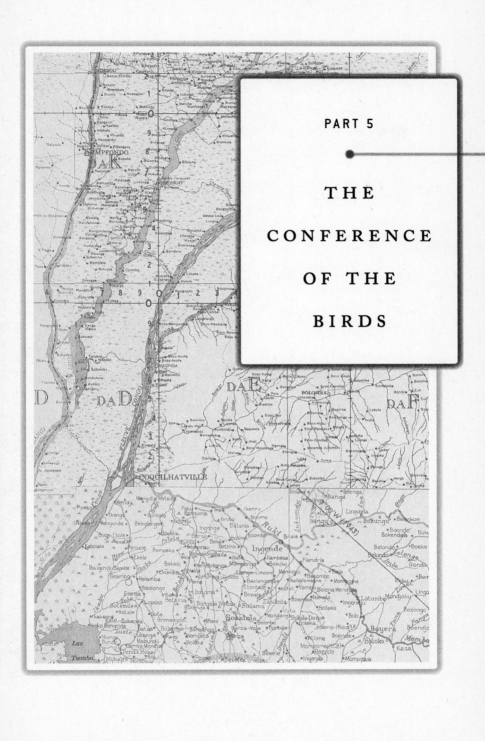

PART 5

THE

CONFERENCE

OF THE

BIRDS

NEW JERSEY

August 10, 2010

All that night, Radar scoured the land. The blackout and the ensuing curfew lent an eerie post-apocalyptic backdrop to his searchings. He dodged police barricades and wove around checkpoints, using his recumbent's low profile and the cover of darkness to glide through the abandoned streets undetected. He visited four local hospitals, all of them overrun with patients and non-patients simply seeking out the comforts of electricity's embrace. His father was not among them.

How intimate, to trace a person's geography. It was almost like looking through his father's wallet. Though it was the middle of the night, Radar still followed the route of Kermin's favorite constitutional along the industrial shores of the Passaic, searching for that familiar hunched profile. He rode past the ghostly rail bridge, permanently frozen in a raised salute, but did not see his father seated at any of his customary benches. He visited J&A Specialties Electrics, in Belleville, site of Kermin's semi-frequent pilgrimages for obscure radio parts. He swung by the Arlington Diner, where his father would eat exactly three-quarters of a Reuben and half of his slaw before casually dismissing the plate with a swipe of his hand.

Everything was closed, shuttered, dark. Humanity a distant dream.

He even crossed the Passaic and headed south, to his grandfather's gravesite in Elizabeth, on the off chance that Kermin had sought out his father's resting place for guidance.

Radar's flashlight illuminated the engraved letters of the headstone:

DOBROSLAV RADMANOVIC

1910–1947

A GOOD MAN.

Radar had always found this summary a touch dismissive, but Kermin had explained that this was the state's default epitaph when little was known about the deceased.

"Your son has gone missing," Radar said to the gravestone.

Dobroslav, the good man, offered no reply.

With each successive foray, it became increasingly clear that he was not going to find his father in any of these places—that his father would not be found simply by looking for him. And yet, in spite of this, he kept looking. Just the act of looking made Radar feel productive, even if he knew he would most likely come up empty-handed. It also gave him time to process all that he had learned in that strange little cottage beneath the mall.

Kermin—the international puppeteer. Kermin—the genius designer. His pride at learning these descriptors was tempered by a certain sadness that he massaged with his velocity. He could not help but feel cheated, as if he had never actually experienced the real Kermin. He had only known his father as his closeted, curmudgeonly progenitor—who had gambled on the tiny television and lost, who had built a monstrous antenna in their backyard so he could communicate only with those farthest away from him and in doing so had shut out those who loved him the most. But Radar had never known his father as *this*. As a doer. A *maker*. One who had changed the course of history.

"Oh, Tata," he whispered to the moonless sky. "I could've helped you. We could've done it together."

FINALLY, EXHAUSTED, BLEARY-EYED, he returned home to Forest Street. He looked at his watch. It was just after 2:00 A.M.

He was almost at their driveway when he noticed the white van parked in front of their house. His system went cold and he swerved wildly, nearly crashing into his mother's Olds.

The authorities. The authorities were here. He had left his mother all alone, and now she was being handcuffed and questioned by some secret terrorism task force. He only briefly considered the possibility of fleeing before he took a deep breath and surveyed the situation. *No.* He was the man of the house now. He couldn't leave her. He would claim all responsibility for the blackout. He would take the fall for his family.

Radar hid his bicycle behind the viburnum and quietly unlocked the front door, readying himself to be tackled by a SWAT team.

All was quiet. The house was dark.

"Mom?" he called tentatively. "It's me."

There was no response.

Upstairs in her room, he found the bed empty. Or not exactly empty: his flashlight caught sight of the little wooden figure lying among the sheets.

"Mom?" he said again.

The flashlight's beam searching the room. Sweeping past a sheeted bookshelf.

"Mom?" An edge of panic rising in his voice.

The record player silent on the rug. The burned-out stub of the candle on the bedside table, a thicket of wax spilling down the wood. The darkened hole in the floor.

He picked up the figurine. Carved-out eyes, the hint of a mouth. A ghastly little thing.

"Charlene?"

"Radar?" said a voice.

He whirled around, the flashlight beam finding her squinting at him from the doorway. She was holding a candle in one hand and a fire poker in the other.

"Jesus, *Mom.* You scared me."

"There's somebody out there!" she hissed.

"Where?"

"In the shack. I can see their lights. I was too scared to go outside."

He peered out the window. Sure enough, he could see the glint of light through the shack's open door.

REIF LARSEN

"Maybe it's Kermin," said Radar.

"It didn't look like him, but I couldn't be sure," she whispered. "There's at least two of them."

They watched the shack but didn't see any movement.

"You didn't find him, did you?" she whispered.

Radar shook his head. "I looked everywhere."

"What should we do?"

Radar took a breath. "I'll go down."

"I'm coming with you."

"No," he said. "It's better if you stay here."

She grabbed his wrist. "I'm not letting you go out there alone!"

And so—she with fire poker and he with a flashlight and a hastily retrieved coatrack that he was brandishing like a spear—together they cautiously ventured through the sliding double doors and into the backyard.

As they approached, a figure emerged from the shack. He was carrying a box in his arms.

"Halt!" called Radar. "Who goes there?"

Who goes there? What was this, Medieval Times?

"It's me!" said the man.

Radar peered into the darkness. The voice, familiar.

"Who's *me?*"

"Lars."

"Lars?" Radar sighed. He put the coatrack down in the middle of the grass. "What're you doing here?"

"You know him?" said Charlene.

Lars approached, box in hand.

"I'm terribly sorry to barge in on you like this. As you can see, we're in a bit of a rush."

"What is that?" said Radar, pointing at the box.

"Well . . . After you left, Otik and I had a little . . . tête-à-tête. And we agreed that, despite the circumstances, all of the work we've done up until this point—including that by your father—really deserves to see the light of day. And it's true this ship that leaves . . . well, now it's *this* morning . . . this ship

504

could really be our only chance for a long time. So I—" He stopped himself. *"Apologies.* You must be Charlene Radmanovic." He put down the box and held out his hand. "Lars Røed-Larsen."

Charlene, who was still holding the poker with two hands, did not return the handshake.

"You know my husband?" she said.

"Kermin's been a longtime colleague, hero, and mentor of mine," said Lars. "You and I have actually met once, long ago. In Norway. I was ten at the time."

Charlene blinked, squinted. "That was you? The blond boy?"

"No doubt I was probably up to some mischief when you saw me."

"Lars and I met tonight," said Radar. "At Xanadu. They've been working with Kermin on a show."

"Kirkenesferda," Charlene said slowly.

"Wait—you know about them?" said Radar.

"I've lived with the man for thirty-five years. Some things you can't keep secret forever."

Otik appeared in the doorway of the shack.

"Hey!" he hissed. "What are you doing? There is like eight hundred fifty-five more birds!"

"Otik," said Lars. "Come out and say hello."

"What is this?" said Otik. "We need to move!" He ducked back inside.

Lars held up his hands. "And that's Otik," he said.

"I know Otik," said Charlene. "Has he had his heart attack today?"

"Most probably." Lars smiled.

"So you're taking the birds?" said Radar.

"If we can manage to find them all. Your father caused quite a mess with that little experiment of his."

"But you're taking them without his permission?" said Radar.

Lars bowed. "I realize this isn't ideal. Believe me, I wish things could be different. In truth, I'm not sure how we're going to pull it off without him."

Otik waddled up to them, his flashlight bobbing.

"We will," he said.

"Will we?"

"You make it with what you have. This is always how we do it."

"Yes, but this is Kermin we're talking about," said Lars. "These are *his* birds."

"But after today there is no more ship!" said Otik. "You said so yourself. If we don't go, we kiss all of them goodbye."

"But say we leave and he shows up tomorrow," said Lars. "What would you tell him? 'Sorry, we didn't know where you were, so after ten years of planning we decided to abandon you'?"

"First off, he will not show. You and I both know this." He swung the flashlight to Charlene's face. "No offense," he said. The light swung back to Lars. "On second hand, he would *also* do this. 'The project comes first,' he said to me. *Always, always, always.* It is like this. If I would disappear like him, I would also want you to go without me."

"We couldn't *do* the show without you," said Lars. "You know that. Or without Kermin, for that matter. We need three people, *minimum,* to pull it off. Probably more."

"Not true," said Otik. "I could do whole show myself."

"You couldn't."

"I could."

"What about Radar?" Charlene said suddenly.

Everyone turned and stared at her.

"What about him?" Lars asked.

"He could go instead of Kermin," she said.

A moment of silence.

"Where *is* this show, by the way?" said Charlene.

After a pause, Lars said, "The Democratic Republic of Congo."

"The *Congo?*" she said, eyebrows raised. "Wow. Okay."

"Wait, Mom, what're you talking about?" said Radar. "I can't go."

"Why not?"

"You know I can't go. I have to find him."

She looked at him. "He would want you to go."

"He would?" The words quarrying something small and dense from the depths of his body. He contemplated his mother, wondering if she could be serious. What could compel her to make such a ludicrous suggestion? She *needed* him. And yet, his fingers began to tingle with current. At the mere possibility of going somewhere. He had never been anywhere.

"No, no," said Otik, shaking his head. "No, that is not option. I'm sorry, he cannot. He would be like child out there."

"Hang on," said Lars. He turned to Radar. "Would you consider it? Kermin always said you were the most talented in the family."

"He did?" said Radar. He tried to adjust to this piece of news. Kermin said that about him? "Well, to be honest . . . I hadn't really thought about it."

"Wait, wait, wait," said Otik. "Everyone, hold on to your horse. Let me just say I am lodging immediate formal complaint. This is *not* how we are electing team members. This is very important position. I have no idea about this man's strength in his mind or—"

"Shut up," said Lars. "Radar? What do you think? Seriously. You could really save us here."

All at once, Radar remembered Ana Cristina. The feeling of sitting beside her in the store, of her lips, the temperature of her hands on his. Of course he couldn't go. There were so many reasons he had to stay here, he was surprised he had even entertained the possibility of leaving.

"I'm sorry," he said. "I would love to help you out, but . . . I don't think I'm your man. I can't."

"You see?" said Otik. "Even he knows this is not good idea."

"Why not?" said Charlene. "Why not you?"

"I *can't,* Mom," he said. "You know I can't."

"Why?"

"Why?"

"Give me one good reason. And don't tell me you have to find Kermin, because I can do that by myself. I've been looking for him my whole life."

"Why do you want me to go so badly?" he said.

"I don't want you to go. *You* want to go."

"No, I . . ." He began to protest and then stopped. He thought of Ana Cristina again. "You really think I could do Kermin's job? *Me?* Radar?" He had intended to say his name as a protest, but it came out sounding like a superhero.

"Of course," said Charlene, smiling, hearing this. "You're his son."

He blinked. His eyes burned.

"I'm his son," he repeated. "Radar."

When he said this, it was as if the needle had finally found the groove. A gear shifted, and the machine came to life. Of course. He was Kermin's son. It was meant to be. They all saw it then.

"Okay," said Radar.

"Okay what?" said Lars.

"I'll go. I'll take his place." He felt the tingle of leaving already spreading through his bones. He was terrified, quivering in his boots. He hooked his hands in his belt loops to keep them from shaking.

"You realize what this means?" said Lars. "Once you're in, you're in."

Radar nodded. He feared he might collapse, but instead he closed his eyes and said, as coolly as he could manage: "I'm in."

When he opened them again, he saw his mother dropping her poker and coming to him. Her arms drifted around his neck, and her face came to rest on his shoulder.

"I'm so proud of you," she whispered.

Otik clapped his hands. "*Fine*. If it means we go, then okay, he comes. But just know I am still lodging formal complaint, *and* I am not responsible for him."

"Formal complaint noted," said Lars. "And you *are* responsible for him. We're all responsible for each other. This is how it works."

Radar was looking at his mother. "What're you going to do?"

"What I've always done," she said.

"It could get bad here if the power doesn't back come on."

"Oh, I'll be fine," she said. "I have the Oldsmobile, don't I? And they'll figure it all out eventually. To be honest, I could use a little life without electricity. Maybe I'll even read some poetry. Go back to Coleridge. It'll be good for me. As long as I get my smell back, I don't care about the rest."

"But what about Tata? And his vircator? We need to hide what he's done."

"We can take care of that," said Lars.

Radar nodded, though he was not sure what that would entail. "And what about him?"

"Kermin?" said Charlene. "Don't you worry about him. When he comes back, I'll give him a piece of my mind. I'll let him know where you went. I'm sure he'll understand."

"But he is not coming back," Otik said, and with that, he turned and headed back to the shack.

SO WENT THE NIGHT. Radar helped them load the van with the rest of the bird bodies. There were well over a thousand, and each needed to be hung up in a precise way, according to Otik's instructions. When they were done, the back of the van resembled an avian congregation frozen in time.

"We'll cover up the vircator in case anyone comes looking. You'd better get your things for the trip," Lars said as they slammed the van doors shut. "Pack lightly."

"Lightly?" Radar realized he had never packed for a journey before.

"Does your mother have a cell phone that works?" said Lars.

"I can give her the one I found in Kermin's Faraday cage."

"Good," said Lars. "You can take this one. It should work where we're going. You can give her the number in case she wants to be in touch. Here, it's on this paper."

"Thanks," said Radar.

"But be quick," Otik said, emerging from the back of the van. "We have four hours before boat leaves, and there's still whole house to pack. So no dillydally."

RADAR FOUND CHARLENE SEATED at the kitchen table, an array of her tea jars splayed out before her.

"Hi," he said.

She looked up at him with sad eyes. "I still can't smell anything," she said.

"I'm sure it'll come back."

She nodded. "You're leaving?"

"I don't have to," he said, sitting down next to her. "Truly. I can stay here with you. I can help you find him."

"No," she said. "No. Don't miss this."

"Why? What am I going to miss? Everything I want is here. Everyone I care about is here."

"Radar," she said. "One day you'll wake up and your entire life will have gone by without you ever having lived it. Don't make the same mistake I did. You have to get out of yourself to know who you are."

He thought about this. Wondered if he should add it to his rule book.

"I've never been anywhere before," he said.

"It's not true," she said. "We took you to Belgrade."

"Oh, yeah."

"And you've been to Norway."

The only sound was the ticking of the grandfather clock in the other room.

"You know, he did it for me," he said.

"Did what?"

"The blackout. He was trying to fix me. My epilepsy, I mean."

Her face had fallen. "How?"

"He built a vircator, like what they used on me in Norway . . . and he thought that if he made another one, he could fix me."

"Did it work?" she said after a moment.

"Did what work?"

"Did it fix you?"

"I don't think I can be fixed," he said. "But he did manage to break New Jersey."

He smiled. She saw this and snorted. Soon they were both laughing. They could not help themselves. The laughter was a substitute for sorrow, racking their bodies, great heaps of it rising from the depths. They were left gasping at the table.

"That man," she wheezed. "That man."

"He's a good man," Radar breathed, head resting against one of the radios on the table.

"Yes," she whispered. "He's the only one we've got."

"I should go pack," he said. "Lightly."

"Make sure you bring enough socks."

In the rush of things, he hurriedly stuffed his backpack full of socks and not much else. A sweatshirt. A cowboy hat. A toothbrush. He saw his pink *Little Rule Book for Life* and put that in, too. He knew he was doing a bad job planning for the future, but that took time, and he had no time.

Downstairs again, he saw that his mother had not moved from her spot in the kitchen.

"I almost forgot," he said. He took Kermin's phone out of his pocket. "They gave me one that will work over there. I'll leave the number here. We can do the text."

She smiled. "You finally learned how to say it properly."

"Oh, Mom." He hugged her. "I'll miss you."

She pushed him back. "I wanted to tell you . . ."

"Yes?"

"About before. I didn't want to give you the wrong idea. About . . . T.K., I mean. I've no idea if he's the one or not," she said. "I just wanted to say that. I didn't want you to believe something that might not be true."

He was quiet, staring at the twin radios.

"It's okay," he said finally. "I kind of like the idea of having two fathers."

"You don't have two fathers."

"I know," he said. "Don't worry. I know who's the real one."

He unzipped his backpack again and took out the pink notebook.

"For you," he said, handing it to her. "It's mostly stupid, but there's a couple of good ones in there. Maybe you can read it while I'm gone."

She opened to a page and read out loud: "Rule number forty-five: Cheese is important."

He sighed. "Well, maybe not."

"Rule number forty-six: Everything happens just once, until it happens again."

"Okay, when you read them like that, they sound terrible!" he said. "Just forget it."

"Are you sure you don't want this? You might need it where you're going."

"I don't think a book could help me now."

She smiled, blinked. "I have something for you," she said.

"I have to go."

"I know; it'll be quick."

He followed her up to the bedroom. The stairs creaked beneath them, strange and loud in the darkness. Radar thought of the heavy toe-heel creaks his father made as he trudged up these same stairs. His mother always took the stairs like a bird, but his father's footsteps sounded like those of a sullen pony. He wondered if he would ever hear those toe-heel creaks again.

In the bedroom, Charlene took his flashlight and went over to the hole in the floor. It gaped, darker than the rest of the dark, like a tear in the fabric of the space-time continuum. After rooting around, she came up holding a book.

"Here," she said. "It's for you."

The book looked familiar. After a moment, he realized what it was: *Spesielle Partikler: Kirkenesferda 1944–1995,* by Per Røed-Larsen.

"I just saw this," said Radar. "They showed it to me. It's by Lars's brother."

"I was mailed a copy a long time ago. It's in Norwegian, so I've never been able to read it, but it seems important now, particularly if you're going to go with them. Maybe you'll have better luck understanding it than I did."

"Mom," he said suddenly, the book in his hands. "I'm scared."

"It's okay to be scared," she said. "It means you have something to live for."

IT WAS NEARLY 3:30 A.M. by the time they parked the van next to the little cottage beneath Xanadu.

"Okay," said Otik. "We have three hours. No dillydally."

There would be no dillydally. They feverishly transferred the birds and much of the cottage's contents into a white shipping container that sat on a trailer not far away in the parking garage. There was a lot of equipment. More boxes and tools emerged from that little house than seemed physically possible. All of it was apparently fragile, and Otik would bark at both of them about holding this with two hands, or not disrupting that by rattling it around too much. Radar tried to be helpful, but more often than not he felt as if he was simply in the way.

When they were finished, Radar collapsed onto the ground. He was utterly exhausted. He expected to seize, to pass out, for his body to fail him, but somehow he managed to stay online.

He opened his eyes. Lars was standing above him.

"Congratulations," said Lars. He offered Radar a little white pill.

"What is this?"

"To make it official," said Lars. "It'll make you grow small. Like Alice."

Radar must've looked alarmed, because Lars smiled and said, "It's for malaria. It might give you some unusual dreams, but believe me, the alternative is much worse."

The three of them poured a little coffee into some mugs, clinked them together, and took down the pills.

"To dreams," said Lars.

"To entanglement," said Otik.

"To Kermin," said Radar. As soon as he had said it, a kernel of doubt popped open in his chest. This pill had not been meant for him.

"To Kermin," said Lars gravely. "May we make him proud."

"To boat," said Otik. "We have half hour before it is gone."

. . .

201-998-2666: Ana Cristina, hi it's Radar. I don't have much time to write because I'm on my way to a boat and you probably will never get this anyway since your phone is dead but I just wanted to tell you that I'm going away for a while. My father was supposed to put on this show in the Congo but he disappeared so now I'm going instead of him. Kind of crazy, I know. So I won't be able to meet your Mom right now altho

201-998-2666: Sorry, I guess I reached the limit for a single text. I've never written one of these before. I guess they don't want you rambling on for a long time. So I'll try to keep this short. These buttons are very hard to write on don't you think? I prefer Morse Code. I'll teach you someday, okay? It's not hard, you just have to get used to it. Point is I was so happy when you invited me to meet your mom before

201-998-2666: Wow. Hit the limit again. That's embarrassing. Now I'm not sure I want you to get these. All I meant to say was: I want to meet your mom, I want to eat empanadas with you. I'll miss you. I hope Jersey is okay after all this. Talk to you soon. Xo Radar.

609-292-4087: Radar! Hi!! :)

201-998-2666: Ana C? Your phone works?

609-292-4087: I got a new one :)

201-998-2666: I hope I didn't wake you. It's like 6?

609-292-4087: I couldn't sleep

201-998-2666: Are you okay?

609-292-4087: Yeah my mama is freaking but we r okay! I M so sorry 2 hear about your papa :(I hope he is okay

201-998-2666: Me too.

609-292-4087: You don't know where he is?

201-998-2666: No

609-292-4087: You'll find him :) Everyone turns up

201-998-2666: Thanks. I hope so.

609-292-4087: So r u really going to congo? That's in africa????

201-998-2666: Yes. I'm kind of nervous. We're taking a boat.

609-292-4087: Boat to africa! Like a movie :)

201-998-2666: I'll miss you

609-292-4087: I was thinking about u

201-998-2666: Yeah?

609-292-4087: Did u know yr name is same forward-> RADAR back-> RADAR :)

201-998-2666: Yours is too! At least ANA is. Cristina kind of messes it up . . .

201-998-2666: Just kidding.

609-292-4087: your funny !!!

201-998-2666: Oh. I can't go. I can't leave you!!!

609-292-4087: I'll be here when you get back :)

201-998-2666: You promise? You're like the best thing that's ever happened to me. I feel like I've known u forever

609-292-4087: I know what u mean

609-292-4087: U there?

201-998-2666: Sorry, We're here I think. I have to go. Ahh!

609-292-4087: Don't worry be safe!!! I'll miss you

201-998-2666: I'll try to text u when I'm in the congo

609-292-4087: Okay that would be great :)

609-292-4087: Like my own reporter in the jungle :)

201-998-2666: It's weird how close

201-998-2666: I feel to u now. Just the words between us

201-998-2666: ???

609-292-4087: I know

609-292-4087: Nos vemos radar -><-

201-998-2666: What's this? -><- ?

609-292-4087: I just made it up :) same backward & forward

201-998-2666: Okay. I get it

609-292-4087: Maybe its being close w/o being close

201-998-2666: -><- see you

609-292-4087: -><- x

As dawn broke across the Newark quayside, Radar stood on the dock watching the great white shipping container slowly descend into the hull of the ship. The gantry crane jammed and the container jerked sideways, swaying back and forth against a velvet maroon sky. From inside the container they could hear crashing and splintering.

"Jebi se!" Otik yelled next to Radar. "They are fucking it! Tell them they are fucking it!"

But then the cable winch caught again and the box resumed its graceless plunge into the bowels of the boat.

The *Aleph*—the vessel to which they were about to entrust their passage across the Atlantic—had seen better days. Her hull was pockmarked by welding scars and archipelagoes of rust, and with every meager rise and trough of the sheltered bay, her joints creaked a painful symphony. In an oddly boastful tone for a man revealing his ship's inadequacies, the captain had informed them that she was supposed to carry six thousand tons but in her current state could manage only five, and that even this sank her below her summer Plimsoll.

"But she will not sink?" Otik said nervously. "She floats, right?"

"It's true, she's unhappy with the world," the captain said in lieu of an answer.

Dressed in the crisp whites of his command, Captain Alfonso Daneri was a barrel of a man. He had greeted each of them with both hands, as if he had known them for years. His beard looked like a giant sea urchin hauled up from the depths, and his eyebrows were two monstrous caterpillars that haunted his forehead, undulating with every consonant.

"Some boats are born this way," said the captain. "Some boats learn their misery. She was put on the blocks for two years in Quanzhou, and now she trusts no one." He was rubbing his hands together in slow, languid circles, as if savoring a piece of music that had only just finished.

"*'She trust no one,'*" Otik repeated. "What does this mean? This is something you say and everybody says 'Okay, yes,' but actually no one knows what in fuck you are talking about."

"The sea takes back everything she gives," said Captain Daneri, clearly enjoying himself. He tapped the toe of his boot against one of the kidney-shaped bollards that secured his ship. "She signs no allegiance. She has no kin, keeps no kin, owes no favors."

Radar noticed the captain swaying ever so slightly. He had the sudden urge to reach out and steady him.

Otik scoffed. "This is man who will take us to Africa? Oh, *please*. We make some more chance to swim there."

Lars stepped in, placing a hand on Otik's shoulder.

"Apologies, Captain. We're all a little tired," he said. "What he means to say is only that we're transporting valuable cargo and want to make sure the ship's seaworthy."

Captain Daneri's face grew suddenly serious.

"You see these boxes?" he said, gesturing at the rows and rows of multicolored containers stacked four high across the deck of the ship. "This is the new world. These boxes disrupt space and time. The world is now inside the box."

"I don't know about you," Otik said to Lars. "But if I'm going to die, I choose to die maybe somewhere in the jungle, on land, not in middle of fucking ocean."

"All right, calm down," said Lars. "I happen to agree with the captain. One could make the argument that the world *is* inside the box."

"If it makes you feel better, I've never lost one," said the captain. "There once

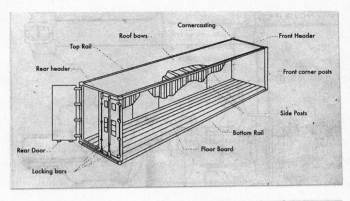

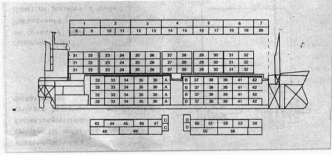

Fig. 5.1. "Parts of Shipping Container" and "How to Load a Ship"
From Peels, S. (1999), *A Short History of Deliverance,* pp. 69, 83

was a group of pirates in Lagos who snuck aboard my ship. They went for one of the boxes sitting on the deck. They didn't know what was inside; they just went for the nearest one with a crowbar. And do you know what they found? *Horses. Thoroughbreds.* We were bringing them down to a race in South Africa. Their trainer was upstairs asleep at the time. But can you imagine? The pirates open this box, they are like boys at Christmas, and what do they find? *Horses."*

"You transport horses?" asked Radar.

"Oh, no. Not anymore."

"So what happened?"

"It was very unfortunate. The horses got loose on the deck. One of the animals went overboard. Another broke its leg. A terrible shame. I had to shoot the beast in the head with a pistol. It looked at me, very calm. It knew what must be done."

"And what about pirates?" said Otik.

"Oh, we caught them. I showed them the box and I said, 'You will never touch another box again.' And then I tied their feet together and I said, 'Go find me that horse,' and I pushed them off my ship."

"You killed them," said Otik.

"No, no, no," laughed the captain. "I gave them the gift of the sea." He made a fist with his hand and kissed it.

THEY WERE THE ONLY human cargo. Radar was not sure whether their presence on board was even legal or whether technically they were stowaways, but when it came time to depart, the captain made a flourish of inviting them to stand on the bridge wing while they pulled away from the docks. A scruffy local pilot, who looked and smelled as if he had only recently stopped drinking, came aboard to guide them out of the harbor. It was clear the captain was none too pleased with the man's brazen intoxication, but he did not protest as the pilot parked himself on the bridge and started issuing instructions.

A black-and-white tug latched onto their bow and began turning up chop as it levered the *Aleph* out of her berth. From the wheelhouse they could hear the pilot rapping out commands in a kind of drunken staccato. Captain Daneri would repeat them, but silkily, like a man cajoling his slighted lover.

"Dead slow ahead!" barked the pilot.

"Dead slow ahead," intoned the captain.

"Starboard five-oh!"

"Starboard. Five-oh. *Please.*"

"Stop!"

"Cut the engines, Mr. Piskaryov."

Drunk or not, the pilot was good. With the tug grumbling by her side, the *Aleph* gradually backed out into the bay. Above, gulls turned circles overhead. Otik was studying them intensely, writing microscopic notes in a journal. He pointed out some element of their flight dynamics to Lars, who nodded, forming his two hands into a diving bird.

A rip from the ship's horn made Radar jump. The gulls scattered. Inside the wheelhouse, Captain Daneri kissed his fist and shot them a grin.

The sky lightened, softening the hulls of the great tankers that lined Newark's port. As they turned, the familiar stench of the Hackensack rose up and filled Radar's nostrils. He shivered, seized by the violent urge to get back onto dry land. Craning his neck, he tried to catch a last glimpse of home, tried to make out the great swath of darkness that encircled the little shack behind his house on Forest Street, tried to see the A&P where she worked, but the sun had already risen and the darkness had fled. Kearny and its mysteries melted into an endless Jersey panorama.

A panic that had been gathering in Radar all night now broke through and overwhelmed him, as if a large animal pelt had been thrown across his back, so thick and heavy he felt he might collapse under the terrible weight of it. He already missed Ana Cristina. He missed his mother. He missed Kermin. He missed everything.

Radar clenched at the handrail of the boat, reeling. He had made a terrible, horrible mistake.

The intensity and vast ballast of this sensation felt very different from the nimble prelude to a seizure. There was no telltale whiff of lemon or cinnamon, but beyond that, he felt much too clear for an electrical malfunction. No: he could tell his body would not let him disappear into an epileptic netherworld. Not now. It held him fast, forcing him to confront his choice, eyes wide open.

What had he done? He was not supposed to be on this ship.

Desperate, he looked back at the docks. The distance between ship and shore had widened considerably. Fifty feet. Now seventy-five. The water white and restless from their maneuvers. He could dive in. He did not know how to swim, but surely he could make it just by thrashing like a dog. How hard could it be? He would not look back at the ship; he would haul himself from the muck and mire, run home, lie prostrate at his mother's feet, and offer a thousand apologies for his madness. Then he would find Ana Cristina and he would hold her, wet and shivering, and he would never let her go.

He released his grip on the railing and stumbled up to Lars.

"I need to go back," he said.

"For what?"

"I can't go."

"You can't go?"

"I need to find Kermin." He willed back the tears. "I can't leave her alone like this."

Lars studied him.

"It's too late," he said. "We've left."

"Please," said Radar. "Tell them to stop the ship."

"She'll be okay."

"She won't be okay. It wasn't me who wanted to go," he said, realizing what he was saying.

"I need to go back," he said quietly.

Lars looked into his eyes. They stood like this, the tug twirling the boat around, and then Lars nodded and walked into the wheelhouse.

As they swung around Bergen Point and headed toward the arched gateway of the Bayonne Bridge, Captain Daneri strode out onto the bridgewing, with Lars in tow.

"What's this I hear about you jumping ship?" bellowed the captain. His posture had changed decidedly. Arms akimbo, he was all right angles and mariner's scowl. His left eyebrow arched and trembling like a flag in a stiff wind.

"I've got to go back, I'm sorry," said Radar, stepping backwards. "I don't want to cause any—"

"May I ask why you got on my boat in the first place?" said the captain.

Radar looked around to see if anyone was watching. "I know, I'm sorry," he said quietly. "I really am, but I've got to get off. *Please.*"

Lars was standing behind the captain, delivering a quiet glare in Radar's general direction. It was the first time Radar had seen this side of him; in all other matters, even during the previous night's gloomier episodes, Lars had been nothing but calm and cheerful, a steady rudder to Otik's mania. But here was a glimpse of the fire within. Seeing that glower, Radar understood how a group as obscure and unfeasible as Kirkenesferda had persisted through the years. It was an indirect kind of rage, a *seething generalis*. He could feel himself shrinking beneath the onslaught.

Hearing the commotion, Otik abandoned his bird-watching and approached their little trio.

"What's this?" he said.

"Apparently your *compadre* doesn't want to voyage with us," said the captain. The eyebrow twitched.

"I told you!" said Otik. "I told you, Lars. He is like the little child. He is half the man of his father. Less, probably. One quarter-half of one percent."

Captain Daneri thrust a finger into Radar's chest. "What's eating at you, my boy?"

Radar opened his mouth but said nothing.

"Go on," the captain said. "What's got you turned around?"

"My father disappeared," he said. "He's the one who was supposed to be here, not me. I can't just abandon my mother in the middle of a blackout. I have to go help her find him."

"She told him to come," said Lars.

"She was probably tired of dealing with him," said Otik. "She wanted him *kaput*."

"She didn't know what she was saying," said Radar. "Please, sir. Let me off. I won't bother you anymore. I just need to go back. They don't even want me here."

"It's not true," said Lars. "We need you. And you need us."

The Bayonne Bridge was above them. The metal laced into a perfect convex, launched lightly from either bank, unequivocal in its conceit. It was a dream of men. Of all men.

The captain went to the railing. He rubbed his beard with the palm of his hand.

"A nasty little strait, this Kill van Kull," he said. "Straits are what get you. Your bow is pushed from shore and your stern is sucked in. You must go straight, but you cannot steer straight. So what do you do?" As he said this, he pointed at the wheelhouse, where the pilot was alternately giving commands and speaking of whores. Yet you could tell that he was completely in control from the ease with which he switched between his story and his directional orders. And so could the captain, apparently, who was comfortable enough to leave the pilot while he lingered out here with them.

"So what do you do?" repeated the captain.

"Sir?" said Radar.

"You don't steer where you're headed." The captain hooked an eye on him. "We aren't stopping. You can jump the Kill, but I don't recommend it. Nasty currents. High traffic."

"But—"

"Once a man signs up, he's one of us. There can be no turning back. You sign up for a reason. You'll get off when you're ready."

Radar was about to speak but realized there was nothing left to say. He briefly had the strange and wild urge to strike the captain, a dose of rage he did not know what to do with. But before he could do anything one way or another, the captain spun on his heel and returned to the wheelhouse.

"Looks like we're stuck with you," said Otik.

"It's really for the best," said Lars.

Radar looked back at the receding bridge, and then down into the opaque green churn of water. He thought of the horse jumping off the boat in Lagos. He lifted one foot onto the railing.

"Don't," said Lars, but Radar knew even before his foot had left the deck that he would never be able to do it. Resolve had never been his strong suit.

Soon they had cleared Constable Hook and found themselves out in the harbor. The pilot had negotiated the portside passing of two giant tankers and nimbly maneuvered around a stalled feeder ship in the Kill's narrows. This balletic performance had done much to revive him; he had discarded his disheveled air, and now went around offering handshakes to the officers with all the gravitas of an ambassador.

"*Bon voyage, bon voyage,* watch out for the pirates," he called. "They will rape you if you give them half a chance."

Captain Daneri clasped the pilot's shoulder and kissed him on both cheeks.

"An honor," said the captain. *"Un piloto y su puerto."* His opinion had evidently softened.

They slowed and pitched as the pilot climbed down the ladder to meet his boat. He offered a final wave to the *Aleph* before disappearing into the boat's cabin.

It was only after the pilot boat had pulled away and was speeding back to shore that Radar realized he could've left with them. Why hadn't he?

You'll get off when you're ready.

The sun had already risen over the flats of Brooklyn, but Lady Liberty's flame had not yet been extinguished. It burned and burned, wary of what the day might bring. She stood, steady and erect as ever, with a clean conscience and an open heart. Behind her gallant robes, the Manhattan skyline paid little heed to their imminent exit. The captain ordered full speed ahead, the engines were fired, and the *Aleph* turned south, to the gates of the Verrazano and the last buoy before the open sea.

Lars had christened their forty-foot container *Moby-Dikt*. On the second day, he even went so far as to paint on a pair of morose whale eyes at knee height, which always seemed to be watching you no matter where you stood. *Moby-Dikt* lay by itself on the bottom floor of the number-four cargo hold, just in front of the bridge castle, a full four stories below the quarterdeck. It was always slightly dank down there, and Radar imagined the steel ribs rising up the sides of the hull as if they were the ribs of a great and monstrous whale. A whale inside of a whale inside of a whale and so on, the universe nothing but a series of matryoshka'd leviathans. His vision was enhanced by the constant, ominous creaking of the *Aleph*'s joints, which would echo and reverberate across the stacks of containers. The ship moaned, complained, howled. But she did not break. Not yet, at least.

Their container had been retrofitted as a hybrid living quarters and workshop, with a firm emphasis on the *workshop* part of the equation. It was packed to the gills with all manner of tools and mechanical detritus, including two soldering irons, a workbench, a wire draw, a hand loom, Otik's vircator, two generators, six large speakers, an electric kettle, three computers in varying exploded states of repair, sixteen reams of old telegraph cable, and a full atelier featuring a band saw, a lathe, a power sander, and a spindle molder. There were also four *djembe* drums and a box of obscure musical instruments, which would occasionally rattle and shake as if of their own volition. In one corner, they had lashed down the gold-and-burgundy theater wagon—the same theater wagon used in Sarajevo. And then, of course, there were also the nearly fourteen hundred mechanical birds they had taken from Kermin's shack, which now hung and swayed from the ceiling. The birds were still headless, their heads kept on six long racks by Otik's cot. Radar never got used to this disembodied gallery of unblinking eyes.

The container actually represented an increase in space from the tiny cottage in Xanadu's parking garage, but it offered precious little maneuvering room when all three men were present. This was not helped by Otik's ongoing seasickness, exacerbated by the minute nature of his work on the bird heads. His pallor, which prior to their departure had resembled the color of unripe melon, had now taken on the hue of the repurposed ham-and-pea puree they used to serve at the Rutgers dining hall. Otik sat there, sweating and breathing heavily, a little moan escaping his lips every so often to signal his body's revolt. He would then rip off his magnifying headpiece, raise his great body out of his chair, and proceed to vomit into a five-gallon bucket set up just outside the container's entrance. The sound of his retching became a kind of metronome for the puppet work in the hull.

Ever since his outburst in port, both Lars and Otik had maintained their distance from Radar, each in his own way. Otik, mired in his nausea, simply chose not to acknowledge his existence. Lars's evasions were more subtle: when addressing Radar, he would often let the ends of his sentences drift off, as if the most important bits could not be said. Radar watched them from his cot, fiddling absentmindedly with one of his father's transceivers. It was evident that they were used to working in tandem. Even Kermin must have existed as a distant moon to their mutual dependence. It would have been more amusing to watch them in action if it were not also a reminder of his alienation.

"I hate you," Otik hissed at Lars, completely unprompted. Yet the line was clearly delivered with such loving familiarity that Radar found himself longing for someone, *anyone,* to hate him with similar affection.

"Is it possible to have them return and perch ten seconds in?" Lars replied.

"Why to perch?"

"A moment of doubt."

"Doubt?"

"Of contemplation, reflection. A prelude before the journey."

"Let me see."

"Ten seconds in."

"This is soon."

"If it's not possible—"

"'Nothing is not possible,' says Kermin Radmanovic, alleged father of *him*." Otik thrust his head in Radar's direction.

"Can I do something?" said Radar.

The two went silent.

"We're okay for now," said Lars. "Thank you."

"We are okay *forever*," said Otik. He grunted, removed his magnifier, and then trundled from the room. They soon heard the familiar sound of gagging.

"He takes a while," said Lars. "But once he accepts you as one of his own, he'll die for you."

"Oh, am I one of his own?" said Radar. "I hadn't realized."

"It's a complicated question for a Serb," said Lars. "But I do know he's been through a lot in life. You must meet him halfway. He has seen enough not to trust another human being on this planet, and yet . . . he does. And he will. Just give him time; he'll come around. He's like an elephant. He never forgets."

. . .

201-998-2666: Hello Mom. It's Radar. I miss you. I tried to get off the ship when we started sailing but they wouldn't let me. I realized this was a mistake. I shouldn't have left you. Are you okay? Did you find tata? I feel terrible. I will never forgive myself for leaving you like this. Please call me. *[Message not sent.]*

201-998-2666: Hi Ana Cristina. I'm on the boat. We left yesterday morning. We're somewhere in the Atlantic. My God I miss you. I feel like I'm the only person on this earth right now. —Radar (lost at sea) *[Message not sent.]*

Soon after their departure, the text messages would no longer go out. They sat in his phone, unsent, left in a state of perpetual limbo. He cursed himself for not giving his mother a transceiver. How had he gotten stuck with cellular communication as his only avenue? Helpless, voiceless, he would stand up on the forecastle deck, feeling the salty bow spray against his skin, and twiddle the dials, catching signal from Montauk, then from Europe, then from a ham in the Azores, in Dakar, in Guadeloupe, in Cartagena. The ionic skip was strange and beautiful out here. He could reach crazy new locations as if they were barely twenty yards away, and yet there were also whole blank spots on the Eastern Seaboard, including his home, that persisted in silence. He wondered about the blackout. How much had come back. That whole world—the swamps, the radio station, Forest Street—it all felt so far away now, separated by a wide and widening sea.

What was this sea? He spent most of his time staring out at its vast expanse. He felt unsettled on the boat, and not because of the vessel's constant roll and pitch. His was not a seasickness like Otik's. This feeling had more to do with absence. An absence of land, an absence of material, an absence of current. The salt water had an electromagnetic frequency all its own, but it was a frequency with which he was not familiar. Its note was singular, ancient, without end. He had come from a symphony, and now he was listening to an old man singing in the dark.

201-998-2666: Ana Cristina, I think about you all the time. Scary how much I think about you and home and everything I had. I wonder if I'll ever see you again. *[Message not sent.]*

201-998-2666: Please ignore my last message. *[Message not sent.]*

201-998-2666: Sorry. It's just lonely out here. I hope the power has come back there. I feel so far away right now. A blackout would be beautiful right now. Out here there is nothing to black out. *[Message not sent.]*

When the weather was calm, Radar—who had taken to wearing a knitted sailor's cap he had found in one of the cargo holds—would curl up on the quarterdeck next to a cargo winch and read. He first looked at the many newspaper clippings in the folder his mother had given him. One would think such a trove of material would be a revelation, particularly coming on the heels of his mother's announcement. Yet soon one article began to bleed into the next. He could feel the writers grasping for something just out of their reach. All they had were a few facts, some names, dates, and places, but nothing more. It was as if they were giving the particulars of an invented character that was him and yet not him. Even the highly technical "On an Isolated Incidence of Non-Addison's Hypoadrenal Uniform Hyperpigmentation in a Caucasian Male," by Dr. Thomas K. Fitzgerald, read as a kind of fiction that had very little to do with who he was. Cloaked within the fancy, medical-sounding language was a blatant absence of truth. He soon lost interest. These documents contained no answers.

He next turned his attention to *Spesielle Partikler.* This book, like the articles, had been fished from that hole in the floor of his parents' bedroom, and just holding it in his hands made him feel close to her. If he closed his eyes, he could almost conjure the feeling of that night, of listening to Caruso in the dark.

The book was a monstrosity. It felt like a brick in his lap. The binding was the color of sand and had clearly been handled many, many times, for the spine was split in two places and a large chunk of pages had come loose from the headband. Radar had to clutch it, lest the wayward leaves decide to up and blow away in the wind. Many of its passages were marked in a soft purple pencil. He found himself wondering about these markings. Who could have taken the care to mark so much of the text? Surely it wasn't his mother, who, like him, couldn't read Norwegian. It must have been the reader before her, or the one before that.

The more he looked at the book, the more intrigued he became, though he could not quite say what drew him to it. Occasionally a familiar name or place would jump out of that incomprehensible sea and there would be a momentary flash of recognition, a pinprick of electricity. He found Lars Røed-Larsen and Miroslav Danilović (who became Otik Mirosavic on page 1184). He found Leif Christian-Holtsmark, the leader of Kirkenesferda, whom Lars had talked about. On page 490 he even found himself, Radar Radmanovic, along with his mother and father. From what he could make out, their visit to Norway was described in some detail.

When he got to page 493, he stopped. There, in the bottom right corner, was a diagram of a man. Except for a strange, slender headband and a boxy arm-strap contraption, the man was incredibly generic, an everyman. He wondered if this could be the diagram of his treatment. The *electro-enveloping,* as Lars had called it. Radar leaned in closer. Four or five strokes of the pen conveyed a subtle look of amusement across the man's lips. Amusement at what? The transient nature of atomic reality? The knowledge that all things must change. Fall apart? Die?

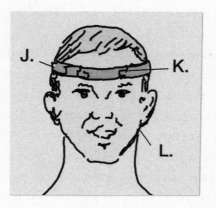

Fig. 5.2. Detail from Den Menneskelig Marionett Prosjektet
From Røed-Larsen, P., *Spesielle Partikler,* p. 493

Was this everyman supposed to be him?

It was preposterous, of course. He had been only four years old at the time, and even now, as a (somewhat) grown man, he in no way resembled this diagrammatic stand-in. And yet he could not look away. He leaned in closer, staring at the simple outline of the man's frame, the hint of tendons in the neck, the twin dips of his pectorals. As he brought his eyes closer and closer to the page, the lines of the man blurred, along with the arrows and their unexplained letters. As their edges softened, he imagined the electricity spilling through this man's skin, unraveling the cells, reversing proteins, morphing colors, peeling back time. The white of the page became him, became Radar the little boy, receiving that pulse, that quiet disaster of a pulse that would forever alter the shape of his story.

"I'm sorry," he said to the man in the diagram. "You're stuck like that."

There were many such diagrams littered across the book's pages. Floating within a sea of Norwegian, these diagrams came to represent little islands of potential meaning. He began to anticipate each image as a shipwrecked man anticipates an approaching shoal. Each one a world. Each one a promise of truth.

Gradually, as he sat with the book, a history of Kirkenesferda began to take shape in his mind, although he could not be sure if this history resembled the real history that had actually happened, or whether he was sculpting a new history, whole in and of itself. He was not even sure such a distinction mattered. He could now picture the four Kirk shows: *Kirk En* was the installation on the island in 1944, with the jars of little people floating in heavy water. One night, Radar had a terrible dream about these jars. He had been having more dreams since he started taking the malarial medication, and he was even remembering some of them the next morning. In the dream, the little people had come alive and were drowning, but he couldn't figure out how to unscrew the tops of the jars, and so he was forced to watch as they slowly died, one by one, their tiny throats filled with the heavy water, stained a terrible translucent shade of yellow.

Kirk To was the Tsar Bomba show on Gåselandet Island in 1961, where the wagon housing the puppet show apparently exploded in the blast wave of the largest atomic bomb ever detonated. The book featured a series of stills from an eight-millimeter film that allegedly depicted the moment of destruction, but Radar had his doubts. How could the camera have survived? And the stills didn't really show anything at all, at least as far as he could tell. *Why show something if you couldn't even tell what you were looking at?* Maybe he just didn't know how to look.

Then: *Kirk Tre.* The horror in Cambodia. He lingered here, knowing what an effect it had had on Lars. Young Lars. Through the palimpsest of diagrams and images he learned about Raksmey Raksmey, who had maybe been found in a hat (?), who had become a scientist (??) in Europe, who returned to Cambodia and somehow survived the Khmer Rouge, and who had then been invited to join Kirkenesferda via telegram. At least this is what he believed had happened. He couldn't ever be sure. Radar studied the diagrams of the complex show, wondered how his father could have helped to create such intricate

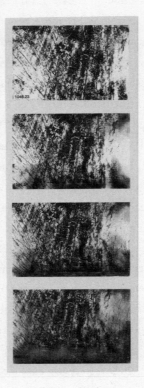

Fig. 5.3. "Gåselandet Still Sequence"
From Røed-Larsen, P., *Spesielle Partikler,* p. 231

creatures. What a production it all was! To put on something that elaborate in the middle of the jungle for Pol Pot and his men. So much effort. And for what?

With a shiver, Radar found the map on page 856: *"Massakren og Escape på Camp 808."* The map depicted the aftermath of the night's bloody ending, in which everyone was shot except little Lars, who escaped with Raksmey, only to see Raksmey die by stepping on a land mine at the Thai border. The maps of course told so little, captured none of the true terror of that night—the smell of death and cordite lingering in the air, the screams, the blood, then the silence, before the buzz of insects slowly returned. The map did not include the sound of Leif Christian-Holtsmark's wet, ragged breath as the last of his life left him or Siri's final glance across the hut to see the blood spilling from her husband's

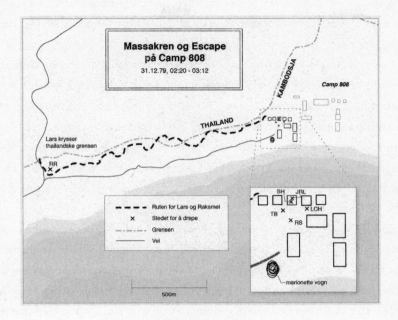

Fig. 5.4. "Massakren og Escape på Camp 808"
From Røed-Larsen, P., *Spesielle Partikler,* p. 856

neck. There was only this collection of dotted lines, a cluster of x's, as if this were from some errant scrimmage in a coach's playbook. And yet, seeing the unspeakable reduced to a simple black-and-white map, Radar felt himself overtaken by a new kind of horror, a horror of viewing but not knowing, of sensing what must lurk in the white spaces between the lines, beyond the boundaries of the map, beyond the confines of the book, beyond even the vast and unnameable sea. Otik wasn't the only one who had been through hell and survived. After experiencing that simple map, in all its silence, Radar made a mental note to forgive Lars for everything he had done or would do.

By contrast, *Kirkenesferda Fire,* the Sarajevo performance, seemed almost tame, though Radar spent perhaps the longest time studying these diagrams, as his father felt most present here. He became frustrated with his total ignorance of Norwegian, with not being able to unravel and savor every detail of the performance. The language barrier felt almost personal; he became convinced that if he could just understand this show, then he would understand everything about his father. He would have to ask Lars to tell him about what had happened, what went wrong, why the show ended early.

Radar did fall in love with a series of images from the performance, although he could not quite explain their origins. The images appeared to have been taken through a strong microscope. In the sequence, a tiny (microscopic?) old man reads a book as he sits amid a lunar landscape. Several frames show him turning pages, until, in the final two frames, he disappears inside a fiery flash of light. Radar could not help feeling kinship with this minute reader. They were not so different. In many ways, he was simply another reader waiting for a spark of light to burn him up.

Radar did not sleep well, perhaps because of the close quarters, perhaps because of the malaria medication's nocturnal effects. He still did not remember most of his dreams, but he often awoke in the middle of the night still caught in the lingering lacunae of their wake, immersed in the feeling of experiencing a horror that could not be known, and such a feeling of unknowing bled into his days. He missed the comforts of his *Little Rule Book for Life* and briefly regretted giving it to his mother. Where would he put all of his stupid little thoughts?

The world had slowly shrunk to only this particular patch of sea. Land became a memory, true and not quite true at the same time. Those afternoons on the quarterdeck with the sun on his face and the seabirds hang-gliding next to the railings as if they were unaware of gravity's embrace—those afternoons flowed together into one long, long day, a day that included all days before and all days after. The ocean of water melded with the text of the book, and he was a helmsman in each, making his way through a vast wilderness to a forever unattainable point on the horizon.

. . .

201-998-2666: Dear Mom, I've been reading the book you gave me. Not really reading, more like taking it in. I don't understand everything (or anything) but it's somehow wonderful. Thank you. Did you find Tata yet? I just wonder what could have happened to him?? He never went anywhere. And the lights? Are they back on? I

left you in such a terrible place. Why did you tell me to go???
[Message not sent.]

201-998-2666: Dear Ana Cristina, do you think we could be happy together? Like really happy? Would you grow tired of me? I would never grow tired of you. I would find something new about you every day. *[Message not sent.]*

201-998-2666: Sorry about the last text. I guess I shouldn't treat these like journal entries. But if you will never get them and if no one will ever read them except me does it really matter? Let's test it: I love you, Ana Cristina, I love you. *[Message not sent.]*

4

When he was not at his spot on the quarterdeck, Radar roamed the many passageways of the *Aleph*. The 456-foot ship was a maze of steam and boilers and valves, and he would wander through it all, laying his hands on random pipes and the walls of containers just to see if he could discern what lurked within. Sometimes the pipes were hot. Sometimes the containers were cold.

The *Aleph* flew a Liberian flag, was owned by a Portuguese shipping company based in China, and was skippered by an Argentinean who commanded a predominantly Russian and Estonian crew. For the number of tons of cargo she was hauling, the number of crewmen seemed ridiculously small—aside from the three of them, there were only fifteen men on board, including a full-time cook. The crew appeared to spend most of their time sanding rust off the decks and painting whatever lay beneath. Sometimes it felt as if the whole boat was made of rust. Radar wondered what would happen if they sanded it all away, slowly replacing the frame of the boat with paint, until she was composed only of latex. Would she still float? Would she still carry five above her summer Plimsoll? Or would she slowly sink—so slowly that no one would notice?

For the most part, the crew ignored him as he passed them sanding down the hallways. He could not read their expressions beneath their ventilator masks, but he imagined that they regarded him like a feral dog that they must tolerate but might eventually have to put out of its misery. One day he, too, would be sanded away.

Only the second mate, Ivan Kovalyov, took a liking to him. Ivan had the face of a baby and the body of a wrestler. He was also missing his left pinkie. He was originally from Vanavara, a tiny town in the middle of Siberia on the banks of the Podkamennaya Tunguska River. He was the only man on the ship, besides Lars and himself, who did not drink.

"Where I come from, if you don't take vodka . . . well, this is actually worse than homosexual," said Ivan. "I am outcast, you see. I am lamb."

His only vice, he claimed, was music, but he pronounced this word as if it had an extra, secret syllable that only he knew about: *myoo-zi-ka*.

"When I was little, I spent all of my monies on compact discs," he said. "Grigor and I would drive down to Krasnoyarsk and get *all* of the latest hits. Like Crash Test Dummies or Midnight Oil. These bands, I truly love. They are like family. Like fathers. Like my sisters.

"Once there was this kid, who gets into an accident and he couldn't go to school," he sang. He shook his head. "That is so beautiful and also so true."

When he was not on watch, Ivan would sit against the bulwark of the poop deck and strum his battered guitar. He had discovered a specific spot where the acoustics caused the music to drift down into the ventilators and naturally amplify throughout the corridors of the ship so that you could hear him playing all the way down in *Moby-Dikt*. Ivan had a surprising number of original love songs in his repertoire. They were named after different women ("Nadja," "Carolina," "Julie Julie"), and they all sounded exactly alike.

"I have only four fingers," he explained, holding up his hand. "So I must play simple songs." He strummed a chord, as if to demonstrate. *"Ooo-ooo-ooo, and her name was Nadja."*

"Have you met all of these women?" Radar asked Ivan.

"Not yet," said Ivan. *"Ooo-ooo-ooo, and her name was Oleana."*

But Ivan did not get many chances to play his songs, because Ivan's true gift was in celestial navigation. Ivan could read the stars in his sleep, and thus he was always in demand on the bridge. Captain Daneri—who otherwise thought

little of his "Red Army," as he called the Russian crew—confirmed the astonishing nature of Ivan's astral gifts:

"He's the best I've ever seen. Sweet Jesus, that boy was born in the sky," he
said.

Radar greatly enjoyed watching Ivan shoot the heavens with his sextant. The
indexing arm slid across the arc, the mirror clicked into place, and the course
was confirmed.

"And what is that one?" Radar said from the deck one night. He was pointing at a star glowing just off their bow.

"That is Sirrah. It looks like one star, but she is actually two stars very close
together, like this. Very close, so from ninety-seven light-years away, we see only
one star. But you have to remember, you are seeing past right now. You are seeing very old light. *Ninety-seven years old*. So this light is from before World War
I, when people still poop in holes," he said. "I always like Sirrah. She is beautiful
because she is in two constellations at once. She is head of Andromeda and she
is also penis of Pegasus. She is both. One day, I will write song about this."

Rarely did an exchange go by with Ivan that did not end in this phrase.

To really see Ivan at work, however, you needed to observe him in the chart
room, with its drawers and drawers of maps covering nearly every coastline in
the world. This was his true domain. Ivan spun his plotters in great pirouettes,
cutting lines with his red pencil, tapping and wrapping the dividers across the
great expanse of depth readings. All he needed was a single star and he could
take you anywhere you wanted. The *Aleph* was equipped with various radar and
GPS locating devices, but the electrical work was shoddy and sometimes the
systems would fizzle out with no apparent warning, leaving them seemingly
without a location. But with Ivan, there was no worry. With Ivan, they would
always have a location, because Ivan did not fail.

"How did you learn how to read the stars?" Radar asked him at dinner one
evening.

"You must understand that in Soviet Union we didn't have very many things.
But one thing we have more than anyone is space. I mean like *literally* outer
space. Our space program was best in the world. We did not fake moon landing
like the Americans. We send up *Sputnik* first and we send up Laika, first dog

into space. And then we send up Yuri Gagarin, first man in space. After this, everyone believed anything is possible. So of course I wanted to be a cosmonaut when I was little. Just like every other Russian boy."

"I'm not sure the Americans faked the moon landing."

"Of course they did. That is common fact," said Ivan, chewing thoughtfully on a forkful of mashed potatoes. "But probably real reason I became interested in stars is because of *the event.*"

"The event?"

"I think this is what you call it in English."

"What event?"

"Tunguska Event. In 1908, there was huge explosion in Siberia. It blew out two thousand square meters of forest, something like this. Eighty million trees destroyed. Center of explosion was seventy kilometers from Vanavara, but the people there, they still felt heat blast all across their skin. The shockwave broke windows, collapsed woodsheds. It blew the men right off their horse. It was powerful, so powerful. Stronger than an atom bomb."

"This was 1908?"

"Yes, 1908. In June. There is a monument in Vanavara, because after this everyone wanted to come to see what happened. Scientists, tourists, acrobats."

"Acrobats?"

"Okay, one acrobat. But he was very famous. He did his Tunguska show, where he launched himself from a wire and disappeared into a puff of smoke. It was very famous and very beautiful."

"So what caused the explosion?"

"Well, that is a lot of debating. When I was little, government report said this was meteor, but many older people who are still religious could not believe this. They said it was God's doing. They said the government had made God angry by mistreating its people and so God is punishing them. I can still re- member this . . . There was line of scientists giving their report. They were standing in these white coats. And I said to myself, *Ivan, if you cannot be cosmo- naut, maybe you can become scientist like these men. These men know about every- thing in sky. Look how clean their coats are! They are so powerful and so clean.* This is what I thought. So I get books and I get chart and I get spotter and . . . I spend time with sky. I spend lots of time with sky. Just watching. In Siberia, sky is amazing. Maybe best sky in world. Like fish eye spinning around and around. You can see stars shoot once every ten seconds, no problem. You look straight ahead and you see more stars in your—how do you call it, on these sides?"

"Your periphery."

"Yes, your *periphery*. Your periphery is having serious party. And when you look there, you see more stars over there, and so on. But funny thing is that when I was looking at stars, it was like looking at myself. At my own hand, but this hand I forget I have. It was like . . . I have to learn this part of me again."

"So you learned all of the constellations?"

"Yes, but not exactly like that. It is like I am becoming familiar *again*, if you understand. But of course I can't see every star. I feel like I know them, but I can't see them. And then I realize: there is *whole Southern Hemisphere* that I have never seen. So this is when I leave Vanavara and my family. To see sky I cannot see. I am not cosmonaut, I am not scientist, but I am next best thing. I become sailor. The sea is my outer space now."

"Rule number two-thirty-nine."

"What?"

"Nothing."

ONE AFTERNOON, Radar was sitting up on the bridge while Ivan was at the helm on the eight-to-four watch. A call came in on an ACR VHF transceiver, but it warbled and fizzled out in the middle of the transmission.

"What did they say?" asked Radar.

"I can't hear. That radio is broken," said Ivan with a shake of his head. "Everything on this ship is broken."

"Not everything," said Captain Daneri, coming into the wheelhouse. "*We* are not broken, Mr. Kovalyov."

"Pardon, Captain," said Ivan.

Radar cleared his throat. "Maybe I could fix it."

"I think it is impossible. Igor tried and he said it is hopeless," said Ivan.

"Igor's a fool," said the captain. Igor was one of those unfortunate souls who had convinced himself that the world was bent on deceiving him. He was also supposedly the boat's electrician. But as far as Radar could tell, he devoted nearly all of his time to hitting the cooling devices on the refrigerated containers with his wrench and cussing in his native tongue. The clang of his wrench had become a common refrain in the ship's painful symphony.

"Well, I could just take a look," said Radar.

"Mr. Kovalyov, would you believe it? Our guest wants to tame the dragon," said the captain. "Our guest is calling Igor *un idiota incompetente.*"

"I didn't say that," said Radar.

"You are correct: Igor *es un idiota incompetente.*"

"If I could just take a peek," said Radar. "I might be able to—"

"He just wants to take a peek," repeated the captain.

"Let him take a peek," said Ivan.

"Please," the captain bowed, and gestured at the radio. "She awaits your intentions."

After removing the front panel, it took Radar barely a minute to discover the corroded transistor switch running off the link board. Telling Ivan and an amused captain that he would be right back, he detached the transceiver from the stack and made his way down to *Moby-Dikt.* Otik offered no response when Radar asked him if he could borrow one of the soldering irons, so he went ahead. Utilizing a spare transistor he found in a drawer, he fashioned a new switch, and what he could not solder he secured with a small wad of well-chewed watermelon-flavored bubble gum.

BACK ON THE BRIDGE, he presented his handiwork.

"It'll run for now, but you may want to get a more permanent solution when you get back to port," he said.

Ivan marveled like a child. "That," he said. "*That* is something incredible. Chewing gum."

"Well, don't tell Igor," said the captain. "Wait, on second thought, let's tell Igor. Let's tell him that *un yanki bobalicón* is doing the job he cannot do."

"One day, I will write song about this," said Ivan.

Later, Daneri would touch Radar's shoulder and say, "You're a part of her now. She doesn't ever forget."

Indeed, ever since offending him that first day in port, Radar had slowly finessed his way back into the captain's good graces. Or maybe it was simply a case of Radar being the only available audience member. It had become clear that Captain Daneri was really just a showman in search of a show. Perhaps this was why he had agreed to shepherd them across the ocean in the first place. Yet in this regard, Otik and Lars were not holding up their end of the bargain. Despite repeated invitations by the captain to join him in his quarters for an after-dinner maté, Otik and Lars consistently excused themselves so as to return to their feverish preparations. Things were not going well with the vircator. A palpable air of panic could be felt inside *Moby-Dikt,* so Radar returned there as seldom as possible now, only to catch a few hours of nightmarish sleep, though even this was proving difficult, as his companions worked all hours of the night. When Radar tried to query them about their progress, both grew cagey, even hostile. Radar was thus left to be Daneri's sole patron.

Entering into the captain's cabin was a bit like entering into a time machine. The room was paneled in a lush African mahogany so dark it appeared almost purple by the light of a candle. At the center of the room was a giant desk of such immense proportions, it was unclear how the piece had ever entered the cabin or how it would ever be removed.

Captain Daneri presided over their evenings together from a body-worn burgundy armchair, sipping his maté out of a calabash gourd through a thick silver straw. Occasionally he would light up a Cuban cigar, although these he dutifully rationed, explaining that his father had lost his entire throat to cancer and did not speak a word for the last fifteen years of his life.

"Do you know what we're carrying right now on this ship?" the captain asked Radar one evening.

"Not really," said Radar, gingerly sipping at his maté. As usual, Otik and Lars had already bidden their farewells, and he found himself wishing they were there to deflect the attention or at least make a pass at one of the captain's riddles.

"Well, good. No one does. At least no one can speak with absolute certainty.

I myself have not opened any of the containers, so I can only tell you what the system tells me, and the system speaks only in terms of possibility. A container does not contain something—it 'is said to contain something'. The same can be said of a good book." He picked up a piece of paper. *"TPMU 839201 3, said to contain 6,800 pounds of frozen chicken; RITU 559232 0, said to contain 14,000 pounds of frozen fish; CSQU 938272 8, said to contain 3,400 pounds of hypodermic needles, pharmaceuticals, and other medical equipment . . . said to contain 6,000 women's long-sleeve shirts . . . said to contain 550 youth bicycles . . . said to contain 55,000 pounds of aircraft engines . . . said to contain 20,000 pounds of computer equipment . . . said to contain 8,000 pounds of unbalanced polymer . . . said to contain 4,000 pounds of gems, precious metals, and coins . . . said to contain 15,000 pounds of barley.* That's a lot of barley."

"It is a lot of barley."

"*If* the barley exists. But even if the barley does not exist, it doesn't matter. Soon the world will not contain anything definitive anymore; it will only be *said to contain* things. We will exist in a system of total possibility. It is what I call *un desdibujamiento*. It's a wonderful word, isn't it? *Un desdibujamiento*. It means 'the blurring of the local.' The lines between here and there have begun to blur, and it is all because of the question of the box." The captain leaned back. "But I can see I'm scaring you. You mustn't let me get started on one of my little rants. Anyone will tell you this."

"*Desdibujamiento*," repeated Radar.

The captain nodded. "Like caressing a woman," he said.

Radar wasn't an expert in caressing women, so he said nothing. They sat in silence. The roll of the ship was causing an imperceptible shift in all the documents around the room. Radar could feel the papers shift back and forth on the desk ever so slightly.

"So tell me," the captain said. "What are you boys going to do in the Congo? Lars wouldn't give me a straight answer."

Radar stiffened in his chair. "I don't really think I can tell you."

"I'm not in the habit of asking people their business, but you look like a man who can be trusted."

"I'm sorry. I would have to ask Lars before—"

"Is it diamonds? Ivory? Ah—" He wagged a finger. "I know. Don't tell me. It's coltan. That's what they're taking out of there now. *Blood coltan,* they call it. For making mobile phones. That's why they have you—*el hechicero de la electrónica*! It all makes sense now. I've seen people do exactly what you're doing before."

"We aren't dealing in those things," said Radar. "We're performers." He caught his breath, but it was too late.

"Performers?" the captain said, raising a gargantuan eyebrow.

"I'm sorry." Radar lifted his hands. "I can't say any more."

"*Well.* My little troupe of performers. What are you performing, then?"

"You can't tell them I told you."

"Go on. *Taming of the Shrew? Parsifal? Waiting for Godot?*"

"I don't fully know, if I'm being quite honest. It involves puppets."

"*Puppets? Ave María!*"

Radar lifted his hands into a pleading prayer. "I'm sorry, I've said too much."

"And where are you performing with this puppet show?"

"Can you please not say anything to Lars or Otik? I don't think they're big fans of me at the moment, and they certainly won't be if they find out I told you anything."

"I like you, Mr. Radmanovic. What did you say you were? American? You don't seem like an American to me. You're too good at listening."

"I don't really know what I am."

"If I may—a word of advice. You've got to be careful where you're going. The system still has its boundaries. And once you get to these boundaries, things begin to get a little hairy. *Un poco peligroso.* In the Congo, the box is said to contain x, but the box will not contain x. The box will contain nothing. Or something else entirely. It will drive a man insane."

"I think that's why we're going there. To perform where the system has broken down."

The captain lifted his arms. "*Performers!* To think, this whole time and I had no idea. Well, I love it. The *Aleph* has never had its own performers, have you, my little darling?" He reached out and tenderly stroked the wall of the cabin.

Suddenly the captain jumped up from his seat.

"Come," he said. "There's something I'd like to show you."

They took three flights of stairs down to the main deck and then out a doorway and into the chilly night. Radar looked up. The stars enveloped them like a casket. He followed Daneri as he wandered through the maze of containers, the captain tapping their sides with his hand as if they were a herd of animals. They wove their way toward the bow and then turned and passed through a doorway that Radar had never seen before. They went down a small flight of stairs to a tween deck below the main deck, where they followed several more narrow corridors before slipping through another doorway and down two more flights of stairs. Radar had long since lost his bearings. If he were not with the captain, he would never be able to get back again. He was not even sure they were on the same ship anymore.

The captain abruptly stopped.

"Here," he said, pointing to a crimson container illuminated only by a dim sea light on the far wall.

"What is it?"

"Open it."

"Am I allowed to?"

"This one doesn't belong to them."

Radar was afraid the box would be either locked or horrendously complicated to open, but he pulled a lever and heard a satisfying click, and the door swung open easily. A familiar smell. A smell of home. He peered into the darkness, half expecting to see his mother, his father, to see everything the way it was before. He squinted. At first he could not understand what he was looking at, but then he saw them. Books. Endless stacks of books. Thousands of them.

"I deliver one of these every time I do the West African route."

"Who does it go to?"

"He's a remarkable man. He has a library in the middle of the jungle. It is said to contain every book in the world. Of course, this is impossible. But it's a noble pursuit. And I'm glad to play my part."

Radar stared at the books, lying, waiting like corpses. The captain swung the door shut.

"Or maybe it's just a glitch," he said. "Maybe the library does not exist. But the system demands it, and I must deliver what the system demands."

5

On the evening of the sixth day, the seas began to swell. An electricity spread through the normally stoic crew. The men chatted nervously in the galley and then dumped their trays and left early to take care of their evening rounds. Hatches needed to be battened, stacking braces secured.

At the officers' table, Radar sensed a palpable air of anticipation.

"We're in for something nasty," Ivan confirmed over his goulash.

"Is this normal for this time of year?" Lars asked politely.

"There's no normal when it comes to the sea," said Daneri.

"The radar didn't see much," said Akaki, the chief mate.

"The radar never sees much," said the captain. "We're in for one tonight."

Ivan, seeing the alarm on Radar's face, leaned over and whispered, "I wouldn't worry."

Back in *Moby-Dikt,* Otik, who had not been present at dinner, had already imploded into the sinkhole of his nausea. He lay on his cot, pale and moaning, one paw gripping the rim of his vomit bucket.

"Please," he mumbled, delirious. "Tell my father . . ."

"He'll be all right," said Lars.

But Otik did not look all right. "Tell my father . . . to meet me at the café," he whispered.

Lars tried to continue at the workbench, though even his normally glowing

Nordic countenance had faded to a pale shade of avocado. The pitching grew worse, and his tools began to slide off the bench and clatter onto the floor.

With nothing else to do, Radar burrowed down into his bed and tried to sleep. As he lay supine, the boat's roll and pitch became magnified. He closed his eyes, trying to reassure himself with the protection offered by these great layers of steel wrapped around his little cot. Surely such an awesome creation of man was immune to the forces of nature? He thought of the *Titanic* and its own claims to invincibility. The *Aleph* was no *Titanic*. She was made of much weaker stock. A shiver passed through him. Outside their container, the ship creaked and groaned. When Radar finally drifted off, his dreams were, as usual, fitful, incomprehensible affairs marked by leaks sprouting in hulls, horses swimming in open oceans, German U-boats breaching the surface in an explosion of foam.

After several hours of tossing and being tossed, Radar was awoken by a sharp, stabbing pain on his forehead. He opened his eyes to find the inside of the container in chaos, the world tipping upward at an impossible angle. It was as if a giant had decided to pick up the opposite corner of the box in order to get a peek at him. The downward slope had caused much of the equipment to come off the walls and the chairs to all slide up against his cot. In his bed he found several tools, including the one that had apparently attacked him: a silver T square. He touched his fingers to his head. They came away wet with blood.

Just when it appeared as if the world could not possibly tip any more, lest the floor become the ceiling and visa versa, they reached a kind of equilibrium point. There was a moment of rest, and then the container began to pitch steadily back in the other direction. The loose tools, the teakettle, and the conference of chairs dutifully complied with this new incline by sliding away to the opposite wall. Radar saw one of his boots tumble by. Again, just when it seemed the container would flip entirely, the angle of repose was reached, and the chairs came sliding back to him. Radar gripped the edge of the cot, transfixed by this display of inanimate migration.

"Help me with . . . would you?" he heard someone shout.

He looked up and saw Lars pressed against a rack of tools. Lars's legs were dancing about as if he were a drunkard, flailing against the extreme rolls of the boat. His furious effort to contain the remaining tools was proving futile.

"What's going on?" Radar shouted. A stupid question.

"It's . . . storm," yelled Lars. This word did not come close to capturing what was taking place inside the container. To be sure, the ship had been engaged in a slight roll and pitch ever since their departure, a vectoring that Radar had steadily grown accustomed to, unlike poor Otik. But this was such a grotesque display of the sea's violence that the situation would have been laughable if it weren't so utterly, utterly terrifying.

"When did it get so bad?" Radar shouted. The container had reached its angular apogee and was now lurching in the other direction, causing the chairs to march away again. More clattering and a crash as the lathe toppled over onto a computer.

"The . . . half an hour . . . so . . . can't." Lars moved to the lathe, trying to extricate it from the IBM.

"What?" Radar yelled. He realized he couldn't hear what Lars was saying because of the incredible racket that was reverberating throughout the container. It was one of the more horrible sounds he had ever heard—a groan sustained and amplified into a curdling wail that came and went, came and went, like the wail of a mother who has just lost her son. Except that this wail came not from any living creature but from the ship itself. The bones of the ship were crying.

"Where's Otik?" yelled Radar over the noise. Otik's cot was empty save for fifty or so errant bird heads, which rolled and tumbled across the sheets.

Lars pointed.

Beneath the terrible yowl of the wind, Radar heard a noise. It was a human wheeze. An escaping of air from parted lips.

"Otik?"

Radar stumbled over to the cot, dodging the minefield of detritus on the move, and found him on the floor, half wrapped in a top sheet, facedown, bird heads all around, a thin puddle of merguez-colored vomit spilling from his mouth like a speech bubble.

Otik murmured something inaudible.

"What?" Radar leaned in. The man's giant back was hot to the touch. The ship reached the peak of its roll, hung, and came hurtling down again, bird heads tumbling everywhere. A chair hit them and Radar winced, trying to shield himself.

"Molim te," Otik wheezed. *"Ja umirem."*

"You're going to be okay, Otik," said Radar, rubbing his back. "It's just a storm. It won't be long now." He had no idea how long it would be. The storm felt like it might last forever.

"I'm dying," wheezed Otik.

"You're not dying, Otik," said Radar. He blundered across the room and grabbed a towel. Scrambling back to Otik, nearly falling into him, he began to wipe at the vomit smeared across the floor.

"Lars!" he yelled. "We need to get out of here!"

"Ostavi me," mumbled Otik. *"Reci im da mi je žao. Reci im da nisam kreten."*

"Don't say that, Otik. You're going to be fine."

"Ja sam Đubre," Otik wheezed.

"You're doing good work," said Radar. "You're doing great work. No one can do what you do."

"Ja nisam dobra osoba."

"Ti si dobar čovek, Charlie Brown," said Radar. It was one of the few lines he could say in Serbian.

Otik opened his eyes and looked up at Radar. He was crying. Radar tried to heave him off the floor. It was like trying to lift a small car.

"Lars!" he called. "We need to get him out of here. The tools—" He ducked as a bow saw came flying off its hook and twanged against the table.

Lars had a rope in his hand and was attempting to lash the lathe to the wall. The lights inside the container suddenly flickered and went out. Radar felt his heart sink. *Not another blackout. Here? In the middle of the ocean? In the middle of the storm of all storms?* He could think of nothing worse.

The lights blinked and buzzed back on again. Radar looked up. The birds. He had forgotten about the birds. They still hung from the ceiling, swaying wildly about, palindroming with the sea.

"Lars!"

"What?"

"We've got to get him out of here!" he yelled.

With much effort, they managed to half-carry, half-drag Otik out the door. *"Ostavite me,"* he kept saying. *"Ostavite me, ostavite me."*

Outside, in cargo hold number four, there were no flying projectiles, but the sound was even more hellacious than inside the container. The wail had turned into a full-pitched scream, and Radar could hear the ribs of the ship straining, their fibers pulled and compressed to the breaking point. It was like being in the belly of a dying whale. At the next roll, Radar tripped and fell and immediately found himself soaked. The floor of the hold was covered in seawater. The water quickly slopped away as the roll reached its vertex and then just as quickly came spilling back onto him. The beams, the bulwark, the very superstructure of the ship screeched in protest. From somewhere ahead, what sounded like an essential support cracked, and the cargo hold around him gave what could only be described as a death rattle.

For the first time, Radar saw what was going to happen: *This ship is going to sink. I'm going to die on this ship.* The idea of his own death did not elicit panic but rather resignation, as if he had known it would end like this the whole time.

"Get him upstairs!" shouted Lars. "There's a lounge on the lower deck."

Radar snapped out of his morose reverie and grabbed Otik's shoulder. Urged on by adrenaline and the threat of a watery grave, they maneuvered themselves to the opening of the stairwell. Radar would have thought it impossible to go any farther, but somehow they pinballed up the four flights of stairs despite his own handicaps, the immensity of Otik's mass, and the heave and throes of the boat. Radar's shoulders were sore from crashing against one wall after another. Yet he had almost grown accustomed to the rhythms of the egregious rolling and pitching. Even if the rules of the world had gone haywire, he sensed a method to this madness. When the boat reached the top of its tilt axis, his body was already readying itself for the release and the counter-tilt.

They slammed against the door to the lounge and then collapsed onto the floor. The lounge was abandoned. *The Little Mermaid* was playing silently on the television. Radar lay there, panting, watching Sebastian merrily sing and leap about on the screen, when a single idea occurred to him: *Ivan*. He need to find Ivan. If he was with Ivan, all would be okay.

"I'm going upstairs," he said.

"Better to stay here," said Lars. "Who knows what's out there?"

The boat reversed its roll. The ship groaned.

"I'm going!" said Radar. "I'll be right back."

Back in the stairwell, he staggered upward. His load was lightened, but it seemed as if the higher he went in the ship, the worse the pitching became. He finally made it to the top corridor, staggering, falling, grabbing hold of a stowed fire hose. He could see the hallway literally twisting and torquing like a Slinky.

Everyone up here must be dead! Thrown overboard or smashed to smithereens!

After some desperate balletics, he managed to make it to the doorway of the bridge and threw it open, expecting carnage.

But there was no carnage. The scene was one of remarkable serenity. And there was Ivan, standing at the helm, feet planted like a matador, nine fingers upon the wheel.

Oh, sweet, sweet Ivan!

Ivan's face was completely calm, his eyes betraying no sense of unease as his gaze held fast into the very depths of the storm. It was a standoff—man versus nature—and seeing him like this, Radar could not bet against man.

Next to him, the chief mate, Akaki, was hunched over the radar, his face barely six inches from the screen. Several paces away stood Captain Daneri in his crisp white uniform. He looked as if he were attending a funeral. One hand firmly gripped the bridge console, but otherwise none of the three seemed particularly bothered by gravity's complete disintegration.

Radar opened his mouth to convey his simultaneous terror and joy at seeing them. He wanted to tell them about Otik, about the water in the hold, about the twisting hallway, about seeing his own death.

"Blow me shivers!" he called out.

The needle in the room did not flicker. No one paid him any heed. Ivan, hands on the wheel. Akaki, studying his computers. Daneri, staring grimly ahead. It was as if he didn't exist.

Radar took hold of a chair, then the bridge console, then made it to the helm.

"Ivan," he said. "Ivan. What's going on?"

"A squall," said Ivan. "Big squall. Radar didn't see it."

"Radar never sees it," said the captain.

"Radar did see it," said Akaki.

"Only once we're inside the goddamn headwall," said the captain. "And then radar sees nothing."

Radar was briefly confused, until he realized they were referring not to him but to the object of Akaki's attention. The technology, not the person.

"How does she feel, Mr. Kovalyov?" the captain said. "Tell me something good."

"She's pushing three, four to starboard. I can hold," said Ivan, gripping the wheel. "But if wind changes we are buried."

The captain nodded. "What's your height, Mr. Akakievich?"

"Twelve meters," said the chief mate. "Fifty-three knots from the north-northeast. Holding. Gusting."

"*Hijo de puta,*" hissed Daneri. He lifted the phone to the engine room and said, "Full ahead, Mr. Piskaryov. Give me more. I want more. We need to cut these down."

"There's a band ahead," said the chief mate, staring at the radar.

The captain hung up his phone. "Keep her steady, Mr. Kovalyov. Pull port if you need, but don't let her get turned. I don't want to lose one goddamn box, you hear me? *Not one goddamn box!*"

"There is a band ahead, captain!" the chief mate said again.

"I don't care what you see on that cursed machine!" shouted the captain.

"I have never seen this," the chief mate said, almost contemplatively.

Radar looked out through the windows, across the great deck of the *Aleph*. The windshield wipers squeaked away, back and forth across the glass—a pathetic show of resistance, given the immensity of the storm that surrounded them. At first he could not see much. The deck lights were all ablaze, but his visibility was still limited by the thrashing rain to a series of glimpses of a huge and unrelenting sea. And then there was a clap of lightning and he saw it all. What before had simply been a series of fantastic rolls and pitches now revealed itself to be a maelstrom of wind and rain and great white-capped waves that rose out of the darkness before crashing wildly against the deck, the stacks of containers lurching and leaning beneath the savagery of the ocean. The ship—once so big in port—now seemed so utterly small and helpless against this raging sea—a slight little dagger of a thing. And then the rain came at them again, pounding against the windows like a volley of bullets, the windshield wipers persisting but doing nothing to dispel the chaos outside. Having glimpsed the magnitude of their foe, Radar saw the odds now swinging back firmly in favor of nature's eventual triumph, even with a wizard like Ivan at the helm.

"*Dios mío,*" said the captain.

Radar looked up. At first he could make out nothing through the blur of wind and rain. The boat bent toward its bow, and it was as if the great sea had taken a moment to rest, a moment to contemplate the extent of its destruction. And then Radar saw it: a mighty, incomprehensible wall of water rising above them, higher even than the bridge upon which they stood, thirty meters above the Plimsoll. The *Aleph,* stupefied, helpless to the world, was headed directly for it.

"Mr. Kovalyov—" the captain hissed.

"I see it, I see it," said Ivan. "What do you want? There's nothing I can do . . ."

The chief mate looked up from his radar.

"*Mater bozhya,*" he whispered.

The boat churned up the flank of the giant wave, doing its best to climb into the sky, but eventually she lost her momentum, for there was only so much her propeller could manage against the laws of physics. The wave, previously content with existing as a mountain of potentiality, finally lost its patience with the ship. The tremendous cornice of white water at its zenith exploded like a volcano and let loose a thundering avalanche of sea down onto the *Aleph*'s deck.

There are few sights as impressive as a wave breaking across a ship. It is the truest of force equations, an honest meeting of liquid and solid, where solid is forced to wonder what liquid might do, where solid resists, re-tabulates, converses, barters, prays, and then reemerges triumphant. Or not. Radar sensed such a negotiation only for a split second before the shockwave from the impact shook the bridge and he was tossed like a doll to the floor.

When he stood up again, he could see nothing through the windows. For an instant, he thought that the boat had simply vanished, that the wave had acted like a giant eraser and banished them from existence, but then he realized that *they* were still on the ship, and *they* still existed, so the ship must exist, too. Maybe she had split off and sunk, taking all of her cargo with her? Maybe they were sinking already and they had precious few moments together before the ocean burst through the windows. But no, there she was: with great effort, the outline of the *Aleph* surfaced from the grim sea like an ancient sea creature heaving itself from the depths. She was still intact. She had made it through.

"How many boxes?" the captain was yelling.

The chief mate was at the window, counting, fingers touching fingers.

"How many boxes are gone, Mr. Akakievich?!"

"At least fifteen, sir," he yelled. "Maybe more."

Radar peered out into the storm, the green and red bow lights still glimmering through the rain. He could see the patchwork quilt of boxes, so small and vulnerable against the sea. Most were still in place, but he could also see what the first mate was looking at: two stacks in the bow were shorter than the rest and now were tilting dangerously with each swell.

"Tell me what is gone!" said the captain.

"I have to check the computers, sir!"

"Hijo de puta."

Ivan was still manning the wheel, his face crooked into the faintest of smiles.

Radar came up to him. "How did you know how to do it?"

"I didn't," said Ivan. "I never know."

Radar looked out across the deck, wet with the sea still churning out thirty-foot waves, though after the monstrosity they had just survived, the rest was child's play.

Through the slashing rain, something caught his eye. He blinked. Just past the gunwales, somewhere over the second cargo hold, he could've sworn he had seen a horse galloping across the decks, weaving around the stacks of containers. He stared out into the storm but did not see the creature again.

"Captain," said Radar, "are any of these containers said to contain horses?"

. . .

THE STORM SUBSIDED, though the seas retained their swell for many hours afterwards. Down in *Moby-Dikt,* the cleanup had begun.

Otik lay on his cot, dead to the world, while Lars worked furiously to restore order from the chaos. Radar picked up the bow saw and began to help him. The precious bird heads, so carefully looked after, were strewn all over the floor. Many had rolled into dark corners, and it took time to find them. And still some had been lost. They had boarded the boat with 1,387; after the storm, they could find only 1,381. Otik, normally so protective of his heads, only groaned.

"I want off," he said. "I want land. I want real land."

After three hours, Radar collapsed into his own cot, exhausted. They had done the best they could. Time would tell whether the storm had doomed the show.

Lars stood by the workbench, swaying, his eyes empty.

"You should get some sleep," said Radar.

"I won't sleep again," said Lars.

"Ever?"

"In the north, you learn to sleep half the year and then stay awake for six months, like a bear."

"Yeah, I'm not quite there yet," said Radar.

"You did wonders today," Lars said suddenly. "We couldn't do this without you."

"Oh? I feel like I'm always in the way."

"You'll see," said Lars. "Otik doesn't forget. Things will be different now."

6

They crossed the Atlantic without further incident. On the tenth day, they stopped in Lisbon, where they unloaded—or supposedly unloaded—50,000 pounds of "lubricated materials," 75,000 pounds of "tractors or tractor equipment," 20,000 pounds of "explosive and/or non-explosive chemicals," 33,000 pounds of semiconductors, 25,500 pounds of "potato product," and 70 tons of flat carbon steel. They took on containers said to contain 1,000 cases of port wine, 10,000 pounds of green olives, 20,000 pounds of leather hide, 2,000 bottles of milk, 15,000 pounds of young wool, 9,000 pounds of "footwear and/ or foot apparel," and a 1976 Mercedes-Benz fire engine.

In the Canary Islands, more containers were exchanged and shifted. Among other things, they dropped off the containers said to contain the milk, the wool, the footwear, and 950 jackhammers. They also dropped off the fire engine, which drove off the docks after sounding its siren, as if in thanks for the safe passage. They picked up 5,000 pounds of live lobster, 22,000 pounds of frozen fish, 30,000 pounds of "cola and diet cola product," 65,000 pounds of "precious gemstones," and 14,000 traffic cones. At no point in the loading and unloading did Radar see any evidence of the horse he had glimpsed in the middle of the typhoon.

They rode the Canary Current down the west coast of Africa, past Senegal, through the turbulent waters of Cape Palmas, and into the Gulf of Guinea, where they stopped briefly in Lagos to pick up five hundred tons of crude oil.

Captain Daneri, nervous about pirates, stationed his crew on the gunwales with high-pressure hoses pointed at the sea while he stalked the bridgewings with a rifle in the crook of each arm. As if knowing who they were up against, no pirates elected to appear. The captain looked almost disappointed at the ease with which they slid out of Nigerian waters.

From Lagos, they crossed the equator, hugging the coast near Gabon so as to mitigate the Angola Gyre working against them. Nearly two weeks after leaving New Jersey, they were forced to anchor just south of Point Noire, next to several Taiwanese oil tankers, while they waited to gain admission into the Congo River.

Captain Daneri fumed at the delay.

"The system crumbles," he muttered into his maté.

While they waited, the tropical sun sent temperatures in the hold soaring. Otik, who had not fully recovered his strength since the storm, tried halfheartedly to work on the damaged bird heads, but the sweat poured off him in sheets and he soon fell back into bed. Radar noticed that he had lost a considerable amount of weight during their ten days at sea, and his eyes now appeared sunken and dull. Despite his pallor, Otik's demeanor toward Radar had softened dramatically. Just as Lars had predicted, Otik now approached him with an almost off-putting tenderness, given his previous vitriol.

"You always remind me of Kermin," said Otik from his bed. "I miss this man every day."

"I shouldn't have left."

"You had to leave, *burazeru*. You had to come with us."

Burazeru. Brother. A word he had heard passed like a secret handshake between two boys while they played soccer on a street in Belgrade. A word he never thought he would hear directed at him. An elusive connection that would always, by definition, exclude him. He was brotherless. Until now.

Burazeru. His skin prickled.

"You mean it?" he said.

"Without you, there can be no show. *Ti si dobar čovek, Charlie Brown.*"

Even if it was not true, it meant the world to him. For the first time in his life, Radar felt as though he might be on the right path.

"Otik, when we were back in New Jersey, you said my father wasn't coming back," said Radar. "How can you be so sure?"

"I didn't know what I was saying, *burazeru*. It was long night. I was tired."

"But what do you think happened to him, really?"

Otik rubbed his face. "I don't know."

"What is it?" asked Radar.

Otik sighed. "There is type of puppet tradition in Java called *wayang golek*," he said. "They are using wooden rod puppets. Very beautiful. When puppet dies in play, the puppeteer hangs puppet next to stage, on special hook, so audience can see puppet. Puppet is not gone. Puppet is still there."

"I don't understand—"

But at that moment, they heard a giant explosion outside the boat. Radar ducked.

"What was that?" said Radar.

"We are under attack," said Otik. "They have come for us."

"Pirates?" said Radar.

More thundering booms echoed from outside.

"What should we do?" Radar whispered.

With a groan, Otik extricated his body from the bed and hobbled out into the hold. Radar cautiously followed.

"Where are you going?" asked Radar. "Don't you think we should stay here?"

"Let's go meet these men who will kill us. Let's shake hands and congratulate," said Otik, and he started up the stairs.

Radar stared after him, shocked. It seemed less an act of courage than a hopeful attempt at suicide.

"Wait!" said Radar, following him up the steps. "Wait for me, *burazeru!*"

They emerged onto the deck to find that it was already dark. They must have lost track of time. Night came quickly in the tropics, always at the same hour. The *Aleph,* contrary to what they expected, was not being overrun by a band of marauders. All was calm on her main deck. They heard the sound of guns again, but some distance away. They hurried to the balustrade and peered out across the water. In the moonlight, they could just make out what looked to be an old man-of-war, nestled in a cove, intermittently blasting its guns into the dark, jungled coastline. Each time its cannons fired, the bush would light up, and they watched as shadows of trees trembled and collapsed beneath the on-slaught. Yet beyond this little war, the forest was endless, unaffected.

"What are they doing?" asked Radar.

"It's Cabinda," said Ivan, who appeared next to them at the balustrade with his guitar. "It belongs to Angola, but it is not attached to rest of country. Same old story. The Cabindans want to be their own people, but they cannot escape their motherland."

"But why are they shooting?"

Ivan started to strum his guitar. *"Ooo-ooo-ooo, Ju-lia, she split me in two, Ju-lia,"* he sang.

"Would you cut that racket!" The captain's voice came from above. His head appeared in silhouette over the bridgewing. "Quit that singing! Respect this night. *Du calme, du calme.*"

Ivan abruptly fell silent. They were left with only the sound of the man-of-war's cannons caressing the darkness and the great silence that echoed from the country beyond.

AFTER WAITING THREE DAYS in the open ocean, they were finally given the crackly go-ahead to enter the mouth of the Congo. The *Aleph* turned, her en-gines fired, steam was applied to valve, and into the continent she went. At Banana Station, they picked up a pilot to help them run the river, but they were barely three miles upstream when a second transmission came over the wireless, this time from a different man: their permission had been rescinded and they were to turn back at once. It was an inauspicious beginning. Captain Daneri raised an eyebrow, looked at the pilot, and then flipped off the radio.

"We never heard it," he said. "If we did not hear it, it does not exist."

They chugged on. Ivan guided the big ship through a snarl of lush islands that looked untouched by man or beast and around an arcing bend carved from a rise of palisade cliffs. A map of the river lay on the table before him, but he did not consult it, nor did he seek advice from the pilot, who now dozed in a corner. They glided by the old river port of Boma, where they saw a handful of children wave at them from the docks, and then they were passing beneath a large suspension bridge. A truck rumbled across. Such a feat of engineering looked out of place amid all this greenery.

"The next bridge is two thousand kilometers up the Congo," Captain Daneri said as they passed underneath its span. "Two thousand kilometers! No bridges for two thousand kilometers! Write a song about that, Mr. Kovalyov. Write a song about Congo, a country of no bridges."

On the right, the sad squalor of Matadi slid into view: a town built on the promises of the sea and the betrayal of a nation. Corroded petrochemical tanks, the burned-out chassis of an abandoned truck cab, clusters of dusty red-roofed shacks rising up into the hills. A dog scratched itself on the riverbank, taking no notice of their arrival.

But arrived they had. Radar stood on the bridgewing, agape at their proximity to what before had only been an idea. This idea had now become a place, though the place felt like a pale imitation of the idea.

"Welcome to Africa," said Lars. "It is the beginning of the end."

"NOW THAT WE ARE HERE," announced Otik, "I can inform you this was also the worst two weeks of my life."

The three of them had been standing on the crumbling docks of Matadi for almost an hour. Before disembarking, they had all donned the bright yellow polyester tracksuit of Kirkenesferda. With one leg in the bottoms, Radar had realized his tracksuit had in fact been meant for his father. He had wanted to disappear then and weep for everything that was and wasn't anymore. But the other two were already waiting for him, so he zipped up the jacket, put on his graffitied trucker's hat—which, as fate would have it, was also yellow—and followed them off the ship and down the gangplank.

"There were some low points," admitted Radar. "But we made it."

"I have lived through war, bombing, everything," said Otik. "And I will never get on another boat again."

"We're getting on another boat, Otik," said Lars.

"Nope. I will walk. I don't care how far it is. I will walk until my legs break off, and then I will crawl."

They stood in a cluster, like a group of cheerleaders with no team to cheer. Radar was still buzzing with the notion that he was actually in a place that could not be called New Jersey. Occasionally, embarrassed that someone might hear him, he would sing under his breath, *"Af-frik-a,"* in what was no doubt a highly dubious accent.

Shortly after their arrival, Captain Daneri had disappeared into the town, along with most of his Russian crew, save for two young sour-faced seamen left on watch. The captain had given no word of explanation or instruction. After such an ungracious exit, Radar wondered if they would ever see him again.

The day wheezed away like a deflated balloon. The sun slinked quickly behind the hills, leaving the river valley in uncertain shadow. The *Aleph,* a modest vessel in Newark Bay, here dominated the quay, leaving room for only one small feeder boat from South Africa, the *Colonel Joll,* which looked as if it had been here for some time. Unlike in the frenetic ports they had visited before now, there was no movement to get the dozen or so rusting gantry cranes to begin unloading the *Aleph*'s cargo. Radar was not sure what, if anything, was to be unloaded besides themselves.

"So what happens now?" he asked finally.

"We wait," said Lars.

The great river flowed by them, carrying all and carrying nothing. A slight breeze brought the scent of burning down from the hills and into the river valley. Radar, despite having stable land beneath his feet for the first time in days, felt as if he were sinking.

Finally, a sweaty man in a beige uniform approached. He looked very, very tired.

"Vos papiers?" he said, although he did not look at them as he said this, but rather at a stain on the dock next to their feet.

Lars handed the man a bulging manila folder with all of their paperwork. He had spent months obtaining the requisite visas, permits, and transport permissions from various consulates, embassies, and government officials. What he could not obtain he had forged. He had even invented several Congolese intelligence officials who had given *"Le théâtre de Kirkenesferda carte blanche absolue"* to pass anywhere within the Democratic Republic of Congo unmolested. These papers contained many official seals. Radar thought it was impressive work.

The man glanced through the folder very quickly. Evidently, he was not impressed.

"Y'a un problème avec vos papiers," he said.

"Quel problème?" Lars asked. His French was impeccable. *"Tout est là."*

"Y'a beaucoup de problèmes."

"Beaucoup?"

"Beaucoup de problèmes," the man confirmed.

"Mais ça n'est pas possible."

"Vous devez venir avec moi."

"Mais que faire de notre conteneur?" Lars called after him, pointing at the boat.

"Il ne bouge pas." The man turned and began walking toward a small, windowless building. What he said was true: the container did not appear to be going anywhere.

THE HARBORMASTER'S OFFICE WAS air-conditioned, but the air conditioner was not working very well. It would make a horrible chattering noise and then proceed to die a dramatic death before repeating the process all over again. The harbormaster took no notice. His desk was covered in a stack of large leatherbound ledgers. The office was completely empty except for the desk and a yellowing poster of the president tacked to the wall. There was no place to sit, so they stood.

The harbormaster selected one of the ledgers from the bottom of the stack and began to write in an entry.

"Qu'est ce qu'il y a dans votre conteneur?" the man asked without looking up.

Lars cleared his throat. *"C'est indiqué sur le papier."* He pointed at the folder on the desk.

The man stopped writing. *"Quel papier?"*

Lars sighed. *"Props. Des décors de théâtre,"* he said. *"Nous sommes des artistes."*

The man resumed writing. *"Il y a un problème. Vous n'avez pas le permis nécessaire."*

"Le permis est là." Lars pointed again at the manila envelope. *"Tout était arrangé avant. Je vais vous montrer."*

"Avant, ce n'est pas maintenant."

"Et c'est quand, maintenant?"

"Ce permis est périmé. Il n'est pas valide."

"What is he saying?" Otik asked.

Lars rubbed his beard. "He's saying he wants some money. *Un encouragement.*"

At this, the harbormaster looked up. His cell phone began to ring. Radar recognized the ringtone as a popular song, but he could not place the title or the artist. All he knew was that the song was sung by a sexy black woman in tall boots. Ana Cristina would know who she was. He longed for her then. Why couldn't she just be here? They would go find a bar and share an ice-cold Coca-Cola. Maybe a Diet Coke if she preferred. They would talk about this woman in tall boots. They would talk about many things.

The harbormaster began to speak loudly into his cell phone and stride around his office, gesturing like a conductor. Radar understood that much of this show was for their sake. When he finally hung up, the phone immediately rang again. He answered and repeated his performance. They waited, watching as this man spoke rapidly in his native tongue. Though his demeanor was aggressive, he was not angry; he appeared perfectly content with this exhibition of verbal combat conducted through his small device. After a long while, he hung up. The phone immediately rang again, but he made a great show of not answering it, throwing it into a drawer before sitting down at his desk.

"Vous comprenez?" he said.

"Je comprends," said Lars. *"Combien pour le permis requis?"*

The man was searching the drawers of his desk. *"Vous avez de la chance que je vous aide. J'ai le formulaire ici."*

"Combien?" repeated Lars.

"Eh bien . . ." said the man. *"Mille dollars."*

Otik snorted. "He is full of shit," he muttered. It was nice to see him back to his old self.

"How much does he want?" whispered Radar.

Lars reached into his pocket and took out a little roll of money. He placed four battered American twenty-dollar bills on the desk.

"*Voici, quatre-vingts. C'est tout.*"

The harbormaster considered this meager pile of money as if it were an insect. He paused, then reached out and took the bills.

"*D'accord.*"

Radar watched as the man filled out the form with great care. Stamping and counterstamping both the back and the front. If this was a bribe, it was an elaborate, well-documented bribe.

"*Dans notre pays, la forme triomphe de tout,*" the man declared. "*Nous avons appris cela des colons.*"

He had become quite cheerful as he showed them outside. It was already dark. Captain Daneri and the crew were still nowhere to be found.

Lars turned to the harbormaster. "*Qui est responsable des trains, ici? Nous devons envoyer notre conteneur à Kinshasa.*"

"*Ils sont morts.*"

"*Mort? Qui est mort? Les hommes ou les trains?*"

"*Tout est mort,*" the harbormaster said, and he smiled in the way a man smiles when he knows more than he says but does not know how to say it. He bade them goodnight and walked off into the darkness.

7

Without anything else to do, they returned to the ship. Lars asked one of the pimpled seamen on watch where they might find the captain.

"*Ya pokhozh na suku?*" The youth smirked. Apparently, he did not know.

They were about to retire down to their den of bird parts for the evening when they heard a whistle coming from the docks.

"HELLO! WELCOME TO AFRICA! HELLO!"

They looked over the bulwark and saw a thin black man waving at them. He was dressed in a simple white tunic.

"Are you speaking to us?" said Lars.

"AFRICA IS THE FUTURE! AFRICA LOVES YOU!"

"Is he speaking to us?" asked Lars.

"YOUR CAPTAIN!" the man said from below. "YOU ARE LOOKING FOR YOUR CAPTAIN?"

"You know where he is?" Lars called down.

"Of course," said the man. "Your captain is my friend. He is at the Hôtel Metropole. Everyone is at the Metropole. I will take you there."

The man's name was Horeb. He was a Muslim. They knew this because these were the first two things he said when they came down off the ship.

"My name is Horeb. I am a Muslim," he said. "I love all people."

"Well, I am atheist," said Otik. "I hate most people."

"It is fate that we met!" cried Horeb, hugging each of them. "How do you like Africa?"

"We haven't seen much of it," said Lars. "Mostly the docks."

"The river's very big," said Radar.

"The river gives life."

"It's beautiful," said Radar, trying to be complimentary.

"Of course. Africa is the most beautiful place in the world. And Congo is the most beautiful place in Africa," said Horeb. He took a step back. "Are you a football team from Europe? No. You are too fat to be a football player. Maybe you are the coach?"

Radar remembered that they were still wearing their matching yellow tracksuits.

"Maybe we should change," he said.

"We do not change," spat Otik. "It is beginning."

"You can take us to the Metropole?" said Lars.

"I can take you anywhere you want, my friends."

Horeb led them to a motorcycle with a small rickshaw lashed to the back by several unsteady-looking cables. They piled into the cart, though Otik took up most of the seat by himself.

"Okay?" said Horeb. He kicked the motorcycle into gear. The engine coughed and spat and then settled into an uneasy putter.

"The fuel is no good here," he said. "They have huge tanks of pure petrol right there, but do we get any? No. It is shipped far away."

"You're from around here?" Lars called up to him.

"I was born in Yaoundé. My father was from Cameroon. My mother was Senegalese, but she was born in Paris. I moved to Matadi when I was ten. In that time, there used to be many more Muslims here. Not anymore. My brother moved to Gabon three years ago. He became frustrated with Congo."

"So you are Cameroonian? Or Congolese?"

"I am African. Most Congolese don't think of themselves as Africans anymore. They only think about their tribe or their town. Or maybe their parents' families. But this is a real problem. We must have a global mind. Only when we stick together will we defeat the forces against us."

"What forces are against you?"

"I fill my moto with dirty petrol, and the tanks are right there. This is a case of bad management. This is a failure of vision. This is a form of warfare on the people," said Horeb as he drove out of the marina. "Tell me, why do you think Islam has been so successful? Muhammad taught us to believe in *universal* humanity. It is not about being from Saudi Arabia or from Egypt or Tanzania. It is about being blessed with life. Africa is blessed with life."

"Africa is blessed with many things—some good, some not so good," yelled Lars against the sound of the engine. "It's a big place."

"Congo is a big place. They call it *le serpent à deux têtes*—'the snake with two heads.' Kinshasa in the west and Kivu in the east. But nothing connects the two. No roads, no trains, only the forest and the river. It's a big place, but people's heads are small. They cannot see past their village, so they turn inside, you understand?"

They wove through the darkened streets. They passed a bar, Chez Maman, with blinking Christmas lights overhead. Loud dance music was blaring from within. People watched them as they went by, but Horeb took no notice. He pointed out the buildings.

"That is the old tourist office. They used to have so many tourists here. *L'entrée de l'afrique,* they called it. And this was where they came . . . That is one of the banks, but it is closed now because they ran out of money . . . That is a Greek restaurant that used to be very good, but now it is very expensive and very bad . . . That is the church. It is the most important place in this town besides the petrol tanks. This is a Christian country now. People must believe in something. When you go to sleep hungry, you must believe in something so that you have a reason to wake up in the morning."

Horeb stopped in front of a statue of a nearly naked man, a quarry hammer lifted above his head.

"He is the African Worker," he said, pointing at the statue. "He built the railroad. Notice his hammer. It is always raised, but it will never come down."

"What do you do when you are not driving us around?" asked Otik.

"I am lifting my hammer," said Horeb. "But it will not come down."

A group of men approached Horeb's motorcycle. They quickly closed around it, placing their hands on the back of the bike and the canopy of the cart. Two of them began to argue with Horeb animatedly, pointing at the three of them sitting in the cart. Horeb shook his head and spat something back. He pushed one of the men away. The man pointed at Radar and then pointed at his own eye. Horeb revved the motor and nosed the bike through their midst. He waved for them to get out of the way. One of the men gripped the cart and started to jog alongside them. Radar thought the man would jump in and possibly kill him, but at the last moment Horeb accelerated and the man yelled and finally let go.

"What was all that about?" asked Lars when they were finally free.

"People don't understand," Horeb shouted back at them. "Everyone wants something, but they don't understand that today is not the last day. There are many last days to come."

L'HÔTEL METROPOLE was a three-story triangular stone building, an impressive colonial edifice whose elegance had dimmed over the years into a kind of ersatz melancholy; the place now felt like a theater set of itself.

"How much do we owe you for the ride?" asked Lars as they extricated themselves from the cart.

"What?" said Horeb, looking shocked.

"For the ride, how much?"

"Oh no," he said. "You have given *me* the gift. Let me show you inside."

Otik and Lars shared a look, but then they followed Horeb through the musty lobby into a large, open courtyard circumscribed by three walls. Inside this piazza was another world, completely removed from the dusty, squalid town that surrounded it. Against a backdrop of potted palm fronds, a mustached man in tails was playing ragtime at a piano that had no top. A white poodle sat by his feet. The floor of the piazza was tiled in a checkerboard pattern, and in the middle of the courtyard a little fountain bubbled away. There were a dozen or so candlelit tables draped in linen, each set for a full meal. The tables were all empty except for one cluster of patrons toward the back. Among them Radar saw Captain Daneri and several people he didn't recognize.

As they approached, Captain Daneri spotted them and leaped to his feet. His face was glowing.

"Ah, welcome, welcome! Have you been exercising?" he said, seeing their outfits.

"We have not," said Lars sharply.

"Never mind then, never mind. *Estaba bromeando*."

"We weren't sure where you'd gone."

"Here, of course. The Metropole. It's my old haunt. Just imagine this place in its heyday," he said, gesturing. "I don't like to spend much of my time on land, but if I had to choose one place besides my home, it would be here. I've lost many a night in this hotel. But come over, *come over*."

The captain eased them past the fountain. "Everyone, allow me to introduce *miei passeggeri*. They are theater—" He clapped a hand to his mouth. "They are here on official business—the nature of which I cannot disclose."

Radar, terrified, looked over at Lars. He wondered if Lars knew that it was he who had given away the nature of their mission. But if Lars was perturbed, his face revealed nothing.

The captain gestured at a strange, withered man with incredibly pasty skin, who, despite the time of night, was wearing a sun hat and dark glasses. A folded parasol rested against his chair.

"May I present Brother Ireneo Funes. He is—"

"Professor," said the man, in a strange, high-pitched voice. "I'm no longer in the order."

There was something wrong with the man's skin. It was stretched thin and almost translucent, as if two or three sizes too small. It reminded Radar a bit of Mikey Melange, the cart collector at the Stop & Shop, who had been burned badly in an auto accident as a child and spoke in a husky whisper.

"Of course, apologies," said Daneri. "Professor Funes is from Uruguay, I am sad to tell you, though he does much to reverse one's impression of that vulgar country. He's a collector of rare books."

"All books," corrected the professor. "Rare or otherwise."

"Yes, rare or otherwise," repeated Daneri. He swiveled his attention. "And this, of course, is the very rare and very lovely Mademoiselle Yvette Michel."

She was lovely indeed. Her short blond hair was covered in a sparkling blue headband, and a thin, lemon-colored evening frock hung from her shoulders. The headband and the dress belonged to another time, but on her it belonged only to this time.

"*Enchantée,*" she said, blinking through a tendril of cigarette smoke. In the candlelight, the color of her eyes was somewhere between blue and green, like the color of the sea on a cloudy day. She smiled and then frowned ever so slightly, and such a juxtaposition managed to convey both an innocence and a knowledge that this place, this evening, this hotel, this world, had been constructed as a stage for her and her alone. Radar could not tear his eyes away from her.

When no one filled the silence, she said, in a velvety French accent, "I like men who dress the same. It is why I married a lieutenant."

"And why did you marry him and not me?" cried a round-faced man with long, sweaty hair.

"*Parce que vous êtes une bête sauvage.*"

Everyone seemed to think this was very funny.

"Yes, this *bête sauvage* is Fabien," said Captain Daneri. "He runs the hotel. Or tries to run the hotel."

"The hotel runs itself," said Fabien. "I just complain."

"Fabien's family came here just after Lord Stanley, isn't that right?"

"My great-great-grandfather was Camille Janssen, governor general of the Congo Free State. He was one of the first assholes from Belgium to arrive on African soil. And now I am one of the last Belgian assholes on African soil, at your service."

"You give yourself too much credit, Fabien," said the captain.

"It's a common habit of an asshole."

"Well, sit, sit," the captain said to his guests. "Join us. We're drinking sixty-year-old Courvoisier."

"The cognac is older than the nation," noted Fabien.

"Fabien also has a legendary cellar of French wine that would be the envy of any restaurant in Paris," said Captain Daneri. "What would you like?"

"I'll try the famous cognac, thank you," said Lars.

"I will have water," said Otik.

"Don't be a fool," said the captain.

"I will have cognac," said Otik.

"Me as well," said Radar.

He had never had cognac before. It had always sounded like a cleaning product to him, something to rid the bathtub of its rings. But if Lars was trying it, then he would, too.

"And some food, if you have any," said Lars. "We didn't get a chance to eat."

"Of course!" said the captain. "Fabien, can we arrange *un petit dîner* for my guests?"

Fabien snapped at a waiter and gave him a series of rapid instructions in French.

"So tell me, what is with these outfits?" asked the captain, who was wearing his crisp commodore whites. "They make you look like American gangster rappers."

"It's not true," said Yvette. "I think they're very handsome."

Daneri held up his hands. "I yield to her opinion on such matters, of course, but I think they are an odd choice to travel in. You are like a women's volleyball team."

"Are you really in the theater?" Yvette asked Lars, leaning forward.

Lars blinked. The question hung in the air. Radar braced himself. He wanted to run from the courtyard. Horeb could moto him to some faraway place so he would never have to see these people again. He was tired of not saying what he shouldn't and guessing what others were thinking of him. He wanted to go back to his little radio station and tend his frequency, free from the burden of face-to-face contact.

"Yes," said Lars. "We are performers."

"And what do you perform?" asked Yvette.

It was clear that she expected answers to her questions. Radar could sense in her a lifetime of getting answers.

"We . . ." Lars stopped.

Otik broke the silence.

"We," he said, gesturing to the three of them, "are the most famous group you have never heard of and will never hear of."

"Really?" said Yvette. "But I just heard of you."

"After tonight you will never know us again," said Otik.

"*C'est une prédiction.*"

The waiter arrived with a tray of snifter glasses. The cognac that was older than the nation was carefully poured into each, snifted, swirled. The scent of time's density.

Captain Daneri raised his glass. "To the most famous group we have never heard of and will never hear of again."

"Hear, hear," said Fabien, sipping at the Courvoisier. "*Eh bien, ça y est.*"

"So may I ask how your adoring audience finds you?" asked Yvette.

"They don't," said Otik. "We have no audience. This is whole point."

"So what you're saying is that it's impossible for me to see one of your shows."

"Correct."

"But it's a pity, isn't it?"

Lars tapped Otik's shoulder. "What Otik means is that our shows occur in a very particular time and space. The staging itself is the art form. They aren't meant to be seen—they're meant to happen."

"If you ask me," said Fabien, "it sounds like a lot of bullshit."

"*Oh, chut, mon chéri.* No one asked you," intoned Yvette. She turned to face Lars. "Pardon me for asking—I have only been to the theater a very few times—but doesn't a show depend upon the relationship between the actors and the audience? Like a *connection.* This is the whole reason for the performance, yes?"

"This is one school of philosophy," said Lars. "That there must be a witness for a performance to exist in the first place. I think for us, the notion of audience is not limited to a group of people sitting in chairs, watching the stage. The universe can also be an observer. The atoms, the quarks, the elemental bonds—all of these can pay witness to the show. There are many ways to alter the course of time."

"*Tu entends ça? Quelles conneries!*" said Fabien.

"*La mécanique quantique sonne souvent comme des conneries pour les personnes sans instruction,*" said Lars.

"You speak French well," said Yvette.

"You speak English well," said Lars.

"I learned it from watching Hollywood movies." She smiled. "Bogart and Bacall are my teachers."

The waiter returned with three steaming plates of food.

"This is grilled catfish with a local vegetable called *tshitekutaku* and cassava cakes, which they call *fufu*," said Fabien. "I thought you might like an introduction to native cuisine. If you don't like it, I will have the chef killed instantly."

"Thank you," said Lars. "That's a lot of pressure."

"We don't do things softly in this country," said Fabien. "It is either the best or the worst. There is no in-between."

"Yes, thank you," said Radar. "It looks wonderful. Please don't kill the cook."

"May I ask how many of these shows you have done so far?" said Yvette as the plates were served.

"Since 1944, there have been four," said Lars. "This will be the fifth."

"*Oh la!* It *is* a true event!" She clapped her hands. "And I suppose you can't tell me where you plan on performing?"

"I'm afraid not," said Lars, taking a bite of his food. "If the show was expected by its viewers, this would change the nature of the performance, you see."

"I do see." She smiled. "Can you at least give me the title? That can't hurt, can it? I promise I won't tell. Will you tell, Fabien?"

Fabien made a fart sound with his mouth.

"This is delicious, by the way," said Radar.

"Good. I'm glad you like it," said Fabien. "I will spare the chef. This time only."

Lars was chewing his *fufu* thoughtfully.

"It's called *The Conference of the Birds*," he said finally.

This was news to Radar.

"Like Attar's poem," said Professor Funes, who had not said a word all evening.

"You know it?" said Lars.

"I'm familiar."

"Professor Funes is familiar with most things," said Captain Daneri.

"Well, do tell," said Yvette. "What is it?"

Funes sipped at his cognac. He tilted his head, as if recalling a distant memory, and then began to speak in his peculiar, high-pitched lilt. "*Mantiq al-Tayr* was written by Farid ud-Din Attar in 1177. Attar himself was not a Sufi . . . but one could say he was heavily *influenced* by the non-dualistic transient spiritualism of Sufism, and this is reflected in his poem."

"Non-dualistic transitory—what is this?" said Fabien.

The professor recoiled at the question.

"You don't know how much your query pains me," he said wearily. "I am trying to deliver you the part, when every atom in my being strains to deliver you the whole."

"*Chut,* Fabien, don't distract him," said Yvette. "Tell us about the poem, Professor. The poem—we want to hear about the poem."

Funes cleared his throat. "I assume you want me to summarize . . . I have learned that this is what most people mean when they say they want to hear of something. Or do you want me to recite the poem itself? It's over forty-five hundred lines long with both prologue and epilogue."

"Correct, Professor," said Daneri. "A summary is in order."

"I would love to hear him recite it," said Lars. "I haven't heard it aloud before."

"You don't know who you're dealing with," growled Daneri. He turned to the little man, whose impossibly pale skin had become flushed and blotchy. "Professor, there will be time to recite it later. For now, a précis; the night is still young."

The professor nodded, coughed into his hand, and began to speak stiffly, as if from a memorized script: "The poem begins with a conference of the birds. They are kingless. The hoopoe stands up and says to those congregated, 'We are not kingless; we do have a king. He is Simurgh. They found one of his feathers in China, and from the majesty of this single feather, rumors have spread throughout the land of his utter magnificence.' The birds are enchanted . . . They want to see their king. But the hoopoe warns them that the path to the Simurgh is fraught with great peril and many dangers. And so, hearing this, the birds begin to come up with excuses for why they can't go on the journey. The nightingale says she is in love with the rose and cannot go; the parrot says his beauty has caused him to be caged; the falcon says he already has a master;

the duck says he cannot be far from water . . . and so on. These are the excuses of life. To each of the doubters, the hoopoe delivers a story, slowly convincing them through his tales that to *not* find Simurgh would be to live a life without meaning . . . to exist without existence. And so, reluctantly, the birds agree to seek out their king."

"It sounds to me as if the hoopoe is their king," said Fabien. "He's the one giving orders."

"The hoopoe gives no orders . . . The hoopoe is the storyteller. He shows them the way by describing those who have denied themselves spiritual fulfillment, those who have lusted after fame, wealth, bodily delights. But he gives no orders . . . The hoopoe is the poet, the guide."

"What is a king but a rotten man with a good story?"

"Go on," said Yvette. "Don't listen to Fabien. He's still mad I didn't marry him."

The professor, looking quite annoyed, gathered himself and again took up the script: "On their way to see their king, the birds pass through seven valleys, each presenting a series of challenges to the flock. First they must pass through the Valley of the Quest, where they see, for the first time, the impossibility of the task laid out before them. Some birds turn back here, others die from fright, but most press on. From there, they enter the Valley of Love, where they confront the dangers of passion. More birds burn up, seethe with lust, or fall under the trance of beauty. Then they enter the Valley of Understanding, where they realize the limits of worldly comprehension—that knowledge is nothing but stones in the palm."

"But do you agree?" said Fabien.

"With what?" said the professor curtly.

"That knowledge is stones in the palm."

"I'm recounting the poem for our guests. It's not for me to comment on the truth of its content. Were I to spend my life commenting on the world that I see, I would never see the world."

"I would just think you would have an issue with such a characterization given your—"

"Fabien, arrêtez-vous! Personne n'aime un trouble-fête."

Funes smiled, slightly. "Soon you'll be nothing but a memory," he said to Fabien.

"The poem, Professor, *please*. What happens in the poem?" ordered Yvette.

He continued, briskly now: "From here the birds, greatly diminished already, pass through the Valley of Independence and Detachment, where they realize the smallness of all things . . . then the Valley of Unity, where they realize the sameness of all things . . . then the Valley of Astonishment and Bewilderment, where they confront the true glory of God's creation. And finally, the Valley of Poverty and Nothingness, where they realize that for all that they have realized, they realize nothing . . . They themselves are nothing. Along the way, many birds perish in any number of ways: they are eaten, frozen, drowned, starved, maimed . . . They die of hunger, heat, madness, and thirst. Of the thousands and thousands that began the journey, only thirty birds make it past the Valley of Nothingness. They step out of this valley, beaten and exhausted, their spirits drained, and they step into the realm of the Simurgh. They are desperate to finally lay eyes upon their king, whom they have traveled so far too see . . . but instead they meet only the Simurgh's herald, who tells them to wait by a lake. This is almost too much to bear for the exhausted birds. They wail and complain, but wait they must, and as they wait, filled with self-pity and contempt for this Simurgh who makes them wait, they stare into the lake. And in this lake they see their reflections: thirty birds, thirty reflections. And then they realize: the Simurgh is them. *Si-murgh* in Persian means 'thirty birds' . . . Their divine leader is within them."

"It's beautiful," whispered Yvette.

"Africa must find its Simurgh," a voice said.

The table turned as one. Horeb was standing only a few feet away. In the candlelight, dressed in his tunic, he resembled a prophet. The sight was startling.

"*Casse toi, bicot!*" growled Fabien.

"He's with us," said Lars.

"You know him?"

"He's our hoopoe," said Lars.

"I am their hoopoe, *monsieur,*" said Horeb. He looked as if he would say more, but then he bowed slightly and receded back into the shadows.

"Well, I think it's a lovely story and will make a perfect play," said Yvette. She raised her glass. "To the thirty birds."

The glasses came together. Clinked, receded. Above them, the night remained.

"What do you think of all this?" Yvette said.

Radar realized she was speaking to him.

"Me?"

"Yes, are you the silent member of the troupe? Harpo to your two brothers? He was always my favorite Marx Brother." She crossed her eyes and puffed out her cheeks and somehow was all the more lovely for doing so.

"Well, I . . ." he stammered.

"What I want to know," the captain interrupted, "is why *puppets*? We had a puppet theater in Buenos Aires, and I'll tell you, it made me deathly afraid as a child. I think they enjoyed frightening children. They had a wolf puppet that gave me nightmares for years. I've seen real wolves, and none was as frightening as the wolf puppet."

Radar felt Lars staring at him.

"Do you know how we might get our container on the next train to Kinshasa?" said Lars. His voice had grown hard.

Daneri sensed his intrusion. He held up his hands.

"Don't look at me," he said. "I'm just a simple man of the sea."

"There hasn't been a train to Kinshasa in ten years," said Fabien. "There are small trees growing between the tracks now. The locomotive is stopped somewhere between here and Songololo. Trains require maintenance, oversight, money. We don't have any of that here."

"So then how do we get our cargo to Kinshasa?" asked Lars.

"By truck. Like everyone else. The road's pretty good except where the rains have washed it away."

Lars considered this. "And who do we talk to about renting a truck?"

"I'm going that way," said Professor Funes.

Daneri snapped his fingers. He pointed at Radar. "Remember I told you about my friend who orders the books? It's him. He's the keeper of the great library."

"If we can fit both containers on the bed of the lorry, I'll take you," said the professor.

"You will?" Lars's eyes brightened. "That would be amazing."

"But no guarantees," said the professor. "The Mitsubishi has seen better days."

"Haven't we all?" said Fabien.

"Of course," said Lars. Then, to Funes: "We're grateful for whatever you can provide."

The professor dabbed a handkerchief against his lips. "I have a small barge just north of Kinshasa. I load up there and then head up the river. But I can drop you in the city or wherever you'd like."

Lars and Otik looked at each other.

"We'll go upriver with you as far as you can take us and then figure out the rest," said Lars.

"But you don't know how far I'm going," said the professor.

"Wherever you're going, we're going farther."

"Oh, a clue!" shouted Yvette. "I *love* clues!"

"I'm leaving first thing tomorrow," said Funes. "Or as soon as I can get those fools to unload the books off your boat."

"Good luck with that," Daneri chuckled. "Work seems to be optional around here."

"It's frowned upon," said Fabien. "If the sun still comes up whether I work or not, then why make the effort?"

Daneri turned to Radar. "Africa," he said, "will make you lose your mind."

"*Mon chéri,* you cannot blame this on Africa," said Yvette. "A man will always lose his mind, no matter where he is."

THEY FINISHED THEIR FOOD, and the plates were cleared. The last of the cognac was savored and dispensed with. Fabien disappeared into his famous cellar and came out with a rifle and three bottles of a vintage Bordeaux, a bottle of

Johnnie Walker Gold, and a metal canteen of some local gin that smelled and
tasted of gasoline.

"*Mais pourquoi le fusil,* Fabien?" implored Yvette.

"*Parce que je suis ton protecteur.*"

At some point, the piano player stopped playing familiar medleys and
seemed to devolve into experimental free jazz. The poodle shifted positions.
Captain Daneri told them a long story about an island off Argentina inhabited
only by women who never aged. At one point a glass was thrown across the
courtyard into the fountain for emphasis.

Fabien waved it away.

"I own this place. I can do what I want," he said, and with that, he stood up
and shot his rifle into the air. Roosting birds fluttered away. The shot echoed
across the courtyard. Lights turned on. A woman stuck her head out the window.

"*Qu'est-ce qui se passe?*"

"*Tout va bien. Retournez vous coucher! Allez, au lit!*" shouted Fabien angrily.

After his sixth or seventh drink, Radar began to lose the sensation in his
fingertips. The night expanded, contracted. The courtyard became all court-
yards that were, that would be.

Sometime past midnight, Otik and Lars announced that they had to be getting back to the boat.

"But why?" moaned Daneri. "Where else would you rather be than here?"

"Tomorrow is another day," said Lars. He turned to Fabien. "*Merci pour la
nourriture et les boissons.*"

"*Merci pour les conneries.*"

"Professor Funes." Lars bowed. "We'll see you at the docks tomorrow. We
sleep on the ship, so we'll be ready whenever you are."

As if by magic, Horeb had materialized again from the shadows.

Yvette turned to Radar. "Are you going with them?"

Radar stood up, slamming his knee into the table. The multitude of glass-
ware shuddered.

"Sorry," he said. "I probably should."

"Oh, don't," she said. "The morning's still not for a long time."

Radar looked at Lars, who raised his hands and said, "It's your choice. We're going, though."

"If it's all right, then, I think I'll stay," said Radar.

"Of course you'll stay," said Daneri. "That's a good lad."

"Whatever you want," said Lars. "But when the truck leaves, we leave. We don't wait."

"Don't worry," said Daneri. "We'll get him back to you in one piece."

At some point, the last of the wine was finished. As if on cue, the man at the piano stopped playing abruptly in the middle of one of his long, spastic compositions. He dramatically threw a sheet over the topless piano and then nodded, formally. Daneri, and Daneri alone, stood up and gave him a long, loud standing ovation. The poodle followed the piano player as he exited stage left.

"It's all so bloody brilliant," said Daneri, collapsing back into his chair.

Radar was just beginning to wonder why he had not gone home with the others when a figure appeared in the courtyard. It was Ivan.

"Ivan!" he cried, waving with both hands. "We're over here."

Radar could not remember when he'd last been so glad to see someone.

"Hello, Radar," said Ivan.

"Yvette, Yvette, Yvette," Radar said. "This is Ivan. He can sing. You should hear him sing. He knows everything about the stars. He's the most amazing person in the world."

"*Quels compliments,*" said Yvette. "*Enchantée.*"

"Madame." Ivan kissed her hand. "*Nous nous sommes déjà rencontrés.*"

"*Vraiment?*"

"*Ça fait quelques années.*"

"*And* he speaks French," said Radar. "So that's true."

"How did your business go?" grunted Daneri.

"What business?" said Radar. "What business, Ivan?"

"Your friend has interests in town. Do you want to tell them, Ivan?"

"This town is no good," said Ivan. "It's dying."

"Careful, Mr. Kovalyov. We're with the locals."

"We're not locals." Fabien lit a cigarette. "You act surprised. This town has been dying a long time. It's our hobby to die. We quite enjoy it."

"Fabien, don't be rude," said Yvette. "They will never come back."

"They'll come back. They are vultures. They pick at the body. Why else would they be here?"

"For a woman," said Daneri.

"We're here to do a show with birds," slurred Radar. He put his hand over his mouth, but it was already too late.

"Yes, tell us more, my little Harpo," said Yvette. "Your friends are so mysterious. What is this all for? And what's this about *puppets*? What are you *really* doing here?"

Radar gazed across the table at her.

"All of us came here not by choice, you know," she said. "No one comes here by choice."

"I come here by choice," said Daneri.

"Vanushka, get him to say something," Yvette cooed to Ivan. "Tell him we want to know the truth."

Everyone was looking at Radar. His head was spinning.

"Excuse me, please," he said.

He got up from the table and began to walk. He was not sure where he was going, but he knew he must leave. He slid through a pair of palm fronds and then up a staircase. There were voices behind him, but he did not stop. Soon he found himself in a long hallway of rooms. He walked past a door that had a little figure made of sticks hanging on it. He stopped, his skin bristling. He raised his hand to knock.

"They haven't been back in a long time," a voice said. "They haven't claimed their things."

It was the piano player and his dog. They were entering a room down the hall.

"Who is it?" said Radar.

"I never knew their names. A man and a woman. They left some time ago. Fabien won't rent it out, though. He keeps it for them. Not that he *could* rent it out. No one comes here anymore."

Radar stood there, swaying.

"I like your dog," he said. "What's his name?"

"Pascal," the man said, and disappeared into his room.

Radar followed the hallway, running his palm along the walls. He found another staircase and went up and up until he came to a door. He assumed that the door would be locked, but when he tried the handle it opened, and he found himself in the cool open air of the rooftop. It reminded him of the deck of the ship. He looked out across the city and saw the *Aleph* lit up at the docks. Suddenly, he desperately wanted to be back there. The ship had become his home now. He could barely remember New Jersey.

One half of the roof was taken up by a giant billboard, illuminated by two large fluorescent lights that buzzed into the night. Insects swirled and dived around the lights in a frenzy. Radar walked over to the front of the billboard and saw a giant smiling man in a tie, talking on a mobile phone. PARLEZ À L'AFRIQUE! PARLEZ AU MONDE! declared the sign to the citizens of Matadi. Radar stepped forward to the edge of the roof. Normally he was terrified of heights, but he felt very calm. He looked down to the street below. He thought he saw Horeb in his white tunic, waiting by his motorcycle.

He placed his toe against the ledge, felt the spot where the building ended and the air began. He knew that if he jumped he would survive. This would not be the way he died—not here, not now, not in a mangled heap next to Horeb's rickshaw. If he jumped, he knew he would get up and walk away from the fall.

"Don't go so close," he heard a woman's voice say behind him.

He turned and saw Yvette standing on the roof. She looked unsteady in her heels. Behind her in the doorway, Ivan appeared. She took a step toward Radar.

"Please, Harpo, *mon chéri,*" she said. "I don't want you to fall."

Instinctively, he inched backwards. Ivan came up beside her.

"Ho," said Ivan. "Come back from the ledge, my friend."

"What's your business here?" Radar said to Ivan.

Ivan took a step forward, and Radar raised his arm by his side, as if he were about to jump.

"Captain Daneri said you had business interests here. What do you do?"

Ivan reached out. "Come back from the edge. You had too much to drink, my friend."

"Please," breathed Yvette. "I don't want you to fall. We only just met."

"What is it?" said Radar again, raising his arm threateningly. "What do you do, Ivan? What did you not tell me?" For an instant he felt himself lose his balance and thought he might actually fall. He flapped his arms, and both Ivan and Yvette flinched before Radar righted himself.

Ivan sighed. He pursed his lips and then looked at the ground.

"I have a child," he said. "I have a little girl. Her mother lives here."

Radar blinked. "What?"

"In one week she will be four," he said. "Her name is Anna, like her grandmother."

Radar took this in. The lights from the billboard buzzed.

"She does not call me her father. For her, she has no father," he said. "I have not earned this, to be her father. It is very hard for me to see her and not to tell her. I can hold her, but I cannot give her what she needs."

No one moved. And then Yvette said quietly, "I had a child. He was taken from me."

She did not say more, and no one asked for more. Then Radar took several steps toward them, and Ivan and Yvette each seized one of his arms. She laughed nervously, and they stood on the roof in silence like this, the scent of burning still around them. The sparse lights of the town beneath, the ship, the river that swallows all rivers, the sky.

Ivan pointed. "It's difficult to see, but there is a star there."

"Where?" said Yvette.

"There." He took her shoulder and pointed. He was pointing with the hand that was missing a pinkie. The absence of the finger somehow made his pointing more precise.

"Alpha Centauri," he said. "It is brightest star in sky. You can only see it here, in the south. I did not see this star until I was eighteen. It was greatest night of my life. I had read about it, but I had never seen it with my own eyes. Seeing it with your eyes changes everything."

They huddled and looked.

"There, do you see? It is brightest."

"Yes, I think so," said Yvette.

"It looks like one star, but it is actually two, Centauri A and Centauri B.

And a little red dwarf named Proxima. All three form star. You can't tell them apart with your eyes."

"Who is little red dwarf?" whispered Yvette, leaning into Radar. "Who is my Proxima? Is it you, Harpo?"

"This is nearest star to us besides our sun," said Ivan. "That light we see is only four years old."

"So young," she murmured.

Radar was staring at the immensity of the sky. "We are really alone, aren't we?" he said.

"Not so alone," said Ivan.

"Come down to my room," said Yvette. "Both of you."

It was not a request. They descended back into the hotel. Yvette's room was decorated with hanging tapestries and various wooden masks. Clothes were draped everywhere, drawers open. A smell of what he realized was her perfume.

"How long have you been here?" asked Radar.

"Long enough," she said.

She fished a record from the shelf and put it on. The vinyl was in bad shape. The dust and scratches could be heard, but the singer was French and sang so beautifully that the three of them sat there in a stunned silence, listening to the little miracles of heartbreak. Then Yvette got up and walked over to the table. She picked up a long tube.

"You don't want any, Vanush?" she said to Ivan.

He shook his head. "I must see the stars."

"You can always see the stars, my love," she said.

All of a sudden, he began to sing. *"Yvette, Yvette, she's loveliest woman I've never met . . ."*

She smiled, clutching the tube to her chest. "Go on," she said.

"Have you two met before?" asked Radar.

"Only once, I promise . . ." said Yvette.

"Someday I'll write song about all this," said Ivan. He shook his head. *"To-night* I will write song about this. Do you have guitar?"

Yvette held out her hands. *"Ma chambre est nue."*

"Okay," he said. "Okay. I will find." He got up and left the room.

Yvette came to Radar and held out her hand. "Come," she said.

"Where did he go?"

"Come."

They parried open the mosquito nets and slinked into bed. She took off Radar's hat and placed it on her head. Even in his drunken haze, he winced, thinking she would be repelled by his baldness, by his tuft, by his Radar-ness. But she only smiled, letting her hand drift down his face before unzipping his jacket and pulling off his undershirt. He was suddenly aware of his skin as a surface that could be touched. She shivered out of her frock and lit a candle by the bedside. He thought of Ana Cristina then. He wondered whether she would be mad or not. It was too late to be mad. It was too late to be anything.

"Have you ever smoked before?" she said. She was wearing his hat and nothing else.

He shook his head, staring into those eyes. What had those eyes seen?

"The flame will bring the smoke to you. Don't breathe too hard. Hold it in. And remember to smile."

She spat on her finger and moistened the tip of the pipe and then brought it to his lips. He shut his eyes and drank in the smoke until his lungs stopped working. When he exhaled, his whole body went up into the ceiling. The smell familiar and not familiar. He had been here before, in this bed, with this woman. He had been here before, but then, he had never been anywhere at all.

"What happened to your husband?" A voice that sounded like his.

Yvette was smoking the pipe. She exhaled, closed her eyes.

"I killed him," she said. She turned and looked at him. "No. It's not true. He walked into the forest and never came back."

The pipe was offered again to Radar. He could barely lift a hand to decline, and so he took more, and the world began to fade.

"I shouldn't," he whispered. "My epilepsy."

"My little Proxima," he heard her say. "Have you ever been with a woman?"

"Yes," he said. Then: "No."

"Would you like to be with a woman?"

He could feel himself sweating. The syrup of his gears.

"There's a girl back home."

"C'est une fille chanceuse."

She came close. He could feel her breath on his neck. He could feel her skin, or the dream of her skin. He opened his eyes briefly, and through the scrim of the mosquito net he saw Pascal, the piano player's dog, watching them.

8

Radar awoke with a start. He blinked at the canopy of mosquito netting above him. A pile of dead insects had pooled in a low spot. The air was thick and damp. His head was pounding. He tried to remember where he was. This could not be New Jersey, could it? He turned and saw her bare shoulder and the night came flooding back.

Shit!

The truck. He was going to miss the truck. *Shit!*

He jumped out of bed, naked, and tried to locate his tracksuit among the jumble of clothes on the floor. There was no sign of Ivan or his guitar.

Yvette stirred in the bed.

"You're leaving?" she murmured.

"I hope," he said. "They might've already left without me."

"They wouldn't," she said, stretching. "They admire you."

He laughed. "Yeah, right."

She wrapped the sheet around herself and put on his trucker's hat.

"Can I keep this?"

He blinked, rubbing his head. "Okay," he said.

"Will you remember me?" she said.

"Yes," he said, jimmying his heel into his shoe. "I don't think I can ever forget."

"Welcome to the Congo, my little Proxima." She leaned in and kissed him. "I hope it's better for you than it has been for me."

He ran through the lobby and out into the street. The rush of morning traffic. Motos and trucks crawling about. A wash of pedestrians, carrying things, selling things. Almost instantly, a crowd of people formed around him.

"Monsieur, diamants? Diamants, monsieur?" The voice was assured, as if they had known each other forever.

"Taxi, caïd? Boss, you need taxi?"

"Croisière de fleuve, monsieur? Très belle, très belle."

"Besoin d'une ceinture?" A little boy held up a stick, from which hung several ratty belts. He was pushed away by another.

"Des cigarettes! Des cigarettes américaines! Authentique!"

"Carottes? Crevettes?" A pot of steaming prawns was thrust into his face.

A gentle hand, pressing at his wrist. *"Des femmes, monsieur? Ladies? Very beautiful . . ."*

Another hissed into his ear: *"Du kif? De la cocaïne? Qu'est ce que vous voulez?"*

He was helpless in the face of their advances. Hands prodded and shoved him, urging him this way and that. Slowly, he was tugged down the street. He was sure he had already agreed to buy hundreds of diamonds, arranged for four taxis, and bought and sold a kilo of cocaine. In the short time he had been outside, he was already a major player in the Matadi import/export scene.

He felt a firm hand on his shoulder and panicked. It was no doubt a police officer, arresting him for his substantial black market dealings. Or maybe it was a rival drug dealer, coming to shoot him for treading on his turf. He turned, fearing the worst.

It was Horeb. *Oh, Horeb! Savior of men!*

"This way," said Horeb, parting the crowd. "Follow me." He yelled something, and the masses began to complain, chastising Horeb for taking their prize. With arms outstretched, he guided Radar to a side street, where his moto awaited.

"Thank you," said Radar. "I didn't know what to say to them."

"There's not much fruit in Congo, so when people see it on the tree, they want to pick it," said Horeb. "Of course if they grew their own fruit, they would have plenty to eat, but conditions make this difficult. We've been taught to make do however we can. It's Article Fifteen."

"Article Fifteen?" Radar grimaced. Now that he was safe in the back of the moto, he could feel the full expanse of his headache. A vast, throbbing tundra. He thought he might be sick.

"A gift from Mobutu," said Horeb, wheeling around the bike. "Article Fifteen is an amendment to our constitution. But it doesn't exist on any paper, only in the mind of the citizen."

"What do you mean?"

"According to Article Fifteen, it's okay to steal a little to get ahead. Not too much, but a little. Because if you do not, you see, your neighbor will. Article Fifteen says that a little corruption is not only expected—it is necessary to survive. Even when Mobutu died, Article Fifteen lived on."

"Do you steal?"

"Stealing is the twenty-third sin in the eyes of God. The thief shall have his hand cut off."

Radar was too tired to point out that Horeb had not answered his question. He settled back into the cart and closed his eyes. He felt exposed and naked without his hat.

"I hope they haven't left," he said.

"You think they would leave without you, my friend? You are one of them."

They arrived at the docks to find a flurry of activity, a stark contrast to the evening before. One of the old gantry cranes was creaking and straining as it lifted *Moby-Dikt* from the hull of the boat. The harbormaster was standing next to Otik and Lars on the docks, watching the crane's progress. Occasionally he would lift his arms and gesticulate, as if giving directions, though no one paid him much attention.

Radar got out of the moto and hurried over to them.

"Sorry I'm late," he said.

"As you can see, you aren't," said Lars. "Things move very slowly in this town. We had to pay our friend here another bribe. *'Des frais de déchargement,'* he claimed. Apparently the first bribe did not cover this fee."

The harbormaster waved his arms. The crane stopped, then started again, belching out thick black smoke.

Captain Daneri emerged on the gangplank of the ship. Next to him was Professor Funes, shaded by a great white parasol. They were deep in conversation, speaking rapidly in Spanish. As they approached, Daneri saw Radar and smiled.

"Our little bird returns! My boy, I heard all about it."

Radar felt himself turning crimson. "Where's Ivan?" he asked quickly.

"Mr. Kovalyov has not been seen this morning. He'll surface. We leave this afternoon, and he does not miss a departure. He, like me, lives to depart."

After some negotiation, it was decided that *Moby-Dikt* would be loaded onto the bed of the tractor-trailer, and the container of books would be bolted on top of this. It was a precarious arrangement, made all the more precarious by the age of the truck. Professor Funes hadn't been kidding. The Mitsubishi looked as if she had been resuscitated from a scrapyard. Many of her parts were in the process of falling off. Yet, like the rest of the country, she endured: when the driver started her engine, there was only the briefest of stutters before she woke up and revved to life. Evidently, she was using the good petrol.

"We must go," said the professor. "It's nine hours to the launch on a good day."

With tears in his eyes, Daneri hugged each of them long and slow, as if he were memorizing the weight of their bodies.

"You're going places where I've never been," he murmured. "I admire you. I admire your course. May we meet again. An honor. *Ustedes son mis héroes.*"

Radar watched as he strode up the ramp.

"If you get lost," the captain called, "you can always follow the water back to the sea." He kissed his fist and then he was gone.

"I like that man," said Otik.

"I thought you hated him," said Radar.

Otik shrugged. "I changed my mind."

There was only room in the truck cab for Professor Funes, his driver, and one more, but Otik and Lars opted to ride in *Moby-Dikt* and continue with their repairs. Time, it seemed, was now of the essence. Radar had just decided that he would join them in the back—not so much to help in the preparations as to sleep off his hangover—when Horeb approached them.

"Pardon me," he said. "But I would like to come with you."

"What?" said Otik, startled. "With us like *how?*"

Horeb bowed. "I would like to be your guide."

Otik exchanged a look with Lars. "Our guide? Who says we need a guide?" he said.

"Last night, you said I was your hoopoe."

"Last night we are saying lots of things. Last night was last night. Just because you give us ride to hotel doesn't mean you are suddenly—"

Lars put a hand on Otik's shoulder.

"Do you know the river?" he asked Horeb.

Horeb shook his head. "I went to university in Kinshasa, but I've never been past there."

"So how would you guide us if you don't know anything?" said Otik.

"I cannot guide you on the river, but I can be your voice. I speak French. I speak Kikongo, Lingala, Kele, and Swahili. And Arabic. And a little Portuguese, too. And I know how to deal with the Congolese mind. The river can be dangerous, not only for the currents but also because of the people who live on it. Some of the villages do not like new faces. This is where I can help you."

"We don't have money, if this is what you want," snapped Otik.

"I don't want money. Allah will provide. I want to help with your show. I'm an actor."

"You're an actor?" said Lars.

"Yes. A very good actor. I've been on television."

"The show has no actors," said Otik.

"Do you have carpentry skills?" asked Lars.

"I have many carpentry skills."

"Can you play the drum?"

"I grew up playing the drum. I learned how to speak on the drum."

"Please, let us confer," said Lars. He gestured for Radar and Otik to join him in conference. Radar was surprised to be included in the quorum and even more surprised when Lars turned to him first.

"What do you think?"

"Me?" said Radar. "I don't know. He sounds like he's telling the truth. I like him. But I don't think I'm a good judge, perhaps. I don't know what you're looking for."

"Otik, what're we looking for?"

"I told you: this is not how we choose our members," said Otik. "We don't even know him. I don't believe he doesn't want money. Everyone wants money."

"How *do* we choose our members? We didn't know Radar."

"Yes, and I lodged formal complaint, if you remember. No offense." He nodded at Radar.

"None taken."

"We have certain standards to uphold," said Otik. "We cannot keep watering group. What about our philosophy? What about Brecht? Artaud?"

"Let's not fool ourselves," said Lars. "A happening is not about what we think before. A happening is about the *happen*."

"Okay, yes, you always say that, but you forget we have planned for ten years to—"

"To what?" said Lars.

Otik was silent.

"This is now," said Lars.

"I know this is now. You don't need to tell me this is now."

"Do we have another tracksuit?" asked Lars.

Otik sighed. "We have another one. There is Thorgen's old suit."

"Radar? What do you think?"

"I say . . . yes. Why not?"

"If we take him, he becomes exactly like us," said Lars. "There's no hierarchy here."

Radar laughed.

"What?"

"I'm just not so sure that's true," he said.

"What do you mean?" said Lars, looking shocked.

"I mean it's you two, then me," he said. "It's not a bad thing, but we're not all equal here."

Otik grabbed him by the shoulders. "Hey. *Hey!*"

"What?"

"*Burazeru,* you must understand. Trust is the most precious. This is why I cannot just say yes to anyone. To be one of us, you must be ready *absolutely* to die. Whole team has died before. But we said, 'Okay we do it again.' Lars lost *everyone,* but he said, 'Okay, I do it again. I believe in this.' Before, I didn't know if you are ready to die. Now I know."

"Okay," said Radar.

"You are like us."

"Okay."

Lars smiled. "So? Otik?"

"I don't trust him," said Otik.

"Why?"

"He is not telling us everything. Why does he suddenly want to come on trip? Suddenly he is actor, suddenly he is very interested in everything we do."

"You heard him—"

"Yes, I heard him, *blah blah blah,*" he said. "And I also do admit, we need two more hands."

"So?"

"Okay. *Okay,*" Otik sighed. "But let me lodge formal request to clarify recruitment process."

"Formal request duly noted."

"Because one of these days we are going to invite real maniac and I will be very upset."

"You want to be the only maniac?" Radar asked.

"I hate you."

"I hate you, too," said Radar, smiling.

The three of them approached Horeb.

Lars cleared his throat. "You will not be our guide."

Horeb nodded, looking defeated.

"We can't pay you anything, either," he said.

"I told you. I don't want money," said Horeb.

"I know. That's why we'd like to invite you to be the fourth member of our troupe."

Horeb's eyes lit up. "Really? Not joking?"

"Really. Welcome to Kirkenesferda."

He bowed. "I am very honored."

"Radar will catch you up on what we do during the drive."

It was time to go. Horeb ran to his moto and picked out a small bag and his prayer mat. Radar looked around for Ivan, but there was still no sign of him. He wrote a quick note and went over to the chief mate.

"Please give this to Ivan," he said. "Tell him 'Thank you, from Radar.'"

Akaki nodded.

"Tell him I will never forget him or his songs."

"Yes," said Akaki. "I tell him."

Radar was not convinced he would, but there was nothing more to do except pile into *Moby-Dikt*. He looked in vain one last time for his friend, and then the doors were latched and closed. The truck shifted into gear and they bade farewell to the dream of Matadi.

FOR THE FIRST HOUR of the drive, Radar descended into a swarthy melancholy, no doubt encouraged by the liquor still lingering in his body. He would never see Ivan again. He had betrayed Ana Cristina. He had abandoned his mother. And for what? He glanced around their little hovel. Otik and Lars had settled down to their respective workstations. Horeb had carved out a space for himself among several great spools of wire and was reading from a book. He had been a part of the team for less than an hour, and already he appeared as if he belonged, in a way that Radar had never managed.

Radar closed his eyes and tried to sleep but could not. One of the generators had been fired up to provide them with electricity, and though a little exhaust fan whirred away in the corner, the room quickly became stuffy and uncomfortably hot.

Otik's motion sickness returned, and he began the now familiar routine of quietly puking into a bucket. Lars and Radar had grown so accustomed to this that they did not bat an eye, but Horeb grew concerned. He went over to the electric kettle and busied himself brewing some tea from several small bags of spices he produced from his knapsack.

"Here," he said, presenting a mug to Otik. "For the stomach."

Otik eyed the mixture skeptically but took the mug and gruffly mumbled a word of acknowledgment.

Horeb came over to Radar with a second mug of the tea.

"Thank you," said Radar, accepting the offering.

"How do you feel, my friend?" said Horeb.

"I've been better. I've also been worse." Radar sipped the tea. It was bitter and peppery, but it reminded him of Charlene and home. "What is this?"

"*Búku oela.* A pan-African tea. I made it up myself. One could say it is *post-traditional*. Rooibos from South Africa, grains of paradise from Nigeria, calumba from Mozambique, ginger from Morocco. It heals the body and brings peace to the soul."

Radar wished he could hear his mother give her olfactory report on the tea. He wondered if she would be able to smell all those countries.

"How did you learn to make it?"

"If I'm being honest with you . . . the Internet," he said, smiling. "The Internet will save Africa."

Horeb glanced over in Lars's direction. He leaned in close.

"I'm very honored to be part of your team," he said quietly. "But I'm not really sure I understand what your team does. Can you explain this to me, please?"

Radar was baffled about why Lars had nominated him to be purveyor of information, particularly because he was the newest member and least qualified to describe what the group did. He barely understood it himself.

"I can try. But I can't promise it will make sense," he said, sitting up. He took another sip of the tea. He already felt better. The post-traditionalism was working.

As soon as Radar started talking, however, he found he had a lot to say. Much more than he thought he knew. At first he was worried that the history he was relating was not quite right—that he was leaving out critical details or shifting dates or mispronouncing names. He kept waiting for Lars or Otik to intervene and take over the role of storyteller. When they did not, he began to gain confidence, and there came a point at which he was no longer worried about whether he was getting it right or not. The story had become his. The story had become more than itself.

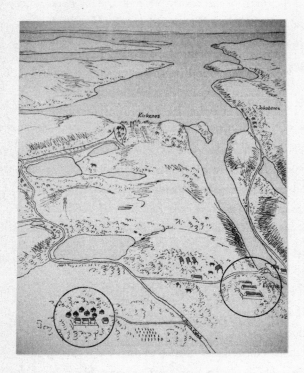

Fig. 5.5. Selected diagrams (1–5)
From Røed-Larsen, P., *Spesielle Partikler*

Using the book his mother had given him as a springboard, he pointed to the diagrams as he told Horeb the history of the group, beginning with the labor camp for teachers in Kirkenes during World War II. The pictures, in their realness, in their little bordered truth, gave him courage.

"They were kept in two camps," he said, pointing at the map of Kirkenes. "Here and here. This was where the idea for the group formed, in the breaks between heavy labor. The science teachers got together and began talking about science, and war, and theater, and they found they had a lot in common. When they were not working, there was nothing to do but talk. And out on the edge of the world like that, ideas can become big things. Ideas can become bigger than reality. And that's why they went through with it. It was also desperately cold that winter. You can see the average temperature was minus twenty. The

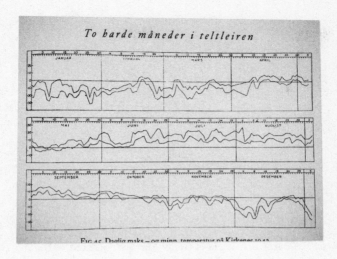

To harde måneder i teltleiren

Fig. 45. Daglig maks – og minn. temperatur på Kirkenes 1943.

mind slows to a crawl when it's that cold outside. But they knew it would one day be spring again. That one day the war must end."

He waited for Lars to tell him he was full of crap. That he was making all of this up. But Lars stayed quiet, and so he went on. He described the creation of

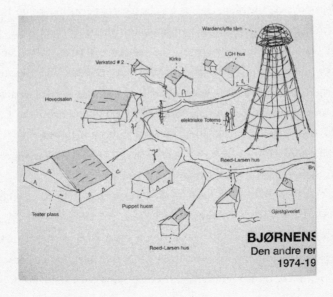

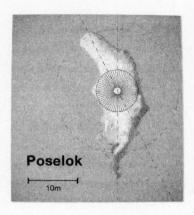

the Bjørnens Hule in the middle of the wilderness, pointed to the map of grass-roofed huts revolving around the Wardenclyffe tower.

"Do you know what a Wardenclyffe tower is?" Radar asked.

Horeb shook his head.

"Nikola Tesla invented it. He was a Serb . . . one of my people. My father used to go on and on about him. Tesla came up with an idea that all electricity could be free . . ." And so on. He talked about the experiments with electricity and nuclear physics, the preparations for the elusive performance on Poselok Island that was only discovered by two Russian fishermen many years later. He described the look of amazement on the fishermen's faces. He recounted the Gåselandet show, destroyed by the massive Tsar Bomba, and the mysterious films of the exploding theater wagon that surfaced and were played at various underground parties to psychedelic soundtracks. He described the films even though he had never seen the films, even though he had seen only a series of stills in the book. But maybe this was enough. Maybe telling a story of the event was more powerful than witnessing it yourself.

"This was their theater wagon," he said. He talked about the symbolism of the wagon at length, what it represented, its history in Europe first as a religious beacon, then as a satellite of safety against the state, then as a vessel of narrative transmigration. He did not know he knew all of this. He did not know he knew the term "narrative transmigration," but out it came with all the rest.

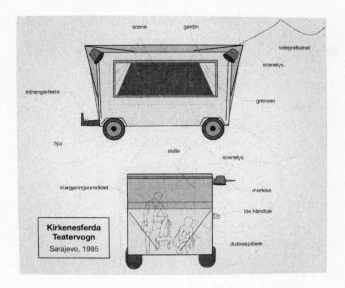

Horeb didn't ask a single question. He kept nodding and saying, "Yes, I see. Yes, I see," though Radar didn't know if, in fact, he actually did see or whether he was just playing along. When Radar got to the performance in Cambodia, he paused and looked over at Lars. But Lars was deeply ensconced in his work with the puppets. If he was listening in, he did not show it. So Radar narrated the tragedy of that night in Anlong Veng as if he had been there himself. He described Siri, Lars's mother, the beauty of a woman who was so gifted and so strong, surrounded by all these men. She was a mother, a craftswoman, a visionary, a beacon of optimism in even the darkest of times. He began to feel his eyes growing misty. He described the sight of the wagon burning, the feeling of watching all that work go up in smoke. He pointed to the map of the killings. The sound of gunshots. Siri on the ground, looking at her husband, their hands reaching out to touch fleetingly before the life left them both.

Radar paused. "I'm sorry," he said. He took a deep breath and pointed to the line on the map representing Lars's escape with Raksmey to the Thai border.

"When they were within a hundred meters of the Thai border crossing, Raksmey stepped on a land mine," he said. "His left leg was torn apart by the explosion. Part of his face was sheared right off. They heard shots behind them, and so he waved for Lars to go on and leave him. Lars tried to drag Raksmey . . . but finally gave up. Those last thirty feet he had to walk on his own."

There was a silence. Radar thought maybe he had gone too far.

"You're a very good storyteller," said Horeb. "You should write this down."

"It's already written down." Radar pointed to the book.

"I mean, in *your* words, like how you said to me," said Horeb.

"I've only ever written a *Little Rule Book for Life.*"

"Like a Koran?"

"Not quite."

"But I'm serious. When I listen to you, I feel your words. You have a gift. When you tell me about this terrible tragedy in Cambodia, it's like I am there. I am remembering, too."

"You remember what?"

"When I was four, I saw a man shoot my father in Yaoundé."

Radar blinked. "Why?" he said.

"My father owned a factory. The man was a Marxist. I didn't know any of this at the time . . . I was just a little boy. All I knew was a man came and made my father fall down, and then my father disappeared and never came back. My mother had already gone back to Senegal, so I grew up with my aunt and uncle. And they taught me Islam. I lost my father, but I found my belief."

"What happened to the man?"

"They beat him to death. They beat him. I was too young to tell them to stop."

Radar looked up and saw Lars standing next to them. He was holding a yellow tracksuit in his hands.

"It's for you. It's our uniform," said Lars. His eyes were wet.

"Thank you," said Horeb, bowing. "I will wear it well. Live long and prosper."

RADAR WAS IN THE middle of telling Horeb about Kermin, the great puppet designer who had resurrected Kirkenesferda from the ashes by organizing the fourth *bevegelse,* in Sarajevo's library, during the middle of the Balkan war.

"And Kermin is my father," he declared proudly.

"And so why is your father not here?" asked Horeb.

Radar opened his mouth and then shut it. He was about to try and explain the blackout in New Jersey when the truck slowed and came to a stop.

The door to the container was unlatched. Professor Funes appeared beneath his parasol.

"A stop," he said. "For petrol. And the calls of nature."

Radar looked at his watch. They had been driving for almost three hours.

They hopped down from the container, some more nimbly than others. Radar blinked in the bright sunlight. The truck was parked at a dusty filling station that housed only a single pump. There were four other trucks ahead of them in line, each stacked high with goods—bananas, furniture, PVC piping. The station was in a town that seemed to consist mostly of tin-roofed houses with a couple of mud streets running between them. A large church could be seen rising above the rest of the buildings. Somewhere, a radio was playing rumba.

Horeb, now wearing the yellow tracksuit, washed his hands and face using a bottle of water and then placed his mat on the ground by a grove of spindly trees. He began to pray.

When Radar came out of the restroom, Horeb was still praying. Otik and Lars were already clambering back inside *Moby-Dikt,* but it would still be some time before they would get fuel, since the line of trucks at the pump had not gotten any shorter.

He did not want to go back inside just yet, so, feeling surprisingly adventurous, Radar ambled down a side street. It was remarkable how even a day in a new place could acclimatize you. Yesterday morning, he would have done no such thing. Yesterday he was a coward who had never been to Africa, who knew only of New Jersey and recumbent bicycles and radio stations. But now? He was an explorer. *A man in the world.* Dusty streets were the new normal.

He came across a group of young boys who were kicking around an old soccer ball wrapped with tape. As soon as they saw him, they stopped and stared.

"Hello," he called out timidly, suddenly aware of himself as foreign.

The kids continued to stare. One boy scratched at his balls.

"Bonjour," Radar tried. "I am Radar."

"They don't see many *mundeles* around here," said Horeb, materializing behind him.

"Mundeles?"

"White people," said Horeb, laughing. "Would you like to play?"

"Play?" Before Radar could say more, Horeb dived among the children and expertly dribbled the ball around the kids with his feet. Soon, the children began yelling and laughing, trying to get it back. But when Horeb kicked the ball to Radar, the kids stopped again and stared.

One of the kids pointed, said something to Horeb.

"They want to know where you come from," said Horeb.

"New Jersey."

"New Jersey?"

"It's next to New York."

Horeb began to talk to the children.

"What are they saying?"

"Children are always so funny. They want to know why you look the way you do. I'm trying to explain to them, but it's not easy. Why does anyone look the way they do?"

All at once, everything felt very familiar. He had been here before.

"Tell them I wasn't always like this," he said.

"What?"

"Tell them I was born black like them."

Horeb raised his eyebrows.

"Tell them." He knew it was impossible, but he had talked to these children before. He had seen these same expressions of wonder. He had stood under this same sun.

Horeb dutifully translated.

"They want to know what happened to change you into a *mundele*."

"Tell them . . ." He was trying to remember what he said the first time. "Tell them it was a machine. Tell them it was electricity."

Horeb shook his head. "These are children. They will believe you. Some of them have never seen a *mundele* before."

"I'm not lying," said Radar. "It's the truth. It was a machine."

Horeb studied Radar's face.

"Tell them," said Radar. He needed the children to understand, just as they had understood the first time. "Tell them I went to Norway, in the north, where there's snow, and a machine changed me. Tell them it also made me very sick. I got seizures. This leg grew weak. Tell them this is why I can't play soccer very well."

Horeb took a step toward him. The sun was hot overhead, and Radar felt his head begin to spin, but he did not look away. The feeling of déjà vu receded. Everything was new again. He could feel the sun, and Horeb was coming closer. In his previous life, this would have been the time when he would have had a seizure and the children could have seen for themselves what the machine had done to him, but now he did not seize. He stayed awake, staring into Horeb's eyes, and he knew then that he would never seize again. He knew he had been cured. Cured by his father's electromagnetic pulse.

Horeb brought his head very close to Radar's until their foreheads were touching.

"Enna lillah wa enna elaihe Rajioun," he whispered. *"Jazaka Allahu Khairan."*

"It's the truth," said Radar. "It's the truth."

Horeb put his hand against the soft part of Radar's neck and then turned and began to speak. The children listened and stared.

"They want to know why you changed."

"Tell them it wasn't my choice," said Radar. "But I'm the same person I was before. Tell them I'm like them. Tell them this never changes."

Horeb nodded. He spoke. He spoke for a while. When he was done speaking, a silence settled over them, until Radar limped over and kicked the ball and the children whooped with delight and easily took it away from him. Horeb swept in and recaptured the ball, and soon it was the two of them in their yellow tracksuits against all of the children. Horeb would keep the ball, pass to Radar, who would lose it, and the children would pass it around before Horeb would win it back again. The simplest of games, but enacted here, it was a pure and untouchable act that superseded all else. Language, color, time, place—none of it mattered when the ball was moving.

"Ahoy! We're leaving!" Lars shouted from the filling station.

Horeb clapped his hands and said something to the children. They came crowding around Radar, touching him, hugging him.

"Mundele ndom, mundele ndom," they cried.

"What does that mean?" Radar asked.

"It means 'the white black man.'"

"Is that good?"

"You tell me." Horeb laughed.

9

It was early evening by the time they reached Kinshasa, though Radar never saw the great city, for they did not stop. He only heard the shouts and the sounds of traffic, the crowds, the cries of anger, the brief caress of laughter, bursts of music from open windows, and the endless chorus of honking. At some point they heard the telltale screech and crash of an accident, followed by screams. For Radar, it was completely and solely an aural city. A city of the imagination.

"It's easy to forget your soul in Kinshasa," said Horeb as they passed through. "I was there to study. I made my brain larger, but sometimes I didn't remember my heart."

"What did you study?"

"Linguistics. International relations. Religious studies. I wanted to be a translator and interpreter for the UN. But I couldn't focus on my work. I was going in too many directions. I lost my way. So I ended up leaving after two years." He looked down. "You must think I'm stupid to throw away an opportunity like that."

"I don't think you're stupid," said Radar.

"I've never been able to finish what I start. It's my curse. I always try to remind myself that when Muhammad started preaching, no one believed him— no one but his wife. Nothing came easy for him. He had to earn it . . . with patience. With patience and wisdom and belief."

They listened to the mutter of a moto approaching and passing their truck.

"When people live too close together, you see the best and worst side of them," said Horeb. "You step over human waste in the street, but you are also given food by strangers. You see people robbed by guns, but you also see young men helping old women carry their bags. Sometimes you see the good and evil in the same afternoon. Everyone understands how difficult it is to live like this. It can make you hard, like a nut, but it also leaves you open for hope, for the words of a prophet—whether this is Jesus, Muhammad, or even"—he gave a little laugh—"one of our presidential candidates. Every nut has a soft inside."

"Is that true? I feel like I've met nuts with no insides."

Horeb smiled. "We need a great leader. We need a young Nelson Mandela in Congo, who can bring the people together. This country has so much. It can be the most prosperous country in all of Africa. It can be a symbol of cooperation. But this leader must not lead because he is seduced by power. He must lead because his only option is to lead, because the world demands him to lead."

"Maybe this leader is a *she*," said Lars without looking up from his work. It was the first thing he had said since giving Horeb the tracksuit. Radar realized he had been listening the entire time, and that what had passed between him and Horeb had in fact passed between them all.

THEIR DESTINATION was a small fishing port called Mikala. The truck rumbled down a dirt track, and when they finally stopped and the doors to *Moby-Dikt* were thrown open, they saw that they were once again on the banks of the great river, though 450 kilometers upstream. The same river but never the same river. The water still as glass and at least three kilometers wide.

Lashed to the docks were perhaps thirty small barges, all in varying states of rust and decay. The beach nearby was covered with small fishermen's pirogues—canoes dug out from tree trunks. The fishermen had splayed their nets across the beach to dry. A single, ancient gantry crane rose above the docks.

As soon as they jumped down from the container, they were immediately surrounded by a crowd. People were pushing and jostling one another to get close, but not too close. Radar noticed that, unlike the scene that morning in front of the Hôtel Metropole, no one was trying to sell them anything. Instead, everyone was staring at Professor Funes, who stood beneath his parasol a short distance away, talking to his driver.

Indeed, as Radar watched, the crowd began to shift toward Funes. The driver immediately brandished a club and blew on a whistle. The crowd halted. The driver started to speak, waving the club above his head. Radar noticed that almost everyone in the crowd was holding a small package. Then a young man broke from the crowd and extended his package to Funes with one hand, his other hand holding the elbow of the outstretched arm. A hush fell over everyone. Radar thought the driver might hit the man with his club, but Funes stepped forward, folded up his parasol, and took the package. He lifted it to his forehead and made a little bow. Funes said a few words to the man in the man's language. The man clasped his hands together and bowed back, beaming. The crowd held its breath and then, with an exclamation, everyone began to push forward. The driver blew his whistle, but no one was listening anymore. Another man held out his package, and again Funes repeated the ritual of receiving the gift and touching the package to his forehead. Packages were being extended from all directions. Funes calmly took each one, repeating his gesture of thanks. The crowd now stretched back off the docks and up into the village. More were coming down from the hills. Everyone was carrying a package.

"What's going on?" Radar asked.

"I haven't the faintest idea," said Lars.

"He's the Tatayababuku," Horeb said quietly, without taking his eyes from Funes.

"The *what?*"

"The father of books. The Tatayababuku is a sorcerer who knows all things. They think his books give him power. So they give him gifts for his library. They think he will protect them."

"Those are *books?*" said Radar. "How do you know all this?"

"Everyone knows about the Tatayababuku. His magic is powerful."

"Why didn't you tell us this?" said Otik, a note of suspicion in his voice.

"Better to see for yourself," Horeb said with a smile.

They watched as Professor Funes received the books. Each book was wrapped in newspaper or brown wrapping paper. More and more people came down to the waterside, and the pile beside him began to grow. The driver managed to keep the crowd mostly at bay, until one woman threw herself at Funes's feet. She was sobbing. In her arms she was holding a small child, whom she offered up to Funes. The crowd immediately grew uneasy.

"Her child is sick," said Horeb. "She's asking him to heal the child."

For the first time, Funes looked uncomfortable. He cautiously touched the child's head and then murmured to the mother. She was led away, weeping but smiling.

"They don't actually believe the books are magic, do they?" said Radar. "How can they?"

Horeb pointed at the crowd. "They must believe in something. I think Americans believe in much stranger things, yes? Guns? Plastic surgery?"

"That might be true," said Radar. "But who told them this? Who told them the books were magic? Did he say this? Who started giving him books?"

"How does anything begin?" said Horeb. "Did Islam begin with Muhammad's first revelation or when his wife became his first believer? You should ask the Tatayababuku about who started this."

The sun began to set over the river. The water turned gold and red and then silver, forming a perfect mirror to the sky.

When there were no more books to be given, Funes raised his right hand above his head and silenced the throng. He produced a small book from his pocket. After a moment's pause, he began to read in his curious high-pitched voice. A poem in French.

"It's Baudelaire," whispered Lars after a moment. "He's reading Baudelaire."

"He's not reading," said Horeb. "He knows it by heart."

Indeed, the book was only a prop. The professor was speaking from memory. The crowd listened intently. When the poem was finished, the professor bowed again, then began walking toward the water, his driver following closely. The crowd shuffled forward. Funes walked onto one of the barges, all the way to the end, and, with everyone watching, ceremoniously ripped out one of the pages from the small book from which he had just read, held the page aloft, and then tossed it into the river. The page fluttered, somersaulted, came to rest on the surface of the water. There was a silence, and then someone from the crowd let out a trilling ululation. A cheer rose up. And now Radar and the others were surrounded by people singing, clapping, dancing.

"What just happened?" Radar asked.

"He released the good spirits into the river," said Horeb. "The bad spirits remain in the books."

The scene quickly morphed into a kind of organized chaos. The truck was backed right up to the water's edge. Crowds of people began to haul the barges out of the way, and from downriver came another barge, pushed by a stout white tugboat—the *pousser*. This tug-and-barge operation, Radar realized, was to be theirs. The barge was guided into the newly vacated space by the docks. Several men scampered up the scaffolding of the gantry crane and into its cab. Radar could not imagine the old rusty creature actually turning on, let alone lifting a heavy container, but amazingly, the crane fired right up. A crowd of men put chains around the container of books on the back of the truck and then attached the crane's hook. The cable went taut, the crane whinnying from the effort of extracting the container from its perch. Radar stepped backwards, sure that the chains or the crane would break, but gradually the container rose and swung perilously toward the barge, hundreds of hands guiding its path. The crowd seemed unconcerned with the danger of such an operation. Everyone wanted to touch the container, to help it on its way. The crane screeched, complained, turned, and—miracle of miracles—deposited the container onto the barge. The process was repeated with *Moby-Dikt*. Many hands guided the box, and soon the two containers lay parallel on the deck of the barge. A group of men went to fetch the pile of book offerings and stacked them neatly next to the first container. Radar made a rough count. Around five hundred books had been given to the Tatayababuku.

By the time all of this was finished, dusk had already settled across the river. The water had turned the color of wet steel. A cloud of mosquitoes had descended upon them, and perhaps this was why the crowd around them had subsided, but Radar still felt eyes watching his every move. Horeb went off to pray, while Funes's driver built a small fire on the front of the metal barge. Radar thought this was a risky maneuver, given that boats and fire don't usually mix very well, but no one else appeared troubled by this incongruity. At least the smoke from the fire did wonders in keeping the mosquitoes at bay.

Professor Funes, who had disappeared into the *pousser*, reappeared in the firelight.

"It's too late to leave tonight," he said. "They don't dredge the channels anymore, so you must know the precise way, and even then there's no telling if it's clear, because the river changes every day. I would buy all the food you need here. Enough to last at least one week. We'll stop only at night, and you can never be sure what will be on offer."

Radar wanted to ask him about what he had witnessed that evening, about the books, about why the people believed in his magic. But before he could say anything, the professor bade them good night and withdrew.

"So what do we do now?" said Otik.

Lars smiled. "Anyone want to go shopping?"

They looked around at the darkness. The eyes watching them.

"I'll go." It was Horeb.

He disappeared into the crowd of faces. He was gone a long time, but when he came back he was bearing two large fish on a stick. Behind him, several men were carrying sacks of rice and three large bundles of bananas.

"Give me forty dollars," said Horeb. "Please."

"Forty dollars," repeated Otik.

"For the food," he said. "I'm not sure it will last us the whole time, but there are villages along the way. You can always buy fish. It's the one thing we do have in this country."

The fish had long, proboscis-like snouts. Horeb expertly cut and cleaned them with a series of easy, precise movements that Radar found mesmerizing.

"What kind are those?" he asked.

"Elephant fish," said Horeb. "Their eyes are small, but they use an electric field to see underwater. They are also delicious."

The fish were tossed into a pan above the fire, alongside a pot of rice and some cassava paste. They listened to the sounds of insects and the silence of the river and the elephant fish sizzling against the heat. The eyes, always watching them.

Horeb was right. The fish was delicious. Succulent and sweet, tasting of river and earth and flesh, it was just about the best thing Radar had ever eaten. He could almost taste the faint hum of an electronic field on his lips. For a couple of precious seconds, he forgot about the mosquitoes dive-bombing him from all directions.

"Let it be known that I am not pleased to be back on boat," said Otik. "But also let it be known that I am pleased to eat this fish."

"Thank you, Horeb," said Lars. "We're lucky to have you on board."

Horeb cleared his throat.

"So I am wondering: what can I do for this team? Besides get you fish." Radar realized that this was the question he himself had not dared to ask. A tinge of jealousy. Through his simple directness, Horeb was already poised to surpass him in the pecking order. Radar needed to learn how to be direct like Horeb. To reach out and point to what you want.

The fire crackled. No one said anything. After a moment, Lars got up and went inside *Moby-Dikt*. He reemerged carrying several drums.

"You said you can play."

Horeb took one of the larger *djembe*s and examined the surface of the skin. He turned the drum around and around in his hands.

"I haven't played this kind of drum before," he said finally. "I usually play the log drum of the Lokele."

"You see?" said Otik. "I told you. He doesn't play. He says he plays so he gets this job."

"It won't speak the same language," said Horeb.

"Try," said Lars.

"Hand me another," said Horeb, and he took the two drums between his knees.

The first beat hit Radar so hard in the chest, he nearly fell backwards into the river. The sound—clean, flat, true—was unlike anything he had ever heard before. A sound to be felt and tasted. A sound that penetrated deep into the marrow of his bones. Then came the next beat, and the next, Horeb working back and forth between the two drums, high and low, the rhythm picking up now, shifting, finding itself, sliding into a groove, pulling back. Horeb paused, took a breath, eyes closed, and then the drumming rolled down again, rising into the night sky, his palms caressing the skin of the drums as if he were conversing with the heavens, fingers flexed up, fingers flexed down, speaking to the night, the beats flying out across the surface of the river.

Radar heard a whoop from their invisible audience. A quick series of ululations. The darkness was filled with people. Otik looked around, his eyes alight. Radar had never seen him like this before. He heaved up his great body and hurried into *Moby-Dik*. He came out with birds in his hands.

"*Lars,*" he hissed. "The scene, the scene. This is happening now."

Lars leaped up and disappeared into the container. He emerged with a large piece of canvas in his arms.

"Help me with this, would you?" he called out to Radar.

Radar held one end of the canvas as they unrolled it against the side of the container. Lars went back inside and came out with several spotlights, which he pointed at the scene. He went back in, connected the cords, and then there was light.

Radar gasped. Such was the magic of the theater. They were instantly transported. A valley surrounded by tall, rugged mountains. A cloudless sky. A sun on the verge of setting. A lazy river. This valley was the world now. He could feel the audience shifting, making room for this new truth.

Otik touched the birds' necks, flicked some switch, and they sprang to life. The crowd murmured as the two birds rose into the air, playing against each other, diving, falling, whirling across the backdrop of mountains. Radar realized there were actually four birds: the two in the air and then their shadows against the backdrop, which were like them but also distinct. The birds' wings were beating to the rhythm of the drums, and Horeb was watching the birds dive above his head. It was as if he were guiding them with his music, high and low, high and low, each bird to each tone. Or perhaps the birds were guiding him—it was no longer clear who controlled whom. Every single eye in the audience watching every single movement of those two little puppets as they united, separated, drifted, spun, circled, floated, soared, plunged. The two birds bound together in understanding, never far from each other, whispering, talking, laughing: *Here we are, here we are,* they said, *know us if you can.*

Radar felt a gear turn in his chest. He knew then what he must do. He ran into the container and fetched one of the transceivers and a speaker. He plugged the speaker into the generator, connected it to the transceiver, and clicked on the radio dial, sweeping the signal across the shortwave frequencies so that scraps of voices, music, static, electricity were scooped from the invisible spectrum and transformed into sound by the radio's internals. Bits of Kikongo, French, pop music, reggae, hip-hop, sermons, all bleeding in and out from that uncertain fuzz. Radar closed his eyes and spun the dial. That little dial between thumb and finger became an extension of him, its sounds his sounds, its search his search.

At a certain point the radio fell upon the sound of drums, and Radar paused there. Horeb's drumming mixed with the drumming on the radio, the beats oscillating and intertwining. The birds and their shadows seemed to respond to this doubling—their pace increased, back and forth, back and forth. At one point they crashed into the backdrop, fell, then recovered, flying high above their heads, out of the light of the fire, disappearing into the vast bowl of darkness.

There was a splash. Horeb abruptly stopped drumming. Radar cut off the radio.

He was afraid to look over at Otik, fearing that he would be furious about losing his birds or furious that Radar had ruined the show with his impromptu addition. But when he finally did steal a glance at him, he saw a broad smile stretching across his face.

"*Burazeru,*" Otik whispered. "I am home again."

Around them, the crowd was silent. There was no clapping—not that there needed to be, but after such an intimate display of aerial courtship, the silence was a bit unnerving. Slowly, though, Radar understood. They had all paid witness. There was no need to say what was already said.

And then he heard it, faint but nonetheless certain: drumming. At first he assumed it was coming from the radio, which he must not have turned off properly, but then he realized it was coming from the opposite bank. First in one place, then drums all up and down the river, carrying out across the water.

Horeb was sweating, smiling above his drum, the spotlight illuminating him from below.

"They heard the message. They are calling back to us," said Horeb.

"What are they saying?" said Radar.

Horeb listened. "They are speaking a different language," he said, closing his eyes. "But I think they say, *We see you, we see you, we see you . . . He is coming, he is coming, he is coming.*"

10

Radar was awoken by a great commotion outside. He opened his eyes, his head still lingering in a dream he could not remember. The other cots in the container were already empty. He leaped through the mosquito net, tripped, and ran to the door. Blinking against the morning sun, he saw that the *pousser* had started to pull the barge out into the river. The docks were crammed full of people waving, crying, shouting, clapping, dancing. Funes was at the stern, holding a book, waving back at them. Radar had to admit, it was nice to have such a send-off, even if the attention technically wasn't directed at him. He gave an embarrassed wave and then went over to where Horeb, Otik, and Lars stood watching.

"If they think he will bring them better life, they are getting big surprise," said Otik.

"They want to believe," said Horeb. "A better life can only come through belief."

"Belief is for stupid people. I can believe this book will save me with all of my heart, and I will still be majorly fucked."

"What do you believe in, my friend?" said Horeb. "Why have you come all this way?"

Otik started to answer but was interrupted by a long, withering blast from the boat's whistle, which scattered the crowd.

The *pousser* spun the barge around and pointed them upstream. Soon, the town and its crowds of people disappeared around the bend, and just like that, the river and the jungle became the entirety of their existence. A man whom Radar had not seen before was standing at the bow of the boat, holding a long striped pole, which he would dip into the river every five seconds while shouting, *"Ah yeah mayee!"*

"What's he doing?" asked Radar.

"He's measuring the depth of the river," said Horeb. "Without him, we are in trouble."

"Ah yeah mayee!" called the man.

As they went on, the constant rhythm of the sounder's declaration, coupled with the little expert dip and twirl of his canary yellow pole, became the measure of time's passage. That pole, plumbing the distance between surface and bottom, was the engine of their progress. If the pole stopped twirling, so too would they.

"Ah yeah mayee!"

Professor Funes had retired to his cabin in the *pousser* and would not emerge for the rest of the day. Radar found this strange, but he did not have long to contemplate his absence, for there was much activity around the container. After the previous night's performance, both Lars and Otik were visibly excited.

"How did you know to do this?" Otik asked Radar. "With radio signal?"

"Ah, have you *met* my father?" said Radar. "I grew up with radio signal. I was taking apart radios before I could speak."

"It is perfect. It is so fucking perfect. It is just what we needed and we did not even know it! Kaprow calls this 'art of life.' But we must have many radios. How many do you have?"

"Three."

"No, it won't do. It won't do. We need at least fifty. Maybe eighty."

"Where are we going to get eighty radios?"

"Was the drumming okay?" Horeb asked

Otik ignored him. "We must rehearse!" he cried. "We must make wagon!"

Otik, now manic, hurled himself around the barge like a loose rhino. He seemed no longer bothered by the fact that they were on a barge, though the river here was decidedly calmer than the open ocean. Together, the four of them pulled the theater wagon out of *Moby-Dikt* piece by piece and constructed it on the bow of the barge, attaching the top, the wheels, the curtains, the spotlights, the wings, and the scrim. Radar had to admit it was an impressive sight, a sight that beckoned with promises of a show as the river flowed beneath and the lush landscape slowly spun and revolved around them.

But plans to rehearse quickly receded as technical problems arose when the vircator was installed inside the wagon. Something was wrong. The chips would no longer entangle. Unlike the pair last night, the birds refused to fly. They lay motionless on the deck, appearing as if they had all fallen out of the sky at once. Even Horeb's beating of the drum would not coax them out of their stillness.

Otik—sweating profusely and cursing a beautiful blue streak (*"Jebeni kuch-kin sin! Serem ti se u carapu!"*)—retreated back into *Moby-Dikt* and began to furiously tinker away. Any offers to help were venomously rejected.

"Let him be," said Lars.

"He doesn't like me," said Horeb, staring after Otik. "What did I do?"

"It takes a while," said Radar. "Believe me. It's nothing personal."

"He'll come around," said Lars. He handed Radar a straw cowboy hat. "For the sun. It can be bad. You've got to protect yourself."

Radar took the hat and sheepishly put it on.

"Thanks," he said, aware of himself and all that he was not.

"Nice," said Horeb. "Like John Wayne."

"You know Morse code, correct?" Lars said to Radar.

"I found Xanadu, didn't I?"

"I didn't want to assume. It is a dying language."

"You think I could grow up in Kermin's house and not learn CW?"

"It would be unlikely," Lars admitted. He handed Radar a Morse key. "We'll set up a station for you, stage left. You'll be the one who sends out the opening sequence. We begin every performance with that line from Numbers—you know, 'What hath God wrought?'"

"Baltimore, 1844," said Radar. He plugged the Morse key into the radio and then clicked out the message: •— •••• •— — •••• •— — •••• ——• ——— —•• •—— •—• ——— ••— ——• •••• — The rhythm of dits and dashes flashed out across the water and over the green islands of floating hyacinth.

Horeb, who was sitting nearby, hit the drums in precisely the same rhythm, alternating the high and low drum for each dit and dash: ↓↑↑ ↓↓↓↓ ↓↑ ↑ ↓↓↓↓ ↓↑ ↑ ↓↓↓↓ ↑↑↓ ↓↓ ↑↓↓ ↓↑↑↓↓↓ ↓↓ ↓↓↑ ↑↑↓ ↓↓↓↓ ↑

"What language is that?" he asked Radar.

"It's Morse code. Each letter has a different coded sequence," said Radar. *"W* is *di-da-da*. Short then long long." He demonstrated: ●——

"Ah, in drumming it is different. It is not letter by letter. The drum is speaking the same words you speak with your voice."

"Wait," said Radar, turning to him. "You're actually *speaking* with the drum? I thought you were just drumming."

"Of course I was speaking," said Horeb. "Did you not hear it? Why do you think they were answering me last night? I wasn't sure if they would understand, because I was drumming in Kele, which is an upriver language, but they heard me and answered. They were drumming back in their local language— I think some form of Teke or Lingala, but I could still understand what they were drumming." He demonstrated. *"'He is coming, he is coming.'"*

"But how did you learn how to speak on the drum? I thought you said you'd never been up the river before?"

"I haven't. I learned to drum-speak while I was at university in Kinshasa. I was studying linguistics, you see, and there was a drumming club. We met in the cafeteria in the evenings. I think it was formed to preserve and study the drum language of the river tribes. You know, most of these boys are not learning the drums anymore. They have mobile phones, they want to get to the city, they don't care about the old ways," he said. "But I've always liked languages. I'm good at them. I can imitate almost anything I hear. My aunt and uncle used to call me *le perroquet* when I was little. One of the students in the club, Boyele, he was from the Lokele tribe, near Kisangani, and he knew how to talk with drums. He is the one who taught us. He is an amazing man—I think he is the first person from his village to go to university. He always said he was going to go back and build a hospital there . . . I don't know what became of him."

"This is where we're headed," said Lars. "Maybe we'll see his hospital."

"This area is very famous for its talking drums. But the Lokele don't use skin drums like these. That's why I was wondering if it would work. I learned on a drum made from a log with a long hole cut out of it. They call it a *bongungu*."

"But how do they talk with it?" asked Radar.

"The drumming language is like speaking words. When you play, you sound out a word. Like *lisaka*."

He played: "Li-sa-*ka*." Two taps on the low drum, and then one on the high drum.

"But Kele is a tonal language. A lot of African languages are. Depending on how you say *lisaka*, it can mean different things. Every syllable can be soft or hard, and this changes the meaning. 'Li-sa-ka,' each syllable said soft, means a puddle, or like a wet piece of land. 'Li-sa-*ka*,' with the last syllable hard, means a promise that you make to someone. And 'li-*sa*-*ka*,' with two syllables hard, means poison."

"Seems pretty easy to screw up."

"For people not used to tones, yes. When you drum, all you can drum is the soft and the hard, not the actual syllable. The drum has a soft tone"—he played the low drum—"and the hard tone"—he played the high drum.

"Like the dot and the dash."

"The Lokele call it the male and the female . . . But because you cannot *say* the word, only the tones, when you drum this"—he hit *soft soft hard* ↓↓↑—"it could be 'li-sa-ka,' as in promise, but it could also be 'bo-son-*go*,' the river current. So you must say more than just the word. You must talk *around* the word to let the others know what you mean. So 'moon,' which is normally just *songe*, becomes '*songe li tange la manga*,'" he drummed this out, "which means 'the moon looks down at the earth.' Or if you want to drum 'don't worry' which is *owangeke*, you must actually drum '*sokolaka likoko lya botema likolo ko nda use*,' which means 'take away the knot of the heart and throw it up into the air.'"

"Don't worry," Radar said, and tapped out the Morse code: —•• ——— —•
——— —•—— ——— •—• •—• —•—•

"*Sokolaka likoko lya botema likolo ko nda use*," beat out Horeb.

Lars, who had been watching them, jumped to his feet.

"This changes everything," he said. "Horeb, you'll be our chorus. You'll nar-
rate the story with the drum. Do you think you can do that?"

"I don't know that many phrases in Kele. I only went to drumming club for
one year."

"It doesn't matter. Use the words you have. That's all we can ever do. Radar
will fill in the gaps with Morse code, yes? But I want people to hear the story
before they see it. I want people to *feel* it before they know what it is. Radar,
you'll do the equations as well. I've got them here."

THEY PRACTICED. They practiced that day and the next. Radar worked his
radios, scrabbling up sequence, tapping out code. His stage-left station became

Fig. 5.6. "Projected Flock Equations"
From Radmanovic, R. (2013), *I Am Radar,* p. 620

an elaborate array of Morse bugs, keyboards, speakers, cables, and shortwave radios. Otik finally got the vircator up and running, and the birds leaped off the barge and began to fly again, first in pairs, then in groups of four, and finally in great swarms. Lars set up a projector that sent out images of diagrams and equations. In the evening, as the birds flew across the beams of light, you could see snippets of these equations come to life, the bodies of the birds a flickering canvas that would materialize out of thin air like wisps of smoke. Occasionally, actual birds would come to investigate the swarm, perhaps thinking there was a school of fish to feed on, but after a moment of confusion, in which they would recognize something familiar in the strange puppet forms and yet also sense the distinct shroud of otherness, these living birds would lose interest and fly on.

Meanwhile, Horeb was studying the text of Attar's poem, working out the words and phrases, taking breaks only to sleep, eat, and pray. With his limited vocabulary on the drum, he did his best to translate the story of the birds into music, his beats intertwining with the Morse code beeps until the two of them had developed a sonic rapport that wove open the night:

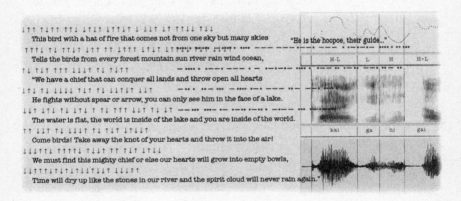

Fig. 5.7. *"Conference of the Birds, Drum/Morse/Radio Palimpsest"*
From Radmanovic, R. (2013), *I Am Radar*, p. 621

As darkness fell on the river, the *pousser* would slow and they would search out a calm area where they could shelter for the night. Their barge would soon be surrounded by men in pirogues offering fish, dead monkeys lashed to sticks, baby crocodiles, cassava, reed baskets filled with squirming fluorescent caterpillars. And books. Books and books and books. As in the first village from which they had launched, everywhere they went these neatly wrapped books were paddled out and offered to Funes, who emerged from his *pousseur* to receive them, foot braced against the bow railing, hands extended as if he were a king surveying his domain.

That first night on the river, one of the villagers, after spotting the theater wagon on the barge, asked Horeb what it was for.

"A performance," Horeb said in Lingala. "These men have come from across the ocean to put on a performance."

The villagers interpreted this to mean that the performance was meant for them. Word spread through the village, and soon everyone was on the beach, ready for the show.

Radar looked over at Lars.

"What do you think?" Lars asked as they gathered in conference.

"They are waiting. They will be pleased," said Horeb.

"Seems okay to me," said Radar.

"We see it as public rehearsal," said Otik. "We don't get too upset. We don't get mad."

"It's not traditionally what we do," said Lars.

"What is tradition? Shitty rules made by shitty people," said Otik.

"A debatable point, but I see what you mean," said Lars.

They assumed their positions: Horeb at the drums, Radar at his console, Otik at the vircator, Lars with the lights, the projector, and the hand crank for the scrolling backdrops and the shadow puppets. The show began in total darkness, and then the lights rose across a barren desert and they were off. The shadow puppet of the hoopoe appeared, and then the birds—great swarms of birds encircling him, encircling the boat, the village, everything. A barrage of drumbeats announced their entrance. Radar found a radio station of a man humming to himself—he could not imagine who this was or where this man must be humming, but there it was, and there it was now on the stage.

Hmmm hmmmm hhmmmmmm.

Radar listened to the drum, nodding his head, and then he began to tap out code on the Morse bug. As they had before, Horeb and Radar slipped into mutual understanding. Not that Radar could tell exactly what Horeb was saying with his drum, but he knew without knowing as he introduced another radio signal, this one full of static and what sounded like a sermon. He tapped his key alongside Horeb's drum, as if they were strolling down a path together. For a moment, everything meshed perfectly. The birds overhead, thousands of wings engulfing them, flashing into the light, melting, everyone listening to the hoopoe's story. The villagers oohing and laughing as the projectors lit up wing and beak, equations dissolving and evolving. Desert melted into the first valley, the Valley of the Quest, and the backdrop scrolled, then suddenly a light fizzled and popped. There was a shower of sparks on the boat, and a clump of birds plummeted out of the sky like stones into the river. They heard Otik swear loudly from behind the wagon.

"Cancel this show, cancel this fucking show!" he bellowed. "Stop! Stop! Stop! I hate this motherfucking shit. *Nabijem na kurac ove jebene ptice!*"

Radar stopped keying and turned off his radios, but Horeb did not stop drumming. Radar looked over at Otik and Lars, knowing they would not take well to this act of insubordination. But then he heard the people. Unlike the crowd the night before, the people of this village seemed to love what they were seeing. They whooped and cried, and several drums were brought out onto the beach and played, and Horeb began to match the beats. As Otik retreated into the container and Lars worked to fix the broken lights, women, men, children began to dance. Leg, hand, limb flashing in the firelight. Whistles of delight, ululations, catcalls, a shiver of chest, a pounding of feet into earth. Circles formed around the best dancers, and above them the birds still flew, diving, dipping, as if egging the people on.

After it was done, they were mobbed by the villagers coming onto the barge, shaking their hands, hugging them, smiling. A crowd of boys came to Radar and touched his radios. He found a station that played some kind of African soukous hip-hop, and the kids all showed him their moves, brushing hands against face, popping shoulders back and forth, jumping onto and off of knees.

Horeb said that they had been invited to meet the chief of the village.

"I don't want to meet any chief," said Otik, still toiling away at his vircator.

"It would be rude not to accept this invitation," said Horeb.

They made their way through the village, lit only by the bright blue glare of the occasional battery-operated fluorescent light. A smell of charcoal and meat cooking. The forest open, breathing around them. In a large mud house they found a man in blue jeans, T-shirt, and a dinner jacket seated at a plastic table. A radio sat on a shelf.

"Bonjour," he said. *"Je suis le chef."*

Horeb spoke with the chief for a long while. Outside, the entire village was watching them through the doorway.

"He says he is grateful for this gift we have given his people," said Horeb. "They will never forget it. They want to give us a goat as a sign of their appreciation."

"Tell them we don't want any goat," said Otik. "Tell them we want to buy that radio. We need radios."

Horeb spoke with the chief.

"He says he's sorry, but he cannot give you his radio, because it is important for the protection of his people. He listens to a radio station called La Voix de la Rivière, and this is where he gets the news for his village. This is how they find out if the rebels are coming back."

"The rebels?" said Lars. "What rebels?"

"He cannot give you the radio, but he offers you a goat."

"We don't want any goat," said Otik.

"I am telling you . . . it's very rude to refuse a goat," said Horeb. "Usually, a goat is only given as a wedding gift. So you see, it would be unwise to not take the goat."

They took the goat, though the goat was not pleased to be taken. He bleated and wailed.

On their way back to the barge, Radar noticed several of the children who had danced to his radio, standing and staring at him, hands on their heads.

"Bonjour," he said. "You are good dancers."

They giggled and hid their faces. One boy jumped out again and began to gyrate, to the great amusement of all. He was wearing a dirty grey sweatshirt that read NY GIANTS SUPER BOWL XXXV CHAMPIONS, 2001. Though it must be said that Radar did not know much about sports, he was fairly sure the Giants had not, in fact, won that year. He remembered this because he had eaten too much guacamole at a Rutgers alumni Super Bowl viewing party, and his sense of loneliness after the game was matched only by the curious postmortem displays of despair by Giants fans, who looked and acted as if a loved one had just died a horrible death.

"His shirt is wrong," he whispered to Horeb. "The Giants lost the Super Bowl in 2001."

"This happens," said Horeb. "Someone once said Africa exists in a parallel world. When they have a big game like this in America, they make winning T-shirts for both teams. It is America, you see—they must plan for all possibilities. The television cannot wait for the people to go back to the factory and say, 'Oh, so-and-so has won, please print this shirt.' And everyone waits patiently on the field. No . . . this would not happen in America. So they print both shirts, but only one team can win, and so afterwards they send the shirts of the losing team here. They donate them to the starving Africans and they feel very good about themselves. So you see, there are many little boys and girls running around with a different history on their chests."

"Should I tell him?"

"I think he already knows," said Horeb. "He knows which world he lives in."

AND SO IT WENT. Up the great river they chugged, past a forest without end, spending long days in the sun, broken only by brief and torrential rainstorms that forced them to head for shore, the rain lashing at the theater wagon and the two containers. They would throw tarps over the equipment and run for cover.

During these storms, Radar would curl up in his cot and listen to the rain pound against the metal roof of the container. He could feel the doubt creeping in then, the little parakeets of discontent imploring him to say what precisely he was doing here. The sky poured buckets, and he was left to wonder if it had all been a mistake.

· · ·

201-998-2666: Dear Ana Cristina, I miss you. I have come to see life as a collection of diminishing failures. I know this sounds depressing, but I don't mean it like that - to fail less badly is something to aspire to. Also, I have begun to write. R

He waited in the doorway of the container, watching the rain fall and waiting for the message to not send. But instead of dying in his phone, the icon changed to a checkmark. The text had gone through! Tiny miracle of miracles! Maybe it was the rain. Maybe the ladders of water were conducting his messages into the heavens. Suddenly he felt guilty. He considered texting Ana Cristina and telling her everything that had gone on in Matadi. But some messages, he realized, could not be sent.

· · ·

201-998-2666: Mom! I'm here! I'm okay. Everything is fine. Have you found Tata? I hope you get this. Love, love, love, RADAR.

This, too, was released. He waited, but no answer came back.

THEY STOPPED BRIEFLY in Mbandaka, a forgotten river city, both bigger and smaller than it ought to be. They purchased supplies and diesel for the *pousser*'s engines and for their own generators, which they were now running day and night, since it was the current from these generators that kept the birds alive and on which their entire show depended. While in Mbandaka, they heard about the unrest upriver. A rebel group had come down from Ituri to take control of a new diamond mine near Basoko. There were stories of mass rape. Whole villages disappearing.

"We cannot be sure what is true," said Horeb. "That region has been stable since 2002. I'm not saying it is impossible that this is true, but in general, you must say the rebels are interested in the two heads of the serpent and not the body. The war has changed recently. It is less political, more like an exercise in capitalism. Capitalism without regulation. These rebel groups, they are like start-up companies in your America. They want to make money. So if they are killing people, it is for an end."

"That doesn't sound like a start-up company," said Radar.

"I cannot guarantee your safety, but I would not worry. It is your choice."

Radar worried. Professor Funes emerged briefly to collect his books and then disappeared back into his cabin before they could ask him about the rebel situation. It had been like this ever since they had left. Not once had their host come out to watch their rehearsals or shows, to investigate the action occurring on the deck of his barge. At first this behavior had struck Radar as most unusual, but soon his absence blended with everything else that was strange on the river. It simply became a part of the reality.

And so, as the sun rose in the sky, they pulled out of Mbandaka as if nothing had changed, as if that which had been said could not be known and so had not been said.

11

For such a grand river, the Congo had surprisingly few boats navigating its waters, bar an occasional fisherman's pirogue. On the third day, they passed a barge full of perhaps three hundred people and animals that had gotten stuck on a sandbank, but the *pousser* did not stop, and they chugged on past.

The sounder, always, swinging his pole: *"Ah yeah! Mayee! Ah yeah mayee!"*

Once, they passed a hand-painted sign sticking out of the water: LE SAND-WICH, it read, in careful sans serif. An arrow pointed upward.

"It is unlikely," said Horeb.

Radar tried to monitor his radios for news of the rebels, though he could not understand the language. Nor was he ever able to locate La Voix de la Rivière.

Yet even if he could not understand what exactly the radios were saying, he made several breakthroughs with their transmission. On the third evening, he figured out how to wire the radios to himself. Using very sensitive electrical nodes adapted from a heart rate monitor he had found in a forgotten drawer inside *Moby-Dikt,* he connected the radios to several contact points on his temples, wrist, and chest. It took him a while to adjust the sensitivity of the connection and to figure out exactly how he could control the dials without touching them, but once he had determined the correct voltage and resistance, the rest came fairly easily. It was as if the radios had become a natural extension of him. All he had to do was simply envision the radio switching channels and it would change, just like that. When he came upon something in the spectrum that felt right, the radio would hold, as if it too knew what was needed for the performance. This freed up Radar's hands to flutter across the Morse key and the mixing board.

Horeb was impressed. "I cannot drum with my mind," he said.

"Not yet," said Radar.

. . .

201-998-2666: Ana Cristina, I've become the radio and the radio is
me! When I get back I have things to tell u. How are you? I think
of u everyday. Of your lips and the sound of your voice. I'm
trying to remember everything -><-

The birds, for their part, had also gone through a kind of evolution. The first few days, they had flown only when called upon and then they would dutifully return to the wagon and fall quiet. But gradually they had developed a mind of their own. They now roosted all over the boat, in the container, on the roof of the *pousser*. They always traveled in pairs. At all hours of the day and night, you could invariably spot a few pairs flittering about here and there, even in the pouring rain. Otik, who had begun acting more and more erratic with each passing day, did not seem to notice or care about the unraveling of his flock.

"They are entangled," is all he would say.

"I still don't know what this means," said Radar.

"I believe also two people can become quantumly entangled," said Otik.

"Two *people*?"

"Yes, two people. These two people are two people, but also same person. Everything that you do affects other person, even if you never meet him."

"Okay," said Radar. "So have you ever been entangled with someone?"

"Not anymore," said Otik. "Once, but not anymore. It is *un*tangle that hurts."

Though they resembled live birds in beak, wing, and feather, the puppet birds continued to project a muddled signal of sentience. They would sit huddled and quivering, staring at Radar with empty eyes as he entered *Moby-Dikt* and lay down on his cot. Several pairs of birds had even taken to nesting in bed with him. He would reach out in the darkness and touch their bodies, feeling the quiet churn of their gears. They were warm to the touch, but not with the warmth of life. Radar tried to figure out what was required for something to be considered alive. Was it sufficient to just appear alive? If no one else could tell the difference, wasn't that enough?

Order had not completely disappeared, however: when Otik fired up the vircator, the birds would still respond to their creator, leaving their perches to converge upon the wagon, forming a great mass that, as soon as the drums began, swarmed into the air as if on command.

"It *is* command—of course it is command. They are electrical, I command them," said Otik when pressed, though the precise degree of control he exerted over them was becoming less and less clear. Increasingly, pairs of birds could be seen breaking away from the pack in the middle of a rehearsal and flying off across the river and into the jungle. The flock was still large, but there were noticeable gaps now. Radar wondered what a man might think wandering through the jungle and coming across the carcass of a bird puppet.

"Why do they fly away?" asked Radar.

"This is malfunction—of course there is malfunction," said Otik. "Everyone malfunction—you malfunction, I malfunction. Remember, what we are doing is very complex and even crazy. More crazy than rocket science, more crazy than human clones."

.   .   .

201-998-2666: Hello Mom. The smells! I wish you could smell these smells! R

On the fourth night, they had again moored near the bank, though this time no village was in sight. A couple of pirogues approached from downstream, the men offering a meager assortment of fish that Horeb examined and declared inedible. The men in the pirogues presented no books, which by now was highly unusual. Blasphemous, even. Indeed, the country in these parts felt swollen with a sinister brand of quiet. Like a recently abandoned crime scene. Except that there was no body, no crime.

Another coal fire was lit on the deck of the barge to discourage the mosquitoes, and chairs were pulled round. Lacking any other food, Horeb went about making *fufu* paste in a pot. Radar sat near one of his radios, writing in his journal. Lars and Otik sat together, quietly arguing about some obscure dramaturgical point, a conversation that had no doubt been going on for years. The man with the sounding pole huddled just on the edge of the firelight, smiling at something small and precise and entirely his own.

They had all settled into a strange routine, the kind of routine men fall into when they are trapped in the pursuit of the divine. Nearby, their goat, whom they had named Bertolt Brecht, bleated softly, homesick. And still: a hundred or so birds shivered and watched them from all around the barge. Not quite watching. *Waiting.* For whatever would come.

Radar found himself looking up at the vast compartment of stars above. He thought of Ivan then; wondered whether he was back across the sea already. Whether he would ever see his child again. He tried to find Alpha Centauri, with its A and B and its little Proxima, but one star blurred into the next, and when he found what he thought must be it, he was immediately consumed with doubt. What he lacked was Ivan's certitude. To be certain was almost better than being right.

Suddenly, Professor Funes appeared in the firelight. The sight of him caught all of them off guard. Lars and Otik stopped talking. Horeb looked up from his cooking. Radar lifted up his pen in the middle of the sentence. Funes stood there in hat and dark glasses, his blanched skin glowing in the light of the flames.

And then, before anyone could say anything, he spoke:

"Come you lost atoms to your Centre draw,
And be the Eternal Mirror that you saw:
Rays that have wander'd into Darkness wide,
Return, and back into your Sun subside."

A rustling from the birds. Bertolt Brecht bleated quietly in the shadows.

"The last lines of Attar's poem," said Funes. "FitzGerald's translation, 1887. I've wanted to tell you this for some time."

They stared at him. No one spoke until Radar got up from his seat.

631

"Would you like to join us?" he said.

Funes shook his head. "I can't."

More silence. Radar pressed his luck. "We haven't really seen you around much," he said.

"You must understand that everything is quite painful for me."

Radar peered at the professor's skin. It was stretched too tight in places, and had grown lumpy in others. The skin did not match the man.

"Are you ill?" he asked. He was immediately ashamed of his impertinence, but Funes did not look offended by the question.

"In a manner of speaking," he said. "Though in all of human history, my condition has been documented only once before."

"What's your condition?" said Radar. His forwardness was quite out of character, but then, he boasted a condition that had never been documented before in human history.

After a moment's hesitation, Funes sank into Radar's vacated chair.

"I've taken this river hundreds of times," he said. "It is never the same river twice."

"It's my first river," said Radar. "Well, if you don't count the Passaic, back in New Jersey."

"It counts. If it's watery and it flows, it's a river," said Lars.

"Barely water. Mostly toxic waste," said Otik.

"It's getting cleaner," said Lars.

"Clean, my asshole," said Otik.

"No, thank you," said Lars.

Radar could see that Funes was growing uncomfortable.

"You've lived here a long time?" he said, trying to include him in the conversation.

Funes said nothing at first. They all watched the bent frame of their host. His eyes were transfixed by the fire's glowing coals. Radar was just about to fill the space left behind by his silence, but then Funes began:

"I am from Uruguay," he said. "I grew up in a modest house not far from the river in Fray Bentos. My mother was a washerwoman. Her name was María Clementina. I never knew my father. My mother rarely spoke of him. You can find all of this in the archives of Fray Bentos. I was unsettled as a child, but I had a good mind for names and places . . . I could tell you the time without the aid of any watch. It should not come as a surprise that I was able to read from a very early age, even though my mother herself was illiterate. When I was seven, I fell off a horse and was badly injured. To this day, I carry a limp on my left side and my knee aches when the weather changes."

"Me, too," said Radar.

Funes glared at him. Evidently this was not a dialogue. He resumed: "My mother sent me away to Catholic school in Montevideo, though how she found the money for my tuition I still don't know. But I did well there . . . I was good at following instructions, and I didn't ask many questions that did not have answers. When I turned eighteen, I swore my life to God: I became a monastic. I joined the Benedictine order at the Abadía de San Benito, in Luján. This too can be confirmed in the various public records. After two years in Luján, I heard about an opening at a monastery in Africa. Knowing this might be my only opportunity to see the world, I jumped at the chance. This is how I came to Zaire. The year was 1971. I joined the Monastère du Quatre Fleuves, near Kisangani. I barely spoke a word of French when I arrived, but the brothers took me in. There were ten of them. This has been recorded in several sources as well. They were kind men, with patience that could last one thousand years. It's a pity our bodies and minds abandon us so soon—only the soul can take advantage of such patience. Soon after my arrival, Mobutu started his campaign of Zairianization. This was a difficult time for the young country . . . The government seized all properties from foreign nationals and former colonials and gave them out to Mobutu's friends. Some would say the country was already lost at this point, though the end would not come until much later. Luckily, we were sheltered under the church's wing. It was a kind of immunity, but we all knew it could not last forever.

"I had noticed during my time in Kisangani that the town did not have a proper library, aside from that at the college. Books had always been a refuge for me, perhaps because I had always been an outsider wherever I went. And so I decided to start a small library for those who might take similar comfort in the realms of the imagination. . . . At first, it was mostly exegetic and hermeneutic texts. We had various translations of the Bible left behind by missionaries in transit, but I made an appeal to several schools in Paris and Montevideo and also New York City to send us their old secular books. I didn't expect any response, but soon the books came—at first just a few, but then more and more. A woman in Paris sent us three hundred detective novels, which the children of course loved. We still had a reliable post system back then . . . The river was open, and the mining companies had regular flights. It was all quite sophisticated. Our little library grew. I housed it in the old greenhouse in the back of the monastery, and the children would come. Many of them began to work for me as docents, organizing the books, making library cards, resealing bindings. We had all kinds of books. Lots of poetry, travel novels, plays, American literature—Melville, Twain, Steinbeck. I will not recount every title at La Petite Bibliothèque de la Connaissance, but it was well used. The sign above the door squeaked in the wind—I can still hear it now. . . . I will tell you that some of the other brothers in the order disapproved of the library. They claimed I was wasting my time. They didn't consider the contents appropriate, but I was of the mind that God was in all books, and we should not bar the path to spiritual awakening, for there are many ways to climb up the mountain and feel His glory. At least this is what I told myself."

He paused as a pair of birds flew out of the darkness and settled in the space beneath his chair. Funes looked down at them and then continued:

"Then the day I knew was coming finally arrived. The rebels came from the jungle and attacked the people. They were upset with the way the country was being run—or not being run—and they held us colonials responsible. I was, as usual, in the library . . . I heard the shots. And my first instinct, I'm ashamed to admit, was not to go to my brothers' aid but to protect the books. I locked the door and put a chair against it. But it was not enough, for soon the rebels came for me . . . They shot down the door. They rushed in; they were so angry, swearing, cursing—it was as though they had been looking for the books this whole time, as though they blamed the books for their misfortune. None of them could read or write a word, but here they were, standing in my little library, fuming at the idea of such a place. One of them held me while they sprayed gasoline all over the shelves. *What a waste of gasoline,* I thought. I asked them why they were doing this, but all they said was 'Be calm, be calm, Papa.' They made me watch as they lit each shelf . . . I couldn't bear it. I broke away from my captors and I ran . . . I ran straight into the flames, and the last thing I remember feeling was not the presence of God, as I might have expected—no, I was overwhelmed by this great sense of human effort . . . to write, to live, to destroy. So much effort in the world, and in the end, all for nothing."

"These don't sound like the words of a monk," Lars said from the shadows.

Professor Funes nodded slowly. "You're right. I was never a monk. I only came to realize this much later."

"But you survived?" said Radar.

"I awoke several days later. I had never expected to wake again, of course, but the family of one of my docents had found me in the library alive. He had gone into the flames and rescued me. I was badly burned, very badly burned, but alive. The books had collapsed on me, you see . . . It turns out books are actually quite difficult to burn because of their thickness, because of their density, and so they formed a kind of shield around me. The father of this docent was one of the village healers. He wrapped me in aloe vera and sandalwood leaves and gave me a narcotic to chew for the pain . . . Still, I could not move, as nearly all of my skin had peeled off. The ash from the books had cured into my flesh. It was like a balm. Even as I lay in such a painful state, I could also see how very lucky I was. Undoubtably, I was and remain grateful to the docent and his family, who risked their lives to shelter me. Soon after I awoke, it did not take long for me to discover that everything was different. Everything was not as it was . . . Time had disappeared."

He stopped speaking. Bertolt Brecht gave a little yip. The sounder was gently singing to himself.

His high-pitched voice began again: "Time, of course, had not disappeared. It was I who had changed—irrevocably. It took me a while to realize how, for once one changes, there's no way to compare what it was like before the change, because you, the one who must compare, are already different. Bertucci called this 'the conundrum of self-parallax' in his *Treatise of the Psyche*. But eventually I came to comprehend my condition. Put simply: the fire had gifted me with the capacity for perfect and complete memory. Or cursed me, as it were. I had gained entrance into the Akashic Records, the record of all records. As unbelievable as it sounds, this has been my reality from that moment forth. I have become a catalog of existence. During those long months of recovery, while I lay in bed nursing my wounds, I remember every single crack in those hut walls . . . I can draw them for you now. I remember every single call from the yellow-throated cuckoo that presided over the acacia adjacent to my window . . . I gave him no name, knowing it would only deepen my curse. I remember every smell that came in from the cooking stove behind the little garden. I could re-count every single meal during those three months, though every meal was the same. I remember every bee, every millipede, every lizard that crossed my sight and even those that did not. Before, I had only the slightest grasp of the Kele language of the natives, but, lying in bed and hearing them talk around me for perhaps a week, I already knew over a thousand words and could speak them perfectly . . . If I wasn't quite fluent, then I spoke as if I were one of them, as if I were a mirror. What, then, is the difference between this and fluency? I real-ized we were nothing but imperfect copies of those around us.

"And then there were the books. The first thing I did when I was well enough to speak was to demand books. Now that the library was gone, these were hard to come by, but they were brought in from the college, which was under government protection and had been spared from the rebels' assault. I opened each book I received and just as quickly shut it, for I had already ab-sorbed its contents. It was a kind of constant torture—reading no longer yielded the pleasure it once had for me: I was invariably hungry for more, and yet my hunger could never be satiated. I read every book in that library before I could even rise from my bed. I read and read and never reread, for once was more than enough. When I had read all the books in Kisangani, I had them send for more from Kinshasa and from South Africa and Kenya. I wrote letters to all of my contacts in Paris, in London, in New York, in Buenos Aires, anywhere I could find . . . I explained what had happened; I explained that I needed more books, that I would die without my books. All this before I could walk. The books began to come . . . My friends around the world took pity on me. And I read like an addict, like a man gasping for air." His voice fell into a kind of trance. "I read Homer and the plays of Euripides and Aristophanes. I read Plato and Aris-totle and Lucretius and Cicero. I read Virgil and Ovid and Sappho and Seneca. I read Saint Augustine. I read the Koran and the Torah and the Talmud and the Bible again for the first time. I read Dante and Machiavelli and Chaucer and Marlowe. I read Dogen and the Sutras. I read all of Shakespeare. I read Bacon and Milton and Dumas and Vaughan and del Castillo and Swift and Cervantes and Diderot and von Kleist and Goethe and Corneille and Mistral and Rochefoucauld and Molière and Rousseau and Voltaire and Burke and Pelayo. I read Khāqāni and Rudaki and Rumi and Khayyām and Hafiz and Saadi and Attar. I read Defoe and Asturias and Sterne and Stendhal and Verga and Carducci and Blasco Ibáñez and Hugo and Verne and Balzac and Zola and Flaubert and Baudelaire and Sand and Verlaine and Paz and Maupassant and Ibsen and Wordsworth and Austen and Coleridge and Shelley and Keats and Blake and Scott and Carpentier and García Márquez and Puig and Cortázar and García Lorca. I read Dickens and Stevenson and Eliot and Wilde and Cabrera Infante and Onetti and Thackeray and the Brontës and Proust and Borges and Carroll and Trollope and Ruskin and Hoffman and Nietzsche and Emerson and Dickinson and Whitman and Melville and Hawthorne and Shelley and Poe and Gogol and Pushkin and Turgenev and Dostoyevsky and Tolstoy and Blok and Leskov and Chekhov and Pessoa and Thoreau and Alcott and James and Twain and Naipaul and Calvino and Nabokov." Horeb began to beat lightly on his drum. "I read Fuentes and Valéry and Machado and Malraux and Ionesco and Levi and Robbe-Grillet and Duras and Breton and Camus and Stein and Yeats and T. S. Eliot and Dos Passos and Shaw and Hardy and Kipling and Conrad and Vargas Llosa and Ford and Wells and Lawrence and Auden and Huxley and Achebe and Gordimer and Soyinka and Tutuola and Perec and Sartre and de Beauvoir and Rimbaud and Gautier and Waugh and Beckett and Joyce and Woolf and Bishop and Rilke and Kafka and Brecht and Andrić and Kundera and Hamsun and Laxness and Ekelöf and Brodsky and Schulz and Hesse and Grass and Singer and Stevens and Cather and Wharton and Williams and Pound and Plath and Ashbery and DeLillo and Mailer and Salinger and Bellow and Hughes and Welty and Faulkner and Fitzgerald and Hemingway. And I read them in that order."

He stopped. A cavity where drum and voice had once been.

"The small house where I was staying was overrun with books. Thousands of books. My hosts were gracious, as ever, but they had grown weary of these deliveries. Their son, my docent, was doing his best to organize the books, but their sheer volume was already putting them in great danger if the rebels should ever return. I could no longer look my hosts in the face, because I already knew too much about them. From that very first look, I knew them better than they knew themselves. Memory is a weapon too powerful for any one man to wield . . . I have come to realize that forgetting is our greatest gift. This is one memory I shall never have: the memory of how not to remember."

His face suddenly looked stricken. He tapped his parasol against the barge. The birds fluttered beneath him.

"One day they asked me to leave . . . Of course, knowing them, I already knew such a request was coming. I already knew everything that was coming before it came, because the future always arises from the past. I managed to thank my hosts, and then I fled to the jungle with my books. I did not even pay my respects to my brothers' graves or the burnt ruins of the monastery. I was too distraught. You can still see these ruins on the banks of the river. But I soon found I had other troubles. After the fire, my skin had become extraordinarily sensitive to the sun. The ash had turned me the most terrible color of white . . . Well, you can see for yourself what I have become. Before, I was dark, almost like a Peruvian. But now . . ." His voice drifted. "Their son, the docent, insisted on coming with me. I forbade him, but he would not hear of it. He was to be the first of what would later become an army. Together, we built a large, five-walled structure by the river—a pentagon. The perfect repository for my books. I thought it would hold all the books I could ever possibly want. I set about writing a hundred letters a day, asking for more books. More books for my African library. I gave gentle instructions for the books they might want to send. *Get me Krleža and Slaveykov and Ōe,* I would write, and the books continued to come, but there were not enough. There were never enough. The more I read, the more I knew I had not read. And so I realized something must be done. I left my library in the hands of my docents and spent one year traveling the world, telling my story, showing my burns. I pleaded for more books. I negotiated the donation of 573 libraries and private collections—in Murmansk, in Bulawayo, in Alta, in Akron, in Havana, in Bangalore. I met with publishers in Madrid, New York, Frankfurt, Milan, London. I asked them to send me anything they could spare. This was the same year I met Alfonso Daneri in Buenos Aires. He agreed to be one of my shepherds. . . .

"You can't imagine how painful this travel was . . . One year in the world for me was like ten thousand lives lived for other men. I can now easily draw a map of every city in the world. I can recount house numbers, the arrangement of flowers in the windowsill . . . the shape and make of door knockers, mailboxes, linden trees, sewer grates, traffic lights. I can never forget any of it . . . It's torture, *torture* . . . I can't convey the torture. But it was worth it, this pain of remembering. It was worth it for the books. You see, people took up my cause with great enthusiasm. Each of them thought that they, and they alone, were saving my library—and they were right, but what they did not realize is that there were thousands like them, each believing they were making the world whole again. And so: the books came. They came by the crateful . . . by the boatful. So many books . . . fourteen thousand boatloads. As the country collapsed, my library grew and grew. Suddenly the problem became not where would I *get* the books but where would I *put* them. I had to build another pentagon. And another. My team of docents grew. I don't know how word spread, but they came from all over the country. You will meet them . . . soon. I trained them in the arts of classification, and it became their enormous task to organize all of these books."

"How many books are we talking about?"

"The larger the library, the more uncertain the collection . . . This is the third law of accumulation, as stated by Jarmuch Hovengär. Even I do not know exactly the number of books we have. Of course, we also started to amass many copies of the same book; we had over four hundred copies of *Anna Karenina* alone. We had thousands of Bibles, all editions, all translations. We continued to accept donations, but I also had to become more selective. At a certain point, I already had most books. So I started to fill out the edges of the collection. I made contacts with liaisons working in different countries, in different languages, and they would ask me what I wanted and I would simply say, 'Get me one of every book.' People like it when you tell them this. It turns them into bloodhounds . . . They would send me the most spectacularly rare books for free, to the middle of Africa! For many of them it became a religion."

"What did people think of it here?" Radar asked.

Funes nodded, as if he knew such a question was coming. "As big as Congo is, there is only one river to the ocean. Stories started about the library, about what kind of place it was—perhaps my docents were the ones spreading these stories. It does not matter. People started to make pilgrimages. First only a couple, but then they came in streams. They came if they were sick. They thought the books held powers . . . They would go inside the stacks and pray. I claimed no power, of course. I was happy for my docents to show them the books and the catalog. As long as they didn't harm the collection. Many who came to the library claimed they had been cured. Of what I cannot be sure. I did not lead them to this conclusion, but then, I did not dissuade them from believing in it, either.

"And then came the wars. For many years, the river was impassable . . . It was too dangerous, even for me, the Tatayababuku, as they now called me. Kisangani was in very bad shape. Many people died. There was fighting all around. I heard gunshots every night and the collection lay stagnant—only a few books trickled in here and there, through clandestine channels. But the library was never harmed. Even the rebels knew that they could not touch what lay inside. And after the war ended, the local people began to give me books."

"Why? You didn't need books."

"I don't claim to know the African mind. I have played along, but I have never deceived anyone. The library is part of this country's history now. It's a part of the world's history. And I can tell you, I was the first to get back on the river after the war was finished. Even when the UN would not run their boats, I was there. The people knew who I was. They saw my crates. And my crates gave them hope."

"So how big is the library now?" said Radar.

"Neither I nor anyone could say for sure. What I can say is that it is by far the largest private collection of books in the world. Over the years, we've built sixty-one interlinked pentagons. Each pentagon holds one hundred twenty thousand books, give or take. We've carved out the space from the jungle and still we don't have room . . . We must always build more. Three hundred and fifty docents are under my employ—they tend the collections, fight the collections. Knowledge is transient. We battle the insects, the humidity . . . The books themselves are always expanding. They can never be happy with the space they have."

"Do any scholars come to use your library?" asked Lars.

"If they came, we would not turn them away. Our location is not the most accessible, I admit, but a library must be open to all who wish to use it. I'm not foolish enough to believe it's simply about preservation. It is also about use. A library dies without use."

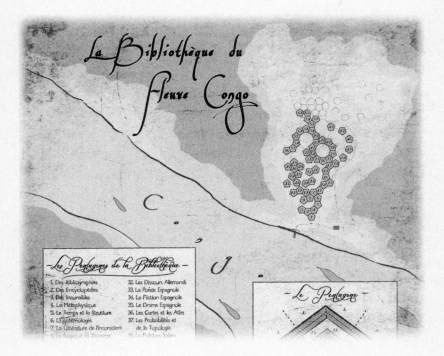

Fig. 5.8. "La Bibliothèque du Fleuve Congo"
From Radmanovic, R. (2013), *I Am Radar*, p. 705

"You're already dead," whispered Horeb.

"I'm sorry?" said Funes with a smile.

"I said, 'What of the African authors?'" said Horeb. "Are they in your library too?"

"Of course," said Funes. "Pentagon forty-eight, sections fourteen and fifteen are devoted to African literature."

"Two sections only?"

"This is not my doing; I'm only the vessel, not the contents," he said. "But I don't find it a coincidence that this is the same continent that housed the great library of Alexandria, the closest we have ever come, until now, to a universal library. This continent is where knowledge was born and where it shall die."

Radar got up, went into the container, and came out bearing a book. He handed it to Funes.

"For your library," he said.

Funes studied the book carefully. He examined it as a doctor examines a patient, touching the cover, the spine, the tips of its pages.

"I've never seen this before," he said. "It's quite unusual to find a book I've never seen. *Per Røed-Larsen*. Who is he?"

Radar gestured at Lars. "His stepbrother."

Lars shook his head. "I have no stepbrother," he said.

"An author who doesn't exist?" said Funes.

"Why do you need the author when you already have the book?" said Lars.

12

On the eighth morning, Radar awoke, shivering, entangled in the lingering tendrils of dream panic. In the dream, he had been seated at the dining room table with his parents. They were all very thirsty—none of them had had anything to drink for days and days. The only way to get water was from a small bird, which they passed around and squeezed, pressing their thumbs into the soft tuft of its belly. If you squeezed hard enough, a single drop of liquid would come out of the bird's beak. It was barely enough to wet the tongue. Radar was caught between the desperation of his own thirst and not wanting to watch his parents die of dehydration. When it came to him, he squeezed the bird and nothing came out, not even a drop. He squeezed harder and harder, until he began to feel bones breaking . . .

He sat up in his cot. He was thirsty. His joints ached. Like Funes, he had inherited a body sensitive to changes in weather. Perhaps a storm was coming. Or perhaps this was the first sign of malaria. Or sleeping sickness. Or any of the hundred maladies, known and unknown, that he might catch out here.

Outside, he could hear the steady throb of Horeb beating his drum. And then he heard something else: a faint beep. An unfamiliar chime. He searched through his belongings and found the source: the cell phone. A battery icon was blinking in the top left corner. The phone was dying. He realized that Lars had not given him the charger. The phone had subsisted this whole time on a single charge and was now signaling its inglorious death.

The phone beeped again.

"What is it?" he said.

He examined the pixelated screen and saw another icon blinking. An envelope. The number 4. Hands trembling, he thumbed at the buttons. The messages must have arrived in the middle of the night, in the middle of his dream.

The first two were from Ana Cristina:

. . .

```
609-292-4087: Radar! I thought u died or something! When i got
your text i literally jumped up n down :) javi laughed at me :O
how is congo???? Can't wait 4 u to get back! My mama and her
empanadas will b waiting :) xo ac

609-292-4087: Also lights came back on!!! All of a sudden like they
were never off! 4 real so weird! PS what are u writing???? -><-
```

He read and reread and re-reread the messages. He wanted to swallow this collection of pixelated words and live off their nutrients forever. If his life stopped here and now, he would have no complaints.

He finally flipped down to the third message. It was from a strange number.

. . .

```
387-33-275-312: MY SON IS BORN. RADAR RADMANOVIC. MOTHER IS FINE.
BABY IS FINE. I AM FINE. KAKAV OTAC TAKAV SIN. 73, K2W9
```

"Tata?" he said. *What the hell?*

Frantically, he pressed the call button, waiting, praying that somewhere in this jungle there was a cell tower that could propel the call into the stratosphere. The long-distance connection sputtered, clicked, engaged, the heavens parting. A single ring. His cell phone went dead.

"No!" he yelled. "No!"

He cradled the device. He had not even gotten to the fourth message! The words somewhere inside this plastic shell. His father had texted him? From where? And what could this text mean? "My son is born"?

"Lars!" he shouted. He kicked open the mosquito net, tumbled out of bed, and tripped over a bucket of electronics before emerging from the container. "Lars!"

As soon as he stepped outside, however, he sensed a difference in the air. A heaviness. The river was cocooned in a haze, the banks on either side barely visible.

He found Lars drinking coffee by the fire pit. His eyes were puffy. He didn't look well.

"Do you have the charger for this phone?" he asked, holding up the mobile.

Lars gave him a weary look. He shook his head. "I think I left it in the van," he said. "I'm sorry. We could probably cook something up."

"Are you okay? You don't look so good."

"I feel a little off. Something I ate, I think. I'm sure it'll pass."

Radar drifted up to the side of the ship, where Horeb was drumming. He looked out at the hazy sky.

"It's foggy," he said to Horeb.

"That isn't fog," said Horeb.

Professor Funes, whom Radar had not seen again since his speech several evenings ago, emerged from the *pousser* in the shadow of his giant parasol, his driver in tow. They made their way out onto the deck of the barge. The professor did not acknowledge Radar or Horeb as he and his driver spoke rapidly in Lingala, gesturing at the horizon. Radar realized this was the first time Funes had been outside in the daylight since their departure.

The birds flew overhead. Of the thirteen hundred or so that had once made up the original flock, there were only a couple of dozen left. It seemed this last night in particular had taken a toll. The few that remained appeared especially restless, flitting this way and that.

Funes walked to the head of the barge. A few birds dived and tried landing on his parasol, bouncing awkwardly off its dome. He lightly jiggled the umbrella as if shaking off a layer of rain, but otherwise he ignored the creatures.

"What is it?" said Radar, approaching them.

Funes continued speaking with the driver for some time before breaking into a wet, hacking cough. It was a cough that came from deep inside the lungs, a cough that instantly revealed the extent of the decay within. The parasol trembled as Funes doubled over, scattering a few lingering birds into the air. Finally, when he had regained his composure, Funes turned to Radar. His face was blotched in an irregular pattern, like the map of a coastline.

"Smoke," he whispered hoarsely. "That is smoke."

By the afternoon the smoke had enveloped them. The air was thick with ash; it smelled as if the sky had been expelled from the inside of the earth. No one on the barge spoke. Otik retreated to the theater wagon and the malaise of his vircator. Perhaps he was trying to beckon the few remaining birds, who now seemed to have little or no connection with the performance and only hung around the barge out of reluctant familiarity. Lars, complaining that he felt unwell, stayed inside the container all day, making little notations into a black book that he kept by his cot.

Radar tried listening to his radio for some news of the smoke, but he heard only the usual hodgepodge of sermons, rumba, and indecipherable mutterings. He made an attempt at jerry-rigging a power cord for the cell phone, but the voltage was not right, and when he connected it to the power source he smelled the telltale scent of burning circuitry. He quickly unplugged the phone, but it was already too late. He would now have to dismantle the chassis and examine the motherboard. This would take hours. He halfheartedly started in, but he found his momentum had been sapped. He couldn't concentrate. He went up to the bow again and tried joining Horeb's drumbeat with his radios, but Horeb waved him away.

"I need to speak alone," he said. As he said this, a distant drumming rose from the northern bank. Horeb's head shot up like a rabbit. He listened, then answered on the drum:

↓ ↑ ↑↑ ↓↓↑ ↑↓↑↓   ↓↑↑↑ ↓↓↑↑↓↑↓   ↓↑↑↑↓↓↑↑↓↑↓

"What're you saying?" asked Radar.

"I'm saying: 'He is near, he is coming, get ready . . .'"

"Who is near?"

But Horeb had gone back to banging out the same pattern on his drums. Again and again, the mantra was repeated, dismantled, copied, and dispersed into the haze.

At some point, they entered the magical hour when the tropical sun began to tumble from the sky, the story of the day draining away into nothing, light becoming shadow and shadow becoming light. Standing at the stern, Radar reached out and caught a piece of skin floating through the air. It was a page, charred, still warm to the touch. For a brief instant, Radar could almost read the text on its face, but then the paper dissolved in his hands. He looked and saw that the river was full of these ashen pages, floating like lily pads. Pages drifting through the sky. It was snowing in the jungle.

"Ay yeah! Mayee! Ah yeah! Mayee!" called out the sounder.

They came around a bend in the river, and then there it was. The source of all things. The fire. The world was on fire.

He could hear the flames. He could hear them because the *pousser* had cut its motor and the sounder had gone quiet. They glided toward the fire, which arced up forty, fifty feet into the air, the smoke so thick and black it looked as if it were made of hair. The current began to slow their progress, pushing them away, the river urging them not to come any closer. They reached a standstill, an equilibrium, and for a second it felt as if they were turning back, but then the *pousser* fired its engines and pressed them forward, toward what Radar now knew could only be the library.

From the deck of the barge, they watched the world collapse. Even from this distance, the heat curling the hair on their skin. A heat like no other. A heat of creation.

"Lars . . ." Otik called, and Lars emerged from inside, woozy. He stopped and stared.

The barge slid up against a sandy beach. A fireball exploded into the sky. The gangplank was extended, and Professor Funes limped down it, stumbling, coughing in the smoke. He was without his parasol. His hat blew off into the reeds, revealing a stark white skull. Once on the riverbank, he started to move toward the fire, shielding his face from the waves of heat.

Radar looked and saw that the woods were suddenly alive with faces. They watched as Funes walked down the beach toward the flames. Above him, the birds were gathering, following.

Horeb was standing at the bow with his drums, drumming to the faces in the woods. All at once, Radar realized he was the one who had told them to do this.

He is near, he is coming, get ready . . .

Funes had reached the flames. He paused. The birds overhead, waiting as one.

"The show," said Lars. "It's now."

SELECTED BIBLIOGRAPHY

Amundsen, S. S., J. Bjørnstad, and A. Dyrhaug (1946). *Kirkenesferda 1942.* Oslo: J. W. Cappelens Forlag.

Andrić, I. (1959) 1977. *The Bridge on the Drina.* Trans. L. F. Edward. Chicago: University of Chicago Press.

Artaud, A. (1938) 1994. *The Theater and Its Double.* Trans. M. C. Richards. New York: Grove Press.

Attar, F. (1177) 1889. "The Bird Parliament." Trans. E. FitzGerald. In vol. 2 of *Letters and Literary Remains of Edward FitzGerald,* ed. W. A. Wright. New York: MacMillan, 431–482.

———(1177) 1984. *The Conference of the Birds.* Trans. A. Darbandi and D. Davis. New York: Penguin Classics.

Bajac, V. (2008). *Hamam Balkania.* Trans. R. A. Major. Belgrade: Geopoetika.

Baudelaire, C. (1861). *Les Fleurs du Mal.* Paris: Poulet-Malassis et de Broise.

Beardsman, T. (1956). *A History of Illumination.* New York: Henry Holt.

Benefideo, C. (1993). *The City of Falling Water.* Anchorage, Alaska: Arctic Dreams Press.

Bertucci, B. (1969). *Treatise of the Psyche.* London: Hamish Hamilton.

Bohr, H., and H. B. Nielsen (1977). "Hadron Production from a Boiling Quark Soup." *Nuclear Physics* 128: 275–93.

Bois, Y. A., A. Rudenstine, J. Joosten, and H. Janssen (1995). *Piet Mondrian: 1872–1944.* London: Bulfinch Press.

Borges, J. L. (1949). *El Aleph.* Buenos Aires: Editorial Losada.

Bozović, M. (1993). "Ja nisam takav sin oca." *Naša Borba,* April 4, 1993, 5.

Brook, P. (1968) 1995. *The Empty Space: A Book About the Theatre: Deadly, Holy, Rough, Immediate.* New York: Touchstone Press.

Carrington, J. (1949). *Talking Drums of Africa.* London: Carey Kingsgate Press.

Caruso, E. (1960). "Una furtiva lagrima." Words and music by G. Donizetti. From *The Best of Caruso*. Originally recorded 1904. New York: RCA Victor, 33⅓ rpm.

Cohen. M. (1995). "Khmer Shadow Theatre." In *Performance and Play in Southeast Asia*, ed. J. Connolly and K. Williams. Chicago: University of Chicago Press.

Coleridge, S. T. (1834). "Kubla Khan: Or, A Vision in a Dream. A Fragment." *The Poetical Works of S. T. Coleridge*. London: William Pickering.

Conrad, J. (1899) 1992. *Heart of Darkness*. New York: Penguin Classics.

de Broglie, H. (1880). "Le Destin d'Angkor Vat au Cambodge." *Le Petit Journal*. 27: August 10, 1880.

de Broglie, R. R. (1974). "On the Electroweak Interaction of Neutrinos with Quarks via Z Boson Exchange." Unpublished dissertation, École Polytechnique.

de l'Épée, C.-M. (1776). *Institution des sourds et muets: par la voie des signes méthodiques*. Paris: Chez Nyon.

Dickens, C. (1853) 1993. *Bleak House*. London: Wordsworth.

——— (1859) 1992. *A Tale of Two Cities*. London: Wordsworth.

Fitzgerald, T. K. (1976). "Notes on the Fitzgerald Classification." *Archives of Dermatology* 112 (3): 343.

——— (1979). "On an Isolated Incidence of Non-Addison's Hypoadrenal Uniform Hyperpigmentation in a Caucasian Male." *Journal of Investigative Dermatology* 72: 349–351.

Fitzgerald, T. K., ed. (1973). *Dermatology in General Medicine*, 2nd ed. New York: McGraw-Hill.

Gogol, N. (1842) 1971. *Dead Souls*. Trans. G. Reavey. New York: Norton.

Hamsun, K. (1890) 1998. *Hunger*. Trans. S. Lyngstad. New York: Penguin Classics.

Hasert, F. J., A. Rousset, et al. (1973). "Observation of Neutrino-Like Interactions Without Muon or Electron in the Gargamelle Neutrino Experiment." *Physics Letters* 46B: 138.

Heidegger, M. (1927). *Sein und Zeit*. Tübingen, Germany: Max Niemeyer.

Heilpern, J. (1977). *Conference of the Birds: The Story of Peter Brook in Africa*. Indianapolis: Bobbs-Merrill.

Hilgendorf, W. (2001). *A History of Figure Permutation: From Antiquity to Modern Times*. Boston: Uhuru Press.

Homer (1260 B.C.) 1965. *The Iliad*. Trans W. H. D. Rouse. New York: The New American Library.

Horwich, R., and R. R. de Broglie (1978). "Effective Mass of Up Quarks in a Baryon Gluon Field." *Pakistan Journal of Pure and Applied Physics* 21: 59–72.

Hovengär, J. (1911). *Accumulation & Disintegration*, 3rd ed. London: Pimlico Press.

International Tribunal for the Prosecution of Persons Responsible for Serious Violations of International Humanitarian Law Committed in the Territory of Former Yugoslavia Since 1991 (2006). *Prosecutor v. Stanislav Gorić* (Appeal), IT-98-29-A. November 30, 2006.

Jackson, J. (1975). "Jesse Jackson, Mayor Abe Beame," *The Alex Bennett Show*. WPLJ, April 22, 1975. Radio broadcast.

Kamm, H. (1998). *Cambodia: Report from a Stricken Land*. New York: Arcade.

Kant, I. (1977). *Prolegomena to Any Future Metaphysics That Will Be Able to Come Forward as Science.* Trans. J. Ellington. New York: Hackett.

Larsen, H. I. (1979). *The Last Boat to New York.* Oslo: Oslo Forlagstrykkeri.

Larsen, R. I. (2009). "It Will Happen Again: Report on Kirkenesferda Fire, Sarajevo 1995." *Tin House* 11, no. 4: 48–61.

Lewontin, R. (1972). "The Apportionment of Human Diversity." *Evolutionary Biology* 6: 381–98.

Malick, T. (1978). *Days of Heaven.* Hollywood: Paramount Pictures.

McCall, L. (1990). "Something's Fishy on Times Sq. Jumbo TV." New York *Daily News,* December 17, 1990, 3.

Melville, H. (1851) 1979. *Moby-Dick; or, The Whale.* San Francisco: Arion Press.

Milišić, M. (1993). "And Outside." In *Stains.* Trans. M. Herman. Zagreb, Croatia: Croatian P.E.N. Centre & Most/The Bridge.

Mindlin, A. (1975). "Jersey Freak of Nature: White Parents . . . Black Baby!" *New York Post,* April 18, 1975, 12.

Mladinov, T. S. (1962). *Židovstvo u južnoj Dalmaciji,* vol. 3. Ljubljana: Knjiga.

Møller, D. (1980). "Vi kjente aldri Raksmey, Raksmey." *Profil* 21: 99–102.

Naipaul, V. S. (1979). *A Bend in the River.* New York: Knopf.

Pavlović, R. (2005). "Stani, stani Ibar vodo." Music and lyrics by D. Nedović. *Uzivo Raša Pavlovic.* Belgrade: Renome, CD.

O'Connor, A. (2003). "Thomas Fitzgerald, 83: Treated Skin Diseases; Invented Classification." *New York Times,* August 23, 2003, B16.

Peels, S. (1999). *A Short History of Deliverance.* Rotterdam, Netherlands: Hongerigevrouw Uitgevers.

Popper, N. (1975a). "Caucasian Couple Give Birth to Black Newborn at St. Elizabeth's." Newark *Star-Ledger,* April 18, 1975, A1.

———— (1975b). "Doctors at a Loss to Explain Child's Appearance." Newark *Star-Ledger,* April 20, 1975, A7.

Pynchon, T. (1966). *The Crying of Lot 49.* New York: J. B. Lippincott.

Radasky, W. (2005). "Non-Nuclear Electromagnetic Pulse Generators." *Journal of Electrical Engineering* 27: 24–31.

Radmanovic, R. (1994). "Ciphers and Cryptography in Renaissance Europe." Unpublished term paper, Rutgers University.

———— (1995). "A Comparison of Geo-magnetic Readings from the Solar Storm of 1859." Unpublished thesis, Rutgers University.

———— (2013). *I Am Radar.* Unpublished novel.

Reprezentativni orkestar Jugoslovenske Narodne Armije. (1973). "Marš na Drinu." Lyrics by M. Popović, music by S. Binički. From *Koračnice.* Belgrade: Produkcija gramofonskih plošč Radio-Televizije Beograd, 33⅓ rpm.

Retour, V. (1999). "Schéma et l'agencement du composé de Pol Pot 808." *Revue de l'Indochine* 78: 126–30.

Ritz, T., S. Adem, and K. Schulten (2000). "A Model for Photoreceptor-Based Magnetoreception in Birds." *Biophysical Journal* 78, no. 2: 707–18.

Røed-Larsen, P. (1968). "Hva er Kirkenesferda? Mysteriet avslørt." *Orientering* 15: 38–49.

——— (1969). "Den Menneskelige Marionett Prosjektet." *Norsk Filosofisk Tidsskrift* no. 3 (1969): 154–60.

——— (1970a). "Gåselendat: Teorier om ikke-deltakende Drama og Sensation." *Tidsskrift for Nord Teater* 1: 65–78.

——— (1970b). "Figurteater som protest: Kirkenesferda og intervensjonsteater." *Mot Dag* 8: 37–49.

——— (1971). "Usynlig Teater, Installasjon, eller en Happening? Norsk teaters tilstand." *Tidsskrift for Nord Teater* 2: 24–33.

——— (1972a). "Filmer av Tsar Bomba: En forbigående hendelse." *Kunst/kultur* 3: 41–53.

——— (1972b). "Opptog uten tilskueren: Kirkenesferda og null teater." *Tidsskrift for Nord Teater* 3: 132–46.

——— (1973). "Har Kirkenesferda saken?" *Kunst/kultur* 4: 59–64.

——— (1974a). "Teatervogn av Kirkenesferda." *Tidsskrift for Nord Teater* 5: 335–51.

——— (1974b). Unpublished letter to B. Tofte-Jebsen. October 30, 1974.

——— (1975a). "Tofte-Jebsen er ikke et sannhetsvitne." *Orientering* 22: 287–93.

——— (1975b). "Verfremdungseffekten av Kirkenesferda." *Tidsskrift for Nord Teater* 6: 117–226.

——— (1975c). Unpublished letter to B. Tofte-Jebsen. August 21, 1975.

——— (1976a). "Konseptualisme og avstand i eksperimentelt teater." *Tidsskrift for Nord Teater* 7: 214–39.

——— (1976b). Unpublished letter to B. Tofte-Jebsen. February 12, 1976.

——— (1977). "Hvorfor et publikum? Tanker om vitne." *Orientering* 24: 239–44.

——— (1978). "Levetiden på sannheten." *Norsk Filosofisk tidsskrift* no. 2 (1978): 67–72.

——— (1979a). "Jeg er Tofte-Jebsen." *Vinduet* 32: 123–29.

——— (1979b). Unpublished letter to B. Tofte-Jebsen. August 2, 1979.

——— (1982). "Oppdagelsen av øya Poselok." Unpublished article.

——— (1985). "Gjensyn med øya Poselok: Teori, Kontekst, Struktur." *Tidsskrift for Nord Teater* 16: 97–112.

——— (1996). *Spesielle Partikler: Kirkenesferda 1944–1995.* Oslo: J. W. Cappelens Forlag.

Røed-Larsen, P., and J. I. Bjørneboe (1976). *Levetiden på sannheten.* Oslo: Gyldendal.

RTV Sarajevo (1987). "Robot Dječak," *Vijesti iz kulture.* March 2, 1987. Television broadcast.

Schlemmer, O. (1961) 1996. "Man and Art Figure." Trans. A. Wensinger. In *The Theatre of the Bauhaus,* ed. W. Gropius. Baltimore: Johns Hopkins University Press.

Scott, J. (1975). "Easter Miracle in Area New Jersey Hospital." *The Record* (Bergen County), April 19, 1975, 2.

Shirokorad, A. B. (2004). Вооружение советской авиации, 1941–1991 (Vooruženie sovetskoj aviacii, 1941–1991). Минск: Харвест (Minsk : Harvest).

Simatović, F., S. Radić, et al. (1995). *Policijski izvještaj o smrti Miroslava Danilovića, 2.1.* August 27, 1995.

Slovene Philharmonic Choir (1972). "Uz Maršala Tita." Lyrics by V. Nazur, music by O. Danon. *Tito med nami.* Ljubljana: Dopisna delavska univerza, 45 rpm.

Snyder, T. (1975). "Black Baby's Condition Remains a Mystery." *New York Post,* April 25, 1975, 34.

Tofte-Jebsen, B. (1970). "Kirkenesferda er en fiksjon." *Orientering* 17: 23–35.

———— (1973). "Hver dukke har en stemme." *Vinduet* 24: 255–68.

———— (1974a). "Elektrisitet og metafysikk i postmoderne litteratur." *Edda—Nordisk tidsskrift for litteraturforskning* 60: 201–22.

———— (1974b). Unpublished letter to P. Røed-Larsen. October 10, 1974.

———— (1975a). "Svart-hvitt barn født i New Jersey under strømbrudd." *Bergen Arbeiderblad,* May 2, 1979, 3–4.

———— (1975b). "Brev til redaktøren." *Orientering* 22: 314–15.

———— (1975c). Unpublished letter to P. Røed-Larsen. September 5, 1975.

———— (1976). Unpublished letter to P. Røed-Larsen. February 21, 1975.

———— (1979a). *Jeg er Raksmey.* Oslo: Neset Forlag.

———— (1979b). Unpublished letter to P. Røed-Larsen. August 20, 1979.

———— (1983). *Foredrag ved Offentlige Bibliotek.* Lecture, Bergen Public Library, April 21, 1983.

———— (1990). "Kirkenesferda er død." *Historisk Tidsskrift* 90: 234–40.

———— (1996). "Bokanmeldelse av Spesielle Partikler." *Vinduet* 47: 56–62.

Tolstoy, L. (1878) 1965. *Anna Karenina.* Trans. C. Garnett, ed. L. J. Kent and N. Berberova. New York: Random House.

Velikonja, M. (1992). *The Atlas of Noncontiguous Territories.* New York: Viking.

Von Kleist, H. (2009). *Selected Prose of Heinrich von Kleist.* Trans. P. Wortsman. New York: Archipelago.

Von Luschan, F. (1897). *Beiträge zur Völkerkunde der Deutschen Schutzgebieten.* Berlin: Deutsche Buchgemeinschaft.

Wagner, R. (1973). *Der Ring des Nibelungen.* Orchestra of the Bayreuth Festival. K. Böhm, with T. Adam, G. Nienstedt, H. Esser, W. Windgassen, et al. Recorded 1966. Germany: Philips, 16 sound discs, 33⅓ rpm.

Wharton, E. (1920). *The Age of Innocence.* London: D. Appleton.

Whitman, W. (1891). *Leaves of Grass.* New York: McKay.

Whitney, T. (1973). *The Atlas of All Oceans.* Boston: Houghton Mifflin.

Yorn, T. (1974). "Sunspots and DXing" *QST,* December 1974, 34.

ACKNOWLEDGMENTS

A book is a touched thing. Countless hands contributed to making the object you now hold in your hands—some knowingly, others unknowingly. This project, in particular, drew upon the expertise of many generous people who helped fill in the landscape when my own brain failed.

First and foremost, I feel incredibly lucky to be teamed with my incredible agent, Denise Shannon, who has always been my champion and confidante. I also hold much admiration for my editor, Ann Godoff, who possesses a rare and steady wisdom and trusts in the often messy process of creation. Thanks to the entire team at Penguin Press, who put up with all of my tiny demands and sailed the ship safely into harbor: Benjamin Platt, Veronica Windholz, Claire Vaccaro, Meighan Cavanaugh, Will Palmer, Sofia Groopman, and Darren Haggar, for his astounding cover. A special thanks to Stuart Williams, my editor at Harvill Secker, who read the book many times and always found ways to make it better. And to my other genius, generous editors: Hans Jorgen Balmes, Maggie Doyle, Lidewijde Paris, Elena Ramirez, and Nicole Winstanley. Thanks also to my agents Dean Cooke and Judith Murray.

I traveled a lot to discover the invented places in this book and was offered much guidance along the way. In New Jersey, I'd like to thank Stuart Engelke, Bob Janney, Jim Wright, Lilo Stainton, Tony Dee, and Gary Hanson. In Norway, gratitude goes to Solgunn Solli, Stine Qvistad Jenvin, Karin Johnsen, and Silje Bekeng. In Serbia, I was welcomed like a long lost relation. Thanks Darko Radulović, Jasna Novakov Sibinović, Vlada Bajac, Igor Cvi, and the entire Geopoetika team. In Cambodia, Tararith Kho,

ACKNOWLEDGMENTS

Proeung Pranit, and Sreang Heng took me to the borderlands. At CERN, Ariane Koek, Rolf Landau, Barbara Warmbein, Joe Incandela, and Katie Yurkewicz all put up with my ridiculous questions. In the Congo, Horeb Bulambo, Pascal Bashombana, and Stewart Lunanga showed me the best and worst that humanity has to offer. And thanks to others for arranging and advising: Bent-Jorgen Perlmutt, Elyse Lightman, Harlan Lane, Matthew Cohen, Avery Gilbert, Bert van Der Hove, and Bryan Mealer.

Some of this book was written in the rare territory of the Netherlands Institute of Advanced Study, where I was the writer-in-residence. Thanks to the wonderful people I met there: Nadège Lechevrel, Ianthi-Maria Tsimpli, Louise Mars, Jos Hooghuis, Kahliya Ronde, Saskia Peels, Joy Connolly, and, in particular, the crazy Balkanians, Mitja Velikonja and Dino Abazović, who offered me such valuable insight and invited me to be an honorary member of their clan.

And a huge thank you to the multitude of readers that took the time to read this project in some ragged form and offer me their invaluable advice. Without all of you, I would still be lost at sea: Alena Graedon, Mike Lukas, Ian Cheney, Marijeta Bozovic, Konrad Ryushin Marchaj, Meehan Crist, Elliott Holt, Rains Paden, Niek Miedema, Manfred Allié, Dagfinn Møller, Nadja Bruner, Jordan Alport, Sarah Fornace, Hannah Pascal, Harrison Holt, Henry Rich, Akira Yamaguchi, and Maria Cristina Rueda, who also did such a beautiful job bringing the images into focus.

Finally, I would like to give a standing ovation for my endlessly supportive parents, Peik and Judith—you taught me how to be human and are the main reason why I write these words. Thank you, Jasper, for putting up with your tiresome, artsy family.

And thank you most of all to Katie and Holt, who form the rest of my solar system. You supply the gravity that keeps me on this planet.

Gassho.

IMAGE CREDITS

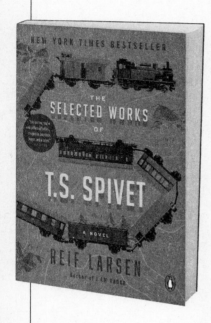